The Rat Machine

For Bob,
my good friend
Kent

The Rat Machine

Kent Harrington

A Market Street Book

The Rat Machine

The Rat Machine is a work of fiction. Names, places, characters, and incidents are either products of the author's imagination or used to further same. Any resemblence to actual events or to persons alive or dead is coincidental.

For information please contact:

www.kentharrington.com
info@market-street-books.com
socialmedia@kentharrington.com

Cover and book design by Stephen Finerty

ebook ISBN: 978-0-9858083-7-2

paperback ISBN: 978-0-9858083-1-0

Library of Congress Control Number: 2012915485

Edition: 10 9 8 7 6 5 4 3 2 1

First Edition

I once had a dream, while in high school, where Anne Frank and I were riding on my motorcycle on the way to Point Reyes for a day in the sun. I'd always wished I could have been at the top of the stairs to stop them from taking her away. This book is dedicated to her memory.

Acknowledgement

I would like to thank my beautiful wife Susan Harrington for putting up with all the thick old history books scattered around the house while researching for this novel! And, also, for her listening to me go on about the most obscure details imaginable concerning: World War II and the Eastern Front, the Sicilian Mafia, the CIA, the drug trade etc. Only someone who truly loves you could put up with that! Thank you for that, and so much more.

I also have to thank several truly wonderful people for being there for me with: help, advice, real-time history (invaluable in this kind of book), comments, or just their support, either for the novel, or this novelist. In fact, *The Rat Machine* could not have been written without their collective help: My amigo Dennis McMillan who had the patience of Job while going over the manuscript. James Campbell who told me about things you cannot learn from history books. Stephen Finerty for caring about the cover as much as I did—which was a lot. Nordine Haddad for pushing me a little bit further with the cover. Tom Towler for sharing this artist-life foxhole and always having my back. Clair Lamb for taking my crazy calls. Aldo Calcagno, a true friend and supporter since way back on Beverly Boulevard! To Dr. Lou Boxer—The Man—who read the book and emailed: WOW. And finally, to Mike C. for calling, years ago, and saying: "Don't give up, Kent!" As you can see, I took his advice.

Other Books by Kent Harrington

Dark Ride (1996)
Dia de los Muertos (1997)
The American Boys (2000)
The Tattooed Muse (2001)
Red Jungle (2005)
The Good Physician (2008)
Satellite Circus

I went down, down, down,
and the flames went higher...

Johnny Cash - "Ring of Fire"

1

1980 ■ SAN BERNARDINO, CALIFORNIA

A brand new pickup truck, radio blaring, sat in the middle of a huge Southern California Ford dealership at 1:30 A.M. on a Sunday morning. The radio was on because Chip Rogers, the owner of the dealership, had been demonstrating to his sales manager, Fred Cooley—a tall, good-looking black man—what a fully-loaded Bose package could do when you "cranked the motherfucker *up*, baby. ...You can sell this rig to the *deaf,* man!" Chip had joked, punching his friend Fred playfully on the arm. The men were waiting for Chip's dope connection, because Chip Rogers, besides being a major Ford dealer, was also one of Southern California's biggest heroin dealers, and Fred was his lieutenant in both enterprises. The Rogers gang broke down kilos of high quality heroin into ounces for sale to street gangs in the Greater Los Angeles area. Demand was high and business booming as heroin use had been steadily rising all over Southern California for the past decade or more. Chip's dope business was protected by a corrupt group inside the San Bernardino County Sheriff's Department, who not only provided him with the heroin, via a trusted and secret source, but got a slice of Chip's action, too. It was all good. And if you screwed with Chip Rogers, you were screwing with a guy who could call The Man down on you; what Chip liked to call his personal "Noriega Corps."

Less than an hour later, Fred Cooley was lying on the clean showroom floor, bleeding to death, while the same Bose speakers wailed a new song crystal-clear and mostly unheard: *turned your back on hu-man-i-ty ... talkin' 'bout you an' me ... and the games people play.* Fred watched the blood from one of his wounds roll under his chin, inky-looking. He could still smell cordite from the short but brutal gunfight that had wounded him in the stomach. And sadly, he could feel himself "walking towards the Lord", as the preacher in his black church would say, six days later, when Fred's mother buried him in a Montgomery Ward suit she bought on credit. His mother insisting that the undertakers put a smile on Fred's twisted face, because Fred wasn't smiling when he died, that's for damned sure.

That Saturday night Fred was lying gut-shot, unable to move, realizing just how

1

fragile life is when you get right down to it. What Fred desperately wanted was to stand up and run home and be safe—the way he'd done when he was a kid. But that was impossible. He felt the fingers on his outstretched right hand getting warmer from the blood pooling under his fingertips. He realized at that very moment that he was probably going to die, and the enormity of it terrified him, as death had been the furthest thing from his mind only an hour ago, when life had seemed so very good indeed.

Fred had woken up that Saturday with a coke hangover and a lot of cars to sell. He had marched through the day like the tall, competent man he was, cracking the whip on his sales force, most of whom respected and liked him. His salesmen—a lot of them Vietnam vets—walked customers through a carefully-crafted process designed to get resistant buyers to sign a contract with every possible extra thrown into the deal—it was the American Way. Now Fred was bleeding-out on the highly polished white linoleum floor of the dealership, eyes bugged-out in shock, his mouth twisted in pain, as he watched the little shit who'd shot him in the stomach moving slowly toward the tall glass exit doors.

The twenty kilos of pure heroin—the root of all the murder and mayhem—were stacked neatly right beside Fred on the floor, three bales high and wrapped in green plastic. The body of a man, one Willie Cole by name, was lying face up on the heroin, stone dead. They'd all just been getting to the pay-for-it part of the transaction, with Chip walking toward his office to get the money out of his safe to pay Willie Cole, Sheriff's Deputy and secret member of the Vagos motorcycle gang. The deputy had been talking to Fred, whom he knew very well from their days together in high school. Everything had seemed so normal.

That's exactly when Tommy Joy came on the scene. Tommy was a young ex-con who'd happened to overhear Fred talking on his telephone that morning while getting a blow-job from his Mexican-American girlfriend, who just happened to live next to Fred's condo unit. The flimsy walls in modern condominiums, it could be said, were the basic cause of Fred's problems later that night. Tommy had overheard the whole conversation between Fred and Cole, which sounded to him like a dope deal, and from which he developed his simple plan. *Rip the sons of bitches off.* Then he'd muttered "Oh yeah," for two good reasons.

Tommy Joy, nineteen, walked into the scene that night using the dealership's employee entrance, carefully easing past the shuttered and dark Parts Department. As soon as Fred saw the showroom's side door swing open, he knew there was some bad shit coming down. Fred pulled a twenty-two caliber Saturday Night Special and opened up like he was starring in a TV Western. There was a moment when Fred and

Tommy were looking at each other, firing, trying to kill each other in the worst kind of way, but neither one was a good shot. Tommy, who was no coward, walked straight towards Fred and Willie Cole, firing the 1911 Colt .45 that he'd bought two days after getting out of prison at a gun show in downtown Los Angeles—ammunition extra. His father had loaned him the hundred and twenty bucks to buy a fresh start in life.

Now the corrupt sheriff's deputy was dead and Chip was, too. Chip's body, half-kneeling, was propped up against his big black jeweler's safe. He'd been shot in the head, his lower jawbone exposed by the bullet that had killed him. Yet somehow the now-exposed muscles in Chip's face grotesquely animated his dead lips—twitching them obscenely. Chip Rogers was trying—it appeared—to explain just exactly what had gone wrong with his plan.

Tommy Joy, who'd shot them all and was going outside to die on the asphalt of the thousand-car parking lot, had thought that Chip had definitely opened the safe. But Tommy had shot Chip "one turn of the dial too soon." A good title for a country song, but the end of Tommy's dream of instant riches. An overweight San Bernardino city homicide detective had sung that lyric to everyone in Chip's office that Sunday morning as he questioned them. Chip's office was, by then, full of cops, including some of the Sheriff's Department's finest, but they seemed preoccupied, angry, and not in the mood for dumb-ass jokes from the homicide guy, who was not part of their crew anyway, but who had figured out what had gone down—*almost.* The homicide cop may have been fat, but he wasn't stupid. It was that same day, too, that the detective figured out that the San Bernardino County Sheriff's Department had some serious problems and was probably bent as all hell. He told the DA about the situation a few days later, but was waved-off, as the DA was up for re-election and didn't want any trouble with the Sheriff, a two-pack-a-day leathery old cowboy type who never spoke an extra word about anything, let alone corruption. He rode a white horse every Fourth of July in Apple Valley's well attended parade, holding a giant American flag and wearing a white Stetson cowboy hat. For a lot of people the Sheriff *was* America.

What the homicide detective's reconstruction had missed was that Tommy had fired at Chip only because Chip had tried to kick him in the head. Tommy was nervous and wounded in the liver and right kidney when he left Chip's office. Mistakes happen, especially when it feels like your insides are being sucked out through your asshole, but that was a big one, not having checked for sure that the safe door was in fact open, before he shot Chip dead. He'd walked over to the brain-splattered safe and tried to open it and couldn't believe that the asshole car dealer he'd just killed had *lied* to him. The safe was still locked with the money inside, and that was the way it was going to remain. Even Tommy Joy knew that jeweler's safes were impossible to peel unless you were a real box-man, and Tommy was basically just a strong-arm robber with a big set of balls for a kid.

"Is that it?" he'd asked Chip, who had made a show of turning the dial on the safe and pretending it was open.

"Yes ... that's it. ... It's open," Chip had said, making eye-contact with Tommy, looking straight at the kid, still on one knee. Chip was a car salesman, so lying came naturally to him and he was good at it. Chip's plan had been to step away from the safe and then go at the kid anyway he could—he sure as hell wasn't going to give up two-hundred and fifty G's in cash without a fight. Chip had studied karate on Friday nights at a local dojo for years, working up to a brown belt, and thought he was bad. His plan quickly failed, however, when it lost "operational flexibility," as they say in the military. Translation: Tommy shot Chip in the head after just managing to duck a round house kick aimed at him from the enraged car salesman. It was a "Game over"-type head-shot.

Tommy, despite knowing better, out of frustration, which isn't uncommon with men of his type, tried to work the safe's brain-splattered handle a second time, just in case, hoping for a miracle. His shoes were getting spongy from the blood running down his leg. One of Fred's twenty-two caliber slugs had bounced off Tommy's third rib and torn through his intestines before taking out the kidney where it was presently lodged.

The linoleum floor around the safe was slick with a mixture of Tommy's blood— originally similar in viscosity to car oil, but already starting to congeal—and a goodly portion of what had recently been Chip's grey matter. Tommy, frustrated and in pain, now finally realized The Plan would have to change and he would have to drive himself to the hospital and go back to jail. That would be the case if he were really *lucky*, he thought. It had all seemed so easy that morning, sitting there with his girlfriend, eating cornflakes in their clean underwear, both of them happy and red-faced from having sex all morning.

His girlfriend, Carmen, worked at the "Jag in the Rag," as the local high school kids called Jack in the Box, and she asked if they could go out after Tommy got back from the robbery—after all, it was Saturday, and she felt like doing some partying. Tommy had said *Why the hell not?* He liked to party as much as anyone else, especially since he'd missed a lot of his youth stuck in the penitentiary for holding up a 7-Eleven when he was drunk, all that time and effort to bag a whole nine dollars! He'd been seventeen when he went to the joint.

"Mother *fucker!*" Tommy looked down at Chip, who he recognized from his thousands of appearances on late-night television commercials; at his half-a-skull with the trademark long blond hair still attached to what was left of his head. He'd shot a minor celebrity! "You stupid fucking lying sack of shit!" Tommy had said out loud. Then he'd turned around and made it out of Chip's tidy, grand, well-lit office, complete with a big plaque from the Better Business Bureau that said Chip Rogers was an upstanding member of the community. Tommy had left a trail of bloody footprints on a brand-spanking-new and very expensive oriental carpet. He headed back out toward the brightly-lit showroom, with its spotless cars and bleeding guys lying on the floor, the green bales of heroin looking like a playground "Jumpy." Tommy heard the radio playing a different song, now, and he was starting to feel woozy and weak and a little sick to his stomach.

"Okay, Tommy, get your ass to a hospital, because you fucked this *way* up." He said it out loud over the music. He'd started talking out loud to himself when he was in lockup for days at a time in Chino State Correctional Facility for fighting with his fellow Hispanic prisoners because he was white and that's just how it was there at Chino. Tommy started to walk by Fred, who looked like he was about one short minute from having his show cancelled, but he stopped, trying not to step in the growing pool of Fred's blood that reflected the showroom's high ceilings, festooned with "deal banners," American flags, and interest-rate offers. Tommy stepped into the reflection so he could see himself, too. He was a good-looking kid, blond and stocky. Girls thought he was cute. He tried to stop his own bleeding by pressing his left hand over the small hole in his side.

"I was just going to steal the money, man. I didn't even want the fucking dope!" Tommy said, looking down at Fred, who tried to say something back to him. Tommy spoke earnestly, as if telling this particular fact to the dying black man on the floor was going to change anything, now. "I got nothing against *you*," he said as an afterthought. Then Tommy passed the big knuckle-head whom he *had* intended to shoot, right after he'd seen the scary motherfucker pull up to the back of the dealership and unload the drugs from a brand new white van, deciding right then that *that* fucker was no civilian and would have to go pronto. The big white guy had died coming at him saying he was a sheriff, no less, reaching for his ID and apparently expecting Tommy to believe him. Tommy fired a tight group of shots into Sheriff Willie Cole's white T-shirt just above the heart, knocking him back onto the heroin bales and killing him almost instantly. *There* was the proof, some of the cops said later, that the 1911 Colt .45 was worth the extra you had to pay for one.

Tommy Joy, his blood pressure plunging dangerously, pushed through the big clean glass doors of the Ford dealership and out into the warm August night. Little white moths were flying everywhere, and the air felt soft and was perfumed by the nearby orange groves, but that bit of nature would soon be removed, after the orange trees were bulldozed to make way for a new Wal-Mart where Tommy's little sister would work for the next twenty years without a raise, finally becoming a meth addict. He could feel the heat on his clean-shaven young face. He'd taken a shower and put on a pair of new jeans and a stylish "Madres" shirt before he'd driven down to the dealership with all the hopes of a quick score and the excitement the young bring to most endeavors. He headed toward his pickup, which he'd parked on the street. He thought that, if he ignored absolutely everything, he might make it to the hospital. But there are some realities in life that put an end to wishful thinking, and Tommy dropped to the ground halfway to his truck, his plan collapsing with him.

Tommy, who was no stranger to bad situations, sat for a moment on his knees and envisioned himself getting up, but his blood pressure had zeroed out and the last few molecules of O_2 passed to the active frontal lobes of his brain. "It's true what they say," Tommy said out loud—now clinically dead. He was seeing people he'd known as a child: his grandma, who'd been a Dust Bowl Okie, carny whore, and "paper-hanger," who had raised him and been very loving, the way some people can be despite grinding poverty, bad lawyers, mean cops, and stone-hearted judges she'd faced all of her life, all of them seeming to hate her for one simple reason: she'd been born poor. But Tommy was very sure she hadn't come with him to the dealership. Then Tommy died, still on his knees. The next morning, on the way to the new drive-in church, a new wrinkle in mass-religion that was getting very popular, whole families saw Tommy kneeling like an altar boy, frozen in time, staring off towards Los Angeles. A lot of people thought he was praying. A billboard with Chip Rogers' face plastered on it sat directly above Tommy. Chip was smiling down at everyone who passed. "Jesus, folks ... drives a Ford," the billboard said. It was a lie, of course. The fact was that Jesus Christ, son of a carpenter, didn't give a good god-*damn* about The Ford Motor Company.

6

2

■ "GATE SIX" SAUSALITO, CALIFORNIA

A girl, maybe twenty-five, slight, and very pretty, Malcolm Law thought, was looking at him from inside her houseboat. She was dressed in white jeans and an orange Mexican peasant blouse. She had spotted him as she poured herself a glass of white wine. Lifting her glass, she looked directly outside and at him—each staring at the other. Malcolm waved as if they knew each other. He looked for a front door on the houseboat, but like most of the boats at Gate Six—half-boat and half-house—the houseboat's front door wasn't immediately apparent to him. He dropped his eyes to look for a door bell, missing the point about Gate Six completely.

The girl crossed the living room and came to a sliding glass door that served as the houseboat's entrance and slid it open. Malcolm, smiling, was standing on the dock in front of her. He was in his late fifties and was well dressed. Despite his obvious middle age he was still quite handsome. *In a Robert Redford way,* the girl thought, studying him, wine glass in hand. She thought right away that it had to be her new boyfriend's father because the resemblance was that striking.

"Permission to board?" Malcolm said, with a show of bonhomie as soon as the door slid open. It was six in the evening and the warren of docks near the freeway had not yet been hidden in fog that was pouring in now over the hills above Sausalito, hauled in on the wind covering the town. The girl's houseboat was at the very end of the dock, and had big views of the San Francisco skyline and Angel Island. The man seemed completely at ease despite the fact that he was over-dressed for the houseboats, which were known as a notorious hippie enclave and small-time Sodom and Gomorrah. Straight people only came out to score something illegal. The feeling of a Casbah-on-the-water was heightened by the fact that the police didn't bother with the Gate Six at all; it was just too difficult to patrol and *impossible* to raid. The man seemed to the girl like a visitor from another planet. It was a planet where men still wore suits and ties and went to work in the morning, their hair slicked down and their middle-classness wound tightly around them.

"Do I know you?" she asked, then smiled. The suit and the overcoat reminded her of her father. The same father who had sent her to the "Left Coast" after catching her shooting cocaine directly into her right arm. The needle was still in her arm when her father unexpectedly walked through the door of her bedroom in the family mansion, which was located in Dallas's tony Sugarland neighborhood.

The coke alone would have slammed her heart into overdrive, but seeing her father come through the door on top of her drug rush—well, she nearly died on the spot. And she would have died feeling six years old again, panicked, wanting to run down to her mother and safety in the kitchen. *He never came home before eight in the evening!* Her irate father had grabbed for her "works," aggressively pulling the syringe out of her arm when she was only half-done with her fix; the syringe had sprayed blood and drugs onto her father's hand, in fact. Her high spoilt now, her heart pounding near its breaking point, she'd been forced to grab the arms of the Louis XIV-style chair and simply look at him defiantly, speechless, as there were no other emotions left for her to respond with other than simple defiance. Her last defense was the stubborn look of a selfish, self-absorbed junkie, and it was plastered all over her young, pretty face.

"Is *this* what I raised!?" he'd screamed. *"This?!?!"* He stepped on her syringe. Its tube cracked under the weight of his heavy wingtip.

She couldn't answer him; the very ability to speak was denied her at that crucial moment in their relationship. By then the rush of cocaine, that had nearly stopped her heart, and that made her feel like a river of adrenaline was coursing through her, pounding on her ear drums, had overpowered her. Instead of speaking up for herself and somehow defending her actions, she was reduced to gripping the chair's arms for dear life as the freight train she was riding ran full speed by all her emotions.

Then suddenly, in the blink of an eye, the ice-cool that cocaine gives you when you shoot it swept through her entire being, and she was transported from a fearful caught-doing-a-bad-thing little girl to feeling the kind of resentment only grown women can muster.

Her father, an exceedingly wealthy oil executive, thought her present state was simply another instance of his daughter's stolid insouciance; the main and most irritating aspect of the bratty girl, *par excellence*, that he'd come to know. And who he believed was poisoning his two other daughters as well. He took her silence as an added insult, and it finally diminished the love he had for his oldest daughter; a love that had held through countless other scenes: black boyfriends, shady lesbian college roommates in Austin who he was convinced had "spoilt" his daughter for a normal marriage—*What good had the expensive cotillion been?* he'd kept thinking as she'd spiraled into a frightening world of drug abuse and other bizarre behavior. Since she'd graduated from college she'd disappointed his wife and himself at every turn. And no amount of expensive psychiatric treatment with Jew doctors seemed to matter. For all these reasons, and others that were not as justifiable, even to himself, he slapped his eldest daughter hard across the face and then stormed out, refusing to ever see or even speak to her again. He'd reached the end of the line. The line he'd believed he would never cross, but, in fact, even parents cross at times. He acted, from that day onward, as if she was a financial obligation and not a single thing more.

It was the older man's "power-suit" that made the girl, Patty Montgomery, recall her past, all in a timeless instant, standing there, glass of wine in hand. She took the man standing in front of her for the same kind of man, certainly from the same class of people who had sticks up their asses that reached to the center of their brains. She'd come out to California and become a hippie so that she would not have to look at men like her father. She could sleep with whoever she wanted to, and do whatever she wanted— including take all the drugs she wanted.

"Sorry, I have all the life insurance I can use," Patty said, half-joking; it *was* meant as an insult. She was barefoot. It was almost six in the afternoon in August of 1980. She'd already had a glass of wine, so it was easy to be catty and smile, too. She just hated the Establishment, no matter what form it took.

"Not selling anything," Malcolm Law said. "Came to see Bruce. We have an appointment. He wanted to meet me here."

"Bruce and you?"

"Yes." She'd seen the resemblance of course: they were both handsome like blue-eyed Dutchmen. She wasn't deceived by the man's lie. The older man was bigger and tougher-looking than his son; he looked like the Bar Harbor yachtsman that he in fact was, right down to the weather-beaten face.

"Are you his father? You look like him," Patty said. The man seemed to think about that for a moment, as if he didn't understand what she was talking about.

"No." He lied expertly, without a trace of nerves. "Can I come in?" She thought he was lying. The "no" had been a little too deliberate and helpful-sounding. She was usually good at spotting lies. The man smiled the way salesmen do, when they're interrupted in mid-pitch. "No ... my name is Rod Clark. Bruce asked that we meet out here. Is he here?"

"No.... Are you a cop?" she asked.

"*No!* Close, though—a lawyer. ... Bruce had a traffic accident last month; he rear-ended somebody. They're suing, I'm afraid. I'm going to be defending him in the case."

"Oh," she said. "My brother is a lawyer."

"Is he?" Malcolm Law said, looking at her very carefully, now. She had not asked him in. He noticed the tracks on her arm, and that she was wearing stretch-pants

9

that showed off her ass. She was actually very attractive—slender and tall. His taste in women ran elsewhere, but he noticed her Art Nouveau-poster body. Her strawberry-blonde hair made her look like Anne of Green Gables, who had gone bad, and now lived on a houseboat in Sausalito.

A dope fiend, Malcolm thought. *Typical.* He immediately discounted her, sliding her into a kind of mental plastic bag of Types he was all too familiar with as a long-time intelligence officer. Malcolm Law disliked people who'd lost control of themselves. And, perhaps at the top of that list were dope fiends; it went very much against his Calvinist nature. He was an expert at twisting those kinds of weaknesses, however. Exploiting people's weaknesses and vices had been, in fact, his stock and trade during his entire career as a spy, and he was very good at it.

"My brother is an asshole, though. Are you an asshole, too? You're dressed like all the assholes I've ever known," Patty said. She was looking at him, still smiling, but it was a clever smile that some pretty girls develop when they want to distance themselves from everyone else.

"No ... I don't think so. ... a bit of an ambulance chaser, actually ... when I was younger. I don't need to, now—thank God!" Malcolm said, feeling like an ass. He took the opportunity to step by the girl, as if she'd invited him in. "Thanks, it's freezing outside."

"Drink?" Patty said, watching the big man survey her digs as he walked onto the houseboat. He walked on into the living room, then stood in the center of it like a rat-catcher might, as if he were waiting to hear, from her personally, where she'd seen the last one, so he could get to work.

Patty Montgomery, whose grandfather was a major stockholder in the Phillips Petroleum Company, had one of the largest boats at Gate Six. She'd had it towed from a boatyard in Richmond, California, where she'd had it built to order. It had two floors and its inside was "conventional," in that it looked like any suburban house. Her father was the long-time CEO of Phillips Petroleum and he had paid for it. He also faithfully sent Patty a check for six thousand dollars every month for "living expenses." In exchange, she was to stay away from the entire family; indefinitely. Her brothers and sisters had been told by her mother and father that she was not to be contacted. Their oldest sister, her father had explained to them at a well-staffed Thanksgiving party, was now to be considered *dead* to them, and he wasn't joking. As a born-again Christian with a past drinking problem he was actually afraid of his daughter—something that he never admitted, even to himself. The little girl, who could be seen on the family's Super Eight films playing in the park-like backyard of their mansion, swimming in the beautiful Olympic-sized pool back in 1970, and being toweled off afterwards by a sweet black nanny called Georgia, was gone forever from their lives. She didn't miss

Texas at all, though: she called the state "Devil's Island."

"A little early for me," Malcolm said. He spotted the bong and the orange Zig Zag rolling papers on a dusty-looking low, hand-carved Indian table surrounded by pillows that were strewn on the floor in the middle of the living room. The pillows were orange and red; the furniture had come from Cost Plus in the City. He turned around and caught a glimpse of the girl's breasts through the thin material of her blouse. They were small and made her seem even younger to him.

"Sorry. ... Was that a 'no' to the drink? Out here we start early. So you don't have to worry," she said. "I promise not to tell your boss at the insurance brokerage. Isn't that kind of work boring?"

"No. Thanks," Malcolm said, smiling. "What a remarkable view ... Angel Island, isn't it?"

"Yes." She took another sip from her glass of wine. "You aren't some kind of weirdo, are you? Are you, *Rod?* Should I be afraid of you? You're not going to pull out your dick and wave it at me, are you?"

"No! Most certainly not! Bruce will vouch for me." He seemed truly shocked that she would think that of him.

"You're lying, though ... I mean, about being Bruce's lawyer," she said, stepping into the living room, her body-language not showing any fear of him at all.

"Why do you think that?"

"I don't know ... you just vibe shady," she said. "No offense, really. I mean I suppose that lawyers lie for a living. And God knows I'm surrounded by shady types out here."

"May I sit down?" Malcolm glanced at his watch. He was getting tired of having to be charming to the young dope fiend but he decided to keep smiling because he didn't want to set off any more alarm bells. *Soldier on.* "No offence taken," Malcolm said.

"Is it all very secret ... what you've come for, then?"

"Not really," Malcolm said, sitting down on a tangerine-colored couch. "Is this marijuana?" He picked up a joint lying in an open cigar box on the table and looked at it. He'd smoked marijuana as a kid in Tangiers while in the Army. It had been in a Foreign Legion brothel right after the war. He hadn't liked it. He preferred a good Bourbon instead.

"Yes, Rod," she said. "That ... right there ... in your hand ... right now ... is a marijuana cigarette. ... I believe from Panama. And very good, too. Would you like to try it? It's on the house."

He put it down. "Fascinating. ... Really? ... Panama? No, I'd better not. After all, I'm here to work, aren't I," Malcolm said, smiling quickly.

11

3

■ SAUSALITO, CALIFORNIA

Alex Law, CIA officer, twenty-eight years old, drove into the muddy parking lot at Gate Six past a motley collection of mostly older cars and hippie vans. A few were newer European models: Mercedes sports cars, and even a new-looking yellow Lamborghini that belonged to a big-time dealer. He parked next to a VW bug plastered with Barbie-doll heads that looked like a voodoo altar on wheels. Alex was not looking forward to seeing his father. So, as a way of making it hard on his father, he'd suggested that they meet out here, at his girlfriend's houseboat. It would be hard to find for the "Old Man," and also from his father's point of view, very much in "Indian Country." He climbed out of a Hertz rental car that he'd already banged up driving stoned, and locked the doors. He was carrying a fully-loaded Walther P-5 Compact with a back-up clip in his jacket pocket. Like a lot of people who lived out on the houseboats, he was armed at all times. Unlike the others, he had a license to carry the weapon and had been trained in its use by some of the best killers in the world. In spite of the training, his instructors had uniformly opined that he was only a fair shot at best.

The Gate Six houseboats were home to dope dealers, anarchists, flight attendants, male and female whores, extremely wealthy trust-fund babies like his girlfriend Patty, ex-cons of various stripes, dope fiends, and every conceivable oddball, loser, sex-freak, sex "instructor," con man, artist, runaway, guru and/or "professor"-without-classroom or portfolio, all living alongside big-time Hollywood scriptwriters, incredibly successful rock stars who had wanted, and got, a front row seat to Sex World, where the streets were paved with cocaine and eighteen-year-old girls searching for rich guys. The young women hung like low fruit ripe for the picking.

More 1920s Weimar Berlin in feel than 1980 America, it was where all kinds of people, good and bad, sought refuge from the "straight world" that depressed and bugged them. If you were not liked by your neighbors, or caused the drug dealers who ran the place *any* trouble, your houseboat was burnt down to the waterline, and you could consider yourself officially evicted. Teenage girls from all over the country—mini-skirted Sirens with very few inhibitions—could be found on any given summer afternoon, lying out, adorning The Man's houseboat or deck, catching rays *au nature,* bongs in hand, a ten-thousand-dollar Macintosh stereo playing "Hey Joe" in the background. Rich hipsters and movie producers that came to score drugs would pick the girls up in Sausalito, and a week or two later put them down in some mansion in New York City, Tangiers, or LA, where their careers as international "party girls" would begin in earnest. Some even became movie or TV stars with big careers; the ones who knew how to please the right men and just what to say to them at exactly the right time. Specifically, when to say the most important line they would ever deliver: "Baby ... I'm all yours."

Alex, having grown up at the opposite end of the social spectrum in a leafy power suburb of Washington, D.C., and at various private schools, including Exeter, liked the place a lot. He thought he might even buy a houseboat there himself and leave the Agency, retiring there on the Outskirts of Civilization at the Edge of the Western World.

"Really, man. You should go out there some time. It's wild. It never stops." He'd said that to Butch, his partner, that week while they were training at the DEA's extensive gun range at Moffett Field.

"Alex—you fuck girls that don't shave under their armpits, man—*Jesus!* All right, I'll come out there ... but you know I don't like hippies. They used to call me a baby killer when I got back from Nam. Do I look like a fucking *baby killer?*" Butch had said defensively, knocking out shells from the .44 magnum "hand cannon" that he planned on using in LA when they were finally let go to run the operation. Having survived the Tet Offensive because he had *not* run out of ammunition, he was taking their ordinance situation very seriously, not wanting to ever be out-gunned by the bad guys on the streets of LA, where he knew that they were heading very shortly.

The place Alex Law was going to meet his father belonged to his girlfriend of almost a month—a twenty-two-year-old freckled-face girl from Dallas, Texas, with short blonde hair who looked innocent but was definitely not. She was the daughter of a socially prominent oil family, had no obvious means of support, and had a pretty good drug habit. That was just about all he knew about her, except that she was a hell of a lot of fun to be with and she never asked him anything personal about himself, so he didn't have to lie to her. She only knew him by his cover name: Bruce Tucker.

He'd met her in a bar called Smiley's in Sausalito after a long day of simulated combat in a series of buildings the DEA used out at Moffett Field. The DEA officers insisted that they complete both the shooting and unarmed combat course before they "disappeared" into their actual operation.

Alex was no good at the unarmed combat, which consisted of mostly judo moves. His instructor was a heavily scarred, bullet-headed ex-Marine who wore old-school grey sweats and told him at the end of the training: "You punch like a fucking chick, man. That's the truth, no offense—I wouldn't want you as my partner out on the streets; no way." Alex was used to being told he was no good at physical things and blew the sergeant's comments off. It was true: in fact, he'd been born-to-the-manor, not to the streets, and on top of that he only weighed 150 pounds, which in Cop World was considered "small." Yet ironically the agency had chosen *him* to follow Butch into the LA underworld, and not a hundred other, "tougher" young intelligence officers. He had no idea why he'd been chosen, and in fact had thought about lobbying to get out of the assignment. All it would have taken was one call to his father, who was still head of the Agency's clandestine services. He much preferred the embassy in London, where he'd spent a very happy year chasing debutantes and learning to fly small planes. Spying on the Russians— most of his targets were in his own age group so that when he *did* turn someone it would seem natural to be seen with them— became almost beside the point.

He walked to Patty's boat, went up to the door, and saw that the lights were on. There was a certain place on her boat that he liked to make love, a kind of elevated cabin at the top, with a waterbed and portholes all around so you could see the Bay at night. He could get his feet on the wall for purchase, and with the marijuana and a little brandy, it felt like maybe she and he had no beginning, middle, or end at all. Just one entity, united by houseboat-love-making. No inhibitions, no tomorrows, no yesterdays: it was complete, as if the normal physical world had stopped and they had discovered and operated by new laws of physics. He was looking forward to that now because he was going to leave for LA soon and knew he couldn't come back here, as it would put Patty in danger, he supposed, and he liked the girl. She was what his mother would have characterized as "silly," and destined to self-destruct like a poorly-built toy that kids get as a present and finally break from over-use. But he liked that very thing about her: She was a startlingly beautiful moment in time and space but would soon be over, no doubt.

"Where's Patty?" he asked, glancing at his father without saying hello. Alex looked around the spacious houseboat wondering where she was. The houseboat smelled of salt water, old carpets, and marijuana. His father was sitting in the living room. Malcolm Law ran the entire clandestine services of the Central Intelligence Agency and was a very important man, but the public would never read about him in the *New York Times*.

"Hello, Alex," his father said simply, as if they always met there.

"Where's Patty?" Alex said again, not smiling.

"She's gone. Said she had to go out. It's better that way."

"Don't tell me *she* is part of this?" Alex said. It dawned on him suddenly that she *could* have been—after all, it was *she* who'd struck up the conversation with *him* at the bar.

"No," his father said. "No, not at all."

"Just checking. With you guys you never know." Alex threw a small plastic bag of weed he'd recently bought onto the kitchen counter. He wanted to shock his father, if that was possible. The baggie rolled a little and stopped on the dark brown tiles with dirty white grout.

"Coals to Newcastle. She's got plenty," his father said.

"... Bay Area? Not your scene, is it? Not exactly the 'right people?' ... What is it you had to see me about?" Alex said. He couldn't say that he really even *liked* his father much any more; not for a long time now, in fact. It was true that at one point he'd loved his father very much; maybe when he was about ten. It had been a simple-minded child's love, before he'd actually gotten to know the man. Now he felt ambivalent, both about his father, and, in fact, his entire family. Even about his mother, who turned a blind-eye to most things; most things but her afternoon cocktail hour, which started at exactly 4:30 P.M. with a Mexican maid bringing a tray of drinks to the living room in Washington, D.C. The Cocktail Hour tended to stretch way past the Dinner Hour, so by eleven you could have told his mother you'd just put a fork through your hand and she would merely smile and say that "the gardener had been late again," that afternoon, or that she "hoped the rhododendrons wouldn't disappoint this year." He supposed that anyone who'd had to put up with his imperious father for so long would *need* to drink, and heavily, too.

"I wanted you to know what this was all about. Before you get started, I want to tell you myself," Malcolm said. "*I* was the one who chose you and Nickels for this assignment."

"You? Directly? I'm honored. But isn't it against the rules somehow? Nepotism, or something like that?"

"Yes."

Alex had joined the CIA only because it had been expected of him, by everyone, but he regretted and resented his decision now. His father had been an original member of Wild Bill Donovan's OSS and a *bona fide* War Hero, parachuting behind German lines into Poland where he'd conducted sabotage raids, and he'd been highly decorated for those efforts. Alex had let himself down by not seeing that it was a trap—trying to recreate his father's war-hero record in the Vietnam era, going to a dirty colonial war with no obvious good guys or bad guys. The truth was, he didn't *like* intelligence work and was in fact really not much good at it. People like his father were *very* good at it; but he wasn't. He didn't have the attitude a person needs for tearing people apart psychologically. That's what turning people was all about; lying and manipulation and oftentimes some kind of physical coercion in the end. It was a world where anything and everything was justified to get the wanted information—including state-sponsored murder. He had gone to Vietnam in the hope that it would "make him a man," but it hadn't. The obscenely wanton and arbitrary daily violence had only spoilt him for a "normal" life, blunting his humanity and knocking him off balance, in just about the same way it had Butch Nickels, his new partner. They had *that* in common, no question about it. Exposure to high-grade industrial-strength slaughter changes people in ways that are unexpected. Normal emotions are tethered and put away, sometimes for good. In Butch it had made him feel guilty on some level and he was now hostile to any form of authority, not unlike the girl from Dallas. Alex knew that in his own case it had simply made him hate himself, in general, so that at times he could be self-destructive in a very quiet and stubbornly methodical way.

"It's going to be dangerous in Los Angeles—you might even be killed." His father, taller than Alex, and now completely grey, looked at him in a way he never had before, as if he knew he was doing something very wrong to his son, but couldn't stop himself from doing it anyway.

"So why send *me*? I was very happy in London. ... The parties were great. The girls were cute and the work was light."

"Stop being a child, Alex. This isn't about you and me. Do you understand? I had to do it. I need someone I can trust *absolutely* and without question." Alex looked closely at him for the first time since he'd entered the houseboat. His father's expression was that of a tired, middle-aged man who was going over the hill fast. In fact, he *was* getting old, and Alex realized it there and then. His father didn't look like the confident Cold Warrior and Red Basher he been ever since Alex could remember. Something had happened to that supreme confidence. Something was terribly wrong.

"I want you to find someone called Sonny Delmonico because I trust you. You could hardly be ... Let's just say ... there are people around me that I can't trust any more. And the only way to get this done is by you personally going to Los Angeles and convincing everyone that you're in the heroin business. When you find him—this man Delmonico—I want you to let me know. I do *not* want you to go through normal channels via the DEA or anyone at Langley. Do you understand? You're to call me directly when you find him."

"That's it? That's why we're going to LA? To find this Delmonico?"

"Yes."

"Why can't you use the 'normal channels'?"

"I can't tell you—not right now. You just have to trust me. This is the most important assignment I could give you."

"We're not supposed to be operating inside the U.S.," Alex said. "Why are we doing this?" He walked to the counter, opened the bag of weed, and poured out the contents onto a spread-out San Francisco *Chronicle*. His father watched him start to pick out the stems and seeds. Alex took the package of Zig-Zags out of a fruit jar that Patty kept on the kitchen counter.

"Because ... well ... sometimes we *have* to." His father watched him roll a joint, stick it into his mouth, then lick it closed, holding it unlit between his lips, all the actions done very quickly.

"Are you doing a lot of that?" his father asked, seemingly surprised. The girl had been one thing, but seeing his son roll a joint in that expert way seemed to him altogether too jaded and sad.

"None of your fucking business, old boy. Your people dragged me out of London, where I was perfectly happy *not* pulling my weight. ... So please, don't complain about the end result. I've been carrying a shotgun all day today while being told I'm a faggot-and-a-half by a bunch of moron 'experts' and 'instructors.'"

"Alex, I don't know why we can't—"

"I'm your employ*ee*, that's why ... so let's keep it to business. Can you at least tell me who this Delmonico *is*?" Alex lit the joint and took a long pull, liking the sudden hot feeling of the hit in his lungs.

"He's a drug middle-man who works closely with the Sicilian Mafia; has for years. He comes to the U.S. on occasion to arrange shipments, sort out problems, that kind of thing. But he uses a host of false passports and we can't keep track of him all the time, day and night. He's in Spain right now. I'm fairly sure of that, at least."

"I still don't understand what this is *about*," Alex said, examining the joint. "Why can't you just approach him in Europe if you have to? It shouldn't be difficult. It seems crazy for me to go to LA just to find him." He spoke without exhaling.

"Because I need a cutout and you're going to be it. Between him and me. Someone I can trust." It was all starting to sound very strange, Alex thought. Certainly they had CIA officers, or their agents, in Europe who could contact the man, and in a matter of hours, too. Why go to such great lengths to hide the contact? And why him, of all people, a junior officer with a reputation for being the boss's son and someone with very little "street" experience. Hardly a good choice on the surface of it, he thought.

"I don't want anyone to know we've approached him. Inside the agency, I mean."

"So he's more than just a dope dealer?"

"Yes," Malcolm Law said. His father had on an expensive wool overcoat and his tie and tailored blue shirt were perfect. Alex stopped the "run" that was burning quickly up the side of the joint. He wet it down with saliva to make it stop. "I chose you, because I can trust my own son. I need people I can trust right now, Alex."

"What about Nickels? He seems an odd choice, to me. Not exactly a 'company man.' He's quite insane, in fact. He should be in treatment, really. He should be in a psychiatric hospital, not out on the streets," Alex said. "He's really crazy, by anybody's definition."

"He's there to protect you, I hope. He's not important; I can get someone else if you prefer. I just wanted you to have someone like him in LA. with you. You'll *need* his type of muscle there."

"A violent sociopath with a drug problem and a contempt for human life ... *and* a death wish. ... Excellent." Alex said.

"Oh yes. And he's dishonest, too—he's stolen from the Marine base in San Diego. Some kind of ordinance; hand grenades, I think it was," Malcolm said. "I received a report on it a while back."

"Yes. Well, he's a real Boy Scout-type. No ... I like him. He stays. So how do I go about finding this Delmonico? Los Angeles is a big city."

"It's important that *he* find *you*; because of the reputation you'll build up. If we're lucky he'll try to sell you drugs, or rather, probably somebody close to him will. That's what I'm counting on that he contacts *you* at some point."

"And then?"

"And then you call me at home. In fact, I want you to leave a message with your mother. Don't even try to tell me directly, just call and tell her that you want to go to Rome for the Christmas holidays. *Her* place. Just say that and I'll know you've found him."

"And that's it? That's all you can tell me?"

"For now, yes."

"Find this guy Delmonico and the Western Democracies will flourish and be free of Communists. And everyone will get to eat apple pie. And drive two cars ..." Alex said, holding his breath, his lungs full of weed smoke. "... No—I won't do it."

"What?"

"You're lying ... I can tell." Alex exhaled. "I've been trained—remember? Micro-expressions, body language and all that. And I don't feel like being made a fool of by my own father," Alex said. "In fact, I'm thinking of quitting entirely. The whole show. I want to be a hippie. They have more fun," he said.

"Don't be ridiculous."

"... Try me."

"All right! There's a scientist in the GDR who wants out. He's very, *very* important. He's developed a breakthrough in missile technology—in laser targeting, specifically. He's sent us a message. It's important I get him out, but I have to be very careful.

I'm afraid there's someone very high up in the Agency who might be on the KGB payroll. I haven't found him yet, but I know that, whoever it is, is privy to everything that comes into my office. I can't take the risk that the Russians or the East Germans discover the guy I'm trying to get out."

"How did you get this far with him? I mean if he's that important ... Why isn't he already dead? Or in some laboratory in Moscow chained to his desk?"

"I've known him for a long time. I met him right after the war, briefly. He wrote to me at my house, not the Agency. Well, his daughter did, actually—she passed the note. She's working at the UN in New York for the East German Legation. Alex, I *have* to get him out of Europe, and *soon*. And I want you to help me. You see now why it has to be someone I know isn't compromised?"

"Well, you never know ... *I* could be your mole," Alex said.

"No, it's not in your character to be a traitor. And this person is high up. *Very* high up."

"Your scientist ... he's really important? Not just some file clerk who's tired of the cold?"

"Yes, really. ... And if we fail to get him out safely the Russians will succeed in developing this technology first, because they're already ahead of us right *now*. The man's family will be. ..."

"Liquidated," Alex said. He was completely stoned, now.

"Most definitely. His daughter will be in danger, and her children, too. She just had another baby, in fact."

"Well, I like babies," Alex said. "Who doesn't?" He intuitively thought his father was lying to him but didn't care as much now that he was stoned.

"Good. Now learn the heroin business, Alex. The DEA believes we're tracking an international crime syndicate and will help us out, but I've told them to leave you completely alone in LA so you can operate freely without them knowing exactly who you come into contact with. You have to convince the underworld people in LA that you and Nickels are gangsters. My guess is that Nickels will go off the reservation and that's going to help. Don't try to stop him if he does. I'm *counting* on him turning into a bad actor—in their eyes, that'll help prove that you couldn't possibly be DEA agents."

"We *are* ... aren't we? Gangsters—of a sort?" Alex said. Stoned now, he saw a bit of Marlon Brando's Godfather in his own father—that is, if Marlon Brando had been a Calvinist who's father before him was part of the American Plutocracy, as the Laws most certainly were.

"No ... you're an *intelligence* officer," Malcolm said. "There *is* a difference."

"Really? I'll remember that the next time I see someone thrown out of a helicopter because they won't answer one of my questions. How is mother, by the way? She must be getting ready for the Chelsea Flower Show. No, that's in May ..."

"She's fine."

"Send her my love, then. Tell Mom her son is? ... What does she think, I wonder? I've forgotten what I told her ... A trade delegate at the State Department, right?"

"Alex, this may seem unimportant to you, but it *isn't*. This operation is of the utmost importance to the security of the United States. What you're going to be doing in LA, I mean. This man Delmonico and my scientist are connected."

"Oh ... I'm sure it is. After all, how often is it that I see my distinguished father in the flesh?" He was very high now, and the dope had broken down the door to his resentment. The truth was, he envied Patty her liberation from an inherited membership in a class that he was beginning to despise. He envied even Butch his working-class-hero ignorance about the world and his simple desires for sex and money. After all, didn't *everyone* want to be a combination of Rockefeller and Mick Jagger—two high points of Western Civilization?

"I've got to go," his father said. "This is going to be very hard. You *understand* that, don't you?" His father approached and gave him a hug. It was stiff and very strange and out of character, as he never did things like that. He'd never hugged him, even as a child. Then his father, looking very much the spy-master in his dark overcoat, left without another word. Alex watched him leave, walking down the dimly-lit quay looking like a fish out of water.

He realized, as he watched his father disappear, that at the present moment he didn't really care about anything but smoking weed and getting laid. And all the Great Big Things that his father represented—that, in fact, his whole family represented—that had sucked him into a life he hadn't really wanted, and that was completely unimportant to him now—were all absolutely meaningless to him. *Fuck the Russians and fuck the Americans, too,* he thought. Then he rolled another joint—a bigger and fatter one—and waited for Patty to come back. While he was working at rolling the joint it crossed his mind that he didn't want the East German woman that he'd never met, who might or might not be a bitch, to catch a bullet in the head because her father had an itch to leave his Red buddies behind. It was odd, he thought, that somehow her very existence had made him care. He *did* like babies, and idly wondered if he'd ever have one of his own. As he smoked the second joint he contemplated his future as would-be daddy and hippie living with Patty somewhere where they could be left alone. Haiti? ... Hawaii? ... Why not?

There were a lot of things that Malcolm had wanted to tell his son but hadn't been able to bring himself to, and he thought about them as he left. He had not told him the whole truth. Nor could he tell him that he was truly scared by what he'd discovered over the last months: A cabal of people who'd been roped off inside the Agency, protected for years now, along with a bunch of former Nazis who'd been brought over after the war to work for the U.S., were running large criminal operations independent of the Agency. That the group headed by the former Nazi general Reinhard Gehlen—until his recent death, head of West German intelligence—in the post-war years had managed to burrow into national intelligence agencies all over the globe: American, French, British, German, and Russian among them. Gehlen's group now seemed to be acting in a supra-national way, running a dark, covert empire, while hiding in—and subverting—every major Western intelligence service. He no longer knew where the CIA ended and the Gehlen Network, as he called it in his own mind, began. The man in the GDR *did* know, and was trying to get to Malcolm to warn him and help him destroy the network.

The man's hand-written note had been very short and very chilling to the old Cold Warrior:

> *Dear Malcolm Law,*
>
> *I am Captain Christophe Neizert. You probably remember interviewing me for project Paperclip at Dachau in December of 1946. My rank in the Waffen SS was that of Captain; my SS number was 45345. I was to be hung for war crimes committed at the Peenemunde V2 laboratory and the nearby Dora camp.*
>
> *I am presently working in the GDR in Berlin and my daughter works for East Germany at the UN in New York. It was she I used to get this message to you.*
>
> *That day at Dachau I warned you that things were not what they seemed. There is a group that has grown out of German Army Intelligence run by Richart Gehlen and hired by the West during Operation Paperclip. This organization now has intelligence assets across the globe, and on both sides of the Iron Curtain. They are very capable, and in the process of becoming a force that will run entire countries—including your own from within, and for their own purposes. I have information about them that I want to share with you in exchange for getting me, as well as my daughter and her family, into the US. My daughter knows how to contact me, but she knows nothing about Gehlen and his network, as I've kept it all from her for her own safety.*
>
> *Hauptmann Neizert*

Malcolm had reached his car. He opened the door and sat for a moment without starting the engine. He knew exactly what Operation Paperclip was, as he'd worked vetting Nazi scientists as a young intelligence officer for the OSS, deciding who—like Von Braun—would be brought to America to work for the Defense Department, which was gearing up for the then-new "Cold War." He remembered Hauptmann Neizert, too. He finally turned on the engine to his rental car. The headlights automatically flashed on. A group of young people were caught in the beams that crossed in front of him. And it was just at that moment, seeing them suddenly surprised that way in their callow youth, that his own youth, which had been brought up short by the war, all came rushing back to him.

"Night and Fog," he said out loud. They were the first words he'd learned in Polish. *Night and Fog.* And he saw again in his mind's-eye what he'd seen that night so long ago: a sudden signal, three flashes of light below their plane. Then he heard the jump master's voice suddenly yelling "Go!" And with that last word, he'd jumped into the Eastern Front, behind German lines, and everything changed for him; he was never young again.

4

■ SAN FRANCISCO FEDERAL BUILDING

Butch Nickels—newly-minted CIA officer—was drinking a Pepsi out of a paper cup. It was three-thirty in the afternoon. He and his partner, Alex Law, had just completed a grueling six-week "undercover" course taught by senior DEA officers with years of street experience, having served in various precursors to the DEA. Their current assignment, according to what little DEA had been told by the Defense Department, was to investigate a major narcotics ring "based abroad," but operating in the U.S. And that's *all* the DEA had been told. Why the Defense Department would be involved in DEA work was not explained to them. Nor had the DEA been told that the two young trainees were in fact CIA officers, or that the CIA was running the operation in clear violation of the law—embodied in the CIA's founding charter, in fact, which prohibited it from any and all domestic activities. A law the CIA had willfully and sometimes blatantly ignored since the moment it was founded.

Butch's eyes were badly bloodshot from smoking weed at breakfast. He hadn't shaved in several days. It looked like he hadn't slept much lately, either. A girl he'd slept with two nights before had said that he smelled like "a donkey in a barn." He was wearing a yellow Players' Club windbreaker with an ink stain on one of the pockets. People said he looked like Tom Jones's ugly big brother. He was not in his right mind, not even close, and had been suffering from PTSD for several years after enduring two combat tours with the First Marine Division in Vietnam. His symptoms were steadily getting worse in fact, but no one knew he was in full psychological meltdown. It didn't help that he was experimenting with LSD, either, albeit in "manageable" doses, as well as snorting coke and taking pretty much any other party-drug handed to him in any one of the multiple bars he'd been frequenting in North Beach after the long days of training. He was pretty much a bottle of nitro that was being shaken violently by his work as a CIA officer in the Agency's covert directorate. Perhaps it was the idea that he was going back out into the world, into a kill-or-be-killed situation, yet one more time, which made him sweat in the wee hours. He did large amounts of drugs in the hope that it would stop the marvelously good feeling he got when he wrapped his hands around any kind of weapon—a knife, a pistol, or just a simple iron bar. There

23

was, inside of him, a raging battle between the forces of homicide and suicide. No one could have said on any given day which one would finally win.

Butch Nickels had been recruited by the Central Intelligence Agency at the age of twenty-four on the strength of his service record in the Marine Corps, which they considered to be sterling. They were also impressed by the initiative and bravery he'd shown during the Tet Offensive in the battle for Saigon. At one point in downtown Saigon, on a side street quite near the US Embassy, it had gotten down to Butch and just six other Marines—including two Korean Marines who were both killed—standing between the Embassy and two platoons of North Vietnamese regulars. The guy who'd ended up recruiting Butch had watched the firefight from the upper floor of the Embassy, and liked what he saw.

Butch had accepted the CIA's offer because he'd heard that their supply of "ring-tailed motherfuckers," as his contact with the Agency called them, was running short. It was either go with the CIA or go back to Pittsburgh and work in the steel mills there, like his father and grandfather had before him. He knew he could never fit back into that kind of civilian life after Vietnam. It just wasn't going to happen. He would rather have killed himself than return to the mundane world of mindless soul and body crushing labor that was the world of the steel mill.

Butch was resting one of his jungle boots—he was already wearing the undercover garb he'd use for the next six months in Los Angeles—on the front bumper of a very clean 1979 black Mustang, "fully loaded" with built-in eight-track tape recorder plus several tapes, including Santana's "Soul Sacrifice" and his personal favorite, Ike and Tina Turner's "Proud Mary" thrown helter-skelter into a box on the floorboards. Butch had turned thirty years old just three days before. The Mustang's former owner, a guy from Cleveland named Johnny Southgate, was now pulling twenty-five to life in Leavenworth for possession of a warehouse full of Bolivian marching powder and would no longer need his hot car, currently owned by the US government.

They were standing in a garage in San Francisco used exclusively by federal cops of all kinds: FBI, DEA, ATF, and some Defense Department spooks, too, who were monitoring Left-wing organizations in the Bay Area, despite all the laws prohibiting that kind of activity by persons of their ilk. The packages of heroin were a light green color. Some of them had dried blood-splatter on them and you could easily see it—the blood stains dull red on the plastic.

The heroin had come into the US via Caracas, crossing the US-Mexican border at Nogales, and had then been brought up to southern California in a horse trailer by two attractive, well-to-do couples. The bundles were tight—professionally packed—and hadn't been opened since DEA agents had lifted a corpse off of a deal that had gone bad down in San Bernardino, right by the freeway in a Ford dealership showroom. Four men had died of gunshot wounds: a black car salesman—a very tall guy who'd played professional basketball in Europe after college; the owner of the dealership, one Chip Rogers, normally seen all over southern California on his TV commercials; a Sheriff's Deputy, who was reported to have been a customer of the dealership; and a very young white recent ex-con, who the cops said had been responsible for the deaths inside the showroom, and who was also suspected of being a major heroin dealer by the same San Bernardino police authorities. The investigation was still on-going.

The packages of junk had little stickers on them: smiley faces, no less, which little kids in Italy slapped on their school books. No one knew what that marking meant *exactly*. Robin Stuckie, one of their DEA instructors, told them they were probably lab marks. "If there happened to be a fuck-up with a particular batch in the lab, they could then trace the shipment back to the place where it had been produced. The stickers were the lab's brand, like logos." Robin had said, trying to stack the packages of junk so they would all fit into the Mustang's trunk.

"Did you say there was no one left alive that had anything to do with the deal?" Butch had asked. He looked like a cop himself, and had fit in very well during their training with the DEA guys. There had been a cop-type chemistry between Butch and their DEA instructors. It was something Alex hadn't been able to generate because he just wasn't physically a cop-type at all. Their instructors were not Alex's social class, either, no matter how hard he tried to play-off his elite background, and the cops all sensed it. The DEA guys smelled the rich-guy on Alex like dogs smell other dogs' assholes. Butch, on the other hand, looked like a cop, talked like a cop, and fit right in. He'd liked the DEA guys and they'd liked him. Butch was very *simpatico*, their instructors thought. Alex, on the other hand, they thought was probably a faggot, but in any case, definitely a pencil-neck and hence worthless.

"Nobody. Just four dead shot-up motherfuckers on the dealership floor and in the parking lot. Place was quiet by the time we walked in. You could hear the Coke machine go on and off. The dope was stacked up neat on the showroom floor. The black guy shot the John Doe—some kid. Got off a good fucking shot, a real three-pointer with a .22 pussy gun, but it did the trick. You know how a .22 bullet bounces around inside somebody's head or body." The DEA guy made a zigzagging pattern with his index finger circling his slight paunch.

"What happened? Why didn't they have any security?" Alex asked. The DEA guy looked at him like he was asking him why men like blow-jobs from girls with heart-shaped asses, big tits, and long legs.

"Who the fuck knows? It's the dope business ... people die. Shit happens. Bad guys do bad things. Someone looked like he was going to do something ... maybe he farted too loud." He shrugged his shoulders. "Then ... *bang!*" Alex didn't think the story added up, but didn't say anything else. These cops were good at breaking down doors, but not too good at comprehending their often morally ambiguous role in the "War On Drugs." Alex understood, in fact, they were *all* only cogs in a monstrous and *very* profitable machine. "The John Doe tried to rip them off, is what *I* guess," one of their instructors, a black guy, said. The black guy had been quiet, just watching the kilos being stacked in the trunk. He was a weight lifter and had a neck that was too short for the rest of his body, like he'd been hit on the head with a sledgehammer in a cartoon, and it had collapsed his neck down a couple of inches. Alex referred to him as "no-neck" behind his back. He weighed three-hundred pounds at least, all of it solid muscle.

"Bad *juju*," Butch said, lifting his jungle boot off the fender. "Blood all over the shit—damn!" Then the white guy, Robin Stuckie, finished loading up the last of the kilos and pushed the trunk lid down with the flat of his palms, making sure it locked. He looked wistful, and already seemed to regret losing control of the dope. Robin had them sign for ten kilos of heroin that had been produced by some of the best mafia chemists in the world, in a laboratory hidden in the middle of a well known Italian industrialist's 500-acre deluxe estate near Palermo, Sicily, where the island's most important pols met in secret. The DEA had traced the heroin all the way back to Italy using chemistry markers, which differentiated it from, say, Hong Kong smack, or Mexican smack, which smelled like wet donkey-shit mixed with burning tires when you smoked it.

"What happens, like, if we're a kilo short when we get to LA?" Butch said, joking. Butch signed the form with a stubby pen, then passed it on to Alex, who also signed it.

"... Then your ass is *mine*, boy," Robin said. The crop-haired 40-year-old, sporting the classic law-enforcement buzz-cut, took the clipboard back. His black partner, Lee Van Steeps, who'd served in Vietnam in the 101st Airborne before joining the DEA, suddenly smiled big. He was a violent man, and Butch felt it when they looked at each other.

"*You* sign for it because *we* had to sign for it; those are the rules. You might lose it before you get to LA. Then management might just look at us funny," Steeps said.

"How would you lose it?" Butch said. "It's locked in the fucking trunk."

"Well, there's one way," Robin said. Then he gave them a cop "got-you" smile.

"The same way the last guys lost it, dumb-ass," Steeps said. Both cops laughed in a way that's reserved for special jokes that have to do with dying on the job and the mayhem that usually goes with it.

Alex decided that he didn't care what was in the trunk, or where they were going, or much about anything, except maybe playing the hell out of this guy called Bruce Tucker, which was his cover name for the operation. Because he was tired as shit of being who he really was. He was really tired of it all; especially their two instructors in all-things-California-underworld. *Fuck you*, he thought, and got into the car.

They drove out of the garage and took off for LA an hour later, complete with their DEA-issued weapons and plenty of ammunition—something Butch had insisted on—plus a few extras in the car: two automatic shotguns and a "Carl Gustav" Swedish M/45 sub-machine gun (because of its proven accuracy), some hand grenades, an M16 with a rocket launcher—acquired at Camp Pendleton by Butch—and an extra array of pistols, including a .44 Magnum which Butch had bought with his own money and called the Eastwood. They also had on board a DEA-produced boiler-plate intelligence report with critical details about their first deal, which was supposed to go down three days after they arrived in LA. The report included many personal details on the players they would be dealing with. The deal had been set up by a DEA informant: they were to sell five kilos of heroin, with the price pre-arranged. They pulled out onto Polk Street Polk from the bowels of the parking garage and into a stone-cold winter day. The blue sky clean, as if all the morning's clouds had been squeegeed off.

"I'll take the car," Butch said. He pulled over to the curb.

"I thought we were supposed to go to LA?" Alex said, dumbfounded. "You know ... they're called 'orders.'"

"I want to get laid," Butch said matter-of-factly. "Before we die, too ... because that's what's probably going to happen in LA. You and me are going to die. It's that simple. We don't have any idea what we're doing, you know that! And management isn't telling us *shit* about *why* we're doing this. So I smell a rat. A really big one. They're just building our cover for something else. We're like the pig the Indians in the Amazon put in the pit to catch the panther. The pig always dies," Butch said, turning toward him. He revved the Mustang's engine just for the hell of it. "I'm not in a hurry to die just yet, really—are *you?*"

"No," Alex said. He was wearing a fringed "Wild Bill Hickok" coat that was grating on him, but it was all part of the "look" that they were supposed to have, according to the DEA intelligence officer, a woman who Alex had his eye on, as he was definitely not a homosexual, despite the rumors that the DEA morons had started about him.

"I'll pick you up in the morning, okay? *Fuck them*," Butch said. Alex thought about the sudden change of plans and decided he didn't care, really. What difference did it make if they went today or tomorrow? The fiction of the rules they normally operated under seemed to disappear all of a sudden. He realized that, indeed, they were on their own now, like kids without their parents' supervision, let loose on the world for the first time.

"... Okay, I'll go out to Gate Six, then," Alex said. "I suppose."

"Okay," Butch said. "What's her number? I'll call you in the morning."

"Yeah. ... Where are you staying tonight, in case? ..."

"Don't know yet," Butch said. He was intent on taking some drugs and wanted to be alone after he busted a nut. Alex wrote down Patty's number on a white paper bag they'd used to carry doughnuts in that morning. He dumped white confectioner's sugar all over the Mustang's clean black upholstery as he wrote the number. By the time they finally returned the Mustang six-months later, the car's interior was full of beach sand, blood, traces of heroin, and pubic hair from the many surfer girls brought to a glass-scratching climax in the car's back seat by Butch. It was a six-month period that neither one would ever forget, and that would forge a life-long friendship that most people who met them would never understand.

"Nice," Butch said. "We should try to keep this *clean*." Alex handed him Patty's number.

"In the morning, then." Alex climbed out of the car. "Are you *on* something?" Alex asked, leaning in through the open passenger door. They were still on Polk Street. Alex had parked a rental car that he'd been using in a lot on Van Ness, and had intended to turn it in that afternoon. "You can tell me. ... If you want to forget all this ... We can tell them ..."

"Fuck no, I don't want to forget all this! Why should I? I need the job, man."

"You think it's bad luck that somebody's already died? You know ... behind that shit?" Alex said, thinking that maybe the blood-stained heroin bundles were the problem. Butch shrugged his shoulders and gave him a sideways glance. Alex thought it was rather a cold look to give a new partner you were going to be working with under only God-knew-what type of conditions. Life and death situations everyday, probably, as they'd constantly been reminded by the DEA. They were to have no backup support at all and would be working completely on their own for the entire operation.

"What the fuck *difference* does it make. Man, we're FUCKED!" Butch practically shouted. Then he pulled away from the curb, burning rubber, and turned into traffic, heading for an Oriental massage parlor he'd seen on Jones Street the day before. It was called Bangkok Delight and had a little orange neon sign that blinked on and off 24 hours a day, reminding you that you could have sex any time *of* the day or night with an eighteen-year-old Asian girl, usually called Sally or Kathy. The place had free parking—that's why he'd chosen it, as there were about five places on Jones Street you

28

could get laid if the Bangkok Delight didn't suit your needs. *If you're going to pay to bust a nut why pay for parking, too,* he'd wryly thought. He pushed in the tape of Ike and Tina Turner's "Proud Mary" and lit a joint from a stash he'd lifted from the DEA's evidence locker—good shit, too.

*   *   *

Butch chugged the half-pint of Southern Comfort he'd bought around the corner from the massage parlor, standing in the doorway of a Vietnamese grocery. He made small talk with the clerk, enjoying his beverage while still half-in the store. The clerk noticed that Butch had thrown the bottle's screw-off top on the floor like he was back in Vietnam in the middle of jungle, and in a way, he was. The whole "Tenderloin" neighborhood was full of Vietnamese, and Butch felt comfortable there. It was a lot like Vietnam, in fact, only better, he thought, looking out onto the street with its pedestrians, whores, Asian gangbangers, and everyone in between. Then he walked back across Jones Street and made sure he'd locked the new Mustang, sitting there sticking out like a sore thumb in the massage parlor's four-car parking lot. Then he went downstairs and was buzzed through the first of three doors that led to the Bangkok Delight, with its pink-painted walls and host of bad smells from the mixture of sex, Oriental food, and dirty carpets.

The massage parlor had a guard that the customers couldn't see, stationed in an anteroom and armed with a sawed-off shotgun. The man could see every client as he walked in via a one-way mirror. This was something Butch didn't know for sure, but suspected very highly because of his experiences in the past. Massage parlors and whore houses were pretty much the same all over the world—only the prices were different, really.

Butch was still wearing the jeans and t-shirt he'd had on when they'd loaded up the Mustang, except that now he'd also put on a funky, stained Army jacket and was wearing his .38 back-up weapon in an ankle holster on his right ankle. The guy behind the one-way mirror thought Butch looked mean, and duly noted him as a potential problem, having watched him walk from his very desirable car, which he'd first seen pull into their parking lot on a black and white monitor attached to a video camera that was focused solely *on* the parking lot. The TV monitor sat on an otherwise empty desk, and the guy with the shotgun was sitting on it, too. Mr. Shotgun was already making a call about the Mustang to a friend he knew who boosted muscle cars for a living, taking them to Stockton and selling them to a Mexican gang there who then took the cars down to Mexico and sold them to rich kids and dope people.

An older Vietnamese woman peeked out from behind the last door that separated the street from the parlor. She was about forty-years-old. Butch smelled cooking oil and fish; it was a special aroma that he associated with his years in Vietnam, and it was oddly comforting. The truth was, he missed the war. What he really wanted was to go back to war, *any* war; it didn't really matter to him where it was or what it was "about." He just missed the life and death action; everything else since Vietnam had seemed bland and uninteresting and void of life to him.

"You want massage?" The woman looked at him, a veteran herself, and just as hard as he was.

"I'm not here for the Sunday Brunch," Butch said, after being buzzed through the last door into the inner sex sanctum. "So I guess I want to see Sally."

"Okay. Sixty-dolla for one hour. Good massage; nice girl. Real good ... Thai massage. Deep tissue," she said, not smiling, but judging him by her own standards as she spoke.

"As long as I come," Butch said. "I'm not going to be here an hour. It never takes me that long." Butch had learned to bargain in Vietnam. It always got his goat to see Alex never bargain with *anyone*. It annoyed him that Alex would leave big-ass tips at restaurants. Alex always stayed at the best hotels, and had plenty of money for weekend trips to cool, rich-guy hangouts with friends who had icy East Coast rich-guy-sounding names. Butch realized partway through their DEA-training that Alex had a private income of some kind. Butch's father, a steal worker, who had always lived paycheck to paycheck, used to try to bargain even at Sears, which was impossible, of course, but he'd try it anyway, over a Craftsman wrench, insisting that he'd seen the item on sale in the newspaper, which was usually a lie. It was all right to lie to Sears, his father would tell him: "Because they lie to us *every fucking day*." Then his father would ask to see the manager if he didn't get the knocked-down price he was after. "Fucking Sears is always trying to fuck me! Why should it be a one-way street?" his father would say in the car on the way home, usually having had to pay full price in the end, and angry as hell about it.

"Okay, fifty-dollar ... 45 minute," the woman said.

"Okay, okay—How long can it take to bust a nut?" Butch said. The older woman, with a good rack on her, Butch noticed, was wearing a shapeless, cheap-looking polyester sarong with no bra.

"I got nice girl for you," she insisted. She turned around and he followed her into the smells-like-fish-head-soup hallway. And it all suddenly got very close and thin-feeling from the liquor and the weed. He peeked into one of the rooms and saw a girl giving a guy a blow job. The guy's white underwear was pulled down to his knees. His fat knees were facing the ceiling. The girl looked up at Butch, surprised.

"*No!* Not there!" the madam said. She pulled him out of the room by his coat. He was in the mood to fuck with people, and he broke out in a laugh like a high-school boy; even the woman smiled, but it was a pissed-off smile.

"Was that Sally?" Butch asked, "Or Cindy?" He followed her down the narrow hallway past several curtained-off little cubby-hole fuck rooms. The madam was annoyed now, but not mad enough to throw him out, *yet*. He was sure that if you got her really mad you'd know it. And then some gook would be coming down the hall with a flame thrower.

"You take shower?" she said, stopping in front of a blue-porcelain nightmare bathroom with a few ragged-ass yellow towels that looked stiff and stained.

"Why not?" Butch said. "Sounds good. I'll soap it up." The madam opened the door for him and waited for her money. He got out the cash and counted out two twenties and two fives. He tried to hold a five back, over-counting the way he'd learned to do in Saigon from the street hustlers; not putting the second five down, hoping she'd take the other bills and not count them. But she caught him, and a distinct dislike for him crossed over her wide face. It was like what a barracuda does when it sees something it wants to eat. They looked at each other like two people do when they pretend to like each other, and he gave her the last five and winked. She took it and he walked into the bathroom and started to take off his jungle boots. He undid the ankle holster and looked for a place to stash his weapon. *Fuck it,* he thought, and he put it where he could see it, and, more importantly, get to it. Since leaving Vietnam, and even after he'd joined the Central Intelligence Agency, in or out of the U.S., he usually carried a weapon and felt strange and very vulnerable without one. He didn't like that feeling, so he was never far from one if he could manage it. "Barroom or bedroom, it's coming with me," he told one girl he'd meet at the Fillmore Auditorium when he went to see Van Morrison, whose music he really loved. He'd fucked the girl's brains out with the pistol lying right next to them on the bed.

He was getting blown in the shower by a girl who looked Korean and was tiny and uninterested in his orgasm when he thought he heard the sound of a muscle-car engine starting up. He'd grown up in a neighborhood of gear-heads and car buffs and he knew the sound of a eight-cylinder engine when he heard one. If they hadn't been fucking in the bathroom he would have missed it, but the bathroom had a tiny window that looked right out onto the parking lot. He jumped out of the shower and boosted his naked-ass up into the high little window in time to see the Mustang being stolen by a short Oriental kid who was backing it up at full speed. They stared at each other for an instant—the kid couldn't miss Butch's yelling and of course the fact that he'd punched out the tiny window with his fist. The kid stomped on it and went fish-tailing out into traffic, backwards. Butch was wet, and he still had a hard-on, so it was difficult to get up far enough to see well, and the window was filthier than shit to boot. He lost the car's image and dropped back down to the dirty wet rug, his right fist bleeding pretty badly from punching-out the thick old glass.

He dropped down prone onto the floor and grabbed the hammerless .38 he'd placed in the fold of his jeans. The Korean girl was still in the shower and when she saw the gun she screamed, loud. He didn't think she had that kind of scream in her. By the time he was up off the floor and into the hallway it sounded like she'd been stabbed in the guts and then branded with a hot iron while being raped by the Devil, judging by the sounds she was making. He saw curtains moving to his right and a young girl poked her head out and he almost ran into her as he started down the hall, his mind going full tilt. *Jones Street to the freeway; he has to go down Jones street ... there's a light at every fucking corner.*

He got to the door at the bottom of the narrow hallway that led out into the anteroom; he saw the madam quickly slip out of what looked like a laundry room. She swung a steam iron at his head as hard as she could, the flat part towards him with the steam coming off the iron's steel face. He ducked and elbowed her in the jaw, hard, and she went down. He hit the door and stepped out into the anteroom. A curtain opened across the red-tinted room in front him and he saw the kid with the shotgun who'd watched him come in. The kid thought just seeing the shotgun would be enough to stop him because it always *had* worked for him in the past. Butch fired immediately, charging. The bullet hit the kid in the right chest area and he collapsed. Butch ran right up on him, grabbing him as he fell, and fired point-blank into the kid's left eye, sticking the barrel of the gun deep into the eye socket; his gun shots were loudly barking over the screaming in the hallway behind him as the kid's body went limp in his arms with his brains now splattered all over the wall.

Then Butch was gone, out the main door, going up the littered concrete steps to the sidewalk. He didn't feel the cold or the pain in his feet when he stepped on a small shard of glass from a broken bottle of Muscatel that cut two of his toes to the bone. He turned down Jones Street running like he was back at college on the football field and he saw the Mustang at the light, two blocks down Jones Street, at five in the afternoon, was a choke point of double-parked delivery trucks, pedestrians, whores, and taxi cabs picking up fares. It was a tangled mess that he'd been counting on to slow the Mustang down on its approach to the freeway and a clean getaway for the thief.

Butch was running so fast downhill that he felt weightless, and remembered as a kid loving the feeling of running fast down steep hills, and how other kids would be afraid of losing control. He'd *wanted* to lose control—that had been the fucking point—to *get some air*. He hit the intersection of Jones and Geary and blew by a limo then a Porsche with a gay thin-faced accountant looking with stunned awe at Butch's johnson swinging in the breeze

A delivery truck, double-parked, was just below Gary on Jones, and was fucking everything up on the entire street. He saw the Mustang try to pull around the delivery truck, but a taxi cut him off. He saw the Mustang's break lights go off as the driver, thinking he had all the time in the world, now, waited for a clearing so he could pull around the truck. Butch felt his feet leave the concrete of the sidewalk. He saw faces and people jumping out of his way. He hit a mailman's pushcart and knocked it over—his knee bashing it hard, forcing him to land half-whirlybird, half-man, just managing to keep his forward momentum and not fall down.

When he hit the intersection at Jones and Geary he thought that he might be hit by a car, and almost was, but he managed to jump on the hood of a Volvo driven by a black lady who saw him butt-naked clear the car's hood with one giant stride, not even denting it. The light had gone his way and he was booking it again, hitting the curb at almost full-white-man speed. He could start to hear his breathing then, deep and ugly from smoking too much weed now for years. His lungs seemed to him to be full of phlegm and filling up fast. What people on the street saw was a big, naked white guy with wet, black, thinning hair, holding a pistol at his side and running like he was completely out of his mind, arms pumping like the Devil himself was trying to crawl up his asshole, the wet hair shapeless, giving him a maniacal vibe. They saw the little pistol—some of them, anyway—and the ones that did turned and went in the other direction, both young and old; they didn't have to be told that this man was a full plate of crazy.

A motorcycle cop getting on his bike on Geary Street after coffee at David's Deli saw Butch break through the intersection and run down Jones. The cop ran to his bike and jumped on. He'd missed the gun, but had seen that the man was naked. He bounced onto the Harley's black, fat seat and kicked the motor over, hitting his radio to report a 5150 at Jones and Geary. "Naked white man ... a 5150 ..." he said again, the radio call-sign for an insane person. Then the cop barreled down Geary on his Harley, swaying around traffic, his shoulder dipping as he brought the hog into a full ass-hauling out-of-my-way jackboot-black-leather cop mode.

What the young Vietnamese guy driving the stolen Mustang saw first, in his rear view mirror, just an instant before he died, was Butch catching up to him at the delivery truck, thanks to one more yellow cab driven by an angry old black man with a brown porkpie hat that took pride and satisfaction in cutting off young Oriental fucks in fancy fucking cars. What the kid saw exactly was a naked man in mid-air going too fast to stop, raising his gun hand and firing the first bullet, blasting out the Mustang's rear window; then a bullet hit the side-post of the car, and he heard that chunk-metal sound of the hollow body-post being punctured. His mind finally registered fear, and he saw Butch continue to fire as he ran past him. The third bullet hit the kid an inch up from his left ear and blew off a good junk of his skull, but it didn't kill him right then and there. He actually got to feel it; part of his skull being blown off. The Mustang did stop now, in mid-street, as the driver, desperate to live, crawled toward the passenger-side door, not realizing how badly he'd been hurt as yet; then he saw the car seat filling with arterial blood-splash, and he knew. Butch hit the delivery man in an attempt to slow down; it worked, too, up to a point. But he had road-burns for weeks afterwards, on his ass, and on his side as well, from skidding and rolling on the concrete and gravel and general bullshit that always exists on Jones Street sidewalks because they never, ever, wash them. There was always a lot of sand and pigeon and human shit from the drunks. Ugly stuff they had to pick out of his skin at San Francisco General, later, as all kinds of cops got involved in "the incident." The Vietnamese kid bled out on Jones Street, waiting for an ambulance that was stuck in the horrible traffic. No one opened the trunk, and the Mustang was delivered, intact, to Butch at the hospital. The operation had big-time coverage in Washington. So big, it seemed, that Butch could shoot and kill two upstanding citizens and he hadn't even gotten a ticket for running naked in public. But if you were the Central Intelligence Agency and you could give LSD to prisoners in several states and run MK Ultra in direct violation of the CIA charter and import Nazi war criminals to run the US space program, you could certainly cover up some silly shit on the streets of San Francisco. And that's exactly what they did. They even had the Mustang's back window replaced before he and Alex left for LA the next morning—ass-burns or no ass-burns, they were heading South!

5

■ MOTEL "CAPRI" MALIBU CALIFORNIA

The sixty-two-room motel had been built in the mid-fifties and sat just back off Highway One at Malibu with motel-style courtyard parking. It was a two-story stucco building, painted sea-blue, with white trim. It sported a classic neon sign facing the highway; a sign that depicted a girl in a one-piece swimsuit diving into the world of perpetual fun that each and every guest would find at the Capri.

The motel had been owned by a Texas oilman and major shareholder in the Zapata Corporation, an oil service company famously used as a front for the Central Intelligence Agency. The man, J.H. Preston, had been implicated in a shadowy network of people that had facilitated the movements of Lee Harvey Oswald around Dallas just prior to the assassination of President Kennedy. Preston had been an old school chum of Allen Dulles at Princeton, and Dulles had been a sworn enemy of Joe Kennedy. Preston was a multi-millionaire and extreme right-wing fundraiser who had worked tirelessly to elect Ronny Reagan President of the United States despite the rumors in Hollywood about Reagan and his "special" friends. Preston had transferred the deed of the motel—for the sake of Operation Cerberus and as a personal favor to Malcolm Law—to someone called Bruce Tucker.

The transaction's trail, if you bothered to follow it, dead-ended in a white-shoe law firm in downtown Los Angeles with three hundred smart lawyers and an ice cold receptionist. It was a law firm with close ties to the Shah of Iran and the Standard Oil Company. The law firm had taken care of the Shah's personal business, and huge personal fortune, since he'd been booted out of Iran and gone to ground in Cuernavaca, Mexico. Five-hundred-dollar-an-hour lawyers wearing gold cufflinks and silk ties had set up something called the "High Street Corporation," which owned the Capri Motel. And, since August, High Street was controlled by the same Bruce Tucker, a resident of Los Angeles; documents on file confirmed. The purchase of the motel had required no loan; it had been an all-cash deal. Malcolm Law had accomplished the whole thing with a phone call to Preston, who was now retired and living with a twenty-year-old stripper in Dallas.

Butch unrolled his works, which had been wrapped in one of his T-shirts, and

35

looked at the plastic syringe, spoon, and various hunks of cotton. He'd never shot cocaine before, but he'd heard Alex's girlfriend from Sausalito extolling the pleasures of shooting rather than snorting it at Smiley's bar before they'd left San Francisco, and her spiel had piqued his interest in trying it. He knew he didn't want to go to battle sober, as he'd learnt long before that when sober he wasn't as good as he was stoned. He also knew that coke had a special quality that allowed him to think calmly and react fast—albeit brutally. He imagined that shooting the drug would only enhance those powers. They would be going to breakfast soon and he decided that he would shoot some right now before he and Alex left. He crossed the room and picked up the phone and dialed Alex's room number. Alex was staying in one of the bottom rooms, near the manager's office. There were in fact two managers who had a connection to one of Langley's secret bases that were maintained in various cities around the country. Both men had been told to treat the two like guests and to never interfere with them under any circumstances and to answer the phone and tell any other would-be guests—should anyone want to actually stay at the Capri Motel—that the hotel was booked for a large wedding. For appearance sake, a young Mexican maid had been hired to push a cart from room to room and clean every day.

"It's me," Butch said, when Alex picked up.

"You about ready?" Alex said. "Did you shower, man? ... Because damn, man, you stink."

"I need you to come up here," Butch said.

"Why? ... Can't you tie your shoes this morning?"

"Very funny. I want to shoot some coke and I've never done it before. If I OD, I want somebody here with me," Butch said matter-of-factly.

"Say *what!*"

"I *said* I want to shoot some drugs *intravenously* and I want *you* to be up here when I do it."

"...You're joking?"

"Fuck no, I'm not joking. Why would I joke?"

"We're going to be going into the ghetto and selling drugs and be dealing with, I'm sure, dangerous types of motherfuckers. Maybe you should reconsider that impulse?" Alex said, stunned.

"Okay—fuck it; I'll do it without you. Fuck you." Butch put the receiver down. "Got to do everything by myself, even jacking off last night. Shit." He slid off the bed and opened the works he'd bought at Gate Six from a guy who dealt out of a boat three down from Patty's place. He'd bought an ounce of coke at the same time, trading the guy a hand grenade he'd stolen from Camp Pendleton for the drugs. The guy was an old-school dealer and very relaxed about the transaction, as he'd already decided right away that Butch was no cop.

"Pharmaceutical grade is what I have right now. I've got a doctor at Marin General that steals it for me," the guy had told him. The dealer looked like James Dean, if he'd made it to fifty. The guy was called Jesus (because he could send you to heaven)—his name around Gate Six—and he'd been dealing drugs in the Bay Area since the Sixties. He was as lean as a whippet, with long, prematurely grey hair, and both of his pierced ears sported diamond earrings that caught the light. He had a very clean houseboat that had a view of the 101 Freeway and the Bay. "Jesus" was a meticulous man—anybody could tell that from his place.

"The secret to shooting drugs is keeping your works clean," Jesus had told him, after Butch had admitted that he was a novice at geezing dope. He sold him a pharmaceutical syringe, and gave him a spoon, a Bic lighter, and some cotton, showing him how he had to use the cotton to filter anything and everything that he drew up into the syringe before he stuck it in his arm. "Otherwise you get impurities and God knows what else and it could be harmful." Jesus told him not to do more than "two match-head-sized hits" of coke under any circumstances.

"You do *three* and you could blow a valve. Your blood pressure just gets too high," Jesus said. "Sex on coke is great, but forget coming—you won't be able to."

"No shit!" Butch had been momentarily taken aback by *that* revelation.

"No, man; you'll need two, or even three girls, if you're going to do some screwing; it's not fair to the girl to just have *one* there; you'll wear her out like a cat in a dog fight." Then Jesus grinned. It was like the devil had a pencil-thin, mischievous little brother who had escaped from Hell and was now in the drug business at Gate Six giving friendly advice to would-be dope fiends.

"Okay," Butch said. "I've got it. ... Two match heads ... Two girls."

"You know, I mean the *size* of a match head." Jesus said, trying to be exact. Then smiled again, that same ironic and devilish smile. He then went out to some secret place in the vicinity of his crib, got the dope, and came back in.

"What's the grenade for?" Butch asked, handing it over. He'd kept it in the pocket of his windbreaker during their conversation.

"For kicks," the guy said. "And you just never know. I got a place in Mexico. It's crazy down there. I'll find a good use for it, I'm sure." Then Jesus showed him how to slap a vain to bring it up big and ready for the geeze.

Butch unrolled the works he'd wrapped up in the new Giant's T-shirt he'd bought at a ballgame and looked at the syringe. It *looked* clean, anyway. He took out the baggie of coke and examined it. He thought about what he'd use to scoop out the drug and then saw the wooden coffee-stirring stick provided for guests of the motel sitting on the counter by a tiny coffee maker and went over and took it and dipped it in the bag. He heard a knock on the door and walked over and opened it.

"Okay. I'm *here*," Alex said, standing there looking at him. Butch caught a glimpse of the Pacific Ocean behind Alex. The second-floor rooms had the best views of both the beach and the motel's parking lot.

"Okay, man—sit down. I got to figure this out. Never actually *shot* any drugs before—I always just snorted 'em." Butch looked at him. His partner was wearing jeans and a black T-shirt and was barefoot. His already-thinning black hair was still wet. He was letting his mustache grow to make him seem older and look even more like a cop, or a biker.

"What is it?" Alex asked, closing the door to the room.

"Coke."

"You're going to shoot *that* into your arm?"

"No, I was going to shoot it into my *dick!* But I'm a novice, so I'll start with my arm." He smiled impishly and then went back over to where he'd laid down the baggie. He found the stirring stick and dumped some coke into the teaspoon he'd bought for that purpose.

"Come here and hold this shit for me." He had Alex hold the spoon. "Don't drop that—it's about a grand-worth of coke." Butch crossed the room and filled up an eyedropper with water at the small sink. He took a wad of cotton from a package and tore off a chunk about the size of a walnut; then he sat down on a chair by the door. "Bring me the spoon there, buddy." Alex had looked at the white powder in the spoon. He'd been angry when Butch had called, but now he wasn't. He was just curious. "Does that look like three match-heads'-worth of coke?" Butch asked, looking up at him.

"What do you mean?"

"... In the *spoon*. ... Does that look like three fucking match-heads'-worth to you?"

"I guess. It *might* be more, even."

Butch wrinkled his nose. "Well, let's find out," Butch said. He dropped water into the spoon first, then flicked the Bic lighter on and held the flame under the spoon. He signaled Alex while he heated up the drugs the same way Jesus had shown him, so the coke would dissolve in the water. "The syringe is on the bed, man."

Alex walked over to the unmade bed and saw the plastic syringe with its attached needle and brought it over to him.

"Hey, can I have your shit if you die?" Alex asked. He smiled. The whole thing seemed surreal: the room, the way Butch's hair was plastered down, still wet from the shower, even the look on his face, like a kid in chemistry class, the big .44 magnum lying on the pillow where he'd slept.

"NO. My *parents* get my shit. *You* don't get my shit. You can have the hand cannon, though—how's that?" He lit the Bic lighter again and held it under the spoon.

The water and coke mixture began rocking slightly, almost imperceptibly, really, from the heat of the flame. The coke disappeared as it mixed with the water in the spoon. Butch dropped a pea-sized ball of cotton into the mixture.

"Okay. ... " Butch stabbed the cotton with the needle and sucked up the liquid until the spoon was almost empty; then he let a little dribble out of the tip of the needle, with the "works" pointed upwards, the way Jesus had shown him. They both watched a bubble rise in the syringe, traveling toward the top. A drop of water emerged from the needle and ran down the side of the syringe, dribbling away.

Butch turned to look at Alex, his eyes wide. "Here—hold this." Butch handed him the syringe and he tied off his arm with his belt. He slapped at his arm hard and then took the syringe back from Alex. "See you later, partner," Butch said, smiling like a rube. Then he found a big blue vein and hit it.

For some strange reason, when Alex started the car in the Capri's parking lot, he thought of those "perpetual-motion" stainless steel balls that a lot of executives kept on their desks. Once the balls started they weren't supposed to stop. He heard their click-click now as he turned the car onto Highway One and into the surprisingly cold morning of the Southern California coast in the dead of winter. The car seemed to want to run fast by itself, and he found himself speeding. There was a lot of dope in the trunk, and also two automatic shotguns on the floor of the back seat with big 24-shell magazines. He had a bad feeling about the whole operation again, but decided to ignore it. *Why would you think about things you can't do anything about, anyway?*

They went and had breakfast, and then picked up a guy called Flaco who was supposed to stamp their ticket to the LA underworld. He'd been the cell-mate of a snitch that the DEA had successfully used several times in Oakland, and who'd been in custody when the snitch was told to call Flaco and tell him that two friends of his were moving to LA and were in the heroin business. There was light fog offshore that morning that seemed to make things more quiet than they usually were; the silky-looking fog just sitting there on the water, diaphanous and peaceful. The car radio was playing "It's a Man's World," Alex looked over at Butch.

"Hey! Are you in there?"

Butch looked at him. The song changed to "Windmills of Your Mind" as they approached the beach. *Butch thought he saw a gook climb out of a sewer drain while he was shouting orders and looking for ammunition for his World-War-2-era Tommy gun that he'd found left over from the Diem years lying where someone had dropped it during the battle. The dead littered the front of the embassy like a scene from a horror movie, some on the way to death, others wounded and trying to crawl away from the fighting, leaving blood spoor like shot animals. Vietnamese ARVN, Korean Marines, and U.S. Marines in filthy uniforms and frightened faces, all mixed together.*

"Yeah," Butch said, coming back from his day-mare, his hands resting on the knees of his rolled-up-cuffs prison-style jeans. He had put on a white bowling shirt that had "THE DEVIL'S HARDWARE STORE" chain-stitched across the back.

"This guy said he'd meet us at Dunkin Doughnuts," Alex said.

"Okay." Butch was looking out at the beach hoping he'd see some girls in bikinis, but it was too early in the morning for that. There were only a couple of surfers riding the puny SoCal waves.

He remembered that there had been a Dunkin Doughnuts near his grandfather's house in Pittsburgh He and his friends in high school would go in there and see old steel workers sitting around, their big hands holding tiny Styrofoam cups of coffee, all of them with blank, used-up looks on their used-up faces; faces that had looked into life's blast furnace for too long, the snow of the elderly falling in their eyes. He'd left Pittsburgh and joined the Marine Corps after going to College at Notre Dame and had been back home only a few times since. He called his grandfather from Saigon once and they'd spoken. His grandfather asked how he was and there had been a long silence, both of them realizing that he was not the kid who'd left, without any more words passing between them.

"Okay, I guess—I'm still jacking off," Butch had said.

"Good," his grandfather had said. "You're doing better than me, kid."

They saw a small Mexican-American in jeans and a white t-shirt standing in front of the Dunkin Doughnuts and picked him up. He jumped into the back seat of the Mustang without saying a word.

"I feel lucky," Alex said. "I read my horoscope this morning. ... It said ask for anything you want and you'll get it."

"No shit? How would you like a Hawaiian punch?" Butch asked. "I promise you'll get that if you want it."

"... Yeah. Libra are attractive. Lot of girls love me. We don't like noise or crowds. I looked it up," Alex said.

"Yeah? I'm a Leo. We're bad motherfuckers," Butch said. Then he gave what would come to be known in the future, to Alex anyway, as a Butch Special Smile; a look that telegraphed his "I'll-do-anything-you-can come-up-with" attitude, and to a casual observer, made him appear as a half-outlaw biker, and half-escaped-mental-patient-on-a-full-load-of-drugs. Alex looked at him evenly for a moment.

"Anyway, they said it was going to be a great day to be a Libra," Alex said.

"I hate all that astrology shit," Flaco said from the back seat. He'd done time at San Quentin and looked like the village idiot's much smarter brother. They'd forgotten he was there because he hadn't said shit since he'd explained that the DEA were the dumbest fuckers in the world, second only to the FBI, who he said were not only suit-wearing clowns, but also chicken-shits. And that if they'd gotten all their training from those two piles of pig-shit they would *certainly* die in some alley with their throats ripped out and their tongues hanging out of their assholes.

"... And that's the *good* news," Butch had said. Then they'd all laughed, even Flaco. "So you know that we're cops."

"Yeah. There are no secrets in the joint, amigo. My pal warned me. So what is it we're doing this morning?" Flaco said.

"We're selling some heroin to some black gentlemen who supposedly run a thriving business," Butch said.

"Black gentleman? You mean you're selling some geese to some spear-chuckers. How much?"

"Five kilos."

"Oh, fuck! We're all going to die," Flaco said. "Who gave you the connection?"

"The DEA. They set up the buy. Their informant set it up," Alex said.

"Like I said—let me out," Flaco said.

"*What?*"

"I said let me the fuck out of the car. *Right now.* Shit, do I look stupid to you?"

Alex pulled over at a strip-mall, the car rolling to a stop in front of a surf shop. Flaco jumped out of the car like his ass was on fire.

"Good luck, fellows. Remember—don't give them the dope 'til you get the money."

"You ain't going anywhere, man." Butch pulled the .44 magnum off the floor and pointed it at him.

"Do I look like a lost motherfucker to you?" Butch said

"No," Flaco said.

"Do I look stupid?" Butch said.

"No."

"Well then, if you try and split on us I'm going to shoot you. Do you understand that?"

"I understand, man," Flaco said. He climbed back into the car's backseat. Butch turned in the seat and reached over and punched Flaco in his left eye for good measure—a straight-arm punch that caught Alex by surprise. Butch had his grandfather's huge hands and the punch rocked the tired-looking kid backwards. It

41

hadn't hurt Butch in the least. It was as if his knuckles were made out of a combination of leather and Titanium. Alex watched Flaco's head snap back and flashed on the Zapruder film.

"*Jesus!*" Alex said.

"Do we have an understanding, now?" Butch said. He didn't even seem angry, just inquisitive.

"Yeah ... Yeah ... fuck—you hurt my eye, man," Flaco said.

"Did I? Sorry," Butch said. "But sometimes I lose my shit."

"Let's go," Alex said. "Like I said, it's going to be a wonderful day to be a Libra."

When they all got out of the car in the Denny's parking lot off Wilshire, the Mexican bolted across the busy boulevard and disappeared. He was their last connection to the DEA and any kind of cover or authority. Butch thought about chasing him but finally decided it wouldn't be worth the effort.

The first thing Butch thought when he saw the big black guy with the Afro sitting in a red leather booth in Denny's was that the Afro was big enough to hide a midget with a gun. The black guy was that big. He didn't stand up, but just nodded to them. The Denny's smelled like syrup and coffee. The booth the black guy was sitting in was near the door and had a view of the parking lot. They'd spoken briefly on the phone and the man called Lucky had told them he'd probably be the only black guy in the place. He was right. They were in a tony part of LA near Westwood that didn't have many black people in it.

"How you all *motherfuckers* doo-in?" Lucky said. He was wearing a Jimi Hendrix-inspired multi-colored bandana around his neck with a red-silk shirt that most likely came from Fredrick's of Hollywood. Butch could see bits of curly black hair on his chest, as his shirt was unbuttoned to the navel. There were serious pec muscles under the shirt and the guy's chest was massive. He was six-five, at least, and right away the guy seemed nervous in a quiet sort of way. Butch thought that the entire situation was all fucked-up. It was the same feeling that he used to get when he was in high school and his football team would take the bus into the heart of the city to some black school in the ghetto and he knew, just *knew* beforehand, that the game was going to be very hard-fought. No quarter would be given white boys against black boys until someone, usually a quarterback, was carried off the field and the game ended as the second string quarterback suddenly got "ill."

"Grand Slam. Get the Grand Slam, guys ... It so good it make you want to slap your momma," Lucky said. Mr. Lucky looked up from his huge breakfast and eyed them both a little like a cat does mice.

For fuck's sake—we're going to go into the hood with this guy and come back out with our money? Shit. No way. The DEA are dicking us, Butch thought to himself. They slid into the booth, which immediately seemed too small for the three of them.

"How about some blow?" Lucky said. He picked up the butter dish and dumped out the contents—the little plastic containers of butter dropped out onto the sticky Formica table top.

"Why not?" Butch said. They watched Mr. Lucky tap out some coke from a pill vial onto the butter plate. Butch reached over and snorted up the line of coke with a rolled-up dollar bill. Alex waved off the offer. Lucky tapped out some more coke and hoovered it up like they were in someone's living room instead of the middle of a restaurant on Wilshire Blvd.

"I want to change the playbook," Butch said, moving around in the booth to face Alex. They were waiting for Lucky to make a call at the pay phone by the bathroom to set things up.

"What?" Alex said.

"I want to change the play. I'm calling a new play," Butch said.

"What the fuck are you talking about?" Alex said.

"I want to change the plan," Butch said.

"You want to change 'the plan'? There *isn't* any 'plan,' and you know it, really."

"Yeah," Butch said. "I've been thinking about it since we left the motel."

"Thinking about *what?*" Alex looked out across the busy restaurant, trying to spot Mr. Lucky.

"I don't want to give them the dope."

"You don't want to give them the dope," Alex said, not believing what he was hearing.

"Right," Butch said. He turned and looked at Lucky talking on the phone at the other end of the restaurant. He looked even bigger from across the dining room.

"Sorry, but I didn't sign up for that," Alex said.

"Okay, then don't go. I'll go by myself," Butch said.

"Our orders are to build a business. We're not supposed to rip off the customers."

"Why not? Our orders are to establish a name for ourselves in the underworld ... and that's all," Butch said.

"And what if our friend over there objects?"

"I don't care," Butch said.

"And what if we get a reputation as rip-off artists?"

"I don't care about that, either," Butch said.

"You 'don't care.' ... That's your answer?"

"Yeah. Pretty much." Alex looked away and out onto Wilshire. It was busy, and moving at a good pace, but the traffic seemed to slow down slightly near the restaurant because of the light.

"I'm going to rip them off—you can do what you want," Butch said. "We're outside the law now, so why don't we make it pay? *They* won't care."

"And how are you going to do that?" Alex said

"I guess I've got to kill them all and take the money," Butch said, picking up his coffee cup and taking a sip. It was too-full and he was shaking, not from he coke, but from all the coffee he'd drunk.

"You're crazy," Alex said. He wasn't joking this time when he said it. He looked toward the pay phone. Mr. Lucky seemed to be taking a lot of time to make a simple call telling "them" he'd seen the stuff and the deal was on.

"How much money does your father have?" Butch asked.

"What kind of a question is that?"

"He's rich, right?"

"Yes, he's rich," Alex said.

"That would make *you* rich, too, right?" Butch said.

"No—not exactly."

"Yes, it does. It *does*," Butch said. His eyes had gone very cold and mean.

"Butch ... We've got a job to do. Orders. A game-plan. People are counting on us."

"*Fuck* them. I don't care. I want that guy's money. *My* father isn't rich. And I want to buy a house. I haven't been able to buy a house. You've got a house yourself, right?"

"He's coming back," Alex said.

"Good for him. He should enjoy his life. Because he won't be alive tomorrow," Butch said. Turning to look at Mr. Lucky coming down the counter with a smile on his handsome face, Butch turned back around. "You've got a nice girlfriend, too. ... *I'm* going to get one of those. Someone to come home to, you know? Someone to cook me dinner and tell me they care whether I live or die," Butch said. "That would be nice. Right? And a couple of kids."

"It's on, *amigos*," Mr. Lucky said as he reached their table. Butch could feel the booth move under his added weight as he slid back onto the seat and tucked into the rest of his breakfast. He'd gotten the Grand Slam: scrambled eggs, bacon, and pancakes. He still had a stack of pancakes to "mop up right quick."

"Good," Butch said, watching him eat. "Good." The three men exchanged glances for a millisecond. Mr. Lucky, his Afro big and glossy from something he'd sprayed on it that morning, looked up from his forkful of pancakes. It was the black guy who felt the atmosphere had changed slightly. He'd survived twenty years in the

LA underworld *because* he had good radar, and something had just gone across his screen and registered, if only slightly. A blip had happened, right then and there. But he decided to ignore it this time, thinking it was the coke he'd just snorted and not his shit-detector going off. Everyone makes mistakes.

"... I'll have to get that next time," Butch was saying. "The Grand Slam." Mr. Lucky looked up again and smiled, swallowing a mouthful of pancakes; looking at him with a straight face.

6

■ LOS ANGELES

"Let's just follow the script," Alex said, trying to be the voice of reason, thinking that approach might work. They were heading east, down Santa Monica Boulevard, the traffic still heavy at 10 A.M. William Morris agents in dark suits turned off toward the William Morris Building's parking lot, worrying about their next move. Assorted low-wage workers were stuck in traffic, waiting for the light to change, dull-eyed and motionless within their cars, marking time. All of them were tired of the "gas crisis" that was making life miserable for Angelinos that winter. Mr. Lucky was ahead of them, driving a white 1979 Cadillac Eldorado with black and white fuzzy dice hanging from the rear-view mirror. It was an easy car to follow. Mr. Lucky's Caddy was brand-new and very clean.

"We'll split the cash fifty-fifty," Butch said. "That's two-hundred and fifty-thousand dollars *large, baby!*" He said this in a very loud voice, as if he were talking in a crowded bar.

"I don't want the money," Alex said.

"No, what you mean is, you don't *need* the money," Butch said.

"Stop it, man," Alex was feeling his face get warm now, partly in fear of what would happen if he couldn't stop their operation from going off the rails, but partly just from being "the rich guy." The bad coffee and the joint they'd just shared had made his mouth taste like dirty pennies. "You have no idea what we'll find at the buy," Alex said. "And we have *no* back-up. You understand *that*. ... No intelligence about what we're walking into. There is no one *out there* for us. So we can suspect that their buy-money is well guarded. We have no way of estimating who we'll face. There are just two of us. Last time I checked, anyway. ... It's *suicide, man.*"

"You're just a *pussy*," Butch said. He had taken off his jacket and was wearing just the bowling shirt with a black T-shirt under it. Despite everything that had happened in San Francisco, and then in his motel room, he seemed fine. He lit a Marlboro with a yellow Bic lighter. "We have better ordnance than those simple fucks. What's wrong?" Butch said. "What the fuck are you *afraid* of? You've gotta die *some* time ... *Vive Le Mort.* That's my motto."

"You're fucking nuts. That's what I think," Alex said. "Literally nuts."

"So? You're a fucking *queer. Dick-sucking motherfucker,*" Butch said.

"So I'm supposed to go get killed to prove to *you* I'm not a faggot? Is that it?"

"Yeah," Butch said.

"Fuck you," Alex said. Butch looked over at him, seeing that he was serious and pissed off.

"... Everyone says you're a pussy. Prove them wrong, man. Behind your back they call you a pussy ... ever since I've known you. No shit. A straight-up pussy dick-sucker-motherfucker," Butch said, taunting him. Alex looked at him. He couldn't believe what he was hearing. Butch looked at him, the dare on his face, then he turned his eyes back onto the traffic. Alex, driving, pulled through the light, still directly behind Mr. Lucky's car.

"I'm *not* a pussy. Okay? I'm just not *stupid.* There's a *big* difference, you dog-fuck *asshole.*"

"The DEA guys all said you were a faggot, from the very first day," Butch said. "I always stuck up for you. Maybe I was wrong."

"Guess what—I don't give a shit *what* those dickheads think. How's that grab you?" Putting up with Butch was starting to irritate him in a way it hadn't before. He suddenly felt betrayed and angry. *What kind of partner was this fucking guy?*

Butch took a long pull from his cigarette and rubbed his palm on his knee very slowly. "Why is it your hands are always sticky after you eat at Denny's?" He opened the glove compartment. They'd been issued several hand grenades. Well, "issued" is what Butch had told the DEA, but the fact was that he'd stolen them from a locker when they'd been training at Camp Pendleton, along with two M203 single-shot 40mm grenade launchers that would fit on the two M-16s that they *had* been issued by the DEA. Butch had put in for the M203s but was told by the DEA assholes that there was no need for such heavy ordinance, as they "weren't going to war." *Well then, where exactly* were *they going?* he'd thought. So he'd taken care of it himself when they went for training at Camp Pendleton, where he still had lots of friends.

"All right. Look, I took this fucked-up assignment because I wanted to make some money," Butch said. "And that's the *only* reason." Alex looked at his partner in shock. They had known each other in Vietnam, it was true, but not well. Butch had been in the Marine Corps at the time, and Alex had been working for the Defense Department, before they were both picked for recruitment by CIA.

"Just a business opportunity, is it?"

"Yeah ... that's right," Butch said. "I figured that: One, We were being set up to take a fall, somehow. Whatever this *is* about, it doesn't make any fucking sense. Why would the CIA want to send two officers into the dope world *in the United States* and not explain what it is we're supposed to be *doing,* exactly. Besides making ourselves well known to gangsters in the greater Los Angeles area—*that's* fucking crazy on the face of it. Number two: What's all this shit got to do with the *spy* business? And by the way, just in case you don't already know it, we're not supposed to be operating in our own fucking country, ever and at all!"

"I don't know," Alex said. But it all sounded like bullshit even to him; he had to admit it.

"You're fucking *lying,*" Butch said. "You're *management.* The one thing my old man taught me is that management always knows why you're getting fucked out of whatever it is they're trying to fuck you out of." They pulled up to another light. Mr. Lucky's Cadillac had gotten through before it changed. "And that's the other thing: Why would they send a golden boy like you into the field with the likes of me—a guy who's hanging on by a thread at the Agency because I stole a few thousand dollars from a dead guy's house in Chile? What difference did it make to the *dead* guy, huh?!"

Alex watched Mr. Lucky's Cadillac turn left onto Rodeo Drive. Butch knew that Alex was being groomed for management, while he'd been sent to carry water for death squads and assassinate uncooperative union leaders who'd questioned why Uncle Sam was crawling up their country's asshole with a pitchfork. He'd worked all over the Third World while Alex had been posted to the London Embassy, a posh job where he was able to run a fast social life while "fighting the Cold War" on brief excursions out from gambling clubs and on up-scale weekend fuck-parties. But Butch knew, mostly from Alex's own accounts, that he'd been chasing ass and getting laid by socially prominent young English women, working as little as possible, and getting away with it.

"My guess is that these people, Lucky and his crew, already know that we aren't who we say we are, because your old man, who happens to be the director of the Central fucking Intelligence Agency's clandestine directorate, isn't going to see you get shot dead in some parking lot over some skag. That's what *I'm* thinking," Butch said. "Am I right?"

"We don't know that."

"No, we don't," Butch said. "But it's what I'm going to bet on."

"You're going to bet your *life* on *that?*"

"Why not? Am I right?"

"No. I saw my father before we left. You're wrong." Butch looked at him, surprised. "What's all this fucking *about,* then?" Butch said.

"It's about some East German scientist who's trying to defect," Alex said.

"*Scien*tist? ... East Germany?"

"That's what he said."

48

"No shit?"

"No shit. So whoever Mr. Lucky is, he's for real," Alex said. He watched Butch throw his cigarette out the window. They went through the intersection and saw that Lucky's Cadillac had slowed on Sunset Boulevard. It took off again when it saw the Mustang had caught up. The Cadillac turned off of Sunset into a typical Beverly Hills neighborhood and they followed it. They were suddenly passing mansions in the beautiful light of late morning. Latin maids, in crisp grey and white uniforms, were out walking big family dogs and looking lost.

"Okay. Do you believe him?" Butch said. "Your old man, I mean."

"Yes. He hugged me."

"*What?*"

"My father ... he hugged me."

"What the fuck does *that* mean? What's that?—some secret Law-family *queer* code?"

"He's never done that before in his life. ... I think we're on our own out here. I don't think we're going to have *any* backup. I think the cover story is so important to them that they won't risk it."

"He *hugged* you?"

"Right."

"No shit?"

"No shit. He didn't hug me when I graduated from Yale. Or the day we graduated from the Farm, either."

"Okay, I get it. Okay ... Mr. Lucky might be for real. ... It doesn't matter. Our mission is to establish ourselves in the underworld, right?"

"No—our mission is to establish ourselves as heroin dealers who are moving weight in Southern California."

"Okay. Stealing this guy's money should do that, don't you think?" Butch reached over and honked the Mustang's horn, then put his arm out the window and made a "pull over sign" with his hand. Alex saw Mr. Lucky's Cadillac pull over to the curb ahead of them on this quiet, wealthy street, and roll to a stop.

"*Fuck, Butch!*" Alex said. Butch turned and looked at him.

"You do this for me, man, and I'll have *your* back. I promise you. We'll do what they want, but we'll do it our way. Okay?" Butch was looking at Alex, his eyes big from the dope and the painkillers and probably a not-insignificant amount of fear. Alex pulled up behind the Cadillac. The taste in his mouth had gotten worse. "... Listen— you're rich; you don't understand."

"I understand that you're fucking crazy and that you're going to get me killed," Alex said. Butch opened his door and started to get out of the car.

"Are we going to be partners or not?" Butch said.

"Okay. Once." Alex said. *"Once!* Understand that, dog-shit." He wasn't even sure why he'd said it. The fact was, he thought, looking out at the Cadillac's brake lights, that he didn't *really* care that much about any of it. Not even his own life. He'd realized that one night in the houseboat lying there looking at Patty while she slept. Something had gone cold in him and for some reason being with someone that was so alive—crazy, yes, but so alive—only made him realize it that much more. He wasn't happy, and he hadn't been for a very long time. His whole life he'd done what his parents had wanted, and now suddenly the thought of how he'd lived made him angry as hell. *Why had he done it that way?* Why was he sitting in this car with a crazy man wearing a Wild Bill Hickok jacket and not in New York like his Sister, working on Wall Street at his uncle's big-time brokerage firm? He'd never wanted to be a CIA officer. Why did he care that dumb-ass cops who would never know a Degas from a horse's ass called him a faggot behind his back? He was tired of it. Tired of his privileges—all of them. Unlike Butch, who he suspected of actually being afraid of dying, he had the startling realization that he was NOT. ... *I'm the suicidal one.*

Butch, Alex realized, was only grieving for the death of his innocence; the death of the person he was *before* the war, the college boy without a care, the working-class hero who came home broken and had to face the truth: he was no longer the "nice," clean, boy scout he'd once been. But he, Alex Law, wasn't grieving for anything at all. He was already dead in many ways; in almost all the ways that once mattered to him, in fact. The girl in Sausalito had shown him that much, anyway. He just wanted out from under the weight of being "Alex Law," now. The idea of death's silence was not that bad a thing. It was the first time he'd admitted to himself how he really felt about his own life. He would almost welcome death, the way he felt right now.

"All right, then ... I'll be right back. Don't move, *partner,*" Butch said. Alex watched him walk toward the Cadillac as the whole world seemed to spin more slowly. The weight of his despair had finally been thrust on him: articulated at last, it sat with him in the car now, lonely and alone.

Butch trotted toward the Cadillac with his handgun, the ridiculous one he'd thrown on the front seat of the car that morning at the motel, the .44 magnum, pressed to his right thigh, as concealed as he could get it given the situation. Alex turned on the radio and heard Tom Jones's "I Who Have Nothing" play. ... *I who have nothing ... I who have no one.* Patty had asked him once why he didn't love her. It was only three weeks after they'd met and he was unable to answer her question. He just sat there like someone hunkered down, living underground in a bunker somewhere inside himself.

"I *know* you don't. ... I mean, I've been with guys that did love me, so I know ... but you *really* don't." Alex had looked at her. She was sitting at the Lighthouse, a coffee shop on Bridgeway in Sausalito. They'd been going out now for three weeks and she had decided to tell him how she felt.

"I'm in love with you," she'd said. "I am. We come from the same kind of people, you and I. I can tell. I think maybe that's part of it. I know who I'm talking to."

"How do you know that?" Alex said.

"I just do. You've got all the signs. Private school is printed all over you, and I've noticed you always pay, but you don't have any kind of a job from what I can see." It was true, he always paid for them and never thought anything about it. Why should he? There wasn't a time in his life he hadn't had money, or the things it bought. Or ever even worried about it. It was always just there for the taking.

"Do you think I'm just a silly girl; is that it?" Patty had said.

"No."

"I'm not just a silly girl you're fucking over at Gate Six," she said. Suddenly she was talking to him in a different tone of voice. She was stone sober. "Okay. Do you understand? I take drugs—Yes. Because they make me feel good and I don't want to go home to Dallas and die at the country club when I'm forty from cirrhosis with a fat husband who won't give a shit one way or the other. And I don't care who wins the next election for President because I know it's a big joke, Okay? It won't matter who wins because people like my father will tell the President what to do. I've heard him do it. But I'm not just a silly girl you're *fucking*. Okay? Give me that much, at *least*. I mean if you can't love me back. At least give me that. Give me credit for not being a complete fool."

"Yes. Okay, I will," he'd said. He nodded to the waitress, uncomfortable, and asked for the check. She brought it. He paid for their breakfast and then they left. He never said anything about the conversation again. He couldn't say he loved her, so he didn't. He was so far away from being able to love himself that loving anyone else was simply impossible.

Butch opened the Cadillac's passenger door and slid in next to Mr. Lucky. The car smelled like pine trees.

"Keep your hands on the steering wheel, my man, or I'll have to shoot you in the head." Butch pointed the .44 magnum at him. He loved Clint Eastwood movies and thought it was funny that he could live like Dirty Harry for real and get paid for it.

"What's wrong, brother?" Mr. Lucky said.

"Nothing. Does it look like anything is *wrong*? I guess so, doesn't it? I had to stop you so I can explain something."

"You don't want to kill me, man."

"I might," Butch said. He saw Mr. Lucky turn a kind of grey color; he remembered black men would get that grey look in a firefight and afterwards look like cold ashes had been smeared onto his face. He could see the big man's pulse ticking in the vein in his thick neck. He was going into that "fight or flight" physical state that made people very dangerous. His body was preparing for battle. As Butch noticed the change he pushed the barrel of the gun into Lucky's neck.

"Okay. This is the deal. I'm the Man. Okay, well, a special kind of Man. And I know where you live. You live at 2314 West Florence in South Central ... with your mom. Right? Now. You have a girlfriend that works at the Hartford Insurance Company downtown. I have her phone number at work—all your numbers are tapped. Her work number is 310-334-0098. You did time at Chino State Prison for armed robbery when you were eighteen. Since then you've gotten smarter and left the small time and moved into the big time working for some gang out of San Bernardino. White guys, in fact. Am I right so far? Your real name is Clive Robert Johnson." This really did shake Mr. Lucky up. Butch could see it. He nodded and his Afro gleamed in the morning sun. "The gang uses you because they want everyone to believe it's a Compton, South Central, black-run set-up. But it's not; it's a San Bernardino, all white, set-up."

"Okay," Lucky said. "You're the Man."

"Now here's the good part. I'm going to offer you a way out of this terrible situation you find yourself in today," Butch said.

"What terrible situation, *man?*"

"Out of me shooting you in the fucking head and leaving you here in Beverly Hills for the garbage men to find. I bet it's garbage day, in fact. I saw a garbage truck back there at the corner."

"What *kind* of Man?" Lucky said. "... You can't just *shoot* a brother for nothing!"

"DEA. ... Now here's the deal. I want to steal these fuckers' buy-money. Me and my partner need a little help. You tell me where we're going, and who's going to be there, and who's holding the money, and I don't kill you. And, if you're thinking about fucking with me, I'll come to your house, drag you out into the yard, and kill you in front of your momma. And I'll do it with a squad of DEA officers and the LA Tac Squad helping me out for good measure. We'll call it resisting arrest and we'll wait to call the ambulance until we're sure you're fucking dead. How's that for a plan?" Butch said.

"You're a crazy motherfucker."

"Yes, I am, sir. Yes I am."

"... ... You're really the Man?"

"Yes, I am."

"Fuck me. I thought so. I thought something wasn't right with that little blond boy. He's no dope dealer. He looks like a faggot, man—your partner. Why the fuck didn't I listen to myself?" Mr. Lucky pounded the steering wheel with his palm, hard. The whole dashboard jumped. Butch lifted the muzzle of his pistol and stabbed it into Mr. Lucky's thick neck a second time. He buried it into a throbbing vein and pulled the hammer back for effect. It worked. Mr. Lucky stopped pounding the wheel. He moved the pistol's muzzle an inch deeper into Mr. Lucky's neck in case he tried to swing at him, There was just no way the bullet would miss killing him even if Lucky managed to hit him.

"... Are you in ... Or are you out?" Butch said.

"What the fuck do you think. ... I'm in. Shit."

"Where we going, then?"

"The Nickel."

"That's downtown, right? ... Why are we up here in Beverly Hills, then?"

"Cause I wanted to see if you had a tail, dumb-ass honky *bitch*."

"Do I look like a monkey ... Okay ... that makes sense ... We don't have one. Now where are we going? Exactly."

"The Nickel. I just told you, motherfucker." Mr. Lucky was getting angry now that he thought he was past getting killed on the spot.

"Where, *exactly*? I need a street address," Butch said.

"Wall Street. It's in the first block," Lucky said.

"And who's going to be there?"

"Some guys."

"Exactly how *many* guys? And where are they going to *be?*"

"Two L.A. County Sheriffs in a patrol car," Mr. Lucky said.

"Excuse me?" Butch said.

"These guys use the L.A. County Sheriff's cops to make the deals and pay the money in L.A. County. That way they won't get ripped off," Lucky said.

"L.A. County Sheriff's officers? *In uniform?*"

"Yeah."

"No shit. I'm impressed," Butch said.

"These white boys ain't no joke. They hooked-up, man."

"Where exactly is this supposed to go down, again?"

"In front of the Carlton Hotel on Wall Street in the fucking Nickel. They'll be there soon. They'll expect to see me first. If they don't, they'll just drive away. So this nigger better not die."

"Okay . Let's go. We'll follow you."

"What you going to do?"

"I'm going to kill them and take the money—Why?"

"You're a cop and you're going to do some *other* cops?"

"Some other *bad* cops, but yeah. Why not? They won't just give me the money if I ask 'em nice for it, do you think?"

"I want to make a call first," Mr. Lucky said.

"Who to? Your grandma can't help you now, baby."

"I know somebody at DEA and I'm want to call them and make sure I'm not bein' fucked with. I call them now or you just go ahead and shoot me, because that's what these white boys gonna do when they find out you weren't really the Man. And you have to *arrest* me, too."

"Okay," Butch said. "You're under arrest."

"How much I get? My cut?" Mr. Lucky said.

"You get to *live*, you stupid fuck! *That's* what you get, motherfucker." He pulled the pistol out of Mr. Lucky's neck and cracked open the door of the Cadillac.

"Well ... when you put it like that, man. I just thought, hell, you know, a brother got to eat. ... "

"Breakfast was on *us*, wasn't it?" Butch said as he got out of the car. "We'll follow you to a gas station so you can make your call. If you fuck with us I swear I'm going to kill you. I just want to make that *very* clear," Butch said. "So there's no misunderstanding on your part ... I kind of like you, actually, and I don't want to have to do that, but I really will," Butch said, and he meant it.

Alex had watched the whole scenario of Butch and Mr. Lucky from the Mustang's driver's seat; he'd seen Butch shove the pistol into Mr. Lucky's neck, and his stomach churned as he thought that Butch might in fact shoot him right there on the spot. He was relieved when Butch finally got out of the Cadillac and walked calmly back toward the Mustang, opened the door, and slid into the passenger seat next to him.

"We're fine. He wants in. He's got to make a call to see if we're really undercover cops."

"Make a *call?*"

"He knows someone at the DEA that he can call and find out whether I'm telling him the truth about being cops."

"You *told* him?"

"Yeah ... I had to. Go ahead and follow him to the gas station." Alex watched the Cadillac signal and slowly make a U-turn. Mr. Lucky, his big afro filling the driver's-side window, shot them a look of fear-tinged-with-respect as he passed them and headed back out of Beverly Hills.

"Mr. *Lucky* thought you were a faggot, too, by the way. For the record, in case you have to end up shooting him," Butch said. "You won't *feel* so bad about it, maybe. ..."

"Thanks for sharing that," Alex said.

"Do you think maybe you might like having sex with Mr. Lucky, old son?"

"No, I think I want to start with you," Alex said. "Just to see if I like it—I'll skip the blow-job and go right to the good stuff, though."

"Promise to be gentle," Butch said. He opened the glove box. "The people picking up the dope are L.A. County Sheriff's deputies," he said. "Pretty smart. Sounds like something the CIA would do. ... Hey, wait a second—I guess when I was dressed like a priest down in Guatemala that was pretty much the same thing—right? Kind of? It's a fucking crazy world, right?"

7

There had been nothing more to say, Alex thought. He'd agreed with himself to commit suicide and that was that. It was pretty clear to him that he and Butch had little chance of living through the day.

"There, that Union Oil station. ... Pull in there," Butch said. Butch had been watching the Cadillac very intently. Alex waited at the stoplight. Mr. Lucky's Cadillac pulled into a Union Oil gas station on Sunset and drove toward a bank of pay phones at the back. They saw the Cadillac's taillights go off. A sign in front of the station informed the public that they were out of gas.

"I'll listen in," Butch said. Alex nodded, but he wasn't really paying attention now to the *strum und drang* generated from their momentously stupid decision. Instead, he was thinking of Patty and what she'd said in the café. She'd seen it in him; what was wrong with him. He hadn't understood that until now—*today,* in fact, at the moment he'd agreed to let Butch get them killed.

"I'm going to make a call, too," Alex said. He pulled into the gas station and stopped next to Mr. Lucky's Cadillac. He got out at the same time Butch did. Alex walked right on by Mr. Lucky, who stood stock-still and stared at him as he held the pay phone receiver. Alex went to another pay phone and started feeding it coins. He dialed Patty's number in Sausalito. It rang. While it was ringing, he turned and watched Butch, who was now standing next to Mr. Lucky, listening in on his conversation, standing *very* close, in fact, to the point of being actually partially inside the booth with him. The two big men looked comical standing in the booth together.

"Hello." Patty finally picked up the receiver on her end. "It's me," Alex said.

"Hey, you—where the hell *are* you?"

"I wanted to call," Alex said.

"Are you coming over tonight?" He hadn't even told her he was leaving town.

"No ... I can't." There was a pause; she was obviously disappointed. Before his "death epiphany," he wasn't going to call her at all, thinking that it would be better if he just disappeared without any explanations or good-byes. But suddenly, driving to the gas station, he decided he couldn't leave it that way, unfinished. He'd realized that she deserved more from him—at least a small lie to soften the truth if nothing else, and maybe a good-bye of sorts.

"…You didn't call last night," she said. "I waited up. … Where are you?"

"Sorry. I had to go out of town." Alex turned and saw Mr. Lucky speaking on the phone with Butch also holding onto the receiver. It looked strange, like they were brothers talking to their parents on the same line. But of course they weren't brothers, because Butch had a pistol stuck in Mr. Lucky's guts.

"What did you mean when you said we were the same? You and me?" Alex asked.

He heard a gunshot and looked through the dirty glass of the booth's partition. He saw Mr. Lucky sagging down, but his legs were moving wildly like he was dancing. The bullet had hit him squarely in the chest and he was dancing, trying to run away from Butch but in the wrong direction, trapped inside the phone booth as he died. Alex heard another shot and saw the glass of the booth in front of Lucky shatter as the bullet blew through his face and out the back of his head, smashing the glass the split second after it exited his skull. Alex stood stunned as he watched Butch step back out of the phone booth and look over at him, motioning toward the Mustang with his free hand. Alex saw the phone booth plastic only a few feet away sprayed and dripping with blood and brains. Lucky sagged to his knees and disappeared from view. Butch walked backwards from the phone booth, the big revolver still in his hand, the barrel obscenely long.

"Bruce … *Bruce* … *Bruce!?* What was that!?" Patty said. Alex slowly hung up the black receiver. For an instant he didn't know exactly what to do. The sight of the bloody mess now lying in front of him on the asphalt froze him in place. The bullet-smashed booth articulated in pieces of ruined human flesh. He looked out at the gas station and saw people crouching by their cars, most of them staring towards them. Some secretaries who'd been on their way to work somewhere on Sunset were running away. He saw Butch run toward the Mustang and get in, taking the driver's seat. Butch backed up wildly and then threw open the passenger door, waiting for Alex to jump in. Alex stood there as if he were a witness to what had just gone down, and not a participant. Then Alex felt himself running, his breath sounding loud and harsh in his ears. The next instant they were out of the gas station and speeding down Sunset Boulevard—real criminals at last.

Butch drove for the first five minutes as if they were being chased, running red lights all along Sunset, with the cross-traffic on several occasions nearly hitting them. L.A. isn't really a town to run red-lights in. The sound of car horns blared everywhere around them. Butch drove like a crazy man, with his hand almost continuously on the horn, too. At one point, they were forced to drive up on the sidewalk to just miss being hit head-on. The gratingly loud cacophony of the horns, the screeching tires, the Mustang going sideways through a major intersection—none of it seemed real to Alex. They were in a silly movie that he was watching, but also happened to be part of, somehow. He thought they would soon be killed, or at least hit, but they weren't, and Butch was able to pull the car back off the sidewalk and onto Sunset and race on toward the freeway on-ramp. There was a bank robbery going on right then in Westwood, complete with hostages and wounded passersby, and it made it possible for them to leave the scene while the LAPD were busy surrounding the bank, tying up all their available units in the area. There was no question that protecting the Bank of America's money took first priority—much more important than some "gang beef on Sunset," as the dispatcher had it.

They hadn't spoken a word since he'd gotten back into the car at the gas station; there'd been too much adrenalin and fear to talk before they finally made it onto the freeway.

"What happened to *Lucky?*" Alex finally said, once they were several miles down the 405.

"He was lying. The area code he dialed gave him away. It wasn't 310. The DEA offices are in L.A. County." Butch was totally matter-of-fact.

"So you shot him?"

"I sure did," Butch said. "I warned him. He dialed a strange area code."

"What if he was calling the guy at home?"

"I couldn't take the chance," Butch said.

They parked a block down on Wall Street and stopped. Butch could see the Sheriff's car stopped on the street, two men in it, double-parked just down from a seedy SRO, the Hotel Carlton. It was almost noon. The street smelled like piss and was covered in decades of broken wine bottles of all colors, a strange multi-colored mosaic glittering in the sunlight, surreal. They could see a gaggle of whores milling on the corner, just down from the Sheriff's car. There were yellow shades drawn down on most of the hotel windows. He saw a young black girl on the third floor looking down on the street while she talked on a phone, some kind of bright-red "scrunchie" in her hair.

"I'm thirsty—are you thirsty?" Butch said. Alex didn't answer. "We should have stopped for a soda or something."

"Shut up," Alex said. Alex took off the ridiculous Wild Bill coat he'd been wearing. He didn't want to be found shot dead in *that* thing, he thought. He stripped it off and threw it into the back seat of the car.

"Fuck it—I'll go," Butch said. "It's my thing." They were both looking at the teeming street through the Mustang's dirty windshield. Alex could hear the Mustang's souped-up engine throbbing loudly.

"I think I fell in love," Alex said, "with that girl back in Sausalito." Butch looked at him and wiped his face with the tail of his shirt. It was a strange remark to be making under the present circumstances, but he was used to guys saying weird shit after a gunfight. He took out some pain pills from his jeans-pocket and downed a handful. He just casually shook them out and tossed them back into his mouth.

"Yeah, Patty. That's nice. I like her," Butch said. "A good-looking girl."

"Yeah ... it is. If I do this with you. ... We're *partners*, right?" Alex said.

"You don't have to. I'll do it myself," Butch said, thinking maybe he'd been an asshole to Alex before and now regretting it and feeling like doing the job himself.

"No, I'm coming with you," Alex said. "If something bad happens, call Patty's number that I gave you and tell her that she was right about me," Alex said. "Now pull into that lot. ... I've got an idea." Alex turned around and dug into a duffel bag he'd brought down from San Francisco. "Pull into the fucking lot, man!" He said it again. His tone was different this time, a take-charge tone Butch would hear many times over the next 20 years, but it surprised him right now, coming from the Alex he thought he knew. Butch watched him digging in the bag while he pulled to the right and into a driveway that led into an empty garbage-strewn lot next to the hotel. "Go all the way in so they can't see the car," Alex said.

Butch pulled into the lot where there'd once been a building, torn down by a redevelopment agency for "the good of the community." Alex finally found what he'd been looking for. He'd taken a dress that Patty had left in his rental car. He was going to throw it out but he remembered it had been the dress she was wearing when he'd literally bumped into her in the crowded bar on Caledonia Street on the Friday night they'd met. It was the dress he'd pulled off of her the first time they'd made love. In the moonlight on her boat, her thin waist and soft hair had completely intoxicated him; her skin had smelled like Dove soap, and her climax eternal and all-encompassing.

"What the fuck are you *doing, man?*" Butch said as he watched him.

"You and me are going to be a *couple*, baby," Alex said, still with the odd tone in his voice. Alex got out of the car and pulled the dress over his head and then told Butch to open the trunk. Alex looked down into it at the two automatic shotguns with canister-style magazines.

"What's the plan?" Butch said, stepping up to him and getting an eye-full of Alex in a granny dress. With his long blond hair, he looked a little like a girl. "*Damn, bitch.*"

"We go down there and kill them," Alex said. "That's the plan. It's simple."

"I like simple," Butch said. "Simple usually works." Alex wrote Patty's number with a ball-point pen on Butch's palm. Butch lifted the two shotguns out of the trunk. Alex looked around and saw a putrid-looking vomit-covered pink blanket hung-up on the cyclone fence that ringed the lot—he took it down and they walked out towards the street.

The two walked out of the lot onto Sixth Street. What the Sheriff—a big white guy with a military buzz-cut, who was driving saw, was two faggots sharing a filthy pink blanket—one of them was kissing on the other one and the sight disgusted him and made him want to barf. There was a cardboard box from Safeway with 250,000 dollars on the backseat of the Sheriff's car.

"Hey, look here," the hairless sheriff said. The other guy, his partner for five years now, was a smoker—a thin and pale guy with a black mustache that he told the Orange County girls was a "pussy tickler" with a completely straight face so they'd laugh at him. Even his partner called him "the loser" behind his back. The small one was genuinely feared in the Nickel because he was known to rob prostitutes for petty cash and slap them around if they didn't come through when he shook them down.

"When is that *fucking* nigger going to get here?" the loser said. He looked at his watch—his mother had given him a Timex with a Spandex band for Christmas that year.

"Well ... He better get here pretty quick because I want that Grand Slam breakfast and they stop serving it at noon at this Denny's downtown here." The big sheriff glanced in the mirror as the two faggots, in some kind of faggot-dream heaven, were walking up behind the squad car wrapped in a pink blanket that looked like it might have pieces of dried dog-shit hanging off it.

"Faggots are proof that dogs fuck kikes," the loser said, turning to watch them pass. That was the last thing he ever said. The multiple twelve-gauge blasts rocked his skinny body like he was dancing an ugly jitterbug.

They got the money. It was blood-spattered, though, because the big hairless one had tried to come out the back window. He died on top of the box of cash minus a real head; there was just a kind of bloody pellet-destroyed blob with hair on it still partly attached to the body.

A clerk from the hotel was the one that saw the Mustang leave the lot and nearly sideswipe a delivery van. The desk clerk walked over to the Sheriff's car and saw the dead officers, the broken thick glass from the windshield where Alex had stuck the shotgun in, trigger down, watching the big Sheriff die. The clerk, terrified at the carnage, ran back into the hotel to call the cops. He'd managed to catch the Mustang's license plate number and wrote it down on the desk blotter while he dialed, his hand shaking like a leaf.

That night, late, Alex called Patty. His room at the Capri was bare. Butch had gone out. They'd gotten a call from their contact in the DEA asking about a shooting in downtown L.A. and Alex had taken the call and lied, standing there with a towel wrapped around his thin waist, having just gotten out of the shower. The desk clerk at the Hotel Carlton who called the LAPD had gotten the license plate number of the Mustang, though. The DEA chief who called the Capri knew that the two men, who were posing as officers in the DEA, were in fact *not* officers in the DEA, and so he decided that for his own good, and the good of his career, he would pretend the lie Alex told him was the truth.

Asked how they had gotten the license plate number, Alex was told immediately. And then the head of the DEA's field office hung up. The head of the DEA's entire Southern California operation immediately tore up his notes containing the hotel clerk's information, and the truthful eye-witness account of the shooting, including the Mustang's license number, which the LAPD had traced back to the DEA. The DEA officer then called his contact in the LAPD and said that his office had looked into the recent shooting at the Carlton and had checked all its sources and had no information regarding the shootings of the two officers. He suggested that perhaps they should check the dead officer's bank accounts for large cash deposits? The hotel clerk disappeared, leaving Los Angeles after receiving a threatening phone call from an unknown person who suggested he forget what he'd seen. Six months later the DEA chief was promoted to a post in Washington with a favorable letter in his file at the CIA noting him as "a friend of the Agency." Everyone was happy.

The phone rang at the houseboat but Patty was out. Alex let it ring for a long time, just lying in bed listening, hoping she'd pick up. She did finally pick up at 2 A.M. She jumped on a plane the next day for Los Angeles. Alex picked her up at LAX and got a room for them at the Beverly Wilshire. The day after that was the first time Alex did heroin. They shot heroin at the Beverly Wilshire hotel, cooking up a spoonful from the kilo bag they'd broken open. She showed him all about how it was done, taught him what different kinds of works consisted of, how to dissolve the drug, and making sure she cut it with some baby laxative. "You'll never forget this first time," Patty had told him. "No one ever forgets it. And you'll never feel this good again, no matter how much you take—you should know that before I do you up ... " she said as she unbuttoned the cuff of his shirt and rolled up his sleeve. He'd watched her eyes as she'd cooked the dope in the spoon, standing there half-naked, the curtains to the balcony and the little terrace open, sounds of the people downstairs in the pool area where they'd been earlier having breakfast on a red table cloth drifting into the room on a light breeze.

"Are you *sure* you want to do this?" she'd asked five minutes before. They had made love and then gone down to the pool for a swim like a couple of tourists. After they finished their swim he went out to the Mustang and pulled a kilo of heroin out of the trunk and brought it up to the room to show her. While he was carrying it up in the elevator a Rabbi and his kid got on and just looked at him. They were both Hasidic Jews who wore the big hat. Alex smiled at the father and the man smiled back. "There was a wedding tonight," the Rabbi said, grinning, "for my daughter."

"*Mazel tov*," Alex said, holding the kilo of junk in a brown-paper Safeway grocery bag.

He'd laid the kilo on a glass table in the middle of the expensive suite and waited for her reaction. She was wearing a white bikini, and looked like she was a normal college girl out for the weekend except for the marks on her arms. She was drying her hair when she came out of the bathroom topless, wearing just the bikini bottom. She was sexy, he thought, looking at her, and that was for sure. In an hour he wouldn't care about sex because of the heroin. Sex would be the last thing on his mind in a very short while.

"I'm in the dope business," Alex said. "That's a kilo of almost-pure heroin. This is my business. It's why I'm here in LA." She stopped drying her hair, then turned around and looked first at the kilo of junk, then at him.

"I thought you said you were in the Merchant Marine," she said. She still held the towel up by her ears, but her arms seemed frozen in place, now.

"I want you to stay down here with me. In LA., I mean," Alex said. She put the towel around her shoulders.

"... That's a lot of heroin," Patty said.

"Yeah," he said. "There's a lot more in the car, too." Her jaw dropped.

"*More than* that?"

"Yeah. ... Lots more."

"Okay. Why not?" Patty said. An hour later she was easing the needle underneath his skin for the first time, and three hours later they did some more. The phone in their room rang several times but they didn't bother to answer it, being too busy at the time wrapped in their separate cocoons of smack and the rock music that was playing on the clock-radio by the bed where they were lying.

Butch had been slapping him hard across the face for some time now, trying to get him to wake up. Alex wasn't able to feel much physical pain, though, in his present state. He did sense Butch lifting him up off the bed, as if he were weightless, but he still mostly existed in another world, a dream-world, far away, practicing his guitar while sitting on the bed in his room at Exeter, the prep school he'd attended years before. He liked the guitar itself, as an object, and he liked playing it, and he was concentrating on *that* as Butch slapped him again, bouncing him up and down violently on the big hotel pillows. Alex could see himself in his prep-school room sitting on a neat, well-made single bed. He could see shelves lined with his school books. He was in his underwear and holding the Gibson guitar his parents had bought him for Christmas that year. The guitar's neck felt slick in his hand. He could hear the notes of a Sibelius piece he'd been struggling with. And then, suddenly, he could feel the slaps. They were very hard. And then he could feel his body leaving his room at Exeter, as if some force were dragging him away from the problems of gripping the neck of the instrument, the tips of his fingers still trying to press the correct strings ... the feel of the steel strings on his fingers lingering for an instant. He heard someone calling his name from down the hall. A friend? An enemy? *Is someone angry with me?* Alex wondered.

"She's dead. Wake up! Wake up! Wake the fuck up ... God damn you! What the fuck!" Alex opened his eyes and was looking straight into Butch's face; a face that was very close to his. Butch's hand was raised up ready to slap him again. Alex saw that his face was red and his eyes big.

"I said wake up, *motherfucker* ... what the hell?" Alex could hear himself breathing and then realized that he was choking and trying to breath, but couldn't. Butch dragged him up, raising him out of the covers and sliding him out of the bed as if he were nothing but a rag doll. Raising him up higher, he laid Alex's shoulders against the headboard and then let him throw up. The vomit came out in small coughs. His diaphragm pushed out the vomit until he could clear his throat, and then he could finally inhale some air.

"What the fuck did you *do?*" Butch said, watching him cough, then finally resume breathing almost normally. Alex turned and looked at Patty's body lying next to him. He wiped vomit residue off his mouth with his hand. He turned and touched Patty's shoulder. He pulled his hand away from her body very quickly, scared shitless by its lifelessness.

"She'd dead, man. You od'd her! We've gotta get out of here!" Butch said. "Jesus H. Christ! ... Fucking amateurs." Butch walked to the curtain and opened it, tearing it across the glass door. The yellow LA afternoon sun poured into the room. Then he went to the Servi bar and took out two beers, twisting the caps off each bottle in turn as he walked over to Alex, holding one of the bottles out to him. Alex was still too stoned and couldn't even manage to grab at it, so Butch took his hand and wrapped his fingers around the bottle and made him take a swallow like a baby, holding the bottle *for* him.

"Here. Drink something, for fuck's sake—it'll help." Alex felt as if he were in a dream, not quite alive, yet not quite dead, either, but somewhere in-between the two states.

"What happened to her?" Alex said, finally speaking, feeling the cold bottle pressed into his hand.

"She od'd," Butch said.

"I don't get it ... ?"

"Too much junk, man. Heroin. ... You remember what *that* is, don't you?" Butch said. Butch drank his beer straight down and threw the bottle on an orange sofa nearby. "She fucked up on the amount. ... I guess," Butch said, looking at her. He'd seen enough dead people to know that she was gone as soon as he'd walked to the bed and looked at her pale face. He'd gotten the maid to open the door for him after knocking very loudly and not getting any response.

"No!" Alex threw himself on Patty's body. She was naked and he realized that he was, too. He held her, gripping her around the waist like a child. The full impact of what had happened was starting to sink in. He didn't really believe she *could* be dead. He had nodded out. She'd been talking to him; that was the last thing he remembered. He felt Butch grabbing at him, and Alex turned and punched at him, but he missed. Butch backed up.

"Hold on, soldier. Hold onto your shit, man! We've got to get the hell *out* of here." He heard himself yelling Patty's name at Butch. But that, too, somehow, seemed strange, as if he were hearing someone else yelling it. His nerves were dead, his soul frozen by the horror of it all, now.

"Get an ambulance ... come on, call one ..." Alex said. He turned and looked at Patty again. "Patty, come on. ... You're all right." Alex turned her over and saw that she'd thrown up, too. He tried to wipe the vomit from her mouth and neck. The tears were coming down his face unexpectedly. "Patty ... come on ... come on. COME ON ... GET UP, PATTY!"

"You got about two minutes to get your shit together, man. Those county cops are coming after us. They followed me here. Two sheriffs in uniform, but driving an unmarked car—and they didn't come to help. ... I'm pretty *sure* of that. My guess is they'd like very much to kill us, and right now!" Alex looked at him, snapping out of it.

"... Yeah—that's right. They're downstairs right now! I saw them talking to the desk clerk, asking him questions. I bet they'll be up here in about two seconds with the manager telling him we're—I don't know, take a fucking guess. But I bet they have your name and my name, so ... " Alex saw that Butch had his .45 automatic stuck in the front of his jeans.

"Where's my pistol?" Alex said.

"How the fuck would *I* know?"

"She's dead, " Alex said, looking at him blankly.

"Correct. *Dead.* There's nothing you can do now. You have to get up, man."

Alex felt himself exhale. He was holding the beer now without Butch's assistance. He drank it all down and slid away from Patty's body, not wanting to look at it anymore. Then he felt guilty and forced himself to stand up and look back down at her. He grabbed the blanket and pulled it up over her shoulders as if she were just sleeping. He knelt on the bed and kissed her on the forehead. He wanted to say something, but he felt Butch pull him by his arm and when he turned around Butch was holding his Walther and his jeans out for him to grab.

"So, I'd like to *get the fuck out of here!*" Butch said. He threw the jeans and Alex caught them, just barely, still physically and psychologically drained. Butch tossed the weapon on the bed next to him.

"All right ... shoes," Alex said. He sat on the edge of the bed just looking at his weapon, then pulled the slide back and thumbed off the safety, noticing as he did so that his hand was still slick with Patty's vomit from when he'd wiped her mouth off.

"Housekeeping" Alex looked up at the door. "Housekeeping." A woman's voice was somewhat muffled by the door but was still quite audible. Alex looked at Butch. He remembered their instructor's words at Moffet when they were going through a drill in one of the empty "fight" houses. *"Stay away from the door if you know the bad guys are on the other side."* "Housekeeping. ... Can come in?" He heard the key turn in the lock and looked for Butch, who was behind a wall next to the door, his pistol out, ready to fire. The door opened to reveal the maid, a tiny Latin girl, very young, standing in the doorway looking at Alex.

"Sorry sir ... I'll come back." She couldn't see Butch, but she was staring at Alex, who looked half-dead to her.

"Okay," Alex said. He watched her close the door. His pistol had been lying between his legs like a dead fish, but now he jumped up in an adrenaline-fueled rush, quickly pulling on his jeans, lacing up his shoes, and looking for his wallet. He found it on the nightstand and shoved it into his pocket.

"You ready?"

"Yeah," Alex said.

"We'll take the stairs," Butch said. "They'll probably come up in the elevator, don't you think?"

"Okay," Alex said. The looked at each other. Butch nodded and headed toward the door and walked out. Alex turned and looked back at Patty for moment, and instead of immediately following Butch, went back to the bed and pulled the cover completely over her face, found her wallet and took out her driver's license, placing it on the nightstand next to the bed so she'd be identified immediately and her parents would be notified. Then he walked out of the hotel room and into the hallway.

Standing in the Beverly Wilshire's security office, the two deputy sheriffs were looking at the closed-circuit view of the hallway and saw Butch and Alex leave the hotel room. After the shooting in front of the Carlton Hotel, the gang working from inside the San Bernardino sheriff's department had called a meeting at a Pizza parlor near department headquarters and decided that whoever had killed their bag men would probably strike again, so they started turning over every junkie and any other type of contact/informant they had in the Southland's underworld. It was a secretary in the DEA's field office in San Diego that said she'd heard that two DEA agents were working undercover in L.A. County and had probably "gone rogue." Two phone calls and a ten-thousand-dollar bribe later they had the story from one of the DEA instructors, a no-neck in the Oakland office who told them everything he knew about the two, including their names, the license plate number of the Mustang, the motel where they were staying in Malibu, and the fact that they were not in fact DEA officers at all, but probably from the Defense Department, part of some new anti-drug group. The sheriffs had never faced that kind of penetration before and had a second meeting where they decided to back off, themselves. They would have to hire outsiders to kill these assholes. There were plenty of people in L.A. who would take the contract. They decided to give it to the Vagos Motorcycle Club, who they planned on keeping in the dark about the two men's actual identities, for fear they wouldn't take the contract if they knew the truth about them.

The maid came back into the room twenty minutes later and found Patty and called 911. Patty was still breathing when the paramedics found her, but she was just barely alive. The two Sheriff's officers decided to let Butch and Alex go. They were satisfied that the license number matched the description of the two "rogues". So they let them leave the hotel parking lot and watched them drive off; observing their departure from the hotel security office's cramped space, chock-full of small video screens and room service coffee cups.

8

■ STANFORD, CONNECTICUT

The nuclear scientist, well into his seventies, was named Carl Issac Smith. He had been a physicist and had worked for the Department of Defense at the U.S. Army's White Sands Proving Ground in 1952. Before that, he'd been at Los Alamos, and was credited with helping to design the first working "trigger" ever used on an atomic weapon. Smith was also one of the scientists that the OSS had employed to secretly keep tabs on the Nazi scientists the U.S. Army had brought to White Sands from Germany under the aegis of "Operation Paperclip," which included the most famous one of all, Werner Von Braun; the man the *New York Times* had called "the father of the American space program." What the *New York Times* had forgotten to mention was that Von Braun had been a confirmed and enthusiastic Nazi party member, an SS officer, and a war criminal, responsible for the deaths of thousands of slave laborers at a camp very close to the Peenemünde V-1 and V-2 missile test center on the Baltic Sea.

Smith had been listening to a recording of Ella Fitzgerald's "Blue Sky," and turned the sound down on his record player when Malcolm Law walked into his elegant room at the expensive retirement home in Connecticut. It was four in the afternoon and they were already getting dinner trays ready for the "guests" out in the well-scrubbed hallway as Malcolm sat down.

"My name is Law. We met a long time ago. I was using a different name, then, though. I think it was Mr. Picture, actually." Law smiled. "You *might* remember me, but I doubt it, really. Las Cruces, maybe?" The old folks home was near Stanford, Connecticut, and full of wealthy old people who wore very expensive watches and talked about how much their grandchildren loved them and what their kids were getting up to on Wall Street or in the State Department. Smith had made a lot of money in the 1970's working for GE as one of their chief engineers and a Cold Water Reactor specialist. You had to have money to end up in a place this nice, Malcolm realized, when he drove through the gate; he was all too familiar with this type of place. He'd had his mother in one and had hated like hell having to put her in a place like that, no matter how "luxurious" it was, physically. It had felt like a kind of final rejection that was totally unfair to her, but "necessary," like so much that goes on in life.

"Oh, yes … Malcolm. They told me you'd be coming by. I got a call from Randy. He's at Lawrence Livermore. Some consulting or something like that. Of course, I'm too sick to look pretty for the government meetings nowadays. But sometimes Livermore calls me about the old days at GE. They usually put me on a speaker-phone …if they have some questions about how we used to do it—that kind of thing. Otherwise nobody calls me, now," Smith said. He was wearing a "leisure suit" circa the early 1970s that sported a gold buckle. It had obviously been well-pressed. He had to breathe using an oxygen canister and had air-tubes in both nostrils. He still had steely-blue eyes, but his hair had almost completely disappeared from his scalp, depilated by the ravages of age and various skin cancers and psoriases stemming from his radiation exposure at White Sands and afterwards working at GE. His skin looked like that of a person who's almost just drowned and at the last instant been yanked from the water, shriveled and sopping.

"Right. Thank you for seeing me. May I close the door?" Malcolm said.

"Dear, I'm way past that … I never think about sex before a martini, now." Smith smiled beatifically. Malcolm smiled back. "But go ahead, if you must."

The room smelled of roses. A large spray of orange-colored roses sat on a coffee table nearby. There was a big picture window with a view of a grove of poplar trees, quite beautiful, in the style of a Japanese print come-to-life, the barks of the tress appearing very white with dramatic black calligraphic squiggles running down their trunks.

"Nice room," Malcolm said. "My mother was at the place down the road."

"*Was she?* …Yes. Well, I'll stay until the money runs out, or I die. I hope it's the latter. At my age, I'm sure I'll get my wish, don't you think? I mean before I'm 'turfed out' as the English say. … Congestive heart disease is the diagnosis—I smoked for years. Being a scientist I've read all the literature, of course. It's gruesome, really … problems of the heart, and *not* the kind I *used* to have, either. … Well, sit down, young man. … I'd offer you a drink, but alas … the nurses are quite thorough, here. They've discovered all of my hiding places, I'm afraid. I've no one to call any more, either. No children; the curse of the gay man. It's lonely at the end. Everyone's gone who might be pressed into smuggling me something to *drink*. Do you have any children?" The old man seemed voluble and angry. Malcolm's mother had been the opposite; barely speaking but lovely about everything. But also disinterested in life at the end of it all.

"Yes," Malcolm said, "two. A boy and a girl. Grown now, of course. Out in the world."

"You're very lucky, you know. … You'll have someone that'll come and bring you what you ask for; what you *need*. … "

"I doubt that'll happen," Malcolm said. "I don't think they like me very much, really."

"Oh … *that'll* change; believe me. Everyone mellows with age. … Even I did."

Malcolm pulled up a chair. He had not been called a young man in a very long time and he enjoyed it, smiling when he heard it.

"I want to talk to you about Paperclip."

"Yes, I thought that's why you'd come. You're with the spies. ... I remember *you*."

"Why?"

"Well that's how we met the first time, isn't it?"

"Yes."

"I thought so. I'm good with faces. And yours was *very* handsome. You've aged, I'm afraid."

"It was in 1952. March, if I recall. You'd sent out an SOS. ... And it was me they sent," Malcolm said. "I was twenty-eight at the time it was a very long time ago."

"You were so beautiful I think I fell in love with you. How could I forget? Like Thor. I *wanted* to fall in love back then. I was lonely on that base. ... You can't imagine how lonely ..."

"Carl, when you sent the SOS, it was about a man named Hans Kamptner," Malcolm said.

"Yes. That prick... What a fucking Nazi. He was a ring leader there at White Sands, selling all kinds of black market things on base: Marijuana, boys, girls. In fact, anything Hans *wanted* to do, he seemed to be able to get away with—without any official consequences. But I told you all that back *then*."

"I need to walk over that ground again. What happened with Hans?" Malcolm said. "I'm afraid back then. ... "

"You boys didn't give a shit—I know that. Why didn't you care? I was onto them. They were *so* obvious. Their little Nazi cabal."

"Because things were changing. ... The cold war was starting up. ... My bosses wanted to get out of that business and into a new business in Asia," Malcolm said, which was the truth.

"Are you still with them? The cloak and dagger boys?"

"Yes," Malcolm said. "I've postponed my retirement, for now, at least."

"Randy says you're one of the top dogs. That's what he'd heard."

Malcolm didn't answer the question.

"Congratulations. You were a bright penny when we met. Going places even back then; I could tell. Full of piss and vinegar."

"Thank you."

"All right, fire away," Smith said. "Do your best. I'm not going anywhere."

"You contacted your case officer, an FBI agent in Albuquerque, and said that you thought that Hans Kamptner was involved in criminal activity, and that he was blackmailing the base commander. Is that true?"

"Yes. And nothing came of it, except I was drummed out of the Army for being a 'practicing homosexual,' as they termed it, which was very funny at the time, as I was hardly practicing. I had no one to practice *with!* Las Cruces didn't even have one gay bar!"

"Tell me about Hans Kamptner. Why did you believe he was blackmailing the base commander at White Sands?"

"Okay. For the *second* time, thirty years later ... Well, first of all he was still an outright Nazi and very proud of it. I saw his CIC file. I had access to the files of all the Nazis that were brought onto the base, their QVs were stapled to the back of their de-Nazification files. Kamptner's was a phony—I told the FBI that right up front. He was supposed to be some kind of high altitude expert—a big Luftwaffe scientist—but I can tell you that that was *all* a lie. He never produced any work at all while at White Sands—at least not *scientific* work. We were working on the U2, then, and he contributed *nothing* to the project—no work at all. I doubt he knew anything about high altitude issues accept when he was drunk."

"When you contacted us you said Hans was spying on the other Germans at White Sands ... and maybe some others on the base, too?"

"Yes. Well that's what it seemed like to me at the time. He had card games in his room; they all went there. He had whores from off-base, which was prohibited but somehow he managed it, and I think he was pimping them. And then there was the question of the Commander. There was something not right there. Hans was screwing his wife—I told you that back then. I knew the girl, we were good friends, and of course I speak German. That was the main reason you boys wanted me to watch the German gang in the first place. But I told you all this way back then. Why would it matter *now?* Everyone is dead and gone, for God's sake!"

"The base commander's wife? You were friendly with her, you told me."

"Yes. Until she *disappeared* ... then they found her *murdered.* We were pretty close, really. You see, she was German. The base commander had gotten married in Berlin and brought her home with him to the States. But she barely spoke any English at all, and she was *much* younger—just eighteen, I think—when she married the old goat. She obviously married him to get the hell out of Berlin. If you'd only listened to me then maybe things would have been different."

"And when she disappeared you called in the SOS."

"Yes, well, first I called the imbecile FBI agents who I'd been instructed to contact first if anything 'untoward' ever happened. They were two simian police-types used to chasing communists, at least the ones they sent out to talk to me were—just loathsome men; disgusting. They said they couldn't legally follow the German scientists, also that they didn't have the manpower to do it, and it was up to the *Army* to track their comings and goings. And as far as the missing girl went, they could have cared less. So I gave up on the FBI and sent out the SOS to you people. And then *you* showed up. ... But it was already too late. She was already dead by then, *wasn't* she!?" The old man looked at him and took a deep breath through his nose, obviously aware that he needed the oxygen to live. His rheumy blue eyes had turned steely, despite his age. Malcolm heard the oxygen machine make a loud spitting noise across the room.

*　　　　　*　　　　　*

1952 ■ LAS CRUCES, NEW MEXICO LA POSTA RESTAURANT

"Do you know that one of their test rockets misfired and shot over the border into Mexico. I think those guys did it on purpose—the Germans, I mean, just for laughs. I think it hit a rancho just outside Juarez and killed several people. The U.S. had to pay blood-money to the families, to keep it quiet." the young man, Carl Smith, smiled crookedly as he spoke. He was, Malcolm knew, one of the youngest atomic physicists in the country, and considered brilliant in his field. He'd studied in Germany, where his father had taught physics at the University of Heidelberg, and then later at Harvard. The father had changed the family name from Groettrup to Smith after the start of the war. The young man was thirty-three years old, blond and blue-eyed, and looked like Leslie Howard, the film star. He'd read Smith's file before flying out to Las Cruces from Washington. Both Smith's father and Carl were working for the US government. The son was still a Warrant Officer in the Air Force.

Malcolm's cover was as a recruiter for the University of Michigan's fledgling nuclear science program. He and Carl were meeting in one of the few restaurants that existed in Las Cruces, La Posta. Malcolm's cover name was Frank Picture, which had been a good joke in the office that handled Operation Paperclip. Paperclip's head offices were actually located in a hotel in New York—to be exact, they were on the fourth floor of the Alamac Hotel, near Broadway, not far from Times Square. They were one of the newly-created Central Intelligence Agency's various satellite offices in the city. He'd been stuck working on Operation Paperclip after his work interviewing POWs in Germany for the War Department's de-Nazification program had been termed "complete": his bosses seemed to think that putting him on Paperclip was a logical follow-up assignment to his work in Europe.

He had tried desperately to get transferred to the CIA's new Directorate of Plans that was being organized by Bedell Smith—a personal friend of his father's—in Washington, but he'd been held back from that because his boss in New York, who answered to the National Security Council Office of Special Projects—and stuck with the oversight of Operation Paperclip—was facing the fact that all the young OSS officers who had any intelligence/talent were trying to get into the clandestine service of the newly-minted CIA, especially young men like Malcolm who had combat experience during the war. His boss had begged Malcolm to go and interview the "fairy" out in Las Cruces before he was released from Operation Paperclip and sent to the U.S. Embassy in Bangkok, a career move that was, Malcolm hoped, going to get him back into the field. He'd agreed to go interview the man, but only in exchange for a two-week vacation, as no one wanted to tramp out to New Mexico to interview a scientist in the middle of the desert in the middle of July about an operation that rumor had it would soon be shut down and handed over to the U.S. Army and private industry. The fact was, the new CIA seemed to not care much about the Nazi scientists on the U.S. payroll who'd been brought into the United States to work on various scientific projects in both private industry and for the U.S. Defense Department. Paperclip—a legacy from the old days of the OSS—was very soon to become someone else's problem, Malcolm had heard.

"All right; if you would, could you tell me exactly what you believe happened to the young woman—the base commander's wife?" Malcolm said. It was hot in the restaurant and noisy, and men from the base were two-deep at the bar on a Thursday night and well into their cups. The jukebox was playing Bill Haley's big hit "Rock The Joint".

"I think this Hans person had something to do with it. ... Her death, I mean," Smith said.

"Why?" Malcolm had to speak loudly to be heard over the music.

"Because she was having an affair with Hans."

"You're *sure* about that?"

"Yes, Carla—that was her name—told me that herself. She was infatuated with him; Hans the Nazi. She *loved* him."

"She admitted *that* to you?" Malcolm signaled for more iced tea; it was a hundred-and-five in the shade that day, with eight percent humidity, and still very warm in the restaurant at nine o'clock at night. Outside in the parking lot, the heat radiating up from the asphalt made it feel like the door to a blast furnace had been opened.

"You people don't seem to care *what* these guys do," Smith said.

"That's not true, at all," Malcolm said. For some reason, he felt he had to stick up for the system. "They're important to America, now, with the situation developing like it is …with Russia and everything. What they've brought to us in terms of scientific expertise. We *need* them." Malcolm parroted what he had been told since Paperclip started.

"Yes. Yes. I know the speech. I've given it several times myself at the Rotary Club. Please spare me that crap. The fact is, several of them are lying about their qualifications. That's something *else* I've told those idiots at the FBI—when they bother to call me back, that is … " Malcolm ran his fingers through his hair and waited for the waitress to fill his glass with iced tea. When she'd left the table, he started up again.

"I'm not here to judge that. I'm here because you said that Hans Kamptner is spying on the other Germans at the base. That's *all* I'm here for. Do you have proof of his activities?"

"Yes."

"What—*exactly?*"

"We have cubby holes for incoming mail for each department in the main office. I've caught Kamptner putting mail back into boxes that didn't have anything to do with him or his department. Obviously he'd taken the letters and opened them and read them. … And there're other things, too. He's always slipping around, reading things on the sly while people are gone; he's constantly wandering around the base in places where he has no business being, then making up stupid excuses, using that pretend-bad-English like a shield. He doesn't fool me for a moment."

"*What* other things?"

"I think he has some kind of control over the Commander of the base. He's got something *on* him, and he's even allowed to live *off-base,* now. This is unprecedented, as far as I know. … And I know for a fact that several of the other Nazis are visiting him regularly at his new digs, here in Las Cruces."

"How do *you* know all this?"

"Because Carla and I were close … and she told me."

"Why would she confide in you? After all, you weren't her lover …were you?"

"God, no! Not my type. I tend to go for the less-feminine types," Smith said. Malcolm felt his jaw muscles tighten up—he had no use for queers, and Smith had struck him as probably "in the closet" since they'd first started talking; small mannerisms and gestures gave him away, and it was in his voice, although he obviously tried to hide it. He thought about the two weeks he was going to get for talking to this creep, who he now flatly disliked. He couldn't think of anything lower than a homosexual unless it was a truly committed Red.

"She confided in me because he was two-timing her. She used to come to my bungalow to talk about him and listen to records. She was obsessed with Hans and

73

followed him to his house, here in town. She used to park and spy on him, and she was sure that he had another girlfriend."

"And she told you that other Germans from the base were coming to his place?"

"Yes. It was a regular beer-hall. Several of the Nazis in the program went almost every night. I knew the ones she mentioned. They were all the worst brutes, bragging all the time about their glorious SS and how the Jews were running the world and all the rest of it. Mostly they raved about getting back at the Jews for what they'd done to Germany. I'd like another drink, if you don't mind," Smith said.

Malcolm signaled their waitress and Smith ordered another gin and tonic "Let's get back to Hans," Malcolm said.

"...I think she confronted him, and then she disappeared. That's what I think happened. That was three weeks ago, when I called the FBI. They said she probably ran away and that she was fine. Wives, these geniuses said, run away all the time. That was before they found her body, of course. Maybe she shot herself in the back of the head, too—do you think? I don't know. Is that something young despondent wives do all the time, too? It seems rather a difficult thing to pull off without help, actually."

"You're saying she was murdered."

"Don't be *stupid*—of course she was murdered!"

"What did the police do?" Malcolm said.

Smith laughed. "This is New Mexico, my friend. ... Most of the police are ex-GI's that fought in Europe. They *hate* the German community here, especially the Nazis at the base. They won't investigate at all. That's my guess. They said it was probably a robbery that went bad and passed it on to the MP's, who are under the direct command of Carla's husband. ... So nothing has happened except a well-attended funeral. They found her body on-base in a ditch, by the way. She'd been raped, badly beaten, and then shot in the back of the head." The young man looked at him. The intelligence in his eyes came out with a literal brightness and intensity that startled Malcolm. "The last time I saw her was here in this restaurant. She told me she was going to leave her husband and go back to Germany. She said she hated New Mexico. She hated the desert and considered America a kind of clean Hell. She said that Hans was going back with her and that she was madly in love with him and that she was going to have his baby."

"Here, I've brought something for you." Smith slid a file-folder across the table. "It's Hans' original CIC file from Berlin. I brought it because I wanted you to see it. The one the CIC did in Berlin, mind you, right after he was arrested. His *original* file. I wrote a friend in Berlin and asked him to pull some strings to get it. It's completely different than the file we have on record here at the base. Hans Kamptner was an intelligence officer in the *Wehrmacht*, and not a scientist, according to this original file. Notice the date: it was put together in June of nineteen-forty-seven at Dachau, where they were sending war criminals at the time for prosecution. He'd been caught in the French Zone in Berlin by the French police and was arrested because his identification papers were phony. Proof enough, I hope, that he was already a spy and was probably working for the Russians even then. Hans isn't a scientist at all. He's a *spy.* ... That's what I've been saying since he got here. Read it for yourself," Smith said.

Malcolm opened the file and recognized the material. He'd worked on several high profile files like it, helping to document various German prisoners' war records by cross-referencing SS files, *Wehrmacht* files, and any other material that had been found in a Berlin bunker complex right after the war. Most of the records had been kept in bomb-proof containers and were intact and extensive, going all the way back to the early 1930s. He even recognized the name of the CIC officer who had put the file together. In fact they'd worked in the same office at Dachau. Then he looked at the abridged file that had been done up by the Army after Kamptner had arrived in America, probably in some office in Washington.

"He went from being a nasty Nazi intelligence officer working in Russia and Poland ... *Abwehr*, SD, the whole thing, to an aeronautics scientist, *magically*. Notice he was in Moscow at one point, having been arrested by the Russians, and then was mysteriously let go by them. Odd, don't you think? How many German intelligence officers do you think the NKVD let go?"

"I see."

"Good. *Finally* you see what's been going on, here. It won't do Carla any good now, though, *will* it?" Smith said.

"Is there anything else I should know?" Malcolm said.

"What do you mean?"

"About you? You seem to have paid a lot of attention to Kamptner. Is there any other reason for that attention? Did you. ... How should I put this ... ? Is Hans a homosexual? Is there something you haven't told me?" Malcolm said, looking at Smith.

"I don't date Nazis. Is that what you're trying to ask? I draw the line with war criminals. ... And, yes, I'm a homosexual. Look it up in the dictionary. We're next to Lucifer's entry. According to Webster's Third a homosexual is a moral pervert, a communist, and an anti-American ... When we take a break from eating little children, that is. We're very busy all the time as a result. Hardly have *time* for a social life, you see?"

"I had to ask," Malcolm said. He took a swallow of iced tea and thought for a moment about what he'd seen at Dachau, at some of the war crimes trials that he was forced to attend. Mostly it was young men who had shown no remorse at all for the atrocities they'd committed in the name of their hare-brained Hitler and Fascism. Then he ordered a hard drink and wished to God he were anywhere else. He wanted to get on with his life, the war was over now. He wanted to put it behind him and go on to Asia and something new.

"I can show you where he's staying … Hansi. I think he should be arrested," Smith said. "For espionage at least. And probably for Carla's murder."

"And you think he's got something on the base commander, too. What, exactly?" The waitress, a tall redhead from Texas with big breasts, brought Malcolm a bourbon and soda.

"How the hell should *I* know … that's why I called you spooks in, isn't it? That, my friend, was the second stupid question you've asked tonight. *Please* tell me this new CIA isn't like the FBI." After dinner, they drove by Kamptner's bungalow on the outskirts of Las Cruces. There were several cars parked in front.

"All those belong to Germans from the base. I recognize all the cars," Smith said. "Maybe they're starting an Oompah band, eh?"

Malcolm was looking at Hans Kamptner through the dirty old screen-door of his rented bungalow in Las Cruces. It was nine in the morning— early. He had not been able to sleep the previous night: the memories of his time in Berlin and the trials at Dachau had come back hard and made sleep impossible. Maybe if he hadn't actually been to the trials and heard the testimony in person he would have felt differently. He'd decided he didn't like Kamptner without ever having met him.

"Hello, my name is Mr. Picture—I'm from the Defense Department. Can I speak to you for a moment, Mr. Kamptner?" Kamptner looked tired; as if he'd been drinking all night. He had a day's-growth of beard and dark circles under his eyes. He was handsome and dark-haired and very tall. He looked mean as hell, and about forty years old.

"I was just going to post office … and I'm late for work."

"It won't take long," Malcolm said. Kamptner didn't move. He just stood there looking at him with hooded brown eyes; eyes that seemed very still, more like the lenses of a strange dual-aperture camera that were about to snap his picture.

"Is it important?" Kamptner said, looking first at him, and then past him out at the street through the screen door.

"Yes," Malcolm said. "It's about Carla O'Sullivan's death. … Out at the base." The eyes took their picture of him and then he heard the hook being removed from its eye and the screen-door was opened.

"Thank you," Malcolm said.

"Yes, please come in," Kamptner said. His American accent was good; he'd all ready ground-off the worst of his guttural German accent, a sign of someone who was trying very hard to blend in, and Malcolm noticed it immediately. Kamptner, like a lot of Bavarians that Malcolm had met, were surprisingly dark-complected. He was wearing suspenders over a sleeveless T-shirt and dark-brown cotton pants. There was a suitcase on a couch with the top open and clothes neatly stacked on a dining room table nearby. "Come in. ... Come in, then, sir."

"This won't take long," Malcolm said.

"May I make a call first?" The German said.

"Of course." Kamptner went into the kitchen and dialed a number. Malcolm could hear him speaking in monosyllables. And then he was back with something between a smile and a smirk on his face.

"What can I do for you, Mr. Picture?"

"I understand you knew Carla O'Sullivan?"

"Yes. I knew her. Very sad."

"How well did you know her?"

"Casually... We met at a parties on the base, several times. And at Colonel Sullivan's house, of course."

"She was a German national, wasn't she," Malcolm said.

"Yes."

"I was told you and she were having an affair," Malcolm said.

"Ridiculous."

"Is it?"

"Yes, quite ridiculous, in fact."

"I spoke to the neighbors, and they said they've seen her here, parked nearby." Malcolm lied, but the camera eyes were looking at him again, taking him more seriously, now.

"They'll say anything about us Germans. ... She had a crush on me—it's true. I tried to avoid her as best as I could, but the girl made a fool of herself on more than one occasion, coming here."

"So you did know her more than casually?"

"Why do you want to know?"

"Captain. That was your rank in the SS, wasn't it, before you were sent to military intelligence because of your Russian language skills? I believe your father was Russian?" Malcolm had called an ex-girl friend in London who was working for MI6 about Kamptner to see what the English knew about him.

"I'm a scientist ... I was never in the SS. I'm afraid you've mistaken me for someone else, maybe with the same name. It's all in my file at the base," Kamptner said.

"Then let me examine your right arm," Malcolm said. He knew that most SS

77

men, officers especially, had their blood type tattooed under their arm: it had been mandatory.

"Are you going somewhere?" Malcolm said, looking at the open suitcase.

"Mexico, after work ... for the weekend ... with some friends from the base," he said. A car pulled up and two MP's got out and walked toward the house, and after them a squad car from the local police department pulled up, too.

"Now maybe you explain to the military police who *you* are, *exactly*?" Kamptner said. Malcolm tried to grab him by the arm to look for the tattoo but was stopped by the MP's.

9

1980 ■ SAN BERNARDINO, CALIFORNIA

The neighborhood was white and working-class. From the street, the Vagos clubhouse was unimpressive, slightly derelict in feel. It shared the block with a motley collection of one-storey older homes and commercial buildings dedicated to light industry. Their parking lots were all protected by chain-link fences, some with helices of razor-wire on top. The clubhouse's cement-block exterior had never been painted, which made it look like something the city might own. The front yard had uncut grass, was full of dog shit, and a black Weber barbeque grill lying on its side was immediately in front of the door. The fact that it had been left pushed-over as a way of ending a party spoke to the Vagos' casual attitude toward everything but violence and crime. The front yard on Friday afternoons was the site of beer parties thrown to hopefully attract young girls. It seemed that San Bernardino had a limitless supply of good-looking eighteen-year-old girls, attracted by the Vagos myth, who wanted to sleep with a bona fide "full-patch" motorcycle gang member.

Inside, though, the space was big and clean and well maintained. In the main hall there was a banner strung across one wall that said: WE GIVE AS GOOD AS WE GET. There was a new bright-green—the club's colors—linoleum floor that one of the members had installed for free, as his family owned a successful flooring business in L.A. There were six brand-new, huge, "slick" dragster tires, that a member was temporarily storing, stacked in one corner. The tires were so new you could still smell the acrid chemical "new-tire smell" that they gave off. Otherwise, the large open room, its block walls painted white, could have been a Veteran's Hall or a Toastmaster's meeting place; except for one thing—there was only one window in the front side of the building, and it was a transom-type, up high and above the steel front door. It was obvious that the Vagos didn't want anyone to see what went on inside their clubhouse. What they didn't want people to see were all the things that revolve around any headquarters of a sophisticated criminal enterprise with interests in prostitution, drug dealing, extortion, stolen cars, stolen motorcycles, and their fastest-growing profit sector—murder for hire.

There were now Vagos chapters as far away as Germany, Italy, and Spain. Foreign chapters paid a licensing fee to the San Bernardino chapter. The Italian chapter had brought the heroin connection that was making the Vagos Southern California club very wealthy—in fact, changing it from a collection of psychopathic killers and wannabes into something even more disturbing.

"These fuckers—who*ever* they are, have to go down," Tony Da Silva said. He was the chapter's president and also the liaison with the San Bernardino Sheriff's Department, who had two officers who were also Vagos "full-patch members" albeit secret ones. The cops were members that never wore their jackets on the streets for obvious reasons. One of the two was now deceased, having been shot at the Ford dealership six months ago.

The Vagos had a lot of smart people running the club, and Tony Da Silva was one of them. This was a fact that the FBI never understood about the Vagos, nor did they fully appreciate what they did understand of the club's organization and place in the underworld. The members may have looked like tattooed, jean-clad gorillas, who swilled beer day and night—which was true in general—but that didn't mean they were incompetent or lacked intelligence. Tony, at forty-one years old, was 6'3" and weighed in at two-hundred and twenty pounds. He'd taken the standardized IQ test in high school and scored 145, one of the highest ever recorded in the school district. As a result, no one, not any of his teachers or his school counselor, would believe he was essentially evil. And, because of his test scores, they were convinced that he could be changed for the better.

Tony had been spotted by the school district's psychiatrist as a possible clinical psychopath after having been interviewed by the doctor at the juvenile hall where he'd been taken during his junior year after assaulting a girl in the women's bathroom of the YMCA. When asked by the doctor why he'd attempted to rape the girl, Tony had said "Because she asked for it." Even the psychiatrist had felt gooseflesh rise on his arm. The doctor had taken the trouble to call Tony's parents to tell them he thought that their son was *very* ill and should be put on medications for his own good. Tony's mother, a long-haul truck driver and Benzedrine addict, had laughed at him and hung up. The fact was, she was afraid of her son and stayed out of his damn way. The rape charge was dropped because of a legal technicality. Some people said it was because Tony's uncle was on the police force, but things like that can't ever be proved. Because the girl was black the case caught no attention from the press.

Everyone at Tony's high school seemed to think that having a high IQ somehow served as a moral prophylactic. After the school's principal was assaulted by Tony in his office and beaten so badly he lost control of the entire right side of his body, that notion was finally put to rest. Tony was sent to the California Youth Authority for 3 years, and the attitudes there were quite different about bright hoodlums. Tony was often handcuffed and shackled even when he was on a routine trip to the dentist to get his teeth cleaned. It was at the CYA that Tony found out that he had leadership qualities. Or, as Tony said to his cellmate, "You don't have to *like* me, motherfucker, you just have to do what I tell you." He was spotted as a "prospect" by the Vagos as soon as he got out of the penitentiary the *second* time. He'd always enjoyed riding motorcycles.

Tony was talking to his two most trusted lieutenants. One of them was Kevin Irons, thirty-two years old and the club's Sergeant of Arms because he could box and had been a Golden Gloves champion. Irons had a murderous reputation for stomp-you-to-death violence; he was a good-looking guy with jet-black hair and green eyes who had gone to Cal Berkeley for a year before dropping out and coming back to his hometown of Bakersfield. He'd never fit in with the middle class kids on the Cal campus and felt isolated and lonely there. He told his mom that the kids just spoke another language and he didn't understand it. Irons had been recruited by Tony himself, who knew that the future of the club lay in becoming both more daring, but at the same time more careful, two apparently opposite ideas that he knew always worked in tandem; the knowledge of which spoke to Tony's criminal genius. The Vagos began to recruit inside the Sheriff's Department using young girls and sex parties as a sure-fire way to get men to want to join the club. If they could have a teenaged girl as a "sex slave"—who could say no to *that?* Tony asked the members. Of course, he'd been right, and they had no problem recruiting members of the Sheriff's Dept.

The other lieutenant in on the current confab was Malinda, Tony's wife, who was a lawyer, and a very good one. She was a petit redhead and liked to wear all black leather when she rode behind her husband on "runs." She'd gone to a third-rate law school in Los Angeles at night. But she had studied hard and understood, on a profound level, that the law in the United States was in large part about money, connections, and straight-up lying under oath. She had a profitable criminal practice, now, that defended a lot of outlaw bikers in Southern California—even bikers who were sworn enemies of the Vagos would show up at her office because they knew that not only was Malinda Da Silva a good lawyer, but she was a fixer, too, "bringing solutions to high risk enterprises," as she told her clients. In other worlds, she could have witnesses disappear for good—for a price. There were a lot of people buried on a certain ranch near Tucson, for example. And there were some younger judges that received "anonymous" favors from eighteen-year-old girls who showed up mysteriously on their front porches when their wives were at PTA meetings. Girls who'd been around the block a few times.

81

"Who *are* these two assholes?" Irons said.

"I don't know," Tony said. "Two faggots, is what I heard on the street."

"Something's not right. ... Why would they shoot down L.A. County Sheriffs? That's just asking for trouble—*no* one does that." Irons said.

"No shit—well, that's why we got the contract," Tony said.

"Only we shouldn't take it," Malinda said. "We're in over our heads on this one—I just feel it." Her husband looked at her carefully. "I think the DEA did it," she said. "*Their* guys did it ... and now they're trying to cover it up."

"How *can* they cover it up? They fucking shot two LA County Sheriffs?" Tony said.

"My sources inside the LAPD said that someone reported the license plate number of the car at the scene of the shooting," Malinda said. "LAPD traced it to the DEA. And then nothing? Now, the LAPD doesn't want to press this case because they found out the two Sheriff's Deputies were both dirty. Both had cash in the bank that way-exceeded their incomes by hundreds of thousands of dollars. The fed's are charging their wives with tax evasion because they filed joint returns. That kind of stuff looks bad at election time for the L.A. County Sheriff," she said. "So suddenly no one is jumping up and down about their two fallen comrades." The two men looked at her. Malinda had a natural authority and wasn't afraid of anyone, including her husband, which was saying quite a lot.

"Well, we *aren't* taking the fucking contract from the LAPD. ... We're taking it for San Bernardino guys, our friends and associates," Tony said. "We've got to do *something*! After all, that was *our* nigger they killed."

"I don't like it," Malinda said. "Something is wrong with this whole thing. I've heard these guys are robbing heroin and coke dealers all over Southern California. These two "faggot" white boys. ... And on top of that, they're selling high-grade heroin by the kilo at a good price. Now who does *that* kind of shit? Sells kilos and then rips people off when they feel like it?"

"Are you saying that these are some DEA guys that've gone rogue?" Irons said. He had a secret crush on Malinda but had kept it to himself, even though he'd just as soon have killed Tony as not if it'd just been up to him.

"That would explain it, maybe. They don't get to keep the money unless they *steal* it from dealers because they have to account for all the heroin they sell—but not for the cash they rip off. And for some reason their bosses can't stop them—or don't *want* to." She threw a pen on the table. "That's the part I don't get. And when I don't get something, I don't like it," Malinda said. "I've got to go to court after lunch, so let's rap this up soon, okay? I say we don't get involved at all, or we're going to be involved in something we don't understand and can't control the outcome of."

"They're offering a million dollars to ... solve this," Tony said.

"There is *one* way. Get Italy to send some people," Malinda said.

"We sell the contract?" Irons said. He was looking at Malinda and undressing her in his mind. She had a tight ass that belonged on a sixteen-year-old, and it had been driving him crazy for some time, now. She had what was known in biker parlance as a "one-hand ass."

"Why not? Keep five-hundred and pay the Italians five-hundred, and that way it can't splatter all over us, if it's actually federal cops we're talking about. Just make sure when the sheriffs pay you, it can't be traced back to us. Have the Italians credit us the five-hundred toward our account, and that way there's no record of a payment. Have the cops pay the Italians directly."

"Now *that's* fucking smart," Irons said. Malinda smiled. She had grown up with an abusive father, and had learned early-on to think three steps ahead of most people. She'd be long gone by the time her father's drunken punch went by her head.

"Why do you think I married her?" Tony said. "*Sheee-it.* Okay!—let's get a hold of the Dagos."

"One other thing—why don't we contact them ... these guys? If they're selling heroin?" Malinda said. "I heard their shit is primo and they're selling kilos for a damn good price. ... I mean before they die."

"Shit, you an *evil* bitch," Tony laughed. "But you're *my* evil bitch."

"Okay, I've got to go to court," Malinda said, getting up. She picked up her briefcase from the floor.

"Hey, baby, say Hi to Judge Phillips for me—that fat-ass motherfucker," Tony said. "We went to junior high together. I used to steal his lunch. He always had the best shit for lunch," Tony said to Irons. His wife walked up behind him and ruffed up her husband's hair. They were a good couple, and actually quite happy, keeping their marriage together in a difficult social environment.

*   *   *

The three of them—Butch, Alex, and Patty—were lying out on the beach at Malibu right below Highway One, just below a famous health food store with juice-bar where Warren Beatty hung out. Patty had been revived by two beefy, gay firemen from New York who were vacationing in L.A. and had run into the hotel room after hearing a maid screaming bloody murder, after she'd walked in and seen what she thought was Patty's dead body on the bed. But Patty hadn't been dead; rather, her pulse and vital signs had gone into a kind of hibernation as a result of the overdose. The firemen had recognized her symptoms immediately, having worked in Harlem, and had pounded

Patty's chest so hard that she had bruises for a week. But they'd brought her back from the dead, or almost-dead, anyway. Alex had gotten a call at the motel and thought it was an auditory hallucination—some kind of a waking nightmare—that he was dreaming the whole conversation as it happened.

"It's me," Patty said.

"*Patty?*"

"Yeah. Thanks for splitting on me, babe. ... "

"I ... *Patty!?*"

"I know, you thought I was dead ..."

"*Jesus!*"

"I'm at the L.A. County Hospital, Room 345. Come and get me. I don't like green Jell-O very much."

"L.A. County?"

"Yes. Hurry."

"Okay. I thought. I mean, I checked ... "

"It's okay ... Everyone makes mistakes. ... Just come and get me ... all right?"

"Yeah. Okay."

Now the three of them were passing a joint around and watching the surfers shuck their wet-suits, standing bare-ass naked to dry off in the sun. A kid about sixteen with long blond hair was throwing his "boogie" board on the wet sand nearest the water, and skimming it for 20 yards at a stretch. The surf sometimes flowed over his feet in cool waves.

"Hey, they don't have any respect," Butch said. He whistled and waved at one of the surfers who'd dropped his swimsuit and was standing naked, his butt turned towards them. "Hey. ... We got a lady here, partner!" The surfer looked back toward Butch. He was a big kid; he flipped Butch off and turned around and bent over, showing them his ass as a joke.

"Wow! Wait a second!" Butch said.

"Butch, why do you get so excited all the time?" Patty asked, passing him the joint. "That's not the first asshole I've seen, and it's not the biggest, either." Alex laughed. Patty was wearing jeans and a white bra. He face was very pale from the meds they'd given her in the hospital. She was thinner than when she'd gotten to L.A., and as a result looked like a waif in some Bergman movie.

"Because he's stone-crazy," Alex said. He'd been subdued since he'd picked her up at the hospital, feeling guilty for having left her behind at the hotel. "I keep telling everyone that, but no one believes me." It was just past noon and the sun was starting to get hot. It was going to be a hot June day, the air still and sweet, a sea-salt smell in the air. Two seagulls stood guard on the sand nearby, eying them.

"I don't think he's crazy. Are you crazy, Butch?" She asked. Patty looked at Butch. She liked him. He was the big brother she'd never had and he was sweet to her, not caring about her problems, or judging her. In fact he'd been nice to her since the first day that Alex had brought him around to her boat in Sausalito. Butch's child-like sincerity and his bursts of enthusiasm over things that other people seemed to take for granted, she had picked up on and enjoyed.

"NO. I'm not crazy! Everyone else is crazy, baby," Butch said. He took the joint, careful not to smash the wet end flat, and inhaled.

"Where are we going for lunch?" he said, exhaling.

"I like The Source ... organic is good for you," Patty said. "I'm going totally organic and maybe vegetarian, too. I don't want to eat anything with a face on it," she said. Butch laughed. He'd shaved for a change. He'd taken his shirt off and his white skin was getting red. He had a broad chest with a simple classic Marine Corps tattoo on his right shoulder.

"Me, too," Alex said. "Except pig's feet. ... I can't let those go. I like'em cold. With that jelly all around the toes."

Alex was wearing over-sized surfer shorts he'd just bought and a wife-beater; his small chest and arms were long and scrawny-looking in comparison to Butch's. Patty, laughing, reached over and kissed him. Butch watched them kanoodle. Then he broke up their kiss by passing the joint back, forcing Alex to grab it. He was jealous, as Patty was adorable and he was attracted to her death-spiral, but he'd not let on. A large wave crashed on the beach, with that pounding sound that was both atavistic and enthralling. The sound, perhaps, of the womb. Patty looked down the beach and saw little dots of color and movement, people—bright specters—moving in the glare of mid-day.

"I love that sound ... the sound of the waves pounding like that ..." she said, taking a hit. They were all silent for a moment. Another three waves hit in quick succession, making the same flat, pounding sound.

"I'll never stop shooting dope," she said, out of the blue. "No one can make me. ..." Alex looked at her. He had spoken to her about stopping, and thought that she had listened to him, because she hadn't said a word after his well-planned lecture on how she had to stop. He was holding the joint and looking at her, now. She was no different than Butch, he realized, looking at her. She was out of control and *crazy, too* "Why should I?" she said, almost to herself, watching the surf slide up the beach.

"Well, maybe because you almost died?" Alex said. The kid with the boogie board picked it up. Alex turned and saw the goopy sand-pocked underside of the boogie board. The kid hurled the board in front of him again, and took off after it.

"It's bad if you do too much," Butch said. Another surfer, part of the group in front of them, dropped his shorts and began to towel off.

"Hey, asshole ... there's a lady here!" Butch said. The kid didn't even turn around.

"I love it here in LA.," Patty said. "It's warm all the time and you feel like walking around naked. ... It doesn't matter."

"Yeah, I like it too," Butch said. He had turned and looked at the group of surfers, their boards strewn on the sand around them. "I like Malibu. I'm going to buy a place. But I can't afford the beach. You want to come look with me?" Butch asked.

"He's been saving his pennies," Alex said. "He's very frugal."

"That's right. ..." Butch said, turning around and looking at them. The expression on his face had changed. It was harder now, not relaxed. "I'm like the broom in *Fantasia*. ... I've been cleaning up!"

"I love that movie!" Patty said. She reached over and put her hand on Alex's thigh, and when she did her white stomach made a knot, and Butch could see her twist, and he thought he liked her more than he should so he looked away. "I made my father take me back three times," she said.

Alex was looking at her. He stood up suddenly and knocked the sand off his knees and walked down the beach toward the gang of surfers, all bigger than him. They had done so many crazy things, so many dangerous things in the last three months, that he'd gone a little crazy, too, he realized. And now he wanted Patty to stop taking drugs but was afraid that she wouldn't and that next time she wouldn't come back from the dead. He wanted to tell her he loved her but couldn't do that, either. He wasn't sure he knew what it meant to love someone.

"Put your pants on, *asshole*," Alex said.

"What?"

"You heard me, faggot." The bigger one that had flipped Butch off looked down the beach at Butch and Patty and then flipped Alex off, deciding they were just hippies and harmless. The guy standing in front of him was no threat, he decided.

"Go fuck yourself, pencil neck," the kid said.

Alex pulled a small Beretta out from behind his back and hit the big one in the face with the butt, knocking all his front teeth out. Then he turned, holding the pistol out at the same time that he pulled the hammer back, and pointed it at the group of boy-men. He made the rest of them put their pants on. They thought, now, they were looking at a crazy man who might pull the trigger. Even the big one, his mouth bleeding, big drops of blood falling onto the dry golden sand, climbed into his swimsuit, afraid of Alex. The pain in his mouth was excruciating; his teeth were lost forever.

"Look what you've done," Butch said to Patty, watching. He slapped on the cowboy hat he'd recently taken to wearing, and stood up.

"...What have I done?" Patty said.

"Can't you see ...? That shit has spaced you out—he's in love with you," Butch said. He got up and walked slowly towards his partner. He felt obligated to walk over there, now they were in fact partners in a very serious way. And, he figured, looking at Alex as he walked down the beach, that they would soon both die here in LA and never grow old. He was grateful for that, actually. Not since Vietnam had he felt much of anything. That thought—of a mystical doom hanging over the three of them—was satisfying for some reason; there was a completeness to it and an odd integrity. He watched Alex hold his gun out all crazy-like, his bird-legs limned by the sunlight. Butch had six hundred thousand dollars in cash, now; more money than he'd ever thought possible to have at one time; more money than anyone in Butch's family had ever seen before. And he was grateful to Alex in a way he'd never been before to anyone else.

"What did I do?" Patty called after Butch. "Huh? ... I didn't do anything." Butch didn't answer her. Like all opiate abusers she was busy building her wall between her and the outside world higher and thicker.

"You got everything under control here, chief?" Butch said, walking up behind Alex.

"I think so," Alex said. Then Butch went over and decked the kid who had flipped him off, knocking him out cold, his big body crashing to the ground like he'd just been shot. His legs twitched weirdly, his heels pushing at the sand in little jerks.

"From Pittsburgh ... with love," Butch said.

*   *   *

"I didn't think you guys would still be ... you know, be alive...?" Flaco said. Alex realized that Flaco looked a lot like Cantinflas, a Mexican movie star and comedian his nanny loved to watch on television when he was a little boy.

"No thanks to you, *motherfucker*," Butch said. They had set the meeting up at Brent's Deli in the San Fernando Valley.

"I got some people—they want to buy three kilos," Flaco said.

"You got some people?" Butch said. His tone was supercilious and threatening.

"Yeah. What's with your partner, man?" Flaco said. He was a meth addict and was just having iced tea. He was sitting on the "shoulder" of his high, uninterested in spoiling it with food.

"What *kind* of people?" Alex asked. He and Butch had ordered lunch.

"Good people." Flaco said. The Mexican sucked on a big red over-sized straw, chewing on it as he sucked.

"Looks like you suck dick, to me ... you do that so well ... *cabron!*" Butch said, glaring at Flaco. He was still obviously angry, and had only been convinced by Alex to take the meeting because Alex had assured him there was money in it for them.

"They'll pay twenty-three large a sack," Flaco said. The Mexican was afraid of Butch, no question about that. He had come across Butch's type before and knew he was a stone killer. There are some people that leave no doubt about that in your mind, and the big white guy was one of them; he'd decided that back when they'd first met—it was the main reason he'd run out on them that first time, in fact. Flaco had grown up in the heart of the barrio and knew a real killer when he saw one, white, brown, or black.

"They aren't 'sacks,'" Butch said aggressively. "Only a *faggot* would call them 'sacks.'"

"*You* know, *kilos. Jesus, man* ... what's eating you, dude? Give me a fucking break, *ese.*"

"Do you know these people ... *personally?*" Alex asked. Somehow it sounded like a stupid question even to him, but he asked it anyway. He glanced over at Butch, who was busy staring two holes right *through* Flaco.

"Yeah. Sure I do. They're cool. They're 'Valley guys.' They run some titty bars out in the Valley. *You* know the type. "

"Who are they, *exactly?*" Alex said again.

"Just some *people*, man. ... What the fuck? Do I look like their lawyer? ... Do you want to do this or not?" The waiter brought Alex and Butch their orders. The waiter was an old Jewish guy who gave the impression that he was both suspicious, and also somewhat fearful of them. He laid their orders down on the table, gave them a curt "knowing" look, and abruptly left. The waiter had been in a concentration camp as a kid and knew right away when he was looking at police of some kind.

"Where are we supposed to meet them?" Alex said, moving his plate closer.

"At a titty bar out here. You go in and pick up the money. ... Leave the junk in the back seat of your ride. ... Someone will go take it out while you're getting your money. Then you drive away." Flaco looked down at his iced tea and grabbed the straw with his teeth. His teeth were very bad in the way of meth addicts who smoke it. "It's an easy deal," Flaco said.

Alex turned and looked at Butch. Butch was still staring at Flaco. It suddenly seemed very quiet in the restaurant. Alex noticed the water-sweat on Flaco's red plastic over-sized glass and then glanced down at the sandwich he'd ordered; it looked so perfect that it almost didn't look real when you were as high as he was right then.

"Okay—we'll do it," Butch said. "But you're coming in with us. You're going to be in the bar *with* us."

"That's not part of the deal, man," Flaco said. Flaco suddenly looked bewildered.

"... And if you try running *this* time ... ... You'd better be faster than a .44 magnum bullet. Is he *that* fast, Bruce, do you think?"

"No ... no, I don't think so," Alex said. *"No* one's that fast."

"Why you being like *that,* man ...? I'm just trying to help you dudes out, is all," Flaco said.

"'Why you be like that, *man'* ... Because *I'm* making the rules, *bitch.* ... That's why." Butch parroted Flaco's whiny dope-fiend tone. Then he picked up his three-inch-thick Ruben and started to eat lunch like he'd never eaten a sandwich before in his life. Flaco wasn't much on conversation after that. He kept glancing at the door while they ate.

10

DECEMBER 1, 1946 ■
Dachau Concentration Camp
US Army 7th Division
Headquarters
Lagergeld Werkstatt Section – C

They'd driven through the east gate of one of Hell's masterpieces, Dachau concentration camp, at nine that morning. The barbed-wire was snow-covered, and made for strange white parallel lines that ran along the side of the road. The camp's gate was still decorated with an enormous Germanic eagle gripping a swastika in its talons. The huge eagle was ridiculous in the present circumstance, but nonetheless still disturbing, as were all the Ruritanian symbols that had been employed by the Nazis—designed to galvanize a simple-minded German public, inviting them to join in the ritualized fantasy and militaristic blood-lust that had, up until the creation of National Socialism, been the exclusive reserve of Europe's aristocracy, rife with all its attendant diseases and mental disorders.

It had been lightly snowing when Malcolm had gotten up that morning, with the snow lingering and swirling on a dirty little street in front of the small hotel where he was billeted in a suburb of Munich. It was the city that had given birth to the Nazi Party in the early 1920s, and as a result was lying now in complete ruin—a grim and just payback for its political recklessness.

Captain Malcolm Law, serving in the OSS's Counter Intelligence Corps, had been picked up at his hotel and driven to work by a coal-black corporal from Detroit who would later become a famous jazz musician. His driver took him into the former concentration camp and down *Lagerstrasse* road to a wooden building that the OSS was using to conduct interviews in their search for Nazi scientists to send to America. They rode, as they had every morning for several weeks now, through the snowy silence, past "roll-call square," past the "infirmary" and the "experimental Station," and alongside the numerous now-shuttered "barracks" and the myriad "workshops" where the prisoners had toiled for the glory of the Third Reich. All of it perfectly "legal" under Nazi law, of course.

They never spoke to each other while driving down the *Lagerstrasse*; perhaps out of a mutual respect for the dead. The camp, having now been turned into a U.S. Army base, was flying the stars and stripes that morning. Ironically, once again, military men strove for order and regimentation within the confines of the former concentration camp. But of course even the grim dirty snow, still holding the ashes of the recently murdered, would frustrate that longing for "order," and—like it or not—produce a weirdly hostile silence that Malcolm would always associate with the place, even years later.

The "work room" at Dachau that Malcolm had been assigned as an office had been used to produce *"Lagergeld,"* and was located on the west side of the camp, just below the main barracks, near the first high fence, and close to Tower B, where the last German SS guards were shot down by the American GI's who liberated the camp.

Lagergeld, a fellow OSS officer and friend had explained over drinks one night in a Munich bar, was a type of money paid to the inmates by the camp administration. It was a scrip that could be exchanged for commodities: food, tobacco, medicine, even sex. It was a refinement to the camp's protocols, introduced by the psychotic, mild-mannered and devout Catholic Himmler, whose idea it was to "pay" the concentration camp workers with the "special" scrip. Himmler's idea was that the use of this internal-money would add to the Nazi's pseudo-legal order, where all notions of morality and decency were trampled under by über-menschen cruelty, dressed up as Reasonable Authority.

There were still boxes of new, unused *Lagergeld* lining the long wooden tables where prisoners with engraving and printing skills had only months before worked to make the camp's "money." Malcolm walked to a wooden box and looked down at the neatly-stacked red bills printed on cheap paper. He picked up a fifty-pfennig note. The side he looked at had two German soldiers standing on either side of an eagle. He noticed it was a replica of the same Nazi eagle he'd driven under that morning on the way to work. He waded the note up and threw it on the floor, then glanced at his watch. His sergeant knocked and said he had the first prisoner in the hallway. Malcolm went back to the long ink-stained table and told the sergeant to bring him on in. It was ten in the morning and he was looking forward to a weekend with a French girl he'd met who worked for the Red Cross in Salzburg, Austria, a city with few signs that the war had touched it, and which already seemed to him to have a sense of "normalcy," which he craved like a drug just then. He wanted to have sex, get drunk, and be as far as possible from this stinking death camp.

A slight young man walked into the room. Malcolm knew from the file on his desk that he was *Hauptman* Christophe Neizert, an SS officer and engineer with the American equivalent of a PhD degree from Heidelberg University and also a post-doctorate degree from the prestigious Karl Wilhelm Institute. He had Neizert's official SS file, which had been retrieved from Himmler's headquarters, where the CIC had found tens-of-thousands of records directly relating to Waffen SS and SD divisions; the depository being a testament to German record-keeping and the Germanic penchant for meticulous detail and order in all things.

As he watched the prisoner enter, Malcolm remembered the first prisoner he'd interviewed shortly after arriving to work at Dachau. That man, an SS doctor, was going to be tried for war crimes. He'd been a tall, very thin, dark-haired man in his forties, with an aristocratic dueling scar, who chain-smoked and had tried to convince him that the Waffen SS were actually *"chivalrous."* He'd actually used the word *"gallant,"* his eyes bright with pride as he said it! The German phrase came back into to Malcolm's head as his sergeant brought Neizert into the room and sat him down. The doctor had been hung after a trial where he'd used the phrase again, several times, to no effect. Even hardened combat veterans from both the British and American sides had been so shocked that they broke down and cried during some of the testimony delivered by maimed and disfigured women who'd survived the doctor's "care." When they heard the man use that word there was an audible shifting of weight in chairs throughout the room, and a general anger that could not be concealed—a kind of hate-electricity that was charging up the spectators. Malcolm had not attended the doctor's hanging, but was very glad when he heard the news that he'd paid for his crimes on the gallows. And at exactly the same place where thousands before him had died without any hope of ever being avenged. It seemed fitting that the doctor's last view of this world was of the camp itself— his own little preview of Hell.

"That will be all, Sergeant. You can wait in the hall. If this prick does anything crazy come in and shoot him." The anger he felt right then had surprised him. The prisoner hadn't even spoken yet, and he wanted to punch him out, knock him down on the floor and kick the shit out of him. His experiences in Poland with the partisans had made him very hard, indeed, and he was having trouble now at times containing his hatred for the Germans, even the ones who hadn't been directly involved in the war; it came out as uncontrollable bouts of anger and violence. He'd become dangerous when he drank too much. He'd seen things—things the Waffen SS divisions had done in their scorched-earth policy—that were beyond anything he could conceive of human beings doing to one another, no matter how much they hated "the enemy."

The slaughter of civilians, Jews and non-Jews, on the Eastern Front was like no other in the history of the world, and he'd seen it first-hand, having parachuted into Poland in 1944 with a squad of OSS commandos.

"Yes, sir. Gladly, sir," the sergeant said. Captain Neizert looked first at Malcolm and then at the sergeant, who was a Jew from Milwaukee and part of the 47th Rainbow Division that had helped liberate the camp. The sergeant had personally shot three guards—who had come toward him with their hands up—stone dead, in a red-rage, fifteen minutes after he'd come through the main gate, having first passed the train carriages nearby with their open doors, the carriages heaped with dead, naked bodies—women, children, fathers and mothers, all of the dead emaciated and horrific looking.

"*Ich spreche Englisch,*" Neizert said, turning back towards Malcolm. He was wearing civilian clothes and looked like a young professor; certainly not a former SS officer. He'd been arrested in Berlin in the French Zone. Only twenty-two years old, he'd been turned over to the Americans because of the underarm SS tattoo with his blood-type, which was the hallmark of SS officers. All SS troops got those tattoos as soon as they'd been accepted by the SS.

"Well, aren't *you* special," the sergeant had said. The sergeant, whose last name was Birnbaum, had fought in the Battle of the Bulge, where his platoon had been cut off by a Nazi spearhead and he'd thought he was going to die in a very bad way as they ran out of ammunition and had heard the rumor that the Nazis—an SS tank battalion—were shooting all prisoners whether they were in uniform or not. Birnbaum's father was a rabbi and a socialist who had been hounded and harassed during the red scare of the 1920s. The sergeant had, despite his father's high-standing in the community, been a troubled kid who hadn't done very well in school, spending more time in the downtown pool halls with the black kids than in class. The war and the Battle of the Bulge had changed him for good. He'd seen his best friend freeze to death. The sergeant saluted and left the room, pulling the door shut behind him. He was a killer now, and he walked like one.

"I'm here to amplify your military record. My name is Captain Law and I'll be making a recommendation for further investigation regarding your Nazi party involvement to the prosecution at your trial." He didn't mention the fact that he was also part of a top secret OSS campaign that was seeking to recruit important Nazi scientists and keep them out of the Russian's hands. The Russians were also furiously trying to collect the same scientists: those that had worked either on the Nazi V-2 rocket program or on the Luftwaffe's advanced new jet fighter that the Germans had miraculously put into production very late in the war, and which had been a true breakthrough in aeronautical engineering. The race to collect those men, estimated to be about a 1000 in number, was intense and on-going.

"I understand," Neizert said.

"You worked at Peenemünde Aerodynamics Institute and at the Luftwaffe's offices at Kaiser Wilhelm?"

"Yes."

"Your specialty was in electrical engineering, or so it says here."

"Yes. And light dynamics," Neizert said.

"And you got your post-doctorate degree at the Kaiser Wilhelm Institute of Physics—is that correct?

"Yes. In 1940. I graduated on April 3." Neizert was looking at him as he made his notes. Malcolm looked up from the file and into the young man's eyes. He realized they were about the same age. It was the first time they made actual eye contact. There seemed nothing overtly crazy in the SS captain's eyes, the way there had been in the doctor's he'd interviewed the week before. The SS doctor, who had conducted "experiments" for the Luftwaffe to determine the effects of salt water on downed airmen, had been an obvious sadist and insane to boot. This guy, Malcolm thought looking at him, was different. A very cool customer.

"You were an SS officer candidate—is that correct? And graduated in 1941 with a commission in *Deutschland* regiment of the *Waffen SS?*"

"Yes. Right here, in fact, in Dachau. Our ceremony ... This was the first SS headquarters," Neizert said. Malcolm ignored the remark about the camp's history, which he knew to be correct.

"You were a Nazi party member. You joined while you were attending Heidelberg University in 1938, and had party number 1210456." He looked down and saw a party stamp on Neizert's university transcript that had been found and forwarded to OSS headquarters at Dachau by OSS officers working at all the important German universities, cross-checking to make sure only vetted and confirmed scientists ended up on their list of candidates, who would then be searched out, and if found suitable, recruited for work in the United States. The Nazi party blue-stamp, Malcolm imagined, was to signal to anyone who read the student's transcript that Neizert was a party member and should be treated accordingly.

"Yes. But only because it was mandatory for students at the Institute to be party members."

"But you joined the SS of your own volition?"

"Yes." There was a pause, but no prevarication at all. Despite the fact that SS officers like him were being tried for war crimes by Military Tribunals there at Dachau, in some cases solely *because* they had been SS officers. It was more common to hear that the accused had been "forced" somehow to join the SS.

"Why?" Malcolm said, putting down his pen.

"Because I wanted to be a soldier. My father was a soldier in the *Wehrmacht*, a colonel, who served under General Hauser. They had fought in 1915 together in the same regiment; Hauser and my father were training the new SS regiments. My father was killed in Poland in 1940. He'd been a soldier his whole life. He was a brave man."

"Why didn't you join a *Wehrmacht* division? The *regular* army, then?" Malcolm asked in German.

"Because I was very young and stupid. I believed what General Hauser said about the new *élan* and spirit that he was building into the *Waffen* SS. He often came to our home. It was romantic. I was not *political*—not at all. I had every intention of joining the army when I graduated from Kaiser Wilhelm. My father had been killed and I wanted to revenge his death, too. As I said, anyone who wanted to graduate was expected to join the party. The party meant nothing to me, nor did Hitler, for that matter."

"Romantic?"

"Yes ... at the time. I had not yet been to war; I'd never even fired a pistol. I was nineteen. I was a student. I had nothing to do with the camps ... the Jews. *Nothing.* There is no reason for me to be here, or for me to be tried as a war criminal. I was a soldier and nothing more. My division, *Der Führer Regiment,* was a combat division. That is well known. Ask anyone. We fought the Russians."

"... What about your rocket work at Dora Concentration Camp?"

"I was never there. I knew about Dora's existence, of course. But my work was at Kaiser Wilhelm Institute, where I worked ever since I was reassigned and taken from the front in 1944."

"It says here you were working on the V-2 rocket. ... Is that correct?"

"Yes. ... If there were questions concerning the guide-beam, my department at KWI would be consulted, because it was an electronics problem. We also worked at perfecting the *Wasserfall* missile, but not in time to make a difference."

"When did you leave the *Der Führer Regiment?*"

"After I was wounded in the East. It would have happened anyway. ... My professors at KWI had been trying to get me released for a year to help in the research for the Luftwaffe, which was a top priority project for Hitler. I was in the hospital in Krakow when I received the orders to return to Germany."

"You were doing what in Poland—your exact duties?" Malcolm asked.

"SD Detachment," Neizert said.

"That's not listed." Malcolm was surprised that Neizert would confess to being part of the SS's intelligence unit, the SD. The *Sicherheitsdienst.*

"That alone could get you hanged," Malcolm said. "Much of their work on the

95

Eastern front was illegal and had to do with rounding up Jews and Communists."

"Yes, I know that. But I was in a counter-intelligence unit. We had nothing to do with killing the Jews or any of that. We were charged with countering the NKVD spy nets left after the German occupation in the East—especially in occupied Russia. ... There is something you should know, Captain," Neizert said, leaning forward.

"What?"

"There is a group ...even now, that are going to work for the Russians. Here at Dachau."

"They're locked up. So what can they do? ... That's not my problem," Malcolm said.

"No. There will be a transfer for many of them. That is the rumor," Neizert said.

"Did you have anything to do with *Einsatzgruppen* activities?" Malcolm said, ignoring him again.

"No. Nothing. We were a counter-intelligence unit; we concentrated on NKVD agents and networks, and that's all we did. Reinhard Gehlen was our boss. The *Abwehr* was receiving our reports as well as the SD. It's Gehlen who's still working ... but ..."

"Who is Gehlen?" Malcolm said, not bothering to look up from his notes.

"He was head of intelligence on the Eastern Front for the *Wehrmacht.*"

"Never heard of him. If he's not on my list ... I don't care. ... But you knew about the Jews? The mass killings?"

"Of course. ... *Everyone* knew. But I had nothing to do with that." Malcolm tapped his pen on the desk and decided that he was probably lying, but it would have to be looked into via the SS Regiment's records. He wrote: *Cross reference SD/Neizert records.*

"You said you were in the hospital? Where were you wounded?" Neizert picked up his right hand; it was mangled and scared, two of his fingers completely gone, the flesh of the hand pink from a severe burn.

"There was a partisan attack on our car. ... That's when I got orders to go back to KWI. I would have been sent back to Germany in any case, at least until I recovered. ... I could spy on these men here if you want ... the ones that are going over to the Russians, I mean. There are already Russian spies here in Dachau. Some of them work for Gehlen and his network. I have ... "

"Like I said, *so what?* They're locked up. *Fuck* them. What are they going to report about?"

"You don't understand! They're not *really* working for the Russians. *Or* for the Americans, either. Not really. ... They're all SD intelligence officers. They're working for *themselves,* including Gehlen. They think they can save themselves and then go on. ..."

"On to *what?*" Malcolm pushed back his chair.

"To re-group. They don't care about either side; not really, Russians, Americans,

French, Brits. Everyone thinks that they're going to work for *them* ... but they don't understand—they have their *own* network, and their own goals. Gehlen is at the center of it, " Neizert said.

"Either side of what?

"Of the war that's coming, between the Americans and the Russians."

"...Would you consider going to the United States to work on your specialty? Your research at KWI is important to us," Malcolm said.

"Yes—of course." The question didn't seem to shock him; he'd reacted as if he were expecting it.

"Because you were in a SD unit you'll have to be vetted again," Malcolm said. "We'll have to review your unit's activities in Poland and Russia. So, in the meantime, you'll be held here. Your trial will be postponed."

"There's no time for that—I might be taken to Russia at any time, now. The Russians have my name on a list. They want all of us that worked at KWI. Let me out of here and I'll explain everything I know to you about Gehlen and his organization," Neizert said. "I'll tell you all about them."

"I told you, Gehlen isn't a name on my list. I don't care about him."

"Let me out of here—I don't want to stand trial for things I didn't have anything to do with. And I don't want to go to Russia. Some are going to the gallows even if they had nothing to do with the Jews. I'm a *scientist* and a regular soldier. I'm not guilty of killing Jews or any other 'war crimes'!"

"...You mean an *intelligence* officer—that's not a 'regular soldier.' And as far as *I'm* concerned, every fucking German is guilty—you all knew what was going on and went along with it; an entire country of barbarous, murdering, Nazi morons, as far as I can see. ... But I'll see what I can do for you. ... In the meantime, it's out of my hands. My job is to discuss you going to America and putting you on the list for further vetting. And that's all. Good day, Captain," Malcolm said, breaking eye-contact and turning his head down to look at his notes. "Sergeant! ... You can take the prisoner back to his cell now."

"Tell them I know about Operation Rupert. ... I tried to help. I worked for the NKVD. If Gehlen finds out. ... The NKVD passed on my reports to your people. They know I helped."

"Who is Rupert?" Malcolm looked up again. Neizert didn't answer.

"It's important you act *now*. The Russians have asked for me and several others. ... I'm telling you this, *now*. Because I helped with operation Rupert, I could be killed immediately. Gehlen doesn't trust me. He'll have me killed."

"I said I'd do what I can. That's all ... Captain."

"You don't understand. ... *Gehlen has fooled you all!* You've got to believe me!"

"I said that's *all,* Captain." The sergeant stepped into the room and that was the last he saw of Hauptmann Christophe Neizert, who, with several other inmates at Dachau, became part of a high-level exchange of prisoners. The exchange took place over the heads of several top-ranking officers of the Army's CIC division. The group of former SD officers was handed over to the Russians for "war crimes committed on Russian soil," according to what Malcolm learned later when he tried to follow up on Neizert's file. There was a lot of dickering over prisoners of this type, with the French striking a deal to have all of the French Vichy prisoners returned to France for trial. Someone above Malcolm in CIC had decided that Hauptmann Neizert wasn't very important, so he was handed over to the NKVD as part of the exchange. All this was secretly arranged by the new Gehlen intelligence organization, now working officially for the U.S government, providing intelligence on the Soviet Union from an office in Bavaria, working closely with the U.S. Army's newly formed task force preparing for all-out war with the USSR.

1980 ■ ENGLAND, CORNWALL PENJERRICK GARDEN

"And that's why I came to you," Malcolm said. "Because I knew I could trust you. I have to trust *someone.*" He had taken the Concord flight from New York to London and driven out to see Mary Keen, not telling anyone in the CIA's London station that he was in the country on purpose. Mary Keen was thirty when he'd first met her in London in 1952, and had been the 'older woman' in his life. A Cambridge don, she was a researcher at MI6 and had given a lecture to CIA and MI6 officers on the transition of the NKVD into the new post-war KGB. Her lectures had been on the NKVD's purges and the fallout from them, which had sewn serious discord at the new KGB. This happened in October, and Malcolm had been pulled in from Bangkok to hear what turned out to be a series of three brilliant lectures.

Mary Keen had been a tall English rose and all the men in the audience, about twenty young Englishmen and Americans, fell in love with her on the spot, not just because of her physical beauty, but they were smitten as well by her natural aplomb and obvious intelligence. She spoke fluent Russian and was encyclopedic in her knowledge about the new KGB. The two of them had had a short affair after Malcolm was surprised to be invited by her to lunch to "discuss Thailand." They had remained friends during the intervening years. Mary Keen had married Lord Ingram, a peer who was an important member of Parliament and an arch-Conservative.

Mary had retired to Cornwall and had a family, all girls, and played the part of the Lord's wife, showing up on his arm at important Tory functions. She was on the board of the Royal Horticultural Society now, and ran the Penjerrick Gardens in Cornwall as well as writing for their magazine's famous "Garden Profiles" series. Lord Ingram had died a few years after the two were married in a small-plane accident in India. Malcolm had read about it in the *New York Times* one day at breakfast and had actually been shocked by the news. He'd almost picked up the phone to call her then, but didn't allow himself to make the call, realizing that he was still in love with her and it wouldn't be right, as he was "happily" married by then himself.

"Why the interest in *that* particular Nazi?" Mary asked. She was wearing green Wellingtons and had taken him for a walk in the Gardens; they were well known for their varieties of rhododendrons and many types of giant ferns that had been collected in Chile the previous century. Her Wellington boots were wet, as were his dress shoes. She was older now, of course, but still beautiful, her blonde hair streaked with gray. He had been madly in love with her when she'd left him for Lord Ingram. She'd never explained anything about her motives or feelings to him; she just came to a tryst near Piccadilly and said that it was over between them, all very calmly. She'd said that she was getting married to someone else, but never mentioned the man's name. It was all settled, and she hoped he understood. It was done with a kind of calm, even a coldness, that most upper-class Englishwomen can muster, apparently at will—suddenly cutting off all emotions—a kind of ripping of the emotional tendrils that bind two lovers. It was as if their affair had existed outside of normal time and space, confined to a parallel universe that had been bracketed by various anonymous hotel rooms. She told him as he'd dressed, completely gob-smacked by her news, that she loved him, but that it would never work for them. She didn't want to "marry an intelligence officer and tramp around the world after him," she'd said, pulling on her coat. She had left first. She was married two weeks later, and the wedding had been covered in all the major newspapers.

"Because Neizert contacted me personally. He wants to come to the West," Malcolm said.

"*Has* he?" She seemed to enjoy holding his arm. The garden—acres of it—was almost totally empty in mid-week. It seemed to him as if they were in some rainforest in South America where time had stood still for eons.

"Yes. And I've been digging, too. The Nazis were on the verge of abandoning the first guidance system for the V-2 for a new one based on light. They had already made the first working lasers and planned on using them to guide anti-aircraft missiles. Those records were destroyed in an air-raid so we didn't know how far that research had gotten back then," he said. He wondered if he should tell her the whole truth about the Hauptmann. Everything he'd written in his note to Malcolm.

"Dear Malcolm ... you didn't come all this way to talk about lasers and old Nazis with me, I *hope?*"

"Yes.... No. But I need your help, Mary. Your mind."

"My *mind!* That's not what a girl wants to hear, *darling.* Have I said I was sorry for marrying Bertie...? God bless his soul."

"No."

"I am, now. I used to dream about us, what we could have had. Back then ... for years afterwards, in fact. That's why I've stayed friends ... you know ... Little calls. Christmas cards. Invitations when you and your wife were in London," she said. "I was so ... I don't know, *sure* that it would go wrong because I was older and you seemed so young—that was the *real* reason, you know—or at least I told myself it was, back then. You seemed *so* young to me, then—it seems so funny, now. Then after the wedding I was sure I'd made a terrible mistake. It was really quite horrible. Like stepping into an elevator that plummets straight to the bottom. I never loved Bertie; not really—not the schoolgirl kind of love, where you're just head-over-heels mad for the chap. It's quite frightening for a woman to realize you've married the wrong man. It took me by surprise, really. You see, I thought I *should* be Lady Ingram. It seemed ... I don't know ... I can't remember exactly *why* or what came over me, now. Perhaps it was Bertie's *house,* it was quite grand, you know." She laughed and squeezed his arm.

"Why didn't you write and tell me?" he said.

"Because I was sure you hated me after what I'd done to you. I *was* a bitch that day that I ended it. *Wasn't* I? It took me ten years to call you, didn't it? And I was pregnant all the time and none too attractive at first. And then, when I'd finally screwed up my courage to call you, I found out you'd gotten married. ... Well, by then it seemed hopeless, really. So I went back to the Service. It was good for me. I'm the type that likes cross word puzzles, and the Russians always had a new set of clues ... 20 down ... Who's calling the shots in Georgia these days? I loved it."

"So, will you help me?"

"With your Hauptmann?"

"Yes. And wherever it goes after we get him over here. There are things Neizert wrote ... in his note. Things he said to me back in 1946, that I'd forgotten, but now make a lot more sense to me. He told me about Gehlen back then. I didn't know about the Gehlen Network, then. And I was in the CIC. They were keeping Gehlen's existence from CIC, even."

"Did he? Well," Mary said.

"Yes. But I hadn't heard of Reinhard Gehlen when Neizert told me about him. I did a few months later, though, but almost by accident."

"Well, Gehlen was your side's big fish, wasn't he? What did he have to do with Hauptmann Neizert?" she asked. Mary stopped in front of a huge rhododendron. "This is 'Penjerrick Cream'... It was first grown here. I wanted you to see it. The garden's creators—the Fox family—brought it. They owned a shipping company, and had it brought from India. It's just *glorious*. It's my favorite," she said. He noticed that her blue eyes were still bright and clean and alluring. She took his hand. She was wearing an old raincoat, and all the dew and rain had made it shiny, and her hair was wet. "The truth is I haven't ever stopped loving you," she said. "When I heard you were coming, I cried. ... I'm a stupid girl." She turned to look at him. "Are you happy? I mean ... you know ... with ... ?"

"No."

"Will you kiss me?" she said. He did. It was as if time suddenly had a hole in it and they'd dropped back into London and it was October 1952 again. She called him darling. "We can go to London. Tonight ... I have a flat. Will you come?" He nodded.

"What about your girls?" he asked.

"Not there. No one will be there. They're all off at school. Oxford, two of them ... Both hippie Greens. With blue stockings!" He smiled at the term. "One of them—the oldest—is in our game. She's in Egypt: she was the first woman ever to take the SAS exam, in fact. Frightening!" They laughed. "And she's quite beautiful. God! A real Amazon."

"Will you tell me everything you know about Gehlen? It's the early years I want to know about, really," Malcolm said.

"If you promise to come to London with me," she said.

"Yes. All right. I promise," he said.

"I'll ring ahead so they'll pull the sheets off and fill the cupboards with things. Wine. Lot's of it."

"Good," he said.

"Your Nazi captain, is he that important to you?"

"Yes, *very*."

"Well, lots of them made good over in the States, didn't they?" She said. "Ours did, too. All over the place. Chemicals, pharmaceuticals. Where is he now?" she asked.

"I can't say."

"Oh, dear. He *is* important, isn't he ... ? A great pooh-bah of some kind, I

101

suppose, by now."

"Yes, I suppose he is," Malcolm said.

She looked at him a moment, deep into his eyes. "You've gotten wet. ... I want to show you something before we leave, though." She led him down the garden path towards an *orangerie* that the Fox family had built for warm-weather plants that were not strong enough to survive the English winters. It was painted white and was constructed of iron and glass in the Victorian style. They walked through the door. The glass room smelled of wet earth. On one entire wall was red Lapageria that was climbing the length of the building and in full bloom; its bell-like flowers were dramatic and startlingly beautiful and totally unexpected—like walking suddenly into a summer's day.

"Good Lord, it's huge," he said. "My mother tried to grow those in Maine. Hers were always tiny, though."

"Yes, I know. I planted this one myself. Here, they're my specialty. I mean, they're what I'm known for in gardening circles. Please don't laugh, remember we're English; we take all this *so* seriously. ..."

"I'm not laughing at you," he said.

"I planted it when my last daughter was born." She went up and took off a flower that had dropped onto an antique marble garden-table. "You have to be careful, though—they can drip a nectar that causes damage." She turned and looked at him again. "Have I gone too far? I feel stupid, suddenly ... all this happening at once. Me and you again."

"Let's go to London. ... You'll feel better," he said.

"I know all about Gehlen. ... He was a very nasty piece of business. But I'm sure you already know all that," she said, her tone changing, the professional intelligence officer in her rising suddenly to the surface.

11

■ SOUTHERN CALIFORNIA
"CITY OF INDUSTRY"

Malinda da Silva had contacted the Vagos chapter in Italy sending a three-word fax to the Italian Vagos club "president," Heinrich Vincent Ricci. Ricci owned a motorcycle shop in Palermo that had been bought for him by a politician in Prime Minister Aldo Moro's Social Democratic Party—no questions asked. Ricci's father had been an important member of Benito Mussolini's PNF—*Partito Nazionale Fascista*. As an officer working in military intelligence during the war, he had worked closely with the Gestapo in their frustrating attempt to round up the Italian Jews, most of whom were being protected by the general population, who had refused—*en masse*—to turn Jews over to the Nazis.

Malinda's fax said simply: *Need some help*. She was instructed by Ricci to phone a New York contact who was already known to her, and also a contact the San Bernardino Vagos used in their heroin business. The connection in New York was a direct go-between for the smugglers in Italy and the San Bernardino Vagos chapter, coordinating deliveries and payments for both sides. Malinda had been taught some simple counter-intelligence practices the Italian Vagos had learned from Italian intelligence officers who, on occasion, used the gang to break up left-wing demonstrations, as well as other jobs given to them to carry out secretly. In fact, the connections between the Italian intelligence and the Italian chapter of the Vagos were well established now and went back almost to the club's founding. The use of a cutout in New York was fundamental to keeping the actual drug connection tucked behind a labyrinth of legitimate businesses in New York—including some locally famous pizza parlors.

The Italian dope-connection cutout lived in the Bronx and was the cousin of the Sicilian mobster who coordinated the actual smuggling of heroin into the Untied States. Later this heroin connection would be made famous by the press and called the "Pizza Connection." Malinda had left a message asking the cutout to call her at a payphone two blocks from her office in California on a Monday afternoon in early July. She'd had to wait at the phone booth, marking time, pretending to look something up in the Yellow Pages that hung from the telephone box by a wire cord. The pay phone finally rang, and she quickly grabbed the receiver off the hook.

"Hello," a man's voice said.

"Hi. Thanks," Malinda said.

"Yeah?" the man said. He had a heavy Italian accent.

"I need some guys ... for a problem I'm having here ... in LA," she said.

"Yeah. Okay. I'll check with my people."

"But, *good* guys. You know ... *Good* at what they do," she said.

"Yeah ... Yeah. ... No problem—I know some very good guys. They'll be in touch." She heard restaurant and street noises in the background; customers talking, she thought, and traffic. All the sounds mixed together, and it seemed to her that the phone call was probably coming from inside a busy restaurant, as in fact it was, but one with side-walk tables, located in Little Italy.

"How are things?" she said, not wanting the call to seem strange to anyone who might be listening in on the line.

"Yeah. Tings dey's good. Business good. We talk later, then." The man hung up. A Penn Register installed at a listening post by the Manhattan Field Office of the FBI had recorded the call from a third-floor apartment in Little Italy across the street and above an Italian pizzeria called Original Rays Pizza. The recorder caught the brief conversation from the pay phone outside of Rays, which was a known Bonnano crime-family business. The call was logged-in, as was the pay phone number originating the call in L.A. The FBI field agent, who was keeping a close eye on several men that worked in the café in Little Italy, had watched through his binoculars as a middle-aged man came out of the pizzeria and made the call to L.A. This particular man was unknown to him. The agent knew that most of the men using that pay phone were Sicilians, and were using it to call all over the United States and Italy. Later, the recording of the call was played again, and it was considered important; obviously a cryptic communication between major players. But, as the call was to L.A., and the FBI was stretched thin in Los Angeles between spying on left-wing organizations and a recent spate of bank robberies, no one from the FBI's field office in downtown Los Angeles was able to go by the phone booth in the industrial suburb for two weeks.

Finally, a young black agent was sent out. The agent took a photo of the empty phone booth and noted that there was a tremendous number of small businesses in the immediate area. He wrote in his report that any surveillance of the phone booth would require a storefront location, as the booth was in a bad spot for clandestine observation from a car. That was the excuse the L.A. field office would give for dragging their feet on any follow-up. The fact was, there was no money in the budget for an extended stakeout of a phone booth, and no L.A. juice for a wire-tap on a New

York case. The call made to the booth two weeks before slipped off the Manhattan field office's radar and was forgotten. L.A. didn't want much of anything to do with a New York case that had nothing to do with anything the LA office was currently investigating, so they buried it. Unlike what most people have been led to believe by the media and movies—that the FBI was a cold and highly efficient modern machine of police investigations and procedures—the opposite situation was more often the case. The FBI was plagued by petty rivalries and private struggles for advancement effecting how a case was handled—if it was handled at all. In *that* respect, the FBI was extremely typical of US government operations in general, and so was fraught with petty intrigues.

*   *   *

The *La Loca* strip club was on East Valley Boulevard in The City of Industry. Before the Vagos bought it, it had been a bucket-of-blood Mexican Dance Club. The Vagos decided they would keep the signage because it was a landmark in the neighborhood and everyone agreed that the famous neon sign from the 60s showing a sleeping Mexican leaning against a cactus should stay, so it did.

They'd left Flaco locked inside a utility room at the motel in Malibu, handcuffed to a pool pump. He'd been given a bucket to shit and piss in, a six-pack of Coke, and told to relax. Alex and Butch had driven by the club the night before around midnight just to check the area out. It was obviously a biker bar, and there were ten or twelve hogs parked in front as they drove by. They could hear loud rock music blaring out the front door. There wasn't much they could learn about the inside of the place from the street because the club's big picture-window had been painted flat-black so that a potential customer had to pay to see the girls.

Butch had gone into the club and ordered a watered-down well-drink and watched a collection of very thin girls, mostly meth freaks, gyrate topless on a badly lit stage under several dim spotlights. Bikers crowded the place but left Butch alone because the Vagos owned the club, and "real" customers—orders had come down from the top—were not fair game for cons or scams. A Mongoose member *could* be shot or stabbed on sight, but there was a tentative truce in force between the Hells Angels and the Vagos in the San Fernando Valley. That truce was currently being strained by the desire of the HA, as they were known, to absolutely control the Valley's meth business.

Some of the Vagos at the club thought Butch looked like a potential recruit to the club because of his size and the crazy vibe he was putting off. But he had no bike out front, so there were whispers that he could also possibly be a vice cop who had parked nearby and walked in. To be on the safe side, the manager made sure that offers for blow-jobs and "private dances" were stopped until Butch left, as he'd made Butch as a cop for sure. A blonde girl with stringy hair and pimples covered-over by make up saddled up to him and put her arm around him, feeling for a gun, but came up empty. She made a sign that the guy was clean. Butch studied the counter-intelligence measures that the Vagos were taking: cameras had been placed near the stage to make sure that the cops couldn't make up charges about the girls touching the customers. All their measures had apparently worked, as the LAPD had come in to hassle them very rarely since the cameras had been installed.

At 2 P.M. the next day, Butch and Alex got into the Mustang with Flaco the dope fiend and three kilos of heroin, ready to go out and do business. A young real-estate agent had come by the motel to see Butch and had had him sign an offer on a triplex in West Hollywood; it was the first piece of real-estate Butch had ever owned. In the car they had talked about Butch's new triplex, which Alex and Patty had helped him pick out, both of them excited and happy for him. But in the excitement and the weed high, they had missed the white dodge van that had pulled behind them, and that followed them down the freeway toward the Valley.

The three men in the van had been watching the motel for a week, and were getting to know the Mustang and its occupants very well indeed. Two of the men were experienced Mafia hit men from Sicily who had come via Caracas, Venezuela, where they had been driven up through Mexico with a load of heroin and crossed into the U.S. using Venezuelan passports, expertly forged by the Cuban government printing office, which, after all these years, was still deriving a goodly income from selling false papers to whoever in the world had the cash to pay for them. Only one of the Sicilians spoke any English. One of them had been an officer in the Italian army for several years. The other, the younger one, was a street kid from Palermo who had come up the hard way, learning his trade from the old-school shotgun killers out in the Sicilian countryside, who, in turn, had survived countless blood feuds and were renowned triggermen. The L.A. *Cosa Nostra* provided a safe house and a driver for the two Sicilians. The American Mafia had never really liked the Sicilian mob, but had leased the U.S. heroin business to the Sicilians after a famous meeting in Palermo in the late 1950s that had been chaired by Lucky Luciano. Luciano had been released from prison on orders from American Navel Intelligence, which had employed Luciano and his gang during the war, turning them into a kind of intelligence network that kept the docks safe and free of German saboteurs. It had been the beginning of a long-standing connection between American intelligence services and the U.S. Mafia.

The Sicilians had learned that L.A. was a nightmare to navigate, and had used a local driver until they had a plan and a place picked out and were able to rehearse the hit several times. They thought they had a plan, now—just eliminate all three targets— the girl as well as the two men. And now that they were a little more acclimated to L.A., they were getting more confident they would find the right place to do the job soon enough.

The younger one, who was riding in the back, came up with a suggestion as they drove down the freeway following the Mustang.

"We hit them at their motel, in the parking lot. ... We're just two regular guests loading our car, *u capisti*?"

"No one ever *uses* the motel parking lot. ... It's always empty ... " the older one said in Italian, watching the Mustang ahead of them.

"Maybe the place has fleas," their American-born driver said in Italian. The two hit-men laughed, as the American had grown up in an Italian family and spoke their lingo well enough, but with what they considered a "bad" accent, so they laughed at his joke *and* at his Italian.

"Naw; we shoot them from up on the balcony, in a cross-fire. When they come back from the beach ... they go to the beach every morning, right? They walk across the road and then they screw around and then they walk back and go to lunch. We kill them as they walk back into the motel from the beach. ... What do you think?" the older one said.

"... Okay. Yeah, why not?" the younger one said in Italian. "We kill a couple of fleas. I want to go home ... shit ... this country ... it's all fucked-up, man, nothing but freeways and signs I can't read!" he said in Italian. "A crazy fucking place—who could live here? All this smog and bad food," the kid said, proud of the fact that he'd come up with a good place for the hit.

"Hey, it's not so bad. I grew up here," the Italian-American said. "I take you to a good place tonight to eat. My uncle Carlo has a good place; you'll see—real good." The two men from Sicily didn't say anything. They knew it was Italian-American food and they hated it, but didn't say so because they didn't want to insult someone's family business.

"What about the little Mexican?" The Italian-American said.

"No ... they paid for two and they're getting three ... and that's all they get," the older one said. The kid from the Ardizzone family in L.A. didn't like the idea of killing the pretty girl, too, because he thought she looked like Kristy McNichol, only a lot hotter. He'd had several fantasies about her already, masturbating to images of her as soon as he crawled into bed at night. He thought of a way of warning her off, but decided against it. When you watch people like that for a week or two you think you know them somehow. *Fuck it*, he thought to himself. *She's got to go, too, I guess.*

*   *   *   *

"I don't want to give them the drugs," Butch said matter-of-factly. "I got to do termite work on that place. You saw that report, right? The whole front of that building needs work, man. And the stairs are shot, too! I should bring my old man out here to fix the place up, really. And I want to re-do the kitchens in all three units, so I can raise the rent. Shit!" Butch said proudly. It wasn't really unexpected, Alex thought. Butch would always wait until the very last moment to decide whether they were going to actually sell the drugs or just rip the people off. This time out there was a very good chance they'd die, and he wondered why Butch didn't see that; or, if he did, why it wasn't apparent to him somehow in Butch's speech or physical state—he seemed as relaxed as ever. Maybe, Alex thought, it's what Butch secretly wanted: to die and get it over with.

"These are bikers," Alex said as calmly as possible. "I'm sure they aren't going to let us just walk out of there if we don't give them the drugs." Flaco started to groan.

"Shut up. Make another motherfucking sound and I'll shoot you," Butch said to the Mexican. "No; I got this. You go in and take the money. I'll go after the person who takes the drugs from the car. It's easy. They'll see the drugs leave the car, and that everything is cool. But I'll be in the trunk. If it goes bad somehow, I'll come in and get you," Butch said.

"You'll come in and 'get me'... ? Holy fuck, man. ... *That's* your plan?"

"Yeah. What do you say? You game for it?" Alex thought carefully about his answer. He had his share of the money they'd stolen lying in Safeway grocery bags in the closet of his motel room. He hadn't touched any of it. Truthfully, he had no real use for it. There was nothing he really *wanted*, for that matter, that money could buy. He'd thought about buying a houseboat, but he wasn't that motivated to move ahead on that front now that Patty was with him. He liked the idea of just drifting the way they had been. He was even getting to *like* L.A.; that loose feeling that the great weather seemed to give everybody that lived there.

"Okay—but what about Flaco?" Alex said.

"He's still got to go with us in case it's a set-up. You know *that*." Butch looked at Flaco in the rearview mirror. The speed freak was in bad shape because they'd kept him locked up at the motel overnight and he'd been unable to cop any meth that morning. He looked like he was going to die from fright right at that moment, and was sitting there drenched in what looked like corn syrup, but which was actually thick, foul-smelling speed-freak sweat. They drove on in silence, then, with the white van keeping it's distance and going un-noticed.

*   *   *

■ LONDON

The hotel was located near Harrods and was owned by the Sultan of Brunei's sister: The Chelsea. It was very hip and quite new. Most of the desk staff were young and French; they'd been chosen for their looks and an ability to speak some Arabic. The maids were all from sub-Saharan Africa, mostly Congolese. The maids never spoke unless they were spoken *to* and they all looked permanently scared-to-death. Many of them had been forced into paying for their jobs by one of the managers in the internationally-accepted coin: sex.

"I'd rather not talk about my wife, if you don't mind," Malcolm said.

"Have you been faithful to her—I mean until *now?*" Mary asked him. She'd gotten back into bed after finding a white terrycloth robe in the sumptuous black marble bathroom. He'd watched her walk naked to the bath and enjoyed the hell out of it. She'd kept her figure, yes, indeed.

"Yes." He lied, but only because he felt he had to; anything else seemed mean, both to Mary *and* his wife. He knew he wasn't a "playboy," but he sensed that if he had told the truth about his many other affairs over the years Mary would hold it against him for some reason. Women, he knew, wanted to believe in Love: the idea of it being the ultimate moment that would both define and fulfill them. He thought men were a different breed, especially ones from his class, who generally defined themselves, not via equality in their relationships, but rather by their ability to control relationships— intimate ones, as well as others—because of their financial success—which always gave them what they desired most of all: authority.

He looked across the expensive London hotel room; they'd decided against going to Mary's flat for their tryst, not wanting to risk bumping into her daughters. Instead, they decided to try out a brand newly-built, ultra-modern place, with a view of Harrods and, as far as he knew, no connection to CIA whatsoever. From what Malcolm observed in the lobby, the Chelsea was filled with the sons of Saudi royals on shopping and whoring sprees, Colombian gangsters from Latin America there in London to visit their bank accounts, and an assortment of other *nouveau riche*, mostly

109

from the Continent. He wasn't like most tourists, of course; he noticed all the details that most of them would have missed. For example, the professional security teams used by the Saudis to watch all activity in the lobby. Some of them were American ex-Green Beret types, their military haircuts, gaunt faces, and rough battlefield gestures betraying their origins immediately.

"I'd rather you lie," Mary said, "if it's going to sting." They were lying in bed. It was late, after one in the morning. They'd had dinner in their room and made love by the gas fire. It had been very relaxed: almost as if all the years between their original affair and the present hadn't rolled by and changed them both, making them not only physically older and not as pretty as they'd been back then, but emotionally wrung-out by so many disappointments in life. With younger women he always felt uncomfortable, and he usually had little to say, as if he worried that they might suddenly bring up the age difference. But with Mary it was different; the whole situation felt completely natural, and even "normal," somehow. It was easy for him to be with someone from the same generation who also shared the spy business and their youth. It was like coming into on a movie during the second act; one you'd seen several times before, where you could pick up the story line right away.

"I can sense you want to grill me about your Hauptman. You can, you know." Mary said. She'd put on the white terrycloth robe and was holding a brandy perfectly balanced on her still-flat stomach. He wondered for a moment if he could feel about her again the way he'd felt when he was twenty-five—or feel that way about *any* woman ever again, for that matter. Mary had a classic profile; he turned and saw it now and reached for her through the robe and held her close for a moment.

"I do ... I want to talk about Gehlen and his organization, actually. Before he went to the GDR, I mean. We took him to Washington first, you know, and debriefed him. I found out that U.S Counter-Intelligence—I was working for them at the time, you know—had been kept completely in the dark about the entire Gehlen affair. They put him back on the list of wanted war criminals, too, so that everyone thought he was still free and running around somewhere in Europe when in fact we had him right there in Washington! He became a mystery wrapped in a morass," Malcolm said.

"There's a myth about Gehlen," Mary said. "I suppose I can tell you *this*—what possible difference could it make, *now?*"

"Tell me, then."

"You know dear, Reinhard Gehlen, stayed head of intelligence on the Eastern Front for the duration and he was ours after 1944. All those things you heard about him burying his files in the woods ... none of that was true—it's all pure poppycock. We Brits got there first, before the war even ended. *We* got his files. He didn't trust *your* lot. He wanted a letter from Churchill—he actually *admired* Churchill, can you imagine *that*!?—a letter promising him that when the war ended he could leave Germany and come to England and live. And he got it, too! We sent it via our embassy in Bern. There was a line opened by German intelligence through our embassy in Bern as early as 1944. The German Abwehr had a pretty good network in Bern—they all knew the war was going to end and they were going to lose it; lose absolutely everything, probably, since Hitler was taking the whole country down with him, the fool. I actually read the letter. Churchill was very warm. For *him,* anyway ... he actually wrote it himself, and it was passed on through Bern and got to Gehlen in Germany without any real trouble; Gehlen was running a network that could move in almost any capital of the world: Brazil, Mexico, the U.S.; quite successfully, too. Gehlen understood that the end was coming after the failure at Stalingrad and the loss of the oil fields in Georgia and Romania. It was clear to him, and to most of the Abwehr personnel after 1944, that the USSR would win the war because the Americans were supplying them with massive amounts of fuel, and of course armaments, too. German intelligence understood that Hitler would be defeated in relatively short order. And of course it was all true. Gehlen was absolutely right. The war ended within a year."

"So why did he go to Washington, then?"

She laughed.

"The Americans paid him a great deal to work for them. It's that simple, really. *And,* he learned that we were almost broke and that Churchill probably wouldn't stand for reelection, so he panicked, thinking that a Labor Party victory in London would mean that his network might be compromised by Communists, who he felt would be part of any Labor government. He feared the Communists above all else, wher*ever* they were. He loathed the English Labor Party. He said they were full of Communist agents with direct links to Moscow, and that if they got into power he'd be turned over to the Russians immediately. As soon as he thought Churchill was through politically, he switched sides, to *your* lot. Gehlen was a survivor, no matter what. He was personally terrified of the Russians because he thought they would shoot him immediately. He had too many enemies in Moscow ... although he did have a few friends there, too."

"So he reneged on your deal?"

"Well, not really. We had his original files, with all the network's contacts inside the Soviet Union, and we kept that fact from your government. Gehlen continued to keep us informed about what he was doing for the Americans once he saw that the Labor Party wasn't really going to take England Communist. By the way, his contact was Kim Philby, no less. Gehlen was building networks that were burrowing into various intelligence agencies around the world: ours, yours, the French, Spanish, Italian, Greek... the list goes on and on. Our relationship was kept secret until Kim Philby found out, and then of course *he* told the Russians about *our* deal with Gehlen. It was Philby that warned us that the Gehlen network was really working for itself, playing both sides against the middle and getting rich in the meantime. And, I think he was sincere about helping West Germany rebuild after the war. What does Gehlen have to do with your Hauptmann, anyway?" she asked, taking a sip of brandy.

"I interviewed the captain at Dachau in 1946 . He said that Gehlen was working for both the Russians *and* the Americans back *then*. I think that's what he was implying to me, then: that the Gehlen network didn't "belong" to anyone but was really only working for itself—to what end, I still don't know. ... I hadn't even heard of Gehlen back then. Frankly, I thought the Hauptmann was running a dog and pony show to keep himself from the gallows. I couldn't have cared less at the time. He was just one more Nazi scientist that was on the list for Paperclip. I had to vet *scores* of them. He wasn't that important."

"So what happened to your Hauptmann?"

"He was traded for some high-level French prisoners that the Russians had captured at the time. The NKVD got him a week later, all very hush-hush. And they sent him to the Russian zone."

"And your lot wanted him?"

"...We were looking at him for Paperclip," Malcolm said.

"It all seems ages ago, now," Mary said. She turned toward him. He could see the girl he'd once loved and he felt the spell again. The tug. It was cozy in the room, far from Dachau, far from all the strange and violent places he'd been since. He wondered what his life would have been like if he hadn't gone on into the new CIA. If, rather, he'd just gone home to New York after the war and played golf like his father, who'd been very happy just being rich and doing nothing at all.

"Do you miss it? The game?" he asked. She looked up at him, her silvery-blonde hair thick. She brushed it away from her face so he could see her blue eyes looking at him.

"Yes." She couldn't tell him the truth—that she'd never really left it. Not really. No one *really* leaves the spies once you are high enough in the ranks. Maybe he caught something in her look, something telling, something she wanted him to know without actually saying the words.

"...You *didn't* leave, did you?"

"... ... No," she said. "No, I didn't. I took a break, but I never really left."

"I imagined that having the children and all, you *had* left. You were never there when I visited. I asked around and everyone said you'd left ages ago," he said.

"I had gone away for a while; I got very bored as *just* Mummy," she said. "And they needed me. And we don't tell you Yanks *everything*; you should know that by now...

We're as bad as the Russians, we Brits—we lie a *great* deal."

"... I want to keep this about the Hauptmann a secret, Mary." He regretted now having told her the situation, thinking that she'd been out of the game for a long time. He'd been trying to keep all this about Neizert a secret from CIA ... but now? He'd never imagined she was still at MI6 and in the game.

"I told you, I love you," she said.

"I don't understand."

"I won't betray your secrets, Malcolm. That's what love buys you." He realized that it was she who had picked out the hotel. He'd let her. He looked around the room with different eyes now, wondering if he *could* trust her.

"Are we safe here, Mary? I have to know. I can't have anyone looking for my Hauptmann right now. Everyone wants him, and he's gone missing," Malcolm said.

"Yes, dear. Safe as houses," she said.

"... This isn't some kind of listening post, is it? This hotel?"

"No, it isn't. It's full of disreputable people just like us," she said. "Whores and pimps and con-men; that's why I choose it. You're afraid your Hauptmann was telling the truth—is that it?"

"Yes," he said. "I want him to come and tell me his story himself. I want to hear it. There are things that have happened. Things that I can't understand and I'm hoping that Neizert might be able to explain. ... Let's say he's very valuable ... for a lot of reasons," Malcolm said. "I'm guessing that he was recruited by the KGB. He was, after all, an SS intelligence officer during the war. Somehow he must have come to understand things we couldn't see at the time. Things about Gehlen."

"Well, these boffins often are, aren't they. Funny—they sit in a laboratory and fiddle with things, writing on chalkboards and the next thing you know people like us can't live without them. I'm hungry," she said. "Shall we go out for a snack?"

"Mary, was Gehlen a spy all along for the Russians? Is that it? A double-agent? Is that what we didn't know?"

She slid out of bed. "It's hard to say, dear, about Gehlen. He's a mystery, really. And that's the way General Gehlen wanted it. But I wouldn't think so, no."

The phone rang. She picked it up and put it to her ear. It was the desk. Someone had left a message for her.

"It's my daughter. ... I have to ring her back. ... She's probably wondering where the devil I've gone to. ... We were never really sure about Gehlen—he and Philby were close. I got the impression that Gehlen was working for himself, really—that their whole network was. And we couldn't tell you lot about *that,* could we, if we weren't supposed to be working with him. I told you we lied about the whole thing from the beginning. That's what spies do, dear, after all. Lie." Then she rang her daughter back.

Mary drove him to Heathrow in a white Jaguar the next morning to catch the Concord back to New York. He asked her to help him find someone called Sonny Delmonico—a contract agent known to have worked for MI6 in the past and who he had heard via the DEA was now living in Spain. He told her he couldn't explain why, and while they were sitting at a red light near the airport, she turned and looked at him.

"I need this Delmonico to contact someone in the US. A Bruce Tucker, in Los Angeles. This Tucker wants to buy heroin from him in the worst way. Buy it from *him* directly." He wrote a phone number down for her in her day-planner.

"Buy *what?*"

"Drugs. Heroin."

"... What's this got to do with your Hauptmann?"

"I can't say right now," he said. "Will you help me?"

"Yes, dear. I'll help," she said.

12

■ LOS ANGELES, SAN FERNANDO VALLEY

Butch had geezed a load of coke immediately after breakfast, using the Denny's men's room where they'd eaten breakfast. And now he was acting like someone whose ass was plugging an active volcano.

"This don't seem right," Butch said indignantly, reaching for the rearview mirror and adjusting it for the fifth time since they'd gotten into the Mustang. Butch hadn't cut his hair since they'd come to LA, so it was getting pretty long. He'd let his mustache grow, too. Unshaven, and wearing a black leather vest with no shirt under it, he was looking very much like a Southland bad-guy that particular morning.

He was looking into the rearview mirror watching two hulking motorcycle riders turn onto Valley Boulevard behind them. The bikers' hands were placed high on their butterfly handlebars. They were still several miles from the strip club and had been refining their plans for a rip-off, which to Alex—who was feeling the Valium and some kind of painkiller that Patty had given him as he walked out the door of the motel room—seemed to boil down to shooting everyone in the place with automatic weapons if things went down badly. Addled by his own drug-taking that morning, Alex wasn't sure exactly *what* the plan was, now. They'd picked up the two motorcycle tails on the freeway, Alex was sure of that, anyway. And he was sure that they were still behind them. Outside of that, the morning seemed indifferent, and the desire to close his eyes was suddenly overwhelming. Only twenty minutes before at breakfast he'd felt wide awake and ready for whatever was coming down the pike at them.

"It *could* be a coincidence," Alex said, glancing—his eyes half-open slits—into the side-view mirror and seeing the herky-jerky images of the bikers rolling along the freeway. His body felt numb but comfortable. How, he wondered, was he supposed to engage in an all-out gunfight feeling this way? He closed his eyes and saw the verdant, bomb-pocked rice paddy in Vietnam from the open door of a helicopter. He opened his eyes again, not liking what he'd just seen.

"Yeah—I guess," Butch said. Alex turned to look at his partner and thought Butch looked like one of those outlaws that you saw on wanted posters in the old west, or in a Clint Eastwood movie.

"Now that's ten pounds of shit in a five-pound sack," Butch said, finally letting go of the mirror.

The morning felt peaceful and quiet, even in one of the ugliest parts of Southern California. This part of the San Fernando Valley was a no-man's land of newly-built tilt-up concrete buildings and old 1920s bungalows; a strange mixture of clean, hastily-constructed modernity laced-in with Our Gang-era houses. Valley Boulevard, at this time of the morning, was jammed with straight people doing what straight nine-to-five types did at that hour of the morning: drive while trying to decide— provoked to anger by the endless views of the traffic ahead—which "drive time" radio station would have the least annoying DJ.

"The valley is *full* of bikers, man," Flaco said from the backseat.

"Shut the fuck up!" Butch said. "I'm not going to tell you again, you little rat-turd."

Butch speeded up and turned the Mustang down a side street off of Valley Boulevard, down-shifting violently. The Mustang's transmission whined and markedly slowed the car down.

They drove into a forlorn working-class neighborhood of small houses with gone-to-seed porches and pie-bald pit bulls defending little patches of dead grass. The Mustang finally slowed down and Butch pulled over to the curb. Alex became aware of the low rumble of the idling eight-cylinder engine. They could hear a sprinkler running somewhere, its peripatetic energetic spitting sound surprisingly clear. Two little Mexican girls, about ten, were playing hopscotch on the sidewalk, just up from where they'd stopped. Their melodic little-girl voices carried down the street.

"... I lied," Flaco said. "They're going to rip you off ... at the bar."

Butch turned and looked at him. Flaco had turned deathly pale and looked like a Catholic saint at death's door.

"I told you. ... He's a piece of rat-shit," Butch said.

"What about *those* two, behind us?" Alex said.

"I told you, man, there are bikers all over the valley. And those weren't from the right club—I could see their colors," Flaco said.

"So what club is it? ... Our buyers, I mean?"

"Vagos. Those back there are HA—red and black—Hell's Angels. They have nothing to do with this deal." They heard the roar of the hogs get louder, then start to fade as the two bikes went on down the boulevard.

"Yeah," Butch said. "Okay. Where's the Vagos' clubhouse?" Flaco hesitated and looked at Alex for help. When Flaco turned back to look at Butch he was staring into the hand-cannon pointed at him—the end of the barrel was only an inch away from his face. Butch pulled the hammer back for effect. Flaco could see the tips of three bullets—out of six— in the pistol's cylinder. He would never forget how big they looked as long as he lived.

"Why?" Flaco said.

"I'm going to pay them a visit," Butch said. "*No one rips us off. We can't have that.*"

"That's crazy, man. ... That's the Vagos *club*house, fool. *Shit! You're a crazy motherfucker, for real!*"

"Unless you want to discuss this with the Devil, right *now*, who's waiting for you, tell me where that fucking clubhouse is," Butch said. He was literally seething from the coke, and his eyes had turned to narrow slits.

The whole conversation was sounding very strange to Alex: the skinny Mexican dope fiend, the feeling of the pain-killers, his hangover, the fact that they were in this poor physical state on the way to rob a motorcycle gang. Alex had to rewind the tape of the last twenty-four hours and play it back on 10x. *Where* was the meeting they were supposed to have about the strip club and its counter-intelligence measures? And where was the step-by-step plan they were going to work out for the robbery? He looked back through the tape in his head and saw no references to any of that. They'd actually planned nothing.

What he did remember was a trip to buy beer with Patty, and sitting in his underwear watching Patty rock out after a hit of slam to a song on their room's clock-radio, "Wooly Bully." He saw her falling into his lap and them fucking, and him not being able to come. Then her face getting red, and then a very deep red, and then her whole body shaking when she came as if she were being hurt. *Wooly Bull---lly—watch it now, watch it! You got it.* She'd sung the lyrics: *Uno, dos, tres, quartro* ... but no plans. No earnest discussions about a robbery at all. He was fucked. They were all fucked. And then Alex remembered that Butch had *just* suggested robbing them—right *then,* for the first time, in the car only moments before. There was no time to even *make* plans for it, not really.

"It's on Albert Street—*Shit*—I'm tired of helping you guys—Lock a motherfucker up over night and shit! It was *cold* down there, man," Flaco said. Alex remembered going down to the motel's boiler/pool-pump room and unlocking it and seeing Flaco sitting on the floor sleeping, handcuffed to the pool pump. The white plastic garbage can they'd left him had three-inches of speed-freak piss in the bottom.

"Where's that?" Alex asked, his voice sounding lethargic and sleepy even to himself. *Had* he been sleeping, just now? He didn't know. Why had he taken that fucking pill! Why was he in love with Patty? Or was he in love with her drug-feel-good death-spiral?

"It's pretty near here, man—just on the other side of Valley Drive over there," Flaco said, gesturing. He was looking at Alex, now, again hoping that at least Alex would have sense enough to object to this course of madness.

"*Butch, ...*" Alex said. He'd used Butch's real name for the first time, too stoned to care.

"Who the fuck is Butch?" Flaco said.

"Never mind. ... Yeah?" Butch said.

"Don't shoot him," Alex said. "It's bad luck to shoot a Mexican-American speed freak before One P.M. Pacific Standard Time." It was getting harder and harder to keep his eyes open. As his eyelids involuntarily closed, Alex saw about half the image of a wounded 18-year-old Viet Cong riding in a helicopter with him.

"Is it?" Butch said.

"Yes. Absolutely. Abort mission and return to base," Alex said, trying to stay awake.

"Why?"

"Because ... there are two little girls over there for starters," Alex said. Butch turned and watched the little Mexican girls playing hopscotch. One of them, hopping on one leg, stooped to pick up a marker, having to steady herself on one foot as she did. She picked up the marker and took off down the chalk-drawn box, obviously having a good time. "He could have taken us there and gotten us fucked up ... but he didn't," Alex said. "We could be looking at a situation. ... "

"Yeah, okay ... One point for Flaco. But he's still two points short," Butch said.

"I was *going* to tell you before we got there—*I swear to God.*" In fact, Flaco was stone sober and had been trying to get the two men's attention all the way down the freeway, but the rock music had been on so loud that he was having difficulty getting through to the two, who were obviously stoned and hadn't been paying him much attention until they'd spotted the two bikers.

"How come you knew what they were going to do?" Alex said, confused.

"I'm supposed to take the Mustang over to their clubhouse after you get out of the car and go inside," Flaco admitted.

"How were you going to do that? I might have taken the keys. ..." Butch said. He laid the long barrel of the .44 magnum between the front seats. Flaco had been put off his game by being the only sober one in the car.

"*Boost* the mother, man. ... I was boosting cars when I was twelve. *Fuck!* What's wrong with you guys?"

"So we come running out ... and no car?" Butch said. He scratched his two-day growth of beard, contemplating the idea, looking at the hopping girl as she turned back around.

"Yeah," Flaco said.

"That's fucked up," Butch said.

"Yeah. Well ... this is LA.," Flaco said. "Your shit can get really fucked up really fast down here, man."

"I say we abort this mission and let's go to the beach," Alex said. "I'm tired, anyway."

"Okay, but I'm going to pay those Vagos fuckers a visit first. Get out," Butch said to Flaco.

"*What?*"

"I said, get out! Don't say another word either, you skinny fucking piece of iguana shit. No!—an iguana would be *ashamed* to have a shit as small and fucked-up as you."

"... Well go ahead then and shoot me cause I can't get out *here*—this is a foreign country right here, dude!"

"What do you mean? ... Speak English, for fuck's sake," Butch said.

"Where you guys from, anyway, man? Shit, this is *LA*, homes, a *vato* can't just be walking around any old place, man... He'll get *shot*, you dig? So *you* might as well do it yourself," Flaco said. And he was serious; his tone was suddenly different. "Go ahead and blast me—I know you can get away with it, and I'm tired of this shit anyway. You think it's *easy* snitching for the fucking D-E-A, man? Bein' an *informant!*? Huh? And I'm a brown man, too. In America—the shithole of the world if you ain't white! An' rich. Shit. Go ahead and kill me, you KKK *motherfucker.*"

"Like I said, ten pounds of shit in a five-pound sack," Butch said. He put the car in gear, throwing the hand-cannon onto Alex's lap. The pistol slid to the floor, as Alex was unable to grab it in time.

"Hey! WAKE. THE FUCK UP, *PART*-NER! *Shit*, I got to do everything my fucking self," Butch said, hanging a U-turn in the middle of the street. "Now where *is* this Mickey-Mouse clubhouse?"

The instant before he fell completely asleep, Alex had the vague sense that things were finally totally out of control in the most awful way possible. He looked out on the wide sun-battered boulevard as they waited for the light at the intersection to change, everything appearing blurry to him. He tried desperately to stay awake, but finally failed. He was out cold before the light turned green.

"Hey, your partner is asleep, dog, ..." Flaco said. "What kind of faggot partner you *got*, man?"

"Yeah ... " Butch said, looking over at Alex, drooling and leaned up against the door, his head almost lolling out the window. Butch shifted, driving back out onto Valley Boulevard.

"Four blocks down and hang a right," Flaco said.

"Okay," Butch said "Okay. ... What's your real name? You know—the one your momma and daddy gave you?" Butch asked. "Nobody calls a baby 'Flaco.' "

"Why you want to know?" Flaco said.

"So I can make sure they get it right on your fucking tombstone," Butch said.

"That's not funny, dog. ... Tomas ... asshole. With an S. Okay?"

"Okay—with a S," Butch said.

"Cause you Anglo white motherfuckers always—you know—fuck that up and use a Z, half the time," Flaco said. He'd become very sober and clear-headed. He sat back in the seat and called out the streets to Butch as they approached them. But as he automatically called out the names, he started thinking about his mother, who had once had such high hopes for him when he'd been in grade school. Both his parents had been from Monterey, in northeastern Mexico, and had come to the U.S. and worked hard at menial jobs and paid for both he and his brother to go to catholic schools. It had been a struggle to afford the tuition at the private schools. His brother had gone to Stanford on a scholarship, and then on to medical school. The brothers didn't talk anymore, although they had been very close growing up. He didn't ever go by his parent's house anymore, either, too ashamed of what he'd become. He hadn't used his real God-given name for years. To everyone on the streets he was just Flaco the dope fiend. Suddenly he started to cry, out loud and uncontrollably; a stone-sober crying, which made it all the worse, in his mind, because he didn't understand what had happened to him over the past years, or even anything about the why of it all. He had *wanted* Butch to shoot him just then. *It would have been a gift,* he thought, watching the tiny single-storey houses go by. Butch looked into the rearview mirror at him and didn't know what to think when the little fucker started bawling out loud like that.

"Take a left here," Flaco said, defiantly wiping away his tears with the back of his hand. "That's their place ... right there. That grey, low motherfucker, right there." The tears from his eyes were still running down his face as he spoke.

"No shit," Butch said.

Butch looked at his watch. It was almost exactly noon. He stopped the car in the middle of the street right in front of the Vagos clubhouse and shook Alex roughly awake.

"Here. ... I'm going to go kill everyone inside there," Butch said, very matter-of-factly. He handed Alex back the .44 Magnum that had slipped onto the floor. Alex wasn't sure he'd heard him correctly, as he'd just been roused out of a such a deep nod. Alex turned and looked at Flaco. The little Mexican just shook his head back and forth in dismay, his face still wet with tears, which puzzled Alex even more. Butch calmly got out of the car and walked to the trunk, then opened it. They both watched Butch reach inside and pull out an M16 with the 203 grenade-launcher already attached to it. Butch stuck an extra magazine in the front of his jeans and another down his pants against the small of his back. He slid the rifle's launcher arm back checking to make sure it was loaded, then he turned and looked at the clubhouse.

Butch walked toward the front door, checking the slide on the launcher again as he walked by pulling it down for a second time. Then he hooked his finger on the launcher's trigger. He stopped on the sidewalk and fired a grenade at the small transom window over the clubhouse's front door. The grenade broke through the glass. There was a terrific explosion inside the building. The heavy steel front door was immediately blown off its hinges and out towards the street. During the blow-back, Alex saw everything as if he were watching a segment of experimental film footage— the colors were off slightly: the heat waves, the blast's shock-wave, Butch crouching down holding his black cowboy hat onto his head; the explosion's glow briefly colored Butch's black leather vest in a strangely shimmering iridescence. The steel door was flying through the air—flying and falling onto the grass of the front yard like it had been killed stone-dead. Then a stream of thick black smoke came pouring out of the open doorway. A burning man—hair, beard, entire head, *everything*—on fire, ran out of the building, incredibly fast. Butch shot him dead as he ran blindly towards him. The man crashed to the ground and landed exactly on top of the door. A second explosion tore through the building when the stored dragster-fuel blew, torching three other people as it did so, essentially vaporizing them on the spot. No traces of their bodies were ever found. Not that the police looked too hard after the fact.

For most people, that would have been enough of a message to send to potential rip-offers, but not for Butch Nickels. For any number of reasons, most probably unknown even to himself, he switched the M16 onto full auto and proceeded to walk straight into the burning building. There were scattered human body parts still on fire as Butch walked in, because a person of now-undeterminable gender had been walking toward the door and had been very near the grenade just as it went off, the force of the blast having torn both arms from the body, as well as large chunks of what had been the person's torso prior to the explosion.

Butch saw someone dart past in a hallway ahead of him. He scanned the first smoke-filled big room and surveyed the carnage: several bodies were on the ground smoking, their clothes still on fire from the second blast: the stored gas' fumes had been ignited by the grenade and had exploded inside the building, creating a conflagration that had rolled as a low wave front of instant immolation across the floor. A huge dragster tire rolled by him cloaked in a surreal nimbus of blue flame. He walked towards the entrance to a hallway that led to a series of smaller rooms and a big kitchen at the very back of the hallway. Thick black smoke from the burning tires filled the room and Butch began to cough as it hit his lungs. Out of the smoke he caught sight of a large man running down the hall at him, screaming and firing from a handgun. The man's face had been burnt bright red and one of his eyes had been completely burnt out of his head, so he was having trouble seeing Butch. Butch caught him with a burst from the M16. The man didn't make it to Butch's end of the hallway. He fell hard, hitting one wall, what remained of his face taking the brunt of Butch's blast—the six bullets drilling into his face and breaking out the back of his skull pitched him into the wall and spun him around.

Butch turned and saw someone getting up from the floor of the big room, putting their hands up. The man's club jacket was on fire, and his hands were both on fire from the gasoline, but his face, miraculously, was untouched by the flames. Butch immediately shot him dead, firing a burst into the trunk of the man's body. He grabbed the spent magazine and dropped it, re-loading from a spare he'd been carrying shoved into the front of his jeans as he walked across the big burning room, directly under a banner that said: WE GIVE AS GOOD AS WE GET.

When he reached the end of the long hall, he threw an office door open to find a woman on her knees, wobbly but unburnt, apparently trying to get her bearings and stand up. He was going to shoot her, too. Butch stood looking at her, rifle raised, his finger on the trigger; the barrel pointed at her face. She looked back at him, still in shock from the blast, her eyes gradually gaining focus despite the smoke that was starting to pour into the room. Butch was now coughing and starting to gasp for breath. He tried to pull the trigger, but it was as if something were wrong with the rifle. He couldn't shoot her. They looked at each other for a long moment through the smoke. He finally slowly lowered the rifle.

"Who *are* you?" she asked. "... The money is in the safe. .."Well, open it the fuck up!" Butch said, glad he hadn't shot her. She staggered over to the safe and opened it, finally pushing the big door open. Butch motioned her away from the safe and told her to get down onto her knees.

"The sheriff will be here soon," the woman said as she lowered herself to the floor. Butch looked at the stacks and stacks of cash in the safe, coughing constantly now.

"Put your hands out," Butch said. She held them out. He pulled a phone cord out from the wall and hog-tied her wrists together. Then he ran out of the smoking clubhouse and back to the Mustang. He ordered Flaco into the house to help him clean out the safe; Butch ripped the Vagos' motto-banner down from the wall and wrapped most of the stacks of cash in it, then made Flaco carry the bundle back to the Mustang and told him to dump it into the trunk.

The Sheriff's Department was in no hurry to get to the Vagos' clubhouse when they were called by various neighbors reporting an explosion and gunshots. The cops knew it was probably a "goat fuck," so they waited as long as they could before sending out the call, hoping that the perpetrators would be long gone before they got there.

*   *   *

"Daddy, there's someone at the door. He says he knows you. ... From the war?" Sal Birnbaum's oldest daughter stood in his home-office doorway. Sal was working at home that day. It was a Saturday; but, like most Saturdays, he'd brought work home and had retreated to his home-office in the six-bedroom colonial that he and his wife had bought in that particular suburb of Chicago. He'd been able to buy the place after he'd made full-partner at the law firm where he had been employed since 1960, practicing corporate law. He was kidded by his wife that he was a bad Jew for working on the Sabbath. He'd married an Irish Catholic girl who had come to work at the law firm, and they'd been madly in love ever since, and very happy together. His three children had, in fact, been raised Catholic. Since the war, and what he'd seen and done in it, it was difficult for him to feel very religious. He'd prayed desperately too often while friends died in his arms to feel close to God, Jesus, or Allah. And then, after what he'd seen at Dachau, his unit having liberated it, he'd given up on religion all together. What kind of god let *that* kind of place exist? He left questions of religion to his wife and daughters.

"The *war?*" Sal asked her.

"That's what he says. He's in the living room. ... He looks rich," his daughter said. Sal nodded and looked out his office window at the leafy street in front of the house. He saw a grey town car with a driver sitting in their driveway. He took off his gold wire-rimmed glasses and stood up. He'd kept up with some of the men in his unit over the years and there was talk of a reunion in Europe, but it had not gotten any further than talk. He followed his daughter out of the room and down the hallway. His wife was out shopping, so just he and his oldest daughter were in the house. His daughter happened to be home from NYU film school that weekend.

Sal saw Captain Malcolm Law sitting in a green chintz-print couch in the big living room and smiled, happy to see his old Captain after all these years.

"Captain?" Sal said.

"Sergeant Birnbaum," Malcolm said, standing up.

"Gwen, this is a *very* old friend." Sal introduced his daughter to Captain Law and they stood for a moment, smiles all around. His daughter was a little confused by the apparent connection between her father and this obviously very wealthy man.

"I ... thought it would be someone from the Rainbow Division," Sal said.

"No. It's me," Malcolm said. "I thought we could have lunch, if you don't have any other plans? ... "

"Sure ... Sure. I'll get a coat," Sal said.

The Italian restaurant—wood-paneled with white table-clothes and red napkins—was near the Birnbaum's home in a strip-mall. It was early spring and the sky was bright blue; the last of the late snows had fallen and the sidewalks had been shoveled-off for the last time—big piles of slushy snow that had been pushed over to the curb by plows were melting and dirty, now. The waiters were standing around in the back of the place when the two men walked in; it was still early in the restaurant's day, not quite noon.

"I'll have a Chianti," Sal told a waiter who knew him and asked about his family.

"Gin and tonic for me, please," Malcolm said without looking at the man.

"We come here all the time," Sal explained. "My daughters actually run a *tab* in here. *God!*" He'd spoilt his two girls and his wife, and he was proud of doing so, as he'd never thought he was going to live through the war and even *have* children, let alone end up being a successful lawyer.

They had spoken in the backseat of the town-car, driving down to the restaurant, catching up on the intervening years, Malcolm asking questions about his sergeant's post-war life, which had gone in a way Malcolm hadn't expected at all. Birnbaum had graduated from college and for a while had worked as a street cop in Baltimore, then he'd gone to law school in D.C. and ended up at a white-shoe law firm run by a friend of Birnbaum's father's, who, before he'd died, had been one of the most influential rabbis in the city. The hard-bitten, very angry young man Malcolm had known at Dachau had seemingly disappeared. In his place, Malcolm was looking at a tall man, physically fit, in full middle age, who, seeing him on the street, you'd never guess was a hardened combat veteran.

"And you have a *driver*. So you're either with the government, or in the mafia," Birnbaum joked. Malcolm smiled.

"I stayed with the government," Malcolm said. Their drinks came and they ordered.

"Any family?" Sal asked.

"Yes. Two kids ... and a wife," Malcolm said.

"Nice ... good," Sal said. He picked up his glass of wine and their eyes met for a moment, almost by accident.

"Your daughter is very pretty," Malcolm said quickly.

"Yeah, they get it from my wife. I want you to meet her."

"I want to," Malcolm said. "You must wonder why I've dropped out of the sky... ?"

"Well, maybe you need a lawyer?" Sal asked. He took a sip and put his wineglass down directly in front of him.

"... I'm after Neizert—remember him?"

"That SS Hauptmann from Dachau?"

"Yes. That's the one," Malcolm said.

"I thought they hung him. *I* would have. Of course I would have hung *all* of them," Birnbaum said. "But that's just me."

"No. He was traded to the Russians, right after I interviewed him. Just a day or so later, in fact."

"Captain ... are you still ... involved with intelligence work?"

"Yes," Malcolm said. "I need your help, Sal. You know what Neizert looks like, and I need someone I can trust."

"I'm a lawyer. I've got a case I'm about to try against *W.R. Grace* for some asbestos miners in Libby, Montana," Birnbaum said. "I'm a little busy, really, Captain."

"Sal ... these guys ... the ones we brought here to the U.S. ... You can't tell anyone, all right? I need your word," Malcolm said.

"It depends on what you're going to tell me, Captain. I've got a family. And I'm an officer of the court. What is this *about*, exactly?"

"Neizert is in Europe. He wrote me and wants to come to the U.S. He has something he wants to tell me," Malcolm said. "Something very important."

"Well it must be *damned* important. I'm just guessing here, but you went from the OSS into the CIA. I saw your name once in the paper as some kind of grand pooh-bah at the State Department. But I knew somehow you weren't flying a desk at State. ... Call me suspicious. Now we're eating a second-rate meal after not seeing each other for thirty-plus years, and you're asking me to help you find some old *Nazi?*"

"That's right—I need your help. I can't do this alone."

"Do *what*, Captain?"

"I can't bring Neizert here alone, to the United States. I need help. Someone that knows what Neizert looks like and isn't afraid. ... I mean if things get rough."

"Well, let's see. ... You've got the largest intelligence community in the world ... so how could an old, out-of-shape lawyer help, exactly?"

"That's just it ... I'm not able to ask the Agency for any help." Sal gave him a long look. Birnbaum took off his glasses and massaged his eyes, then put them back on again. "But if I'm right about him, Neizert is the most important defector the U.S. will have ever brought in."

"... Okay, Cap. What do you need?" Sal asked, tucking into his lunch.

13

■ SOUTHERN SPAIN

Sonny Delmonico was considered to have very reliable connections to both the Sicilian and American Mafias. It was because of those connections that he'd been chosen by Malcolm Law to act as a guide for the Hauptmann, although Sonny didn't know that yet.

Delmonico was having a sherry in the *tapas* bar *Pedro Romero* in the Andalusían town of Ronda, five miles from the new home he'd just built in the countryside. The bar was a small one and smelled of mopped tile floors and frying squid and was directly across from the town's very famous antique bullring. It was kept fairly dark in the bar because the summer afternoon's heat could become unbearable in Andalucía. The harsh Spanish sunshine became so oppressive by lunch time that it forced most people indoors until well after four in the afternoon.

The kids who lived near the bar called Sonny *El Tuerto* behind his back, because he had the use of only one eye, now. Sometimes, when Sonny Delmonico was flush, he was known to hand out ten-dollar bills to the gypsy women who begged on the streets of Ronda. And because of his generosity, he was protected by the gypsies and was considered a friend. When he was very drunk they would make sure he got home safely and was not bothered by thieves. The gypsies have a sense for people that are different and extreme, and Sonny Delmonico was all that and more.

He was one of hundreds of foot soldiers in a very secret part of the Cold War where drugs and drug money were used to forge allies and buy allegiances from South Vietnam to Turkey; most recently with the right wing generals in Colombia. The use of drugs as a political weapon was something American intelligence agents had learned from the English, who had been part of the international drug trade since the East India Company pioneered it, becoming the world's first drug cartel and multi-national corporation all-in-one. The English company—who counted the Royal family as important shareholders—turned China into a country of opium addicts by military intimidation. The French, not to be outdone by the Brits, did the same thing in their Indochinese colonies, with the same kind of state-sponsored trading companies. And the drugs—all completely "legal"—were taxed by the various colonial governments, making them doubly lucrative.

There are always problems in any business, Sonny thought to himself, as he heard the phone in the back of the bar start to ring loudly. It was an ancient black phone with the kind of heart-stopping bell that could be heard a half-mile away. He glanced at his watch—*right on time.*

Of all the important talents Sonny Delmonico possessed—and he had quite a few—the ability to survive in the underworld was his best. He was not only cagey from years in the mafia—having lived through several brutal internecine wars—but also generally very brave, which gave him an edge, even now in middle age. He had a sense of humor that was very dry and English and came from having grown up in the East End of London. If you were looking for the beating heart of the Sicilian mafia and its connection to Western intelligence services, then Sonny Delmonico would be your man.

He was known to both the CIA and MI6 as a "fixer." His MI6 file, which was sixty pages long, said he was a homosexual with "peculiar leanings." He'd been married to an Italian woman, but had left her in 1962 after having two children, both girls, while living in Brazil. The file said he was a "made" member of an important branch of the Sicilian mafia. His father was from Corleone in Sicily and had been a major *caporegime* in the mafia there before leaving for London in 1929 to escape the Italian police, who wanted him on a multiple-murder charge. They said Sonny's father had stopped a car full of special Carbonari that had been sent from Rome by Mussolini to help the local police control the mafia. He'd killed them all with a shotgun. His father had once reenacted the hit for young Sonny in a kind of pantomime while standing in front of the family car, back in 1940, one day when they were parked on a street in the Harold Hill section of London. When his father was finished shooting at the imaginary Carbonari inside the parked car he'd turned and taken a few playful half-steps in the opposite direction, as if he were running away toward central London. Then he turned back and smiled at his young son as if it were all a lark. He'd put both his big hands on Sonny's shoulders and swore him to secrecy about "the event"—son or not.

Sonny's movements, as he prepared himself to slide off the bar-stool and head towards the phone, were those of the studied, albeit confident and well-equipped drunk. If he had a weakness, it was his eye for pretty young men. And it was a young man from Raleigh, North Carolina—a U.S Navy boy, in fact—who had put out Sonny's right eye shortly after the war in a bar in Crete; the kind of bar that back in those days was called an "open" bar. The kid had stuck a fork in his eye and almost killed him. It was one of the few times Sonny's intuition had let him down, and he'd paid for it dearly. He wore a black patch over his missing eye, just like the Arrow-shirt man in the commercials then ubiquitous on American television. Sonny's code-name in intelligence circles, both American and English, was "The Barrow Boy," and that cognomen had been ironically bestowed by none other than Kim Philby, the notorious MI6 double-agent, who had found Sonny useful and employed his services before Philby himself was caught-out and escaped to Moscow.

The morning before, Sonny had received a telegram from his contact in Palermo. It had been delivered to his house, which stood isolated from its neighbors in a field of sunflowers. The message in Italian was succinct:

Schedules upset with personnel difficulties please be available for a call tomorrow usual number. Noon. – Humberto

At eleven A.M. he'd driven into town in his prized green Fiat Spider and parked in front of the bar that served as a kind of office for him in Spain. The bar had a phone he could trust: Sonny's contacts in the Spanish government's intelligence service kept him posted on all on-going criminal investigations and phone-taps in Andalucía, and in Ronda in particular. He would be the first to know if the phone at *Pedro Romero* was being bugged for what*ever* reason. He could have used the new phone line he'd just had installed at his recently completed hacienda, but was chary of changing anything about his work arrangements. Andalucía was quickly becoming a drug trans-shipping point for the new Colombian coke routes into Europe because of its several large and largely unpoliced ports. The Colombians were notoriously sloppy in their trafficking efforts, and had already attracted the attention of the quickly-growing, albeit very recently established, DEA presence in Spain. Sonny knew his new phone line might be vulnerable to American surveillance, the technicians having just been at his house to install it.

He knew that the bar's phone was clean, and that it was used by a great number of different people, which made it even safer. The bartender, a Fascist who'd fought in the *División Azul* for the Nazi's in Russia and still had a slight limp, courtesy of a Russian sniper who'd shot him near Stalingrad, called out Sonny's name. Only he called "Robert Farley" to the phone—one of the many aliases Sonny had used now for years. He left his stool in the darkest corner of the bar and meandered over to the phone. He was wearing a pink cravat with a white t-shirt, white linen jacket, and white pants, looking like the general image of a lost English ex-pat on vacation, rather than an important spoke in the international heroin trade. His black eye-patch made him seem colorful and a bit rakish, but altogether harmless. In fact, he'd survived the Second World War as a infantryman in the British Army and had fought at the second battle of *El Alamein,* when he'd been only seventeen-years-old. Most of his original platoon had later been wiped out crossing the beach at Anzio. He had aged twenty years in a hundred yards, as he'd once told someone, and it was true. He was most definitely *not* "harmless."

"Bloody hell ... what is it, then?" Sonny barked into the receiver. He hated talking on the phone about business, because there was always the need to use funny double entendres and code words. Most times, meanings were encoded in one's tone of voice more than the actual words being spoken. It made him nervous and irritable, even after all these years of doing it.

"We have a problem with deliveries." The man on the other end of the line was speaking Italian, which Sonny spoke like a native, as both his parents had been born in Sicily and he'd grown up with the language.

"Yes, I gathered *that*. If you're *calling*," Sonny said.

"There's some new competition in Los Angeles. They aren't playing by the rules."

"Well ... Who *does*, these days? It's all gone to the dogs, hasn't it? Amateurs everywhere," Sonny said.

"It's a matter of the utmost *concern*," the man-on-the-phone said.

"Yes. Yes. I see."

"We feel it best that *you* meet with them. As they seem *special*. Perhaps it's best if we take them in. Or perhaps something *else* could be arranged. ... "

"*Special*, are they?"

"We think so," the man said.

"Well, everyone is special, my mum used to say. ... I'll need details, of course," Sonny said in English.

"Forthcoming. The usual office," the man now replied in English.

"Right." The man rang-off. Sonny put the phone back down on the receiver. He saw two Guardia Civil step into the bar, their patent-leather hats shiny, their faces red from the sun. They went to the end of the bar, laid their automatic weapons down on the scarred wooden surface, and proceeded to order lunch. One of them looked at Sonny and smiled and nodded. They'd known each other for years; both of them enjoyed the company of men, and especially young boys of a certain bent.

"Buy that big nasty devil a drink!" Sonny said, walking back out towards the barroom.

*   *   *

Sal Birnbaum's wife Catharine, who'd been born in Ireland and had come to the States to study history at Columbia University, was standing in the couple's master bedroom watching her husband pack. She had a look on her face that Sal didn't think he'd ever seen before, except perhaps when they'd been audited by the IRS. It was shock, tinged with fear. When the Irish are fearful, or angry, they wear the same expression, Sal had learned—the hard way.

"I'm trying to understand," she said. "But it's difficult. I mean, one day everything is normal. And now you're leaving and you won't say where to, or why you're going— or even for how bloody long."

"It won't be long," Sal said. He put several pair of dark socks in his suitcase. He was hoping to pack without anyone else in the room because it was always hard to know what to take on an extended trip, and especially this time, since Malcolm Law, who he had not heard from in years, had asked him to go to West Germany, check into a famous hotel in Berlin, and wait for a phone call—all without much of an explanation other than saying it was very, very important.

"Tell me again you aren't leaving me," Catharine said.

"Honey, *please,* don't be ridiculous," Sal said.

"You have a big case. ... You were going to trial *tomorrow,* remember? You've been preparing this case for months!"

"... I know. Yes. I've called the judge, and we got an emergency postponement. I explained to him that I'd had a family emergency and he was very nice about it."

"*What* family emergency, Sal?" Sal was standing by the big, baroque French armoire that he and his wife had bought and that had cost ten-thousand dollars. She liked to buy expensive furniture and he liked to indulge her taste. He'd loved his wife passionately from the moment he'd laid eyes on her. There was something about her hips that he'd loved, and her pearl-white Irish skin; her fay smile and her beautiful red hair. Other, younger, lawyers at the firm had zeroed in on her, too, but for whatever reason she'd fallen for the tall Jewish guy who was ten years older than she was. She told him later that he looked tough, and where she came from in Dublin, that was a plus. He loved her now as much as he did the day they had gotten married. After the war he'd spent a long time living alone, dealing with the depression that came with being a cop who drank a lot to forget what he was doing on a daily basis. She'd changed his life, making it worth living again.

"I told you ... I lied," he said.

"That's what I don't understand. *Why,* Sal!?"

"I had to. ... I've got something I have to do."

"*What,* for God's sake?" Catharine asked. She sat down on the edge of their bed. He thought she was going to cry; her blue eyes were intent and piercing. He pulled out some golf shirts, looked at them, and choosing the dark one, took it to the suitcase and put it down on top of the other clothes he'd already packed. His wife instinctively started rearranging his clothes in the suitcase, tucking them in so they would fit better.

"I just can't say why. You have to trust me, honey," Sal said. They were both in their fifties now, and that was a word that meant more than when they'd been younger: trust. They had daughters and they had a beautiful life they'd built together. All those things were held together by that one word, trust, which became a fragile word at a certain age. They had both seen couples, who they'd known very well, blow-up and destroy everything they'd had together and end up living in separate condos with views of the freeway. There was a heavy silence in the bedroom as he looked at his wife.

"Where are you going? ... At least tell me that," she said.

"I can't say—you see, I can't say *any* thing," Sal said.

"Sal ... Please, this is *crazy*. Does it have to do with that man I met the other day, Mr. Law? The one from your Army days?"

"No," he lied. It was the first time he'd ever lied to his wife in his life, and his face colored a little bit and she noticed it immediately. He was a terrible liar and he knew it.

"You're *lying*, Sal."

"Catharine. We've been married for twenty-five years. ... Right now you just have to trust me. This has nothing to do with *us*." He looked down at his suitcase absent-mindedly. He still had room for his toiletries, and walked to the bathroom to get his kit-bag to put them in.

"What did they say at work?" Catharine asked from the bedroom.

"John said that I could take all the time I needed. And that he hoped whatever was wrong wasn't too serious," Sal said. He spoke while rummaging through a drawer, looking for his travel kit.

"So you lied to John, too?" She said.

"Yes. I did," Sal said, finding his kit-bag and picking up his tooth brush from the bathroom counter. He took a deep breath and walked back out to the bedroom, but his wife was gone. His daughter had to drive him to the airport. He told his daughter that when the Irish get mad there's nothing to do but let them cool off. She agreed with him from her own experience.

"I would say she's three steps beyond pissed at you right now," his daughter wryly commented.

Malcolm Law picked him up at Dulles International Airport in Washington, D.C. They drove to a down-at-the-heels motel out in the suburbs.

131

"Neizert's still in Germany. I'm sure of that. I'm going to send him a message in a day—once you've gotten to Berlin," Malcolm said.

"I take it he's in some kind of danger?" Sal said, keeping his eyes on the road in front of them.

"Yes. Look in the glove compartment, Sergeant." Birnbaum opened the glove box and saw a short-barreled Berretta inside.

"Do you still remember how to use one of those?" Malcolm asked. Birnbaum reached for the pistol. It had been a long time since he'd held a weapon. He was surprised that it felt so good. "Go ahead. Take it with you."

"But how am I going to take it on the plane—I can't pass the metal detectors with it, can I?"

"You aren't flying commercial, Sergeant. You're going to Europe on an Agency plane tonight at eleven. You'll be in Berlin tomorrow morning." Birnbaum looked at him.

"Well ... okay. I'll take a weapon, then," Sal said.

"You need to get Neizert to Lake Como ... *alive,*" Malcolm said as they pulled onto the freeway. He watched the Sergeant take the pistol from the glove box and immediately eject the clip onto his lap.

"Has it been cleaned recently?" Birnbaum asked, picking up the clip and examining it. He heard Malcolm laugh.

"... What's so funny, Captain?"

"I just realized that I picked the right guy." Then he stopped smiling. "You don't have to do this, you know. ... It will be dangerous. I'm sure of that. There are people that want Neizert dead. There're parties that want to stop him from getting here to the U.S." He felt suddenly guilty for having dragged this man away from his family and his comfortable life. And, too, Malcolm realized that, on some level, he was jealous of his former sergeant. Birnbaum had the kind of life most men dream of—a family that was close and a beautiful wife; a thriving career; children who obviously adored him. It was a lot to lose if something went wrong. It was the life Malcolm had wanted for himself, but his children all hated him and his wife had turned indifferent.

"It can't be any worse than the Bulge, Captain," Sal said, looking intently now at the Berretta, holding it in his right hand getting the feel of it. "... Anyway, I needed a vacation," he joked in a put-on pseudo tough-guy voice.

"All right, then, let's do this," Malcolm said, and he proceeded to map out the next four days and how they would stay in touch with each other once Birnbaum arrived in Berlin.

*　　　　　*　　　　　*

"Endless summer," Butch said.

Since they'd beaten the crap out of the surfer, word had gotten around that the three odd-ball hippies were best avoided. As a result, they had a whole patch of beach at Paradise Cove almost entirely to themselves. Butch had gone swimming and was now plopped down on a small towel from the Capri, but his knees had missed the towel and were sand-covered. Alex looked at him. It had been two days since they'd shot up the Vagos' clubhouse. Butch had shot their president stone dead and blown the shit out of their clubhouse, essentially destroying it completely, since the building had been destroyed, only a blackened shell remaining when the fire department arrived on the scene. The psychological aftermath of their attack on the remaining gang was very predictable.

"I saw that movie," Patty said. *"Endless Summer."*

"I saw it in Saigon," Butch said, "at a USO club."

Patty raised her arms like she was surfing, even though she was lying out on the sand in a new red micro-bikini, wearing big, over-sized dark glasses that she'd bought in a second-hand store in West Hollywood.

"I liked the part in South Africa," Patty said. "Cool."

"Yeah," Butch said. "Me, too." They seemed close, Alex realized, like a brother and sister. He knew Butch liked her, but it was a sweet and protective kind of "like," and he approved. And he knew Butch eyed her—like other men on the street—at times, but how could he blame him for it? There were times when she was just so beautiful it was almost painful—the simple things she would wear, a pair of jeans and a wife-beater with no bra, not caring about her arms, which were scarred from drug use. Her hair was longer now and very sun-bleached. Living in L.A. had changed her for the better, actually; she seemed more womanly, and you noticed her freckles more now, made darker by all the sun-bathing they did. The fact was that when he wasn't high, he wanted her—all the time. Sometimes they'd made love in the Mustang out in the parking lot at the beach at night because she liked to do it there: they would drink a half-pint of brandy and then she would undress him and become instantly pliable, insistent on having an in-the-back-of-the-car-palms-on-the-windows orgasm.

"Why don't we go to South Africa?" she said. Patty picked herself up and looked at both of them. "It's got these really *long* beaches, *man*."

"Yeah, why the hell not?" Butch said. "Sounds good." He didn't mention that he'd been there more than once. That he'd been sent to train some of the South African troops that were being sent to fight in Angola against the Cubans who had troops there.

"What happened to Flaco?" Patty said, changing the subject. "He's too much, man."

"Oh, he's around," Butch said.

133

"Let's take him, too," Patty said. "I like him." Butch laughed and looked at Alex. There'd been an uneasiness between them since he'd shot up the Vagos' clubhouse, after they heard from Flaco that they'd managed to shoot dead the Vagos President, not to mention killing several other members of the gang. They understood now that things were getting a little out of control, even for *them*, with all the latitude they had to do pretty much as they wanted when it came to low-life drug dealers. Butch had started carrying a sawed-off automatic shotgun in a duffel bag, even bringing it to the beach, along with his usual side-arm.

"You guys seem different today," Patty said. "What's wrong? Cats on a hot beach or something?"

"It's not easy being a busy executive," Butch said. "And now I'm a property owner, too, and that's *always* stressful. You know ... "

"Why don't we all move into your new place?" Patty said. "I'm tired of living in that motel. It would be fun to be in West Hollywood. Maybe I'll bump into Ryan O'Neal, or Elizabeth Taylor, or some really cool movie star."

"Actually, that's not a bad idea," Alex said. He'd been sitting with his knees gathered up to his chest. He, too, was now finally tan and his hair was very blond from their daily stints at the beach.

"Can we, Butch? Huh? I'll fix it up; buy stuff for it. I'd like to. I'll pay rent," Patty said. Butch turned and looked out at her from the shadow cast across his face by the brim of his cowboy hat.

"Let's talk about it at lunch," Butch said. They decided to go back to the Capri to change, and then go eat somewhere close-by.

14

■ MOTEL CAPRI, MALIBU CALIFORNIA

The two hit-men from Sicily were set up very well and they knew it. They were confident because they had designed a very beautiful crossfire, and it couldn't fail. Above the Capri motel's parking lot, on the second-storey terrace, lying down, the older gunman had chosen a short-barreled Minimi canister-fed light machine gun, of the type often used by infantry troops around the world and known for its reliability. He'd used it before and found it worth the trouble of carrying the long, sixteen-pound weapon because of its rate of fire—700 rounds a minute—a rate that could overwhelm just about anything put up against it. He had two ammunition canisters lying next to him. The canisters fed the gun's ammunition belt automatically. He could feel the pebbling in the concrete pressing against his chest as he waited, his cheek resting on the polymer stock of the machine gun.

The concrete, in the heat of the morning, smelled not too different than fresh fruit for some unknown reason, and momentarily took him back to his childhood in Sicily. He had killed the young desk clerk at the motel with a chopping blow to the third cervical vertebra of the neck, which was in line with the man's jaw. The hitman had walked in carrying a large suitcase and asked for a room. The young desk clerk was explaining that all the Capri's rooms were reserved for a big wedding party. The desk clerk, not expecting the vicious blow, had fallen like he'd been shot, his legs collapsing under him. The chopping blow was always devastating, crushing the vertebra when done correctly. The blow's secret was the palm-strike's follow-through. He'd dragged the convulsing and dying man into the cubby-hole office behind the desk and closed the door. Then the killer calmly took the desk clerk's place, standing and looking out the large picture window, watching the traffic pass on Highway One, waiting.

The young one, Ricardo, killed the maid, just after she'd turned to look at him as he walked in. He'd smiled, which put her immediately at ease. He raised the pistol and shot her in the side while she turned off the vacuum so she could hear what he was saying. The second gunman had walked in the motel room at exactly eleven A.M. The door to the second floor room was open, and the maid's cart was parked out in front on the walkway. He could hear the vacuum running as he stepped into the room. He shot the woman in the upper chest. The nine millimeter bullet knocked the middle-aged Latin woman backwards, tearing through both her lungs. She turned slightly, still standing. The gunman, right up *on* her now, shoved her violently. She hit the nightstand and struck it as she fell, smashing a cheap ceramic lamp, breaking it with her elbow. She fell into the narrow space between the room's two twin beds, not quite dead yet.

The young man stood over her. One of the beds had caught her body and was making her sit up straight against the side of its mattress. She was trying to breathe and looking up at her attacker, terrified. The young man placed the extended barrel of his pistol against her forehead and pulled the trigger a second time. A *pssst* sound was all that came from the U.S government-issue silencer—which had been made by U.S. Colt Arms Corp. exclusively for the U.S. military, especially for its Green Beret divisions. It had been made available to the U.S. Mafia by right-wing Cubans, who had been issued the same silencers by the CIA for their covert work in Cuba and Chile. The high-tech devices dispersed the sound of the nine millimeter round through a two-chamber method. The young gunman looked at the dead woman, her expression in death one of complete shock. A black, quarter-sized burnt divot was left on her forehead when he pulled the barrel away.

The white sheet of the bed she'd been making was sprayed with blood and grey matter now, as was the wall behind it. The young man, very thin, in a brand-new yellow short-sleeved cotton shirt, his jet black hair slicked back, pulled the maid's master-room key from a rubber band around her wrist, breaking the band as he did so. He turned around and walked out, being careful to push the maid's cart into the room and to close the door behind him. It was 11:05 A.M..

The two men had started the operation late that morning, as soon as they'd seen their three targets troop off to the beach at 10:49 A.M., like clock-work. They knew their drill. They would be back between 12:30 and 1:00, at the latest, at which time they would walk across the kill-zone on the way to their rooms.

It was now 12:35, and the older gunman was ready, his big body lying half in and half out of room number 20 on the second floor with it's view of the parking lot directly below. He'd put the machine gun together in the empty stale-smelling room in complete silence. He'd realized then, as he worked, that there was indeed no one else staying at the motel other than the three they were here to kill.

He smiled when he thought of the maid cleaning already-clean rooms. He wondered why again, as he put the NATO-issued machine gun together, having brought it up to the second floor room in its suitcase. It still puzzled him. But their plan hinged on their guess that no other guests were staying at the motel, despite the fact that a desk clerk had been on duty every day. They had watched the hotel for ten days and nights and were as sure of it as they could be. He had insisted to the younger man that, strange as it might seem, that *was* the case, and now he felt vindicated. No cars in the parking lot, he'd told the younger man, meant there could be no other guests, despite how unusual that seemed, or even implausible, especially in L.A. The two hit men had decided that they were dealing with men that were rich enough to own the motel and use it as a cover. Before the older one had walked out onto the terrace, he'd extended the metal legs to the gun's bipod, snapping them into position, testing them once, and then opening the door. It had been exactly noon when he finished getting ready.

On the terrace, the machine gun was ready, the bolt having been pulled back into the firing position, the bipod giving the gun a very sturdy feel. He laid waiting on the narrow concrete walk that overlooked the motel's freshly-asphalted parking lot with new white lines painted in, only two spaces occupied: the Mustang the men drove and the desk clerk's car. The only adjustment he would make when they came in sight would be to push the gun a few inches forward through the two foot space in the balustrade.

The man clicked the cheap walkie-talkie they'd bought; one short click. He immediately heard a click back, signaling that the other gunman—the younger one—was in position behind a low, crudely-painted, ugly block-wall, four feet high, that ran the length of the parking lot and out along the driveway, gradually sloping down to just two feet high when it reached the highway in front of the Capri. Now they waited. The next time his partner would click the radio, it would be to signal that the trio was approaching the kill-zone, and that their escape was blocked at the rear by his young partner behind the wall. A long burst from the machine gun would do the work of killing them in the stretch of open parking lot twenty-five feet below. They both expected that it would be over in mere seconds and that the van they had waiting nearby would pull into the parking lot and pick them up.

The gunmen knew that if one of their targets escaped the burst from the machine gun it would be up to the younger man to kill them, shooting from the wall with a short- barreled AK-47, leaving the protection of the wall if necessary, as he would be covered from above by the machine gun.

It was a classic, two-fields-of-fire ambush—with high elevation/low elevation firing positions—a scenario the older one had used countless times before to good effect. It was the exact tactic used in the assassination of President Kennedy, too, and spectacularly successful that day in Dallas.

And no doubt it would have worked as planned, except for the two unexpected things happening that day that could not have been foreseen. First, Butch had been separated from Alex and Patty, cut off from crossing Highway One with them by one of the young surfers they'd beaten up. The kid, seeing the three of them on the highway in front of him, sped his car up and tried to run Butch over—he was serious about it, too. Alex and Patty had run ahead towards the Capri. Butch had stepped back and let the asshole pass, not wanting to chance that the kid *wasn't* serious and was only trying to scare him. The kid flipped him off as he drove by, grinning ear to ear. The second thing was seeing two Harley Davidson Sportsters parked on the shoulder of the road in front of the health food restaurant they usually ate lunch in, just down from the Capri. The restaurant sat right on Highway One directly across from the beach. Butch had decided that, given what he'd done at the Vagos clubhouse, he should open the satchel he was carrying and take the safety off the automatic shotgun he'd brought to the beach with them every day. He'd done this before he trotted across the highway to warn Alex that there could be Vagos members at the restaurant. Since his rash attack on—and ensuing rip-off of—the Vagos' clubhouse, he and Alex had been lying low, knowing that they'd pushed their luck about as far as it could go, at least until things cooled down, whenever *that* might be. Their attack had even made the pages of the *LA Times*, the article had chalked-off the killings as due to a "gang rivalry" on the back page of the *Metro* section.

"Hogs ... at the restaurant," Butch said, catching Alex and Patty on the sidewalk in front of the Capri. Patty had put on a big straw beach-hat and was holding flip-flops and a towel in her hands. They were all stoned and had been joking around before they crossed the road. The surfer's attempt to run them over had sobered them up, though. Patty stopped and turned to look at Butch. Alex took out the pistol he'd had shoved in the back of his cut-offs. He draped his small motel towel over the Walther.

"What's wrong, Bruce?" Patty said. She knew they carried the guns to the beach, but it was the first time she'd ever seen Alex pull his out, and it frightened her.

"Go on ahead—I'll be right back," Alex said, not looking at her. He'd turned towards the restaurant. Butch, who was standing fairly near them, started walking towards the two parked bikes. His hand was deep in the nylon satchel gripping the shotgun, hard. Patty turned and headed towards their rooms. Her suit was wet and clinging to her ass, and men driving by on the highway were gawking at her as they drove past.

Alex trotted down the driveway after Butch, slipping the safety off his Walther as he did so, his fingers used to finding the roughly-knurled safety by the trigger. It was Alex who first saw the man start to stand up from behind the wall as he passed, catching him out of the corner of his left eye, as he hurried to catch up with Butch.

It was the black paint of the AK-47 that he knew so well from Vietnam, then the weapon's wood stock taking shape in his peripheral vision as Alex turned toward the man, who was just starting to lean on the wall, his weapon pointed towards the parking lot.

Alex instinctively raised his pistol and fired. It was a twenty-yard shot and he fired high on the first round. By his second shot, he'd fully turned toward the man and solidly planted himself. That shot struck home. By his third shot, his wrists were locked around the butt of his pistol. His second shot, although low, caught the man, who was crouched with one elbow up resting on the wall, in the fleshy part of his ass. His fourth shot smashed the man's left femur at the hip. The shooter had started to turn toward Alex, but he was too late. The AK-47 was going off on full-automatic as he tumbled backwards, the barrel pointing up, the shots going wildly into the air. The fifth bullet from Alex's Walther hit the man a second time in the hip, traveling into his lower intestines; none of the shots as yet had been fatal. Alex saw the gunman slip from the wall, with the AK-47 leaving his hands as the man reached for his wounded belly.

Alex ran behind the wall and directly toward the wounded gunman, pistol pointed straight ahead of him, continuing to fire as he moved. He emptied the Walther into the man, several shots striking the man directly in the top of the skull—all kill-shots.

After the first click from the walkie-talkie, and before the unexpected firing out on the highway began, the gunman on the second-storey walkway was concentrating solely on the kill-zone, expecting the girl to be followed closely by the two men, as she had been every morning, their having watched the trio's pattern of movements from a street above the motel for the last two weeks.

His finger had pressed on the trigger, sighting-in as the girl strolled into the parking lot with her hands full. But then, when the two men didn't immediately appear in the driveway behind her, he had only a second to decide whether to fire at the girl, or hold off. He instinctively held off, but when he heard the unexpected shooting, and just before the girl in the red bathing suit disappeared out of the kill-zone, the man let go a short burst from his weapon and saw her tumble to the ground. The sound from the machine gun was so loud that people eating at the health food store, already on the ground by then, thought that the automatic weapons fire was aimed directly at them. It seemed as if a war had suddenly broken out in Malibu, and people in the restaurant started to scream, some hysterically, and a few ran out of the place and across the highway, causing near-accidents and general chaos on Highway One, resulting in several rear-enders that would end up blocking the highway and slowing considerably any Sheriff's deputies coming from Malibu Station, which was actually not too far away.

The gunman on the terrace looked immediately towards the wall and saw his partner—now leaning on the wall—turn towards the highway. Then he saw him fall quickly from view amidst very loud gunfire. Their plan, he realized then, had failed, and failed spectacularly. He had to make a quick decision. Should he try to escape while there was still time, or carry on the attack alone? He saw a blond head appear, running behind the wall towards his companion.

His decision was instinctive. He stood up with the machine gun and fired a long burst at the running man, who was now running crouched down. He saw the blocks on the top of the wall broken and splintering as if someone were hammering at it with a cold-chisel; huge chips were flying every which-way. The bullet strikes followed the bobbing blond head. It was after that burst that he felt the adrenalin rush that every soldier feels in a firefight; the restriction of the peripheral vision accompanied by a kind of light-headedness, even a giddy euphoria—*if* you were 'winning' whatever the encounter was. He waited for a moment. He was exposed now, standing on the terrace, but didn't really think about that. He glanced at the girl lying on the parking lot. She wasn't moving. He fired into her body a second time, in reflexive anger, and saw the fresh new asphalt being thrown up in the air in clumps around her body. He heard the crack of gunfire and instinctively crouched back down. The door behind him had been hit, and then the wooden balustrade was being strafed by gunfire. He was hearing the sharp, cracking sound bullets make when they pass close to one's head.

Still crouching, but resting the machine gun on the balustrade's rail now, he returned fire, cutting a large notch in the wall where he'd seen the blond man firing from. He realized that he could literally shoot the blocks out of his way and reach the man firing at him. He emptied sixty rounds into the top of the wall in a few seconds, knocking big chunks out of it. At this point in the firefight, the first call went out to the Sheriff's Department from the restaurant down the street. The gun battle was just two minutes old. The gunman on the terrace reloaded a second canister into the machine gun; he had just emptied a hundred rounds into the wall in less than twenty seconds.

Alex crawled over the dead man, his skull destroyed, and grabbed the AK-47 from the dirt where it had dropped. There were two extra banana-clips on the ground beside it, and he changed out the magazine. The sound of the wall being broken apart by the machine gun fire hitting just above him was incredibly loud. He was now lying prone, as low to the earth as he could get. Concrete chips were hitting him in the side of the face as the hollow blocks above him were being chinked and drilled by the machine gun's bullets. He crawled away from the spot as fast as he could, clumsily cradling the AK-47, hoping to return fire from another place, as the wall was quickly torn apart. Suddenly the machine gun firing stopped. He decided that the man must be reloading, so he stood up and fired a burst at the gunman on the terrace, who knelt down as he fired at him.

In the harsh sunlight Alex saw Butch, his shotgun pointed straight up, running across the parking lot, having taken the same opportunity to move when the firing from the terrace stopped. When Alex saw Patty's body lying in a pool of blood on the asphalt, everything seemed to stop; time itself hung in a suspended dimension. Then something went off in his brain, a kind of fit fueled by adrenaline and pure rage. He stood up and fired at the man on the terrace again, covering Butch as he ran. He saw Butch reach the other side of the parking lot a few rooms down from the man on the terrace. He saw Butch throw himself against the wall. He looked up at the terrace's catwalk above him. His shotgun was useless because the gunman on the terrace was protected by the concrete he was standing on. Butch waved frantically at Alex to resume firing, which act would allow him to move out into the parking lot again and fire at the man himself.

There is a moment in any battle when the tide changes. The gunman on the terrace had not been able to reload in time to stop Butch from crossing the kill-zone, and he knew it was all over—he was simply out-gunned, now, and it was time to retreat. He spoke into the walkie talkie in a clipped calm voice: *finito*. The van that had been parked on the street came roaring up the driveway. The gunman decided that he could make it to the waiting van only if he could suppress the fire from the wall while he was descending the steps to the second floor that led down to the parking lot. But the steps were attached to the wall, and hence he'd be vulnerable while on them. He tried to think of a way out. He heard a siren and realized that he was running out of time. The police would be here soon. He decided to jump onto the top of the van as it stopped directly below him. It was a twenty-five foot drop—but then it would be easy to roll from the top of the van to the ground. He climbed the rail and slipped his feet over it while cradling the machine gun. He saw the blond head appear again, so he fired, one-handed, at the wall; a long, concentrated burst. He could feel the hot air from the machine gun's breech hitting him in the face while the spent shell-casings fell like rain onto the parking lot below. He finally jumped, still holding his weapon.

Butch stepped out in front of the van and opened fire on the driver with the "Striker." The effect of the automatic shotgun at close range was devastating. Six twelve-gauge blasts in quick succession—windshield, metal and flesh, all destroyed. The driver's face was hit by the first blast. The driver's body slumped onto the horn. The gunman who had jumped from the second-floor was caught by a long burst from Alex, who'd jumped up onto the broken wall and aimed at a point just below the falling man. It worked, but Alex didn't wait to see the results; he'd already jumped off the wall and was running towards Patty's body.

When the first Sheriff's car pulled into the driveway of the Capri Motel they saw Alex wildly beating on a dead man; the one who'd hit the van and rolled away and had by now bled to death from his wounds. Alex was beating the dead man with the now-empty AK-47, down on his knees, using the weapon as a club, bringing the heavy stock down again and again on the man's head; the Sheriff's deputies who'd pulled up and were now protected by their car doors, kept shouting at Alex that they would shoot him, but he wasn't listening. Finally, he stopped of his own accord, his face blood-and brain-splattered; the van's horn still blaring. Butch had his hands up, and had been standing there watching Alex beat the dead man. They were both told to get on the ground, face-down.

"DEA!" Butch finally yelled. "DEA officers—Don't shoot *us*, for fuck sake! We're on your side!" And it was finally over, seven minutes after it had started.

15

■ LONDON

"Sonny Delmonico, Ma'am, is as dirty as they come. There are two pages of *known* aliases, at least. He's been selling heroin since the fifties ... if not before," the young man said. He was slightly freckled and had brown, thinning hair that needed badly to be washed. He was wearing a suit that was verging on trendy and would have been viewed as "light-heeled" in the old days when Mary Keen had first joined the Service, only a few months after the war ended, back in 1946. In those days, MI6 was dominated by tweedy dons and rakish dark-haired colonels with solid war records from "good families" and the odd glamour-boy types who'd been recruited because they were wealthy Englishmen living abroad and were well woven into the fabric of the Empire. There were Eastern European aristocrats, too—with family ties to the seats of power in their parents' home countries—many were White Russians; holdovers from the Czar's time, and rabidly anti-communist.

The boyish-looking young man was perched on a chair across from her and seemed to Mary as if he were still in the 7th form at his public school. He was the type, she imagined, that would be caught "abusing himself," and would cry openly when threats were made about calls home. She couldn't help making snap-judgments these days; her patience with the younger generation had been running very short lately–the mark of true middle-age, she supposed. They all seemed to go adrift, ever since the 60s. In part she was jealous, because she could no longer claim the power of youth–something she'd enjoyed to the fullest when she had it. But hers was a class-bias, too; she preferred the high walls the Service had built before the Thatcher years. Those walls had kept this kind of colorless type out. It was, very ironically, Margaret Thatcher's Tories who had brought this spirit of mediocrity to the spy business.

She and the young man holding Sonny Delmonico's file were sitting in Mary Keen's office at MI6. The file had a white ribbon around it. The older files at British Intelligence, those that pre-dated the computer age, had curious white-ribbon ties; their use dated to before the First World War. And, in fact, the Boer War was when MI6 was officially put in charge of amassing a huge file-system to keep track of subversive Afrikaners, who at the end of the Boer campaign had been rounded up and herded into concentration camps —the first camps ever so-designated by those who created them to segregate their "enemies" from the rest of the "good" population who supposedly all supported the English suzerains.

Sonny Delmonico's file went back to the early 1950s. Mary had asked specifically for the old-school, hard-copy file, because sometimes important bits of pertinent information were not picked up when the files were scanned into the modern electronic file-registry, which was housed on the Department's main-frame computers.

Marginalia, the odd tidbits that had oftentimes been so useful to her generation in the field, were either partially cut-off or a blurry, unreadable mess when the electronic version of a file was printed out. But the original notes, left on the margins by unknown officers in the past, sometimes contained very important information—names, addresses, little things that she knew were important when rounding out a story or a profile. She had grown up in an era of fountain pens and writing-in-the-margins that younger people now viewed as antediluvian, but that her generation did as a common practice. She didn't bother to explain to the young man what she was looking for. She didn't have to, because as head of MI6 research and achieves there were only a few senior people she had to answer to.

"...Go on," Mary said, sitting back in her chair. Her desk was a cluttered mess.

"He goes doggo, for one thing," the young man, whose father was an important Tory politician, looked up at her with a queer, half-vacant look. "He was completely out of the picture for three years in the late seventies. Some kind of problem he had in Italy. Our Sonny crossed the wrong people, maybe? ... Anyway, the file says he simply dropped from sight. Unavailable, even to us. It says he may have been hiding in Brazil. *Brasilia*, specifically, it says here. ... But we gave up trying to find him back then, anyway."

"Is he ours, *now*? Or is he the Yanks'? ... This creature, Delmonico ..." Mary said, gathering herself up. She was sitting at her desk behind a pile of books about the Soviet Union and Eastern Europe.

"Not really; he's *anyone's*, Ma'am," the young man said, looking up again from the open file. He was scared of Mary because she had a reputation for firing people from her section simply because she'd taken a dislike to them. "He's worked for us and for the cousins in the past. He does us favors. But it's quid pro quo and always has been, from what I read here. When he's in a pinch and needs something, he'll ring *us* first, never the cousins. Or Wally Giordano, here in London. Very old-school boys, indeed. Both their parents were Italians. Both were from Sicily. The file says that Sonny's father was an important Mafioso in the Old Country."

"And we own this man Wally, too?" She'd known the answer to the last two questions, but as the young man was new to her section, she was testing his ability to retain facts.

"Yes. Ever since someone called "Jack the Hat" was murdered. An associate of the Krays, actually. I saw something recently about them—the Krays—on the BBC; it was on their Channel 4 show, I believe," he said.

"Jack McVitie," Mary said.

"Yes. Some kind of big-time gangster in the *very* old days. ... This Giordano was going to be charged with his murder. We sent someone from MI5 to speak to him and explain the situation. He's been in the family ever since. Giordano still reports to us directly, in fact. He's one of our eyes on the heroin market, and he keeps it English. MI5 rolls up his competition—mostly Hong Kong Chinese from what I could see, and a few Corsicans. For some reason we want to keep the Chinese out. ... " The young man looked up at her, apparently genuinely clueless. She tapped her pen on the leather blotter and gave him nothing back, sitting there stone-faced and impassive. "... I suppose the money would go to the Reds?" Still she gave him no response.

"And, Sonny?" She didn't bother explaining that the heroin market had been tightly controlled since the end of the war. It had been designed by them and the cousins so that the Sicilians could be well-fed, with the agreement that the Sicilian mob act as their agents in controlling a very real Communist threat in Italy. It was a partnership with a devil, but a necessary one. No one had expected the profits to be as big as they were now, certainly. In order to slow the Sicilian mafia's growing monetary—and hence, ultimately, political—power, the cousins had to set up the South Vietnamese heroin producers as a counterweight.

"Wally and Sonny contract directly with the Sicilians. Wally *runs* England—runs the whole show here—and makes gobs of money off it. But Sonny doesn't work just for him. ... When he works at all, of course. He's a sybarite, *in extremis*." The young man looked up from the file. "A real 'high-stepper,' as my father calls them."

"But they're close? Delmonico and Wally?"

"Yes. *Very* close. He and Wally go back to the 50s, it says here. I pulled Giordano's file, too. It's much thicker. Anyway, they grew up together, and when Wally came to us, he brought Sonny, too, you could say. They're still good chums."

"So Wally is someone Delmonico trusts?"

"Yes. I would think so, Ma'am. As far as people *can* trust, in *that* world." He looked at her, wanting to share a deprecating glance. She didn't give him anything back for a third time. He uncrossed his legs and closed the file, realizing that she probably didn't like him, and his budding career might be doomed because he'd failed to make a good impression.

"... I want this—Roger, yes?"

"Yes, Ma'am. Roger."

"Roger, I want this Wally arrested and brought down to the Yard. His house turned over as well. His wife pushed down on the couch—that kind of thing," she said. "Have them bring a police dog right into the house. Crap on the rug. That always sends a proper message."

"Right. That's for our liaison at MI5. Mr. Billy."

"Yes. What about Delmonico's business?"

"He seems to move heroin for Wally, but various others, too. Canadians; Americans; Irish gangs. Even *Israeli* gangs work with him. I'd call him an expeditor, working to connect the refiners and marketers. He goes to Sicily and arranges shipments after they've been paid for. The Sicilians won't take on a new client unless someone like Delmonico, who they know and trust, vouches for them. In the past he moved some important people for us via the same routes as the heroin. There is mention of the cousins using him to smuggle some unsavory types into Mexico for them in the 60s on a contract-basis."

"Smuggle *people*? When, exactly?"

"In the early 60s he moved two ... " He flipped back through the file, looking for the entry. "Strange ... it was here *yesterday.* " He looked up with a miffed expression. "I read the file from beginning to end, Ma'am. And I remember it because he did it only twice, both times through Mexico, and for the cousins."

"What are you saying? ... That you've lost pages out of the *file?*"

"No, Ma'am. There *are* pages missing, though." He looked up at her in real shock. "I must have left them at my desk. I'm very Sorry." He turned red for a moment. His throat was crimson, as if he'd eaten some hot food.

"Do you remember anything *about* the men ... their names or anything?"

"It was done for the cousins; two Germans. I remember they were German names. Hans ... that kind of name," the young man said. He was still looking down at the file, trying to find the missing pages. Then he shut it and forced himself to look up, afraid now that he'd bungled it completely.

"For the cousins? You're sure that's what it said?"

"Yes, Ma'am. It was our set-up, but it was for the cousins. We were the cut-outs. And we used Sonny. I'm sure of it."

"Find those pages, young man," Mary said. "*Today.* I want to know who those men were. *Names.* I want their names before lunch. Is that clear?"

"Yes, Ma'am."

"So, we've done Sonny some favors? "

"Yes. Twice. In Turkey, in 1969, for one. Seems he was arrested for trafficking narcotics. He was in goal without a prayer. He gave our man a call at the Embassy in Istanbul. He said at the time that it was all done for the Americans, but that he couldn't break his cover, and asked that we intervene from *our* side for him."

"And?"

"We did. Spoke to the Turks' Chief of Intelligence and they showed him the door. Even gave him a lift back to his hotel."

"And ... ?"

"In Cuba, two years ago. A very tight fix there for him. *Very* tight, indeed."

"Drugs trafficking again?" Mary said

"Yes. He was going to be shot at sunrise ... that type of charge. They'd already shot two of his Italian accomplices and a Cuban general who was helping them on the Island. The General's court martial made the international news, actually."

"And?"

"Well, Sonny is 'that' type—*lucky*. He got a hold of the Spanish Ambassador during his trial *somehow,* and then he contacted us. Sonny said he had the name of the biggest heroin dealer in Spain, and he would furnish it if we got him the hell out of the fix."

"Out of his *situation.*"

"Precisely."

"Hard for us to *do,* in Cuba," Mary said.

"Not for our Spanish friends, apparently. It worked out and he threw out a very big name that we passed on to MI5 and took care of some favors we owed on that side. The Cubans grumbled, but he was released to the Spanish. They traded him then for some anti-Cuban living in Madrid. Everyone was happy, I suppose. ..."

"So, he pops up now and then," Mary said. "I'd heard of him back in the Sixties. He was in the Balkans, then. 'Belgrade Jack' was his code name. We had him reporting to us on the arms-for-drugs deals going on with the Turks. He was quite good at it, really. Spying for us, that is." She knew a lot more than she'd said, and was pleased that what she knew wasn't in the file, either. She had removed it years before, in fact. The entire present conversation was for appearances' sake and nothing more.

"Nothing about that here, Ma'am."

"Really? Nothing about Belgrade?"

"No; *nothing.* I read it all ma'am—all fifty pages ma'am as thoroughly as I'm capable of ma'am," the young man said.

"Well ... Very strange, indeed," Mary said. She acted shocked. The young man crossed his legs again, still holding the open file, and looked at her.

"What is it? ... "

"He's an *incorrigible* trafficker ... yet the cousins have a hands-off on him."

"Nothing about Belgrade Jack then, in the late 60s?" She asked the question again, ignoring his attempt at insight.

"No, Ma'am."

"How curious. ... Leave it here then, young man," Mary said, and took the file. "Oxford or Cambridge?" Mary asked, watching him slide the file onto her crowded desk.

"Neither, Ma'am ... Durham, Ma'am," the young man said.

"Right. What's the family name, again?"

"Morton."

"You're new to our section, aren't you, Roger Morton?"

"Yes, Ma'am; I've just been on board two months."

"Well, Roger Morton ... I want you to find out who Sonny shepherded for the cousins in Mexico. I need names. Things don't just disappear from the files, *do* they? Check your office ... check your girlfriend's purse ... or is it boyfriend? ... And I want to find Sonny Delmonico. Give the particulars to our hunters ... everything recent on all his haunts. Where he's roosting. He lives in Southern Spain, the last I heard. Don't ask the cousins. Don't tell anyone what we're up to. Not a *word*, young Roger Morton, or I'll have your balls for earrings. Do you understand? And find those missing pages."

"Yes. ... And what about Wally, Ma'am?"

"Have him arrested. This Saturday would be convenient. Let me know when they have him down at the Yard. I want to interview him myself. You said you've been with us *how* long?

"Just three months, actually—just since the course finished up," Morton said. "Is that all then, Ma'am?"

"Yes, young man, it is. I want those missing pages, though, Morton." She watched him leave, then opened her desk drawer and took out the pages she'd taken from the file the night before and slipped them into her briefcase.

■ LOS ANGELES

The L.A. County Sheriff sent a homicide detective out to the Capri Motel after it was determined that both John Does, and a young woman—who'd been identified at the scene—were dead. The man they sent was an intelligent, old-school detective with twenty-five years on the force, having started out at the County Jail when he was only twenty-two years old, straight out of the Marine Corps. He'd served in Vietnam with the First Marine Division, landing at Red Beach Two, Da Nang, in April of 1965. His name was Warren Talbot. He was overweight and was secretly on a diet. He and his

148

wife collected antiques, which they refinished and resold as a hobby. They had a house in Agoura Hills and were childless and regretted it, but she'd been hurt in a car crash after they were married and the doctors had advised against her getting pregnant. Talbot's wife was half-black and half-Cherokee and worked as a kindergarten teacher. Warren Talbot was not a member of the top-secret cabal inside the Sheriff's Dept. with connections to the CIA's Domestic Division—a grey area under the Agency's charter—instituted during the COINTELPRO program, and very active in L.A. County during the 60s and 70s, having helped spy on the Black Panthers and other subversive groups—the Sheriff's Department fronting for the agency when necessary.

It was decided early-on by the famous E. Howard Hunt, in fact, that both the LAPD and Sheriff's Dept. should have a working group that liaisoned with the CIA and FBI for sophisticated domestic spying operations. COINTELPRO ended up being the most infamous of several such groups that were formed and disbanded over the years.

Det. Talbot had been left out of the COINTELPRO loop because he was suspected of being too much of a by-the-book type to put up with any "top secret" work, which invariably was technically illegal, and in some cases actually involved what was euphemistically called "wet-work," referring to torture and even assassinations by CIA and FBI operatives; the very terminology that came into common usage via action-movie dialog a few years later.

"Where *are* these DEA guys?" Talbot asked.

"We put them in the office," the Sheriff's Deputy who had handcuffed Butch and Alex replied. He'd actually gone into one of the motel rooms at the Capri and brought back a towel so Alex could wipe the brain-matter from his face because it was making everyone on the scene sick just looking at him.

"Do you have a call into DEA about these jokers?" Talbot said.

"Yes, sir—we did that immediately, from the scene, sir."

"What about the dead girl?" Talbot glanced from where they were talking in the driveway towards the body that now had a bright yellow plastic sheet draped over it.

"Not DEA. She was a civilian. Patty Montgomery. We found her driver's license in one of the rooms," the officer said. Talbot nodded. "She's one of the DEA guys' girlfriend."

"And the John Does?"

"No ID at all on two of them. The driver of the van had an ID, though." The deputy dug in his uniform pocket and came out with a driver's license. The Sheriff's Captain had instantly recognized the man's last name; he knew it belonged to an important

Los Angeles mafia family that was well known to the police. It was that clue that helped him organize his thoughts as to how to categorize the gunfight—marital revenge killing; gang-related; serial? He now had a place to work outwards from and toward a mob-related shooting, and that knowledge made him relax a little. He knew instinctively, too, that a drug-related killing was not going to get much attention from the press, because they were common as dirt nowadays. He felt that now he was in familiar territory. He also suspected that the two men in custody *were* in fact probably DEA officers because their names could not be connected to any prior arrest records.

"The guy in the van doesn't have any face left," the Sheriff said. "The other two John Does look like Mexicans to me."

"So we got the girl and the two by the van? Where's my other body? I heard four on the call," Talbot said.

"Over behind the wall," the deputy said.

"The wall?" The deputy pointed out the cinder-block wall that ran down the driveway and was now shot-to-hell.

"... Yeah. ... It's shot to shit," Talbot said.

"What do they say happened?"

"The two DEA guys won't talk to me about it."

"Nothing?"

"Absolutely nothing; not a peep out of them, so far, anyway. They say they want to wait and tell their story to their boss. Top secret, I guess," the Sheriff's Deputy laughed. "Doesn't look like a secret to *me*. It's a fucking blood-bath."

"Yeah. So we'll wait to hear from the DEA about these two. Finish securing the parking lot, I guess, then," Talbot said. "Did these DEA guys have any id's?"

"Yeah. I put them on the counter in the office. Edward Perry and Bruce Tucker. No priors." Talbot nodded and then headed over to the where the dead girl was lying on the asphalt of the parking lot. He stopped, took off his coat, then went back to his car and laid his jacket neatly on the passenger seat of the white, four-door Ford Victoria. *I've got to loose some fucking weight*, Talbot thought to himself as he walked back towards the dead girl. He absolutely *hated* to diet.

"Hey—we got another body!" Someone was yelling from the second-floor walkway. "Yeah ... make that five bodies and counting." An older sheriff—a completely bald guy in his forties—walked to the shot-up baluster where the gunman had set up and looked down at the detective. His gold badge reflected the late afternoon sun, which by then had turned to a surreal reddish-gold hue. "It's a woman. Got a bullet in the head and chest—looks like a maid."

"Shit," Talbot said, under his breath. "*Shee-iiit*. Okay. Go through every God-damned room. Find a master-key somewhere. Look in the office," the detective said.

He bent down and lifted the plastic sheet off the girl. He saw the blood-soaked asphalt around her body pock-marked by the machine gun fire and noted that this was not a run-of-the-mill small-arms shootout of the type that he was so familiar with in L.A. County. This reminded him of Vietnam; the look of the girl's body. He'd seen a lot of dead bodies—women's bodies in black silk, mud-covered and mutilated by the fire from "daisy cutters."

"Jesus," he said out loud, then he dropped the plastic back down on her bullet-torn body. "Jesus. This is like a fucking firefight, right *here!*" He walked towards the van. The engine had finally been turned off. The two bodies had not been touched, other than when a deputy had extracted the driver's wallet from his corpse. The door to the driver's-side of the van was open, Butch having opened it to check for anyone hiding. Talbot looked over the scene. He saw the automatic shotgun where Butch had laid it down. It, too, was unusual—an illegal-to-possess-for-civilians military weapon and very hard to come by even for law-enforcement types. He walked to the front of the van and saw the light machine gun and the second dead man, whose skull had been turned to a pulpy mess. The body was pock-marked where he'd been shot. The AK-47, its stock brain-smeared, was lying nearby. *Now that's unusual*, Talbot thought to himself. He'd heard that one of the DEA guys had beaten the man after he was dead. *That shit is not normal. That's just rage.* He'd seen that kind of thing before, too, but never here in Malibu. He'd seen that kind of crazed, over-the-top violence in Vietnam and noted it now, suspecting that one of the DEA men was a vet, perhaps. Then he glanced towards the Capri's office. Now he was engaged. Had the DEA guys been the targets of an assassination attempt? Had the mob guys in the van intended to kill them? Had they killed the girl—an innocent bystander—and had *that* set the DEA guy off? He looked at the various shell casings on the ground it seemed like there were at least a hundred or more from the machine gun, which he then walked over to and knelt down to inspect without touching it. He looked over and saw a few spent plastic shotgun casings, the tops open now, the ends blackened. Then he stood up and looked at the phone number on the license he was still holding. The picture would help, now, he thought, as the guy was definitely missing his face. Then he walked to the Coke machine standing beside the door to the office. It was completely empty, though. *Strange. Right here on Highway One. There was something else he noticed ... where were the cars? Where were the other guests? It was summer—the motel should be full of the guests' cars.*

Butch was watching the traffic drive along Highway One, passing the motel. He looked down at the weed on the clean counter and dug into his pocket for some rolling papers. He'd tried to push Patty's death away from him in an almost physical manner. But it wasn't working. He saw an unmarked car full of jar-headed federal-types stop and move into the center lane, their car's turn-signal on.

"Hey, you got any rolling papers?" Butch asked. He turned and looked at Alex.

"I have to call my father," Alex said. "I want *out* of this shit, man," was all Alex said. He still had a streak of blood on his forearm where he hadn't quite gotten it scrubbed-off when he cleaned up in the office bathroom. His eyes were very bloodshot.

"They were set up real good. ...I'll give the motherfuckers *that*," Butch said. He'd been digging in his jeans and had come up empty. He now checked the pocket of his black leather vest and found a package of Zig-Zags.

"It's *my* fault she's lying out there now," Alex said.

"I found them," Butch said. "I'll have this bomber ... rolled right quick." He turned and shook out a joint's worth of weed onto the clean countertop. Then he looked for something to scrape it into a mound, but there wasn't anything nearby. So he used the edge of his hand while he licked the glue-end of one of the papers and stuck them together and then sprinkled the weed into the stuck-together Zig-Zags and rolled the joint. He was numb. His own voice sounded far away to him. He was used to this feeling after people he cared about had been killed.

"I lost my hat," Butch said.

"What?" Alex said, looking at him.

"I lost my fucking hat. I think out there." He lifted the pack of matches off the clean Formica counter and was able to strike one of them one-handed, bending just one match out of the bunch down and then using his thumb to rub the match head on the striker. It always hurt when he did that—it usually burned his thumb. He walked out of the office holding the joint and then walked on out into the parking lot. The Capri was now filled with cops of various kinds, some wearing green windbreakers. He saw the four-door Federal car pull into the parking lot, loaded with what he suspected were FBI agents: tough-looking, no smiles. Then he stopped. He saw the overweight Sheriff's Detective sporting a crew-cut, walking toward him in Sears' black shoes with thick soles.

"You one of the DEA guys?" Talbot asked.

"No ... I'm a CIA officer," Butch said, looking over at Patty's body.

"What?"

"Yeah, but you won't be able to tell anyone that after those guys get through here. That's what I'm thinking right now, anyway," Butch said. He took a big hit off the joint he'd just lit and offered it to the Detective.

"What's your name?" Butch said. Talbot saw Butch's First Division tattoo on his shoulder.

"I'm Detective Talbot. What's *your* name?"

"Which one? I'm losing track," Butch said.

"The one ... I don't know. Your fucking *real* name, I guess." Butch watched what he was sure were FBI agents, now walking towards them, all in dark-colored suits and white shirts. He decided he hated the FBI.

"You seen a cowboy hat out here?" Butch asked him. The joint in his mouth bobbled up and down as he spoke.

"*What?*"

"A cowboy hat. I lost it ... Edward Perry. That's my name," Butch said. "It says that on my driver's license."

"What happened here, Perry?" Talbot's tone had changed, because he was talking, not only to a fellow Marine, but to someone who had been in his division.

"What's it look like happened, Detective?" They didn't find the last body—the motel clerk's—until after Butch and Alex had been handed over to the FBI. The Feds took over the investigation after a call was placed to the L.A. County Sheriff from the Director of the DEA himself, who'd been called by the Deputy Director of the CIA and asked to intercede with a cover-story of some kind. The two men—Edward Perry and Bruce Tucker—were working on a top secret drug enforcement project that had been sponsored at the highest levels of government. That's all the Sheriff needed to know, he was told. The investigation of the murders at the Capri Motel were then mysteriously moved into the jurisdiction of the FBI, despite every California law to the contrary.

Detective Talbot's notes were confiscated by the FBI a week later. It was the confiscation of his notes that angered him the most about the whole affair: that, and the fact that a civilian—an innocent girl—had been killed, and apparently no one was going to investigate her murder any further. It *bothered* him, for some reason. It was then that he first suspected that the Sheriff's Department was hiding something about the case. There was a kind of silence that surrounded the shoot-out that didn't make any sense to Talbot, at all. It was definitely not a by-the-book-type case. He asked around and found out that the FBI had yet to actually open a file on the case.

16

■ COUNTY KENT, ENGLAND

"Hello?" Mary's youngest daughter was eyeing him boldly, looking straight at him. She was a strikingly beautiful girl: tall, athletic, very fair, and wearing pressed designer-jeans with a black Macintosh, a chic belt tied tightly around her narrow waist. Malcolm guessed that she was nineteen or twenty. For him, it was like seeing Mary again as a young woman.

"Are you Portia?" Malcolm asked.

"Yes."

"I'm Bill Burns," Malcolm said. "Pleased to meet you." He closed the trunk of his rental car, which he'd parked in front of the Mary Keen's "cottage" on her husband's ancestral estate.

"I don't understand. What are you doing *here?*" the young woman said. She had a Weimaraner pup on a long leather leash.

"I'm an old friend of your mother's. She's allowing me to use the cottage for a few days. I'm having some work done on my flat in London ... I needed some peace and quiet. And she was ... " The girl's eyes were boring a hole in him as he spoke.

"... ... I'm sorry—have we met?" Portia asked, sounding suddenly very formal, as if she were interviewing him for a job.

"No, I don't believe so. ..." They'd encountered each other while he'd been going out to his rental car to fetch something from the trunk and the girl had been coming down the lane that led to the cottage in the drizzly summer morning.

"... Are *you* my mother's new boyfriend?"

"No," he said, and smiled. "No! I'm afraid not—just old friends ... that's all," Malcolm said, lying instinctively. "And I bat for the other team." He threw that in to help convince her he was safe.

"I doubt that," she said, looking at him carefully. The dog sat down at her heel. "You're an American."

"Guilty," Malcolm said. The girl told him that she'd had brought some friends down from Oxford for the weekend and that they were staying in the main "house."

"... Beautiful dog," he said.

"She's my sister's. She's away in the Army. She promised me she's going to show me how to kill people *silently*. ... You look like someone my mother might date." The girl

154

stepped closer. "You're handsome ... though you're rather old."

"Am I? Old? God, I suppose I am," Malcolm said.

"Yes. Like someone from the movies. You're some kind of soldier, I think. I'm told I'm quite intuitive," the girl said. "You're the square-shoulders type." There was something ineffable and starkly impressive about her beauty, like the morning itself.

"Is that a compliment?" Malcolm asked. He had his kit-bag in his hand, and had closed the trunk of the rental car and was walking towards her.

"I think so. ... I'm afraid a tree fell across the road at the gate. ... We're all trapped 'til the gardeners drag it away," Portia said.

"Really? Trapped? Sounds wonderful," he said. "I mean if you have to be trapped it might as well be here."

"Yes, I suppose so. Is my mother inside? She's very strange about bringing men around. She always brings them here to the cottage, never the house. I suppose she's hiding you from us."

"No—I think ... "

"I hope you aren't ... what's the term? An *adventurer*. Is that what you people call it in America?"

"Sorry?"

"Someone who's after her money. She's got a trunk-load, you know," the girl said matter-of-factly. "I think she's one of the richest women in England, really." The dog had been looking at Malcolm, but now it turned nervously away, wanting to get on with its walk. Malcolm and the girl shook hands very quickly. She smiled faintly, as if she'd gotten to the core of things regarding him, and was satisfied with the outcome. The air was cold and it had made her cheeks red. He could smell the wet grass. The main house—a hulking Palladian mansion built in 1798 by the family—was ivory-colored and very grand, with tourists allowed in for tours on Sundays. It stood half-a-mile down the road, just now barely visible in the misty morning.

"I'm a lot of things, but you don't have to worry ... not about that—I'm not an adventurer," Malcolm said. He smiled back.

"Well, you're not a homosexual—I'm quite *sure* of that," the girl said. "My college is simply *full* of them. ... Well, a pleasure meeting you, Mr. Burns. ..." She turned away. "We're having breakfast in the main house soon, if you'd care to join us ... please do. I've brought one of the Dons down, and he's part-American and he needs company because he's old, too ... like you."

"Thank you," Malcolm said. "I think. ..."

"What is it you *do?*" she asked, turning towards him and then walking backwards slowly. The dog had wondered in a circle around her legs, and she had to step out of the leash.

155

"Banking," he said.

"I see. Well, I don't believe anything you've told me ... Not a word of it—I just want you to know that," she said matter-of-factly. "But I like you. I think you're probably some kind of an adventurer and probably a cad. Now that we've met, tell my mother she needn't bother to hide you." Then she turned and walked back up the long drive, that was lined with red trumpet-vines; very red and in full bloom because it was early summer. He watched her walk up the driveway, just as impressed with *her* as he had been the first time he'd seen her mother.

"Was that Portia?"

"Yes," he said. "It was." He'd come back into the living room with its leaded-glass windows. Mary had watched them from the bedroom, still in her robe, and then hurried downstairs to quiz him about the encounter.

"*God!*"

"She's very beautiful ... *and* precocious," he said.

"Yes, I know, extremely. Sometimes a little bit *too* bright for her own good. She's going to get a first in physics. Where did you tell her I was?"

"I played stupid. And apparently I'm 'ancient.'"

"I parked in the garage, just because I knew she might snoop," Mary said.

"Don't tell me you're afraid of your own children, Mary?"

"Yes, most definitely. Aren't you afraid of yours? ... I'm afraid they won't approve. Of what I *do*, personally, I mean. You don't understand; you're a man. It's different if *you* have affairs. I've kept my love life secret all these years." She was sitting at the dining room table now, still in her robe. The "cottage" was actually quite a large misnomer. It was, in fact, a two-storey, vine-covered, four-bedroom stone house and looked like something out of a Jane Austin novel. There was an attached mews that had housed the estate's carriages in the old days and had at some point been turned into a four-car garage.

"There's a problem with Delmonico's file. I've brought it along for you to look over. I'm going to cook you breakfast—what do you want?" Mary asked, as Malcolm came and sat down across from her. "But I warn you, I'm a terrible cook."

"What do you mean, 'wrong'? Cook whatever you like, please. Eggs, maybe? With cheese, if you have it?"

"There are things missing. Things that I know about him myself. And even as recently as this week, someone went into our section and removed things from the original paper file. I went ahead and looked at the new electronic file. There's nothing there, now—it's completely disappeared. There's no electronic file on the man at all. It's been erased. ... Do you think she'll come back?— Portia?" Mary said.

156

"No; they're having breakfast. Don't worry. I as much as told her I was queer. But she didn't believe me!" he said.

"Of course she didn't; *look* at you, and listen to you. Do you think she liked you?"

"No. I don't; not really. I think she knows exactly what's going on, or close enough, anyway," Malcolm said.

"God help me—why didn't I have a *stupid* child?" Mary said. Malcolm was now looking through Delmonico's file. Mary had put it on the table in front of him while they were having coffee. He stopped at a page with some marginalia: *Delmonico came to our attention in Mexico City, August 1965. Mentioned him to the cousins. GC.*

"There was a job he did for your lot then, I suspect. *That* was removed from the file, too."

"Yes. It was in Mexico City," Malcolm said. "I gave him the job. George had sent him to me."

"George Cummings? ... I thought so when I saw the initials. It's why I love paper files. Tell me more, darling."

"Yes. Whatever happened to George?" Malcolm said.

"He was shown the door right afterwards. They suspected him of working for Philby. It was all bollocks of course. He's working for British Petroleum now, I think. He's Head of Security, I believe."

"Why do I think good old George has been here at the cottage before?"

"Because he *has,* dear. So you know all about the job in Mexico?"

"Yes, it was part of Paperclip. It happened just before it was wound-down. I was having trouble getting my man out of Mexico. The KGB wanted him back. He'd run away from them, you know."

"And that's why you want *me* to find Delmonico—so he can smuggle the Hauptmann? Because he's done that sort of thing before?"

"Yes, that's why," Malcolm said.

"You're going to move your Hauptmann using *Delmonico?*"

"Yes."

"Why Delmonico? He's not trustworthy ... God knows *that* much about the man. How do you know he isn't a part of Gehlen's network?"

"I actually met him once, in person. He doesn't like them. The Germans. He landed at Anzio Beach, you know. It was pretty rough—much worse than just 'rough,' really. He has a hatred for the Germans that verges on the pathologic. I'm sure *they* all know that. And he's too low-level. They only recruit important people ... like you and I, my Dear."

"But if you're afraid of your own people? ... Of this secret network? Certainly they'll be able to stop the Hauptmann from leaving, if they're all you said they are."

"Those ratlines are old. ... And Delmonico is just one of *hundreds* of people the Agency ... "

"You're lying to me, darling—that scenario doesn't make any sense; none of it washes, at all," Mary said. "You're forgetting who you're talking to, Dear." Malcolm looked up.

"Okay, I'm lying."

"Tell me the truth. I want to know. If the cousins are being run by some cabal, then we might be, too—*mightn't* we?" Mary said. She was wearing a beautiful white-silk robe. Her hair was falling over her shoulders, grey-blonde. Right then it struck him that she was still as beautiful as her youngest daughter.

"Not '*might be*'—you *are*. I'm certain of it. Or at least you're being used, which amounts to the same thing, in reality," he said.

"What do you mean? I need some proof of all of this," she said.

"I mean that your dear MI6 are in their pocket, just like the Agency is. It's just that *you* can't see them outright because they're so woven into the fabric of your entire organization now. Just like they are at CIA and elsewhere. It's taken them *years* to do it."

"So Gehlen knows all our secrets? ..."

"I think so. *Everyone's*, in fact: the KGB's, the Stazie's, the CIA's, and MI6's, too. Even the Mossad's, by now, I'm pretty sure. I suspect Gehlen has got important politicians in his organization, too. Bought them outright, in most cases. Especially in Latin America. Yes, you can assume he knows all your important secrets, and uses them to the network's advantage when he needs to. It's what makes their network so dangerous and effective, at whatever they want to do with it," Malcolm said.

"And *your* lot. The CIA. Taken over, then? It sounds hard to believe, really," she said.

"More or less. ... Yes. That's what I'm trying to find out. How bad it is. I'm hoping the Hauptmann can tell me. If I use Sonny, they'll of course get wind of it ... I suspect, anyway. I *want* them to know, but I want them to think they found him themselves," Malcolm said.

"I don't understand," she said.

"They've taken over the heroin business for themselves, so Sonny will be very well known to them. That's what I think, anyway. And not just heroin. It's cocaine and other drugs now, too. They're the ones that work to keep it all illegal around the world. It pays much better if it's illegal, and they know it. The U.S. spends billions trying to stop it. A massive anti-drug bureaucracy has grown up since Nixon was in there. Don't you see how perfect a racket it is? They get paid to help stop its production and manufacture *and* they also get paid to produce and distribute it. It's more money than even you can imagine ... billions of dollars, as long as it's kept illegal. The Gehlen network uses the drug business to fund their other operations. It's more than just the drugs ... or the money; think of the political control it buys. The junta in Brazil is *theirs*. Chile. Argentina. Greece. Dictators are the easiest to buy, of course. Ten-a-penny."

"Control of *what?*" Mary said.

"Whole governments. They just buy them and their banking systems, and then, well then they have it all. They control a country without a shot ever being fired."

"That's *ridiculous*," she said. "*Impossible*."

"Is it? I thought so, too ... at first," he said. "But not now. I've seen how things work, now. There are hundreds of millions of dollars pouring into New York banks from the drug trade, *monthly*. I've seen the reports. This drug money is going to the selected banks that have been used as platforms by the Gehlen network. These huge banks in turn advise Chile and Argentina, Brazil, Mexico, and even the World Bank on important economic matters, which in the end shape these countries' politics. Drug money buys the network power. And it's growing. The arms business they control does, too. Once they control a country's politicians they can sell them weapons. What does a country like Brazil need with jet fighters when they don't have schools or hospitals or roads? Who is Brazil going to go to war with, *exactly*? Over what—fishing rights in the Amazon? The United States? Russia? That's what's so ridiculous. The Gehlen network is like gangrene. And it's spreading. Drugs and arms is how they're funding themselves."

"So what about your Hauptmann? They'll come after him, then? And that's what you want?"

"Yes. But I want them to find out that I'm using him on their own—I want them to think I'm trying to hide him. Delmonico is perfect for the job because they know he helped us move people around on the rat-lines back in the day. Someone will snap to it, I'm sure. They'll be watching him—and others."

"But they're liable to kill him *and* your Hauptmann when they find out what's going on. ..."

"Yes—maybe. But I need proof that he *himself* is not just another spy, sent to lie to me. If they try and kill him—really try, I mean ... then I'll *know*, won't I? ..."

"And if you lose the Hauptmann?"

"I've sent someone to help protect him. I'm hoping they make it through all right, but I had to be sure. If I'm right, they'll do everything they can to kill him before he can help me. If I'm wrong, well, then ... the Hauptmann will be safe, and he's just another defector telling lies to come to the West and live the 'good life,' and they won't care."

"Who have you sent? ... Can you trust them?"

"My own son," Malcolm said. She looked at him for a moment without saying a word. Her hands lay folded on top of Delmonico's opened file.

"How do you know *I'm* not with them, darling? ... I could be—after all, I'm the right age and everything else. I actually *met* Gehlen once in the GDR. I was over there at their headquarters in Berlin when he was appointed head of West German Intelligence," Mary said.

"I don't, really—but I can't go on alone, from this point. I had to take a chance because I knew you—and now I know that you're still the same person I loved, back then. And I think I'd already be dead by now if you were with them. Don't you, dear? I took a chance. I'm only one man, after all. I need help."

"You've really sent your *son?*"

"Yes."

"For the same reasons?"

"Yes. I wanted them to show themselves there, too. I had to pretend to be hiding, so that meant I had to bury my son, too, so they'd think they'd found him themselves."

"You are a *very* devious man, Malcolm Law. ..."

"I've had to be. They're very good at hiding—and at finding those who're hidden!"

"Aren't you afraid that it could all go terribly wrong? Your plan, I mean?"

"There's no reason to talk about the obvious, between *us*, especially," he said. "All I want to know is if you can get Delmonico to surface in *Italy*? And meet my son there."
She looked at him from across the table, her blue eyes searching his face.

"... I've got someone I want you to meet. After breakfast. He's an associate of Delmonico's, and I've had him arrested. He's at Scotland Yard right now."

"Was there a storm recently?" Malcolm asked.

"Why do you ask?"

"Your daughter said that a tree had fallen across the road to the gate."

"It's July," Mary said. "Pretty good weather for England, actually. ..."

"I suppose you'd better send some people out to see what's going on. ... About the tree, I mean," Malcolm said. She reached across the table and held his hand.

"I'm in love with you—you know that. I don't want anything to happen to you. You might be out of your league this time," she said. "Have you ever even *thought* of that? Maybe you should stop this, right now, before it goes any further. ..."

"... There's an end to everything ... old trees fall. And it's worth the try, I think. If I don't do this, I think they'll control my country, too—if they don't already, to a certain extent, anyway. And I can't have *that*, can I?" Malcolm said. "It'd nullify everything I've ever done ... *you* know what I mean. ..."

"... The tree won't matter," Mary said, pulling her hand away. "We're leaving in a helicopter in an hour. ... Are you up to tossing a house in Clapham? It belongs to a friend of your man Sonny's." She got up and went into the kitchen to cook them breakfast.

*   *   *

Malcolm was sitting in an anteroom at Scotland Yard where he could watch and hear the interrogation. The room had been very well-designed. A one-way mirror separated him from Wally Giordano, who was still wearing "golfing" attire. Giordano was sitting alone at a small wooden table that had been placed in the exact center of the room.

Malcolm, sitting on a somewhat higher plane, could see Giordano very clearly through the glass; it was as if he were sitting in the interrogation room alongside the man. Giordano had looked once directly at him, for a few tens-of-seconds. And, Malcolm thought, probably somehow realized just at that very instant that he was being watched. Giordano finally got up from the small table, walked over, and knocked on what appeared to be a large mirror that was attached to the wall by screws. He smiled to himself and nodded, looking almost directly *at* Malcolm, who he couldn't see, but was obviously imagining *as* that someone who undoubtedly was on the other side of the reflecting surface. It was uncanny to Malcolm how the gangster had ferreted out his *exact* position behind the mirror so quickly, as there were other mirrors and a few paintings that had been hung "casually" on the four walls of the room.

As he had been instructed to by a police woman in the hall outside the room that *he* was in, Malcolm opened the cover of a baffled-vent, which act would allow him to hear what was said inside the interrogation room in real time, as it was being spoken.

"I'm a friend," Malcolm said with his mouth close to the tube-opening. "We can help you, if you want." Wally Giordano quickly looked around the room he was sitting in as if he'd just heard the voice of God speaking to him. He suddenly turned and looked at the mirror again, then ran over and started lightly beating on it with his large palms—seemingly a just-short-of-frantic rhythm that reminded Malcolm of the syncopated and staccato beats he associated with flamenco dancing. Malcolm tapped once just before Mary Keen opened the door to the interrogation room and walked in.

Wally Giordano had become well-known in London's East-End Italian community by the time he was fifteen because of a job he'd done in Palermo for friends of his father. He'd calmly walked up behind an important *capo de tutti capi* and blown the man's brains out all over a cafe table cluttered with platters of muscles and clams. The shot had splattered the other men at the table's faces with the *capo's* grey matter and blood. It was a clean hit, they'd all agreed.

They said later that the dead man had been so angry that a mere "kid" had shot him that he'd actually stood *up* before he died—a good story, but not exactly true. He was technically dead before his body hit the table, and the force of that falling dead-weight had sent platters of pasta spilling out onto the sidewalk.

The men at the table who had paid for the hit were bloodied, but certainly not surprised. They all calmly got up, wiped their dirty faces off with large white linen napkins and walked away, melting into the crowds walking by on the sidewalk. Wally immediately dropped his weapon, which had been handed to him only minutes before by a very plain teenaged girl with long black hair, who had also guided Wally *to* the restaurant. A few feet away from the target, she'd opened her plastic shopping bag, just as she'd been instructed. Wally had reached into the bag and pulled out an American .357 caliber revolver, never hesitating at all once his fingers had touched the black rubber grip. He strutted confidently up to the table. And, as his heart pounded with excitement, he'd started his new career as a button-man for the Sicilian mafia.

It was calling the man's name that sealed Wally's new reputation with the older gangsters that day. Wally had spoken like an old-time hit man, like he had a personal beef with the guy he was about to shoot.

"Hey ... my friend. *Hey!*" Wally had said. His face was pimply but his eyes were very old. Wally had old-man eyes even at fifteen.

The man he was about to shoot had turned in his chair with a smirk on his face and had looked the kid in the eye. And then Wally capped him. The heavy bullet smashed through the man's teeth and exited the back of his head, taking a back piece of skull with it. Wally had fled back to London with a budding reputation, a young Sicilian girlfriend who he'd fucked standing up in the return-ship's cabin—a second-class cabin that smelled of mothballs—and a nickname that even the police back in London used with respect: "The Cannon." With the proceeds from the hit, Wally set his sights on the heroin business and made good, starting out as an "ounce man." But it was the bludgeoning death of Jack the Hat in his rooftop pigeon coop with a pipe that really changed things for Wally Giordano. It brought Wally to the attention of MI6 in 1967, an important year in the heroin business, which was then just starting to enter its full bloom.

"You're being held under the amended Official Secrets Act," Mary said, after she'd come in and sat down across from him. She'd put her reading glasses on before she'd spoken. She had a small, chicly-thin briefcase with her. She took an envelope out from the case and put it in front of her.

"... And you would be? ... Ma'am?" Wally asked. She finally looked at Wally.

"Well, that depends, Wally," Mary said. "I could be a friend. And we all need friends. Or, I could be the Gorgon bitch that sends you up to Birmingham without a charge. You'll stay there until I've decided you can leave. I'll make sure they put some crazy paddy in the cell with you. Someone who doesn't like Italians. It will be a long way down from Clapham, Wally. I was there at your house this morning." Mary took off her glasses and looked at him. "*Very* nice, Wally, for a poor boy from Harold Hill. Done well for yourself, I see. Indoor pool ... "

"I'd like to see my solicitor," Wally said. Not rising to the bait.

"And I'd like to meet the Queen. ... It's cooperate with me and my bunch or go to Birmingham tonight. No stops on the way, Master Wally. No fish and chips. No visiting that young woman you've set up—very pretty, Wally, by the way."

Mary dug into her briefcase and fished out a photo of the girl who he'd bought a flat for; a Jamaican girl who was a foot taller than Wally and twenty-five years younger.

"... We've been to your house this morning and left it a mess. Your wife is upset and wants to know where you are. I was nice enough not to mention the bird at Forty Dresset Road, Apartment Fifty-Six. How old is she, Wally? Eighteen? I hope she's of age. ... Very naughty, Wally. I could call her, though; your wife. There's still time. I've pictures, too, of you and the girl, all kinds of them."

"Are you with the *Specials* then?" Wally said, ignoring her threat. He tried to keep the anger out of his voice. "Why didn't you just say so, Ma'am? I've always had a good relationship with the Specials. Since the old days. Old friends, aren't we? Always done my bit for England. There's a bloke at MI5 that will vouch for me."

"Well then, we won't have a problem ... will we, Wally dear?" Mary said. "Now, you know a chap named Delmonico. Grew up with him. Bosom pals from what I've heard. Practically shared the same titty," Mary said.

"Sonny? ... Sonny Delmonico?"

"That's right," Mary said. "Where is he?"

"Spain," Wally said. He glanced at the mirror, wondering how many people were watching him. *This is like a bloody film. But who's the good guy?*

"Where in Spain, Wally? I want the house number. Street name. How many flies there are on the wall; what Sonny eats for breakfast. The lot," she said.

"He's in Ronda—somewhere in the South—that's all I know, Ma'am. Damned if the Spaniards have house numbers in the bloody place. It's donkey-country from what Sonny says. The back-ass of beyond."

"... Is he working for you now? Sonny?"

"Sonny ... yes, sometimes. ... Yes. Mostly for the Count and that lot now, though.

He's outgrown me, really. But you know all that, I expect," Wally said. He was looking at her, trying to remember if he'd ever dealt with a woman from the Specials before. They usually came in twos, and were men who looked liked solicitors. They'd made sure over the years that the French and Chinese stayed out of London's drug-scene for reasons that were known only to MI6. With MI5's help Wally and his boys had kept London's drug-world entirely British. She seemed like an extra hard bitch, Wally thought, studying her closely; she had the coldest blue eyes he thought he'd ever seen on a woman.

"He trusts *you* though ... doesn't he Wally?" Mary said. "You're pals."

"I would think so. We go way back, don't we? Just like you said. All the way back to Harold Hill, we do."

"Good. I want you to go home and call Sonny in Spain and tell him that a certain person wants into the game and has your blessing. His name is Bruce Tucker—he's a Yank. Sonny should call Tucker at this number." She slid the envelope towards him.

"I'm not putting my old pal in a tight spot, am I, Mum?" Wally said, taking the envelope. "Is this person a friend of yours? This Tucker bloke?"

"Just make the call, Wally."

"And if I don't, it's the clinker then, Ma'am?"

"That's right," Mary said. "With bowls of shit for breakfast, lunch, *and* dinner, if I get *my* way."

"When I call him ... it's usually on Sundays. This Sunday soon enough?"

"That will be fine," Mary said. He wanted to strangle her where she sat. There was just something about the icy bitch he didn't like. She reminded him of all the snooty upper-class women on the high street when he was a kid and working at Fortman and Masons in the stockroom. He never had liked the police, but it was never personal. Suddenly, for the first time in his life, it felt personal with this upper crust woman.

"Why didn't you-lot just call me? We have an arrangement, don't we? ..."

"I wanted to make a point," Mary said, getting her things sorted again; a pad and her glasses, then sliding them into her briefcase.

"Trouble in the hen house?" Wally said. "... Coppers got glue stuck to their shoes?" She stood up and pressed her hand against her blouse. "Well, you take care now, Ma'am. I'm sure we'll meet again. Maybe dinner?" Wally said from the table. Mary stopped at the door and turned and looked at him very carefully. He was smiling at her as if she'd just bought something in his shop. Something expensive. He picked up the envelope.

"Sunday, Wally. We'll listen to the call. If you should slip up; say what you shouldn't; I'll send the photos. Understood? And then I'll have your ears pulled off."

"Wouldn't think of it, dear. Me, I'm an honest Indian, Ma'am."

Malcolm relaxed—he'd been listening to them and leaning forward in his chair. He leaned over and spoke into the tube that brought the sound of his voice into the interrogation room.

"Tomorrow. Eleven P.M. The Club Colossal in Brixton. Nod if you understand," Malcolm said. He watched Wally look around the room, and then nod carefully. Then Malcolm stood up and left.

17

■ LONDON

Wally Giordano had once kicked a man to death for failing to slow a revolving door for his girlfriend at the dog track. The man had called Wally's new breathtaking girlfriend a "nigger" under his breath and let the door hit her. It was one of those big revolving glass doors. The doors were blocked as they fought inside the small space. The man tried to escape but Wally caught him with a knee in the third rib, which snapped and was driven into his lung, puncturing it. After that Wally stomped him until his jaw broke in two places and his mother wouldn't have recognized him. The door had stopped revolving at all by then. The stomped-man's body was wedging it in place. The girl, who had watched the whole thing through the glass, knew then that she was in for a wild ride and that Wally was a violent man and capable of murder at an instant's provocation. She already knew he was a gangster. She didn't mind that he was violent. She had grown up with violent men in Jamaica and knew how they thought. Sometimes it was just too much testosterone hitting all at once. In fact, Wally had told her that that was *his* problem, and that he'd had a "rotten temper" ever since he was a boy.

Wally was wearing an expensive black raincoat when he emerged from the Club Colossus. The wide-brimmed fedora he wore had a green feather tucked under its black-silk band. The feather shone iridescently in the intense light. Wally had taken to wearing a hat because it had been a very cold and wet winter that year. He wore the same kind of Borsalino that his father had worn in Sicily because that was the hat he'd grown up seeing his father wear, and he had loved and idolized the man. And, unlike some other men in "the trade," he'd never wanted to look like someone from "the City." He hated "City-men" as much as he hated the police. City-men took his money for laundering and looked down on him as they did it. He was proud of who he was and what he'd become: the kind of boss that even City-men came to see when they were in trouble. A car-hop had taken off to fetch his new Rolls, and now drove it up in front of the Club's entrance. The black Roll Royce's headlights were cutting through the heavy, almost silvery rain, which was striking the dark asphalt at a extreme angle, as if it were being fired from the sky by a monstrous machine gun.

After his meeting with the American, Wally was angry in that horrible, quiet way that Sicilian men have; a state of mindless rage that can almost blind them so they become dumb with it, and are unable to respond or speak at all except in monosyllables. He deliberately pushed past two men who were standing by the club's doors waiting for a cab. His authority was bristling and on full display as the kid brought Wally's new Rolls up to the curb. Wally flicked his cigarette butt into the night. The burning end of it shot a yellow-orange streak for twenty feet through the darkness and then disappeared into the rain. The men made way as he pushed past, and he bumped into the larger one a second time on purpose, hoping he'd say something. The blond man he'd bumped was a foot taller, much younger than Wally, and had been an officer in the Royal Navy and considered himself fairly tough. After the second bump, he glanced at Wally and their eyes locked. The ex-Navy man broke-off his gaze first. The look he'd gotten back from the Italian was so murderous and cold that he instinctively drew-back, realizing that whoever this guy was, he was no ordinary punter. Maybe it was Wally's hat that warned him, more than anything else; the way it was pushed back just a little bit on his balding head. Wally wore his hat the way black pimps from Jamaica wore them—pushed up and back on their heads as a sign of arrogance and control of the situation. The Royal Navy officer later told his friend it was the kind of hat that only "dagos" wore and that no "gentleman" would ever own.

Wally fished in his wallet and handed the kid a ten-pound note. But he didn't get in the car right away. He just stood there, trying to take in the conversation he'd had just moments before inside the club. The club's doorman recognized him and walked up and tried to hold an umbrella for him as he stood by his car, but Wally pushed him away angrily, the sight of anyone trying to help him merely elicited an ungrateful angry remark and made his anger spill over the top. It was as if the anger were a separate entity from "him," had its own existence, apart from his, and was trying to crawl *out* of him and kill someone on its own volition. The doorman quickly backed away, thinking Wally was drunk, and let it go. The Cannon—the doorman knew his nickname—was someone he didn't want to rouse, especially not any more than the man obviously already was.

As Wally slipped in behind the wheel, it seemed to him that the rain was making an almost desperate sound; as if the world were ending right at that very moment in a great deluge of metal-colored sheets of water. Wally glanced at the men under the awning for a moment, giving them one hard last look. Then he straightened himself behind the wheel, put the car in gear, and raced off at high speed down the street, like he and the car were both one piece of wet machinery, his neck soaked, still physically very powerful at forty, savvy and full of guile, and with a tremendous sexual energy.

All the Giordano men were physically strong—what English society women liked to call "brutes." He looked like the brute they all feared as he bent the Rolls into a turn and disappeared, leaving the men under the awning staring at his taillights, glad he was gone.

"Who was that?" the Royal Navy man asked the doorman.

"That gentleman is known as 'The Cannon,'" the doorman said.

"Bloody wop gangster if you ask me," the Navy man said.

"You forgot to mention that to him when he was *here*." The doorman, an Irishman, smiled. He *liked* The Cannon. He liked any*thing* or any*body* who fucked with the bloodly *English* and their tight-assed lord-it-over-you-all bullshit, as a matter of fact.

"Where you been? ... You *late*, baby," the Jamaican girl said from the plush living room with the white shag carpet she'd made Wally buy because she loved to walk on it barefoot. He'd laid her out naked on it the day they'd installed it and it was quite a sight, seeing her there bare-ass naked on it. He'd turned up the stereo and had her right then, "on the spot," as the Brits would say, hard. The girl was tall, cinnamon-colored, thin, and stone-beautiful. She was wearing a teal-colored wrap-dress that clung to her body; and it was a body that put most other women's—white *or* black—to shame. If you were a man, and not dead, or moribund, you would dream about that body and her. It was that simple. She was a siren—a voodoo child; the woman you *had to have*, and right *now*, too, the instant you laid eyes on her.

Wally came through the door of the posh six-bedroom apartment near Harrods in Chelsea that he'd set up for the girl and stood there dripping-wet. He'd bought the apartment from an HSBC managing director and heroin addict who was main-lining heroin in his penthouse office throughout the trading day, losing the bank's money at his Bloomberg terminal—millions of pounds an hour as he nodded-out at his desk, oblivious to it all, drool running down his chin from his drug-slack mouth. Wally was also using the man to help launder the growing flood of cash that the trade was bringing in to him every week. Wally had more cash-money now than he knew what to do with, or that his friend and cohort "the Jew" could launder safely. Max the Jew had escaped from the Nazis, fortunately having understood the whole thing that was coming after *Kristallnacht*, and gotten out of Berlin with his life and even *some* assets.

"I saw their faces in *der feuer*—all these big husky blond boys—and they were singing *der Horst Wessel*, and they meant every word of it. I said to myself: Max, that's it ... they're crazy ... insane with blood-lust, like wolves when they hunt together in a pack. I went to my girlfriend's house and *stuuped* all night. She was a German girl and worked in the Hugo Boss factory making SS uniforms—then I left that fucking city and came to London with nothing but my brains and my balls. No one would look at me. When you're poor, Wally, no one wants to look at you. But I studied at night and worked in my uncle's candy shop. I did. I did, Wally ... and I'm never going back to fucking Germany. *Never*," Max had told him when they'd first met. "You know what religion I believe in? The Power of Money. That's *my* religion, Wally. Not any 'God' ... because he'll let you down. Always. He'll let the wolves kill and eat everyone you love. What I believe in is gold. Money never fails you, Wally; remember that." Max said that while sitting at his wooden desk in a low-rent office with dirty windows. He was a small man who wore suspenders and heavily-starched white shirts and had an old-fashioned adding machine. He had millions, in dollars and gold in Switzerland, socked away from his end of the trade. He liked women and was always trying to fuck the young secretaries that Wally sent him from the East End, even though he was well into middle-age. He would playfully chase them around the office, and sometimes the girls would let him set them up in an apartment somewhere. Max always had more than one going at the same time. What had happened in Germany, and the loss of his entire immediate family—father, mother, sister, aunts, *every*one—to the Holocaust— had made him a little "strange in the head," as people said. He was always looking at the newspapers and saying that it could happen again. The whole thing. "The wolves *will* come back," he would tell people. "You can bet on it."

As a chartered accountant in the City, now, Max was the only man who really knew Wally. Wally felt close to Max for some strange reason. He liked him because he felt that Max Salinsky was the only man who, on some level, understood and accepted him for what he was—a balls-to-the-wall straight-up gangster. He never talked down to him, as all the other "gentlemen" did, thinking that he was just another stupid kid from Harold Hill. The Jew wasn't afraid of him, either, he'd found out. He'd lost his temper with him once and Salinsky hadn't budged from behind his desk. He'd just looked at him with those watery blue eyes until Wally was finished yelling and knocking shit over, and then he would ask him again what it was that had angered him. He was the only man Wally knew who could give him advice. The Jew was his go-to guy. His *consigliere*. He was the only man he trusted. Max Salinsky had become important to him, like a second father.

He knew what Max would say now. And yet he didn't want to hear it. He'd become one of the largest heroin dealers in Europe. He'd branched out now into other drugs and was using tugboats to haul the dope into France and Germany, having recently won a war against two other mafia gangs: first some German skinheads, and then some tall, slick Corsicans out of Paris, who'd turned out to be the most cunning people he'd ever dealt with. The Corsicans had tried to kill him *twice*. Once right in his own home, sending a gunman into his house at two in the morning while he was sleeping.

They'd shot it out on the front lawn—his men and theirs—and the boys from Harold Hill had won, using only shotguns. He had bags of cash stashed in a warehouse on Elephant Road in London. So much cash was coming in, *daily,* that it was backing up the "laundry," and had to be stored like you would coffee or rice, warehousing it.

The doorman of the building had asked if he could take Wally's coat because it was so wet, but Wally had walked right by him not speaking a word. He'd gone to the elevator tracking water on the carpet as he walked. He hit the elevator button and then turned and looked at the doorman, and the doorman knew enough to turn his eyes away without saying another word. Wally, the doorman told himself, was in one of his moods.

Now, Wally was dripping on the black marble floor, the tip's of his dress-shoes soaked-through. Even his silk socks were wet. He was an hour late; he'd been at the Club Colossus with an American who knew things he shouldn't; but he'd *known* them, all right. They'd struck a bargain that Wally didn't intend to keep, and he was very angry about it. Like all survivors of a ghetto, he was a paranoid personality. He knew now that he was being somehow offered-up, and he didn't like it; not one bit. *Fuck the American and his bullshit,* he thought.

The girl had been sitting on a sofa drinking a brandy out of a Waterford crystal glass and watching the rain fall, listening to the Animals' *House Of The Rising Sun* on the stereo.

"I had some business. With a Yank," Wally said. He looked at the girl very carefully. He'd "come heavy" to the meeting at the Colossus, carrying a forty-five in a shoulder holster. It had been unnecessary, because the American was too powerful to just kill outright. *That* would have to wait.

"My sister called; she needs some money, Wally. They had a hurricane. Her son got hurt." Bridgette Claypoole trained her big brown eyes on him. He was looking at her like he'd never seen her before, or like she might have suddenly grown two heads.

"... ... I'll send her some money." Wally finally said. His tone was flat; no inflection whatsoever. She'd never heard him sound like that before. He wiped his face with his handkerchief. He started to peel the wet raincoat off his wide shoulders. He took off his hat and knocked the water off it by slapping it with the back of his hand, and the force of the slaps inadvertently knocked it out of his hand and onto the floor. He bent down and picked it up and then placed it on an antique Empire-era chair by the door.

"... Where you been, baby?" the girl said again. "Stop looking at me like that, so mean and all. ..."

"The Colossus ... taking to a Yank. I told you," he said, still staring hard at her.

"Was there cute girls there? ... Next thing you know I'll be out on my ass," she said.

"Don't worry, honey," he said. "... *That's* not going to happen. Not looking the way you do."

He was still so angry he could feel the muscles in his big bull-like neck enlarge to the point where his shirt-collar felt tight again. He finally turned away from the girl and undid his collar, loosening his tie so he wouldn't feel it pinching his neck, like a noose. He liked the girl a lot, actually, but she had everything to do with his present mental state. It had been a shock—what the Yank had told him—and he wasn't nearly over it. It would take him *weeks* or longer to get over something like this—he knew that from past experience. He decided that he really was in love with this girl. His wife had told him that he was, but he hadn't believed her. But he'd realized it when he'd walked out of that club. He really did love her. He was *in love* with her, in fact.

"What kind of business? Why you never tell me *shit*, baby? You come here late and I been waiting for you to take me out to dinner." He'd met Miss Claypoole in an expensive knocking-shop facing Green Park, not ten blocks away. He'd walked her out the very night of the day he'd met her. She was eighteen. That was twelve months ago. He told one of his brothers, the one that held down the old Harold Hill neighborhood for him, that the girl had the ass on her that he'd been looking for his "whole fucking life." It was heart-shaped. He'd used his hands to mold the girl's ass under a streetlight, leaning against his Rolls Royce. "And when she wiggles it, mate ... you know you've met your fucking match! You're done looking. *Finished*. I finally found it. I don't need anything else." He'd punched his brother playfully on the shoulder. His brother had been a boxer called One-Punch Eddy. He'd been a sparring partner of Henry Cooper's—the famous English boxer who'd been the only man to ever knock Mohammad Ali down in a fight, and who'd lived for a while there in Harold Hill.

Then Wally had laughed, enjoying his own good luck. Then he'd tossed his younger brother, who was decked out in black sweats and black trainers, a kilo of pure Sicilian heroin wrapped up in green plastic, and had driven back out of the old neighborhood, straight back to the girl. He always made deliveries to his brother himself, because it gave him a chance to walk through the old neighborhood and see how things were going there. He never used a bodyguard in Harold Hill, because The Cannon didn't need one. Not in Harold Hill, especially. Everyone loved Wally on the Hill.

Bridgette had long, thick hair that she'd inherited from her East Indian grandmother. It felt like silk in Wally's hands when he ran his fingers through it. She used olive oil to make it glisten. When they were screwing, him behind her "taking it home," he'd twist it into a rope that he could pull on like a bridle as they slammed together in a black and white fury.

171

She had come to London as a back-up singer for a Reggae band, and ended up in a place above the Playboy Club giving blow jobs to Arab royals, the occasional American movie star, and English toffs using Daddy's American Express Card, which the madam of course accepted. It was the coke, she'd explained to Wally, who had always treated her well since the day he'd walked her out of the place. "You know the coke is evil, baby. *Evil.* I was just crazy for it." He'd sent her to a famous clinic in Switzerland, where they gave her a cure based on natural medicines and B12 shots and something called *Biostrath*. It worked, because when she came back after three weeks, she was straight, and had never touched any drugs since. They'd flown to the States away from prying eyes, and had lived at the Ritz Carlton in Miami for six weeks, until his business started falling apart while he fucked the girl for hours on end. It was right then that the Corsicans decided to make their move on him—with his wife threatening to leave him and take his sons with her, too. His kids were ten and twelve, and she said they wanted their daddy back, and begged him on the phone to come back to England. The girl was that kind of woman; you just didn't want to get off of her, ever. He decided one day while they were counting money at his warehouse on Elephant Road that she was like a drug to him, and he could only take her in small doses, then he'd have to lay-off until the next dose. Otherwise he'd just fuck himself to death, literally. Now he knew that he had to kill her, and it didn't sit well with him. He wanted to call Max about it for some reason, as if she were an accounting problem that he could sort out without coming up with a negative balance. Twice he thought of picking up the phone and calling Max to ask what he should do. But even Max wasn't smart enough to fix this problem, he finally decided.

"We got to go out," Wally said. "Pour me a drink first, hon." Bridgette looked up at him. She was barefoot. He had a tonsure, the top of his bald head shiny; but she liked it. She had grown up in Trench Town, where men like Wally caught respect. And she truly loved him. He was looking at her in a strange way and she noted it. But she knew she could handle his bad mood in the bedroom—she always had before.

"Something wrong, baby?" she said. "I'll get the drink ... brandy?"

"Yeah." He watched her go into the kitchen, and remembered how happy she'd been the first time he'd brought her up here. He owned London and then he owned her, and she liked it that way. And now he supposed he had to kill her. He looked at the phone as she poured him his drink. He thought one last time of calling Max. He thought the Jew might understand why the hell this *was,* happening all of a sudden to his world.

*   *   *

"My name's Burns—Bill Burns," Malcolm said, sitting down. Wally was well known at the Club Colossus, as one of his top lieutenants owned it. It was a strip-club with rooms in the back for blow-jobs and lap dances—if you had eighty pounds minimum and twenty minutes to spare. The girls were mostly all London girls, leggy blondes with Nordic-looks who'd never left the Second Form. The drinks were watered-down and the clientele was middle class. Men from the City liked the dim lights and the prompt service, and of course, blondes. If it had been out in the East End the lights would have been turned up and the service slower, but no one there would have accepted watered-down drinks, especially the Irish. No one dared to try *that* in the East End. And there would have been black girls and East Indian girls, because the working-class Irish, Turk, and Italian men liked dark skin and exotic eyes.

"That was quite a show at the factory. Speaking up," Wally said. "Took me by surprise—the way you did it."

"I thought you could use a friend," Malcolm said.

"Are you with *them*, then?" Wally asked. "The Specials, I mean ... I've always had good relations with the Specials ... it seems that things have changed, though, lately. I tried to tell the lady copper that, but she didn't seem to want to listen. ..."

"My bunch is different. We come from across the pond," Malcolm said. He thought Wally looked bigger than he had at the Yard, maybe it was the raincoat—it was broader in the shoulders. He was formidable, no question about it; the kind of man you wanted next to you in a fight.

"I see," Wally said.

"I'm here to help you," Malcolm said.

"Help *me? Wally?*"

"Yes," Malcolm said. They'd been seated in the back against a wall. The place was full of men in grey suits and blue ties; City men. The booth was black leather, rolled-and-pleated, festooned with gold buttons. The thick fug from curling cigarette smoke made the overhead spotlights focus a tarnished ashy-yellow light on the stripping "nurse," her head bent down to the stage to show off her small, shiny, white-girl ass, marked-off by a white garter that was still wrapped around the top of her left thigh. She was leaving nothing to the imagination for the men sitting behind her. Then, suddenly, music started to play—Ike and Tina Turner's "Proud Mary." The nurse stood-up straight and began to shimmy across the catwalk like she was dancing past the doorway to Hell. Wally watched the girl perform. She took off the pink nurse's hat with finality and tossed it out into the crowd. It was about the last thing she *could* toss.

"She's still got the garter," Wally said, almost to himself.

"The woman who interviewed you today," Malcolm said, ignoring the show.

"She's a bitch," Wally said, turning back toward him. A waitress brought them their drinks: two whiskeys straight up, "compliments of the management," the girl had said. Wally picked up one of them as soon as she put it down on the table.

"I want to make a deal with you," Malcolm said.

"Are you a policeman?" Wally asked.

"Yes. You could say that—a kind of policeman."

"But an American. FBI?" Wally took a sip.

"It doesn't matter who I am," Malcolm said.

"It does to Wally," he said. "I want to know who I'm doing business with. You could be *anyone*, really. You could be the fucking janitor who cleans up down at the Factory," Wally sighed.

"...You have a girlfriend named Bridgette Claypoole, born in Jamaica. She works for MI5. You took her out of a cat-house. She reports to someone called Hector twice a week, meets him at the grill in Harrods. She tells him everything you do. What time you shit, what time you screw. Every conversation you have about the heroin business. She tells them about someone called Max the Jew. He's the mastermind of your laundering business, which is run out of New York City. She recently told the police that you are overwhelming your ability to cope with the cash. She is a material witness to several crimes, including a murder at the dog-track. Seems you stomped someone to death at a dog race for insulting her. She says she loves you—by the way."

"Well, you're not the fellow who cleans up then, are you? ... He called my girl a nigger," Wally said. He finished his drink and put it to the side. He took off his *Borsalino* porkpie hat and laid it down, too. It was warm in the club. He unbuttoned his raincoat and slid it off. He was built like a bull; a dimpled chin and not much neck. *You would have to shoot him to knock him down,* Malcolm thought.

"Is that what you wanted to know? ... They've bugged all your phones, too."

"Thank you," Wally said.

"I want a favor in exchange," Malcolm said.

"Yes, sure, anything I can do for *America*," Wally said. "I like your new president—Reagan."

"I want to make sure that Bruce Tucker is not someone Sonny Delmonico fucks with."

"That's what this is about? ... That bitch's Yank?"

"That's what this is about," Malcolm said.

"Right. I've gotten the message. Why the dance of the seven veils, though? Aren't the Brits and Yanks working together anymore? They were always deeply in love, before," Wally said.

"Let's just say we have *our* secrets and they have *theirs.*"

"Understood, mate. What's a man without his secrets, eh? Why *me,* though? Why the girl? I've always told them whatever they wanted to know. They should have left her alone."

"I suppose they just don't trust you. You've gotten 'too big', I suppose. ... If it makes it better, they told her they'd send her back to Jamaica. She didn't mean to hurt you— you should know that."

"And I suppose you know yesterday's blue-eyed Tory bitch at the Factory?" Wally said.

"Yes."

"I don't like her. She bothered my wife. Could you speak to her? Maybe get her to stop bothering my wife and kids. Stop her from coming to my house?" Wally asked, sincerely.

"All right, I'll try. But you never saw *me*—understood?"

"... Tell her there are some things that are sacred. Even in *our* business," Wally said, looking back at the stage.

"I'll see what I can do," Malcolm said.

"What's this all about?" Wally said. "I mean, I feel like the rules have suddenly changed for old Wally."

"There are no rules in this game. Didn't you know that? You're just a convenient tool both to them *and* to us. Don't forget that and you'll probably still be okay."

"Well ... You mean they don't really *care* about old Wally, then?"

"No. ... Not that at all, really. They certainly care if you become too expensive. Perhaps you already have. ..."

"I've killed people for them. ... Did the bitch tell you *that*? People they didn't like. Irish thugs. Nigerian ministers who showed up in London on the run. 'Get Wally on the blower' ... that's what they do."

"Of course they do. What did you expect ... a free ride?" Malcolm said.

"How about your lot? ... Need a Wally, then? Any odd jobs for me lying around?"

"Yes, I think so," Malcolm said. "One more thing. How long have you known her ... the woman from yesterday? If you lie to me, I'll have you killed. It will only take one phone call. I promise you that." Malcolm picked up his drink and tasted it. "This is very badly watered-down," Malcolm said. He looked straight *at* Wally and didn't avert his gaze until he'd replied. The nurse left the stage and another, even taller blonde, in a Catholic-school-girl get-up walked by her on the stroll, half her ass already showing.

"Strange how it's always dog-eat-dog," Wally said, staring back. "I suppose it's the way it has to be? ... Life in London. ..."

"It's the way it *is*, Wally ... everywhere. And I'm the biggest dog," Malcolm said.

"Right, then. I want to get along with America; I'm just a businessman, after all. And especially if the rules have suddenly changed with the Brits."

"Again, I'm asking you: How long have you known the woman who interviewed you at the Yard yesterday?"

"You mean Mary? Quite a while, really."

"So it was all just theater ... for my benefit. And just now?"

"Front row seat ... just for you. 'Bowls of shit' and all that. Opening night."

"Do MI5 know about you and Mary?"

"No. She came to old Wally years ago ... alone, without the other members of the tribe."

"Sent by whom?"

"By Count Cici."

"What does she want with *you*, specifically ... with Wally?"

"What does she *want* with me?"

"Yes. What is it that she *does* with you?"

"You're kidding, mate?" Wally started to laugh. He started laughing so hard that men nearby turned to stare at them. Malcolm watched him, his thick neck turning red. His eyes were watering from the cigarette smoke. He noticed then that Wally was wearing a pistol under his jacket. He caught a brief glimpse of it, and confirmed what he'd only suspected earlier, from the way the man had carried himself when he'd walked into the club.

"Did I say something funny, Wally?"

"What she *does*? ... *Mary*? ... She's up to her eyeballs in the trade, is all. In Sicily. In Colombia; in Mexico; even behind the Iron Curtain. ... That's what she *does*, old man. She's the *boss*. Cici works for her, now, from what I've heard. We *all* work for Mary and her gang now, I think."

"Just heroin?"

"Yes, mainly. But she's branching out and wants me to sell the marching powder, too. I had to take it on. She says it's going to be big. Bigger than anything we've ever seen before. I had to go see some wogs in Bogotá for an *abrazo* and a pig dinner. I had to pay them so I could have the franchise. Pleasant enough country ... if you like mad-dog killers and parasitical worms in your water. Their women are pretty, though; I'll give them that," Wally laughed again. Then he spotted the waitress, waving to her and signaling for another round by holding up two fingers. It was now Malcolm's turn to be, not surprised, really, but angry that he'd been right about Mary Keen from the first. He'd thought it had all been too quick and easy with her.

"How do I get a hold of you?" Wally asked. "She's going to find out I told you, and then there'll be Hell to pay. *Won't* there?" Wally said. "I would be very careful now, if

I were you. ..."

"Are *you* going to tell her about our little meeting here?" Malcolm said.

"I won't have to," Wally said. "Mary will know. She wants your man Tucker dead, by the way. Very *explicit* instructions. He's not to make it in to see the Count. I'm to tell Sonny."

"Go ahead, then, tell Sonny."

"If I do that, it won't be easy to fix. ... It's Sicily, after all, you know."

"I see."

"... Your call, Mr. Burns," Wally said. The waitress brought the second round of drinks. Malcolm gave him a phone number at CitiBank in New York and told him to act as if they hadn't ever met. He had no choice, now. He would have to stop the hit on Alex *after* it was ordered, or risk warning Mary. He realized he was being out-maneuvered at every turn. It seemed like he was climbing up the wall of a sand pit and could never quite reach the top before he slid back down again. He was falling backwards, right now, with no traction at all.

"Call Delmonico ... Tell him what she wants done on the call. She'll be listening in, no doubt. If I find out you've told her about seeing me I'll have you killed—is that clear?"

"As day," Wally said. "Is our Mary in trouble then, Bill? Disappointed you, has she?"

"Can you protect Tucker in Sicily? Secretly? Without Mary finding out about it?"

"No, I can't. Mary will hear if I do *anything*. Are we friends, then, Mr. Burns?" Wally asked. "Have the Yanks taken Wally over, now?"

"Yes." Malcolm got up and left. The only solution was to kill Delmonico now, before he could move against his son.

18

■ LONDON

They'd eaten at her favorite restaurant. A good meal, with expensive wine. They were riding in Wally's Rolls Royce. The radio was playing "Knights in White Satin." Bridgette was in a white-sable coat, sitting close to him. She'd worn the fur coat because Wally had asked her to. He'd gotten the coat from one of Max's friends in New York, a furrier who was helping with their cash problems. The furrier was taking two points on the transaction, which Max said was fair, so Wally had accepted the deal. He and Max were air-expressing sacks of cash to the furrier's Brooklyn workshop. The furrier was a young man from Rockaway Beach whose parents were Russian Jews. The young man had a long narrow shop in an old office building that smelled of charred wood. There had been a fire in the building once, years before, and the sweetly-burnt smell still clung to the hallways and offices. The furrier's brother worked at Merrill Lynch, and the brothers would jointly walk the cash into Merrill's big vault near Wall Street on Fridays and deposit it in an account his brother had opened for a "wealthy client." Nobody at Merrill Lynch asked any questions.

The young furrier sold vintage fur coats—both men's and women's—to Jews and black people, both groups traditionally having a penchant for expensive fur coats. The furrier was also known for his innovative designs—sometimes even designing the coats himself. He sometimes used different color combinations and mixed different types of skins in a single coat. Many of his customers felt he was a true artist.

The furrier had taken a shine to Bridgette, as most men did. He'd given her this coat and said that a famous female movie star had recently owned it, but that he'd had to repossess it because the movie star hadn't kept up with the monthly payments. It was a sixty-thousand dollar coat. The furrier told them the story of how he had two guys from the Bonanno family go and collect it from her penthouse apartment in Manhattan. They'd come to her house in the middle of a party she was giving for her boyfriend—an older man and big-time Hollywood director—who was dating her because he thought it would look good in the trade papers. The furrier recounted that the two "Palookas" had to go through the movie star's closet as she screamed at them and they laughed at her. Her boyfriend—ramped up on coke—had come rushing into the bedroom and promptly been knocked-out cold by one of the Bonanno men, who'd blackjacked him in the face and broken his nose. After that he stopped seeing the woman.

Bridgette, in a short black dress, had sat and listened to the furrier's story and then tried on the coat and was enchanted by it. It was truly beautiful, with bits of black ermine in it that made it very dramatic. She walked out of the place sporting it. Wally had made love to her with the coat on back at the hotel on 54th Street in Manhattan. The room had a view of Central Park. It was the best fuck he'd ever had, and he'd had a lot of them.

It had stopped raining. The M4 was cleaned off after the hard rain; the asphalt looked freshly laid and very black. His father, once he moved to London from Sicily, seldom left the Italian enclave at Harold Hill, always staying within the same few blocks. So as a child Wally had been forced to stay in Harold Hill, too, not even going to central London until he was twelve, and old enough to ride the underground with his mates. The first time he rode in his own car he thought he'd gone to heaven.

Wally looked down at the backlit dials that were laid out across the cherry wood dash. It was a brand new car and had cost him a packet. He loved the girl and he loved the car, too, both about the same amount. He had even thought seriously about leaving his wife for her. She'd blown him while they drove past the airport. Her head was in his lap when they passed under a big jet on its way to Paris, lumbering into the sky enormous, as she sucked his cock and made him think twice about everything he was about to do. Everything he was about to do might just get him killed. But he'd learned since that day long ago that he'd hit the Capo in Palermo that the bigger the risk, the bigger the reward. Only big dogs ran the street. The bigger the balls you had, the bigger your bank account. And *nothing* mattered more than money. He'd grabbed her by the coat and felt its furry slickness against his palm as her head bobbed in his lap and he could only hear the plane's jet engines' roar as it flew directly over them, casting a night shadow. He watched the plane's grayish underbelly as its landing gear retracted into the fuselage. He could see the wheels tuck into the plane's belly and disappear from sight. He came—full dick-on as they said when he was in the service—while trying to make the cut off for Swindon, and almost drove off the road. He would miss her; that was for sure.

"Where we goin', hon?" Bridgette asked. Wally was looking normal now. She'd fucked the anger right out of him. She was thinking to herself that she knew how to handle him. *A good blow-job would usually take the nasty right out of him.* And it had seemed to. He was wearing the hat he'd worn to see that American, Burns, but tilted back on his head, now. He'd made some decisions. The first one was that he had to kill Bridgette. Then there was the matter of Mary Keen. That was a very hard one. And there was that fucking American who'd threatened him. Now, when the *police* say they're going to kill you, it's no empty threat. He'd learned that as a boy in Harold Hill. There was more than one copper that would make good on that promise and no one would stop them. Hadn't they tossed old Tony Santini for not paying the beat-cops for the right to pimp when they were just kids; throwing Tony off the top floor of a twelve-storey estate? The coppers' joke—told later on the beat—was about how Tony could fly, but only for the first eleven floors.

"I'm going to send 50 G's to your sister," Wally said, while they were in the Brynglas Tunnel. The headlights of the Rolls swept the walls. He was driving faster than he should have, but he enjoyed that. Taking the engine up to 120 kilometers per hour out of the tunnel and passing other cars like they were standing still.

"I love you. You know that. ... I know you got another woman. Is it that bitch that comes around to our place, the old upper crust English one? Old bitch," Bridgette said.

"No." Wally smiled.

"I don't like her," Bridgette said.

"I don't, either," Wally said.

"What she do for you baby? Old worn-out white bitch. I can do it better and longer." He turned to look at her. He wondered if the sex-kitten role was Bridgette's real personality or if there were another Bridgette in there? Had she gone to Cambridge? Was she a real copper? He wondered if she even dressed differently when she met with the coppers. Black suits and a string of pearls. *Was she even Jamaican?* "Where we going?"

"We're going to Swindon," Wally said.

"Why?"

"I've got some business there," Wally said.

"I'm glad you took me with you tonight. I was scared the way you were looking at me ... when you came in I thought it was over. ... What's in Swindon, hon?"

"You know where they smash the cars?"

"Yeah. Your uncle's place."

"Yeah. Uncle Nick. I got business there," Wally said.

"You got some business in the car first," Bridgette said, and had him pull over and she fucked him hard—for good measure. Just in case.

*   *   *

Malcolm had thought the apartment the Agency had procured for him was a good one. There was a doorman who was armed, and a call-box if there was problem, that went right to the American Embassy. They'd never had a problem there, though. It was on a quiet street across from the Hotel Green Park and quiet comfortable. He had stayed there often over the last ten years, whenever he was in London, and it always felt safe to him. That was a mistaken feeling. A team of men snatched him right out of his flat.

"Who are you, mate?" A man asked, pointing a gun at him. They'd had a key, and had made no noise when they'd come in.

"Bill," he'd said. They'd walked him past the doorman, who'd been shot dead, and was laid out and bleeding at the closed front door. *How had they managed it?* He'd glanced at the white phone on the small lobby table as they'd hustled him out the big glass-door, with traffic on the street passing by and everything looking totally normal. It was almost one in the afternoon. A few people looked casually at him as he was tossed into a cab. Had the people on the street thought he was being arrested by the police? Maybe; probably. He'd yelled-out even as he was pushed into the car, but it appeared to have no effect. All cities are the same, he thought. *Anonymous. Murders, rapes, kidnappings—they all happen anonymously in the midst of millions of people, in any big city in the world. No exceptions.* They traveled in silence across the city, a man on either side of him. *How many times had he done this kind of thing himself to others?*

They'd walked in while he'd been sitting there talking to his wife on the phone back in Washington. The big pistol that was pointed at him said it all. The man had simply signaled with his hand that he hang up. He'd rather abruptly told his wife that he needed to go and had hung-up. The man with the gun was wearing a dark-green trench coat almost identical to the one he wore.

He had been handcuffed to the chair he was sitting on with two pair of handcuffs. One ring of each cuff had been slipped under each of the chair's two front legs.

"Is your name Bill?" the man who'd been questioning him had asked.

"Yes."

"You're lying." The two men who had ridden with him were gone and had been replaced by two other men. They seemed very professional, and had worked him very calmly—so far, anyway. They were both wearing suits and looked like business executives. One had not shaved recently, and his beard shone blue-black. He smelled of deodorant when he took off his jacket.

"We're from the police," one of the men said. "You should tell us the truth."

"I did." He realized that the men were not English or American, but were speaking English with accents that he couldn't immediately identify, despite his years in the game.

"Your name is Malcolm Law. We know exactly who you are," the man said.

"No; it's not. My name is Bill Burns."

"Yes it *is*. Why are you lying to us?" There was an accent all right, but he just couldn't tell exactly where it came from. Maybe German; or Hungarian, even. He tried to mentally go to a place he'd culled-out for himself when he was in Poland during the War. It was a place of calm inside himself that he had created that he could use in the midst of a battle. He went there now. It was a sealed-off place where death was expected—even welcomed, and it didn't mean anything any more; nothing did, in fact, in that place.

"Who are you? I'm sure this is all illegal," Malcolm watched himself say, from a great interior distance, like watching a movie where a character named "Malcolm Law" played his part, just as the others played theirs. "I'm an American citizen. I have rights." Both interrogators noticed that his voice had suddenly changed tone, and was now colorless and indifferent.

"That doesn't matter, here," the one who'd taken his jacket off said. The man unbuttoned his shirt cuffs and then rolled up his sleeves. His arms were hairy. The hair was coarse and dark. Despite the glare of a desk lamp that was pointed directly at his face, Malcolm saw that the man's fingers were thick—*a peasant's fingers*.

"It does to me," Malcolm said, watching him. He was slapped suddenly, very hard, by the other man. He hadn't seen it coming because he'd been looking down. The desk lamp had been placed very close to his face so that he'd be looking straight into the bulb unless his head were tilted to one side or another; or up, or down. It was an effective interrogation procedure because it made him squint and look down at his knees most of the time making him feel trapped like an animal. After a moment of silence from the interrogators, he decided to close his eyes and try to think this through. *Who was he facing, exactly?*

He heard his pants buckle being undone. He briefly opened his eyes. He saw a pocket knife pierce his right pant leg at upper thigh-level and then cut down through the fabric to the knee. First the left pant leg was cut, and then the right, so that both his knees were exposed. He saw the hairy man's thick fingers lift the elastic band of his underwear and cut through it down the front so that his genitals were exposed. He realized then that he'd been pulling desperately on his wrists, which were handcuffed to the chair's legs. Each cuff was locked to a chair's leg—both left and right. The cuffs now were biting into his wrists, cutting him. He tried to go back to that calm place at the very center of his being. He felt fingers touch his scrotum and pull it so that he yelled-out, very loudly, at the sudden and excruciating pain. *What was it they wanted? Who were they?*

"Tell us who you are?" Thick Fingers said.

"My *name* is Bill Burns, for God's sake! I work for Citibank. I'm a Vice President. I work in New York. I'm here for a meeting with my British colleagues." He felt the man pull on his scrotum, yanking it again very hard. He screamed. He had to stop talking: the pain was intense and deep, and ran up to his chest in a wave. The man pulled on his balls a third time. He tried to stand up. The pain was overpowering and he crashed to the surface from that deep place inside him that he could no longer hide in.

"You're lying! Your name is Malcolm Law and you're a spy. I'll cut your balls *off* if you don't tell me your name." The man slid his knife under Malcolm's nut-sack. He could feel the coldness of the blade.

"... I'm Bill Burns ..."

There was a commotion in the room: someone had come in and walked behind him.

"Do you remember someone called Anna Maximovna?" His heart went cold. It was Mary Keen's voice. He had not been able to see her because of the light in his face. But it was her; he was sure of it. He tried to look around the white bulb, but when he did the man holding it moved the light right back in front of his eyes, almost covering his face with it, the lamp's hot bulb burning his cheek.

"*No.*"

"You're lying, dear. Did you ever meet with General Maximov in Moscow?" Mary said. "Put that away." She was speaking to the man with the knife. Malcolm felt the blade withdraw.

"I don't know who you're talking about. ..." Malcolm said. "Why *you*, Mary? What happened to you?"

"Dear, you must talk to these men. I'm afraid that you've gone too far, this time. I've come to help you."

"Mary? ... There's still time to come back. Don't do this."

"*Back?*" she said. "Why would I want to do that, dear? I'm afraid that you'll have to use *that*," she said to the men. "Turn him over, then."

He tried to fight them when they slid the handcuffs free from the chair legs but they immediately pulled him up to his feet. There were three men now, and much stronger than he was. He was jerked by the handcuffs and then dragged to a desk and thrown over it; one man pulling him forward by the cuffs so he was forced to fall on the desk, chest first, then dragged forward so that he was lying stomach-down on the desk, with his feet still on the ground. His hands were re-cuffed in front of him to the desk's drawer-pulls by a new, third man, younger than the other two, who'd apparently come in with Mary. He could see and feel that it was a metal desk. They'd got the cuffs locked-down to the drawer-pulls. He felt his underwear being ripped away. He tried to look behind him, then. The light had been taken away, so he was able to get a better picture of the room. It was some kind of large office. The venetian blinds were drawn. But he could see that the setting sun was painting them orange. He saw Mary standing to the side, watching; a very cold look on her pretty face.

"It's called a Hot Shot 36," Mary said. "It's actually American. We first used it in Sicily. We found it useful in dealing with the hard-cases you find there." He felt a hand on his ass. He tried to roll off the desk, but he couldn't because his hands were held-fast by the cuffs. Mary crouched down and showed him the device; it had a long wand and a red tip "It has a trigger, you see. It's used on cattle to make them move along," she said.

"Mary, *don't*. It doesn't have to be like this."

"I'm afraid it does, actually," she said. "Now ... who is it you sent to pick up Neizert, and where is he now? I must have him, Malcolm."

"I don't know where he is."

"You're lying."

"You're with them. With Gehlen," he said.

"I'm an independent business woman," she said.

"Why did you do it?"

"Because my husband turned out *not* to be rich. ... Not at all what I'd thought—just an old, broken-down aristocrat with bills like anyone else. And he was with them back in the Nazi era ... even before the War. A bloody Nazi spy for the German's from the start. They came to him, Gehlen did. Fabulous money from the very beginning and everyone was looking at Philby; never at us, you see. Now where is Neizert? Dear," she said. "When it goes up your rectum it won't hurt at all ... it's when they pull the trigger ... that's when you get the electrical charge, you see. The current goes everywhere because of the intestinal tract's moisture content. The shock will run up to your stomach, even, and most people have found it quite painful." She walked around the desk and leaned down and looked him straight in the eye. "You see this long part that we stick up there. ... You see?" He realized now that she was truly angry and wanted to hurt him, probably badly, no matter what he told them. "Is it General Maximov? Is that who's helping you? You had to have *some*one—I *know* that."

"No."

"I don't think you'll be able to stand it, really. We'll inject you with methamphetamine to keep you awake. You'll soil yourself. The smell is terrible, but the pain won't stop. You'll have a heart attack in the end from a combination of the drug and the current. That's usually what happens," she said.

The edge of the metal desk was cutting into the thin flesh across his pelvic bone. His hands had gone numb from the tight cuffs, and the position of his shoulders, as his upper body had been forced to hang over the other edge of the desk. He remembered once seeing a German soldier who'd been taken prisoner by the Polish resistance being tortured for information. They'd started by cutting the man's ears off and showing them to him. They had had no mercy whatsoever. The soldier had been a *Hitlerjugend*, only about seventeen, from the infamous 12th Panzer Battalion. The boy had begged for his life. He really *had* no information to give them. The men had been driven crazy by hatred after seeing so many innocent Polish women and children casually slaughtered by the Germans. They'd ended up burning the kid-soldier alive in a barrel inside a barn that had only a partial-roof, he remembered. He'd said nothing about it at the time, as he was not in command, but had been sent only to help with logistics and intelligence, using a radio to report to OSS on German troop movements. He'd briefly tried to stop them but they'd pushed him aside.

"All right; do it. Find out where Neizert is," she said, speaking to the men.

"Mary!"

"Yes, dear?"

"I'm going to find you and kill you myself," he said. "I promise you. *Do you hear me?!* I'll find you no matter where you hide." Then he felt something cold go up his rectum. When they got the cattle prod well up into his small intestines, they pulled the trigger and he heard himself scream, his whole body spasming and jerking like a marionette whose puppeteer had lost control of the strings. Then they turned it off for a moment. He heard the door close. Someone turned on a radio and searched the dial for rock music that would partially cover his screams. Cream's "Rollin' an' a-Tumblin'" began to play. He tried to concentrate on listening to the music as a way of holding on to Neizert's whereabouts.

When I woke up this morning all I had was gone ...

*   *   *

There was a crazy, shiny mound of used hubcaps, maybe six feet high, and yards wide, that marked the turn-off to his uncle's car-dismantling business. Wally slowed and turned down a narrow tree-lined lane. The road was very dark. The asphalt had long ago broken and been pitted by the heavy trucks bringing jalopies and other wrecks to "Clyde's Car-Crusher." His uncle had bought the property—a hundred hectares—from an Irishman who had run the business before him.

The asphalt—or what was left of it—ended, and their car was forced onto a rutted dirt-track. In the distance, they could see a large and relatively new white trailer with lights on inside it. They had to cross a stream on an ancient-looking trestle-bridge that seemed too rickety to have survived the tons of worn-out cars that had been driven across it over the years. The Rolls bottomed-out twice as its undercarriage scraped the surface of the dirt road just before they drove over the wooden bridge.

The first thing a person noticed were the bright tower-lights that were pointed down on the huge crusher, which was almost brand new and painted a bright canary yellow. Its metal slot-mouth stood empty and was hanging open. The gate to the business was wide open. There were several new trailers scattered near the crusher that served as parts' warehouses. Some of the more valuable cars were parted-out before being crushed and were lined up around a cyclone fence. Cars, once they'd been crushed, were sent out of the yard as four-cubic-meter squares of metal and other detritus that ended up in the Peoples' Republic of China to be melted down and made into toys and guns.

"Why come so late?" Bridgette said. Wally drove the Rolls up to the lit-up trailer and put on the parking brake.

"Wait here. I'll be right out," Wally said ignoring her. It was raining slightly; almost a fog, rather than a real rain.

He walked up to the trailer's door, but his uncle Nick pulled it open before he could knock. His uncle was from Sicily and had been in England since the late sixties. His English was still spotty, though. He was wearing a wool cap and grey overalls that were stained with grease. The business was owned by the Sicilian mafia, and his uncle had been sent to run it and to work for them distributing heroin. No one noticed the comings and goings from the place, so it was deemed a perfect spot to break down large shipments of heroin. The car dismantler was a legitimate business and operated alongside the heroin trade. It was his Uncle Nick—a "made man" in Palermo—who had recruited Wally for his first hit as a teenager.

"Come in," his uncle said in Italian. Wally stepped up the metal stairs into the trailer. His uncle looked out at Wally's Rolls Royce and the young girl who he'd met before.

He hugged his uncle. He smelled of garlic and car lubricant. *"Como vie?"* Wally said.

"Crushing cars," His uncle said, and hugged him back. They hid large shipments of heroin by burying them in a container that a Chinese company sent to be filled with crushed cars.

"What is it?"

"I want to crush my car," Wally said. His uncle smiled, thinking he was joking, turned away and went back to a small table and sat down. He was eating. He had sausage and pasta on a glass plate and a loaf of French bread with a kitchen knife stuck in it. There was a small ceramic cup of coffee that was stained around the top from having been used thousands of times.

"Yeah, I want to crush my own balls sometime, too," His uncle said. He picked up a fork and began to eat standing up.

"No, I'm serious," Wally said. "Right *now*. ..."

"Why are you going to do that?" His uncle looked up. He was cutting a piece of bread off the loaf.

"Because I want it to hurt. I'm going to have to do something, and I want it to hurt me, too." His uncle gave him a funny look.

"Wally, why you come here and talk crazy?" He sunk a fork into a piece of sausage and put it into his mouth and chased it with a piece of bread.

"How you do it?"

"Do what?"

"Crush the cars; how do you do it?" Wally said.

"I pick it up with the fork lift and I push it into the crusher's mouth," his uncle said.

"Okay," Wally said, nodding.

"That's a new Rolls Royce, Wally. ... Give *me* the car—You crazy," his uncle said.

"No. It's got to hurt. If I gave you the car it wouldn't hurt, *would* it?"

"Shit. ... You on drugs? You fucked-up on-a someting? I tell your father."

"No. I want to do it myself—pick it up with the lift and put it in the crusher. A hundred-and-fifty-thousand-dollar car," Wally said. His uncle looked at him and stabbed a second piece of sausage and shook his head. He knew his nephew was crazy, but this was beyond anything he'd ever done. He assumed he was high on drugs, and was disappointed because he loved his nephew.

"How you and the girl get home?" his uncle said in English, his mouth full. "You think of that? Huh?"

"She's not going home," Wally said. "... She's staying here with the car. You got the handcuffs we bought—if we ever had trouble?"

"Yeah." His uncle put down his fork. "I got them. You going to crush the girl, too?"

"Yeah ... I'm going to crush the girl, too," Wally said. "Find the handcuffs, uncle Nick. ... Please."

"I thought you liked that girl? What she do? She that Cuban girl, right?"

"She's Jamaican. ... Just find the bleeding handcuffs." Wally walked up to a cardboard box and started rummaging. He was looking for the handcuffs. The trailer had scores of grease-stained boxes full of scavenged car parts.

"I finish eating first. Maybe you wake the fuck up and stop this bullshit talk," his uncle said. Wally glanced up from the box for a moment and then went back to looking.

"Wally ... why?" Bridgette said.

"I had a drink tonight with a Yank. Maybe you know him. Mr. Burns?" Wally said. "At the Colossus." Wally had handcuffed the girl to the Roll's steering wheel. She had stopped fighting him. He'd had to slap her once to get her to stop trying to move her wrists to avoid the cuffs.

"He told me you've been singing to the coppers." Wally was leaning through the Roll's driver's-side window. He heard his uncle Nick bringing the big forklift, a *Kamatsu* #10. They used it to snatch cars off of the flat-bed trucks and then run them over to the crusher and into its mouth. The forklift was loud and huge; the driver's seat was enclosed by a cage. His uncle, a small man, almost looked comical in the cage. He pulled the forklift up a few yards behind his nephew. Wally had explained that the girl might be a policeman, and any sympathy the uncle had felt earlier for her was now gone.

"Is it true?" Wally said, turning back to look at Bridgette. "... Who are you, really— tell me, *now!?*"

"It's true, Wally. The Americans arrested me in Chicago. ... The DEA. I was a drug mule for a gang in Trench Town that sent me to Chicago. They told me I had to work for the DEA or go to jail for a long time. I was addicted. I couldn't even talk I was so scared. The DEA brought me to London and told me to work where you found me that night. They wanted me to report on who came and went from the knocking shop. They were interested in a one guy—a Saudi Prince who wanted me to be his regular. When you took me home that night they weren't expecting it. ... It wasn't planned. They'll know, Wally ... If something happens to me," she said.

"Will they? I doubt they'll care much, hon. The coppers don't care about people like us. People in the game. We're just not all that important. You know?" He looked at her. She didn't believe he'd kill her.

"Wally, listen to me. I can help you. I love you—you know I do. ... Don't do this. *Please!*"

"Was it all a lie? You being an addict when I met you?"

"*No*. It was true. I was addicted to blow when they arrested me in Chicago. They told me they would arrest me for selling heroin. They know all about you. What it is you do. Everything. I was frightened, baby. I didn't know what else to do. They said that all I had to do was tell them who you spoke to and what you said. That's all. Half the time I didn't tell them anything because I'm in love with you. That's the truth. It is."

"I was in love with *you*. You know that. ..." Wally said. "Why didn't you tell me the truth?"

"I was afraid you'd hate me. Kill me. ... I'll make it up to you. I'll lie to them. I'll disappear if you want me to. I'll stay if you want me to. Just tell me what you want me to do, *baby*. *Please*. Just *tell* me!"

Wally locked the driver's-side door and turned around. His uncle Nick got off the forklift, jumping down from the cage. His face was dead and cold-looking. He jumped into the mud and stood by the forklift, the engine idling loudly even in neutral.

"How's this thing work?" Wally asked, climbing up into the driver's compartment. His uncle climbed up alongside him and showed him how to lower and raise the forks.

"So what do I do?" Wally said.

"You pick it up with the forks, tilt the bitch back, and then you run it over there," his uncle said. "Shove it in the crusher, lower the forks so the car sits in the mouth on its tires and then pull back. Then we turn it on and the mouth closes."

"Okay," Wally said. The lights from the tower were cold. He slid the hand-brake off and lowered and raised the forks, getting the feel of the machine. The heavy forks clanged when they hit the ground. He stopped and looked at the girl. She was screaming at him from inside the car. He gunned the motor and pulled forward and let the forks drop suddenly to the ground; he tilted them level as he moved. The forks drove into the mud and acted like plows as he came forward. His uncle stepped back and watched him slide the forks under the car and tilt the Rolls back slightly. His uncle turned and walked towards the crusher, a large, yellow steel-box with a jaw that was hydraulically operated. He went to the control panel on the side of the crusher and hit the start button that lowered the "jaw" down to ground-level so a car could be slid into its mouth.

His uncle turned and saw the forklift holding the Rolls Royce—the car's black passenger door reflecting an image of the crusher. The girl had managed to power one of the windows down and was screaming at Wally as he bounced across the muddy field, the Rolls tipping slightly on the two forks of the lift. Nick powered-up the second panel of the crusher's controls, which opened the jaws; left, right and top—increasing the size of the crusher's mouth to twenty-five meters wide and ten meters high. Once the mouth's jaws closed, the top and sides of the crusher would push in using thousands of pounds of force to compact a sedan down to a cube of plastic-veined metal.

"GOD! WALLY PLEASE ... PLEASE ... PLEASE." Bridgette was hysterical. Wally's face showed the strain. He sped up. The Rolls was threatening to tip off the forks because he was moving too fast. His first attempt failed as he gouged a fork into the side of the jaws. He had to back up and approach the mouth again. This time he slowed it down and he managed to enter the crusher dead-center with the Rolls. He stopped the lift and backed up slightly, lowering the car back onto its tires. The car now sat in the crusher. Bridgette was hoarse from screaming. You could hear her all the way back by the hubcap pile, almost two kilometers away, but there was no one on the deserted road *to* hear, because they were surrounded by dark countryside.

"Wally! God! *Please!*" She'd stuck her head out of the window, now in a total panic, and then she was trying to climb out of the Rolls' window, her left foot first, and then her right, so that she managed to drop out of the car, her face still facing the steering wheel. The sable coat had been pulled down off her shoulders, and was hanging halfway in and halfway out of the car, making it harder for her to free herself.

Wally stopped the forklift and hopped out and walked in the mud up to the crusher. Bridgette, exhausted now from screaming, and her arm hurting, tried to turn to look at him. He walked over to the machine and nodded to his uncle who hit the "On" button. The crusher's "jaw," which had been retracted, started slowly to move up. Its bent and banged steel lip pushed hydraulically. The jaw caught Bridgett's foot and she was able to stand again. But she realized that the machine was closing in around her.

"*Wally ... please. God help me!*" He'd never heard a person scream like they were calling from the grave before. He'd killed lots of people but it always was quick. This was scaring even him. The sound of her voice was child-like in its fear.

"Are you telling the truth about being forced into it? You're not a copper?" Wally looked at his uncle. "Can't you make this move any quicker?"

His uncle shook his head, no. Suddenly Wally leaned over and stopped the machine, banging his palm on a big red button. The hydraulics slowly stopped moving. They both heard her whimpering like a child; she was trying to get inside the car again, frantically thinking that it would somehow help her to be inside the car, but the sable coat had gotten bunched up around her shoulders and she couldn't manage to get back through the open window.

"Hey. Hey!" Wally said. "Answer my question!" She stopped whimpering, realizing that the machine had stopped. She was shaking, trembling; he saw her knee shaking as she tried to balance on the edge of the crusher's metal lip. The sable coat was a mess around her face, her wrists still fixed by the handcuffs that were locked to the steering wheel. He saw that her wrists were bleeding from tugging frantically on the cuffs.

"Wally ... baby ... *I swear to god. I'm not a policeman!*"

"Turn it back on ... " Wally said "Turn it back on. Bitch, I don't believe you!" He reached over to hit the bright red ON button. "Who is this Mr. Burns?"

"I don't know, Wally!"

"Why *you?*"

"They targeted you. They knew you liked black girls and they put me in your way."

"DEA?"

"Yes." She managed to turn around, but her high heel slipped off the metal lip and she fell inside the box hanging from her wrists. Wally walked over and grabbed her foot and got her back up so she could stand on the lip.

"And what is all this about?" he said. "Why *me?*"

"It's about the trade. They want you to stay on top. I was the guide. They're helping you stay on top. The Americans."

"... No—the Yank Burns. What's *he* got to do with it?"

"I don't know," she said "I swear to you, Wally, I don't know. He came to the last meeting I had with the DEA. That's all I know. He never spoke a word."

"I *loved* you," Wally said. She looked down at him.

"Let me go, Wally ... I'm beggin' you. Let me go."

"I wanted you to love me, too," Wally said. "I would have done *anything* for you."

"I will. I swear to you. I love you, too—you know that."

"I don't believe you," Wally said. "... You work for them. You *can't* love me."

"I'm yours. I swear to God, Wally. I won't go back to them. I swear it. It can be like it was." He stared at her. He pulled his hand away from the fat worn-looking "ON" button.

"When I was a boy I had a favorite pigeon ... I sent it out one afternoon. I remember this hawk got it right above the car-park across the street. It came up from the car-park. Usually the hawks sat over in the trees by the roundabout. But this one didn't. This hawk was different. The pigeon wasn't looking *below* her, you see?" Wally said.

"Hon. ... I'm sorry. Don't kill me," Bridgette said. He turned his back on her and hit the ON button and then turned and watched the jaws close down. Then all at once it seemed all the crusher's motors came on and started their work. He watched a big stainless steel elbow move—pushing the sides in. There was the sound of metal-on-metal as the car—as strong as it was—finally began to be crushed from above. He watched for a second more and then hit the OFF button with his palm. He couldn't do it. He reversed the engine with a switch and watched the jaws open again.

19

■ COLMA, CALIFORNIA

Black sheep, whether artists or dope fiends, especially once-socially-prominent ones, usually have very quiet funerals with few in attendance. The socially prominent want nothing to do with those that stray from the gilded script. Patty's funeral in San Francisco was typical in that regard. She remained an outcast even in death. A week before her funeral her father did get out the Super 8 movies and played them—sitting alone—late at night, in the family room against the wall. The small projected square of color and movement was all that was left of his pretty daughter. Then he destroyed the small cans of films, too. He didn't want Patty's sisters and brother to remember her in any way, afraid that they'd blame him for her death somehow later on, after they'd grown up.

Patty's funeral service was held on a Friday in the city of Colma, just south of San Francisco. It was a city built solely for cemeteries. It was a foggy and cold day in a remote part of the Bay Area, in a white stone chapel decorated to give off a stiff non-denominational vibe that somehow still, nonetheless, kept a Western God at the center of it all. There was a marble statue of a white angel, very large, off to the side of Patty's closed and very expensive bronze casket.

Her casket was left out for exactly half-an-hour by the attendants and two gardeners who had been dragooned into carrying it into the chapel; a task usually reserved for family members, or loved ones. But there *were* no family in attendance that morning. The gardeners had grayish mud on the edges of the soles of their work boots, still there from earlier, when they'd dug Patty's grave. The men had been curious about the girl they were to bury, as they'd heard from the front office that she'd been some kind of gang member à la Bonnie Parker, and possibly a hooker as well. Like most crime stories, the facts had, in a very short time, been spun beyond recognition and had taken on a sensational and sexy life of their own. The men had taken their hats off when they finished the grave; the act of respect for the dead was customary and traditional, and still held, even in the upside-down world of 1980. The biggest Irish laborer even shut up long enough so that they could hear the wind in the cypress trees. The practice of taking a moment to reflect on the insignificance of man's life in this world would finally end a few years later, when the mostly-Irish grave diggers were replaced with Mexicans, who were more casual about death in general, and had never paid any attention to Edwardian formalities.

A few people, mostly young, had signed the "mourners' book" in the chapel. Two of them were girls who had met Patty when she'd taken courses at the College of Marin, and she'd had affairs with both of them. One of the girls had fallen in love with her. The other one was going to become a nun as a result of bad experiences inside the drug culture out at Gate Six, and just wanted to do the right thing by Patty, who she saw as the ultimate Lost Soul–somehow Catholic piety with all its grand and empty ramshackle nonsense made life bearable and now made some kind of sense to her. She'd come to equate sex with evil. The girl would later be killed in Central America, very ironically at the hands of the Salvadoran Army in a hail of gunfire, not unlike Patty.

Patty's drug connection—"Jesus" Kennedy—attended in a surprisingly natty dark suit, his long grey hair pulled into a pony tail for the occasion. He was old-school and a devotee of the obituary page of the *San Francisco Chronicle*, where he'd seen the three-line mention standard-death-notice: *Patty Montgomery, daughter of Lisa and Douglas Montgomery ... formerly of Dallas, Texas, and Sausalito, California, will be buried on Friday at 2 p.m. at Cypress Lawn.*

Bruce Tucker and Edward Perry didn't bother signing the book, as they had been ordered not to come by the DEA, but they were both there when the gardeners and the two older men in dark suits and white shirts from the front office carried Patty's casket in and placed it onto a kind of dais in front of the thirty metal folding-chairs sitting there on the bright-green AstroTurf. The chairs that had been put out for friends and family of the deceased.

Alex and Butch each came from different parts of the world. So that made five people who sat there in an uncomfortable silence wondering where the hell Patty's *family* was. The ugly truth hit everyone at about the same time: they weren't going to show at all. Not one. It was Butch who finally—after twenty minutes of total silence— stood up and walked to the front of the cold chapel and decided to say a few words, because he'd been brought up as a Catholic and he expected words to be said over the dead, *no matter what*. He'd spoken over the dead many times in Vietnam and was used to it.

And, as it turned out, he'd taken Patty's death very hard—surprising even himself, as a veteran witness to so many meaningless deaths in the past. He'd drunk only a half-pint of Southern Comfort in the taxi from the airport so was—for Butch, anyway—

stone sober. He had replayed the scene of the shoot-out in the Malibu sunlight from beginning to end in his mind many times, and had come to the conclusion that they'd killed Patty out of spite. He'd seen plenty of that kind of killing and understood it well. He'd seen Marines do it, and the VC do it, too. Everyone does it. Patty was the kind of girl he'd want to marry, Butch had thought when Alex called him and told him he was going to the funeral. Butch said he would go, too.

"Well, if no one is going to say anything, I will. I knew Patty in LA," Butch said. "Not too well here in San Francisco. I didn't know her for very long. ... She reminded me of those girls you see at college and are afraid to talk to because they're so damned pretty and you think they're going to be up-tight and stuck-up because of it. But she wasn't either one." He looked out at the few faces looking back up at him, most of them blank, since they didn't know him and had no idea who he was to Patty, exactly, thinking finally that they'd probably been lovers. But they all seemed grateful to have the silence finally broken by someone.

"Anyway, we went to this store in L.A. together and there was a hutch she wanted me to buy for my new place and I told her I couldn't afford it but I liked it because it looked expensive and had class. I forgot about it. Two days later I got a call saying that the men from the store were parked out in front of my new place and wanted to deliver a piece of furniture and I told the movers, when they called, that I hadn't bought anything and the guy insisted the delivery was for me. Patty bought me the hutch. I drove down to the place and saw it and I thought wow she bought it. It had a big teddy bear that came with it and said that I was supposed to give that to my kid when I finally had one and say it was from his aunt Patty. ... Anyway, I liked her because she liked to do things like that. She didn't care about money, really. I liked to be with her at lunch, too, because she would tell funny stories about the people she grew up with acting out funny events. ... And I'm sure if they were here they would say what a nice young ... well, that Patty was a good person." Butch Nickels, the man who had never cried, at least not for the last ten years of his life, started to weep, openly and unashamedly the tears running down his face, no attempt to wipe them away. It was as if he were someone else; a man who'd fallen in love with a girl he would only touch when helping her into a car, or by accident, waiting for lunch in line at the health food restaurant; but he'd fallen hard for her and she'd died and she wasn't ever coming back into his life and he was not able to deal with it; not at all. "Sad" was a feeling that he didn't think he still had in him; not after Vietnam and everything else. He thought that he was only capable of a slow-burning anger most of the time; "quietly angry," as he thought of it; angry for a lot of reasons; angry mainly before this,

194

though, because many of his best friends had died *for* nothing in a war that *meant* nothing. Zero.

Butch suddenly stopped talking, because the last things he'd said struck him as having gone too far. Everyone listening to him by now knew that her people must be the biggest assholes this side of Nixon. Butch wiped the tears off his face and looked at Alex, who hadn't said a word to him from the moment he'd sat down, sliding in next to him wearing a blue Nordstrom suit, with his very blond hair cut short now, and looking like an investment banker or young doctor. They hadn't said a word to each other since they'd been taken to the airport with tickets in their hands by officers in the Domestic Service of the CIA, who'd picked them up at DEA headquarters in downtown L.A. eight hours after the shoot-out in Malibu and then dropped them off at LAX. All Butch knew was that the operation in L.A. was being "closed down," and that was it. He was to go back to Pittsburgh for a much-deserved furlough and would receive further orders in due time. He'd bought Alex a drink in the airport bar and got on his plane dead-drunk—the smell of cordite and blood still on his clothes. The last he'd seen of Alex was him sitting at LAX in a large tarmac-facing bar. When he saw him get up and leave before the men came to take the casket to Patty's final destination, Butch somehow knew that he would be at a similar bar later and, sure enough, he found Alex sitting at an airport bar when he walked into SFO three hours after she was put in the ground.

"Where you heading?" Butch said when he found him.

"London," Alex said. "I like it there. What about you?"

"I don't know. I doubt somehow that they're finished with us. Something tells me they *aren't*, you know what I mean?"

"What did her headstone say?" Alex looked up at him. He was drunk, but level; a term Butch had heard when he first joined the Marine Corps, and which came from Marine pilots. It meant that you weren't out-of-control—yet.

"It just said "Patty," with her dates. That was it."

"No last name? She *had* a last name, you know," Alex said

"No last name."

"She had a *last name*. It was Montgomery. Is that *our* doing, man? Did we do *that*, too? I mean, besides getting her killed. Did we steal her *name*, too?"

"*We* didn't get her killed—don't even tell yourself that, man. She was already going down a steep street when you met her," Butch said. "She was going to have a short life no matter what—you know that! She didn't sign up for a long pull." Butch took the shot of tequila that Alex had bought him and then tried to get the bartender's attention again. "Where're *you* going?" Alex asked again. He would never mention Patty Montgomery's name again over the next twenty years.

"Central America. Just got the word," Butch said. "The Embassy in El Salvador. I'm an AID official called Mark Miller ... A *banana* expert, of all things. Shit. ... Do I look like a fucking *banana* expert to you? A *fuck*-around expert, maybe. Right."

Twenty minutes later Alex was gone. Butch struck up a conversation after he'd left with an Army Colonel, but found himself looking for Patty in the crowded and noisy bar. In six-hours and forty-five minutes he was in El Salvador, a hot wind blowing in his face, standing there on the tarmac of an airport that the Contras would shortly be using as a transshipment hub to bring cocaine into the United States.

20

The girl who waited for Malcolm Law that Sunday in the second-class hotel, Anna Maximovna, had grown up privileged in Moscow because her father was a very important KGB general. It was the girl's day off. She worked at the Russian Embassy on *Vasconcielos* a block down from a Sanborns restaurant. It was the same embassy that Lee Harvey Oswald had allegedly walked into a few years before.

Anna Maximovna had wanted to be a ballerina and had been accepted by the famous Bolshoi Ballet School at the age of six. But her neck was judged to be just two centimeters too short when she was sixteen years old—the age when cuts were made, based on a variety of physical and mental factors. Russian prima ballerinas had to conform to a strict physical ideal. Anna was sent home one Wednesday morning the week after the Easter recess after a routine evaluation, with no warning whatsoever. She was devastated. She had just turned sixteen.

She had grown up at the School. She needed the right length of neck (measured from the chin to the clavicle with a tailor's tape) but didn't have it. That is what the woman who evaluated all the sixteen-year-old female dancers said to her while she made a note on a clipboard and ended Anna's career. Male dancers were of course exempt from that particular measurement; their measurements were taken at the buttocks, which were expected to be large and capable of providing lift. The older woman had commented that it was too bad, because Anna's other proportions were perfect, and she was very pretty—she had long legs and arms. "You can go now," the woman had said, rolling up her tape, as if Anna had just been visiting there at the School for the last ten years of her life.

Anna had looked around the big room wearing her black leg warmers and black tights, bought in Paris while on a trip there with her father. The other aspiring ballerinas, watching her, were sitting in terror because of what they'd just witnessed. Several shrank away, afraid they would be next. Anna was sure it was a nightmare and she would wake up in her parents' apartment in her large bed, with the ornate tin ceiling painted white. Instead, the school's director, a pleasant former ballerina herself, was called into the practice hall to collect her when it became clear that she had not understood that she was being asked to leave the school—*forever*. She was walked out in a hush; her childhood dreams of being a prima ballerina who would headline at the Bolshoi were over and would not live another day.

She'd gone home to her parents' apartment and stared at herself in a large mirror, trying to see what was wrong with her neck, examining it from every possible angle. Then she'd broken down and cried in the bathroom, with its high ceilings and prewar fixtures. She'd tried to choke herself an hour later. She'd wanted to break the neck that was the cause of her problems and sudden misery. She was never the same afterwards—everyone agreed that her spirit had been broken. You could see it in her eyes.

She'd become, by seventeen, unstable, anorexic, and dysmorphic; hesitant sometimes to go to school, hesitant to eat, hesitant to even speak. She would spend hours in her room examining herself for other "flaws" that she'd missed and that she was sure would come to the fore and create problems for her. What she began to see in the mirror was a monster—the reflection of a hideously deformed monkey. Her mother kept a canary in a cage in their kitchen. Anna would take it out when her parents were gone to work; her mother was a doctor. She would follow the bird around the apartment. It would hop innocently about the room, its green and yellow wings clipped, unable to fly. She finally killed it by smothering it with a towel while telling it that it was flawed and must be destroyed for its own good. She'd clasped it to her chest while wearing toe shoes and doing spins while holding the dead bird. Anna was enrolled in a top school were she did well academically but failed socially despite her great beauty, which ironically only intensified through her adolescence. Her father, desperate to help her after she graduated with a degree in English from the University of Moscow, got her a job at KGB headquarters at the Lubyanka because of his pull. He'd been a hero in the "Great Patriotic War"—a famous tank commander in the battle of Kursk—and he was greatly respected throughout the entire country. He was, in fact, third-in-command of a secret army that was organized to protect the Kremlin in case of social unrest. He'd become a personal friend of Khrushchev's as a result. They often played racquetball together in the Kremlin's underground gym.

Anna's psychological problems, and her visits to a sanitarium on the Black Sea while she was still at university, were kept out of her KGB application, nor did they come up during a cursory interview with KGB recruiters. Her father simply lied for her, walking into the interview to "check in and to see how things are going." She was hired on the spot and taught to type, as well as the use of intricate procedures for cabling top secret communications. Coded messages were the backbone of the KGB's extensive communications networks around the globe, and a very important job. Because of her intelligence and ability to type ninety-five words a minute, she was sent first to the KGB's Budapest Station to work in a sealed-off room with twelve other young women who sorted files, typed top secret reports and ran the cable traffic for the KGB's Eastern European operations. Her father expected that she would marry soon, and that his daughter would leave the KGB and become a house-wife and things with her would return to normal. Somehow her father believed that motherhood could cure her psychological problems. But she refused to date, despite most of the men at the embassy constantly trying to seduce her.

The Budapest Station had been, since the end of the war, one of the KGB's largest posts. It was there that she first came across what she called "the problem." A file concerning an ex-Nazi scientist who had been sent from Germany immediately after the war to the USSR—a highly-sought-after war criminal's file—had gone missing and she had been blamed for its disappearance. There were rumors about her erratic behavior, and people gossiped about her love of foreign films, especially the French "New Wave." She was arrested and returned to Moscow. It was only because of the direct intervention of her panicked father that Anna was saved from being summarily shot after a kangaroo-trial conducted inside Lubyanka prison. The prosecutor had called her a traitor to the Revolution and "a girl with petty bourgeois tendencies, unfit to work for the Motherland in any capacity, let alone do top secret work as part of the KGB." The Nazi scientist's file was "found"—it had been locked inside another desk in the Budapest station's cable room by a new girl, who had reported the situation immediately to Anna's father—she'd known through the grapevine who he was—and helped saved Anna's life at the eleventh hour. All was forgiven. As a "recompense" to make up for what she'd been put through, Anna was allowed a trip to London, and a sum of money to spend there however she chose to. But the trip didn't make her forget what had just almost happened to her, and for no real reason whatsoever. She had been just one hour away from execution and, because of her previous mental condition, the experience had oddly cleared her mind, which she realized then had been befuddled, to a greater or lesser extent, since the day she'd been ousted from the school. On the cusp of death, she'd found herself again. She saw her country clearly for the first time—it was merely a giant gulag full of frightened sheep waiting for their next order from above. She was certain that the file had been taken from her locked desk by someone in authority at the embassy who had forgotten to return it and then had blamed her *simply because they could*. She told her father her opinion and analysis about what had really happened to the file, but he told her to not mention it, just to try and get along, saying that mistakes happened even in the KGB. He secretly believed that his daughter *was* to blame for the missing file, and was terrified that she was losing her mind. She finally went back to her job in Budapest, with her salary having been substantially increased. She swore to herself that she would get even with her superiors at the embassy for what had happened to her. *And* that she would defect to the West the moment it was possible. She would not die in Russia. She would get to the West and freedom, which she believed really existed there after having been to London; a place that had seemed to her like Paradise Attained.

When a colleague of Malcolm's in the American Embassy first saw Anna Maximovna's photo, he had said she was "Love's Young Dream." Another man on the CIA's team running her described her as "a fucking sexy Amazon," which might have been crude, but was more accurate. The surveillance photo showed that Anna Maximovna was a very pale blond; tall and thin; twenty-two years old; very pretty, narrow-waisted—some might say "boyish," in that respect, but still very feminine. She had small breasts and very long legs. What the photo couldn't show was that, like her father, she was very strong physically. The day she came to meet her case officer, she was wearing nylons and a teal mini-skirt that set off her crystal blue eyes to stunning effect.

She was sitting across from Malcolm Law in a second-class hotel room near the Archeological Museum. The Russian girl's hair was long and parted in the middle because she'd seen a photo of Marianne Faithful while in London and had been impressed with the singer's hair-style. She'd spent a great deal of time on her hair that morning, getting it just right before leaving her apartment. She'd become an anglophile in most things.

This was the second time they'd met. Malcolm thought she was fairly complex for a Russian, as he'd come to think of most Slavs—he'd come to know many Slavs quite well during the War—as an intelligent and a pragmatic race in general, but blunt and usually very aggressive, like their new Katyuasha rockets. He was one of the few in the CIA who had gotten to know the Slavic culture in any depth, and he even spoke some Russian. They made good wrestlers, spies, frontline soldiers, and classical musicians. *And they have some very, very beautiful women*, he thought, looking at the girl—*the kind that you find yourself staring at whether you want to or not.*

He knew, too, that they—the Russians—didn't like to be crossed. Malcolm had learned that in Asia, during the time that he'd been battling the KGB across several countries there, from Japan to Australia, for the past five years. They would come after you *personally* if they thought you needed to be taught a lesson, or if you'd broken the rules both sides usually lived by. A CIA officer who had tried to recruit a KGB officer's young and very pregnant wife had been found with his head submerged in a shit-filled toilet in a Bangkok apartment with a view of the river. The water from the toilet had over-flowed for two days around his bent-like-a-paperclip dead body. Everyone at the embassy got the message—"Don't fuck with their wives." And after that, they didn't.

This particular Russian girl, named Anna, struck him as different somehow from the first time he'd interviewed her at the Sanborns on *Benito Juarez*. She'd been sent to him via another important female agent the CIA had recruited from inside the KGB: a blowzy fifty-something woman who'd had the temerity to walk into the U.S. Consular office in Lyon, France wearing rouge and a heavy coat. The woman had plopped herself down in front of a young man fresh from St. Louis and said— clutching her black handbag as if she thought it might be stolen—"I want to talk to someone from spies," very matter-of-factly. The woman, Cerenia Kalakova, had been born in Hungary and had supported the 1956 uprising, and was very angry at the Russians for interfering in her country's internal affairs. It turned out that she was the personal secretary to the head of the KGB in Paris, and all the alarm bells went off at once. They'd had to get her out of the Consulate in Lyon immediately, and had hustled her off to a safe-house in Madrid until they could determine that the woman was *bona fide*; then they'd rushed her back to Paris—all during her three days' off. She began recruiting for the CIA amongst the clerical staff at each embassy her boss was moved to. Kalakova had been moved twice, and was now in charge of all the clerical staff at the KGB's Mexico City station, which was technically a *Pravda* bureau. As was the case in the CIA, newspapers—like the *New York Times* or *Pravda*—were merely covers, with their "correspondents" more often than not actually spies.

Malcolm had been moved from Southeast Asia to London the year before. It had been decided that the London Embassy's Russian Desk, which was expanding along with the Cold War, was a necessary stop for all CIA officers who were expected to go on into high positions. London was a make-it-or-break-it assignment; fail there and everyone back in Washington would know it. Malcolm was expected to go all the way, now, and he wasn't even forty yet. He had the perfect pedigree: a war hero and the son of one of the richest men in America, who was an important contributor to the Republican Party. On top of it all he was engaged to: the daughter of a Democratic Senator who was a plutocrat from a Virginia tobacco-farming dynasty, who'd voted against the Civil Rights Act and was constantly bragging about it to the press. Malcolm's soon-to-be father-in-law was Chairman of the Armed Services Committee, the most important post in the entire Congress according to the insiders, because that's where the *real* money was handed out to American corporations that made war matériel.

"Are you hungry?" Malcolm asked.

"Why?" Anna said.

"I just thought you might be; it's two in the afternoon, after all," Malcolm said, "and I was late. I'm sorry."

"Yes? I think so," the girl said, smiling slightly. They were quiet for a moment. The funky motel room resonated with the sounds of the afternoon traffic outside.

"Okay, we can go out. ... Do you have something, Anna ... *special* for me? Is that why you're so nervous. ... Is that it?" Malcolm asked the girl. She was obviously keyed-up; he could tell from his experiences with the hundreds of agents he'd worked with in the past. The girl's blue eyes were easy to read. People, when they betray their country, can sometimes change very suddenly, he knew, become paranoid, or just the opposite: feel all-powerful, invincible. Sometimes both states happened in the space of a single interview.

It was warm in the city, and he'd taken off his white seersucker sport coat and had laid it on the couch next to him, as the Russian girl closely watched him. She had been promised escape to the West in exchange for spying. She wanted to go to Los Angeles after her work for them was finished. They'd promised her a job and an apartment there. She was a small victory in a noisy and dangerous capital city that was at the heart of an economically-booming Mexico. The Russians were working Mexico hard because Mexican politicians were notoriously corrupt and hence easy targets. The idea was that if Mexico could be brought into the socialist camp America would be profoundly embarrassed, and even feel threatened. Mexico was a big prize and a very high priority for both sides in the Cold War.

Anna Maximovna had received an envelope every week with a thousand dollars in it in exchange for specific information provided to her handlers. A month ago, Malcolm had been added to the team that was "working" Anna. Since they'd first met he'd been haunted by her vulnerability and youthful beauty. Today, while riding up to the hotel room in the confined old-fashioned elevator to meet her, he had admitted to himself, finally, that he was attracted to the Russian girl sexually. Sitting across from her now, he felt suddenly guilty as well: he knew that the KGB would eventually discover she was betraying them and arrest her. His team had discussed that very possibility that morning over coffee. But the men had decided, nonetheless, to press on with turning Anna. It was, Malcolm knew, a callous decision; and he'd help make it.

He felt that the sexual attraction was mutual, too; that, or she was a very good actress. There had been something about the way she'd glanced at him when she'd opened the door to the room. Standing there at the door, Anna had smiled at him in a knowing way, as if they were already lovers. They had reached a kind of unspoken intimacy now, all of it communicated during the long silences, and unguarded looks that had passed between them during their meetings in this very hotel room.

If she were caught, her life expectancy would be very short indeed. She knew that, and so did he. She'd been turned by Cerenia Kalakova, who had made a point of targeting Anna because of her strange behavior and aloofness from the rest of the staff.

"Yes. Yes," she said.

"They have something like an Automat nearby; we could go there? ..." Malcolm suggested in English, which Anna spoke very well.

"What is an Automat?" Anna asked. He smiled. He was sitting in a big club-chair on the other side of the spacious hotel room that had a slight, old cigarette-smell to it.

"It's a restaurant with little cubby-holes, and you pull out what you want to eat from them. There's a famous one in New York." She shook her head as if the idea was silly, and then she smiled. It was a half-smile, as if she had something else entirely on her mind.

"No. No, I don't ... I don't understand." She smiled again, more broadly this time, and he let it go. He saw how beautiful she was when she smiled. "They've set out to find a man," Anna said. "Someone they want who's passing through the city ... a German scientist. I think they want to kill him. I just typed-up the orders that came from Moscow by cable. There were three copies: one was sent to the head of station—Cerenia Kalakova's boss. Another one went to the hunters, who're at a desk in the Embassy that is designed to spy on us, the Russian employees. But they are also trained to find people in foreign countries if necessary. The third one, and this is the one that I came to tell you about, was to be cabled to the GDR. I didn't understand why we would be sending a copy of an order to anyone in the GDR. This is unusual. It would normally have been sent from Moscow Center, and never from a station, like us."

"Do you have a name? The officer to whom it was sent to in the GDR?" Malcolm said.

"Yes; the officer there is called Colonel Heinz Beck. It was to go directly to him, and was for his eyes only," she said. There was something about the girl's posture that excited him: she sat so ram-rod straight, *like a soldier,* Malcolm thought.

"... Are you going to be my case officer?" she asked. "I don't want to be handed-off to somebody else—I feel comfortable with you."

"You won't be handed-off; I promise you." That was a straight-out lie. He knew he was scheduled to return to Washington in another week and then he'd be assigned to oversee the South Vietnam desk at Langley. It was a big promotion. He'd come to Mexico to help get the German scientist, who'd somehow managed to escape from a lab in Moscow, safely into the United States. He'd known the man personally, having interviewed him once at a Red Cross station immediately after the War. It was actually *the* specific reason he'd been sent to Mexico. Interviewing the girl was something that had been suggested once he'd arrived in Mexico.

"... Are you married?" Anna asked.

"No," he said, sticking to a practiced script. He'd been trained to answer all personal questions with a lie, but to remember the lies consistently and use a well-rehearsed cover-story. In this case, for Anna, he was Peter Buck and was from San Jose, California. He had gone to UCLA. Peter Buck was recently engaged, not married. Using this methodology, he could share intimacies with an agent, and hopefully not get caught-out by some little detail wrongly-remembered from the false life that he was "sharing" with the agent. He could converse about the normal things people do; talk about their families, etc, and further seduce the would-be spy so that they believed their case officer was also their friend. They were *never* in reality their "friend," but rather it was more like the relationship a prostitute has with her pimp. It could and would turn ugly if it needed to, to get the job done. But, in exchange for *complete* obedience and loyalty, they would be protected and paid.

"Why?"

"My career," Malcolm said.

"Are there no attractive women, then, in America?" she asked from across the room.

"Yes. Several million." He smiled. He had been in the hotel with her only fifteen minutes at that point. They had each come separately to the room. Each had ridden the rickety elevator up alone. Each had gone down the long quiet hallway and used an old fashion heavy key to open the door to the room.

"Are they all film stars, then?" She was joking, now; it was the first time he'd seen her smile in a natural, unselfconscious way. She folded her hands on her skirt. She had very pretty legs, he thought. She was twenty-two, he was thirty-eight. He'd been seeing a girl from a rich Mexican family and having sex with her on a regular basis, usually at her apartment. They were Spaniards; her father had made his fortune in the bread business, of all things. She'd recently divorced her bullfighter husband, and had two children that were spoiled rotten, and that he couldn't stand to be in the same room with. They had met at a party thrown by her father. He didn't really *like* the girl or her brats, but she had an incredible body, and he'd chased her. He liked this *Russian* girl, though, already. She had an inner calm that was mysteriously attractive; that, coupled with her incredible beauty, of course, was extremely seductive. He'd wondered if the Russian girl could, somehow, revive his own youthful innocence just by being girlish and profoundly quiescent.

Recently, he'd been questioning his own marriage choice. His fiancé—he was engaged and the wedding had been scheduled—was a distant and uninteresting young woman from his class, a Sarah Lawrence girl, who had ticked off all the right boxes. But, like so many people from the upper classes, he had sensed a great void in her personality. When he tried to describe his wartime experiences to her—and how they had changed him—she would be completely at sea. She was certainly pretty, and typically *always* happy. Sex, too, he realized, was something she seemed to prescribe for them, as part of her version of the Love Dream, but not really *need*, the way he did. He'd known too many women during the war that were like himself—using sex to escape to some other place—so his fiancé paled in comparison there, too. He was surprised himself and confessed to himself one morning while shaving that she was useless in *everyway*.

"Are you able to send any money home?" he asked.

"No," she said quickly. "Of course not. How could I? My father is a general. Russia is not *free*. I work for the KGB. They would know at once if I did anything like that— don't be ridiculous. Do you like me?"

"Yes," he said. He was careful with the tone of his voice. But he couldn't help himself in answering her truthfully.

"Would you consider sleeping with me?" she asked.

"Yes. Of course," he said automatically. She'd asked the question as if it might be a hardship for him.

"I don't think I'm going to live very long—do you?" she said. Her question sent a chill through him; as if a window had been left open in the middle of Winter. But this was Mexico City in June, and it was very warm out. "I won't ever see Los Angeles. ... Is it beautiful?"

"No. ... The beaches, maybe. But they've ruined it with too many cars," he said. "Why do you say that?"

"Because I saw a girl dragged away once in my apartment building. We all have to live in the same apartment building, once you come to work for the KGB. It's because it's bugged so completely. Even the showers, and where you ... " she bit her lip. "I'm afraid they're going to find out I've betrayed them and kill me." She suddenly burst into tears, and sat there with her head lowered, sobbing uncontrollably.

He stood up and walked over and sat next to her, and she put her head on his shoulder like a school girl. There is a moment when good spies take the initiative and when ordinary people give comfort. He was a spy to the bone, so he used the moment, holding her against him, the smell of her hair very lush and womanly. He knew that even this "seduction" would be used against her, and yet he felt guilty now, for the first time since he'd started thinking about sleeping with her. Had she somehow returned something he'd lost about himself? Something younger, something he'd had in him before the War? *A desire to be happy, maybe?* The War had taken that from him, utterly. His six weeks at Dachau had robbed him of it, and it had never come back in the intervening years. He'd gone cold; emotionally cold, and he hadn't even really realized it, or missed it; he never thought about it, in fact. The war had killed part of him off.

"Is there something about this man that makes you afraid—the scientist, I mean?"

"They want him very badly. The head of station is very angry that he escaped and he knows that if he doesn't capture him and get him back, he'll probably be shot. Everyone is scared in our section, right now." She kissed him then, and he kissed her back. It was a tentative kiss at first—*not the kiss of a vamp or a whore*, he thought. He'd had plenty of those in Vietnam and Thailand. They were always too big and too forward and too eager to get to the scheduled transaction. Not this one. This one was an offer of love, and somehow a chaste kind of love at that. An offering of purity and intense intimacy—a real giving. *Venus would arrive*, he thought.

"Will they shoot you if you fail?" she asked. Her arms were around his neck as she asked him that question.

"No," he said. "No, of course not. This is the *West*. ... We don't do that kind of thing." She looked at him a long time, then, as if he might be lying. She unbuttoned his shirt, starting with the tie, pulling the knot gently back and forth to loosen it, all the while looking at him, taking him over so that he was looking into her eyes, connecting with her, the woman-girl who he'd only met a few times before, casually, really; just four times, in point of fact. She'd been so frightened at her first interview, they'd had to call a doctor in to give her something to calm her down so they could talk halfway normally.

"Will you protect me? Could I go to America? I want to be a wife. Maybe yours? I'm pretty—aren't I? I could be a wife there ... I speak English. I'd speak it better if I practiced more."

"Of course you can, and you will ... " There was something about her tone of desperation that was scary and disturbing to him. She held his hand and kissed it, kissing each of the fingers in turn, brushing her lips against them. He saw the part in her hair; how straight it was as she lowered her head. He watched her unbutton his shirt, and tried to protect himself from feeling too much. It was always better if you didn't. He'd heard women talk like that during the war, when they would pass through villages with the partisans. Woman offered themselves in order to go with the soldiers, afraid of what would happen when the SS came back to their village. Some women were taken along; the unlucky ones were not. She lifted the shirt away from his chest and kissed his neck near his Adam's apple. *He'd entered villages where every woman and child had been shot to death by the Germans and left to rot in the snow.*

"I've thought about you, you know," she said. "I know you are a good man. Kind. A kind man," Anna said. He knew himself that he was no longer kind *or* good.

He heard a car horn blare through an open window. The sound drilled through him. They were on the fourth-floor of the hotel, in a corner room that they'd used once before. He saw her unfasten his belt buckle and then zip down his zipper. He heard it as she pulled it down—a "plastic" sound. The hotel was in San Angel. It was a tony part of the city, green and leafy and lush, with wide, tree-lined *avenidas*, from another, much more elegant, era. They were the wide streets of the well-to-do. It was a CIA hotel, actually owned by a front company of the Agency. Counter-intelligence ran bug checks there frequently. Everyone who worked at the place had to pass a strict background check. Many had been brought in from the States. Even the restaurant staff was run by the Agency. He was uneasy that that his superiors could receive dirty black and white photos of him fucking this girl ... her blowing him, or whatever else they did to each other. Which, by the time she'd unbuttoned his shirt, he knew he was powerless to stop, or even had the least desire to stop, despite any consequences. He felt her kissing his stomach.

Suddenly something let go inside of him—whatever the last vestige of foolish concern for his career that had been holding him back— broken down by lust—and he went for everything he wanted. It was as if she'd unchained a wild dog searching for something.

The rest was a blur; an entire day spent in that hotel room exploring each other, until he knew her *completely*. She was the prettiest girl he'd ever been with. And yet, she never lost that innocence, and it seemed to him as if she were doing it all for the very first time. And, in fact, she was. But *he* didn't know that, and never would. He would never know that it was the great gift she had not given to anyone before him. She'd only had sex once before, raped in the Lubyanka by a guard never telling anyone even her father. When they went out very late that night, she made him stop in the lobby. The street outside was pitch-dark, and the intimate small lobby was totally quiet.

"I never sent that cable to the GDR. They'll know about that soon. They'll find out," She said.

"I need to know if they suspect the scientist is here ... in the city ... the man they're looking for. Can you find out Anna?"

"Yes," she said. "I think so—yes. ... I love you. I'll do anything for you," She said.

21

1965 ■ MEXICO CITY

"They're looking for me. ... my own people. And I've got a leak, somewhere. Quite a bad one," Malcolm said. He was standing up and looking out the office window of the British Embassy's eighth floor. "You know that part, I suspect. What you don't know is that they've sent out the hunters for me. *Langley* has, that is. I'm to be arrested immediately for not reporting the whereabouts of my scientist—L21."

"Is that his code name? Your scientist's?" the man behind the desk asked, smiling.

"Yes, George, it is." Malcolm turned around. "It's the one he was given when he contacted us. I shouldn't tell *you* that, of course, but now you know. You should also know that I've hidden him and I'm not telling anyone where he is until I get him somewhere safe. And there's a girl ... a Russian girl who's in danger because she's an agent of mine. And it's *complicated* with her. ... I slept with her today, in fact."

"I see," George said. George had been a captain in the SAS in Burma and had fought with the famous Chindits—operating behind the Japanese lines—commanded by Orde Wingate and lived to tell about it. He knew Mary Keen's brother, who had *not* come back from Burma alive. George had first met Malcolm in Mary Keen's apartment in London before she was married. Neither one knew the other was a spook until they met in Hong Kong five years later and were presented to each other at the American Embassy.

"I've got no choice, George. *Do* I? ... If I hadn't gone doggo and reported his whereabouts, then the Russian's were sure to have heard about it and snapped him up. Someone there at Langley has gone over to the other side you see; someone in the chain of command. I've got an idea about who it might be, but I'm not sure yet. It *could* be from some other source, even—I can't totally rule out that possibility, yet. In the meantime, I'm in trouble and my career is now in flames."

"And I thought *we* were bad ... the nancy boys spilling the beans to the Russians and all," George said from behind his big and very orderly desk.

"If I can just get him to the States. ... He should be safe there. I'll deal with the political problems afterwards. But I need your help. You're the only one I can trust right now, here in Mexico. I can't go back to my embassy right now."

208

"Yes, I know. Well, they contacted us today and said not to communicate with you if you should show up here. Seems your lot is quite angry with you. Want you shot on sight, that kind of thing. Where is he now? Your boy?"

"I've got him here in the City. I'm waiting to see if it's safe to move him. I doubt that it is, right now. The KGB have been turning over our hiding places, one after another—that's why I know there's a leak. Some of the safe houses, even. They want this guy back in the worst way. Anyway, George, old boy, can you help me get him out of the city?"

"There's a man in jail here who's connected to the Sicilian mafia. He's what we call 'qualified,'" George said.

"You're joking," Malcolm said.

"Not in the least, old man," George said. "You wanted our help. We don't normally use kindergarten teachers."

"A drug dealer, eh?" Malcolm said.

"... Heroin. He's a conduit for it into the States. He's quite an expert at it, really. 'Belgrade Jack,' we call him."

"And you want *my* Russian scientist to be handed over to someone in jail here?"

"It's an idea, anyway. I can't very well call London and ask them for help, can I? You and I are on our own with this one, I suppose. Our man called us yesterday; he's been picked up here in the city. It seems he shot two men who had tried to kill him at his hotel. It's all part of some kerfuffle back there in Palermo."

"You trust him?"

"Of course not. But from what I've heard from my friends in Rome—unofficially, mind you—he's very good at moving anything you want moved without the authorities getting wind of it."

"What's his real name?"

"Delmonico, Sonny. He's very well known to us. I called London about him and they said to spring him if at all possible, as he's a friend. So, there. Ready-made."

George looked at him. He was what his former English girlfriend Mary had once called a "bounder." He had more lovers in London than there were taxis, she'd said. He wasn't handsome, but women almost always noticed him, and liked to be in his presence. He was not the bureaucrat type at all. And, as MI6 became more and more like the Foreign Service, he was finding it harder and harder to exist in a job that was being overrun by accountant-types.

"Would you like to meet him? See if you two can strike a deal? All on the qt, of course," George said.

"What can *I* offer *him*?"

"Don't worry about that. I'll scare the piss out of him. I have the other parties'

209

phone numbers that are looking for him," George smiled again.

"I see."

"Yes. Never trust the English, old man—we're a shifty lot. Believe me. He's a nancy boy, our man Delmonico is; at the head of the line, apparently. He once lost an eye by asking the wrong question of an American sailor, I believe."

"I don't care about that," Malcolm said. "Let's go meet him, then."

They had to wait for Sonny Delmonico to be brought out of his cell and to a low shed that was used for conjugal visits and interrogations, and to arrange bribes. There was a semen-stained mattress and a window just above head-level covered with wire mesh. George and he both had taken off their ties and jackets because the shed was stuffy and cloyingly sweet-smelling, like a cheap brothel. They'd been talking about the Eastern Front, with Malcolm describing his fighting experiences to him. How they'd all had to learn to use German weapons because the partisans had no others. How they'd come upon whole villages that had been razed, the occupants slaughtered wholesale by marauding German troops that were terrified of the partisans. George had listened attentively. Malcolm could only tell his war stories to fellow soldiers like George. That was the main reason they'd gotten on so well in London and become good friends.

"Have you seen Mary?" George asked, while they waited for Delmonico to be brought in "... Since she got married to Lord Asshole, I mean?"

"No."

"*I've* seen her. She even asked about *you*, specifically," George said. "They passed through here not too long ago. She's with child. Can you even *imagine* that? Our Mary a mother?" It hurt him to hear she was pregnant, because that meant there was little chance, now, that she would ever leave her husband.

"He's a shit—her husband, of course. ... Silver spoon shoved up his arse so far you'd never be able to find the handle," George said.

"I never met him," Malcolm said.

"I don't think she loves him. I always thought she was in love with you," George said.

"Then why did she marry *him,* for God's sake!?"

"Money, I suppose. I never thought of Mary as the gold-digger type before, though. But if it wears a skirt it's a mystery to me," George said, and ground-out his cigarette on a piece of tin foil. "I suppose you were in love with *her,* too. There's our man." The door had opened, and a slightly overweight man in his early forties, wearing an eye-patch, a dirty white suit, and badly in need of shave, was standing in the doorway.

His hands were manacled in front of him, and a grubby-looking prison guard was standing behind him.

"Is this the club bar, then, gents?" Delmonico asked. "It's been days since I've spoken the mother-tongue. Seems like all they do here is speak in grunts." His jacket was stained in front where a fellow prisoner had thrown some kind of bean gruel on him. It also looked like he'd been shit on.

"Come on in, then," George said. "*Gracias. Por favor, amigo, quítele las esposas.*" George ordered the guard, speaking in Spanish, to unlock the man's manacles. Delmonico smiled as his hands were freed.

"I can't recommend the place, really," Sonny said as they were unlocked. "It's the waiters. ..." He smiled as if he didn't have a care in the world. The guard closed the door behind him. He walked into the room with short little hopping steps, and they both noticed that his legs were shackled in old fashioned leg-irons, which it then became obvious to them was the reason that the guard had been unarmed. Delmonico been hobbled more or less like a horse. He couldn't have actually *run* two feet without falling flat on his face.

"Well ... we meet. I'm Mr. Jefferies, and this is my friend, Mr. Long," George said.

"I hope you're from Her Majesty's government?" Sonny said.

"We are," George said.

"Excellent. May I sit down, then? It's been difficult standing so long with all this jewelry on—we dress for dinner here, you know," Sonny said.

"Of course, old boy. Make yourself comfortable," George said, smiling. He was much more comfortable with Sonny's type than with his own bosses.

"You can call me Sonny." Sonny turned to look at Malcolm, trying to gauge him. He smiled, then hopped to the table. Malcolm stood and gave him his chair, then went and stood himself by the camp-cot. Their was a filthy mattress on top of the cot which had been ruined by an ugly charred-black hole where someone had left a cigarette burning after their connubial bliss had been consummated with one of the local girls that worked the prison.

"Well, Sonny it is. ... Here you are, then," George said.

"Yes, sir; here I am."

"I'm afraid the Mexicans don't like you right now. You've shot two men. Fortunately for you they were only visitors to this fair country. Italian citizens, in fact, it seems. One ... " George opened the file he'd brought with him, "... Lugia Bagaballia, and a Mr. Enrico Stenso. Is that true?"

"Sicilians, sir. Hardly the same thing as *real* Italians." Sonny smiled tightly. "Might I have a fag, sir?" Malcolm gave him a cigarette that he fished out of the pocket of his jacket, which was hanging over the back of the chair in front of him.

211

Sonny looked up at him.

"Are we American, sir? ... Marlboros ... I just thought ..." Malcolm took his pack out of his coat pocket and slipped it into Delmonico's.

"And what *is* it you want us to do about your troubles, Sonny?" George asked.

"Well, Governor, I was hoping you might have a word with the authorities on my behalf. Tell them I've done work for Her Majesty and that I was a war hero and all that."

"A *war* hero?" George said.

"Yes, sir; I got the Cross for doing my bit at Anzio. Taking out a German tank seems to have helped quite a bit."

"*Really?* ... I say. Well, *Sonny.* ... Bravo," George said.

"Also, sir, the two men had been sent to kill *me*, sir. An honest subject of the Queen, I am."

"Self defense was it, Sonny?" George said.

"Yes, sir. Most definitely self defense."

"They say you went up to the men's room—at the *Hotel Presidente*, no less—and shot them dead with a shotgun in their beds as they slept. I hardly call that 'self defense,'" George said. Malcolm saw that Sonny and George were really basically the same kind of men. Both had become first-rate killers during the war and had found it hard to go back to being "normal" men afterwards. They recognized that in each other the moment the door opened—and something else, too, perhaps. There were rumors about George in London regarding his not being picky about who he slept with, gender-wise. Mary had dropped a hint that George was what she called a "typical public-school boy and a sexual rogue-elephant."

"I was trying to reason with them, but they wouldn't have it," Sonny said, drawing hard on the cigarette. Malcolm burst out laughing. It was strange. Perhaps it was all the tension around this meeting, as he saw now that he could be arrested himself, and perhaps brought to this very place if he *were* caught. And he knew that it was probably only a matter of hours, not really days, before he would be found.

"Is there something funny, sir?" Sonny turned his hand holding the cigarette.

"No. ... No, I'm sorry. It's just that I was told they were both shot while they were sleeping," Malcolm said. "Sorry."

"No, sir. That's not true. ... I woke them up when I came in." Sonny winked. "In my world, it's dog eat dog, I'm afraid."

"Well, old man, we've a proposition for you," George said.

"A proposition, sir. From the Crown? I'm the first to fight for the Queen, sir."

"Listen here," George said. "My friend here, Mr. Long, has someone he wants to end up in the States, but the man doesn't have a passport and doesn't have time to wait for one. We were wondering if you could get him across?"

"Into the United States, sir?"

"Yes, that's the idea."

"Well, sir, that's my specialty. Moving things about and all."

"Then you'll do it? Of course, we'll clean this mess up, here; have you released."

"Thank you, sir. Of course. Any help I can give to our American friends."

"If you fuck it up, Delmonico, I'll take your other eye," Malcolm said, walking up behind him. "Just so there's no misunderstanding, here."

"... Is it just the one man, sir?" Sonny ignored the threat, which seemed very pedestrian and totally predictable to him.

"Yes," Malcolm said. "Just the one."

"... Shouldn't be a problem at all, sir. How much longer do you think I'll have to stay here?" Sonny asked.

"It shouldn't be long. We should have you out by dinner time," George said.

"Well, there's always a silver lining, isn't there ... sir," Sonny said. He looked at Malcolm with a long gaze. "... Fancy a fag, sir?"

"*What?*" Malcolm said.

"I thought you might like one ... A *fag*," Sonny said, and then smiled. George looked at Malcolm and burst out laughing.

"Our American friend here shops at the other store," George said.

213

22

1965 ■ MEXICO CITY

"You are Anna Maximovna?" The young KGB officer was questioning her from behind his cluttered desk. "... Sit down, please."

"Yes, comrade." Anna looked around the small office as she took a chair across from him; there were stacks of *International Herald Tribune*s as well as *The News*, an English-language newspaper published in Mexico that was funded covertly by Radio Free Europe, a propaganda arm of the U.S. State Department. There were assorted Mexican dailies, too; the newspapers and magazines stacked between old Styrofoam cups of cold coffee that hadn't been cleared away yet. The coffee cups all had iridescent oil slicks on the top that reflected the overhead lights.

"You say your *father* sent you?" Zaytsev asked, either feigning or actually surprised.

"Yes," Anna said.

"Your father is the famous General Maximov?"

"Yes. My father said that I should take this information directly to you. We spoke on the phone. He remembered your name from the academy," Anna lied.

"I don't understand," Vlad Zaytsev said. It was a Sunday afternoon, late, and Anna had walked into the *Pravda* offices in Mexico City. They were in a two-storey building which served a variety of functions. The Central Committee of the Communist Party of Mexico used the building, as did its newspaper. The Party's newspaper was funded directly by the USSR. The KGB had total control of the paper's international content, because the paper used *Pravda* much as U.S. newspapers used the AP. Both wire services were used by their respective intelligence services to leak stories into the mainstream press that were either "black," or more or less true, but part of some larger disinformation campaign. The difference was that everyone expected it from *Pravda*'s wire service, but not from the AP, which made the AP's propaganda much more effective. Or so most of the people running the larger show thought, anyway. Of course, the AP stories were carried in hundreds of newspapers around the globe just because it *was* an *American* wire service, and hence thought to be somehow intrinsically "better" than other countries'—in that respect, the U.S. propaganda machine was currently winning the "war of words" between East and West.

"Please explain," Vlad Zaytsev said. He looked at her with cold blue eyes. He was only twenty-eight, but was rising fast in the KGB, having recently come to Mexico from Cuba. It was rumored that he was in charge of counter-intelligence at the Embassy. He happened to be in the office that Sunday only because his West German girlfriend from Berlin, who was studying at the Cuernavaca Language School, had been hit by a motorcycle in a crosswalk and had been hospitalized as a result. Her leg had been broken and she'd been sent to the American hospital—known to be the best in Mexico City. As a KGB officer, Zaytsev couldn't be seen in the place, as it was also used by all the American Embassy officials and their employees. So, very much to his chagrin, he'd been forced to stay away—not even being able to call the girl on the phone.

"I wanted to report this," Anna said. She handed him the cable from Moscow that she'd been asked to forward to the GDR. She looked at the young KGB officer, who her father had in fact never mentioned to her before. She knew his name because she'd forwarded coded cables from the Embassy to his attention here at *Pravda's* offices. She was taking a risk, she knew—a very great one, in fact—but the plan had come to her as she walked the streets back to the Embassy after her tryst with Malcolm. It was, she'd thought, the only way to do what Malcolm had asked of her within the short time-frame he'd allotted for the job. She expected to be arrested at any moment, but was now in a state of mind where she was no longer frightened by the prospect of arrest, or even death.

She watched the young man read the cable. His hair was blond with dirty brown streaks in it. He read carefully, holding the paper directly in front of his face, with his elbows resting propped up on the desk. He was wearing a sharp powder-blue suit with narrow lapels and no tie—very *au courant*.

"I've sent a coded copy to you, of course," Anna said when he'd stopped reading.

"Yes." Zaytsev looked at her. "I still don't understand, comrade. ..."

"My father said that there might be people in the KGB that are acting independently of the Party, and if I was to find any document that supported this, I should bring it to you *immediately*. My father has been following your career comrade. ... and so have I," she said, as if she were part of some top-secret cabal herself. "I understand that the man you're seeking is an important scientist and that the operation to arrest him is top secret."

"Yes. I'm glad you've come to me," Zaytsev said. He looked at the attractive girl. She was stone beautiful, and reminded him of the American film actress Lauren Bacall. He had noticed her working in the Embassy building. All the men working at the Embassy, young *or* old, knew her name—for several reasons it had flown at the speed of light through the building as soon as she'd arrived. Her father was a hero and

215

famous KGB general, and also a personal friend of Nikita Khrushchev's. And, she was one of the prettiest girls any of them had ever seen in their lives. It was well known at the embassy that she'd once been within minutes of execution at the Lubyanka for a KGB mistake. If it hadn't been for her father's call to Khrushchev she'd have been executed and the truth about the affair swept under the rug. Khrushchev had gone to the Lubyanka himself to make inquires into the case—a first, as far as anybody in the KGB knew.

"I studied under your father at the Academy," Zaytsev said. "I was very sorry to hear about what happened to you ... a terrible mistake," he said.

"Mistakes sometimes happen," Anna said.

"Yes. Unfortunately, they do," Zaytsev said.

"Have you found your scientist?" She asked it in a way that she hoped would be judged as ordinary professional curiosity.

"I'm sorry ... I can't say," Zaytsev said.

"I understand," Anna said.

"I found the request to forward this cable to this certain person at Stasi headquarters highly unusual," Anna said.

"I understand." He was staring at her now, and she told herself to meet his intense look evenly. *Make eye contact.*

"I haven't read it," she said, after a moment of uncomfortable silence.

"I see."

"I don't want to be sent to Lubyanka a second time," she said firmly. She was sitting with her hands folded in her lap. Her father had once told her what the trained KGB officer looked for when interviewing a prisoner: there were body cues he'd once explained to her playfully at the dinner table. Hands in the lap was a position signaling emotional neutrality. Palms held up—fingers clenched—indicated a good possibility that the interviewee was lying through his teeth. Any covering up of the face—no matter how fleeting, was a sure sign the prisoner was lying. The lowering of the head onto the hands was a proven sign of guilt, or submission. These were general "rules," but one could usually go on them, unless one was dealing with a highly trained agent.

"I understand," Zaytsev said. "I will look into it."

"I mean, really, why would we forward information like this at such a crucial time in the investigation? I find it very strange, indeed," Anna said, asserting herself.

"You did the right thing, comrade."

She stood up. "There's a rumor in the typing-pool that the scientist has already been caught and sent back to Moscow. I want to know if this is true or not, in case I get more misleading information. I suspect a certain person in the typing-pool of working for foreign agents. That was why I was arrested in Budapest, *we* suspect.

Please. I must know the truth about this," Anna said. The young man sat back in his chair. "My life might depend on it. If I should forward a cable from a spy—well, I doubt I'd be given a second chance, after what happened before. ..."

"I understand ... Anna. Sit down, please." She noticed that it was the first time he'd used her Christian name. "The man in question is still at large, and we must guard against any attempt by Western intelligence agencies to wreak havoc on our attempts to capture him," Zaytsev said. He was enthralled by her beauty, and it showed for an instant on his young face. She could tell he was opening up to her, now.

"... Thank you," she said. She sat down again. She made sure she kept her hands below her waist.

"What if I were to tell you, comrade, that we, too, suspect someone here in the Embassy of spying for the Americans? That in fact you are probably correct," he said. She didn't answer at first. She felt a cold fear sweeping over her and she wanted to bolt, straight out the door. "A woman ... someone you must know."

"Who is it, comrade?" Anna asked.

"Cerenia Kalakova. We were warned about her just yesterday. ... We are opening an investigation. She's been arrested, of course."

"The secretary to the Head of Station? Of course I know her," Anna said.

"Yes. Her boss may be involved, too; it's not certain. I'm afraid the search for the scientist is taking precedence at the moment," he said.

"Was she responsible for this strange cable request? Cerenia Kalakova?"

"It's possible," he said. "We'll know more soon enough." Anna wanted to stand up, but felt she couldn't. It was as if she'd been punched in the stomach and was still reeling from the blow.

"Is there something wrong, comrade?"

"No. It's just that ... I know her quite well—she's in charge of our typing pool."

"Yes, of course. It's always a shock when something like this happens." He looked at her. She seemed to him to have suddenly gone very pale. He stood up and went to her side.

"Are you sure you're all right?" he asked

"She may be the one that almost. ... She's the one that *may* have had me sent to Lubyanka from Budapest. ... I never suspected Cerenia Kalakova at all," Anna said.

"I see. It's quite possible, I suppose."

"I was afraid to speak about my suspicions to anyone but my father, before." Anna stood up. "I will tell my father that you are the man he thought you were."

"Thank you, comrade."

"Yes, of course. ... Could I *see* her? She might ... as a woman, she might confess if she were guilty ... to someone like me, I mean."

"She's scheduled to be moved back to Moscow tomorrow morning," Zaytsev said.

"I would like to help," Anna said. "Perhaps Cerenia Kalakova knows something about this scientist—if she's the one behind requesting me to send the cable to the Stasi ... ?" He looked at her for a moment. "I remember that she mentioned it to me. I didn't think about it at the time. ... She said that it was a high priority that we find him. She wanted to know if I'd received any cables concerning him or his whereabouts from Moscow. His suspected location ... anything like that," Anna said, lying again.

"A familiar face—someone that she will not fear? A girl from the typing pool ..." Zaytsev pondered the situation.

"Yes. I will lie and say that he's been caught and confessed to us about who has helped him and that I will help her if I can. It may work." Zaytsev looked at her a moment, impressed with her deviousness. "That I've been arrested again, too. That will make her even more likely to confess," Anna said.

"Brilliant, Maximovna," he said, and picked up the phone on his desk. "You'll call me immediately if she says *anything* about the scientist, then?" He sent her in a car to the apartment where Cerenia Kalakova was being held.

Anna was searched in the hallway outside by a male guard, and was then allowed into the apartment. There was a women KGB officer sitting in the small, bare-walled sitting room.

"My name is Anna Maximovna. I was sent by comrade Zaytsev," she said. "He asked that you wait outside while I conduct the interview." The woman, middle-aged, showing thick ankles in her nylon stockings, looked up at her. Anna could tell that the woman was bored and disinterested, but still suspicious. Why would counter-intelligence send a mere girl over to interview a prisoner?

"Yes. He called. There is a suicide-watch in effect," the woman said matter-of-factly, putting down the Mexican movie magazine she'd been flipping through. Anna had previously heard that the woman was an outrageous lesbian who coerced sex from the Mexican office girls at the Embassy, threatening their jobs if they didn't submit to her desires.

"Nonetheless, those are his orders. I'm from the Ministry. ... I've been sent out from Moscow by counter-intelligence." It was a lie, of course, but she'd told so many in the last two hours she saw no reason to stop now. She stood in the doorway. "My father is General Maximov" The woman put down the magazine. "I'm used to getting my way," Anna said, bluffing.

"... You will take complete responsibility for the prisoner's safety?" The woman said.

"Of course—where is she?"

"Lying down; she was sedated again this morning. To inhibit her from any rash acts."

"I understand. Now, please, leave us, comrade, so I can do what I have to do." The woman, twice her age and wearing a shabby Moscow suit, got up and walked past her, out of the apartment. Her hair was cut very short, and she looked extremely man-like. When Anna heard the door close she almost lost her nerve. It would not take the woman long to find out that she'd lied. She turned and walked down the hallway and stopped at a closed door. She prepared herself for more lies, and then opened the door. The room was dark. She snapped on the light switch. She hadn't expected to see the woman's face bandaged. Cerenia Kalakova was sleeping. She walked to the side of the bed. There was a glass of water, and, surprisingly, a photo of Saint Barbara in an antique gold frame. She shook Cerenia Kalakova awake.

"It's you. ... " Kalakova said, finally waking up.

"Yes," Anna said.

"Anna ... how?" Anna held up her finger to her lips. And pointed to her ears. Kalakova's eyes were blood-shot.

"Are you injured?" Anna asked.

"No. These are the bandages they use when they wheel you through the airport. They don't want the American spotters to see me when they take me through customs," she whispered. She held out her hand and Anna took it.

"I'm frightened," Kalakova said. Anna brought a chair to the side of the bed.

"The scientist. ..." Kalakova took her hand again and pulled her very close, until Anna could smell the older woman's perspiration. She'd been sweating because of the drugs, and the sheets smelled slightly sour.

"Behind the headboard." Kalakova whispered. She nodded. "Look. They thought I was asleep." Anna stood up and peered down between the wall and the headboard. There was a listening device attached to the back of the headboard. Kalakova handed her one of the pillows and Anna wedged it between the headboard and the wall, covering the device.

"Okay," Anna said. "We don't have much time—what happened?"

"I don't know."

"Someone informed on you?"

"I don't know, Anna."

"Have you told them about me?"

"No. No. But that will come at Lubyanka, later. They've kept me isolated in here and asked me only a few questions, so far. They know I was working for the Americans, though." Her eyes were terrified. It was an expression that Anna had never seen on another human being's face before—raw terror and the fear of imminent death.

219

"Who was it that told them?"

"I don't know. There is something I have to tell you, Anna. ... Something I was working on. Your father should know—I want you to promise to tell him."

"Tell him what?"

"There is a syndicate inside the KGB. It's run from the GDR. We've been compromised. They do whatever they want. And they do it for money. And for drugs and other things. One day they will bring down the USSR. They want to take over—everything."

"Who? ... Do you have any names?

"Yes. Hans in the GDR is their connection to Gehlen. Reinhard Gehlen had his hooks into the NKVD as far back as the Great War. We didn't know it, then. It was during the War, before my time. But I'm sure that's when it started."

"Who is Gehlen?"

"A Nazi. A German. Your father will know of him. Tell your father that Gehlen is back. Tell him that. He'll understand. Tell him that Demitri Osmorof in the Kremlin is Gehlen's man and that my boss is, too."

"Are you sure?"

"Yes. My boss has me set up meetings with someone called Hans in Germany. They go for the weekends to Bavaria. To the Chalet Gloria. The Americans, when I reported it, said that the Chalet belongs to West German intelligence and to find out more about Hans. I confronted my boss about it, hoping to turn him for the Americans, threatening to report the meetings to the KGB. He confessed it all to me himself. That he worked for the Gehlen network in West Germany and that they were infiltrating all the intelligence agencies in the West and that I could join and I would be made rich beyond anything I could even understand. I refused. Gehlen was a Nazi. My parents were *killed in front of my eyes* by the Gestapo," she said. "I've always hated the Nazis and everything they stood for. ..."

"Has he been arrested? Your boss?" Anna asked.

"No. He disappeared yesterday, just before I was arrested. Don't you see—it's the Gehlen people that told the KGB about me. They've gotten my boss *out*. He must have alerted them, and they've somehow gotten him out of Mexico."

"Do the Americans know he's escaped?"

"No. I was arrested before I could contact them. Anna, how in the world did *you* get in to see me?"

"I lied. I told many lies. I said that you would confess to me. Tell me about the scientist and other things they want to know."

"It was the scientist that they want, and desperately, too—the Gehlen people, I mean. It was my boss's contacting Hans in Germany, when he heard that the scientist might be in Mexico, that really caught my attention. I knew the scientist was important, and that it was top secret, but he called a number in *Germany*. It was then that I knew it was all connected, and that he worked for Gehlen."

"Does the KGB know where the scientist is?"

"No. I don't think so—not yet." There was a knock on the door. The female KGB officer opened the door to the bedroom.

"I was just checking."

"Everything is fine, comrade," Anna said. "Thank you."

"They're coming for her. We're to get her ready."

"I need ten more minutes," Anna said. "Is that understood?"

"Yes." The woman shut the door.

"If I go to Moscow, they will torture me. I'll tell them everything, I know I will. ... You have to help me, Anna, please!"

"What can I do?"

"...You must kill me, right now." The words went through her like a spear. Cerenia Kalakova's green eyes peering out of the bandages were wet and imploring. "Please ... Anna, I want to see my parents. I am alone here. I know they're waiting for me in heaven. Please. *I beg you. Help me.*"

"I don't understand." Anna said.

"You must. You must. *Please.*"

Anna looked around the room. Cerenia Kalakova glanced at the nightstand beside the bed and picked up the framed picture of her parents, which had been taken before the War. "I've no children ... help me. You're like a daughter to me, Anna."

"... ... Yes. All right." Anna touched the top of Cerenia Kalakova's head instinctively. For a moment the two women looked at each other. Cerenia Kalakova shut her eyes. Anna took the pillow out from behind the headboard and placed it on Kalakova's face and pressed down until she began to fight for her life. She pressed down with all her might knowing what the woman faced if she lived. In a moment she went suddenly limp, and the one arm that had still been up slapping Anna's face finally dropped. Anna felt for a pulse in her neck and found none. She was dead. When it was over she took the pillow off Cerenia Kalakova's face and turned quickly away, not wanting to look at her, now. She waited a brief moment, composing herself, then strode out the door.

She walked down the very quiet and narrow hallway keeping a close watch on the door at its end. She could feel her heart beating. She thought of Malcolm Law for a moment. She had to live to see him again, she thought, if for no other reason. She stepped through the door and walked out into the hallway of the apartment building. The guard and the woman officer were talking. They turned to look at her.

"Call the doctor immediately. I think she's had a heart attack," Anna said. *"Hurry, you fool!"* The older woman ran past her and into the apartment. "I must report this at once," Anna said as she turned away and went down the stairs, expecting the guard to come rushing after her, but he didn't. She caught a taxi, telling the driver to take her to the Archeological Museum, then she turned to watch to see if she was being followed.

23

1965 ■ MEXICO CITY

Sonny Delmonico had on a clean, light-green linen suit and a blue shirt. He had shaved and gotten a haircut at the hotel and looked entirely different than he had at the prison. He walked through the enormous private garden towards the pool house after a taxi had dropped him off in front of the mansion, which was located in the *Pedregal*. The guard at the gate and been told to let him in. It was a foggy, overcast morning in Mexico City, causing his new shoes to pick up dew from the manicured grass as he walked across the lawn. George had given him the address in the *Pedregal* where he was to meet Malcolm. The Englishman had been waiting for Sonny when he was released from the prison and he'd driven him to the Marriot Hotel where he was furnished with a new suit and a thousand dollars in cash. They had a quick conversation in Sonny's hotel room before George left him. He told Sonny he no longer existed as far as the Embassy was concerned.

The enormous "pool house" where Malcolm was hiding out with his German scientist was on the estate of the wealthy Mexican woman he'd been seeing and who had gone to Spain with her father for the winter. It was completely unknown to anyone at the American Embassy and was very well-guarded because the woman's father was one of the richest men in Mexico.

He'd learned over the phone from George that he was now suddenly in trouble with his bosses. London suspected him of being in with the Philby Network and he was to be flown back to London that evening—a complete surprise to everyone at the British Embassy. There was no arguing about it or he, too, would be arrested, he'd told Malcolm during the call. It seemed more than odd to Malcolm that only twenty-four hours after his having walked into George's office, his friend—a career intelligence officer and a war hero with a sterling record—was now being ordered back to London under suspicion of treason.

"So you're on your own now, then, amigo," George said, seemingly unfazed. He was calling from a well known bar in the Mexican capital's financial district, where he was getting drunk and trying to pick up one of the younger women that filled the place at happy hour looking for wealthy businessmen. "I've got friends following me that I didn't have a day ago. ... They think I'm going to bolt for Moscow, I suppose—can you imagine that!? I suppose my knighthood is out, now, too," George joked.

"I'm sorry," Malcolm said. "Do they know about our friend S?"

"No. Nothing about him. I've blotted him from the record. Even his call into the Embassy. Totally erased."

"Thanks, George."

"Good luck then, old boy," George said. "... For the record, I never liked Philby. Didn't trust him," he said, and than rang off.

"Well, sir. Your man? Where is he?" Delmonico asked. He'd been waiting, sitting patiently on the couch while Malcolm had been on the phone with George. The view out the pool house door was of a half–an-acre of well-trimmed lawn, ending at a wall with elephant-ear plants growing up over the top. The top of the wall was covered with shards of broken glass to keep people from climbing over.

"Shut up," Malcolm said. He was in a foul mood now with the recent news of George's troubles, which he blamed on his own bungling, somehow, even if he couldn't see just *where* he'd bungled the situation to bring down this degree of wrath from above.

"Sorry, sir. Bad day at the office, is it?" Delmonico said. Sonny lit a cigarette and dragged over an ashtray from one side of a long white marble coffee table.

"Are you always so flippant? ... It's annoying," Malcolm said.

"Mum's the word," Sonny said, "if that will make you feel better."

"I don't trust you." Malcolm said, "... fucking drug-pusher."

"Well, sir, there's not much I can do about *that*, is there?" Sonny smiled. And the insouciant smile at just that moment made Malcolm even angrier.

"No ... I don't suppose there is."

"The fact is that most people in my line ... Well, we're actually quite reliable. The penalties are much greater ... should we disappoint, you know. ..." Delmonico pinched a piece of tobacco from his tongue and dropped it in the ashtray.

Malcolm was wearing swimming trunks and a white T-shirt. He'd gone to the pool and read a *Time* magazine he'd found in the pool house while he waited for Delmonico. He was to be married in just a month to a young woman—ten years his junior—who he didn't really love. Everything he'd told Anna Maximovna had been a lie. He was only marrying because she was the kind of girl he was *expected* to marry. In the eyes of the Agency, he was "getting on in years," and without a wife further moves up the management ladder would be difficult. Hints had been dropped about his marital status, suggesting that it was time that it changed. In point of fact, he had spent the night thinking about the *Russian* girl. He wanted her again as badly as a heroin addict wants/needs a fix. He was sexually infatuated with her. And he was attracted to her emotionally, as well as physically; attracted by the idea that she might need him. He'd realized she was a woman and not just an addition to his résumé.

The escaped German scientist, a middle-aged man named Max Keller, had slept in the pool house's single bedroom with Malcolm—on the floor. The man had kept him awake most of the night, talking in his sleep. Malcolm had sat up in bed smoking and thinking about Anna Maximovna; seeing her again—naked, willing, supremely girlish, looking at him intently while he made love to her. He'd never known a woman quite like her. Her sadness—so "Russian" to his way of thinking—had harpooned him through the heart. No matter what he wanted sexually, she gave it to him with a passion he'd rarely encountered before—as if she were pushing him on towards some kind of ultimate climax. Some bridge he had to cross that would be blown up behind him and then he would be hers forever.

Sonny glanced at his watch. "You wouldn't have a drink, sir? Would you? Since I was sprung this morning it's been rush-rush. I'm afraid your pal was in quite a hurry. Hotel for shower and a change of clothes, then a quick haircut. Now here you go—off with you, now! It's all been a bloody mystery to me."

"Tequila?" Malcolm said. He was suddenly no longer angry at Delmonico. He'd neither done or said anything "wrong," Malcolm decided, looking at the one-eyed man. He was a well-groomed survivor in an unholy world. He was a criminal, yes, but what about *him,* himself? Wasn't *he* smuggling war criminals? What did that make *him?* Suddenly he realized that he was no better than the man sitting in front of him, who he'd been morally looking down upon just a moment before. The thought scared him, in a weird way. He could no longer lie to himself that what he was doing would "matter." Had the H-bomb really mattered? Was the world any better off for what he'd done—the little part he'd played in bringing *that* hellish monstrosity into the world— so "the West" could have it first, just slightly before the "enemy" Russians got it?

"Thank you. Yes. Please," Sonny said.

"He's here. In the other room, there. Your package," Malcolm said, walking into the small kitchen.

"Your man?"

"Yes," Malcolm said.

"Who is he, sir, if I may ask? I hope he's not been *too* naughty ... if you catch my drift. The Mexican police are not as flat-footed as they're made out to be in American films," Sonny said.

"Never mind who he is," Malcolm said. He poured two-fingers' of tequila into a water glass and brought it out to the living room and handed it to Delmonico.

"Thank you, sir ... Cheers. We'll need to be shoving off soon, I'm afraid. So, if you would get your man ready? He won't be able to take any luggage. Hardships of the road, and all that," Delmonico explained, downing the drink in one swallow.

"When will he be in the States?" Malcolm asked.

"In about fifteen days, sir. He'll call you. Do you have a number you can give me?" Sonny put the glass down on the table. Malcolm gave him a number at an import-export company in San Francisco and told him to leave a message there saying his old friend was in town.

"Secure route?" Malcolm asked as he wrote the number down.

"Very. I'd take my grandmother on it. Very picturesque. See a bit of old Mexico along with way," Sonny said. "Done it all before, several times, no problems."

"Do you care anything that you sell poison?" Malcolm asked, handing him the phone number.

"I don't really think much about it, sir. I suppose there are worse jobs. Intelligence work, for example. I've heard you have to deal with all types, some of them quite unsavory," Sonny said. "You never said exactly what business *you're* in, sir?"

"... I'll get him, then," Malcolm said, ignoring the question. He walked into the bedroom and woke the ex-Nazi. The man had barely spoken to him since he'd been picked up in Vera Cruz. *"Machen Sie sich berei ... macht schnell,"* Malcolm said in German.

"No. ... I won't go—with that man," Keller said in English. He was sitting on the unmade bed. "I don't know that man. The one outside." The seedy-looking German, Max Keller, in his late forties, his black hair greasy-looking, was terrified. He was wearing cheap pants that Malcolm had bought for him in the market near *Chepultepec,* and a white *guayabera* shirt. The suit Keller had been wearing when he'd stepped off the boat in Veracruz was exactly what Malcolm thought the Russians would be looking for. He now looked like the millions of down-at-the-heels foreigners that lived in the city from hand-to-mouth.

Malcolm walked to the closet and got out the revolver he'd laid on the top of his suitcase and came back into the room and placed the barrel of the pistol directly against Keller's heavily-lined forehead. Keller had worked—like so many taken out of Europe by Malcolm—on Hitler's rocketry program, or at least that was what he'd told his CIA contact in the GDR who had referenced the name the man had given him. Max Keller's name had been found on a list of former Nazi scientists who'd been captured by the Russians in 1945; a list that had been kept by American intelligence since the end of the war. He had been gladly accepted as part of Operation Paperclip.

"You will do exactly what you're told. Do you understand me?" Malcolm said.

"I'm afraid, sir, that we're about out of time," Sonny said from the doorway. He had opened the door to the bedroom and was looking in on them, a bemused expression on his round face. "*Ich bin deine Freund*," Sonny said in German. "*Was Sparte?*"

"*Das Adolf Hitler Sparte*," Keller said, "*und du?*"

"British Army. *Ich bin Englischer. Engländer*," Sonny said, the smile leaving his face. He glanced at Malcolm for a moment. "Oh, what a tangled web we weave, sir. My, my." Sonny walked across the bedroom. He went up to Keller, put his hands on the German's shoulders as if he were going to kiss him on the cheeks then very quickly pulled the man up to a standing position and kneed him hard in the balls, viciously— *twice.* Keller sagged to the floor and began to writhe in pain as if he'd been shot. "You're being too nice to him, sir, if you don't mind my saying. ... It's all these Nazi-types, understand, isn't it? I don't really *like* them. The Germans, especially. They tried to kill me more than once. Every time I stuck my head up in Italy, in fact. And I was just a wee lad, too. ... May I, sir?" Sonny asked.

Delmonico took the pistol out of Malcolm's hand. "It might come in useful ... where we're going, you know. And I seemed to have lost mine along the way. ..."

"All right, *Fritz.* It's you and me, now, dearie." Keller, still on the floor, had stopped squirming in pain long enough to look up at Delmonico, and it was as if he were looking at the Devil himself. Sonny bent down, got his face very close to Keller's and whispered something Malcolm didn't catch, then helped Keller up as if it had all been a terrible mistake. In a few moments they were gone. Fifteen days later Max Keller was left at a hotel in downtown Tucson, Arizona, were he was picked up by Malcolm himself. The room contained 20 kilos of Sicilian heroin and one former Nazi scientist. Malcolm later told a friend at Langley—where all had been forgiven—that Sonny had left a note pinned to a bound-and-gagged Keller, as if he were just another bale of dope. *Call anytime, Dear. Yours, S.*

*   *   *

The hotel they'd checked into was in Cuernavaca near the famous Diego Rivera murals. It was a very expensive hotel called *Casa Colonial,* and Malcolm had chosen it because it catered to both rich Europeans and Mexicans. It was not the kind of place that American tourists liked, because the menus weren't printed in English and there were no TVs in the rooms. But it was a good place for him to hide with the girl. He was waiting for a message from Delmonico, telling him that Keller had been crossed into the States. As soon as he got news that Keller was safe, he planned on turning himself in to the hunters, not really sure what would happen to him for what he'd just pulled.

Anna Maximovna was watching him towel off. She was lying on the bed, looking out at a huge orange bougainvillea that was growing down onto their private veranda, the two French doors were open wide so that they could smell all the garden smells; a redolent mixture of climbing roses and sweet honeysuckle.

He knew that their relationship would have to end soon, but he just didn't know how to tell the girl; and, he needed to know what she'd found out about Keller, if anything. She hadn't mentioned a word about the assignment he'd given her since they'd come here. And he was getting anxious about it, now. After a weekend of love-making and intimacy and real happiness, the spy in him had re-awoken. He couldn't help himself: an agent of his, a person who he was using to gain advantage over his country's enemies, had information, and he wanted it. All these thoughts went through his mind as he looked at her. Her face was still flushed from their love-making. It made her look just that much more beautiful. He was on the verge of falling in love, of being completely out of control, and that was something he couldn't allow himself, he decided—if, indeed, he had a choice in the matter. Not with her, anyway, of all people. Bring her to America and marry her and his career would be over—a Russian girl, and one whose father was an important general in the KGB, no less. *Did she know that, too? The impossibility of it all?*

"I want to tell you that your agent—Cerenia Kalakova—is dead," Anna suddenly said. He was toweling off his hair. They had decided to go to lunch at the hotel restaurant; it was "late" for lunch—way past one o'clock. He had intended to ask her then what had happened after she'd run away from the Embassy. "Have you lied to me about being married?" Anna reached for his shoulder, then touched it. "Everyone lies, don't they?" she said. She had fallen asleep while he'd been in the shower and dreamed of the day when she'd been waiting to be shot at the Lubyanka. It was a reoccurring nightmare for her. She'd woken with a start and then heard Malcolm in the shower and had then gotten up and walked naked out onto the veranda, her heart still pounding with fear.

She could hear children playing in the hotel pool on the other side of a tall hedge. The hotel had a large pool with a slide. They'd seen it the night before when Malcolm had taken her out very late for a swim. They swam naked in the pool, its underwater lights on. They'd both been drunk, and it was the first time in as long as she could remember that she'd been truly happy. It was as if everything in her life had changed for the better, finally. For one single moment she saw a wonderful future with this man she'd really only just met. She had fallen in love for the first time in her young life, and allowed herself to feel hopeful.

She had not thought once about killing Cerenia Kalakova in her bed while she'd been in Malcolm's arms. Rather than the killing being a terrible memory and frightening her, it had felt as if she had been instantly reborn—she could never go back, now, no matter what. Even during the horrible moments when Cerenia Kalakova's was fighting her during the last seconds of her life, she knew that what she had done was right and good. Anna looked down at her hands. She had used all of her strength to suffocate the woman. An orange blossom blew in the door and onto the white rug. She bent down and picked it up; it was paper-thin—translucent—and very beautiful.

She turned and looked through the hedge and caught glimpses of families enjoying themselves. Because it was a Sunday, the pool was crowded. Even when they'd been making love—a very intense and sometimes almost brutal love-making—it was there, that sound in the background: children's happy voices crying out in a strange but somehow perfect juxtaposition to their passionate gasps. It reminded her that she would most likely never have children of her own. It was a strangely haunting thought that she'd first had at the Lubyanka as she'd been prepared for execution—a day that the prison was covered in a very white and clean newly-fallen December snow. The same stark prison courtyard that had for forty years, and more, been the scene of countless executions. Most of them unrecorded, after quick and terrifying drumhead trials where the sentence was always "death." Prisoners whose names would be lost to history faced their unknown accusers with the blank faces of the doomed. Few had ever lived through one of those trials to tell about it.

The courtyard where she was to be shot had been shoveled-off the first thing that morning by tattooed prisoners in blue prison garb wearing old-fashioned fur hats. Her cell had a perfect view of the yard through a narrow window. The cell was known by the guards as the "death cell."

They had taken away her jewelry and the clothes she'd been arrested in two days before in Budapest and given her a hospital-like smock to wear. A warder was brought to sit in the cell with her as she waited to be taken down. The warder was dark and from Tashkent in Central Asia. The woman had become inured to death, so was of little help, emotionally. She'd only spoken once to Anna, saying: "It will not hurt, and it will be over, soon. They always execute before the dinner hour."

It was there in the cell, waiting to die, that Anna went over the things she'd missed in life. Sex, children, Christmas morning with a husband. As a child, she'd loved December. That day was, in fact, the fifteenth of December, and the streets of Moscow near the Kremlin had been decorated with lights. She was unaware that even then Nikita Khrushchev—recently ousted from the Politburo—was in the prison with her father and that there would be no execution. As the minutes ticked by, Anna prepared herself to die, watching the desultory snow fall across the grey empty courtyard below like sand through a giant hour-glass. She found herself thinking of the day she had been measured at the school. She felt the tape on her neck, and even recalled the smell of the woman's perfume who had measured her. She saw herself in the mirror across the huge dance studio, a skinny young girl who just wanted to dance. It was her father who had then suddenly pulled the cell door open and told her it had all been a mistake, a horrible mistake. She had run to her father's arms and they both cried together.

"... I suppose," Malcolm said. The bed was luxurious, and many times later in life he would remember that hotel room in great detail, because he, too, had been happy there. You never forget where you've fallen in love. The bright orange color of the bougainvillea; the smell of Anna's hair; her whimpering orgasms. The girl, so extremely feminine and yet so physically strong beneath him. In the shower he had contemplated what he was doing: smuggling a Nazi war criminal into the United States; a man that his government needed to help so it could put the entire world at risk with a bomb that Edward Teller was working on. It seemed to him, looking at the girl now, utterly insane. Everything that had happened to him since the day he'd jumped into Poland in 1944 seemed insane—all of it. Just simply *crazy*. Would Nazi scientists save the world for democracy? He'd been ordered to bring them to America, but it seemed wrong, somehow. He'd never been able to admit that to himself until now. Had the girl done that to him? Had something about *her* sparked a latent reaction in him? Had her sexual willingness pulled him into the deep end of the pool? *Why*? *How*? He had an impulse to get away and leave her then and there, but he couldn't bring himself to act on it.

"Is it lies that drive the world, do you think?" Anna said. "Lies that governments tell their people, and lies that we tell each other to gain things. I thought when I was a child that grown-ups never lied. Isn't that strange. I thought only children lied."

"My parents told lies all the time," Malcolm said, and laughed. He was feeling guilty about abandoning her. He felt like a coward for the first time in his life.

"What do you mean that Cerenia Kalakova is dead, Anna?"

"I killed her," Anna said, sitting up, her small breasts like sculptures, white, the darker nipples perfect. She didn't try and cover herself after her admission.

"Just tell me one *true* thing," Anna said, ignoring the killing she had just confessed to. "One. Just one."

"What?"

"Please ... I beg you to tell it to me."

"One true thing? You're the most beautiful woman I've ever seen in my whole life."

She blushed. "*Did* you actually kill Cerenia Kalakova, Anna?"

"Yes. Yesterday. She'd been arrested by the KGB. Someone told them she was working for the Americans." Malcolm was shocked, because the CIA had done everything they could to keep Cerenia Kalakova's identity a secret. Only people with the highest clearances at Langley knew of her existence and her identity. There could have been no more than a dozen people who knew she existed. And he'd thought all of them were completely beyond suspicion when it came to being a traitor.

"She *asked* me to do it. She begged me!" Anna said. She looked at him. Her blue eyes were quiet; she was resigned to the reality of what she'd done.

"... To *kill* her?" he said, trying to keep the shock out of his voice. Anna nodded.

"Yes. She was afraid of going to the Lubyanka ... What they would do to her there. I know what that place is like. I understood her. I would want the same."

"How did you manage to see her if she was under arrest?"

"I told lies. That's how the world works, doesn't it? You lie to me about not having a wife; I lie to the Embassy's counter-intelligence chief, who wants to sleep with me, and it works—as if everyone involved were children. He actually thinks I want to sleep with him. He's a fool. I hate him. I hate all of them." She kissed his neck and pulled the towel off his shoulder and pulled him down towards her on the pillows with her arms around him.

"Cerenia Kalakova told me there is a cabal inside the KGB ... a man, a German named Gehlen, controls it. She said that *her* boss works for this network, too. She said that someday they will defeat the Revolution and bring down the Soviet Union. She said that this network exists on both sides but is not truly loyal to either us *or* America—only to itself. She called it the 'Gehlen network.' ... *They* sent you that precious scientist. He's one of them, Cerenia Kalakova said. They wanted him to be in America, and made it possible for him to escape. He works for them. He's to report to them when he gets to America. Now I've told you all my secrets. ... Will you tell me yours? *Are* you married?"

"No, but I will be soon. When I go back to Washington." He told her the truth, and it made him feel better.

"Do you love her? Is she very pretty?"

"No. No, I don't love her. But I have to marry her. It's for ... my career," he said. He said it as if he were talking to himself.

"Do you love me?"

"Yes. I think so. Yes. I've never felt this way before, " he said, without thinking. But it was true. It was his turn to confess. She let go of him then, letting her arms move down to the warm sheets.

"I want to go with you. Wherever you go ... take me with you," she said.

231

"All right. I want you to be with me," he said. "I won't go back. I won't. I'm finished now with all that," he said. "With lying."

She told him to go down to lunch because she wanted to dress up for him and look pretty. She would be there soon. But she never showed up. After half an hour of sitting there, watching couples and families in the crowded restaurant, he got up. At first he walked, not wanting to draw attention to himself. But in the long hallway he ran as if the devil himself were after him. When he got to the room she was gone. The towels they'd left on the bed were still there. Much later, he found out that the Russians had taken her. She was shot in Lubyanka prison a week later, on a beautiful June morning. The patch of sky above her head was bright blue. She'd seen a starling cross the sky just before they put the hood over her head. There was nothing her father could do to stop it.

24

1980 ■ CENTRAL LONDON

"And what do you want us to *do* with them, George—*exactly?* Shall we cashier them?" the man on the phone asked.

"I would prefer that they get posthumously elevated to the highest possible rank. After having been killed by the guerrillas. Appropriate, don't you think?" George told the Nigerian Head of Intelligence. "... A tidy ending is what we need."

"George, do you mean we should ... ?" The man interrupted his old friend, who they'd all called "Bumpy" at Cambridge. He'd been a hulking boy, and his father was one of the major Yoruba chiefs, and also a Christian.

"Precisely, old man," George said and hung up the phone and looked for his cigarettes.

It had been a busy morning at George Cummings' office in Kroll's London headquarters. George had been tasked with an important private intelligence operation for Royal Dutch Shell. Shell executives were trying to mitigate the corruption the company faced from inside the Nigerian army. Nigerian generals had been sending army personnel disguised as anti-government guerrillas onto Dutch Shell oil rigs in Nigerian waters as part of a shakedown of the company. The phony "guerrillas" would demand money from the company while holding the oil rigs hostage and shutting down production. The gangs had killed several European workers and had already been paid millions of pounds. Royal Dutch executives had come to Kroll for help in stopping the raids and the payments.

It was George who had discovered the plot by a few Army generals. He was now trying to pay off other important members of the Nigerian government who in turn would round up the generals who were responsible for the raids and hopefully "neutralize" them. So far, George had had to buy two members of the Nigerian government outright: the Head of Naval Operations and the head of the Nigerian intelligence services—Bumpy—who George had known since before the War. This morning he was hoping to finish up the deal, with yet a third high-ranking government official, who was to call him directly to see how much Royal Dutch was willing to pay to stop the raids. George's secretary had only put Malcolm's call through because he'd said they were old friends and he only had a short stop over in London that afternoon. Malcolm told her they had fought in the War—had been in Burma together—all of it a lie, of course.

He had tracked George down to Kroll, Inc., where he was Vice President in charge of corporate affairs for the entire continent of Africa. Kroll was the closest thing extant to a stand-alone intelligence agency in private hands that had intelligence gathering capabilities on the order of any given Western nation. In the seventies, George had married a much younger woman from a wealthy English family that had pioneered the coffee business in Kenya. They'd met on holiday in Egypt and by now had three children and were living comfortably in London. He'd been drummed out of MI6 for unknown reasons—everyone generally thought it was because he had a gambling problem. But there were whispers, too, about his relationship with Kim Philby, and that the gambling had been used as an excuse; a cover up for the real reason he was let go. He was past fifty now and had given up most of his vices. He still liked to gamble, but he tried to keep his visits to the Playboy Club to a minimum, just as he'd promised his wife he would, and these days he was trying to stick to his promises. It was the roulette wheel he missed the most, he'd told her: "I just love to see the bloody ball bounce, that moment just before—you know—where it's going to land ... there's something about it I can't put into words ... But I just *love* it!" He'd told her that he thought it had something to do with his experiences in the War, but he wasn't sure what; he just couldn't put his finger on it. His wife, a graduate of Oxford and very liberal-minded about such matters, got him to go to see a psychiatrist on Harley Street, and the man told him that he thought George used gambling as a way to re-create his wartime hyper-anxiety. The doctor said that he was unable to divorce himself from his past. "Now why the hell would I do *that?*" George had said, looking at the young doctor with disapproval.

"Well, that's what we're here to find out, isn't it?" the doctor said. "It's why you've come—hopefully to free yourself from these symptoms."

"... Have you ever been to Burma?" George asked the doctor, shortly after they'd first met.

"No," he'd replied: "I did my national service in Old Blighty." George shot him a look and the two smiled at each other. The doctor wasn't without a sense of humor.

"... Have you ever seen someone holding their guts together, asking to be shot?" George said. He took out his cigarette case; the doctor was going to tell him he couldn't smoke in his office, but he held back for a moment because his patient had a strange and pensive look on his face. The egg had cracked. He watched George take the cigarette case out and open it. His hands were shaking as if all of a sudden he was back there, all those years before.

"... No." The young man said carefully. He was sitting in his "doctor's chair," loosely holding a notepad in his lap with both hands. He looked up at his patient and watched him light the cigarette, inhale deeply, and then put the case back into his inside jacket pocket.

"... Well, what if I told you that I had ... that I shot the bloke. A boy from Liverpool, who I liked. He was making too much bloody noise, you see ... and he was going to get us all killed. ... We were out of drugs ... no more morphine. Nothing left. Do you have any pills for *that*, Doctor?"

"No. No, I don't," the doctor said.

"I'm tired of re-living it," George said. "*Very* damned tired of it. I have, you know, just about every day since."

"Is this George?" The voice on the other end of the line asked. He had two assistants; one of them a young man he'd brought with him from BP, where he'd been Head of Security. That assistant came into the office and handed him a cable from Kroll's field office in Kenya marked "URGENT."

"Yes, speaking," George said, glancing at the cable, trying to do two things at once.

"It's Malcolm. ... Malcolm Law, George."

"*Malcolm!* Good Lord, man. ... Where *are* you? And how did you find me?"

"I'm in London," Malcolm said. "It was easy to find you, George, I just asked the nearest pretty girl."

"Oh—still over there at the Embassy, are we? Well, I suppose so. You always did strike me as the career type," George said. His assistant was still waiting for him to read the cable.

"George ... could I see you?" Malcolm asked. George managed to skim the cable. A major coffee executive was sure that there was going to be a second Mau-Mau Rebellion and had wired Kroll with an intelligence report and a stern warning: *And as we continue to see demands by workers across the country for higher wage ...*

"Bit of a ringer today, old man. The Hottentots are not behaving. I've got to call you back. ... How's Saturday? Why don't you come by, meet the wife and kids. ... I've got three—all brilliant, of course, and beautiful, like me."

"... It's a work problem," Malcolm said. "One that can't wait."

"I see. Sounds like old times. Where are you?"

"I'm at the place on Green Park," George looked at his watch.

"I know the address. I'll pick you up in an hour. Lunch at my club. How's that? It's nearby."

"Thank you," Malcolm said.

"Don't mention it. But *you're* paying. I lost a packet on the Derby. But don't tell my wife when you meet her ... *whatever* you do," George said.

"All right, an hour. What are you driving these days, George?"

"A Jaguar. Blue," George said. "I've come up in the world. I've left government work, so I can finally afford a decent car."

George turned the corner onto Chatham Lane and pulled over. He saw a black London Cab parked in front of him at the curb, no doubt waiting for a fare. He noticed a red awning with slightly-worn gold lettering on it touting the building's official name. He remembered the building from the old days. It was a CIA-owned apartment building where CIA staff lived while visiting or working in London. He looked down the street and saw the U.S. Embassy, far enough away from the apartment building to satisfy the CIA watchers who patrolled the neighborhood, and who often followed people leaving the Embassy. He took the car out of gear, turned on the radio, and then glanced at his watch. He looked to his right to see if perhaps Law was standing further up the street. He saw the apartment door open, and was about to smile and honk, but he stopped his palm from striking the horn. He saw Law, who looked older than he thought he should, being held by two larger men. They pushed him into the waiting black cab and drove off. For a moment he thought he'd imagined what he'd seen, it had happened so fast. He instinctively pulled out and followed the cab and turned off his radio. The taxi drove off towards the Waterloo Bridge, then suddenly pulled over at Somerset House and the two men took Law out of the first taxi and to another one that was obviously waiting for them. It was then that Law turned and looked out at the traffic, briefly glancing his way before he disappeared again, pushed into the second London Cab, which immediately pulled out into traffic and went back towards the center of London.

"Bloody hell," George said to himself. "Bloody hell." He followed the cab, letting a few cars get between him and his quarry. There was a moment when two other London Cabs—identically black ones—had simultaneously pulled out into the street, and he had to guess which one to follow.

The cab had stopped in Soho, after turning down a tiny lane off Brewer Street called Silver; a short street lined with shabby, three-storey, second-class hotels, their upper-storey windows uniformly grimed and opaque. George waited at the top of the street and watched the taxi which had pulled over and stopped. They took Malcolm from the backseat of the car into one of the hotels, then the cab went to the end of the

236

lane and turned around, so the driver was looking right at George as he turned out of the lane and back onto Brewer Street.

For a moment George just sat and waited. He let the engine idle for a moment, then turned down the lane himself and parked his car in front of a hotel he noticed called the Golden Tulip. He looked up at the seedy entrance and pulled forward. He rolled to a stop and looked around. He looked in the rearview mirror and saw heavy traffic passing on Brewer. A van drove past and went on down the lane, with a black man behind the wheel. He reached over and pulled open his glove box. He took out a Walther he always kept there at the ready, and laid it in his lap. There was a team of former SAS men that Kroll kept on retainer who were ready to go anywhere in the world at any time and extract someone from any given situation on Kroll's behalf. They worked mostly kidnapping cases, where the clients were so rich they could pay for revenge on their abductors, hiring Kroll to track down those responsible, after having paid their own ransoms and been freed, to make sure that those particular people wouldn't ever work the kidnap game again. He thought about calling that number, now. He wouldn't even have to lie; but instead, he looked at the entrance to the hotel and something told him not to make the call he'd just been contemplating. He glanced up at the rearview mirror again and saw a cab coming down Silver Street. He watched it stop in front of the hotel, and Mary Keen get out, alone, then walk up the stairs and disappear. George looked down at his pistol. He'd had the same one for years. For a moment he simply stared at it, trying to understand what was going on.

"Well," he said, more to just hear the sound of *a* voice, and somehow psychologically break-up the surreal situation he found himself in than anything else, even if the voice was only his own. He dropped the clip out of the automatic and examined the magazine. He'd loaded it himself a few weeks before, sitting at the kitchen table of his home in Bayswater. His wife had stood looking at him, watching him methodically load the bullets into the clip. He'd waited until the children were in bed to do it. Because she was just so *much* younger—she'd only been twenty-five when they were married—he never wanted to talk about the War with her because he thought it made him seem old, and he was very afraid of losing her some day to a younger man.

"Is that really *necessary*, George?" she'd asked dismissively. "Those things are so old fashioned ... aren't they?" He knew his wife could not comprehend the war-time environment that had molded his attitude; a world where a sidearm was not only commonplace, but often decided the quite arbitrary difference between who would live and who would not. Guns to her Flower-Power Generation were just hopelessly foolish toys—end of story.

"Force of habit, really," was all he'd replied at the time, and then she'd gone up to bed and left him there alone in the kitchen.

Why was Mary Keen there? Of all people? And why had Malcolm called him? Was this part of the game? "Trouble at work," Malcolm had said to him. He thought again of calling the SAS men, but there was something strange about what was going on here that compelled him to go into the hotel alone.

Mary—why are you *here? And why is Malcolm being boxed-up like a Christmas package? Huh?* He shoved the magazine back into the pistol, stepped out of the car, and went to see what was going on for himself—all his alarm bells going off at once and telling him that he was doing this the wrong way, but he forged ahead alone anyway; it just seemed "right," somehow, given what he'd observed so far.

"I was an intelligence officer," George said one day, looking at the doctor. "A cold warrior. I loved it. I loved everything *about* spying," George admitted.

"I see," the doctor seemed noncommittal to George, as always, with his reply.

"They took it all away from me. It was the only thing I truly loved, really. I hated what came afterwards. A desk job. A security hack for British Petroleum. I nearly lost my mind doing that rubbish," George said. "Drank like two fishes on holiday."

"Is it the *only* thing you love? ... What about your family?" the doctor had asked him.

"I'm not right for it, really, old man. Husband-hood and all that. I always seem to want to go off the rails, just for the hell of it," George said. "Pushed by demons, I suppose. Spies don't make good fathers, you know," George said. "They deserve better, don't they. ... Time's about up, isn't it, doctor?" George looked at his watch.

"Not quite yet, George. I think we're getting somewhere today, don't you?"

"Where would that *be,* exactly, doctor?" George asked.

George had had his overcoat pockets enlarged so that the Walther could be taken in and out without catching the hammer on anything. He carried the pistol with him every day, even when he was out with the family on Sunday drives. He told the doctor that it just made him feel better to have a loaded gun with him. It had been that way with him for years.

"And why do you think that is?" the doctor had asked. It was their fourth session, and George was finding it horrible to confess that he didn't want a family, that he didn't want to stop gambling, or whoring, and that nothing seemed to stop him from thinking of that day he'd killed the boy in the jungle, even when he was drunk out of his mind.

"I don't know," George said.

"Are you sure?" the doctor said, "I don't believe you." George was looking out the doctor's window toward a cloud-filled sky. He looked back at the doctor.

"I suppose I'm afraid someone will come and kill *me*," George said.

"Who would do that, George?"

"I don't know. I just think they will, I suppose. And I'll be bloody glad to have it if they *do* come. Bloody good and useful things, guns. I don't expect people like *you* to understand that, of course," George said.

"Why, George? Why carry the gun on Sunday afternoons with the family? Your wife isn't going to kill you, surely?" the doctor said. He took his pen and clicked it off. The look on the doctor's face was intense. His father had been a Rabbi, and like his father, he had a religious zeal about the hunt for sanity.

"Maybe it's because I *know* things ... things most people don't know," George said. He wanted to leave. He was tired of dragging out his feelings. Exhausted, in fact.

"Come on, *George!* You sure it's *that?*" The doctor almost barked the question; it was as if he were pushing his patient towards a cliff and wanted him to tumble over the edge. "Are you sure it has anything to *do* with your intelligence work? Or your time in the War?"

"Of course it does. ... Those times. ... In the Sixties—the Russian thugs. In Mexico. They were everywhere. ... Don't look at me like that," George said. "Don't you dare look at me like that. I'm not a child, for fuck's sake!"

"Are you sure it's not because you want to do *yourself* harm? Is it *you* that you're afraid of? Is that it, George?" the doctor said.

"... What do you mean?"

"I mean carrying the gun, having it at hand all the time. Are you sure you don't want to use it on yourself? Isn't that why you keep coming back here even though you'd rather not? You've said so yourself; you hate all this. Everything about it, you told me last time." George didn't answer. Instead, he got up and collected his overcoat, the pistol in the side pocket, and left without saying another word. The doctor waited for a moment. He'd just realized that George had had the gun with him, and that he'd been bringing it to the office each time he'd come. He tapped his pen on the notepad. He clicked it again. The noise of the pen seemed loud now, in the empty office. He made a note: *Patient made a breakthrough today and stormed out. He's faced his fear for the first time, no doubt. Is he in danger of using the weapon on himself? On others? On his family? ... But shell-shocked victims are hard to read. Anger so deep it becomes perverted and poisonous.* The doctor looked up at the empty chair across from him and wondered if his patient would ever return. But he had returned.

George got out of his car and went up the steps leading into the hotel, the pistol in his right overcoat pocket, his hand on the pistol. The lobby was small and its red carpet was very worn and shabby-looking. There was a desk piled with brochures aimed at the mostly young European tourists that stayed over at the Golden Tulip. The young woman behind the desk was an East Indian, plump in a red sari. George smiled as he approached the desk. He noticed that there was a security camera, and TV screen showed an image of the entrance and street outside. The TV monitor was turned so that someone in the anteroom—immediately to the right of the desk— could see who was coming and going without having to actually be *at* the desk.

"Good day," George said, "I'm DCI Filbert." He got out his Kroll ID and flashed it and folded it up again. "The men that came into the hotel a short while ago. Which room are they staying in?"

"Twenty-three, sir. We want no trouble with the police, sir."

"Well, I'm afraid there is," George said. "If you cooperate you should be all right, though. But I'll have to have your full cooperation. Do you understand?"

"Yes, sir." The young woman, a Dravidian he guessed, was in her twenties and had a gold front-tooth. Lower caste Indians were terrified of authority and he knew it. The moment he walked in and spotted her, he'd guessed she would be afraid of a white man in a suit.

"How many men came in with him?" The front door buzzer went off behind them.

"Two others, sir." A group of French girls came up the hotel's main stairs, stopped at the desk to pick up their room key and started to climb on up the stairs, chattering the whole time.

"No elevator?" George asked, as soon as they were gone.

"No, sir. Just the stairs."

"Is there a fire escape?"

"No, sir. Just stairs, sir. That's all."

"How many floors?"

"Three, sir."

"What floor is room 23 on?"

"Second floor, sir, in the corner."

"The woman who came in. The tall, older woman. Did she go to room 23, too?"

"Yes, sir."

"Do you have to connect calls to the rooms through your switchboard here?"

"Yes, sir. No direct dialing."

"All right. Do not connect any calls to room 23. Do you understand me?"

"Yes, sir."

"Now give me the key to the adjacent room."

"I can't, sir; it's occupied," she said.

"Are there guests in the room right now?" She turned and looked at the key cupboard.

"No—the key is gone, sir."

"Do you have their passports?"

"Yes, sir."

"Let me see them," George said. She looked at him a moment. "... Go on—get them for me." She went into the anteroom to the right and came back in a moment with two Italian passports. He looked at both of them. It was a young couple in their twenties. The photos showed a boy with long hair. He gave the passports back. "If they come back and ask for the key, tell them that there is work being done in the room right now, and to come back in half-an-hour. Ring me if they come. Do you understand?"

"Yes, sir ... Sir—what's wrong?"

"A prostitution ring. ... And we suspect the owners."

"The owner is my uncle, sir. There's no prostitution here, sir." He picked up the Italian passport. "This man is a well known pimp. Now you'd better cooperate, hadn't you. For your uncle's sake," he said. "I'll need a pass-key."

It was dark in the hallway. The rug was threadbare and hadn't been changed in years. The rooms all shared a bathroom at the end of the hall. He walked by the room they'd taken Malcolm to and hesitated a moment. He heard voices through the thin door, then went on to the adjoining room and opened the door and flipped on the lights. The phone began to ring the moment he shut the door. He walked into the room looking for the phone, saw it almost immediately by an unmade double bed, and walked over and picked it up.

"They're here, sir."

"All right. Tell them to come back. In half-an-hour," he said.

"They don't listen, sir ... they go up to the room."

He put down the phone and took the pistol out. He went to the wall and put his ear against it. It was as thin as he thought it would be. He could hear Mary's voice. He went out of the room and closed the door, making sure it was locked, then went to the bathroom at the end of the hall, using the pass-key to get in. He saw a young couple enter the hallway and start walking towards him. He stepped from the bathroom and took out his Kroll ID and told them that there was a police operation underway and that they had to leave. The young man looked at him. He saw the pistol in his right hand and took his girlfriend's hand and turned around and the two went back down the stairs without saying a word to him.

He walked back down the hall, and as he did, he heard a scream. His first instinct was to use the pass-key and enter Room 23. But he fought the urge and listened

241

carefully instead. He expected someone from one of the other rooms to rush out into the hallway to investigate, but no one did. It was almost twelve-noon, and most people would be out now, he supposed. He took a deep breath and opened the door to the adjacent room. He walked over to the phone, picked it up, and rang the desk-number that was printed on the phone.

"Call room 23 and tell them that they need to speak to someone at the desk. That there's a problem. Make something up—I don't care what you tell them—anything," George said. He hung up. There was another scream. It was a man's—he could tell, as he'd heard men scream like that in Burma after they were captured by the Japs, and he knew what it meant. This time it was *very* loud. *If I go in the front door they'll shoot me right off.* He went to the wall and put his ear against it. He heard the phone ring in Room 23. It was picked up almost immediately. He heard a groan and involuntarily flinched. He heard the door open and close next door. *There was one less now.* He'd at least improved the odds a bit, he thought. He looked at the door. It was a wide field of fire, as this room would be the same as the adjoining room—*but maybe not*—he couldn't know for sure, because it was a corner room. He'd never be able to cover the whole room in time. He looked quickly around him, feeling desperate now, as he felt that time was running out; that whatever the desk clerk would say would be ignored and whoever they sent would soon be back. He rushed out of the room and went to the stairs, looking down them and seeing no one. He turned around. There was a fire alarm on the wall at the head of the stairs. The kind with the box behind the glass. He took his pistol and smashed the glass and pulled down on the alarm. He stood for a second at the top of the stairs, then turned and walked quickly back down the hall and tapped his gun on the door, yelling:

"Fire! Get out, now! Fire!" He didn't have long to wait. As the door opened, he fired almost point-blank at the man coming at him through the doorway. He got a head shot. He stepped through the door and saw that Malcolm was tied to a desk, turning as he made the identification. The other man was stepping towards him, but his gun was caught in the backup holster he wore on his ankle. He was bent over tugging at it when George shot him through the top of the head. The bullet exited out his nose. He stood up and looked at George, as if to speak. The blood spurted out of the wound like a fountain. George shot him again in the head—dead on his feet now, he fell backwards to the floor.

They'd sent Mary down to the desk. He looked across the room at Malcolm, who was straddled over a desk with something up his rectum. It was the strangest thing he'd ever seen. There was quite a bit of blood on the floor. He went to the desk and tore the tape off Malcolm's mouth, and the two men locked eyes for a moment.

25

"What you need is a brandy, old man," George said. "You've been asleep for a while."

"Nice place," Malcolm said. He was lying in an antique Edwardian bed and didn't remember anything of the past day, or the young Indian doctor who had worked on him, stitching up his anus. It was all a fog of partial memories. He did remember being tortured and the horrible jolt of the rod.

"Wife's rich," George said, pouring a drink for him. "Might as well get a rich wife, I always say. At least *I've* found it very convenient."

"... How long have I been asleep?" Malcolm said.

"A whole day. The doctor thought it best to knock you out," George said.

"I don't remember him, at all."

"A Harley Street man that Kroll uses. Stitches up our boys after a scrap. Raj Gupta. A good man. He takes drugs himself ... but I don't hold it against him," George said.

"Thank you," Malcolm said, "for following them. I saw you when they first put me in the cab." He closed his eyes for an instant and saw the moment again that he'd spotted George pulling over. He felt himself going back to sleep, but fought against it and opened his eyes again.

"Don't mention it," George said. He handed him a drink from a bottle of Hennessey brandy he'd brought in and put on the nightstand. The guest bedroom in the Cummings' Bayswater house was large with very high ceilings and intricate plaster mouldings. There were seven bedrooms. The house had once belonged to a famous turn-of-the-century coal baron. His mines used child labor and he'd been sent to Parliament by the Conservative Party as a reward for fighting the miner's union and the eight-hour day. George's wife had decorated the guest bedroom in red tones and they laughingly called it the "Pope's Room." The four-poster bed was huge, so that anyone lying in it looked like a child. Malcolm took the brandy and pulled himself up further, sitting up in a sea of pillows.

"The doctor said no spirits," George said, "but I ignore any advice about alcohol or smoking. And look at me; I'm the picture of health."

"So do I. ... ignore doctors," Malcolm said. He had a headache from the Haldol the

Indian doctor had used on him. He felt enervated. Everything seemed so impossible now. He was losing the fight and he knew it. It was the first time he'd felt they would win. Something about the orderliness and grandeur of the bedroom told him he was losing.

"Haldol, you said. What the doctor gave me?"

"Yes. Gupta thought they had given you some kind of drug. Perhaps LSD. You certainly weren't in your right mind by the time I got you here," George said.

" I see. ... It was an electric cattle-prod, I think," Malcolm said. "What they used on me."

"Yes. ... The doctor thought so, too. Said it may have burnt your intestines. The small one, to be exact. You *should* go to the hospital and have it checked out. He wanted to take you but under the circumstances I didn't think you'd want to go," George said. "I couldn't protect you there, could I?"

"No. You did the right thing. And who needs an intestine, a small one, especially. ... It wasn't my finest hour, George," Malcolm smiled, trying to make a joke out of it all, wondering how he'd looked when George came into the room.

"... I've already forgotten about it. Sometimes we're not our best, are we? It's the nature of our business," George said. He pulled a chair over and took a drink of brandy. "... My wife wants to meet you. Right now I've told her you're off limits. That you have a drug problem and needed to be brought down. That you're a fabulously rich Canadian friend of mine from Cambridge. Dissolute ... but nice."

"I want to meet her. I wish you would have said something more flattering about me. ... drug addict, huh?" George nodded.

"I saw Mary at the hotel," George said. "She went down to talk to the desk clerk. She killed the girl. I was very surprised. She shot the clerk." He touched his index finger to a point between the eyebrows. "A nice girl, too. Certainly not part of *our* world. ... Why would Mary do that, Alex?"

"It's a long story," Malcolm said.

"Well, I've a full bottle here, and it's past the children's bedtime so why don't you tell me. I love stories."

"It's Gehlen," Malcolm said.

"General Gehlen? What about him? He just died. I read it in the papers."

"It starts with him," Malcolm said. "It starts with him."

"The head of West German intelligence, and Hitler's head of Eastern Front intelligence before that?"

"Yes."

"What about him?"

"Mary is working for him. ... She has been for quite awhile."

244

"For the *Germans?* Our Mary?"

"Yes," Malcolm said. His still eyelids felt heavy and he had to fight to keep them open.

"Why?"

"I'm not sure. ... Money, I suspect."

"Does this have something to do with your Company? Is there some kind of war out there that I'm not aware of? Have Britain and Germany teamed up against the CIA? ... That seems odd, if true."

"George, what I tell you now could ... well, if you get dragged into this, frankly, you probably don't want to be. You have a family, now; you should stay out of it."

"I'm afraid I've already been dragged into it. You're *here,* aren't you? What *about* Gehlen? He was a Nazi general during the war. If my memory serves ... ?" George said.

"Yes. We—OSS—took him over, of course. We wanted his networks in the East. He was head of Eastern Front intelligence for the Abwehr. He came with loads of files: he'd taken all his files, whole networks he could light up again anytime he wanted: Poland, Finland, Hungary. ... We bought him and his people, lock, stock and barrel."

"And he made good, too—everyone knows that. I mean, your lot loved him and he climbed up the ladder. Came all the way back from war prisoner to head of West German intelligence," George said.

"Yes. Exactly," Malcolm said. "We thought he was our man."

"And now?"

"I'm afraid Gehlen created a stand-alone secret intelligence operation that has now matured. They have people buried in all the major intelligence agencies in the world and are running operations that benefit only *their* organization: This "Gehlen network." I think they've taken over, or at least compromised, the CIA. And your people, too—MI6. It's brilliant and they've been working at it for a very long time. Twenty-five years, in fact," Malcolm said. "They've been very patient."

"Surely you're joking. Surely. This sounds like a Ludlum novel," George said.

"No, not at all. I wish I were," Malcolm said. He took a drink. His head was muddled. The events in the hotel room seemed to come and go when he closed his eyes. He'd dreamt it was Mary who was torturing him. In the dream she'd stood behind him and laughed as he felt his guts burn up.

"And yesterday ... When I found you? What was all that about?" George said.

"It was them. The network. They wanted to know what I knew about someone. I'd stupidly gone to Mary for help about it, you see. I can't fight them alone. I need help."

"Our Mary is still in the game from what I heard. At MI6," George said.

"Yes. She's head of research."

"But you say she's working for this network."

"Yes."

"Good Lord. How do you know all this? ... About Gehlen?" George said.

"It took me quite a while to figure it out. There were too many strange things going on, for one thing. I think that when they got rid of you it was part of a purging of officers who might, for whatever reasons, be suspicious of what was going on, too," Malcolm said. "It happened on both sides of the Atlantic. That was Gehlen's first big move. They turned your Philby problem into an advantage for *them*, you see."

"I still don't understand. What would a West German intelligence chief get out of all this ... If it's true?"

"Control of the enemy. The West. The Allies. I think that was his goal all along—to rebuild Germany—unite it again. And now I think that's high on their agenda—a united Germany.

"That's preposterous," George said. "I'm afraid the Soviets might have a word to say about that."

"... Maybe. But in the meantime, the Gehlen people are big players in the drug business because it's so lucrative. And because of that, they can use the money they make to control some major banks, which in turn gives them political influence across the globe. They are interested in power, George. That's what they want—*power.*"

"And all this ... to what end—a Fourth Reich?"

"Gehlen wanted a unified Germany at the head of Europe. And I think they want to bring down the USSR. They want to recreate the Reich again, maybe. Or some version of it, anyway, with Germany calling the shots in Europe again."

"Sounds like a stretch to me, old boy," George said.

"I know. I thought so, too, at first. But I believe it, certainly now that they've tried to kill me! They've gotten very powerful, George, the West Germans have. They're now the third-largest economy in the world. Right?"

"What are you going to do, now?" George said. "It seems you have some very dangerous enemies—whoever they are."

"I don't know. Can I stay here for awhile? Did Mary see you at the hotel?"

"No."

"George—you *should* throw me out. They could come here. I don't know if they were able to tap my phone at the bank. It's very possible that they know I contacted you for help, even. They *could* come here."

"Frankly, I think Mary would come to that conclusion herself," George said. "She's terribly bright, you know."

"She will kill you outright, then. And maybe ..."

"... Yes, I understand. I've got some young chaps downstairs right now that I trust.

Former SAS boys. They're Kroll men, now. Very nasty boys if they want to be. You'll be quite safe here, I should think; for a little while, anyway."

"Do you believe me? What I told you?" Malcolm asked him.

"What is it Mary *wanted* from you?" George said.

"There's someone that I'm bringing out from East Germany. A scientist who contacted me and said he knew which people inside Langley were Gehlen's people."

"And you believed him?"

"Yes. He worked in the Abwehr, was a former SS man, too. I first met him in Dachau during Operation Paperclip. He was supposed to be hanged there, but he escaped due to some Russian shenanigans. I suspect that a lot of the Nazi scientists we brought to the West *were* secretly part of Gehlen's network. After all, they were all German army or SS officers; almost all of them, even Von Braun.

"The Gehlen network rescued this guy from the hangman—he's a Hauptmann named Neizert—and he went to work for the East Germans, and I suspect also for Gehlen. He contacted me directly just recently. I know what you're thinking, George. That this all sounds incredible—I understand completely, believe me." George looked at him and picked up a Waterford lighter and lit a fresh cigarette, taking one from a silver case that Malcolm remembered from their time in Mexico. He still had it.

"You know it was Mary who accused me of being a traitor ... of being part of Kim Philby's KGB network," George said. "It was absurd. We were in such a state then, right after Philby left for Moscow, that *everyone* was suspect. Half the people in the Circus had gone to school with him, after all. She came to me and told me that I should quit before I was accused. That she would fix things with the powers that be, in Whitehall. Her husband would, anyway. She said she wanted to help me because I'd been friends with her brother. She spread a rumor that I had a gambling problem and was a security risk."

"And you believed her... ?"

"She knew that I had gone and secretly made my own accusations about one of Philby's associates; I'd come across the man in Suez during the crisis. A very fishy fellow, always taking off and disappearing during the worst of it. So I decided to follow him one time. He had a dead-drop. *I* picked up the message, however. It was a nice little map of where our boys were going to land. I knew that map was top secret. I told the station chief and expected the git to be arrested. He ended up being transferred to Germany, though. ... Bonn, in fact." George looked at him. "I made a full report—in triplicate, and sent it to London and said that he was spying either for your lot, or for the KGB. I was told to mind my own business, that it was "operational." So I assumed he was working for your lot and London didn't care. Or couldn't complain about it if they *did* care, you know.

I could see that something was terribly wrong in the Service after I got back to London after Suez. There was a strange nervousness, suddenly—in-fighting, closed doors, and a real fear that we were losing the Cold War. I was glad to go to Mexico when they sent me. Then in Mexico I got the order to go back to London under a cloud right after I saw you. All the men I knew during the war were gone and a new crop of young Turks had taken over after Philby. Overnight, really. I was alone and I knew it. Mary just pointed to the obvious. It was as if there had been a silent coup of some kind. I thought that it was because of Philby's betrayal that they'd cleaned house. And as I was seen by them as one of the old lot ..."

"So you left."

"Yes, but not before I was invited to go down to Mary's place for a weekend. The house in Kent. A very strange weekend it was, too," George said.

"What happened?"

"It was there she advised me to leave the service. That they knew about me, or suspected me of being a traitor. She asked me to stay on and root out the problem. To report to her directly. She said that there were a lot of KGB spies and that Kim Philby wasn't the only one. She wanted me to spy on people I knew from the old days. I told her no, I wouldn't do it. I left. I turned in my paperwork that week. I stuck to the gambling-problem-story and everyone bought it."

"Did you sleep with her?" Malcolm asked.

"Yes. Of course," George said. "Well, she'd come to my room. I thought that was why she'd invited me down to the bloody opulent place. I think now it was all just part of the show. To get me to believe in her—if we were having an affair, how could I refuse her and rot like that. ..."

"So she forced you out when you refused to cooperate?"

"Yes. ... All very nice and quiet, too, if you know what I mean. ... I haven't forgiven them, you know. ... So maybe you're right. It explains a *lot*, anyway. Another drink? ... I think I will," George said. "Doctor's orders."

"Will you help me, George? I know I've no right to ask, especially in light of what you've just done, and how far you've been sucked into it already, but still. ..."

"Why not?" George said refilling his glass.

"Would you deliver this Hauptmann Neizert for me ... to Sonny Delmonico?"

"The poof from Mexico."

Malcolm smiled. "Yes; the same."

"Still around, is he?"

"Yes, he is. They'll come after you, George, with everything they have. They want their Hauptmann back. Very badly."

"Right. Well, it can't be *that* hard, old man," George said. "Where is he? Your fellow?"

"In Berlin right now. He's with someone I trust."

"And where do you want him taken?" George asked.

"Rome."

"My pleasure, old man." George smiled. "What about our Mary?" Malcolm didn't answer. "I see. Can't say she doesn't deserve it. Do you have a man for that?" George asked. "It won't be easy, I don't imagine. ..."

"Yes, I think I do," Malcolm said. A young and very attractive woman opened the door. She was striking; very tall and regal-looking.

"Dear ... come in. Come in. I want you to meet my old pal ... I say, I didn't catch your name? Did I?" George said. "You see, dear, it's been years and I ..." She looked into the room, gave her husband a curious look, smiled at his guest, and closed the door again.

"I'd say that went very well. Don't you think?" George said.

26

■ RONDA, SPAIN

The hard and dry Andalusían landscape had changed, becoming a faded purple color as dusk fell; everything was receding and diminished, no longer the blurry, sun-dominated fortress of brass-colored hillsides and dark-cloaked masculine oaks that had surrounded Sonny Delmonico's house that noon. The end of the day had also brought a welcome end to the stifling heat. Sonny's new house was something he'd wanted for years, and now that the construction was complete, he felt odd, as if there were still something important missing—some room he'd forgotten, or a view he'd left unexploited.

Perhaps it was just that middle-age had finally caught him there in Spain and, like the dusk, there was no escaping this harbinger of the coming darkness. It was a sense of Time—it was running faster. For long moments while Sonny floated in the pool he thought he might be reaching the end of his run of good luck. The heroin business was changing and he knew it. The Americans had finally waded in full-force, with something called the DEA. The Colombians, unheard of only a few years before, were sending hit teams out across the world to stifle competition. A dirty business had recently gotten even dirtier.

Sonny, his skin lightly oiled, was floating naked, having enjoyed himself all afternoon in the company of two very pretty English rent boys he'd picked up in Lisbon near the Castle de Saint George, while visiting the home of a business associate, an English Lord. The Lord was a very tall man, ramrod-straight, and hatchet-faced. He'd once been a Colonel in the Coldstream Guards, as well as a personal friend of the King of England, no less. The Colonel, a world-class sybarite, had gone into the heroin business directly after his illustrious family's finances had collapsed due to the *Mau Mau* rebellion in Kenya where they'd lost their coffee estates. Like with most aristocrats, questions of money always trumped morality— something that Sonny had noticed was especially true of the British. Lord Hayland had moved on into the heroin business, his ancestors having made their first real money selling opium to the Chinese—so its modern version, heroin, was not really much of a stretch.

Sonny had gone to Lisbon two weeks before to shepherd a fifty-kilo load of heroin aboard a container ship flying a Lebanese flag that was heading for Toronto, the merchandise to be hidden in a shipment of new Fiats. The ship was actually owned by a Greek company. It was said that the Greek company was in turn owned by very important members of the former Greek junta, but of course, that could never be proved. The whole purpose of the Lebanese registry of the ship, as part of a host of other cut-out corporations, was to make precise ownership of the vessel extremely difficult to trace.

Lord Hayland's job was to make sure his contacts inside the Portuguese government and police were paid-off, helping to insure that the DEA, and any other American police agency, didn't get wind of the operation. The new DEA were, in fact, fed disinformation about a possible shipment moving by truck through the Algarve— Sonny's idea, which had worked very well. The heroin that had been flown in from Italy in a private jet was now hidden in new Italian cars being shipped to Canada, all of this happening while the Greek ship had been docked in the Lisbon harbor and the DEA was frantically looking for it in the Algarve. In fact, and to Sonny's delight, the heroin had been loaded in plain sight of the DEA's brand new office in Lisbon, with its view of the harbor.

Sonny, because of rumors of DEA infiltration at the port, had been nervous the entire week he was in Lisbon. He and Lord Hayland—who wore an old-school tie as a belt—sat in a restaurant overlooking the docks and watched their ship—christened The Irene 2— depart for Canada, her running lights quite beautiful as she made her way out of the port late one Wednesday night, their part of the job finally finished. They'd gone back to the Castile and had gotten drunk on champagne and fucked the daylights out of the two rent boys who Lord Hayland had picked up in a bar.

Sonny had brought the two boys back to Ronda because they'd said they were "out seeing the world for a year," and were eager to visit Spain. The two boys were "positively kalokagathic," as the gray-haired Colonel had said of them, lighting a cigarette in bed, using the ancient Greek term, and the two blonds *did* seem to have stepped off a marble plinth in some ancient Greek temple that had been dedicated to Adonis, buggery, and high-living in general.

The two had proceeded to earn their money after lunch, after good-hearted squirt-gun fights and long bouts of guzzling the local wine from Sonny's well-used leather *bota*, which had been passed around several times while they'd all been in the pool. Then, when Sonny judged it was time, he'd taken the two upstairs into his very warm second-floor bedroom, which had a marvelous view of the surrounding hills, for what he called their "close-up." He'd thought they were well-worth the money they'd cost him, as they were not only physically beautiful boys, but quite obviously sexually eager, and really all he could have asked for in the way of whores.

The two, back in swimsuits now, were looking at a Michelin road-map of southern Spain, planning to push-off that evening, when the phone rang inside the house. The two had been calling out the names of towns they might visit, with Sonny giving his opinion of each town while floating face-up on a lime-green air mattress, still butt-naked.

"*Murthia?*" one of the boys said, stabbing at the road map with his finger.

"Gonorrhea capital of the south! ... Has the biggest horse-flies in Europe," Sonny said, while trying to balance a bottle of cold Spanish beer on his stomach. "They sound like the Messerschmitt 109s at Anzio Beach. ..." Sonny made a loud sound, miming the German planes as they strafed the legendary beach at a mere fifty-foot of the sand. "*Raaaaatatatatata.*" He looked up at the boys, who he realized were staring at him questioningly, as they hadn't a clue about that war, Anzio Beach, and certainly not the Messerschmitt 109. And yet it seemed like only yesterday to *him*. Sometimes when he was half-drunk, like this, and happy, his day at the Battle of Anzio Beach would come back to him in all its horror. Without any warning, he would be trying to cross that bloody, gut-splattered, horror-filled beach once more, and be seventeen and scared shitless yet again.

"Anzio ... Is that in Spain ... ?" The slower and prettier of the two asked. He had big girl's lips and a pageboy haircut. He looked up from the map, his expression a pleasant blank. He'd actually been to Eaton. Sonny had made jokes about the school all day, enjoying the idea that he was actually fucking a member of the British upper class. The boy's father was a solicitor and an important Tory politician, no less.

"Valencia? Any better ... Sonny?" the other boy asked, ignoring Sonny's momentary lapse.

"... For *you* two ... a *gold* mine ... believe me," Sonny said.

"*Jerez something de la something.* ... It's near the sea. Could be jolly?" Pageboy enthusiastically chimed in his next query.

"*De la Frontera* ... Grimy peasants! Topless Saudi princesses with Brazilian gigolos. ... Nothing like a Bedouin in the bedroom, ah what? ... The garlic capital of Spain, too. A *must* see for the adventurous-traveler-on-a-budget like you two," Sonny said.

The two young men laughed, genuinely entertained by their roly-poly John's avuncular repartee, and obvious knowledge of the country, unaware that he was simultaneously hearing the sounds of battle and the sounds of violent death—the actual smack that bullets make when they hit a face, or the dull, metallic-whack sound of a helmet catching one. For a moment Sonny disappeared again into his day-mare, his air mattress spinning slowly in the pool. Their host seemed a million miles away, both boys finally noticed, and looked at each other, too young to understand much beyond the surface of things. Then the prettier one splashed Sonny in fun, just as the phone started to ring inside the house.

Sonny immediately paddled to the shallow end, rolled off his air mattress and walked naked, dripping wet, like a strange hairy amphibious queer, on into the house to pick up the phone in the new living room. He put his beer down on the kitchen table carefully, making sure he sat the bottle on a coaster before he answered the still-ringing phone.

"It's Wally, Beer Monster," an Englishman's voice said, over a connection that seemed to Sonny to be at least half-static.

"*Wally?*" Sonny said.

"Beer Monster ... is that you? Listen, someone is pestering me. Needs a bloody Sherpa. I thought I'd have him give you a bell on the old dog and bone." The two men used the cockney rhyming-slang they'd grown up with and that they knew made any wire-tapping of their conversations doubly difficult because their patois was impenetrable to all but a few trained English policemen. For the American DEA it would certainly be a "bag of shit" nightmare, at best.

Sonny had known the man on the phone, Wally Giordano, since he was seven years old. They had grown up in the East End together in the same housing estate. Their two families had been close because both sets of parents had been born in Sicily and come to England at about the same time. Wally had gone over to the Camorra for practical reasons at the age of twelve and was a made-man by his twentieth birthday. Both Wally and Sonny had run with the Kray Brothers, who were Camorra fronts—something Scotland Yard never understood about the Krays, or in fact about the East End drug business, which was all run by remote-control from Italy.

It had been Wally who'd brought Sonny into the heroin business after the war. He'd sent him to Italy to meet Lucky Luciano and to arrange for the sole rights to sell Italian-produced heroin in England.

"Is he safe?" Sonny asked.

"Safe as houses," Wally said.

"You're sure, Wally? There're so many *odd* people about these days ... *you* know. ..." Wally was calling from the apartment on Canary Wharf.

"I *do* need the money, actually. Bit of the *half inch*. Who is he, your bloke?" Sonny asked.

"A Yank. He wants a bell today. He was sent by some friends in spats. A real hoity-toity bitch, in fact."

"... What's his name?"

"Tucker." Sonny moved the phone from one slightly oily hand to the other. "... Yes or no, old boy? I have to know right now. He's a persistent type, this lad. And his friends are a surly bunch."

"... Wally. ... You're *sure* he's all right? Is he a diamond-geezer?" Sonny asked, using an East Ender term for a man who could be trusted completely.

"Yes. Some of the friends don't like him. Say he's a git. Seems he's got a checkered past. But who doesn't? *I could care less,*" Wally said.

"... ... Yes, all right. Have you a number?" Wally gave him one, and he wrote it on the Formica tabletop with a pencil that he kept by the phone. ... How are the boys and Margie?" Sonny asked.

"Couldn't be better. Right you are, Beer Monster. You'll call the man, then? *Now?*"

"Yes, right *now*. If you say so, Cannon." Sonny used Wally's underworld nickname.

"That a boy," Wally said. "Oh, by the way ... I saw that old film ... on the teli the other night ... you know—that one with John Wayne and Rita Hayworth. Lot's of elephants in it," Wally said. "Have you seen it? You should. My kids loved it. ... The elephants; the way they walk about? *Huge.*"

"Yes. ... *Circus World* ... I've seen it," Sonny said. "Saw it once when I was in the nick in Turkey."

"Can't beat those old American films," Wally said.

"... Thanks. Wally. *Ciao.*"

"Don't mention it, you old curry-digger."

Sonny put down the phone and stood there thinking, still dripping wet from the pool but starting to sweat from the close heat of the house's interior. Wally was always clever. He'd managed to transmit a coded message. "Elephants" in their East End slang were important high-end policemen— specifically, MI5 or MI6. John Wayne referred to America, so he was warning him that Tucker was some kind of intelligence officer, most probably DEA. But the shocker was that Wally had said that he could "care less" about him. That was an outright death sentence, and a long-time code in the Sicilian mafia when you wanted it understood that the man in question was to be eliminated, by whatever means necessary. His old friend had gone out of his way to explain Tucker's provenance in a way that very few people would understand. Wally was asking him to kill an American police officer who had been sent via British intelligence—his reference to "friends in spats" being yet another code phrase—and this was something that had never happened before.

Sonny knew that if any of the various police agencies—MI5 or the DEA among them—had listened-in on the call they would have only heard Wally doing what he'd been asked to do by his handlers: act as a gatekeeper, and wave Tucker through to Palermo. But had they ordered a hit, too? Sonny was used to double dealing, especially in Sicily, but for British intelligence to set up a hit on an American? That was shocking, even to him. He picked up his beer, sweating profusely now, and drained it at a swallow. Then he went and toweled himself off, wrapped the towel around his waist, then picked up the phone and dialed the number he'd been given by Wally, listening to it ring.

"Hello," Sonny said.

"I've heard you're an expert." The voice had an obvious American accent.

"Do I know you?" Sonny asked.

"Bruce Tucker. I think we've got some mutual friends ... in the business."

"Do we?"

"Your pal Wally for one. I'll be in Italy in two weeks. I need a good guide—I want to go to Palermo and see the sights while I'm there."

"Palermo?"

"Yes. They say you speak the language. That you're fluent," the American said.

"Oh. ... Well, it's true. I *can* order dinner and not be misunderstood," Sonny joked.

"Is it a date, then?" Alex said.

"If you insist. ... Where do you want to meet?" Sonny said.

"Say the bar at the Hotel Majestic in Rome? Do you know it?"

"Fine," Sonny said.

"Okay, then. I'll be there at around two o'clock, on the sixth of next month," Alex said.

"Fine. ... But I'm an expensive date, you know, *dearie*," Sonny impulsively threw in.

"No problem about that. Wally's explained the rules to me. What do you look like?"

"Yul Brynner ... only with a black eye-patch and much better-looking. And You ... ?"

"The sixth, then." The man hung-up without responding to Sonny's attempt at flirtation. By the time he put the phone down dusk had finally segued into a hard dark. He tied the towel around his waist a second time and walked back out to the pool, sobered by the call. The boys had turned on the pool lights and everything looked perfect. Just the way he'd planned it.

Sonny wasn't surprised that the American had chosen the bar at the hotel Majestic for a meeting place, as it was close to the American Embassy and a known haunt for American intelligence operatives. He'd gone there by train the day after speaking to

Wally on the phone: first to Madrid to meet his MI6 contact and make an inquiry as to who "Bruce Tucker" was, pretending he'd never heard of him before, but explaining that the man wanted an introduction to the Sicilian Mob. He'd asked pointedly if Tucker had CIA protection, afraid he might be dealing with a situation that could blow back at him if there was a misunderstanding between the Americans and the Brits about Tucker. His long-time contact in MI6—a middle-aged woman who spoke perfect Spanish—told him a day later when they met in a working-class bar in the capital—that Tucker was a DEA officer who had gone rogue and was of "no interest" whatsoever to MI6. If there had been any question about Tucker in his mind, it was cleared up by that meeting in Madrid. Tucker had been sent to Sonny to be disposed of, no doubt, because of his drug-dealing. Better that he "die in the line of duty" than be caught some day and brought to trial, possibly embarrassing the DEA. It made sense to Sonny, too, that MI6 would be the cutout and pass the contract on to Wally. It was simply the way business was done. Near Valencia, on the train back to Ronda, Sonny decided to accept the contract on the American.

*　　　　　*　　　　　*

Sonny, standing at the bar dressed to kill, hadn't touched his drink. He had gotten a good night's sleep, too. *If I hadn't spent so much money on that damned house,* he thought to himself, *I wouldn't have to take such big risks now.* He'd just celebrated his fifty-third birthday, and had suddenly realized that he might be getting too old for The Game, which, after all, was designed for the young. And, for the first time ever, too, he had second thoughts about what he was about to do.

He'd arrived early, and was standing at the nearly empty bar nursing a Coca-Cola with a slice of lime in it. In fact, he was stone-cold sober for a change, because he knew now he might be in danger himself, and he needed to keep all the wits he had. He looked at his watch. The whole idea of hitting someone on orders of the Brits was bothering him. A lot. And the fact that Tucker had already escaped death by assassination once—he'd been told that in Madrid—demanded that Sonny respect him. A slight young man in a dark suit ambled casually into the barroom.

The young man looked entirely different than what Sonny had expected. He'd expected someone older, and frankly meaner-looking, given all he'd heard about Tucker. Alex smiled slightly. Sonny waved, as if Tucker and he were old friends. He couldn't help himself from noticing the young man's good looks; he was a kind of more-slightly-built Robert Redford-type, he thought to himself. *A damned good-looking boy. It was a shame he had to die.*

"You were right; you'll need a guide," Sonny told him. "You can't just show up in Sicily without one. I'm afraid that's the rule, young man."

"That's what I was told," Alex said.

"It's mainly because no one knows who you are. *I* don't know who you are—not really—and they *certainly* don't. The Sicilians are a different breed. They get uncomfortable with strangers. It's a terribly provincial place," Sonny explained, taking a sip of his Coke and looking at their dual reflections in the big mirror behind the bar.

"Well, I'm basically just a simple business man," Alex said. "And I've heard you're the man who can fix things ... in Palermo, that is." Alex ordered a gin and tonic and glanced at a group of Pan Am stewardesses still wearing their uniforms, who'd just come into the bar after their long flight from New York. They'd all spotted Alex and were flirting with him from a distance. "I want to meet with Count Cici directly—can I do that?" Alex asked, his eyes still on the girls.

"It depends," Sonny said, raising an eyebrow, "on what it is you want."

"Well, I want to meet him and discuss some business." Alex said as he turned back and looked at Sonny.

"What kind of business?"

"The kind that always makes money," Alex said.

"Heroin?" Sonny said. "... I'm not a fool, young man."

"Yes," Alex said.

"You don't seem the type," Sonny said.

"What's the type?"

"Well, you're not an Italian for starters. I'm used to greasy little men from Detroit or Bayswater. Not blond boys with clean fingernails."

"It's a business my associates and I would like to explore—I didn't know you had to be Italian to be in it," Alex said.

"And your market would be ... ?"

"None of *your* business," Alex said, lifting his glass and spotting a cute brunette stewardess who met his gaze without hesitation. She gave him the green light right then and there. He'd been having lots of casual sex since Patty, in an attempt to forget that he felt responsible for her brutal death. It wasn't working very well, so he drank a lot now as well, in order to forget. He'd done everything he could to get fired from the Agency, too, but it hadn't worked. After the shooting, his father had sent him for a "rest" down to Mexico, thinking the foreign ambience and the trip itself would help. But, as it turned out, it had only allowed him to drink more, without anybody in the Agency finding out about it. He had no idea where Butch was, and had often wanted to call him when he was gassed. They'd last seen each other at the airport in San Francisco. He really missed their time together in LA. What they'd done there had been strangely liberating for Alex. It had been the first time he'd been really happy, too, in a very long time. He'd felt connected to his friends there, in a way he never had before. He'd actually *had* friends for a change; the kind you want to spend time with. After everything that had happened in Southern California, he'd found it almost impossible to return to the straight-and-narrow world of a spit-and-polish intelligence officer; following orders; reporting for duty in a suit at the London Embassy, where everyone said they'd missed him. He hadn't liked any of the men he'd worked with there, at all. L.A. had changed him for good, in many ways.

"I'm afraid it *is* my business, old man. They won't want to give you a market if it's already taken. The Bonannos have the entire East Coast sewn up, I'm afraid," Sonny said, dropping the name for effect.

"Yes, I've heard of them," Alex dryly assented.

"I thought you might have."

"We want Los Angeles, is what it amounts to. We're fairly new to the business. We're a fledgling company," Alex said, "but excited about the opportunities there."

"L.A. doesn't belong to anyone as far as I know. It's an open city," Sonny said.

"What do you mean?"

"No one family controls the business," Sonny said.

"Well, then it shouldn't be a problem, should it?" Alex said. He winked at the girl who had given him the "look."

"You might have to pay a fee ... to do business there. I could check. There is a family in Los Angeles. Everyone gives them a taste," Sonny said. He watched Tucker's face, looking for any hint of what had happened in LA, but didn't see anything, and was duly impressed by the young man's *sangfroid*.

"Thanks for the advice. But I still need to go to Palermo and speak to the Count. I want to do business directly with him if I can. I've heard he's in charge of all product coming out of Sicily. It's almost as pure as the Hong Kong product, or so we've heard. But cheaper." Sonny smiled, as if Alex had asked to meet with the Queen and go riding with her. Or perhaps speak casually with the Pope.

"All right ... I can send a message. ... Did you bring my fee?" Sonny finished his drink. He put down his clean napkin. The barroom was paneled in dark oak and all the lies and all the stories ever told in the Hotel Majestic's bar in Rome—and there had been many—seemed to hang there floating in the chic atmosphere. "I'll have to have your passport for a day or two," Sonny said.

"My *passport?*"

"Yes. They'll need to vet it," Sonny said.

"You're kidding?" Alex said.

"No. You don't expect him to meet with someone he hasn't vetted. You could be a

DEA officer ... couldn't you?" Sonny said.

"All right." Alex got out his passport and put it on the bar. Bruce Tucker was someone who had actually been killed in Vietnam, but when they checked now, they'd find that Bruce Tucker owned two motels in L.A.. He'd been to law school and was now selling large quantities of heroin—all the buys had actually taken place— sometimes he'd bought directly, without any middlemen involved, from producers in Mexico, too, should anyone check that deeply. The rip-offs, however, were not part of the "legend" that had been constructed by the DEA with the help of Langley. Alex put his hand on top of his passport and slid it over to Sonny.

"Your money is waiting for you at the desk. I gave them your name and told them to give you the package. It's all there ... fifty-thousand dollars," Alex said.

"Capital, old man," Sonny said. He pocketed Alex's passport. "Fancy a drink this evening?" The look from Sonny this time was different, devilish. "I know some out-of-the-way bars. You might like them ... if your tastes run in *that* direction ... ?"

"Which direction would that be?" Alex said, looking up at him. The power of Alex's male beauty, and it was a powerful animal sexuality, was obvious to everyone in the room, from old queens to giddy jet-lagged twenty-year-old stewardesses who'd decided to make a play for the blond in the suit and crisp white shirt sitting at the bar. And who, in fact, would end up screwing him all afternoon in that very hotel later.

"To the *queer*," Sonny said, smiling at him. "I mean, dear boy, looks like yours shouldn't be wasted on just *girls*." Sonny had finally let his hair down, letting all the pins fall at once.

"I'll take a rain check," Alex said. Sonny winked, quite an appalling one, because it came from his one good eye, so made it seem like he was playing to the back row. *A queer Cyclops*, Alex thought to himself. *Jesus Christ, make it stop!* "I have a fascination with women that I can't seem to shake," Alex said.

"Oh, that's not a problem," Sonny said. "I've worked around *that* in the past."

"When can I have my passport back?" Alex said, changing the subject.

"As soon as they're finished with it, young man. It shouldn't take long—they have people in the Embassy here."

"In the Embassy?"

"Of course. Half the employees in the building are Italians, aren't they?"

"Sonny?" Alex said. They shook hands, and Alex was surprised to find Sonny's grip surprisingly firm; at least compared to what he'd had in his mind as to what a queer's handshake should be like.

"Yes, dear."

"You wouldn't be planning on cheating me, now? I want to go to Palermo as soon as possible and I want to meet the Count. I'm very serious about this business."

"I wouldn't dream of it, dear boy. I'll leave that to the Sicilians. They're much better at it."

"Good."

"Do you have a death-wish?" Sonny asked.

"Not particularly, no," Alex said. The question took him somewhat by surprise.

"I just thought I'd ask. I wanted to make sure you weren't crazy or something. Sicily isn't like L.A., *at all*," Sonny said, then he left.

A week later they rode the night train together to Palermo. What happened next was unexpected. The first cable out of the CIA's Rome Station read:

Flash Cable

HEAD OF ITALIAN DESK: *A.L. missing ... presumed kidnapped. Palermo ... agents employed ... forward Director of Operations immediately.*

The phone rang at a CIA station in Miami, forwarded from the number at the motor court hotel in Malibu, California, during a shift change at 6 A.M. The man who picked up the line said: "Good morning, Hotel Capri." The man calling the Capri spoke with a heavy accent, and asked to speak to the manager. The man who had answered the call in Miami said that the manager was not in at the moment, but that he could take a message. The message turned out to be very short.

"We have your friend Tucker in Palermo. We'll kill him in two days if you don't send us a million dollars. We'll have someone pick it up here We'll call you just one more time to arrange the pick-up." The voice was a man's deep baritone. The man in Miami held the phone slightly away from his ear for a moment, shocked, yet not quite sure that this wasn't some kind of a joke being played on him by one or more of his compatriots in the Agency. There was something about the gravity of the voice, and it's all-business tone, though, added to the very thick accent of the speaker, that made him pay close attention rather than start laughing it off, as his initial impulse had been.

"Do you understand?" the caller asked.

"Yes. I'll pass it along ... But I'm sure ..." Whoever it was hung up in the middle of his reply. The call was traced later to an Italian number in Palermo that belonged to a phone-booth at the train station.

It took less than two hours for the message left at the CIA station in Miami to get to Alex's father in New York. He was in his office at Citibank when his assistant came in with the message.

"I'm afraid it's about your son," the young man said. Malcolm Law was on the phone with his daughter in Williamsburg. She'd called to ask for an increase in her allowance and to complain that the lawyer handling her grandfather's trust fund seemed not to like her. Malcolm told her he would call her back.

"It seems he's been kidnapped, sir. He was sold to some kind of competing gang in Palermo, apparently by Delmonico. We can confirm that much now, at least. This other gang has called the motel in L.A. and asked for a ransom of one million dollars. They've given us two days to organize it. They'll call again to arrange a pickup in Palermo."

The motel, and everything else that had been so carefully constructed as a front for Bruce Tucker, had been vetted by a Sicilian mafia plant at the U.S. Embassy in Rome, and later by someone at the Bank of Rome who had called a friend of his at Bank of America to see if the motel had ever shown up in their credit card records. And then the shocker, the same man at the Bank of Rome had placed a call to someone at the U.S. Treasury Department to ask if Bruce Tucker paid taxes and were those taxes related to reported income from several motels in Southern California? Had the Agency not done a very thorough job in creating a cover-story, Alex—his father knew now—might already be dead.

"So we're holding? Our cover story, I mean?" Malcolm said. During his long career he'd been involved in so many operations that had blown-up, that even a report about his own son's kidnapping and possible imminent death could be immediately put in a certain place in his mind that he'd created for bad news to keep it from swamping and immobilizing him.

"Yes, sir. Our cover story is holding. For the time being, anyway. They've checked with people in L.A. about Tucker's illicit business there, too."

"Well, you'd better arrange for the money," Malcolm said.

"Yes, sir," the young man said. "I've already started on that."

"Do we know anything about the people who have him?"

"No, not really, sir. Not yet. It appears they've doubled-crossed Delmonico. He'd arranged to have Tucker killed, actually. We've been monitoring his telephone for a while, now. He made a call from the Hotel Majestic in Rome yesterday asking if the job had been completed yet.

"Do you know where Delmonico is *now?*"

"We think he's gone back to Spain. We're checking on that right now, sir. ..."

"Jesus!"

"Yes, sir. It's a cluster-fuck," the young man said. He didn't know all the details of the operation, but he knew enough to understand that whatever Law's son had gone to Palermo for, it wasn't to be kidnapped.

"Those *fucking* Italians," Malcolm said out loud. They were supposed to have picked Delmonico up—arrested him in Rome, in fact—*before* he left with Alex for Palermo, but to allow Alex to contact Count Cici, who was prepared to protect "Tucker" in Palermo and thwart the hit that Sonny had arranged. Malcolm had spoken to Count Cici—a long time important CIA asset—himself on the phone. The two had conspired to make it look, to anyone observing, as if this person Tucker was a bona fide heroin dealer. But the detention by Italian police of Delmonico, and important part of the plan, had failed to happen. Somehow Delmonico had not been stopped, let alone arrested. It was more proof that something was terribly wrong, everywhere. Either Count Cici had joined Gehlen's people—and lied to him—or the Count himself was losing power inside the Sicilian Mob and had decided to back away from the Tucker operation altogether. Nothing was clear, now, except that his son was in danger of being killed, and it was all *his* doing.

"I want you to call this man, Butch Nickels, and I want him sent here to New York *immediately*," Malcolm said.

"Yes, sir."

"He's in El Salvador. ... Call the Embassy there," Malcolm said. "He's listed as an AID officer there." After his assistant left, Malcolm picked up the phone and called a hotel in Berlin and left a message for a Mr. Jones. The message was a short one: "The meeting with our partners has been put back a little bit. Stand still and wait for further instructions." Then he wondered how he was going to save his son. His plan was in shambles and he knew the other side was probably now in control of the situation.

*　　　　　　*　　　　　　*

The last Alex had seen of Sonny Delmonico was on the platform in Palermo's train station. "These chaps will take over now, old boy. You'll be in front of the Count in an hour—good luck, old man," Sonny had said, disappearing down a flight of stairs that led to the street. That had been just after four in the morning.

The men that met their train were young and not much different looking than young men Alex was used to seeing in London or Rome. They wore bell-bottom jeans and T-shirts. Except this group seemed to palpably exude a kind of casual viciousness—maybe it was just their individual postures, taken together, that seemed to somehow radiate a potential for brutality in whatever they were about—a group effect that was obviously designed to send a message to the public at large. They also seemed totally unconcerned about any consequences to their actions, as if they had nothing in the world to fear from *anyone*.

He'd expected to be spirited off to his meeting with Count Cici, *capo di tutti capi*, but by the time they got to the center of Palermo, Alex realized that there was something *very* wrong with the entire scene. The car he was riding in pulled into an anonymous-looking two-storey garage, and he was hustled from the white Fiat he'd been picked up in at the train station to a waiting black Mercedes with an entirely different group of young men inside it. This time his luggage didn't come along with him, though. When he protested about his luggage being left behind, he was totally ignored. It was the case that none of the men in the late model Mercedes spoke English, or they simply didn't want to speak to him at all, if they did. One of them seemed to be in charge because he did speak, but only in monosyllables, and in Italian. That man looked briefly at Alex when he was pushed into the back seat directly behind him. The man now turned and smirked at Alex as if he knew that Alex was now a commodity and nothing more.

"I'd like a cigarette," Alex said. He hadn't spoken since he'd gotten into the first car at the train station. He asked for the cigarette as they sped down a narrow garage ramp and back out into the dawn streets of Palermo. It was going to be a hot day; Alex could tell that from the orange sun-blotches on the walls of the buildings as they passed. He looked up at the sky and saw the edges of roofs, with laundry hung out to dry, all varicolored by the rising sun. And he saw a blue line that was a patch of sky above the narrow street. It was the first time in his life that there was no one he could turn to for help. Even in L.A., when it had gotten bad, he'd had Butch to turn to, but not here.

The one in charge, sitting up in front next to the driver, took out a cigarette, and for a moment Alex thought perhaps things were not as bad as he'd suspected, that he'd misjudged. Maybe his luggage *was* going to follow. And perhaps the men were just being careful that he was not some kind of policeman with a homing device in his bag. The young man turned again and looked at him. He was dark and he was well-dressed, unlike the others. He had a long, vicious face, and contempt for Alex was rising in his eyes. He took the cigarette and flicked it at Alex, hitting him on the chest with it. Alex watched it roll into his lap and then onto the floor of the car.

"Fuck you," the man said in perfect English. He had a New York accent; Brooklyn to be exact. Then the young men in the car all laughed at Alex, simultaneously, as if they'd orchestrated their laughter beforehand, had actually *rehearsed* it; even the driver, who was speeding down the street changing gears, was quietly laughing at him.

27

■ MALAGA, SPAIN

The old Spanish priest who was showing him the weapons cache had a pink birth mark on his forehead the size of an American fifty-cent piece. Butch Nickels was choosing the weapon he planned on using to kill Sonny Delmonico from a large cache kept in the Catholic church in Marbella, Spain. He'd been flown from New York where he'd had a meeting with Malcolm Law at a cover position he used in the Citibank Office Tower in Manhattan. The meeting with Law had lasted all of fifteen minutes. He had been told, in no uncertain terms, that he was to find a man named Sonny Delmonico in Southern Spain and kill him and take a photograph of the body for Law's father to see. It was a startling request. He was also told to find out what had happened to Alex before he killed Delmonico—*exactly* what happened, and where Alex was being kept in Italy, explaining to Butch that Alex had been kidnapped in Palermo with no other details. Butch had sat in the chair and listened to the older man talk without saying more than a dozen words.

Butch was impressed that after nine years in the Agency he was *finally* being noticed by management. But he decided while riding in an Agency Towncar to JFK— with Law's assistant peppering him with details of his cover story while in Spain— that perhaps he'd made too big a jump in status. Now he was answering directly to Malcolm Law, head of clandestine services, who'd made it clear to him that he was to find this Delmonico and kill him. He'd failed to ask if perhaps this Delmonico was not alone, or was protected by the Mafia, who Butch had also heard from Law were the ones who had kidnapped Alex. Law's father had also implied that if he failed in this assignment his career as an intelligence officer would be over, or worse. Butch was told the Agency was fully aware of what he had been up to in Los Angeles where he (with no mention of Alex having been there with him every step of the way) had "gone over to the dark side" and been profiting from the assignment. The Los Angeles District Attorney might be informed about several killings. It could be said that Malcolm Law had gotten Butch's full attention.

"He's as good as dead, sir. I promise you that," was all Butch said, before he left the office. And he'd meant every word of it.

The arsenal Butch had been taken to had been dug under the church's massive golden Baroque alter during the Spanish Civil War and was full of the latest automatic small arms, including the latest bullet-proof vests that were being used by U.S. troops. The Cache was—like others in Italy, Greece, and Turkey—kept as a secret arsenal should Communists parties win any elections and a CIA-supported shooting-war break out. The Catholic priest who'd met him at the airport in Marbella—father Hidalgo—was a cherubic sixty-year old who had fought for Franco as part of an elite group of young Catholic fascists, young men and women who'd been trained by the Gestapo in Berlin. Their Falangist brigade was used to round up Communists and Anarchists after the "liberation" of Andalucía and deal out the fascist brand of justice, which amounted to being marched to the nearest wall and summarily shot, usually in the town square and in front of their families. Usually, this happened because someone in the town had accused them of being a "Red," or having helped the "Reds," as a way of settling old personal grudges or scores, since most of the villagers were, in reality, totally apolitical. The summary executions were right out of a Goya painting, complete with windy skies and family members screaming, pleading to the young Falangists for mercy. Hidalgo called it "God's mercy" and even told the-soon-to-die that they were going straight to Hell, and that Lucifer himself was waiting for them there. Hidalgo was a firm believer. He was a natural and fervent anti-communist. His aristocratic father and mother had both been hung from the rafters of their grand home by anarchists from the printers' union in Valladolid at the outbreak of the Civil War. They had both been left with placards around their necks saying that they had been sent to visit Jesus and were sitting alongside him now on "God's Golden Throne." The anarchists were firm believers, too, but on the other side of things. After the defeat of fascism in Germany by the Allies—something Hidalgo had prayed would not happen—he was eager to help former SS and Gestapo officers escape from Europe along the ratlines that ran out of the Vatican, leading from Rome to Franco's Spain, and from there on to Latin America. It was a common saying in Buenos Aries, capital of Argentina, that after the war all the police in the city suddenly started speaking German.

Butch—posing as a Catholic priest—had been taken back to the rectory in the Marbella cathedral and given lunch. He was wearing the collar and was introduced to everyone there as Father Nickels from Chicago, a Mary Knoll Father who was on his way to Africa to work with the poor in the Congo.

Twelve priests were served lunch in a room with fifty-foot ceilings and *Mudejar* décor. The rectory's interior had been unchanged since Ferdinand and Isabella retook Marbella. Young female acolytes served and were not spoken to. Butch looked hard at one girl, dark-eyed and strikingly beautiful, despite her grey acolyte's habit. He guessed she was probably only nineteen. He felt a very un-religious stirring as he hadn't gotten laid in a while and there was something about his jet-lagged brain and her full lips that did it for him. He was having a roaring fantasy about making love to her on the long wooden table where they were eating lunch while some of the priests were trying to make light conversation with him about Chicago. One thin bespectacled kid from Madrid was asking if he wanted to see the garden after lunch? As Butch had gone to Notre Dame, he knew just what notes to hit with light-heeled priests: it was better to say very little and just nod. He did that now, although Hidalgo, even at his advanced age, looked quite formidable and reminded Butch of some of the old Marines who he'd served with in Vietnam. Some of those older men had been in Korea at Inchon, and some had even served in WWII. The older men had no problem walking up to kneeling prisoners that had been identified as Viet Cong and sending them on to the next world with a few words of encouragement and a kick in the head, just before the bullet. Hidalgo made it clear, as the acolytes were clearing the table and a bottle of port had been put out, that Father Nickels would be traveling with him to Ronda after lunch to see the sights and visit the ancient megaliths there. The bespectacled kid seemed sorry to hear it. Butch glanced at the pretty girl again as the conversation at the table lapsed back into Spanish, and something passed between the two of them that convinced the young girl that, if Butch was in fact a priest, he had the eyes of a young man with unholy and lustful intensions. But she liked the feeling it gave her. It felt natural and good; something she had not felt since coming to Marbella. When it was time for the port to be poured she made a point of leaning in and pressing her thigh into Butch's right arm, which felt very strong to her. He was not surprised.

"*Porto, Padre?*"

"Si," Butch said. "*Gracias.*" And then he saw the kind of smile that all men wait for. It came at the moment she brushed against him, with all those clothes in the way. He thought that Hidalgo had probably noticed, but wasn't sure, and he didn't really give a damn, for that matter. In part because it was possible that he was not going to come back from Ronda, but rather would die there all because of Alex, whose father was in management and wanted revenge as well as answers, not necessarily in that order. He took a drink of the port. It smelled good and tasted somehow of the dry and warm streets of southern Spain. He wondered what the hell Alex had been sent to Italy for, and if he'd already been killed. He'd known so many friends who'd been killed that the idea of another one dying violently was not surprising to him, but it still bothered him deeply, because he and Alex's friendship had come to the point where they knew they could rely on each other absolutely and unconditionally, no matter what the situation, and that was a rare thing to find among players in their world.

He tried to picture the girl without clothes on, and the vision of her as a kind of *Venus-of-Urbino* figure coupled with the sweet alcohol now circulating through his brain made the prospect of dying violently a little less painful. He decided he did care about what happened to Alex, a lot. He'd come through for him that day when he'd needed him in L.A., and he planned to find out what this asshole in Ronda knew about his whereabouts and what had happened to him.

They'd taken a new Volkswagen Beetle out of the gated-parking that belonged to the rectory. A sacristan closed the gate behind them and Butch and Hidalgo drove through the empty streets of Marbella at 2 P.M. The Volkswagen engine burring-rattle sound broke the thin silence of the siesta hour.

Hidalgo was the first to speak. "I've confirmed the address. The parish priest in Ronda, who's with us, will take us straight to his house." He spoke while up-shifting and looking both ways as they passed through an empty intersection. Butch glanced over at the man and noticed a quite raw-looking pink scar on his neck. It was a wound of some kind; Butch was certain of that.

"Have you done this before?" Hidalgo asked.

"Yes," Butch said.

"Good. Sometimes, if it's your first time. ..."

"It's not," Butch said quickly. He didn't feel like taking any advice from old-fart priests. He looked at Hidalgo and tried to make it clear with his expression that he could pull a trigger.

"You know I don't like priests," Butch said. Maybe it was the drink or the way the girl had brushed up against him and made him want her. Or maybe it was that he would soon be putting a bullet into someone and he'd gotten edgy about it. *Or would they put one in me?*

"I don't like most of them, either," Hidalgo said. They both suddenly broke out laughing and the tension between them instantly and totally dissolved.

"I didn't like the little guy with the glasses," Butch said.

"He's a homosexual. We'll get rid of him after a while," Hidalgo said, joking.

"I *did* like the girl," Butch said. "The tall one."

"She wants to be a nun. ..." Hidalgo said, indifferently.

"*Does* she? Why the hell would she want to do that?" Butch said.

"It's a job. She comes from *Murcia*. It is very poor there. Her father was killed recently; he was a truck driver. He left nine children. No money at all."

Butch rubbed his nose; they were on the two-lane road that ran up the coast towards *Jerez de la Frontera,* a main artery. To Butch it seemed like a country road compared to the freeways he'd grown up with in Pennsylvania. The traffic was light because of the siesta hour; there were many tall cranes on the beach below, used for building condo towers. They appeared, to him, like medieval siege towers paused momentarily in the midst of an apocalyptic battle for modernity.

"Are you a Catholic?" Hidalgo asked.

"Yes ... I guess," Butch said. "I was an alter boy and I went to Notre Dame University. Does that must make me one?"

"Good," Hidalgo said.

"Would it make a difference?" Butch said.

"No. But I prefer to work with those of the faith ... under the circumstances."

"Those of the *faith!* Jesus! You're kidding—right?" Butch said.

Butch realized that he was angry not because of the hit he had to perform on some stranger, but because of what he'd grown up with: the incense and all the other bullshit that went with Catholicism in the U.S. It had all come back to him in the rectory. How he'd felt guilty about jacking-off when he was a kid, how he'd felt bad when his mother had told him that she and his father would have gotten a divorce, but were afraid they'd go to Hell if they did. He was also angry because, since going to Vietnam, all he'd believed in, all the things he'd been taught about God and Country, seemed to be not only lies, but even worse—fabrications that were specifically intended to keep you stupid. God allowed little kids to be burnt like match heads in the middle of the day. He'd seen it, many times. God made eighteen-year-old soldiers hold young girls for days in the bush tied to trees and rape them again and again and then shoot them because they couldn't let them live. *God allowed this?* No, he was sure there was no "God." And if there was one, he imagined he was a lot like Father Hidalgo: an old bad-ass with a high forehead and cold blue eyes that knew all the answers. No, he believed in the God that had animated the girl's eyes when she'd looked at him as she'd disappeared into the rectory's kitchen, and did not come back out. *That* was God, and if he got his chance, he was going to commune with the divinity as soon as he got back to Marbella, if he could manage it. Hidalgo turned on the little radio and they rode the rest of the way listening to Spanish pop music. Butch rolled down the window and got lost in the oak trees clustered in groups on the rugged, gold-colored hillsides. Two hours later they drove over the famous stone bridge on the Tajo, and into Ronda, as the small town was just waking up from the *siesta* hours.

*   *   *

Alex noted a strange smell in the room—something like burning tires but more acrid. There was a blood-stained wooden table in the middle of what appeared to be a kind of basement room with no windows.

Earlier, Alex had been hustled through an empty restaurant upstairs from the basement room, where the dining room stood empty and was quite chilly. There were posters of the Coliseum in Rome on the walls of the hallway upstairs. The tables were covered with red table-cloths, but there were no plate-settings at any of them. Alex was thirsty, too, and he'd first thought that they'd brought him here to both meet their boss and to finally get him something to eat, as he hadn't had anything since the night before on the train. He asked for something to drink but was ignored and roughly pushed along towards the kitchen. It was then that Alex had had enough. He tried to stop dead in his tracks, and was in fact able to turn and look at the older tough, the one in the dark suit, the man's shirt looking very white in the half-light of the empty, low-ceilinged and narrow hallway.

"I think you're making a very big mistake," Alex said. The men holding him by the arms heard the angry tone in Alex's voice, and because it was so authoritative, they actually stopped for moment. "If you think you're going to get away with fucking with *me,* you'd better check your facts."

"And what are those?" the rat-faced young man said.

"I'm here to see your boss, and I was brought to you by someone quite well known to him. He's expecting me, and I'm sure he won't like it if I turn up missing. I've been checked out thoroughly or I wouldn't even *be* here—you understand that? And people know that I've come here. People you don't really want to fuck with," Alex said.

" *Wow!* ... Yeah? No shit? Your friend *sold* you to us, dickhead! How's *that* sound to you? And the people you want to see don't want to see *you.* Now go downstairs or I'm going to shoot you in the face right *now.* How's *that* sound, faggot?" The man took out a revolver and put it against Alex's cheek. "How would you like *that?*" The phone started ringing somewhere in the restaurant. Alex still thought this was all a mistake of some kind, that the operation couldn't possibly have gone so terribly wrong. He felt the barrel of the pistol hit him in the lip and then the slap that knocked him backwards on his heels. The man kept his hand in the air for effect.

"I said move, *bitch!*" The phone in the corner by the restaurant's entrance kept ringing. One of the men went and picked it up and said something in Italian that Alex couldn't understand. The man on the phone looked at the boss and nodded.

"There's someone on the phone who wants to talk to you." The boss said something in Italian after that, and Alex was pushed towards the phone. The stinging pain on his face from the slap was still building. Someone put the receiver to his ear.

"This is Michael at the hotel. Is it you, Bruce? Are you okay? ... We're working on the problem."

"Yes," Alex said, "I'm okay."

"We're getting the money. They'll have it tomorrow."

"Good," Alex said. "Make sure you tell *everyone*," Alex said.

"Yes, everyone knows," the voice said.

He was handcuffed to a steel ring attached to a pock-marked concrete wall in a semi-dark room, the air heavy with a peculiar smell of chemicals and shit. They'd taken his watch because one of the men who'd picked him up had fancied it. He had no idea how long he'd been there when the door opened and another set of men came down, pushing an hysterical older man who appeared to Alex to be in his late fifties down the stairs in front of them. None of the group was speaking English. The older man, short and barrel-chested, had been badly beaten, and his dress shirt was blood-splattered. His left eye was bruised and swollen shut. He'd pissed himself as well, and his pants were piss-stained. It was as if Alex, standing there with his left arm handcuffed to a steel ring sunken into the concrete, didn't exist. The man was being led toward a low-sided plastic container. He fought fiercely as the six men dragged him to what turned out to be an acid bath. It was one of those moments when what was going to happen in just a very short time was understood first viscerally, almost telepathically, and it caused Alex to stand bolt upright before he fully consciously understood what the plastic tube was about *exactly*. The man finally stopped fighting and fell to his knees, begging like a child for his life. It did no good, though. The men who'd brought him down snorted some lines of cocaine they'd lined up on the table. Laughing giddily while they hoovered-up the rails of coke, the young men pointed at the vat and staged what was apparently a running-commentary about the man's fate, making various remarks that Alex couldn't understand. You didn't have to speak the language to understand what they were saying while the man begged them to take pity on him in a child-like tone of voice. Alex Law's view of humanity and his own place in it was changed forever by what happened during the next five minutes. Like the man who was pushed and disappeared into the acid bath face first, his legs moving and kicking horribly, something disappeared out of Alex right then, never to appear again in his entire life. They forgot to turn off the light when they left, so he was forced to watch the surface of the acid rippling, its work not quite finished.

*   *   *

They'd stopped at one of the two churches in Ronda. Hidalgo had gone inside, and in a moment he came out with a black priest. The priest was slight, around thirty years old, and with very short hair. Hidalgo was speaking to the man as they walked towards the car. Butch watched as the square near the bridge was starting to come alive after the *siesta*. Shops were opening and a few cars drove by. It was hot and Butch finally stepped out of the car. A laborer walked by in dirty blue coveralls and nodded respectfully at Butch, taking him for a real priest.

"He's probably at home," Hidalgo said, getting back behind the wheel.

"This is father Oni," Hidalgo said, introducing the black priest. Butch nodded as the black man slipped into the back seat. He was tall so he had to partially fold up his legs. His skin was the same color as his black suit. The Volkswagen started up and headed through the mountain town, then down a hill and across a wide shallow creek with no bridge. In five minutes they were in the countryside, east of the town, driving past fields of sunflowers and olive tree orchards without a soul in sight.

"He has a house out in the country," Oni, a Nigerian, explained. He spoke English with a Nigerian accent.

"Is he alone?" Hidalgo asked.

"No," Oni said from the back. Butch's stomach got funny when he heard the target wasn't alone.

"Who's with him?" Hidalgo said.

"He has a boyfriend, but he shouldn't be a problem," Oni said. "An American he picked up." Butch looked at the Nigerian in the rearview mirror, trying to get an idea of him.

"You know him?" Butch asked.

"No," Oni said. "I know the woman that cleans for him." Hidalgo stopped the car in the middle of the road. He got out and opened the trunk. He was sweating, his thick glasses glinting in the sun. He fished out the small leather suitcase and picked it up and brought it with him back to the side of the car. A flock of goats stepped from a pasture onto the narrow dirt road in front of them. Several of the goats had bells on so that they heard an exotic cacophony of bells, a kind of strange field music. Hidalgo handed Butch a forty-five. Butch took the pistol and dropped the clip in his lap. He saw Hidalgo hand the black priest a weapon. The Nigerian opened his coat and stuck a revolver in his pants as if he were used to carrying one. Hidalgo had chosen a revolver, a .357 Magnum, with a short barrel, that Butch recognized as the type he'd carried in Vietnam as a backup weapon. Hidalgo then slipped back into the car himself and laid the revolver on his lap. They had to wait for the goats to cross the road before they could drive on. So, for a minute or two, they did nothing but sit there with the engine idling. The goats—black ones, white ones, grey ones—all looking like Lucifer in disguise, sauntered past them at eye-level. The sun disappeared behind a mountain so that the hills seemed burnished; the myriad oaks ever-receding into growing deep dark blue shade-shadows. It was all very beautiful, like a Romantic Era painting.

Butch cleared the clip to make sure the rounds looked right, then refilled it and pushed the clip home, chambering a round as he did so, then lowered the hammer with his thumb. He found the safety and pushed it to the off position. Had *he* planned it, he thought to himself, they would have brought a hell of a lot more firepower.

28

■ RONDA, SPAIN

A driveway, lined with white-washed rocks, marked the entrance to Delmonico's house. There was a wooden gate that opened on a beautiful courtyard with a pool. Butch noticed a very long TV antenna on the roof as they stopped at the gate. He saw a man in the window and knew it wasn't the man he'd been sent to kill as he was far too young. The young man was looking down at them. Because he saw three priests, he had no fear of them. The young man in fact went to the window and pushed it open all the way and smiled down at them.

"Hello. Did Sonny forget it was Sunday?" the young man asked. The men had stopped at the pool, which was sparkling and brand-new. There were new lawn chairs on the verge and a half-glass of ice tea had been left on a newspaper to keep it from blowing into the pool.

"We're here to see Sonny," Hidalgo said, smiling back, his pistol held behind his back. The three of them were standing along the back of the pool and looking up at him.

"He's down at the river. The gypsies pulled in yesterday and made a camp. Very exciting. He's gone to see them," the young man said. He turned around for a moment as if he were checking on something in the room and then turned back toward them. He'd lost his smile in the interim.

"May we come in?" Hidalgo asked, looking up and smiling like Santa Claus.

"Of course, father," the young man said. It was the way he'd said father, shirtless and probably wearing a bathing suit from what Butch could see of him that made Butch feel in control of the situation. He doubted he was lying. Hidalgo raised his revolver and shot the young man in the face. The sound of the gunshot startled even Butch. Hidalgo had been holding the pistol behind him with the hammer already cocked. The boy fell backward his face a shattered, bloody mess. Bits of teeth fell into the pool. The water was instantly speckled by fragments of teeth.

Oni was already running through the front door. The boy had been lying, and Hidalgo had sensed it. They caught Sonny running across an empty field in his

273

bathing suit wearing flip-flops. He'd heard the shot and already knew what he was in for. He, unlike the young man, knew gunmen when he saw them, and had decided to run for it, asking the kid to stall them. Hidalgo had gone upstairs to the bedroom and Butch heard another shot. Butch, who'd followed Oni out through the back of the house, was standing overlooking a ploughed field and had a magnificent view of the mountains to the south. Oni had caught Sonny running across the open field, and now had the older man by the arm and was bringing him back towards the house in the dusky light.

Butch heard another—a third—shot from upstairs, and flinched. *Hidalgo was a real killer,* he now understood. At the sound of the shot, he saw Delmonico break free and try and run again. But Oni quickly tripped him and hit him once very viciously in the small of the back. *A kidney punch,* Butch thought. Delmonico collapsed immediately and stayed on the ground for several minutes. Oni just stood over him, guarding him to make sure he didn't try any other moves in the way of escape. Then Hidalgo appeared, stepping out of the house and marching past Butch, who watched him lean over and say something to Delmonico. Then the two priests picked Delmonico up and marched him into the house like cops. When they passed Butch he saw that Sonny Delmonico's face was completely drained of blood; grey with fear. It was the kind of fear Butch had seen in many parts of the world; it always looked the same no matter who wore it.

"Would you like something to drink?" Butch asked. He was not usually the one to conduct interviews. In Central America he'd been present at several interrogations, but they were usually handled by some other CIA officer, almost always a "specialist." But he'd seen enough to know that kindness at first helped, as the prisoner would then bond with the "good guy" and relax a little—or so the theory went.

Hidalgo went to the kitchen and got out a pitcher of iced tea from the new refrigerator and brought it to the dinning room table. He sent Oni to find glasses. The dinning room had a view of the fields and the mountains in the distance, too. Hidalgo put the pitcher down on the table. Sonny wiped his face with his dusty T-shirt. It left a streak of sweaty grime on his face. His eye-patch was slightly crooked; it, too, had gotten dirty when he fell. Hidalgo poured them all an ice tea. It was stifling in the house; well over a hundred degrees.

"We aren't to hear this," Hidalgo said. "It's forbidden. We'll go outside on the patio. If there's a problem, I'll kill you," Hidalgo said to Delmonico, "myself." Sonny looked at Hidalgo, but didn't say anything.

"What about the boy?" Delmonico asked.

"He's dead," Butch said.

"Right. ... Sicilian rules ... I suppose," Sonny said.

"What's *that* supposed to mean?" Sonny's comment had already pissed Butch off, given what he knew the man had just done to Alex.

"Well, it means that no one is safe—no one is exempt, even an innocent bystander who has no part at all in what's happening." To Butch, Sonny didn't seem at all surprised or even angry about what had just befallen his paramour upstairs. Hidalgo and Oni took their drinks and walked out towards the pool. Oni glanced back once and gave them both a look that Butch thought was meant to express his authority over the situation, despite the complete silence the African had maintained to that point. "What happened in Palermo—to our man?" Butch asked.

"*Your* man?" Sonny said.

"Yes; Tucker. What happened to him? He's gone missing."

"That's what this is about? *Tucker?*" Sonny was genuinely shocked.

"Yes."

"Oh, Jesus. You must be joking. He's nobody. Some git from Los Angeles who wanted into the business—a fool. I don't understand ... ?"

"What happened?" Butch said. The chairs around the table were ladder-backs, nice ones, new. The lace tablecloth, was new as well. Everything was done-up with good taste and everything appeared to be quite expensive. Butch noticed three joints, nicely rolled, sitting in a porcelain cup on the table. *This asshole has a nicer place than I do,* Butch thought. *Far nicer.*

"I sold him off," Sonny said, lying.

"Tucker?"

"Yes. I have two-hundred thousand dollars upstairs that they paid me for him. I think ... I may have spent a little since I got home. I could give it to you. For an arrangement of some kind."

"Upstairs?"

"Yes," Sonny said.

"Where?"

"In the shower. The soap dish comes off," Sonny said. "And I also have a bank account in Switzerland—a numbered account. We could go there, too." Butch turned and looked out at the pool through the open front door. It was getting on towards dark. He couldn't see Hidalgo or Oni. He supposed they were sitting at the table with the umbrella drinking their ice tea and waiting patiently for him to shoot Delmonico. He turned back. In all his years in the Agency he had never thought of doing anything really wrong until Los Angeles. Sonny was watching him very intently. He'd morally changed in Los Angeles and he liked the change. He had a bank account now, and property, and plans that didn't include him kicking people's asses for a living for the rest of his life. He had *plans*. He wanted a normal life. He picked up a joint from the dish.

"Matches?"

"I'll get you some," Sonny said. Butch nodded and Sonny got up.

"Don't fuck with me," Butch said, "or I'll have that old guy fuck you up real bad. Frankly, I think he'd love to."

"No; no, of course I won't," Sonny said. "Can I ask who you represent? I suppose I badly misjudged Tucker. …"

"Yeah. … You *could* say that," Butch said.

"I see," Sonny said.

"Get the fucking matches, dickhead," Butch said.

"All right." Sonny walked into the kitchen and came out again. Butch had the forty-five pointed straight at his chest. It was stifling in the house and the priest's collar was starting to pinch his neck. Butch pulled it off and threw it on the table. It was soaked with sweat.

"Just matches, old boy." Sonny held up a book of matches with his palms facing outward.

Butch lowered the pistol. Sonny put the matches on the table and sat down across from this man who was rubbing his face in a way that Delmonico had seen men do who were not quite sure of their next move. For the first time since Oni had punched him he thought he might, if he were very lucky, live through this and make it to the other side.

"Where is he? Tucker?" Butch lit the joint and inhaled deeply, the smoke finally pouring out of his nose. He'd smoked a lot of marijuana in Vietnam and had missed it. He found the stuff in L.A. and Central America tame compared to the weed in Vietnam, which was 100 percent shit-kicker dope. Immediately he felt the effect, as if someone had loosened something behind his eyes. *The faggot had good dope, too.*

"I suspect he's still in Palermo," Sonny said. He briefly thought about trying to grab for the man's weapon, but he knew he couldn't kill the others, too, so he put the thought aside.

"*Where* in Palermo?"

"I can make a call. I don't know exactly where," he lied again.

"Who has him?" Butch said.

"I sold him to the Lenzi family."

"Mafia?"

"Yes. One of the less important families."

"Why? Tucker wanted to see the boss. Why did you sell him off?"

"Because I thought he was a DEA plant," Sonny said.

"You didn't think it through far enough," Butch said, looking at the joint. It was burning perfectly.

"I told you—I thought he was just some ordinary policeman. I checked to see if he was important, but I was told he wasn't. Obviously, that's not true. Can you tell me who you represent? Is it someone in New York?"

"You could say that," Butch said, and took another hit. "My gang is bigger than yours." Hidalgo walked into the house. He came into the dinning room, smelled the marijuana, and shot Butch a look as if smoking marijuana were some kind of unpardonable sin.

"*What is it?* ... Get the fuck out!" Butch said. Hidalgo looked at him, placed the empty glass on the table, and went back outside without saying a word. It was completely dark, now. Butch glanced out the window; the mountains far to the south were turning purple, parts of the field already lay in darkness, while other parts were deep purple and turning dark. The room was also darker; to the point where Sonny's face now appeared hooded in a grayish-green light, while his blue eye still shone brightly under his obscene looking balding pate. "Turn on the lights, 'old man,'" Butch said.

"It's getting dark." Sonny got up again and turned on the lights in the dining room.

"What happened to your eye?" Butch said.

"I lost it in the War," Sonny said.

"Yeah? I heard some kid stabbed you with a fork when you offered to blow him." Sonny flipped on the light and stood there, and something briefly crossed his face. He understood now that Butch Nickels was a killer and had killed before. He hadn't been quite sure, but he was sure now, and he tried to factor that fact into the long equation he was building in his head that he unconsciously called: Sonny/quantum/death/life/for/money.

"So you're from *them.*" He knew that only MI6 was privy to how he'd really lost his eye. It was too long ago. Even the people in Palermo thought he'd lost his eye in the War.

"What about our deal?" Sonny asked.

"Sit down. What deal? We don't *have* a deal—do we?" Butch said.

"I give you the money upstairs and you let me go," Sonny said.

"I'm thinking about it. I'll just have to explain it to my boss, you see, and I don't think I can. And I got the priests to deal with, too. Maybe I should just blow your brains out right now and take your money, too."

"...Well, you *could* do that, but I could help you with *that* problem. The men outside, that is."

"You're a helpful sort, aren't you?" Butch took another hit from the joint. "There 's a gun in the bedside table. Together we could make an *adjustment* to this."

"Kill them?" Butch said, still smoking.

"Yes." Sonny looked at him. "We could. If you want to … ?"

He wanted the money upstairs, Butch thought to himself, stubbing out the joint. He definitely needed to build up his reserves, because he sure as fuck wasn't going to be doing this all his life—cleaning up shit for rich people. That was for God-damned sure. He'd had a chance in Vietnam and passed it up when some friends of his in Air America were freelancing; sending Number 4 Heroin over to Hawaii, having stolen it from General Key's little mafia. In L.A he'd started to turn things around, though, but he still had a lot of catching up to do. In Vietnam he had looked the other way and not gotten involved. Now all those guys were out of the Agency sitting pretty, and *very* rich. They owned car dealerships and real-estate development companies and no one seemed to care—least of all the fucking CIA, which wasn't about to go after its own former employees. He'd been stupid and regretted it, now. He had no family other than the Agency, really. And what had his "family" done for him? They treated him like some kind of stupid gorilla, a killer in a suit and tie, who they thought they could unchain at will, and who'd do whatever they told him to. *Fuck them,* he thought. *I like this* new *me better.*

"I want you to find Tucker. Get on the phone with your pals in Palermo and find out where he is. If he's dead I want to know it. What did they *want* with him, anyway?"

"Ransom money. It's what these people *do,* for the most part. Kidnapping. Extortion. It's the bottom rung of the mafia there," Sonny said. He didn't say that they would kill Alex as soon as they'd been paid the ransom money.

"Will they give him back if the money is paid?"

"Yes. Definitely," Sonny said.

"Where's the phone?"

"Upstairs. … In the bedroom."

"All right … let's go," Butch said. "You better hope Tucker isn't dead or I *will* kill you."

There was a very narrow and steep stone staircase with white-washed walls, the stone steps leading up to the bedroom. A nicely-framed poster depicting the famous ancient bullring in Ronda had been hung on one wall. The air in the stairwell smelled of marijuana. Butch followed Sonny up to a master bedroom, which looked out on the moonlit fields. He could see the scratches on Sonny's legs from where Oni had tackled him. Butch walked to the big unmade bed, and noticed that a robe had been thrown over most of it. The robe was fouled with pink and white brain-matter from the shooting. He opened a drawer on a French antique hand-painted dresser. It contained Delmonico's "works"—syringe and dope—wrapped in a handkerchief. Butch picked up the handkerchief and dumped the contents out onto the bed.

"Nice," Butch said.

"On my side," Sonny said. "I keep a pistol there. ... I have my share of vices," Sonny said.

"Fucking people in the ass and shooting drugs for starters?" Butch said.

Butch stopped and looked at him. It was terribly hot in the bedroom. He looked at the pieces of brain-matter freckling the white robe. *Is that the way I'll end up?* And then at Sonny and his fucked-up one eye. Everything seemed snow-white in the room. He was good and stoned, and everything that he experienced as a result was more intense and larger than in "real" life. The whitewashed room's one overhead light reminded him of the day he'd been wheeled into a surgical theater in Vietnam.

"Don't fuck with me. If I open that drawer and there's no gun in there, I'm going to shoot you," Butch said. He walked around to the other side of the new double bed. All the furniture in the house looked brand-new and elegant. He glanced to his left and saw the dead body of the young man hanging half-in, and half-out of the window—what was left of his face lying in a the geraniums. He could see that the back of his skull was missing and what was left was busted-up-looking, like a broken jar. He went to the other nightstand. There was a half-smoked joint lying on the edge of the table, the ash-side facing out towards the window. He opened the drawer, saw the revolver, and took it out. He opened the cylinder, saw it was loaded, then snapped the cylinder closed.

"I want to see the money," Butch said.

"Do we have a deal?" Sonny asked.

"Maybe. Let me see it—then I'll let you know." He followed Sonny into a bathroom located off the back of the room.

"Flip on the light," Butch ordered.

The bathroom was modern, with two sinks and a full-length mirror, It also had an open shower with a red porcelain-tiled pan. He saw a pair of surfer-style swimming trunks hanging over the glass shower door. Sonny stepped into the shower stall and pulled the soap dish off the wall. He put it down at his feet and stuck his hand in the hole. Butch walked up and stuck his pistol in Sonny's side at armpit level and pressed. He was angry and it felt good to finally ventilate it. *I will shoot this motherfucker. ...*

"The money better come out ... and that's all," Butch said. Sonny, sweating heavily now, reached his arm into the hole up to the elbow, then reached up to some kind of platform inside and pulled out a wad of bills four inches thick, held together with red rubber bands.

"Throw it on the floor," Butch said, "then step back away from there. And go sit on the counter with your hands behind your neck." Sonny did as he was told. He slid his ass onto one of the sinks by lifting his right cheek onto the counter, then shifting his weight, putting his hand behind his head. Butch, aiming at him and watching him, reached into the hole himself, wanting to make sure there was no weapon still hidden there. He could feel the ledge that had been built into the wall and the pile of bound stacks of cash lying on a rough board. He felt a splinter stick him in the palm. He started to pull the money out of the wall, wad by wad, letting the bundles fall at his feet until they had covered his priest's shoes with wads of cash, Sonny sitting there watching him all the while.

"Shit, you weren't kidding," Butch said. "Who's the guy hanging out the window?"

"A tourist," Sonny said. There was sweat pouring down both their faces; it was over ninety degrees in the bathroom. It had been a hundred and four in most of Andalucía that day. The brutal afternoon heat had made an oven out of the second storey of Sonny's new house. Butch could feel the sweat literally pouring off him. He suddenly felt sick to his stomach. They hadn't stopped to drink anything since they'd left the rectory, and that single glass of iced tea hadn't been enough to forestall the beginnings of dehydration.

He cleaned out the shelf, then stepped out of the shower, careful not to slip and fall on the dirty-looking wads of hundred dollar bills. It was pitch-dark outside now, the last of the twilight finally gone.

"Now you're going to call about Tucker. I want to know where he is and if he's still alive," Butch said.

"No."

"What?"

"No. Not until you tell me if we have a deal," Sonny said. He put his hands down. His arms were brown and wrinkled from years of sun-bathing. His white cotton shirt was sweat-stained and dirty from his fall, as if an animal had stepped on his chest and left some weird dirty print across the front of the shirt. His khaki shorts displayed his ugly knees, which appeared like two baseballs stuck just under the skin. Bird legs. His one good eye was red and looking at Butch intensely. Cicadas had started up outside and were getting louder by the minute. It was weird to watch one eye stare at you like that, Butch thought. He took a breath and felt his shirt stick to him like plastic-wrap. The dark jacket was killing him. He slipped it off, tossing it onto the pile of money on the shower floor. *Am I going to have to kill this motherfucker?*

"Do you think you can find Tucker and pull him out of the fire that you threw him into?"

"Yes—if he isn't already dead. But don't pay the money. If you do … they'll kill him immediately."

"Swell. You lied to me before."

"Yes. Sorry," Sonny said. "I thought I had to."

"What if they've already paid it?"

"Sicilian rules, I'm afraid. You have to stop the payment. It's the only thing still keeping him alive. Now ... I've told you the truth. I want an answer."

"Shit. ... Okay ... we've got a deal. Now go find out if Tucker is dead."

"I can do that," Sonny said. "Good." Sonny was about to get off the counter, but stopped himself. "I suppose you want the money in Switzerland."

"Fuck, yes, I want it. That's our deal—right? ... Now, just so you understand—if you kill *me?*" Butch said. "And I'm *very* sure it's crossed your mind more than once—you won't live more than a few days—a week, at most. Is that clear? In fact, your only hope of living is if *I* live and Tucker gets out of this alive," Butch said. "Is that clear? They will make you a *priority* if this doesn't happen. Do you understand that? And the Brits won't protect you, not from us. No one can protect you from us. So, is that clear?"

"Crystal clear, old man," Sonny said. "It's the Americans, isn't it? Why didn't Tucker just tell me he was working with *them?*"

"We work in mysterious ways," Butch said.

"What about the others—downstairs?"

"We have to kill them. ... I have to make a call first, though," Butch said. Then he stopped worrying about Delmonico and started worrying about the two men downstairs. Butch walked into the bedroom and picked up the phone on the nightstand. He called a number in London. It rang in an office at the IBM headquarters and was picked up by someone used to getting unusual calls. General Motors. Alcoa. All over the world American corporations had someone that CIA could call. Need a shipment of guns sent to the Congo? Just call the American Fruit company and ask for Paul.

"This is Bill from Intel. There's a shipment of chips that shouldn't be sent out yet," Butch said.

"Do you have an order number?" the man asked.

"Yes. It's 45450," Butch said. Sonny walked into the room.

"Tell them to stand still until I can talk to the boss. I'll call back. But don't send the chips or we won't get paid," Butch said into the phone, then hung up. He looked ridiculous. He caught a glimpse of himself in the full-length mirror, and he looked absolutely ridiculous. He had on a wife-beater and the black priest's pants with the ugly thick-soled black shoes they wore. His brown hair was cut so short you could see the scalp glistening under the harsh room-lights. He looked much older than his 30 years.

"All right, your turn," Butch said, holding out the phone.

"Can you explain to me what this is about? Perhaps it would help," Sonny said.

"Sure. Okay. ... It's about you making that fucking call or I tell that old priest down there to hear your confession," Butch said.

29

Butch turned on the clock-radio by the bed. He was nervous—not about having to kill the two men downstairs, but rather about what would happen to him if it was discovered by the CIA that he'd failed to kill Delmonico. If he could manage to find Alex quickly, he could explain Delmonico's having lived to his bosses. But if he failed to get Alex back, then he was finished, and probably a dead man, too. He looked at Sonny and finally made up his mind. *I'm going to do it—fuck it.* He tossed Delmonico his revolver. A Cuban song came over the radio *"Donde estabas tu?"* Ironically, Butch recognized the tune from his months in Central America, tracking down union organizers and "neutralizing" them with the help of the Guatemalan police and their state intelligence service, G7. They usually just pulled up outside the mens' homes and waited for them to come out in the morning. He was often still drunk from the night before when things went down.

He sat down on the bed. The Cuban music filled the room. He was suddenly tired. He saw his own reflection in a dressing mirror. He was starting to go bald. He was only thirty years old, and he was already losing his hair. Maybe it was there—in Guatemala—that he'd changed? He'd stopped believing he was one of the "good guys," and it had become just a job, like working in factory—just like his father had done. Only *his* product, when he finally faced it—one night in a whorehouse along a desolate highway near the Mexican border—was Death, produced in the early morning hours in little mountain towns, with women screaming horribly when it was carried out. Afterwards, his "fellow workers"/murderers calmly getting into their cars and driving away. *I'm stoned. ... shit!* Butch thought. *Shit!*

"Don't you think they might find that a bit strange ... the music, I mean?" Sonny said, looking at him.

"That's the fucking point, you one-eyed faggot." He was both angry and stoned. He was angry because he was sitting *here* making a life and death decision instead of back in the States with all those other guys he'd started out with in Vietnam that were, these days, all cleaning leaves out of their new swimming pools in some brand-new suburb, watching their kids and wives get everything they wanted. He had no wife, *or* children—why was that? For starters, he had refused to help them sling dope from the Golden Triangle. He was, at the end of the day, mad at himself. He'd believed stupidly in God and Country back then. *What an asshole and fool he'd been.*

"I see."

"How much is there in Switzerland?" Butch asked. He was still looking at himself in the mirror. He turned towards the radio and turned the music up slightly.

"Three million dollars," Sonny said. "My retirement fund. We faggots retire, too, you know. We need the money for all those pink cravats." Delmonico opened the old Webley revolver. There was something about the deliberate way he did it, very *un-queer*, that made Butch realize that Delmonico might be a faggot, but he was no stranger to gun violence and death of the kind they were about to inflict on the two downstairs.

"I want it all," Butch said, "all of it." He glanced at the bedroom door.

"Fine," Sonny said. "What could I do with it if I were dead—right?"

"I need to find Tucker, first," Butch said. "Then we'll go to Switzerland and get it."

"We'll find him," Sonny said.

"How did you get *into* this fucked-up business?" Butch asked. He turned up the radio now a little more to make sure they could hear it outside. He picked up the roach on the night table and lit it with a stand-alone lighter that had been sitting by the lamp, then inhaled deeply.

"Oh, I'm not much good at actually *working* for a living," Sonny said. He moved to the right of the door. "Do you think this will do?"

"Yeah; it'll do," Butch said, holding the weed-smoke in his lungs. He reached over and turned up the radio even more, so it was almost blaring, now, then exhaled. He casually noticed little come-stains on the sheets. *Fuck.*

Sonny moved to the right of the closed door and put his back to the wall.

"... You call Palermo as soon as Hidalgo meets with Jesus. He's the one who's going to come up to check, no doubt. I'll take care of Oni," Butch said, closely watching the door.

"The black one could take the car and get away," Sonny said.

Butch dug into his pocket and dangled the key out in front of him. He dropped the roach and stepped on it. "Always take the key. Rule number one." Sonny nodded, and then they waited. In a moment the door opened. They couldn't hear the footsteps coming up the stairs because the music was way too loud, now. Hidalgo stepped through the door, his face with a concerned look on it. He looked at Butch sitting there on the bed. Butch looked at him and smiled. Hidalgo then turned to his right. Sonny shot him through the temple, blowing his brains all over the new white wall. The Webley bullet punched a hole through a big piece of plaster and grey-colored block from the wall, too. The report from the pistol was very loud. Hidalgo's body fell, his mouth still open, as if he were starting to speak.

Butch stood up. Sonny lowered the gun and looked down at the twitching priest. Butch stepped over Hidalgo's body and went down the stairs, holding his forty-five out in front of him. The back of his wife-beater was stained dark with sweat. As he reached the living room he saw Oni dart along the side of the pool outside. Oni was hard to see because the African was coal black and he was wearing all-black on top of it but he caught a glimpse of the man's white collar. Butch fired and saw his bullet strike the back-lit white patio wall; stucco and concrete bits were spit off and hit the surface of the pool; the bullet had knocked a big chink-hole out of the wall. Butch stepped outside onto the patio and thought he saw just the outline of the African running down the driveway towards the VW. He tried to listen but the sound of crickets and the music were too loud. The music, coming from the upstairs bedroom, suddenly stopped. Butch walked calmly along the pool, but hesitated at the big wooden gate that led outside to the driveway. *Sneaky fucker might be right there.* He looked down the path and saw what looked like the strip of a white collar. And then he was able to make out the outline of a man running towards the Volkswagen. He jogged through the gate and aimed at the dark shape and fired. He heard the Volkswagen's car door open. He moved the barrel and aimed for the center of the passenger door knowing that it would be about gut level on the African, then fired several rounds, each one penetrating the passenger-side door of the Volkswagen. He heard a car door open, but it was getting hard to see anything other than the outline of the car. *Mother fucker!* He thought of not chasing him at all, knowing he was wounded, but he thought better of it and walked slowly, the forty five out in front of him, his eyes straining to see in the darkness.

He walked up to the car and saw blood on the driver's seat. The driver's-side door had been left hanging open. He slid in and put the key in the ignition and started it up. He turned on the headlights and backed up, then pulled forward onto the narrow dirt road. The lights from the car cut through the pitch-black night. He saw a heard of goats suddenly staring back at him, thirty yards ahead on the dirt road. He pulled forward slowly as moths flew by, big ones. He kept the car in first gear, with his left arm dangling out the window holding the pistol. The goats finally parted and he saw Oni lying on the road, face up. He stopped the car, turning off the engine but keeping the headlights on.

He slowly got out of the car and walked toward the goats; the herd started to move their odd-sounding bells tinkling together in a jangled rhythm as the herd moved— dusty-looking, black and white shapes randomly jostling each other in the dark. Some of them jumped over the African, who was lying in the dirt badly wounded.

Butch walked through the herd and stopped. He stood above the African. He could see he was still breathing. He could see the wound leaking blood like a broken hose in the man's gut. Butch's bullets had hit him in a solid group, and he was surprised he was still alive, much less able to make it fifty yards down the road. Oni looked up at him. Butch just shrugged in a kind of explanation. The African, to his credit, nodded back, a kind of good-bye tinged with an odd look of respect. Butch leaned down and put the barrel of the pistol against Oni's head and pulled the trigger. Nothing. Just an empty click. The man was staring at him wide-eyed. Butch knelt down slowly, taking aim while Oni watched him, and then smashed the butt of the pistol down on the man's head—hard, again and again. The goat bells were jingling wildly as the goats left the road en masse and descended into a field below. Butch kept at it until he was sure Oni was dead.

Butch Nickels then stood up, his gun hand wet with blood, his wife-beater grey-matter and blood-specked, and walked back towards the headlights that seemed to capture him. Had anyone been there to see it, they would have seen the face of a thirty-year-old man who had just stepped through a door marked Hell and was well aware of it. His face was frozen in a kind of weird just-having-killed another human being grimace. The last of the goats, shitting in the road, made its way past the dead man and on down into the dark.

Butch had wiped the African's blood off the driver's seat of the Volkswagen with a towel and had thrown the money and a suitcase into the small trunk in the front part of the car. He'd changed his clothes, taking a pair of designer jeans and a Che Guevara T- shirt that he'd found in the dead American's suitcase. He decided to take the suitcase with him, too. He'd thrown the cash into a white plastic bag he found in the garbage. He wedged the .45 into the map pocket on the door. Sonny had showered and shaved, and walked out of the house dressed in a khaki shirt and pants with a blue cravat, totally at the ready, Butch thought, for a stroll down some corner of the British Empire. Sonny turned to look once at the house. They hadn't turned off the lights in the house, so it was all lit up, both floors, and looked impressive.

"I suppose I won't be coming back," Sonny said, turning back to take a look at the place.

"Not unless you can explain all this to the Guardia Civil," Butch said, putting the car in gear.

"I liked Andalucía. It's ... No one bothers you," Sonny said. "Not too bloody likely I can explain all that, though." He said it wistfully—obviously he was someone who had upped-stakes before in the middle of the night. "I spent a fortune on that place, old boy. It was the pool, most of it. Shouldn't have done it. You never know when you'll have to move quickly in my line of work." He turned back around and faced the road. Butch stopped the car and Sonny looked at him.

"You've got to move him. ... I can't drive over him. I mean, it's insulting," Butch said. The Volkswagen rolled to a stop. It was pitch black out except for the car's headlights.

"Right." Delmonico got out, leaving the door open. Butch could hear the loud sound of crickets. He watched Delmonico pull the African's body off the dirt road. The black body was painted yellow by the car's headlights. Sonny lifted one leg up high so Oni's smashed face tilted towards the car. Delmonico let gravity take over and the body slid down a slight embankment and disappeared into the dark. Butch looked at the back-lit dial of his watch. It was 11:42 P.M. Delmonico dusted his pants off and slid back into the passenger seat next to him.

"Is he alive? ... Tucker, I mean?"

"Yes. They haven't been paid yet. He's in Palermo," Sonny said.

"Okay," Butch said. He put the Volkswagen in gear and they started off. The headlights made a tunnel that lit up the road directly in front of them.

"Why do your people care so much about him? Seems like an average bloke to me," Sonny said.

"Do me a favor and shut the fuck up," Butch said. "I got a lot on my mind right now."

"Is something wrong?" Sonny said.

"What the fuck do you *think*? You should be dead, for starters."

"Right. I see," Sonny said.

"I got to explain *that* when I get back there, too," Butch said. " It's a total goat-fuck."

"Hard to do, I suppose," Sonny said. "I mean you came with them, but you're leaving with me." He tried a tentative half-smile. Butch looked at him. He suddenly wanted to smack the man.

"You think? We just killed two priests on top of it," Butch said.

Butch just shook his head and put the car in second gear. When they got to Malaga he checked them into a hotel and made a call to the Navy base at Rota. They left Spain at dawn the next day in a navy C-140. He'd promised to explain in Palermo to the Head of Station in Rome why Delmonico wasn't dead. He was told to wait at the Consulate in Palermo and not to move from there under any circumstances. He had no idea what he was going to say.

Butch had dragged the suitcase he'd taken from the dead American the night before and pulled it closer to him as they'd taken off from Rota that morning. He'd thrown out the American kid's clothes in the hotel room and crammed the suitcase full with the cash he'd taken. Delmonico watched him the whole time and had not said a word except once, when he asked how long he was going to carry the money around with him.

"I could simply have it deposited for you," Sonny said. Butch looked at him.

"Wire transfer, old man—to your account. You're new at this, aren't you? This is Spain." Butch looked at him. Then he went back to carefully stacking the bills up in the suitcase. "No questions asked, ever," Sonny said.

They were in the air over the Mediterranean when the Spanish police were notified of the murder of three unidentified men on the outskirts of Ronda who had been discovered by a goat herd who found the African, the man's face totally fly-covered. Three hours later a cable came across the Italian desk at Langley. *Butch Nickels— presumed rogue—terminate extreme prejudice order Dir. CIA.*

30

■ PALERMO, SICILY

Alex had lost track of time since they'd left him alone watching the vat, the last of the man's body disintegrating, his ankles sinking slowly into the acid as the flesh was eaten away. His leather shoes the last to go, making a strange hissing and bubbling sound when they, too, were finally dissolved by the acid. Alex had shit himself as he experienced an uncontrollable fit of terror while watching the man's body disappear into nothingness before his eyes. It was as if he himself were possessed in some strange way, and he didn't know by what. When he'd heard voices at the top of the stairs he'd been sure it was now *his* turn for the "bath," and he'd lost control of his bowels. It was the *manner* of death that terrified him—it was somehow beyond horrible—a ghastly and total erasure of existence.

Alex watched a young girl of about twenty-two, slightly built, with long brown hair, being pushed down the stairs in front of two young men: the same ones that had brought down the first man. The light bulb in the stairwell was a dim yellow, and as she passed under it, she glanced over at Alex, chained there to the wall. Then she looked at the white plastic bath, situated in one corner of the basement. She froze midway down the stairs and the two men behind her had to push her to make her continue down the rest of the way to the bottom.

The young men were now pulling her towards the acid bath. She said something in Italian that Alex couldn't understand. The young men who had her by the arms suddenly stopped. She got down on her knees; slowly down to one knee, then the other. Alex felt the piss running down his leg. He was shaking, terrified that he would be thrown into the bath and die like the other man. It was as if he were someone else—someone who'd been completely gutted by fear. One of the men pulled the girl's hair back, hard. She was passive, and he slapped her across the face with the back of his hand, enjoying her passivity. He pulled down his zipper. It was clear then what was going to happen next. The other man pulled down *his* zipper as well. Alex watched them undo their belts, one of them standing there with a coke-powdered nose. The one that had chained him to the wall walked toward the girl, leaving him standing, still handcuffed, watching. Alex fell on his knees, not able to watch any more. All his bravado was gone, now—eviscerated by the horror he'd just witnessed.

He saw the girl slip a knife from her bra as she held the man in her mouth; the man's eyes were closed in pleasure. The girl flicked the knife open and quickly stabbed the man in the stomach. The switchblade stuck out of him like some kind of strange new toy. She pulled the knife down hard, ripping a hole in the man's guts several inches long. The man screamed and fell forward, trying to hold his spilling guts in as he fell. The girl quickly stood up, grabbed him and pushed him backwards before he'd fallen completely to the floor, using his own momentum to tumble him into the vat of acid. Before he could react, the girl grabbed the other one by his balls, her fist yanking and squeezing. She stood him up on his toes, and the screaming man followed her because of the way she was pulling him. Then she quickly pushed him backwards, down onto the floor. She grabbed a pistol off the wooden table before either of the men could even *think* of stopping her.

The two were both still alive. The one on his knees, moaning now, with his balls badly injured, begged her now for mercy in Italian, but she shot him, not speaking a word while she fired the entire clip into both of the young gangsters, finishing them off. When it was done she looked over at Alex. "It's all right, comrade; it's all right," she said in Italian. They looked at each other for a moment. She looked for the key to Alex's handcuffs and found it in one of the dead men's pants-pockets, then walked across the room and freed him. She said something to him in Italian that he couldn't understand, and he followed her up the stairs, walking funny because of the shit in his pants that was now running down his leg. He managed to look over toward the vat one last time. The surface of the acid was bubbling a reddish color. It seemed to be alive as it continued to eat the man's body, patches of his skin and gobbets of flesh already floating free of his bones.

They walked out of the empty restaurant and into the mild air of the evening. The girl's blouse had been torn in front, so she had to hold it closed with one of her hands. Alex's pants were piss- and shit-stained. He followed her with his head bent, looking only at the sidewalk. She was still carrying the pistol in her other hand, but now she threw it into a planter that stood in front of a sidewalk cafe and, holding him by the arm, they walked on together up the street, several people looking questioningly at the strange and somewhat frightening-looking young couple as they walked silently by them. The Mafiosos hadn't taken his wallet or his passport. He could feel them in his pockets as they walked down the sidewalk. Suddenly he stopped walking.

"What's your name?" Alex finally managed to stammer out. He was humiliated in front of this girl and wanted to run away and hide from her.

"Gemma," she said.

"Do you speak English?"

"*Si, piccolo*, a little," she said.

"Thank you," he said.

"*Andiamo*," she said. "We must go ... before they come." He took out his wallet and saw the Lira notes.

"Taxi?" Alex said, offering her the money.

"*Si. Andiamo*. Ahead," she said. They walked up another block. The street opened up on a dirty little square with most of its shops closed, but there was one taxi stand. They climbed into one of the parked blue taxis. He could smell himself then; the shit smell. He'd shit himself from pure abject fear, and was mortified. In his mind, it was an awful thing to have done, even under the circumstances, and he was embarrassed. Worse, he felt like a little child in front of this girl. As soon as the shit smell reached him the driver immediately kicked them out of his cab. Alex felt a complete fool. He told the girl to run away, to leave him there, to just go. The girl very calmly told him to wait, and that she would be right back. She went into a small food store and used the phone. In a few minutes a car came for them. It belonged to a grim older man with a day's-growth of beard. He drove them quickly out of the city and into the countryside.

"Communist?" The girl finally asked, looking straight at Alex, who was sitting in the back seat. "*Si?*"

"No," Alex said. "No. ..." He looked out the open window, still embarrassed because he stank, and the smell seemed to be getting worse.

About a half-an-hour after they'd left the city, the man who'd picked them up in the square drove off the two-lane country road and down a long dirt lane toward an isolated farm house that sat on a hill. There were two men standing by a simple gate as they pulled off the road, as if they'd been waiting for someone. One of the men waved them through, smiling. The girl said something to the driver. He made a motion with his hand, patting his coat, signaling that the men were armed, and that made her seem to relax a bit, finally. She turned again and looked at Alex.

"Maybe they follow us," she said. "The Mafia back there."

"I hope not," Alex said. She didn't smile but the look she'd worn on the street of half-terror, half-anger had been replaced with something more normal. She seemed very young to have done what he'd seen her do.

"Who are you?" he couldn't help but ask.

"Communist," she said. "They kill us communists ... the Mafia, for the Government.

I was at university. Make trouble for the Social Democrats. ... The government want us all dead." She turned back around. The car was kicking up dust as it moved across the barren hillside. He could see a few olive trees that had been planted near the front of the house as a kind of hedge. They pulled up to the farmhouse and the car suddenly stopped.

"You can clean here," she said. He was embarrassed, and didn't know what to say back to her. She was beautiful, and she'd seen him back there lose his nerve and shit himself while she'd stayed calm and had survived; in fact, she'd saved his life. He had to stop breathing with his nose because his stench was so rank.

"It's okay," she said. "You alive. It's okay you smell. I smell, too," she said, and smiled at him, making a joke out of it. They'd stopped at the head of the Sicilian Electricians' Union house, where they were fed and Alex was able to bathe and was given a change of clothes: a pair of old jeans and a collarless white shirt that must have belonged to someone's grandfather. He had only understood where he was because the man wanted to practice his English while they'd eaten lunch with his family. He'd called Alex "comrade," and thought he was some kind of syndicalist, too.

"AFLCIO?" the man asked him, wiping his plate with a piece of black bread. His grown children, all four of them—three girls and a boy—were in their twenties, and attending college , and were all seated at the table with them. Alex wondered if the father knew what had just happened back in Palermo. He thought that the man must know.

"No—tourist," Alex said. He looked at Gemma. She looked at him from across the table. She said something in Italian that he couldn't understand and the man looked at him, then shook his head in dismay.

"What do you think of Jimmy Carter?" the man asked. "Why America so. ..." he searched for a word in English, then looked over at the girl for help.

"Mean," Gemma said.

"Yes—to us Italians you be. Huh? We fought with you against the Germans. I was partisan. Here in Sicily." He made a motion of mowing down Nazis and smiled. He lifted up his right hand. It was mangled; some of the fingers were missing. "Gestapo," he said. "They took my fingers to Germany for more questions." And then he laughed loudly. His wife messed with his hair. He smiled, and his wife, a very short woman in her forties, put a *dolce* down in front of him—a delicious-looking confection of figs and cream garnished with mint leaves. "I like Jimmy Carter," the man said. Then they all slipped into Italian, and Jimmy Carter and the U.S. were forgotten. Alex was having trouble eating because of what he'd seen just a short time before. He tried twice to bring the food to his mouth and chew, but he simply couldn't. The wife said something to him with a hurt look on her face. He smiled and picked up his fork and dug into the meal out of guilt, and not to embarrass her, but food was the last thing he wanted. He began to eat and the woman relaxed and turned back away from him. The wonderful flavor of the pasta over-powered the terror that still clung to him, and helped him begin to feel somewhat normal again. They left after lunch, but not before the man walked him to the door and, looking over at Gemma as she picked some lemons from their tree, nudged him, in a man-to-man-way, and spoke to him *sotto voce,* his breath smelling of garlic and wine.

"*Que bella ragazza, no?*"

"*Si,*" Alex said. "*Molta bella.*" Alex looked across the patio at the girl. She was barefoot and reaching for the fruit. Her legs were very brown, and she looked very Spanish, with her thick chestnut colored hair and almond-shaped eyes. He owed the girl his life, and just realized that he'd not asked to use the telephone. He'd seen one in the man's house. He *could* have, but he hadn't. *Why?* He could have simply called the Embassy, and in a few hours they would have come for him; but he hadn't. He didn't feel like himself. Something profound had happened to "him" there in that basement, and he was just starting to try to sort it out, but he didn't seem to have the ready-made categories to fashion those events into some kind of legitimate explanation for his cowardice. Wherever *she* was taking him, he wanted to go; he knew that much, at least. Otherwise, he felt like hiding from everything else he'd ever known until he could put those last hours in that room in Palermo behind him somehow; but he was beginning to suspect that that would never happen.

The fact was that he was deeply ashamed of the cowardice he'd shown in that horrific cellar. He'd turned out to not have been who he thought he was, at all. And, as the car turned off the driveway back onto the road, with the hills sparkling in the sunshine, he wondered what else *wasn't* true about himself.

Two hours after they'd driven from the union boss's home, they left the two-lane asphalt road for a dirt one, and drove for forty minutes on into the increasingly wild countryside. All Alex saw that afternoon along their route were occasional, isolated farm houses; some newer than others, some with older barns attached. There were red poppies and myriad wild flowers growing in the fields that weren't planted with vegetables or fruit trees. At one point they went over a rise and he was surprised to see the sea off in the distance. He'd thought they were much further inland. Finally, they stopped at a farm house that looked as rustic as any he'd seen on their trip. In ten minutes the driver was gone, and they were standing watching his green Fiat get smaller and smaller.

"We must stay here until it stops in Palermo," Gemma said.

"What stops?" Alex said.

"The round-ups," she said. She turned and walked towards the little farm house.

"Stay here?" He looked around.

"Yes," she said, not bothering to turn around. "It's safe here; they won't come here. This valley is anti-Mafia. They are with us, the farmers. She was at the door. There was no lock, and she pushed it open and walked in.

It was a one-room stone farmhouse, probably several hundred years old. There was a wooden table inside, and chairs covered with dust; beyond that was a bedroom with white-washed walls. He turned and saw a fireplace, where the white-wash had been blackened by wood smoke. He saw a mouse run quickly across the floor toward the bedroom and disappear.

"*Topolino*," Gemma said. She put down a plastic shopping bag that the union leader's wife had given her. "We clean." She turned her back to him and took off a sweater they'd given her. She was still wearing the skirt she'd been wearing when he'd first laid eyes on her. And suddenly that put him—without his wanting to be—right back in the room where she'd first seen him, cowering against the wall, shackled like an animal.

"Did they give you a change of clothes?" he asked stupidly.

"Yes."

"Would you mind putting them on?" he asked. He felt that he was on the verge of involuntarily and uncontrollably shaking all over, and he needed to have her do something that would occupy her attention so she wouldn't see him "lose it," if he were going to. She looked questioningly at him and then, after a moment, nodded assent. She came back in five minutes wearing jeans and a bright-yellow T-shirt.

"Thank you," he said.

"*Prego*," she said, looking at him carefully. She picked up a chair and walked it outside, passing very close to him. He noticed how thick her hair was and how slight and girl-like she was.

"I can't stay here," he said. "I mean, my people—they'll want to know where I am." She looked at him from under the arbor that had been built over the stone patio in front of the house.

"No phone," she said. "I find the ... *acqua* ... water." She walked out from under the arbor and disappeared around the corner of the building. He walked outside, too, but still felt shaky. The patio was stippled in shadows from the sticks that covered the arbor, which had been designed to give the patio partial shade during the hottest part of the day. The lines of shadow made dark, parallel lines on the white stones. He stared for a moment at the pattern. *There is something wrong with me, and I don't know what it is or how to deal with it.* He looked at his hands. They were shaking slightly. He felt exhausted. *This is all wrong. I have to call the Embassy.* She came back with a bucket and tossed water all over the chair. He watched the white stone floor turn brown underneath it.

"Does anyone around here have a phone?"

"No," she said. "I don't think so."

"Where did you learn English?"

"New York. In my uncle's house. I went to Brooklyn High—two years."

"New *York?*" he dumbly asked again.

"Yes. ... Chairs." She gestured at him.

"What?"

"Chairs. Bring out the chairs." She smiled. He turned around to go back into the house.

"Oh. Okay," he said.

"Are you okay?" she asked. He turned back around and faced her.

"No, actually I don't think I am—not really." She put down the bucket.

"I make some coffee?"

"No. I'll help you clean up. Then I have to go," he said. He looked out towards the road. She looked at him, concerned. He suddenly went into the house and brought out a chair and helped with the rest of the furniture. She filled an old metal pale with water and repeatedly splashed each piece of furniture in turn while he watched, sitting there on a wall, a strange fear still *on* and *in* him, like some kind of beast that might break out of its cage at any instant. He looked down the road: it was empty, but he kept compulsively looking to make sure no one was coming. She scrubbed the table with an old rag she'd found in the house. They didn't talk for more than an hour. He didn't feel like helping, or talking, or doing anything but watching her. At times he'd turn to watch the road again.

"Why you?' He finally said to her. She was getting ready to put on water for coffee after somehow getting the ancient wood-burning stove lit and going good.

"I'm student leader," she said.

"They were going to ..."

"Yes," she said quickly.

"They did ... a man," he said. "I saw them do it."

"Yes. Comrade," she said.

"I thought. I thought. ..."

"You thought you were going to die in that hole," she said.

"Yes," he said. "At first I didn't, but then I did."

"Are you mafia?"

"No. I'm a *tourist.*" She looked at him and laughed, not believing him.

"Not tourist," she said. She put the water on the stove in an old blue-enameled coffee pot.

"Tourist, yes." He insisted on watching her; on making eye-contact. She shrugged his lie off and put out some sugar and brought him a cup of coffee. They sat under the arbor on the wall, not able to use the table and chairs yet because they were still too wet. A tractor suddenly started up in a nearby field. They could see a man drive it out of a shed and head up the road.

"If they catch you, they kill you—'Mr. Tourist,'" she said. She took a sip from her coffee. "What's your name?"

"Bruce."

"What's your family name?" he asked. He realized they hadn't formally even exchanged names yet.

"Gemma del Torre," she said.

"Del Torre sounds Spanish," Alex said.

"Yes. My father Spanish." She looked at him. "Why you lie?"

"About what?"

"You are mafia. I heard men talk about you in the car. I didn't tell the comrades. They think your father is a brother worker. I said he was in the carpenter union in America. They are afraid that if you go back to Palermo the mafia will kill you." The cups were very old and he noticed that the handle of his had been glued back several times. He smiled. The idea of his father being a carpenter was quite ironic.

"Why did you lie to your friends for *me?*" he asked.

"I feel sorry for you." He turned away. He could imagine what she'd thought of him when she'd come down the stairs and seen him begging.

"I'm sorry you saw me acting. ..." he said. She shrugged.

"I'm sorry you saw what happened, too," she said. "We saw things. We cannot change what we saw."

"It was horrible," Alex said, looking at her. He felt that strange panic again, and didn't understand her calm. He put his cup down, spilling some of the coffee as he did so, and he had to take the old rag from her to wipe it off his hands.

"We're *alive,*" she said. She moved the hair out of her eyes.

"Yes, we are. But I have to go," he said. He looked down the road. The tractor was gone.

"Okay," she said.

"How far is it to the nearest town?"

"Four kilometers. ... walking on the beach. Maybe you catch a ride. If you're lucky," she said. He stood there anxious, uncertain. He couldn't imagine facing anyone else right now. Certainly not any questions about what had happened that day in Palermo. What would his father think of him if he knew what had happened in that room? Alex was surprised that he even *cared* what his father thought, these days, after L.A. His father had been a fucking war hero and his son was ... he couldn't bring himself to say the word *coward* out loud, but he thought it. In fact, he couldn't *stop* thinking it; that was the problem.

He sat down again on the wall and stared out at the empty hills. He didn't say anything else to the girl for a long time.

31

■ ERICE, SICILY

"You haven't left yet. I thought you said you were leaving first thing." Gemma looked over at him and smiled. She had an impish smile, like a little girl that knows something you don't and wants you to tease it out of her. She was sitting up on the edge of the bed, and was already starting to put on her clothes. It was very early in the morning, just after sunrise. There was no glass in the window so it was very cool in the mornings in the room they shared. There was just a very worn, old wooden-shutter for closing off the window opening. The morning sun came through chinks around the window frame, making a pattern of myriad rays of light swirling with dust-motes. Alex looked through them at the red candle by the bed and remembered drinking some brandy and making love after dinner. He remembered the almost total silence of the night and her breathing, and the feel of her small body snuggled up against his, and also the way she'd fired on the men who would have killed him that day in Palermo, a week ago now. When he woke up, he remembered the touch of her hand and the feel of her hair, very soft against his face while she moved towards him. Her hips were tight against his. She didn't feel, look, or act like a killer, but she was, he'd realized. His eyes were finally open, now.

He felt her get up off the mattress. "You say you will leave, but you don't. You say that every day." She crossed the room and picked her bra up off the top of a neat pile of folded clothes on a wooden chair by the window. Her skin was dark; as if she'd been in the sun for a month. Her hair fell around her slight shoulders as she dressed. She was small-framed and wiry-looking. When she'd finished dressing, she opened the shutters, looked out for a minute, then stepped back from the window.

"Did you hear a car last night?" she asked.

"No," Alex said. He got up. He was naked and the worn stone floor of the bedroom was cold to his feet. He walked towards the window and saw a new yellow Volksbus parked in the field in front of the house. Its canvas-sided pop-up roof had been put up. There were curtains—drawn—pulled down over the windows. Gemma went to the open shelf that ran along one side of the wall and picked up the pistol that had been delivered to her by two students who'd ridden their bicycle out to the village a

297

few days before.

"Wait—we'd be dead already if it were them," Alex said. "We don't have a lock on the door; they could have just walked in and killed us, if they'd wanted to." She turned and looked at him.

"Do you want to take that risk?" she said.

"Give me that," he said. He wanted to switch roles, now. After a week of being more or less in a daze and feeling sorry for himself, he'd finally woken up. What had happened in that basement in Palermo had changed him profoundly—he knew that and he couldn't change it. His cowardly lapse had made him question everything about himself. But he was suddenly tired of feeling defined by what he *hadn't* done in Palermo. *Perhaps I was a coward that day.* But he realized he didn't have to be one now, today. He was free to decide if he could mend. "It's time I earn *my* keep around here—don't you think?" She looked at him for a moment, not sure how to respond. He stared back at her. *Did she, too, believe he was a coward—was that it?*

"Come on." He reached for the pistol, pulling it out of her hand. She finally let it go, after a few seconds' hesitation. Something had changed, too, last night. It had just happened after a week of being together in this isolated place. At first he'd slept on the floor in the other room on a mattress stuffed with hay that they'd bought in the village when they'd gone in to buy food. The man they bought it from had brought it down from the village in a red donkey-cart that same day. Last night after the brandy, though, things had changed and he'd slept with her in the main bedroom of the cottage. Now he felt the pistol move from her hand to his. She put her arm around his naked waist. She understood that he had to prove something now, and wanted him to. She was quite aware that he was still afraid. She held him briefly, hugging him tightly. It had all started to change the week before, when they'd gone to the sea for the day. There had been a moment on the beach, lying in the sand there side by side, when he'd reached over and touched her. It had all culminated last night with her pulling him into the main bedroom.

"Go on, then," she said. "Find out who it is." He slipped on a pair of new pants he'd bought in the village, then his loafers, and walked out the front door of the little house without a shirt. He dropped the clip out of the pistol and saw that it was fully loaded, then opened the breech and slid the action back, noting that it had a round in the chamber. It was a nine-millimeter Berretta automatic, just like he'd trained with in San Francisco, firing hundreds of rounds at targets that flashed up from the windows and doorways of buildings at the DEA's training center. He thought back to when he and Butch were running like madmen in and out of the fake houses, their DEA trainers yelling at them as they fired at the targets, some of which were actually designed to move across the rooms as they tried to hit them.

He didn't feel afraid now, though. She had made him feel like a man again; she'd built him up somehow by making love to him the way she had; letting him seduce her while she'd been cooking dinner as he'd walked up behind her and held her close. He cocked the hammer and walked across the field towards the blue-colored, brand-new Volksbus. He felt the early morning sun on his naked back. Halfway across the field, a girl popped out of the bus. She was naked, with long blonde hair, about twenty years' old, slim; obviously a hippy. When she saw him, she froze. Her long curly blonde hair sparkled in the sunshine. He raised the gun and pointed it at her. For some reason it seemed silly to do that, because she was stark naked. He kept walking towards her, not saying a word. The girl quickly turned around and jumped back into the bus and slid its big door closed.

"Shit," Alex said out loud. "*Shit.*" He walked up to the door and thought for a moment of what to do next. He heard the bus' engine start up—the gears were grinding. He saw the Volksbus' back wheels suddenly move. He lowered the pistol and watched the bus pull out back onto the dirt road and then speed up. He saw a young man's hand come up out of the passenger side and flip him off.

He suddenly burst out laughing and couldn't stop. Everything that had happened back in Palermo, that left its pall on him, seemed to finally have lifted and totally dispersed into the clear light of the Sicilian dawn.

32

■ PALERMO, SICILY

"I'm in *Palermo*," Butch said to his emergency contact in London. They'd checked into the hotel *Des Palmas* because Delmonico had insisted on it, giving the taxi cab driver the name of the hotel as soon as they'd gotten into the cab.

"I want to come in and talk. There's been a problem. Don't pay for the merchandise. I repeat, *don't pay*," Butch said into the receiver.

"Hold the line, Perry. I'll put you through. Don't. Move ... from there," the man's voice said. "Stay on the line with me." It was the tone of his voice that made Butch hang up immediately and then stare at the phone like it might be a snake coiled and ready to strike him.

"*Shit*."

"Trouble at the office, old man?" Sonny asked. Their hotel room had two double beds. They'd taken a cab from the U.S. Navy base at Sigonella into downtown Palermo. Sony had insisted they stay at the hotel *Des Palmas* because it had been owned by the mafia since the War and they'd be safe there.

"Yeah. You *could* say that. ... My guess is they want to kill *me*, now," Butch said. He was pissed-off and felt like ripping the phone off the wall and throwing it across the room.

"*Really?*" Sonny said. Delmonico had showered and was wearing a woman's robe with a red-rose print. His eye patch was off, and his bad eye looked strange, a mangled hole, like someone had come at him with a fork and plucked his eyeball out, leaving a fleshy lacuna, which was actually very close to what *had* happened in Crete, all those years ago.

"It looks like you got a second asshole on your face," Butch said, looking hard at him. He was in a bad mood and he didn't like the faggoty robe. If he was going to be gun-downed by his own team, he didn't want it getting out that he died in a second-class hotel with an old queen in Palermo. It bothered him what his friends from Vietnam would say if they found out, and thought he died queer.

"I have a glass eye. But I lost it in a scrape," Delmonico said, offended now. "I have one on order in Madrid. I'm waiting for it."

"Great," Butch said. "I'm happy for you. It can't be easy getting a date looking like that."

"Give me the phone. They won't get in *here*—I promise you that," Sonny said. He looked offended—actually emotionally hurt—Butch thought, because of what he'd said about his missing eye. *The Mother fucking gangster is sensitive.* Butch was amused, but still pissed as hell.

"*My* guys? Oh yeah, they can," Butch said.

"You're in Palermo, old man. I don't think *you* understand. Your fellows can't get near the place without us knowing it *way* in advance, and that'll give us plenty of time to get out of here if we have to. Now please give me the phone." Sonny came over to where Butch was sitting and made a call to the desk and asked for the manager. He spoke in perfect Italian for about a minute, then hung up.

"I ordered lunch, too," Sonny said. "Now a girl has to get her face on. Please don't be mean about my eye." Delmonico looked at him. He'd cupped his hand over the puckered socket. "I know it's not pretty, but a girl has to pretend, sometimes."

"Sorry," Butch said. He sat on the edge of the bed in his underwear trying to figure out what he was going to do next. He'd heard about rogue guys when he was in Vietnam. One had used his connections at the French embassy in Saigon to send bank transfer wires to his account in Chicago, stealing from a bank in Paris as part of a dope operation being run for General Key at the time. He'd tried to run away. He'd been found hung in a pay-by-the-week motel in Perth, Australia. Butch had known the guy real well—he'd *thought*—and had never suspected that he was bent. They called it a suicide in the papers. A few years later he met the two guys who'd hung the errant compatriot. The message they wanted to send was: you can steal, *but don't steal from us.* He looked at the closet door and then at the suitcase. He ran his hand over his balding head and felt where his hair was going thin, and that annoyed him, too.

I'm fucked, now. He got up and took the suitcase out of the closet and threw it on the unmade bed. He unlatched it, hearing it click open. He looked at the stack of bills. It made him feel better to look at the cash. *I can do this.* He closed the suitcase and walked to the window and looked down on the street. A Ford pulled up to the front of the hotel and four men got out and walked quickly up the stairs to the hotel, leaving their car parked in a red zone. Sonny told him they were there to protect them.

They'd driven by the *Giardino Iglese* and turned onto one of the streets behind the park. The next thing Butch knew they were pulling into a gated parking area on a narrow street, the gate—operated electrically—closed slowly behind them.

The men who had brought them there knew Sonny Delmonico well, so the

301

atmosphere in the car had been relaxed. Butch had brought his suitcase along, afraid to leave it in the hotel no matter what Delmonico had said to reassure him.

"Let me introduce you. Don't say a word until I've finished explaining. Do you understand? Not one bloody word," Delmonico said to him.

"Yeah, okay," Butch said. "But I'm taking the suitcase. I'm not leaving it here in the car with these guys." Delmonico rolled his eyes and they both got out of the car in the driveway.

They'd pulled up to a 19th-century Edwardian mansion built by an English viscount during Palermo's heyday as a summer playground before the First World War—a three-storey edifice. The men who had brought them stood in the parking area and one of them pointed Delmonico and Butch toward the front door, which opened as they walked towards it. An older man who looked to be in his mid-sixties appeared in the doorway; grey-haired, wearing a white shirt and dark slacks. He met Delmonico at the door and the two traded the European-style hug of three "false kisses" and embraces. Delmonico stepped back from the man and introduced Butch. The man in the door looked him up and down, smiled slightly, and nodded. They then went into the foyer of the mansion, where Delmonico spoke in Italian, nonstop, for about two minutes to the older man, who didn't inject a word of his own into the conversation. The older man listened with a blank expression on his face, then he suddenly came forward and shook Butch's hand.

"He says that he will help us. Now put the fucking suitcase *down* here in the foyer," Sonny said. Delmonico gave Butch a half-smile. "If you don't, he'll take it as an insult." Butch looked at Sonny and then at the man. The older man was dressed simply, he looked almost nondescript; someone you wouldn't notice out walking on the street. Delmonico said something in Italian and the man nodded; he called to one of his men, and Butch watched the man trot across the driveway and come in the door and take the suitcase out of Butch's hand. Butch let go and the man took the suitcase and walked back outside.

"I've explained that your wife back in the States is going to have a baby and you can't lose that money. He understands that," Sonny said. "Now come on, his girlfriend is serving lunch in a little bit." Butch turned back a moment and looked for the man with his suitcase but he'd already disappeared.

"I speak English," the older man said. It surprised Butch.

"I. ..."

"Thought I was Italian. Everyone does. I *am*—I was born here. Not far from this very place, in fact, in *Castellanmare Del Golfo*."

"Mr. Perry, I want you to meet Joe Bonnano. I think he can be helpful to us," Sonny said.

"... Joe. Nice to meet you," Butch said.

"Ed?" Joe said.

"Yeah, that's my handle," Butch said.

"You have a problem?"

"Yeah. Several, actually," Butch said.

"Don't worry. Everything will be all right. We'll have lunch and kick it around. I'm pretty sure I can help," Joe B. said. Butch looked over at Delmonico. He was hugging Bonanno's *goomah,* a young knock-out blonde, wearing Versace from head to toe, with the best ass Butch thought he'd ever seen on a woman. He felt his face getting warm like when he was a kid and saw a beautiful girl and had trouble keeping his cool.

"Hey! I'm on vacation. ... What the hell," Joe B. said to Butch, conspiratorially, exaggeratedly out of the side of his mouth and under his breath, as if they'd known each other for years.

It was a simple deal, really, Butch thought, sitting on the couch and looking out at a vast expanse of ancient, stained tile roofs; a view that drew his gaze outwards and all the way down to the Bay off *Palermo.* He would do Joe B. a favor sometime in the future, and Joe B. would make all his problems disappear, right *now. Why the fuck not?* Butch thought. What difference would it make if he worked for two "different" mafias?—it was all the same to him. He'd recently come to realize that they weren't all that different anyway; in any respect. In fact, he considered himself a fucking independent contractor at this point in his so-called career in government service, and didn't see that status changing in the future, near- or far-term.

"Where you from?" the blonde asked, bringing him back out of his momentary reverie. She was wearing a wrist-full of gold bangles that tinkled when she moved. They had been left alone together while Bonanno and Delmonico went to meet with the "*mammasantissima*" of Palermo, one Don Aldo, to see if they could find out what had happened to Alex Law. If they were successful, Butch suspected that Alex's father would call off the dogs that Butch knew were now after him. He figured that he had a few days—at most—to live, if he didn't come up with Law's son, alive. He'd had three drinks at lunch out on the terrace, and he was working on a good buzz by 2 P.M.: his very possibly quite imminent violent death had been temporarily pushed away by the red wine and the good-looking girl sitting across from him.

He'd noticed that the girl had looked at him twice during lunch. The first time while she was ostensibly talking to Joe B. about football; he was a big New York Jets fan. Joe had sat at the head of the table regaling them with stories about the racetrack at Aqueduct when he was a kid, and all kinds of sports games his family had rigged, and the money they'd made off those scams. He worked running bets as a kid, and he'd figured out ways to screw both ends against the middle, he'd told them, laughing about the good old days.

The girl was very young. It was the clarity of her blue eyes and her first hard glance that had stuck with him. The second glance had come when she was passing a plate of pasta *al vongole* to him that an old Italian woman, wearing cheap shoes and sporting a thin black mustache, had brought to the table; the pasta had smelled like heaven. That's when the girl had turned and looked at him with the kind of look that penetrated all his defenses. He actually seem to feel something pass between them.

"Pittsburg," Butch said, looking at her like you would a work of art; studying her, in detail. She was wearing gold pants that went with all her bangles.

"You made there? You don't look Italian." She had a Brooklyn accent. Her eyes seemed to dance when she spoke, full of energy and that playfulness that younger women have, that unfortunately time inexorably dims. Butch unconsciously rubbed his nose, one of his sexual "tells," as the implications of her glances at lunch hit him, along with the wine.

"Excuse me?"

"You made 'em there ... your bones—you're one of the guys." She shrugged.

"Oh, no. No—I made 'em in Vietnam during the Tet Offensive. I was stupid enough to stay out in front of the Embassy, holding my dick and a prayer." He bobbed like a fighter in the ring and then smiled, picking back up his wine glass. She looked curiously at him.

"Tit offensive?" she said, and giggled.

"Yeah ..." He said. "It's a holiday ... like Christmas, only they throw hand grenades at you. It's all a lot of fun. Kind of like Fourth of July, only louder."

"My brother died over there. In Vietnam. Well, we think he did, anyway. He was lost," she said. Her expression changed. "My mom and dad got a letter saying that they couldn't find him. He was in the Special Forces," she said.

"I'm sorry," he said immediately. The atmosphere changed. Now they had a connection, if only a negative one. *Special knives and special forks* had been the joke in the Marine Corps, about the Army's much-hyped "defenders of liberty" that could live off the countryside—as long as they could grow bullets, too, as one of his friends had sarcastically commented.

Her expression had changed, the party girl look suddenly gone completely from her beautiful face.

"He was only 20," she said. The words hung in the room. She grabbed the bangles and slid them up and down her right wrist.

It was two o'clock in the afternoon and he was feeling like he might actually live, now. If what was left of the girl's brother was rotting in some godforsaken spot in the jungle and *he* was still alive, when really he should have died countless times over there, why would he die *now*, in Italy of all places? He looked at the watch his father had gotten him when he'd joined the Marine Corps. It had been a cloudy day in Pittsburg, and he'd actually been looking forward to going to war. The truth was, he liked a good fight and he figured Vietnam would be like one long bar fight, but with bigger stools to throw. He'd been sent as a callow first lieutenant with a platoon to the Embassy to augment the regular Marine guard during Tet, and it had ended up changing his life. Only two men out of the platoon survived.

"So you were in Vietnam, too?"

"Yes, I was," Butch said. She uncrossed her legs and looked at him carefully.

"Were you scared? My brother wrote me and said he was scared all the time. He was in some kind of highland or something."

"Just on certain days. And only for a few minutes at a time." He winked at her.

"What time you think they'll be coming back?" he said, trying to change the subject away from her brother and the war.

"... I miss my brother all the time. Funny: you think it will go away—the feeling he's going to call; but it doesn't." The conversation was getting depressing. He never allowed himself to consciously think about the war, although many nights he dreamt about those hours at the Embassy when he was certain he was going to die: *when the mother fucking gooks were running like rats coming up out of the fucking sewers—an unending supply of them.*

"Where are *you* from?" he asked.

"Brooklyn," she said.

"... It's Marie ... right?" Butch said.

"Yeah. My father named me after his favorite saint," she said. Butch nodded.

"How do you know Joe B.?" Butch asked.

"He came into the delicatessen where I was working and ordered a meatball sandwich. Then he came back every day. He said only *I* could wait on him. Everyone in the place nearly shit when he asked me out." She smiled. "You know, he's famous in the neighborhood." The girl moved forward on the couch and picked up her wine glass. It was empty. Butch looked at the bottle sitting on the big heavy white-marble coffee table between them and picked it up. He smiled at her. She smiled back. The bravado-mask-party-girl façade was gone. He felt like he was back in college suddenly.

"You like Joe?" he said, curious, pouring her a drink.

"Yeah, he's nice to me. He buys me a lot of shit. Like this." She held out her hand

and he saw a big yellow diamond ring glittering as it caught the light. "And everyone in the neighborhood is talking about me, now." Butch poured her half a glass of wine. "Thanks. So you aren't with *them*. You know. ..." she said, giving him a knowing look.

"No," Butch said. "I'm with a different gang."

"I thought maybe you *were*. ... The fag is, I know. ..."

"Yeah, he is," Butch said.

"Fags are funny. But I like *him*. He's nice. Even Joe likes him, and he doesn't like fags at all. He calls fags 'butt-chewers;' it's funny."

"Yeah, Sonny's a gas, I guess." He poured himself a drink, too. "Where's the bathroom in this place?"

"To the right and down the hall." She looked up at him. She seemed suddenly apprehensive, as if she knew something was about to happen that was somehow untoward, but exciting.

"Thanks. ..." Butch said. He thought about it again as he got up: since he'd come back from Vietnam, he'd lost the ability to hold back his impulses. Since going to LA, in fact, his desires were taking him over like a fire that spreads across a wooden floor. He *wanted* things and that Want became all he could think about.

"I'll show you." She got up. "It's a big place." He followed her down the hall. Her ass was pressed into her pants and almost stopped his heart right then and there. "Here," she said. He thanked her and shut the door and took a piss. He was washing his hands when she came in and closed the door behind her. He looked up into the big ornate mirror, and noted that it was immaculately clean. He also noted that she was probably a bottle-blonde but he liked the darker moments in her hair.

"You seem real nice, to me. ... You aren't going to tell Joe B., are you?"

"Tell him what?" Butch turned off the water.

"That you and I ... you know. I don't think he'd like it," she said.

"No ... I don't think I *will* tell him," Butch said. She handed him a towel for his hands.

After he had the mother of all orgasms with her bouncing up and down, riding on his lap while he sat on the toilet seat; she covered his mouth with kisses to shut him up. He could see her back in the mirror; it was glistening with honest sex-sweat. He watched himself rub his finger down her spine, relishing the feel of one wet bump at a time. *Fuck Joe B.,* he thought.

33

■ ERICE, SICILY

His career in the KGB had been meteoric. Vladimir Putilin had started out as a minor uniformed policeman tracking down enemies of the state, mostly petty bureaucrats involved in some kind of corruption. Vladimir was born on October 14, 1952, in Leningrad, where his mother had suffered greatly during the Nazi siege of the city, having lost her first-born to diphtheria, when the city was completely cut off by the German army and without medicines of any kind. Her first son had died—a victim of the Nazis—like so many innocent civilians. There had been no time to grieve; the situation had been that desperate. It was fight or die.

His mother had fought in a partisan band and been wounded several times and was decorated for bravery like so many were in those terrible days. She'd become inured to battlefield death in all its forms by the age of nineteen. After the war his mother had not joined the Communist Party, but had urged her son to join the Young Pioneers to "get ahead." Emotionally exhausted by the war, his mother had returned to her job as a kindergarten teacher and had raised her remaining son alone. She'd divorced her husband, an Army officer, because he was a drunkard with no future. Vladimir's grandfather had worked for Stalin as a cook at his Dacha, and his mother used this connection when she needed it to acquire a better apartment or a top elementary school for her son, who his teachers all said was very bright. She was fierce about her son's well-being. When he was ten his mother married an important economics professor, who was also a Communist Party member, and that act made it possible for Vladimir to enter the KGB's Officer Candidate School. He'd been a top student at the Academy, and found a real home in the KGB. At the time of his graduation, he'd thought that there was no higher calling in Life for a young man. Shortly after his graduation, his mother was beaten to death by a drunk in the street—a man who'd stalked her, apparently almost at random, one evening during her walk home from the school where she still taught. She'd been killed near where, as a girl, she'd fought the Nazis in house-to-house combat. Vladimir was in Cuba at the time, working for the KGB; his cover story being that he was a journalist—a *Pravda* reporter, in fact— when he got the telegram informing him of his mother's murder. Through his own connections, he'd managed to have his mother's killer beaten to death, while the man was in jail awaiting trial. He demanded and got a military funeral for his mother, with full State Honors. Six smartly dressed soldiers fired into a cold March sky. A woman who had fought alongside his mother in the battle of Stalingrad made a speech about the bravery of the people of that city, who'd faced the Nazi juggernaut alone in what many at the time thought was Russia's last stand. She reminded everyone at the funeral that simple people, young women and men, without any special training, had defeated the SS elite troops, who were supposedly "Supermen," equipped with the best of everything.

Vladimir Putilin, charged with finding the missing Nazi scientist for the KGB, came into the café in the tiny Sicilian village at exactly noon and casually sat down across from Gemma. His looks were very "Slavic." Of late, he'd become certain that he was being watched by his own side, for no reason that he could think of, and as a result, he was on the verge of a quiet paranoia. The stress of his situation had been growing by the day. En route to the village, he'd pulled into gas stations several times in an attempt to discern if he was being followed or not. In the past few days, he'd had to completely abandon his official KGB networks because he knew, beyond the shadow of a doubt in his *own* mind, anyway, that they were compromised and hence useless in his current efforts; he thought, in fact, that they were probably an actual hindrance to his efforts in tracking down the Nazi. The reports he'd asked for on Christophe Neizert were not appearing on his desk. Officers he'd asked to help in the search for the East German were constantly making excuses as to why they couldn't locate him. For a month now he had been fighting what seemed to him to be a kind of "inertia" inside the KGB itself that seemed to be set on keeping him in the dark about the man's whereabouts, and yet *he'd* been personally charged with finding the scientist. Something was wrong with the system—he was losing control of the operation and he knew it. If he'd ever actually been *in* control of it, he thought to himself. He had a recurring dream, where he was trapped in a maze of high hedges: loud voices on the other side taunted him as he ran to find them. He went deeper into the maze; ever deeper, but he never got any closer to the voices.

Vladimir was not really handsome, but his facial features were regular, and his body was sturdy-looking, and in fact solid as a rock, from so many years of practicing judo. At the age of thirty-five, his blond hair was starting to thin. He was a man under enormous pressure from his bosses in Moscow, who were all sure that this operation was going to lead to big, personal pay-offs.

No one could have discerned that pressure by looking at him, though. *A classic Russian*, was what Gemma had thought when they'd first met. She'd been only eighteen at the time: it had been in New York at a party given for foreign high school students studying in the U.S., hosted by a foreign NGO. She had fallen in love with the somewhat older man immediately; it had been an intense school-girl crush and very much unrequited at the time.

The NGO, legally registered as "ISA," was a KGB front-organization with an office in Bern, Switzerland. The party had been held in a church basement somewhere in Brooklyn, and Vladimir had introduced himself as an ISA official. He'd actually been sent to the party specifically to make contact with her, and hopefully recruit her in some way, as she'd been a "prospect" in the KGB's eyes for over a year. Her father had been a Communist Party member, and had died in one of Franco's jails. She had been heavily vetted by the KGB, and it had been decided that she would probably cooperate with them on the basis of allegiance to "the great anti-capitalist cause." She had gone to Italy as an exchange-student to learn the language, and been accepted into an Italian university in Florence. It was in Italy that she'd agreed to become a KGB operative.

"What did you tell Tucker?" Vladimir asked.

Vladimir had left his coat and tie in the car so he wouldn't look quite so obvious an outsider, walking around the almost-deserted country village. Ironically, the café owner thought he was an Englishman because he and the girl were speaking English. The couple had been noticed by the owner of late. He assumed that they were having a tryst of some kind, because they always sat in the very back of the café and spoke very quietly.

"I told him I was coming in to pay the rent," Gemma said. "I told him to come to town later and meet me here." The fact was, the KGB owned the farm and the house where she and Tucker had been staying, and were ultimately paying for everything. "He doesn't speak any Italian, so he depends on me for everything," she said, almost as an afterthought.

"Good," Vladimir said. He'd ordered coffee, and now he brought the cup to his lips and looked at her. She was the kind of girl who always looked beautiful. Even now, in this shoddy café, sitting across from him in just a white blouse and jeans with her hair down.

He was using the cover name "Oskar Eccoles," a Swedish businessman who bought fruits—mostly lemons and oranges—from Sicilian farmers for export to Sweden, Finland, and the Soviet Union. That practice explained his occasional visits to Moscow, should anyone bother to be watching him. She'd been his agent and he her case officer for over two years, now. She had not been able to squelch her romantic feelings for him since the moment she'd met him. They were totally out of her conscious control. She'd tried to seduce him more than once, but she'd finally stopped when he explicitly made it clear to her that their relationship would always be professional and would never be complicated by any kind of sexual intimacy. Of course, *he* was suspicious of any sexual entanglements because he so often used them in his own work, to entrap and manipulate persons of interest from one of the "other sides." He himself preferred commercial sex, which was more or less risk-free for men like him; men who spent long periods away from their wives—his own wife was an M.D. who lived in Moscow—and who needed actual physical companionship but couldn't risk the entanglements that come with casual affairs. His sexual relations were, like most things in his life, carefully managed.

"What do you make of him?" Vladimir said.

"He's young and seems unsure of himself," Gemma said.

"He's twenty-eight, according to his passport," Vladimir said. "... Not so young, really. ..."

"Immature, then," she amended. "He's afraid to go back to his old life, I think ..."

"Has he talked about it?"

"Yes. I think he would prefer to stay here."

"Why?"

"I'm not sure, but I think he believes he's a coward. It's some psychological problem he has as a result of having been a prisoner in that basement, and seeing that goomba eaten up by the acid; I'm pretty sure that's what it's due to. ..."

"*Really?* That's good; we can use that against him. You're sure about this?"

"Yes. He thinks because he was scared-shitless in that basement in Palermo he's a coward."

"*Was* he? ... " Vladimir asked. He took a sip of coffee, then put the cup down and lowered his head. Gemma saw that he was losing his hair on top toward the back.

"No, not at all. ... He was chained to the wall and he'd seen several people thrown alive into that acid-bath and eaten alive. I think his nerves were completely shot and he was also dehydrated. He'd shit himself. I don't think he's a "coward," at all. I think he's a soft bourgeoisie, but not a physical coward; no. He's just telling himself that *now* so he won't have to go back home, I think. He's not like you. He doesn't love this. What we do," she said.

"Soft—what do you mean, exactly?"

"Yes, soft. He comes from money," she said. She'd grown up in Franco's Spain as a young girl and seen her father taken to prison to never return, like so many other people who had been denounced as a "Red." Many of those "Reds" had no political opinions at all, other than maybe a general hatred of the plutocratic system that held almost everybody down; in fact, most of them were denounced by personal enemies, or by people who'd envied some possessions or status in the community that they'd had, and knew they could get rid of them, permanently, simply by pointing them out to the paranoid fascists as "communists." It was there, in Madrid, that she'd first hooked up with what was left of the Spanish Communist Party—a small group of students that read Marx and kept track of the thousands of political prisoners that were being held without trial by Franco, right up into the 1970s. Most were simply left to rot and eventually die in prison, like her father had been.

"Are you going to tell me what this is all about?" Gemma asked.

"No ... I can't; not quite yet. I'm sorry."

"Who *is* he? *Is* he a gangster? Can you tell me that much, at least?"

"He's an American spy. A CIA officer. The Americans have gone to a great deal of trouble trying to convince everyone, including the mafia, otherwise," Vladimir said.

"You're sure about this?"

"Yes. Are you having ... *relations* with him?"

"Yes," she said quickly, then picked up her coffee and took a sip, but immediately set it back down. "Isn't that what you *wanted* me to do?"

"Yes, Comrade, it was. It's an important part of the assignment." Her cup was a very old and small one, made expressly for cappuccino, and it made a jangly, clattering sound as she put it down on the saucer. She turned her head and looked out onto the empty street. The village had been depopulated over the past few years; most of the young people had gone off to Milan or Rome, or even further into Europe in order to find work, and there were just the old men and women left now, for the most part.

"I'm very impressed, Comrade, with what you did in Palermo. You risked your life, and we appreciate that," he said. He meant it, too, and she knew that. It was just the "we" that she didn't like.

"Thank you. Now can you tell me what I risked my life *for,* exactly?" she asked, again.

"I'm sorry, no; I just can't at this time. Has he tried to call anyone?"

"No. He came to the drugstore one day and I watched him ask for the phone, but he left before he made the call. He changed his mind," she said.

"It's important that he go back to Palermo and then to Rome. You have to make him feel better about himself—build him back up. We need him to go back. He's been here long enough," Vladimir said.

"I understand."

"If he goes, we want him to take you with him. He has to fall in love with you. Can you do that?"

"Yes," she said quickly. "I can—if that's what you want." He sensed her hesitation. Her blue eyes moved to stare at a corner of the bar. He noticed her thick chestnut hair, just how thick it was and how lustrous, and the way she'd parted it that morning, slightly off-center. He was attracted to her, and he let the attraction sweep over him and then pass on. It was how he'd learned to deal with things he knew he shouldn't, or couldn't, have.

"Is there something wrong, Comrade?" he asked.

"No ... nothing is wrong," she said.

"You have to stay distant ... whatever feelings you may have for him. Feelings are not unusual in cases like this. ..."

"I have no real feelings for him," she quickly said. That wasn't true. She had come to know him as a human being. She had made love with him. He had confided in her as any lover would. All of that had softened her attitude toward him. "He's a gangster; why would I have feelings for him? He's a capitalist goon. You just said so." Vladimir looked at her and didn't speak for a moment. Even he could tell she was trying to convince herself that she didn't like him, but her ambivalence was evident in her eyes. People's eyes always betray them, he thought. Hers were passion-filled, not at all cold, as they would have been if she hadn't cared about the man. What he missed seeing were her feelings for *him,* Vladimir. What he didn't and couldn't comprehend was that she'd risked her life for Vladimir—not for the KGB.

"His father is a very important man in the United States—an arch-enemy of the Soviet People and *all* progressive people around the world," Vladimir said. His tone was that of a priest; reverential. "I *can* tell you that." She nodded her head. "His father is a personal friend of the Spanish government. His father has met Franco on several occasions." He told her that just to hurt her. *Was he jealous?* "... Your young man is one of the most important targets we have in Europe at the moment. ... He's coming," Vladimir said.

She turned and glanced out the window of the bar and down the street. Alex Law, his blond hair glinting in the sun, wearing jeans and a T-shirt, was obviously looking for her. He seemed lost; like a boy who's drifted away from his chums and expects to find them again any second.

"He's probably gotten bored and come into town early," she said. She sounded angry that he'd come looking for her. For a moment Vladimir stared out the window. The tone of her voice was different, and he noted it. *Is she falling in love with him?* He noticed how handsome the young American was, and realized that he had a problem, now. There was a part of him that wanted to immediately go out into the street and shoot the man down and get rid of him. It felt personal. He knew that the Americans were still—right now—trying to smuggle in their biggest prize, and if they were successful he himself would probably be taken to Lubyanka prison and shot in the back of the head. He suddenly wanted *control* over the rich American, who looked so young and naïve at that moment. All his suppressed hatred filled him like a venom. He hated Americans, and he hated this particular one especially. And, maybe because they were close in age and because he knew how "glamorous" Law's family was, there was a strange attraction there, too; an attraction he didn't want to admit—one like people have for movie stars: a stupid, child-like caring about what happens to them, as symbols of what they themselves secretly want to be. He fought the conflicting emotions, and simply got up from the table and left without saying another word. Gemma glanced at the man behind the bar, who she knew had been watching them. She called for the bill and he brought it. By the time she'd paid, Alex was standing in the doorway, Vladimir having just walked by him on the opposite side of the street, seeming to pay no attention to him at all. She stood up and put on a smile. She tried to steel herself against the first thought she'd had when she saw him walking in the street. *I want him to find me.* She'd realized that she had feelings, too, for the boy-man, despite trying to keep them at bay. She was confused, now—part of her angry and part of her glad that she could make Alex fall in love with her so she could make Vladimir jealous.

"Is this where you meet? Your assignation?" Alex joked. He was half-smiling.
"Assignation? I don't understand?" It was an English word she didn't know.
"You have a lover, of course. Here in the village. ... Is this where you meet him? Some big, strapping, farmer's son?" Alex said, smiling. "He takes you out to his barn, I bet." He'd been feeling better during the past week. Maybe it was the love affair. He certainly was smitten by the girl, and every time he thought about the basement now, it didn't seem quite so close and horrible. They'd talked about it in bed. She'd explained that his lack of hydration for over twenty-four hours would begin to simulate a psychotic-break, coupled with the extreme stress produced by what he'd been forced to watch. The fact was, he'd been pushed to the limits of physical and emotional endurance, of *any* man. She was studying medicine, and told him that stress of that type was both mentally and physically exhausting. He listened to her analysis, propped up on one elbow, her blue eyes piercing his, her small body exciting to him because she was so energetic; her orgasms incredibly intense. He wanted to believe her. She said she was a third-year medical student—which was the truth—and that her opinion was an "educated one." He wanted to believe her.

His walk to the village in the noontime sun from the farmhouse a few kilometers away had been very pleasant, and after three weeks at the farm he'd finally stopped trying to convince himself that he was a coward. He knew he was in trouble with his father; there was no question about *that.* But he didn't know how far that personal trouble would carry over into his supposed "job," and, if it did, what his father might

313

or might not be able to "fix" about the situation. After all, how could he explain three entire *weeks* without contacting the Embassy, or anyone? He couldn't.

"How would you like to go to Rome with me?" he said.

"Rome?"

"Yes. My mother's apartment. There's a pool there, and of course all the great restaurants. I'm getting a little tired of the countryside. And I'd like to show it to you. ..."

"Are you sure?" she asked.

"I wasn't until just today ... but I think so; yes, I'm sure."

"I just paid the rent on the cottage," she said.

"All *twenty dollars?*" Alex said. She laughed.

"I'll reimburse your comrades," Alex said. "Do I make the check payable to the International Workers of the World?" She didn't laugh at his joke. The sound of the word "comrade" coming out of his mouth was strange. She looked at him a moment. *He's the enemy*, she thought, *and you've been sleeping with him.* What would her father think of what she'd become? *Am I just a KGB whore?* She felt dirty. *Would he hate her for making love with the enemy? ... A CIA man, no less.*

"Yes. I'll go to Rome with you," she said.

"What about your studies?"

"I don't care," she said.

"Is it safe, now? I mean, your friends back in Palermo. Will they be a problem?"

"It's never safe," she said. "I thought you understood that. For me, it's never safe." She kissed him and felt his body through his shirt. He'd lost weight since they'd come to the countryside and was quite thin, now. The fact was, she had very strong feelings for him. The reality of it hit her. She felt like she was losing her mind. *Could she be in love with two men at once?*

"I was afraid you were going to say no," he said, holding her tightly. He looked at the owner behind the bar in the café, who was giving him a strange half-smile. The man thought he was a cuckold, and that the Englishman was having him off. And, in a way, he was right.

*   *   *

"I got a problem, Don Aldo," Joe B. said.

They had interrupted lunch at Don Aldo's villa, and the de facto head of all the mafia clans in Sicily, the *capo dei capi*, wasn't in a hurry. The room they were eating in had housed the Nazi General Staff between 1943-44. Don Aldo was telling everyone at the table that ex-German's staff officers, including ex-Gestapo men on holiday in Italy after the war, often stopped here with their wives and kids, asking to see the place so they could reminisce about "the good old days" during the War. He held up his hands in mock frustration.

"What am I going to do—say *No?!* They served their country," Don Aldo said.

"Don ... this man is a stone in my shoe," Joe B said.

"Is this business?" the Don asked.

"Yes," Joe B. said.

"Sonny, *que va?*" Don Aldo asked, looking across the table at him, ignoring Joe B., who he personally didn't like.

"I'm good, Don. I'm good. Thank you," Sonny said in Italian.

"I knew your father and mother very well," the Don said. "Your father was a good man."

Joe B. glanced over at Sonny, then smiled and then leaned in. They'd been seated at opposite ends of a very long table with other men that Joe B. didn't know.

"I want to find this man, Don Aldo—can you help me?" The Don put down his fork. He was an elegant-looking man of eighty who still kept two mistresses. He'd personally killed thirty-two men in his career, and was most famous for a killing an entire family, up to and including their goats, in retaliation for the head of that family having killed Aldo's brother. Don Aldo was the son of a laborer, and he'd grown up near *Corleone* in a stone house with no bathroom. He'd slit each goat's throat, and then had laid them end to end in front of the dead family's house, whereupon he picked up his shotgun and went home to his mother's house for dinner. Murders, especially spectacular murders like that one, were the key to a reputation in Sicily. After that day Aldo was feared by one and all.

"Sonny?"

"Yes, Don Aldo."

"Is it true? You know ... Sonny tell me. ..." The don tore off a piece of bread and eyed him. He wiped his plate with it without looking down.

"What ... ?" Sonny leaned forward so he could hear the old man.

"Is it true you suck dick like a woman?" Don Aldo asked in Italian.

"Oh. Shit!" Joe B. said, and then sat back and looked at Sonny. Several of the men at the table laughed, but guardedly.

"We had a boy in the village that sucked dick. But I don't think he really liked it. Do you really *like* it?" Don Aldo asked. Sonny looked at him. It suddenly got very quiet. They all heard the clock ticking on the huge mantel. It was an antique French clock that that had been imported from Paris many years before; its second-hand had ratcheted through the time from when the house had been owned by one of Sicily's biggest land owners, one Julius Madrovenni, a man who considered his workers to be

315

only one step above donkeys—and not as smart—right down to the present moment.

"It depends strictly on the dick, Don Aldo." Sonny said it like a choirboy. Then he smiled and winked his one good eye. Sonny—Joe B. thought—was a lot of things, but a coward wasn't one of them. He really didn't give a shit what people thought of him. Don Aldo slammed his palm on the table and laughed.

"It depends strictly on the *dick!* ... I always liked you, Sonny! It depends on the dick, huh, Joe B.?" Don Aldo slapped his hand on the table again, and made the silverware jump this time. All of the men at the table suddenly started laughing, admiring Sonny's sangfroid, and respecting him for it.

"Don Aldo. I got to get back to New York soon. ... Can you help me with my problem?" Joe B. asked.

"When did this man come to Palermo?"

"A month ago," Sonny said. "I sold him to the Lensi Clan. He wanted to see Count Cici, this man Bruce Tucker, and he paid me to bring him here to meet him."

"Why did he want to meet Cici?"

"He wants to buy heroin directly from our organization."

"Why did you sell him to the Lensi's clan, then?"

"Because I thought he was beneath Count Cici, and I needed the money. I didn't trust him, either. I thought he might be a DEA plant. I wasn't sure ... something just wasn't right about him, and it turns out I was probably right," Sonny said. Don Aldo slapped his cheek gently. "You're a smart boy, Sonny. Everybody likes Sonny, Joe. Who is he? This man Joe wants?"

"He's a CIA officer. His father is a very important man in America."

"Yeah. Now Don Aldo, if you can help me get this kid back, I think that I can cut a deal with them, and maybe they'll owe us a favor," Joe B. said.

"They know all about our business, Joe. They've been here many times. Every time there's an election, the American guy comes here from Rome to speak to me about helping get the Social Democrats elected again. And they usually want me to shoot a couple Labor people just for the hell of it." Don Aldo laughed, then tucked into his soup. "... At least they *pay* on time," Don Aldo said, blowing on his soup.

"Yeah, but they could get the FBI to back the fuck off in New York, maybe," Joe B. said.

"Okay. Okay—we get your boy for you," Don Aldo said. "Now you owe *me* a favor, Joe. You got to watch out for Sonny, Joe—okay?"

"Yeah, I know."

"Depends on the *dick*," Don Aldo said again, smiling. Then he stopped talking and ate his soup, relishing every spoonful.

*   *   *

"Is this the motherfucker?" Joe B. asked. He was standing on a beach north of Naples. There were some fishermen down the beach a little ways repairing nets, but they knew enough to stay the hell away. The Mediterranean lapped at the dark sand in the twilight. It was about six in the evening.

The men who'd brought him to the beach all nodded—he's the one. "How do you know?" Joe B. said. The middle-aged Colonel was wearing the uniform of a *Carbonari* officer, and in fact worked for SISMA—Italian military intelligence—who's motto was "Understanding Hidden Things." The joke being that there were so many hidden things in the SISMA itself, you didn't have to do anything but arrest the guy standing next to you to assist Italy in its "war against organized crime." SISMA was heavily penetrated by the CIA, by the KGB; by just about anyone, in fact, including various mafias, both north and south. SISMA was the official, *unofficial* contact between America and the Sicilian Mafia; the cutout. The man on the road above them had a desk in the Falcone's office and was privy to every move the government made against the mafia in Sicily, including actions taken by the FBI in New York as it was building its "Pizza Connection" case.

"What the fuck happened to his hand?" The man was frightened. Bonanno and he exchanged a look. The man had lost several fingers on his right hand—they'd been cut off with a bolt-cutter when he wouldn't talk.

"Where's this fucking American kid?" Joe B. spoke Italian to the man they'd brought to the beach.

"I don't know," the man answered. "He come to the house with a girl. I don't know where he went after that."

"Lying *motherfucker,*" Joe B. said.

"Yes, he knows something," the Carbonari colonel said. "He knows *exactly* where he is."

"I need to *find* this fucking American kid." Bonanno looked at Sonny.

"Bruce Tucker?" Sonny said to the man kneeling on the sand, speaking carefully. There was something terrifying in the way he said it. The man, realizing Sonny would kill him, repeated his story. The Colonel took a pistol from under his coat and put it against the man's forehead. Sonny asked the kneeling man in Italian where Tucker was, and promised him if he told them he'd be allowed to leave and go back home to his family. He swore it.

"Erice," the man confessed, finally giving in. "In a farm house there. A few miles from town. He's with a girl called Gemma. I don't know her last name." The Colonel shot him in the head. Then, with the man's body still jerking on the sand, the Colonel motioned to the fishermen, who came and took the man's body and dropped it out at sea later that night.

"You can't keep her *here!*" Sonny said.

"Why not?"

"Certainly, you're *joking?*" Sonny said. He looked at the girl Butch had brought back to the hotel.

"No. ... I'm not," Butch said. "I'm serious." He was drunk, Sonny realized.

"You're daft!" Sonny said. "That's Joe B's goomah, you stupid man."

"Did you find Tucker?" Butch asked.

"Yes."

"Where is he?" Sonny came further into the room and looked a Joe B.'s girlfriend. She was dressed in the same clothes she'd been wearing earlier in the day. But she was slightly drunk, too. They'd been at the bar at the hotel and both of them were drunk.

"I need my money," Butch said. "And I like her."

"I don't understand. You want to die?" Sonny said.

"I want the suitcase with my money," Butch said. Sonny went and sat down in a leather-covered chair, completely exasperated.

"Joe won't mind," the girl said.

"Shut up, you cow!" Sonny said. "Fuck, I told you Joe B. was taking care of it for you. Now send the girl back to him. I'll take her myself. I'll explain that you two hit it off, that you brought her into town to go shopping. He *may* forgive you. He's not an unreasonable man," Sonny said.

"We fucked," Butch said, looking at Sonny. "Didn't we, Marie ... in Joe B's house in his bathroom," Butch said.

"...Yeah. I like him," Marie said. "He's cute. I like him better than Joe. Joe's, well, he's old and he ... he can't really get it up and he falls asleep early. I'm bored ... you know," she said.

"I got a big dick, too. But I didn't want to say anything about that," Butch said.

"You're drunk. ... Both of you."

"We had some drinks. Yeah," Butch said. "Anyway, she doesn't mean anything to him."

Sonny looked at him. Truly amazed that one human being could be so fucking stupid. "This girl is a *goomah*. You want to die for a *whore?*"

"*Hey!* I'm no whore!" Marie said. She stood up a little unsteadily.

Butch stood up then; he wobbled but managed to right himself. The girl walked across the room and helped him stand. Butch drew the pistol he'd stuck into the front of his pants, pulled the hammer back, and pointed it at Sonny.

"Say you're sorry. ... She's a nice girl. Go ahead tell her you're sorry." He fired the pistol and blew a hole in the wall a foot from Sonny's head.

"*Why?* Are you insane?!" Sonny said, not frightened at all.

"Yeah. As a matter of fact, I am ... She's a nice girl. I knew her brother, or I *could* of known her brother, over there, were I was. A little place you never been ... called Vietnam."

"Vietnam ... What's *that* got to do with it? ... That's Joe Bonanno's *girlfriend*, old boy. He brought her from New York. He paid her way. I'M SURE HE'S GOING TO MISS HER when he climbs into bed tonight," Sonny said.

"He doesn't own me. ..." Marie said. She was helping Butch sit down again. Marie took the gun out of Butch's hand as if they were an old married couple, and he let her take it. There was a commotion in the hallway—someone in the next room reacting to the gunshot that had come through their room. It was a retired American insurance executive and his wife on vacation. The bullet had just missed the man while he was jacking off. The phone rang and Sonny went to answer it. He spoke in Italian, exasperatedly running his fingers through his hair a few times while he talked. He finally put the phone down.

"Let's go tell him now," Butch said.

"Will you *shut up!*" Sonny said, turning to the girl. "Just shut the bloody hell up. For fuck's sake. My God, let me think!"

"She don't want to be there. I'll go see him and explain," Butch said.

"What *exactly* are you going to explain? That you played titties and tummies and now you're sorry?"

"But I'm *not* sorry. Marie and me ... we like each other. I'm lonely. You ever been lonely? I don't like it ... I'm tired of it ... I want her to be with me. I like her," Butch said.

"You're going to go tell him *that?* That you're *lonely?*" Sonny said.

"Yeah—why not? *He's* got a family, don't he. He should understand *that*," Butch said.

"You *are* crazy," Sonny said. "I thought you were a normal person. But you're not."

"Why did you think that?" Butch said. "Shit, I haven't been normal for years. In fact, when you spend three days waiting to die, but you're too busy killing North Vietnamese regulars that are coming out of the fucking drains like rats on a MOTHER FUCKING SINKING SHIP. ... I bet you wouldn't be fucking normal, either! *I'm tired of trying to hide it.* Anyway, you're not much better. You shot a priest in the head." Butch looked at Marie and nodded. "He did, Marie. I saw it. Like he did it all the time. He's a cold-blooded motherfucker," Butch said. "That's right ... he is."

"Stop it—both of you. *I'll* go tell Joe what happened," Marie said. "I'm not afraid of him." Butch started to laugh.

"She's crazy, too; that's why I like her," Butch said.

The girl looked at Sonny and then at Butch, not quite sure she hadn't jumped from the frying pan into the fire.

"I could just let him kill you," Sonny said. "Both of you."

"Well, then your ass is dead, too. I'm the only one that can vouch for you with *my* people. I'm dead ... you're dead. How do you like *that?* Now take me over there so I can explain what happened," Butch said. "Then we'll go get Tucker. Everything will be fine." He grabbed Marie and held her around the waist. She smiled like a teenager without a care in the world.

34

■ PALERMO, SICILY

"Are you a gangster?" Marie asked Butch, for the second time that morning.

They served a big buffet breakfast with all the trimmings at the hotel *Des Palmas,* and for some reason Butch was thinking of his parents and all the places in the world they would never get to see. Maybe it was because the hotel had a busload of well-turned-out middle-class American tourists that had stopped for lunch, having come that morning off a cruise ship sitting in the bay. *They were the type that never had to change their oil out in front of the house,* Butch thought, looking at them. He saw their mouths moving and saw the way the men stole quick side-glances at Marie, who they all would like to see in the way Butch had just seen her: very naked and very ready to jump.

"... Why?" he said, finally looking over at her.

"Well, because I don't know ... and I thought maybe I *should* know? ... I don't care—you know *that,*" Marie said.

"Yes, I'm a gangster," Butch finally said. He gave her a penetrating look which she immediately understood as reveling and honest. He didn't elaborate verbally on it. Instead of explaining any more, he merely slid the short, fat, butter knife inside a thick slice of toast he'd folded over to clean excess jam off it. He was both hung over and angry that he'd lost his money. The suitcase of money he'd lost was driving him crazy, and he couldn't really think straight about much of anything else; even the girl, right now, anyway. And he *liked* the girl, a hell of a lot—but he *wanted* his money, very, very badly. He'd sworn to himself that he wasn't going to be some broken-down old civil servant living in Pensacola, shuffling to the 7/Eleven for cat food, after the Man had used him up. The money he'd made in L.A., and now this bunch he'd taken from Sonny, was a down payment on a shiny new life and a shiny new Butch Nickels.

He had dreamed of buying a hotel, maybe somewhere in the tropics ... *maybe even in Mexico.* He'd liked Cuernavaca. He'd been sent to that lush-life hideaway of the very rich just south of Mexico City to kill two Cuban intelligence officers who'd been procuring guns from the Mexican black market for the rebels in Guatemala. He liked Cuernavaca a lot; it was quiet there, and the houses of the rich were finely wrought and hidden behind thick high walls, all of them on big, flat, lots that had Olympic-sized pools—all the owners' vast wealth and privileges totally hidden from street-view. Everything had seemed big and glamorous to him in Cuernavaca. He'd found the two Cubans in a bar downtown and shot them both off their barstools and then just casually walked on out. Opened-mouthed Mexican men in sloppy shirts were looking at him, still holding their shots of tequila as he passed them on the way to the door, which had a sign over it that said: "No Soldiers. No Whores, No Children."

He'd taken a taxi back to Mexico City and had gotten out of it a few blocks from the American Embassy. Then he'd found a decent restaurant on the walk to the Embassy, and had eaten lunch before reporting in. At one point, while he was eating, he'd spotted a bit of dried blood on his shoe, and had had a shoeshine boy there in the restaurant clean it off for him.

"I guess we fucked up," Marie said. Butch looked at the girl. He'd bought her a dress in the hotel's boutique the night before and she was wearing it now. She was beautiful; a fresh-faced twenty-two-year-old Italian-American goddess even with a hangover: that was what youth bought—you could look good *all* the time.

"I guess we did," Butch said. He took a bite of his toast and dug into his eggs. He was the kind who could still eat after a bout of heavy drinking. His pals in the Marine Corps never understood how he could do it. Marie was having a grapefruit and a cup of coffee, unable to eat anything more substantial.

"I'm going to go see Joe B.," Butch said. "I left something with him."

"Maybe that's not such a good idea," Marie said.

"I got to see Joe," was all Butch said. He looked down at his plate with determination.

"He's not going to like ... you know ... that I left with you," she said. She was looking at him, and he was looking at her blonde hair—how thick it was. *Why is it that a girl can make you forget all your problems: for a little while, anyway?* He forgot about everything else that had been in his mind and just stared at her.

"I know *that. Shit*, do I look that stupid to you?" Butch finally said. "Sorry," he said, then. And he was. He had a way of scaring women off because of his temper, which was usually completely out of control. He didn't want her to go, or to scare her away. He'd been lonely—with a truly aching and agonizing loneliness—and now he wasn't, because of her. He realized now that he'd been very lonely back in L.A. *Maybe the money wasn't as important as the girl,* he thought. *Maybe. ...*

"Anyone ever tell you how fucking beautiful you are?" he said. He wiped his face with a big linen napkin. *"Really* fucking beautiful."

"Yeah, they have," she said, and smiled at him coyly. "But I like it when *you* tell me."

They pulled up in front of Joe B.'s gated-house.

"You sure you want to do this?" Sonny asked him.

"Yes," Butch said, completely sober now, and very caffeinated.

"He's going to kill you," Sonny said. "I can guarantee you that; it's really pretty simple, old man." They were waiting for the gate to be opened. Butch didn't bother to answer. He wanted his money, and that's all he knew. They'd left Marie at the hotel. The gate was opened by a tall, black-haired kid in a suit with no tie, and they drove on up the driveway and then parked in front of the house. Butch got out of the car right away. Sonny followed him; the expression on his face half-bemused and half-frightened, because he had no idea if Joe B. might not be mad at *him* for bringing the crazy man who'd fucked his girlfriend straight to his house! They crossed the driveway and saw the front door open just about half-way. Then Joe B. himself was standing in the doorway, with a look as cold as a day in January at midnight on his face. Butch walked right past Joe B. and into the house as if he'd been invited in and everything was copacetic.

"I'm sorry about Marie," Butch said. He went into the living room where he'd first set eyes on her the day before. The view of the sea out the windows was pale-blue and beautiful. Butch sat down exactly where he'd sat before and watched Sonny and Joe B. follow him into the room.

"Sonny, why did you bring a dead man into my house? Does it look like I'm running a mortuary here?" Joe B. said.

"Now look, Joe ... I want to explain what happened," Butch said.

"You want to explain why you fucked my girlfriend in *my* house?"

"Yeah, I do, and I think you should listen to me."

"Okay, I'll listen—then I'm going to have your dick cut off and shoved up Sonny's ass," Joe B. said.

"She doesn't mean shit to you, really, right?" Butch said, not hearing his threats.

"That's not for you to say," Joe B. said.

"But am I right?" Butch said. "I mean, she likes you and everything; and she's grateful to you, too. ..." Sonny didn't sit down. He was looking at Joe B. and wondering when this interview was going to be cut short.

"... Here's the deal. I'm an officer in the Central Intelligence Agency—the CIA. I want to trade the girl for any favor you want from me. I've killed people all over the world for the U.S. government. I'm good at it, and you can call me any time if there's anyone in the world you want dead. That's what I'm willing to trade for the girl." Joe B. walked all the way into the room, his expression still very hard.

"You're really a CIA guy?" Joe B. asked.

"Yes. And I know lots of people in that world that will help me do whatever it is you want done. You want King Kong to butt-fuck Margaret Thatcher?—no problem.

... But I want the girl. Give me Marie. And I want the money I left here yesterday, too."

"Okay. I want you to kill Sonny," Joe said. Butch looked at him.

"What?"

"You heard what I said, *motherfucker*," Joe B. said.

"Well, shit ... I meant ... you know. ..."

"What did you just *say?*" Joe B. said.

"I know what I just said, but. ..."

"I want you to kill Sonny." Bonanno called to someone in the hallway, something in Italian, and the kid who'd opened the gate took out a pistol from a harness strapped to his chest and crossed the room and handed it to Butch.

"Go ahead, wise guy," Joe B. said. "I want you to shoot the motherfucker right *now*. You can have the bitch."

"Do I get my money, too?" Butch asked.

"Yeah ... why not? Now shoot this faggot!"

"And I get the girl?" Butch said.

"*Yeah!* Now shoot the faggot." Sonny looked at Joe B., and then at Butch.

"Now, gentlemen. Perhaps there's another way," Sonny said. His face had gone as white as a sheet.

"*No!* Shoot this big fucking faggot, God damn it!" Joe said.

Butch stood up and examined the pistol. He opened the slide and checked the action to make sure a round was in the chamber. When he was satisfied, he walked toward Sonny, cocking the hammer as he closed on him.

"Just so I understand this: you want me to drop him here in your living room?" Butch asked.

"Yeah. I want you to shoot him in the knee first ... then the stomach. ..." Joe B. suddenly broke out laughing. Sonny collapsed into a chair, realizing it was all a joke. "Okay, *motherfucker*, you got your deal, but *next* time ... I won't be kidding," Joe B. said. Butch had raised the pistol and had actually pointed it at Sonny's knee, and was looking Sonny in the eye, prepared to shoot him. He was going to do it. He wasn't even going to say he was sorry about it or anything. He wanted the money and the girl: that's all he could think about. He liked Sonny okay, but that was not going to stop him from killing him.

"Look, Sonny's filled his drawers," Joe said, still laughing. "Look at him. ... He's filled his drawers." Sonny, pale, looked at the two of them then, and never forgot the look on Butch's face when he'd pointed the pistol at him. It was by far the scariest look he'd ever seen in his life, and he'd seen a lot of them. He knew then that Butch Nickels was a stone-cold killer of the worst kind.

"This fucking guy is a real crazy motherfucker," Joe B. said to Sonny. "Get him his money and then get the fuck out of here, but you owe me, asshole. We ain't finished." Butch handed Joe B. the pistol. "She gives a lousy blow job," Joe B. said. "I got two other girls do a lot better. ...How do I get a hold of you when I want you?"

"... Call Marie, I guess," Butch said. Then they left.

*   *   *

"Comrade—please sit down." The man—General Baikov, who was second in command of the entire KGB—had come to Vladimir's office in the Russian Embassy in Rome. He was part of the Secretary of Intelligence that reported directly to Leonid Brezhnev in the Kremlin. Baikov was exactly three steps away from the party leader in the Communist Party's chain of command. Vladimir had met the man twice before. The first time had been in the halls of the Kremlin itself, when he was more or less casually introduced to Baikov after a major crisis had erupted in Cyprus, where the Americans had rolled up their entire network on that island. The second time had been in Baikov's own office, where he'd been called to discuss the case of the German scientist Christophe Neizert, when he'd been given the German's KGB file and told to find him before the Americans got to him first.

"How are you?" Baikov said.

"Fine, sir."

"You have a wife? A doctor? Yes?" the General asked.

"Yes. She's very well, thank you."

"And two children. The children ... how are they?" Baikov asked.

"Very well, General. Thank you, Comrade, for asking."

"Good." There was a silence in the office then. Vladimir's office in Rome was in the Russian embassy and was part of the large KGB complex that not only served the KGB in Italy, but was also headquarters for the KGB in all of Southern Europe.

"I came to Italy especially to see you about this swine Neizert. We must apprehend him. Is that understood?"

"Yes, sir."

"Our reports all tell us that he's no longer in the GDR," the General said.

"Correct, sir. I believe he's left the GDR."

"And his daughter?"

"She and her brother were both picked up by MI6 and taken to London three days ago, along with his daughter's child and her husband. At least we assume they've been taken to London," Vladimir said.

"So, we've no one in his family we can arrest?"

325

"No. His wife is dead. His brother immigrated to Canada years ago and died there." The general looked across the desk, his hands folded in front of him.

Vladimir was concerned, perhaps even a little scared, because he knew what this meeting meant in their world. Failure to capture Christophe Neizert would mean that he himself would be arrested and charged with a crime against the Russian People. He'd seen it happen before to KGB officers who'd failed to get an important assignment accomplished successfully. He would be "sedated" against his will and then taken by hospital plane from Rome back to Moscow. He would wake up in a cell in Lubyanka prison. He would not be allowed to see anyone until the day of his drumhead trial, which would be presided over by officials of the KGB, and it would all be done inside the prison walls. He would be found guilty and would be shot the same day. His wife would be notified after the fact and his children would be earmarked as the children of a traitor. Their hopes for good educations would be impossible. He wanted to avoid that outcome at all costs, but he now saw it starting to close in on him; he was simply no longer as sure as he'd previously been that the Americans wouldn't, in fact, succeed in getting Neizert out of Italy. In any case, he personally had no idea where the bastard *was* at the moment. He'd been spotted in Austria, but then they'd lost him, and the trail had been cold now for over two days. He seemed to him like he was chasing a ghost.

"Do you have a plan, Comrade?"

"Yes, sir. Of course I do, sir. I expect him to be picked up by an American agent working for the CIA. We intercepted a conversation between the agent and his case officer at a bar here in Rome. We expect to pick Neizert up when he crosses into Italy. That's why I've come here. I think it's better if we let Neizert come to *us*, at this point."

"Who is this asset?"

"I'm not at liberty to say right now, sir, not until Neizert is captured and returned to us."

"What *exactly* is your plan?" the general asked.

"I'm sorry. ... I'm not at liberty to give you the details," Vladimir said. He looked at Baikov, not sure he wouldn't be arrested immediately, after his refusal.

"You're not at 'liberty' to say?" The general was wearing a new Italian sharkskin suit, which made his body shimmer iridescently in the sunlight from the window as he moved forward to sit on the very edge of his chair. The wooden chair creaked under his weight as he moved. He had a burn-mark on his left hand from a helicopter crash in Afghanistan; the skin was an ugly deep-red color.

"No, I'm not. But I expect to have Neizert in custody by next week at the latest, Comrade."

"Why can't you tell me who this contact is?"

"Because I cannot risk letting my operation be compromised in any way, sir. Not at this critical moment. I'm sorry, sir."

The general's grey eyes—the man was in his seventies and been at Stalingrad—were hard and very clear for a man of his age. He had the eyes of a combat soldier who had faced death many times.

"And you insist in keeping the operation a secret, Vladimir Putilin?"

"Yes, comrade. I believe it would be better for the sake of the operation." Vladimir wanted to add that he would be shot in any case if he failed to capture Neizert, so he was not going to risk the operation being spoilt because some unknown mole in the KGB got word to the Americans or the Brits that he was closing in; had even managed to place a girl at the exact spot he expected Neizert to surface.

He knew, from talking to older KGB officers in Moscow, that in a situation like this, the Americans would most probably go to their old Vatican rat-lines; the ones that ran through Switzerland at Lake Lugano—a route they'd used many times in the past, and trusted. He'd also been warned that those in the heroin trade, the Sicilians, would likely be the expediters, as they had been since WWII. And he was right. The recorded conversation at the Hotel Majestic had been a piece of luck. He'd been right to come to Italy and keep his ear to the ground. He was certain that this man Tucker had been sent to pick up Neizert.

The conversation the KGB had recorded at the Hotel Majestic bar had been all the break they'd needed. It was clear to him that Sonny Delmonico—a known Mafioso in the heroin trade—had come to guide Neizert. Some digging in Moscow had turned up a file on Delmonico. He'd been instrumental in doing this once before in the nineteen-sixties. Why not again? Vladimir had reasoned.

"I suspect that we have double-agents just like any other intelligence service, and some of them may be at the very highest levels of our government," Vladimir said. The General studied him coolly, then held him in his gaze for what seemed to be hours, but was in fact only seconds.

"You're either a total fool or a very smart man," the General finally said. "We will know soon enough, Comrade." He got up. Vladimir knew that the moment of extreme danger to himself had passed. "I'm staying in Italy until Neizert is arrested or shot. I'll give you 10 days."

"Yes, Sir. ... I understand completely," Vladimir said.

"I repeat; you have ten days."

"Yes, sir. I understand."

"You're right, of course ... about spies among us," Baikov said and left.

*   *   *

Alex had resurfaced a week ago, and had taken Gemma to his mother's place in Rome. They'd spent three days in the luxury apartment, totally cut off from the outside world. He'd gotten a call on the third day from his father.

"How did you know I was here?" Alex said.

"I sent that person from L.A. after you. The one from Los Angeles. He's actually traced you down to some damn village in Sicily, but you'd already left. I simply guessed you'd gone to your mother's."

"Where is ... that person?" Alex asked.

"He's in Sicily."

"Send him here," Alex said.

"They said that there's a girl with you—that she helped you escape," his father said.

"I got rid of her." Alex lied instinctively now to protect Gemma. He knew she was the last kind of girl his father would approve of. And he was afraid that if he didn't keep her existence a secret, she would—somehow—end up like Patty had.

"Good," his father said. "... You're okay?"

"Yes, Fine," Alex lied. It was easy to lie, now. His time in Los Angeles with Butch had changed him. Lies were easy to tell. People were easy to shoot.

"I want you to come home when this is finished. Have a good long rest. Go to Bermuda. Then maybe back to London," his father said.

"Fine," Alex said. "When this is finished."

"Good," Malcolm said. "The package is on the way. I just wanted you to know."

"I'll need that other person," Alex said.

"... He's not stable," his father said.

"Yes, I *know* that," Alex said. "Does it matter?"

"All right," his father said. "There are some other people that want the package, too."

"What do you mean?"

"Not just Ivan and his friends," his father said.

"All right."

"They may seem to be one of us."

"All right," Alex said.

"Delmonico is with your friend. I want him to get the package to me here. You must be. ..."

"I'm going to *kill* him—Delmonico," Alex said, very matter-of-factly.

328

"You can't, Alex. I know how you must feel. ..."

"No, you don't," Alex said. "Not in the least. If I see him, I'll kill him *on the spot.* Do you understand?" He hung up the phone.

Alex walked out onto the portico, a huge tiled-space that led down one wing of the apartment, which was actually more like a house. He went to the library, which had a collection of first editions that included Dante's *Divine Comedy.* His grandfather had been a world-class rare book collector. He went out to the breezeway and saw Gemma sitting at the end that opened onto the garden. She had fallen in love with the pre-War apartment and the library. He could tell; it was the kind of place that had the feeling of a kind of "sanctuary," that the ultra-rich were so good at creating. The apartment had been in his family for sixty years, and was three-stories of an opulence and tranquility that she'd never experienced before, and she was drinking it in, lying in bed until late in the morning, reading and making love with him. It had been a perfect few days, and he was feeling almost normal again; or as "normal" as he would *ever* feel again, after what had happened. The idea that Butch and he would reunite and begin to work together seemed reassuring and exciting too.

"That was my father," Alex said. He sat down on the floor of the hallway across from her and leaned back against one of the fat marble balustrades. She closed the book she'd been reading.

"What's he like? ... Your family must be *very* rich," Gemma said.

"He's really very typical of his generation of Americans," Alex said. She shook her head as if she didn't quite understand.

"*Supremely* confident, arrogant about their place in the world; know they're always right ... 'God' is on their side ... all business ... no nonsense. 'World by the balls' bullshit."

"Do you have any brothers or sisters?"

"A sister. She's a year older than me," Alex said.

"What does she do?"

He smiled. "She goes to parties in New York and spends my parents' money on clothes and pretty things. She has boyfriends with more money than God. She comes here, sometimes. She likes it here in Rome because the police don't bother her and her friends for smoking marijuana and taking drugs. The rich foreigners get away with pretty much anything they want to, here. Especially rich Americans."

"Yes, I know," Gemma said. She was holding the book on her lap.

"What did you find to read?" Alex said.

"*The Origin of Species*," she said. She held up an expensive leather-bound edition.

"You *are* different," he said. She was wearing a T-shirt and a pair of jeans and had been walking around barefoot.

"Why?" she smiled. "Because I like to read?"

"I don't know. I've known a lot of girls ... none of them would curl up with Darwin, though; that's for sure." She seemed puzzled by that. She thought rich people spent time in libraries because they had them. The idea that most of those fine libraries were for show, simply expensive ostentations for other members of "society" to be impressed by, as this one certainly was, had never crossed her mind. In reality, the rich preferred to read *Time* magazine and the *Wall Street Journal* and *Who's Who*—the last being a particular favorite, since most of them were personally mentioned in its pages.

"I should go back to school soon," she said. "I've been here three days—I should go back, really."

"I want to take you to Mexico with me," Alex said.

"*Mexico?*"

"Yes. I want to disappear. What do you think? But there's someone I want you to meet. He's truly a Darwinian masterpiece. ... He'll be here soon. Will you go to Mexico with me?"

"I don't know. I want to study," she said.

"Why? I've got money. I'll take care of you. It will be educational," Alex said.

"I want to go see my sister. She's in school here ... in Rome," Gemma lied.

"All right. You want me to go with you?"

"No. It's all right. I'll be back for dinner."

"You'll come back—you promise?" He was surprised he'd said it that way, so earnestly.

"Yes, I'll come back," Gemma said.

"Do you really want to be a doctor?"

"Yes," Gemma said.

"You don't look like any doctor *I've* ever seen," he said.

She smiled. "You don't look like ... I still don't know what it is *you* do?" Gemma said.

"... I sell heroin," Alex said. "I'm a gangster. Do you care? But I want to stop being one. That's why I want to go to Mexico. I want to start over."

"... You're a *gangster*?" Gemma said.

"Yes," he said. "Does it matter?"

She didn't answer.

Butch had the leather suitcase full of money opened up on the bed. He was holding the .44 Magnum in his lap because he knew that they had to be closing in on him, and that he would probably be dead very soon, and he was pissed as hell about it. He'd opened the suitcase to count his money, wanting to make sure Joe B. hadn't stolen any of it. He had laid it all out on the bed, and had been briefly happy just looking at it. It was all there. Neat stacks of hundred-dollar bills.

Marie had just whistled and said nothing as she stood there watching him lay out the cash. Now he'd put the money back into the suitcase, his hands soiled from handling it. Marie was sitting next to the suitcase on the edge of the bed. He felt like having sex right then and not worrying about anything else, but he knew that probably wasn't a good idea. He was trying to think of what to do next when the phone rang.

"This is Mark at Gem Agriculture in Paris. Is this room 1220?"

"Yeah," Butch said, "it is."

"There's been a mistake. ... We're so sorry about the mix up with that order. It's been cancelled. ... You're to call this number and get a credit," the voice said.

"You're sure?" But the man had already rung-off . Butch called the number he'd just been given. He was told to report to Rome immediately, and given an address which he wrote down carefully on a hotel notepad by the bed.

"Yes. Have a nice day," a woman said in a heavy Texas accent, and then hung up.

"Who was that?" Marie said.

"That was someone telling me that they don't necessarily want me dead," Butch said. Marie looked at him and pushed her hair back out of her face.

"You have a hard job, baby," Marie said.

"Sometimes. Yeah," he said.

"What do we do now?" she said. "I mean, are we going to stay here in Palermo?" It seemed to be understood that they were together now and that Marie was his woman. They were both from a class that didn't need to make long speeches about fidelity or passion or loyalty, or to write little poems to each other. A certain kind of look would suffice, and that look had passed between them when they'd been getting dressed that morning. She was his now, and in exchange she expected him to take care of her in an old-fashioned male/female way.

"No. I got to go to Rome," Butch said. "Do you want to come with me? Or do you want me to send you home?"

"Wherever you go. You know. That's how I feel," Marie said.

"... Okay. I got to make a call and see about something. Some people might still try to kill me on the way out of town. They *could* be lying. You never know."

"I don't care," Marie said.

"You're not afraid?"

"No," she said, "I'm not afraid."

"How come? ... *I'm* afraid," Butch said.

"I got to tell you something about my family My dad ... he's a made-guy."

"Yeah?"

"I didn't want you to think less of me because of that. You know. Some people, they don't like. ... You know—to be around my kind."

"Can you use a gun?" Butch said.

"Yeah."

"No shit?"

"It's a long story, but my dad had to take us to the Dominican Republic when I was in high school ... to hide, and well things got rough there, and I learned to help my dad out. ... There's one other thing," she said.

"What?"

"There's something else. Sometimes. ... I ... I don't know how to say this to you. I ... kill people for money. Back home. That's what I do. Me and my dad. I help him out."

"Back home? You mean in the States?"

"Yeah. My dad, he. ... My dad. He used to take me to work. You know nobody is afraid of a guy with a young girl in tow," she said.

"... He'd take you to work?!" Butch said.

"Sometimes. After what happened to us in the Dominican," she said. "You know how it is. He said blood was thicker than water. My last name is Anastasia. Marie Anastasia. My grandfather was Albert Anastasia," she said, finally confessing.

"You mean your grandfather was ..."

"Murder, Incorporated. Yeah. You heard of him?"

Butch nodded his head. "Shit yeah, I heard of him."

"He wasn't a monster ... my grandfather," she said. "I loved my grandfather."

"Yeah, okay," Butch said. "I loved *my* grandfather, too."

"... I'll need a gun, then, baby ... you know. ... If you want me to help you out," Marie said. Sonny walked into the room. He was staying in a room across the hall.

"I just got a call from the desk. There's some men down in the lobby—they want to speak to you," Sonny said.

"Who are they?" Butch said.

"I don't know," Sonny said. "Police, I suppose?"

"I'll go down and see," Marie said. The two men looked at her.

"Would you, dear? That would be wonderful. Just tell us what they look like," Sonny said. Marie got off the bed and picked up the .44 magnum, opened the cylinder, turned it and looked carefully at it, then snapped it closed again.

"Listen—either one of you got a knife? I need a backup weapon," she said, looking up.

"You aren't going to ... you know," Butch said "Down in the lobby. ..."

"Why not?" she said. "It's as good a place as any, I guess."

"Dear girl. ... You don't even know how many there are?" Sonny said, his mouth falling open.

"Well, if there's more than five ... I guess I'm fucked. I'll meet you at that café across the street. ..." Marie went to the window and pointed to an outdoor café down the street a little way. Sonny took out an old switchblade from his pants pocket; it was the old-fashioned, long type. He tossed it to her.

"It belonged to my grandmother. ... So don't lose it, okay?" he joked. Marie caught it. She opened it once to judge its action, then folded it up and put it in the right front pocket of her pants. She got her purse and put the pistol in it and walked out of the room as if she were going out shopping.

"A very interesting young woman," Sonny said after she'd closed the door.

35

■ ROME

"I told him I was seeing my sister," Gemma said. They had met in a café not too far from where she was staying at Tucker's apartment. It was a beautiful, tree-lined, very narrow street near the Villa Borghese.

"Does he believe you?" Vladimir asked.

"Yes," she said. "He has no idea who I am. He thinks I'm a medical student." Vladimir was wearing a well-pressed white dress shirt and dark slacks. It was very warm that afternoon in Rome; he'd left his coat at the Embassy and looked like all the other office workers sitting around them in the cafe. His blond hair was freshly cut. He'd gone for a shave and a haircut that day in the lobby of the Ritz Carlton. But his eyes were tired, there were dark circles under them. She could tell he was under a terrific strain.

"... Has he mentioned anyone called Sonny?"

"Yes," she said. "Sonny Delmonico's supposed to meet him at his mother's apartment tomorrow. Tucker says he's hatched a plot to escape from his current life and go to Mexico. He won't say what it is he does, exactly. But he's been dropping hints that he's some kind of gangster."

"Mexico?"

"Yes. He's asked me to go with him."

"What did you tell him?"

"I said I had to think about it. That it was hard for me to leave everything here in Italy, just like that. I told him that that was why I had to see my sister alone; to discuss it all."

"Good."

"Do you want me to go?" she asked.

"Yes. I want you to stay with him, no matter what he does," he said.

"You've never said why I'm doing all this. ... I would like to know." Vladimir looked at the girl. She looked very beautiful; he'd chosen well. She was the kind of girl you could dress up and she would look elegant. Or, like today, in jeans and a white blouse she would seem bohemian and very young—a Roman student. He understood the

American's attraction. He'd felt it too from the moment they'd met. Today it was almost overwhelming him. He desired her tremendously, and a sudden fit of jealousy toward Tucker swept over him. The feeling that he wanted to sleep with her—to "have her on the spot," as he'd once read in a English novel—was overwhelming all of his defenses.

"If I tell you, you could be killed, if this ends up going badly for me. So far, very few people know about you—I've kept you a secret. You have no name in our files. You only have a number. You're listed simply as No. 24. I'm the only one who knows your real identity in the whole KGB," Vladimir confessed, and it was the truth.

"What do you mean?"

"It means that this operation is *critical* for me—for my career and my very survival, to tell you the truth. And I have to protect it from being compromised. Every officer has people like you. People that he has cultivated but who are kept secret—fenced-off from everyone else. In case there's a penetration by an outsider."

"I see," she said, somewhat bemused.

"If something bad happens to me, you can just walk away. They won't know anything about you. I've even destroyed your recruiting file," he said. She looked at him carefully now, taking in what he was telling her. She understood now that he wanted to protect her, that she could get up and walk away from it all at any time if she wanted to.

"I want to know what it's about, though," she said. "Is it important?"

There had been countless times when he'd wanted to ask her to follow him to one of the safe houses they kept. It fact, he'd felt that way since he'd first met her in New York. There was something about her. She had a solitary quality that he had, too. It was a way of standing apart from the rest of the world, mentally. *He'd* gotten it from his mother, who had suffered so much during the War. Some days, he was psychologically comforted by just thinking about Gemma; just to know she existed made him feel better, even if there hadn't been any recent contact between them, and wouldn't be any for a long time to come, either. It was as if this girl was in possession of some great universal female power that all men were attracted to; driven to want to hold, to protect, to worship, and to love in a blind and mad way. It was silly, "juvenile," but that's the way he thought of her, now. Every time he saw her it was harder and harder not to make a sexual or emotional advance, not to reach out for her in a personal way.

"The Americans have contracted with someone from the Sicilian mafia called Sonny Delmonico to bring an East German scientist to America," he said. "That's what this is all about."

"I don't understand," she said.

"It's someone we need back, very badly. This scientist. He walked away from his desk in the GDR, and I have to get him back. I've been given the job. *I have to succeed*."

"And if you fail?"

"Then I'm afraid something will happen to me—and my family," Vladimir said.

"I understand," she said. "You have a wife, then?"

"Yes."

"And children?"

"Yes. Two; in Moscow," he said, looking at her. Her fingers were wrapped tightly around a small white porcelain cappuccino cup.

"... You could have had *me* anytime you wanted me," she said, very matter-of-factly. It shocked him. They looked at each other for a long time. "I mean, I really am not a communist—not really. My father was, but I'm not. I didn't realize it until lately. I don't even care about politics. Not really. I want to be an artist." She looked into his blue eyes. "It all seems pointless to me. All this ... *politics*—what good does it end up doing anyone, really? Man is corrupt in his most basic instincts, and nothing can change that, can it? Which side will help these people around us, here? Who really cares for us, as individuals? No one," she said. "That's the truth, and you know it. We both do."

"Why did you. ... do this, then?" he said.

"I fell in love with you back in New York. Surely you know *that?*" she said.

"What about this American—Tucker?"

"What about him? ... He's an assignment," she said.

"Don't you have any feelings for him?"

"I don't know, really. ... Maybe I do. ... He's still a boy, but ... *Yes*. I suppose I do. But it's not exactly 'love.' He's too different. It's like being on the moon when I'm with him. He's not like you and I are. You and I are the same, basically. I knew it the day I met you. I felt it immediately, and I think you did, too."

"But you sleep with him?" He was surprised that he'd asked that rhetorical question, since he knew the answer quite well.

His unexpected question made Gemma realize, as she hadn't before this conversation, that, on some level, Vladimir was jealous of this Tucker, and that knowledge rekindled the hope that she'd lost that she could make him hers, eventually, if this played out the right way, in spite of the fact that he was already married and had two children.

"Yes—that's my job, isn't it?" she said. "What you sent me to do."

He wanted to change the subject, now. It was too uncomfortable for him to sit here right across from this woman he desired like a madman and talk about these things with her. He was feeling guilty enough that he'd gotten his wife and children into this horrible position. He *had* to find this Neizert. Whatever he and the girl felt for each other was not important now, in light of what would happen if he *didn't* find him. It simply had to be pushed away and come back to later—if he survived this crisis.

"I believe that this scientist will be guided to America along the same routes the CIA used for Nazi scientists in the 50s and 60s," he said. "They won't change that aspect. The methods and routes are proven. At some point he'll pass through the Vatican, or Vatican hands. And from there he'll be sent on to Mexico."

"... This scientist, he was a Nazi Party member?" Gemma asked

"Yes. And a captain in the SS. But he's a very important scientist, now."

"And Tucker is going to Mexico to pick him up, once he arrives there?"

"Yes, I think so," Vladimir said. "Yes."

"So he's lying to me? About leaving his old life behind?"

"Yes. Tucker is a CIA officer. Don't forget that."

"What am I to do?"

"I want you to kill this Neizert if he gets past us here in Italy—if the Americans are successful in getting him to Mexico. It's the only way to stop him. He will be too close to America once he's in Mexico. You *must* kill Neizert. You have to stop him," he said.

"I'm not sure. It seems real to me; the American's desire to leave his job. To leave the service," she said. "Are you sure?" She was going to use Tucker's name, but didn't. She realized that it would be better if she referred to him as "the American," now.

"He's lying to you. It's a cover story ... nothing more. It's all for *your* benefit. No doubt he cares for you. That part must be genuine—look at you. ... Go with him. When you get to Mexico, contact the *Die Mennonitische Post*; it's a German-language newspaper in Mexico City. Call the office there and ask for Mr. Bretler. Leave a message there telling me where you are and how to contact you. A phone number and an address. I'll call you. If I leave a message for *you*, I'll say it's from Mr. Bretler. Can you remember that?" She nodded.

"Yes, I can remember."

"Neizert *must* die, Gemma. Do you understand? Even if it means killing Tucker, too. Can you do that for me if it becomes necessary?" He reached for her hand and took it. He looked at her and wanted to blurt out that he was in love with her and that she must not let him down, but he didn't. Instead, he concentrated on the sensation of holding her hand; the touch of her fingers, the warmth of her small palm.

"Yes, I can do it," she said. "I'll kill him, if that's what you want." It was the first time since they'd first shaken hands three years before in that church in New York City that he'd touched her.

"Gemma, if you fail, go with him to America ... start a new life. Don't *ever* come back to Europe. Do you understand?" She nodded. He held her hand for a moment longer and then got up and left the cafe without saying another word.

She sat for a moment and watched him leave. She felt suddenly emotionally empty but very frightened. She bolted out of the café and looked for him along the narrow noon-time street that was jammed with tiny cars and scooters parked on the sidewalks. She ran down the street when she saw a taxi leaving, turning right into the Borghese. She ran as hard as she could. But the taxi turned onto the busy street and disappeared. She ran out into the boulevard following it and was almost hit by a scooter, and then another one. Cars whizzed by her on both sides, some honking like hell. She was oblivious. She'd wanted to tell Vladimir that she was in love with him and put her arms around him and never leave him again. She wanted to tell him she was pregnant with Tucker's child, but it was too late. He was gone.

*   *   *

"She's with them," one of the gunmen standing in the lobby said as soon as the elevator door opened. He was dressed in black. He pointed a machine pistol at her and mumbled something about the police and immediately took Marie by the arm. Another three men, well-armed, Marie noticed, walked into the elevator and the doors closed behind them. Marie looked at the man as he walked her into the dining room. He was large and about thirty years old. He had a day-old beard. She looked down at his shoes as he pushed her along. He was wearing black, military-style boots with the captoes polished to a fine gloss. Her father had taught her to look at shoes as a good indicator as to what kind of a man she was dealing with in any given situation. He told her once after a hit in Florida, at a golf club, that looking at a man's shoes was better than any kind of ID. "Better than a driver's license," he'd joked. He told her, too, that Italian men would always underestimate a woman. She decided that this one, an obvious foot-soldier, would be no different.

She felt his hand gripping her upper arm. She let him walk her into the dining room. He pushed her down into a chair. The dining room was completely empty at this hour. A few hotel guests were gawking in at them from the lobby. He took her purse away and opened it. He saw the pistol and then looked at her for a moment.

"Whore," he said in Italian.

She answered in Italian that she wasn't a whore but that his mother was. She looked at him. She hoped he would rise to the bait, as she wanted him as angry as she could make him.

"What's your name, bitch?" he said.

"Marie," she said.

"Are they in the room?"

"Yes," she said. He nodded, not surprised that a woman would tell him what he wanted to know.

"You're in a lot of trouble," the gunman said. She just looked up at him, studying his vital spots the way she'd been trained to. Studying what her approach would be; both psychological as well as martial. He was wearing a holster and belt. She looked at his throat. He had a big Adam's-apple. She guessed he could take a punch. She looked at his closely shaven head, then at the black nylon jacket he was wearing, which was unzipped. She reminded herself that she'd been in difficult situations before. She looked across the dining room at an older couple still gawking in at them.

"What have I done?" she said. She turned back and looked at his weapon. She had trained on a host of weapons, but this one was unfamiliar to her. It looked quite modern, with an extended magazine. The barrel was only and inch or two long as well.

"I said, what have I done?" she repeated.

"Shut up," the man said. "Stand up."

"No," she said.

He let go of his weapon's grip and struck her across the face with the back of his big hand. It snapped her head back and she instantly felt her eyes start to tear-up—the first thing that happens when you're hit on the nose. He pulled her up roughly, the way she hoped he would, turning her around at he same time.

"Spread your legs. ... You know how to do that, don't you?" She'd gotten the knife out as he turned to frisk her while he'd been looking at her upper body. He may have heard it click, as she noticed that he'd started to step back from her and his hand was moving toward the grip of his weapon. She turned quickly, pivoting on her left foot, and delivered a side snapping-kick to the man's right knee, smashing it. She'd been taught by her father that the gun-sling works as an excellent weapon to control your opponent, and she grabbed it now as her kicking foot came down, yanking on the sling as hard as she possibly could. The kick had deprived him of the ability to get a grip on his weapon on his first attempt. It also put him off-balance so that he had to try to both get a hold of his weapon and stand back up, because the sling was around his neck, and her yanking on it was forcing his head and shoulders downward, pulling him even more off-balance, all his weight having to be put onto his one good leg, now. The other leg had been completely put out of action by the kick. She followed through—still holding the strap with her left hand, her right gripping the knife, driving it toward his head as he tried to lift it up. Her own momentum from the side-kick had been stopped by her back foot. She now propelled herself forward, all her weight behind the thrust, driving the knife into the man's throat at the level of his Adam's apple, sinking the blade far enough in to sever his brain-stem. The man fell dead at her feet the moment that vital connection was destroyed. She took the automatic weapon from his dead body, found the safety and turned it to the ON position after firing one burst into the floor in front of her just to make sure that the weapon was functioning properly. She marched back into the lobby past the older couple, who stood stunned, not believing what they'd just seen.

"How many are there?" Marie barked. She pointed the weapon at the desk clerk. He hesitated, and she immediately shot him in the chest and turned to the other desk clerk, a woman.

"*Four*," the woman practically screamed it.

"Where's their car?"

"In front of the hotel."

"Is there a driver? Go see for me." Marie turned and looked at the elevator, it had one of the older-style needles from the twenties, designed so that people in the lobby could watch its progress from floor to floor. It had stopped on their floor and was now moving again—descending. She had to make a decision immediately as she watched the young woman go to the door and look out at the street.

"Yes. There's a driver," the girl said. "I think."

"Go outside on the steps and scream, as loud as you can," Marie said in Italian. She looked back at the needle—it was at the third floor and still descending. She watched the girl go out the door and scream. Marie followed her and waited until the driver had gotten out of the car and was coming up the hotel stairs at full charge. Marie came through the glass door and cut him down with a short burst aimed at this chest. She turned around and went back through the doors past the screaming desk clerk and trotted toward the elevator doors. She walked behind the desk and squatted down. She realized that she was kneeling on one of the dead clerk's thighs, and moved. The floor was slick with his blood. She heard the elevator bell ring and the door open. She waited, counting to three, then came out from behind the desk.

"*FLOOR!*" she yelled. She saw the three gunmen, all dressed the same. They had Butch and Sonny in front of them, and were herding them out of the lobby with their weapons pointing toward them. She screamed it again and started firing. She saw Butch throw himself sideways into Sonny, knocking him down. She fired high, hitting all three gunmen in the head as she swept the lobby with automatic fire until the magazine clicked empty. She ran forward, still holding the weapon, so she could use it has a club if she had to. She looked down at Butch and saw that he was all right. She immediately took a fresh weapon from one of the dead men.

"Okay?" she yelled in English.

"Okay," Butch said.

"Let's go," she yelled. She was in full combat-mode, and the adrenalin rush made her face look very strange. Terrifying.

"I got to go back up and get my suitcase," Butch said. She looked at him incredulously.

"Okay," she said. "Okay, but hurry the fuck up!" She watched Butch jump up and run toward the stairs. Sonny stood up and checked himself for wounds, not believing what the girl had just done. She turned and looked out onto the street. She could see people running away from the sound of the gunfire. She froze for a moment as the adrenalin overwhelmed her nervous system all at once. She gripped her weapon as hard as she could, fighting the desire to run like the people outside. When it finally passed, she started collecting extra clips from the dead men's bodies. A moment later, the three were running down the stairs of the hotel. They took the policemen's unmarked car—the engine was still running—and drove out of the square with Marie behind the wheel and Butch riding shotgun now, holding one of the wicked-looking weapons that was very familiar to him, and much-used in Central America. Marie fished-tailed out of the square, briefly driving up onto the sidewalk, where the rear-end of the Ford hit a café table, sending it flying out into the street, its chairs smashed and going every which way. Sonny yelled from the back to head toward the bay.

Later, when they were safe at a country estate owned by Count Cici, ten kilometers from the hotel, Sonny asked for his knife back. Marie just looked at him, and then climbed out of the car without responding. Butch made sure he carried the suitcase of cash with him from then on.

They learned later that the CIA had called off the hit, but that the Italian Army's Special Forces, who were assigned with the task of eliminating Butch, hadn't gotten the message in time.

36

■ MOSCOW

"Comrade Vladimir, you understand why you have been arrested and brought here to the Lubyanka for questioning?" The KGB officer was a huge pocked-marked man in his forties with grey hair. He wore a hammer-and-sickle pin on his lapel. As soon as his plane had landed in Moscow, they'd taken him to KGB headquarters on the third floor of the Lubyanka, and he and is interlocutor were now sitting in a small interrogation room in the infamous prison. He'd gotten a call from his wife at the *Pravda* office in Mexico City telling him that his stepfather had died, and that he should come home immediately for the funeral, if at all possible. It was a total lie. His stepfather had been arrested, too, and his children had been threatened, to force his wife to make the call to Mexico. The KGB's plot to lure him to Moscow had worked perfectly.

"No," Vladimir said. This was his third interview in as many days, and he was sure, now, that they didn't know everything he'd done to keep Gemma's identity secret. He'd put her under three layers of security. The first had been to remove her from his list of agents, where her name had once appeared. The second had been to create a cut-out: he'd created a young woman like Gemma from whole cloth and had inserted her "stats" into his agent file, with Gemma's name attached, so anyone looking for Gemma would be sent in a completely wrong direction. The third and last layer was himself. Only *he* knew the truth about who she was and what she had been doing in Italy. The KGB had breeched the second layer and now there was just his own knowledge protecting Gemma from them.

"I was close to capturing the traitor Hauptmann Neizert," Vladimir said. "I insist on knowing why I was arrested? And on whose authority?" He had asked each of his interrogators the same question, and it was an honest one. "Why have I been relieved of duty at this critical moment?"

"We've told you since your arrest, Comrade. This is a question of your agent in the field; a certain person that was found to be receiving money from your account at the Embassy. We have photographs of her." The man slid a photo of Gemma over to him that had been taken outside a café in Rome. The photo showed the two of them meeting. It had been taken from outside the café by a passing car, but it clearly showed them sitting down together at the same table.

"Who is this girl? And why have you kept her a secret?"

"She's a woman I was seeing; I've told you. We were having a sexual affair. She's an Italian student I met named Adrianna Sturialie," Vladimir said. "I broke it off with her recently. It was nothing. Only sex."

"Why can't we find this woman?" the man said.

"How the devil should *I* know!" Vladimir said. "She was unstable mentally—that's why I stopped seeing her. She took drugs for fun. She could be anywhere in Italy for all I know!"

"We believe that you were meeting with this girl and she was your CIA handler. We now believe that she works for the Americans," the man said.

"That's totally ridiculous," Vladimir said.

"We believe that you have been telling the Americans everything you know about the scientist Neizert and our search for him. Is that not true, *Comrade?*"

"No! It's *not* true," he said. "I protest this absurd accusation! I'm a loyal citizen, and I've always worked to further the cause of the Motherland. My own mother was a Hero of the Great Patriotic War." He saw the interrogator smirk.

"Are you *loyal,* Vladimir Putilin?"

"Yes."

"Tell us the girl's real name and who she is working for, then."

"I told you her name and why I was seeing her—that's all I can *do!* I've told you that for three days now."

"You paid her money; is that not true, Comrade?"

"Yes. All right; I paid her money, that is true. She needed money for her studies and, I suppose, drugs. I gave her a thousand dollars."

"Money that belonged to the people of the Soviet Union," the man said.

"Yes. But I paid it back ... out of my own salary. Go see for yourself. It's all accounted for. Go check my records." That was a lie, but he knew that he'd kept his accounts messy, and he'd often taken money from his *Pravda* expense account to pay for incidentals for agents he was running at the time. He'd made tens of thousands of dollars of direct-cash payments to various Italian politicians who were constantly demanding money from him. All of them were scoundrels of the worst kind. He had purposely made it hard for anyone in the KGB who might be after Gemma's identity, to wade through his *Pravda* cash-accounts. He knew there were moles and double agents everywhere, and he was determined to keep them in the dark about the girl, even now.

"Your trial is tomorrow, Comrade. My report will not be favorable," the man said.

"What am I charged with?"

"Treason, Vladimir Putilin. You will be found guilty, I'm sure. You know what that means, of course."

"Yes. It means that I've been *used*. I was close to capturing Neizert, and someone wants to stop me. Why don't you ask yourself *why, for God's sakes!*" He realized that he was shouting. It was the first time he'd raised his voice since he'd been arrested at the airport. "... I'd like to see my family before the trial," he said. "I would like my stepfather released. He's innocent of any wrong-doing and he's an old man, now, and no threat to anyone."

"All that could be arranged, Comrade. *If you'll tell us the name of the CIA agent who was your handler.* Here is her photograph. Who *is* she? Where is she *now*? What did you tell the Americans? ... How much were you paid, and where is the money now?"

He stopped listening. There was a window behind the pocked-marked man, a long and thin window with thick glass that had been heavily scratched over the years. He could see the snow falling outside. Sometimes it briefly turned to rain. He remembered sitting in his stepfather's *dacha* on a couch as a young boy and watching the rain fall on the winter wheat that peasants planted across the road from their country house. The wheat was so green, it had seemed iridescent to him. He loved to watch the acres of winter wheat in the rain of early fall, the grand beauty of Nature in it.

He loved to watch the comings and goings of horse-carts on the road, too; the mud-splattered horses, the men with their pipes in their mouths, their dogs following behind. For a long moment he was again in that house, hearing the sounds of the fire behind him, the family dog that would bark in the front yard at the passing horse-carts, the look of the white Fiat 124, his stepfather's most prized possession, parked in the front yard, a mark of his stature in the village.

His stepfather had been a college professor who taught economics. He'd been an assistant to Kondratieff, but he'd escaped the purge of economists who had helped produce Krondratieff's report to the Politburo on economic cycles, which Stalin had tossed into a trash bin with disgust. Stalin had had Kondratieff shot. His stepfather had been a prudent man, and had taken the vacant post telling the Politburo the lies they wanted to hear about the Second Five-Year Plan, none of it remotely possible to achieve given the horrible state of the country after the War. The Nazis had taken whole factories back to Germany with them. His stepfather had been rewarded for his lies, and like so many others of the Communist Party elite, he lived very well. His mother had met his stepfather at a mutual friend's house and they'd fallen in love. It was the first time he'd seen his mother happy. Like so many combat soldiers, she'd suffered psychological damage and had been strange sometimes, drinking too much, and often wanting to be alone. He would find his mother in her bedroom smoking and looking as if she were about to burst into tears. One time he'd asked her what was wrong, and she'd just swept him up in her arms and hugged him tightly, tears streaming down her face. All of that stopped after she remarried, and he was grateful to his stepfather for everything he'd done for them, including getting him into the KGB immediately after graduation from Moscow University. He realized now that his stepfather might be somewhere nearby in one of the other cells. The thought that that kindly man, now in his seventies, was in jail because of him, pained him greatly.

"Is my stepfather here at the Lubyanka?" he interrupted the man's questions. He could tell from his look that he'd guessed correctly.

"You haven't answered any of my questions, Comrade," the man said, staring at him. "I will have to report to the court that you've refused to cooperate and are no doubt guilty of grievous crimes against the Revolution." The door to the interrogation room opened. An older man stepped through. He was dressed in a dark suit and wore several combat medals; one of them was the gold star, designating a Hero of the Soviet Union, the highest award given in, or out, of the military. He recognized the old Army general, who'd been a regular speaker at the KGB Academy when he was a student there.

"General Maximov." The interrogator stood up quickly and saluted. The general—in his sixties now—looked at the man and then at the prisoner.

"I'm here to interview the prisoner," Maximov said.

"Yes, sir. On whose authority, sir?"

"The Politburo has sent me," the general said.

"Yes, sir. I see."

"He is to come with me. Here is the order." The general handed the man a yellow half-sheet of paper.

"I'll have to confirm this, sir," the pocked-marked man said.

"Go on, then. Be quick about it!" the general said. The interrogator left the room. For a moment they were silent. The general went to the window and looked down at the courtyard, his back to Vladimir. He was a big man. He'd heard at the Academy that the Nazis had offered a reward of 50,000 Deutschmarks for anyone who would assassinate Maximovna. There had been two attempts during the war, but both had failed. The general had killed one of the Nazi assassins himself. He turned around.

"I'm innocent of all these charges, General." Vladimir looked at him. The general held his finger up to his lips and signaled that they were being recorded by pointing to the ceiling.

"You recognize the lane," the general said. They were driving in a Soviet Zis limousine with the window-curtains pulled back so they could see the countryside.

"Yes, of course," Vladimir said.

"Your stepfather's *dacha*," the General said.

"Yes. Yes," Vladimir said. The village had not changed much. There were more cars now than when he was a boy, though. It was late in the afternoon, close to sunset, and many who worked in the Soviet-run Fiat plant nearby were home by now. He saw some women in long dresses and coats digging in the gardens of their houses, scarves on their heads.

"During the war this village was famous for its vodka stills," the General said. "They were very productive. I was stationed with my brigade, nearby." Vladimir looked across the seat out to the pond he remembered as a boy. It was still there, but it seemed smaller now, with the surface reflecting great white clouds and patches of very pale blue sky.

He'd heard the stories about the Nazi *panzer* force being stopped only a few miles away back in 1941.

"They still make it. Vodka," Vladimir said. "In their homes."

"Yes, but they fail to tell the authorities about it," the General joked. "Some things in Russia never change. ...The peasants don't like the State—they tolerate it," the General said. "During the war everything changed, all the repressive anti-*Kulak* laws were dropped. We depended on the people to fight the Nazis, not bureaucrats, huh?" Maximov smiled wistfully. "They died for their stills, and their gardens, and their children with mud on their boots ... believe me, they didn't die for Stalin or Lenin or any of that crap. What makes a man fight is his women and his children."

"Why am I ... why did you bring me here, General?"

"I want to help you, young man. And to explain some things, too."

"How?"

"I want you to find Hauptman Neizert and protect him. I myself was instrumental in getting him out of East Germany. Right now, Neizert is on his way to the U.S., as you well know," the General said. "That's what is important to me. There's no time to explain why. But you have to believe me it's for the good of Russia that Neizert succeed and escape, and that he be protected from the KGB until he arrives safely in the U.S."

"You want to *protect* ... Neizert?" Vladimir said, shocked. Maximov shook his head, yes.

"Yes, I understand that Neizert was an SS officer who was to be hanged in Dachau in March of 1945. Yes; I've seen the file—Stop the car—but he worked for *us* during the war ... that's what is not known by most in the KGB. He was a double-agent and his identity has been well-guarded. He maintained his contact with the Nazi networks after the War. They believed he was still one of them all this time." The car stopped. "We'll walk now. Stay behind us," he told the driver. "Come on, young man. Get out. Let's get some fresh air."

They got out of the car and began to walk along the muddy, narrow road, with the limousine idling along behind them. The sun was setting, casting an dirty orange hue over everything. Vladimir had been given a long Army overcoat, as it was cold and he'd had nothing but a light cotton suit on when he'd been arrested at the airport. He turned the collar up.

"... Here ... brandy," Maximov said. "Go on, drink. It'll do you good." The general handed him a silver flask. "Drink." Vladimir took a drink and handed it back to Maximov. "There are people in the KGB that know we are slowly being taken over by foreign forces. These people—and I am one of them—must keep their identity secret." Vladimir looked at him.

"So you understand that I'm innocent," Vladimir said.

"Yes, of course!" the general said. "You were arrested because corrupt elements in the KGB did not want *you* to find Neizert before *they* did. They were afraid that he would reveal to you what he knew about KGB corruption."

"I don't understand ... ?"

"Neizert was sent by loyal elements of the Revolution to the West. He knows the names of important people in both the East German government and the Soviet state who are members of the Gehlen network and are now under their orders, following their own program."

"The Gehlen network?"

"Why do you think you met with so much frustration while you hunted Neizert? Why were you forced to use the Italian girl *secretly*? Keeping her out of the normal channels? Because you had guessed that the KGB—in the person of some high-placed mole—was trying to frustrate your search; so you decided to bypass them all. It was very clever, but it could have cost you your life. It almost did, today. They were going to shoot you at the Lubyanka tomorrow morning."

"You know about Gemma?"

"Yes, we know about her. I've watched you. I've read everything you ever put into your files. I knew your mother and I'd hoped that you would join our cause."

"It's true, what you say. I found many who seemed to be totally uninterested in catching this man, Neizert. It was very strange. They would say one thing ... but do another. And I knew I was being watched. In Italy, especially. I thought it was some mole or moles working for the *West*, though, who were trying to stop me from catching the Hauptmann."

"Yes—I'm not surprised. It's why they had you arrested, finally, Comrade. You were getting too close and they couldn't trust you to fail."

"They couldn't trust me to *fail!* I'm a KGB officer. My mother was war hero like yourself. What did they expect?!"

"Exactly. They judged you to be *too* loyal. Do you remember the offer of money in New York? From a certain German women?"

"Yes. I thought it was just a test being done by our counter-intelligence to root out traitors. I ignored it—and thought I'd passed," Vladimir said.

"It was indeed a test. But from Gehlen's people," the general said. "We've sent Neizert to explain to the CIA that the Gehlen network is about to take *them* over as it already has *us*. We're offering to help them stop this secret network. We understand it more thoroughly than they do. And we can help them. They must be stopped before they gain control of both countries."

"I don't understand, General? How is that possible?"

"We believe the Gehlen network—a kind of "fascist international"—has taken control of positions in our party leadership, including planting important men in the Army and the KGB," Maximov said.

"Gehlen?" Vladimir had heard the name and knew he'd been—until his recent death—the head of West German intelligence, and before that a Nazi general in Hitler's high command. He only knew that because at the KGB academy all students read the biographies of important figures in the Western intelligence services. He knew as well, for example, that George H. Bush had been a long-time high-ranking CIA officer—now head of the U.S. delegation to the UN—since the War. It was something that had been kept secret from the American people, but was well known to the KGB.

"Yes. Gehlen was a genius; and he swore that he would destroy Russia. It was really Russia that he hated the most. He blamed us for destroying the Reich on the battlefield because he knew the truth—it was we Russians, on the Eastern Front, who stopped them."

"But Gehlen died a few months ago," Vladimir said.

"Yes, yes. But he created a stand-alone secret network that lives on, a super-national intelligence operation. A 'Fascist International' that now answers to no one but itself," the general said. They stopped for a moment as a motorbike went by them, the two young women astride it passing on by, not giving them a second look. One, a redhead, rode sidesaddle behind the driver.

"And what do *I* have to do with all of this?" Vladimir asked.

"You got in their way. These corrupt elements in the KGB are now completely in the hands of the Gehlen network. They had you arrested because you might have stopped Neizert and learned the truth about why he was on the run."

"Neizert is *your* man, then?"

"Yes. Our man since 1944. You couldn't be allowed to capture him, you see. The network wants him executed on the spot. You wouldn't have done that, and that was what was so dangerous to them. Neizert in custody might have convinced you to contact us. Believe me, they're looking for him all right, but if they find him, they'll kill him immediately. They would *never* bring him back to Berlin or Moscow for questioning."

"You're telling me that the KGB is in the hands of traitors?"

"Essentially, yes. ... But there is a resistance to this catastrophe. It's why you're here with me and not in the Lubyanka getting ready to be executed! We still have some power. But it's less every day. We believe that you are an honest man who believes in the Revolution and will join us and stop them before it's too late and we are all killed."

"I don't understand? How did this network manage all this?"

"Money. They've totally corrupted us. They have enormous amounts of money from the drug trade. They're running the world's heroin business, and have for years. It wasn't that difficult ... They started out early with penicillin, in fact, and quickly moved to heroin back in the 1950s. Neizert is important because he understands their various networks and who in the Western intelligence agencies are working with Gehlen. He's fooled Gehlen himself for all these years. He's a very clever man."

"And this network ... It's why I was kept away from. ..." the General stopped speaking. He got out a cigarette case. Vladimir saw that it was very battered.

"My daughter gave it to me as a present," he said. "Comrade, the Revolution is in grave danger. Do you understand? It's possible that they could actually turn our country over to the West, lock, stock, and barrel—destroy us from inside. That was what Gehlen wanted more than anything else, even during the War." The general offered him another drink from the flask, but Vladimir waved it away. He watched the general light his cigarette and start to stroll along again. "Gehlen had vowed to destroy the NKVD, and later the KGB. He was obsessed with it, in fact."

Vladimir looked down the road and saw his stepfather's *dacha*—one of three on a slight rise above the road a kilometer or so away, now. He could see that the lights were on inside the house, and a car he didn't recognize was parked in the driveway.

"Does Gehlen work for the Americans?" Vladimir asked, trying to understand it all.

"He seemed to us at first that he did, but he always had a German network with a secret fascist agenda. It's grown, of course, and they've become much more powerful over the years, and in fact employ all kinds of people, nowadays. We know that they've made inroads into all the important intelligence services in the West: French, British, Italian, American—all of them.

349

"I've had your children taken to Paris. Your wife is in the *dacha* waiting for you," the general said. "She should be there now. The children are staying with a friend of ours in Paris. You're to call them from here." He dug in his pocket and handed him a phone number.

"I don't understand all this," Vladimir said. "It's all happened too quickly for me to take it in. ..."

"You and your wife will be picked up at your stepfather's *dacha* in twenty minutes by a woman in a Red Army jeep. She will take you to an Army airport near Moscow, and from there you'll be flown to France by our people. Once you've settled your family in our safe house, I want you to help Neizert escape from Europe and get to America. It won't be easy, because *you* will be hunted by the KGB yourself. But, if I understand what you've done correctly, your network, whoever they are, will help you out on this. We have money for you, and it will be given to you in Paris. But you *must* find Neizert and help him get him to America. And you *must* help us bring down the Gehlen network. Do you promise me that? It's the one condition I've placed on your freedom. You must give me your word."

"Yes," Vladimir said. He really didn't have to think about it. Based on what the general had just told him, everything suddenly all made sense to him: all his years of frustration and strange feelings he'd had about the direction the KGB was taking, and even about the Soviet Union in general.

"Good."

"But ... I don't understand how I can just walk away. Certainly they will want you to explain why you let me go? ... "

"You must kill both the driver and me," the general said. He took a puff from his cigarette. Vladimir stopped dead in the road as if he'd just been slugged in the gut. "It *has* to be this way, my boy. They must think you escaped alone and without my help," the general said. "I've got a pistol in the pocket of my overcoat. The safety is off. I'm going to turn around and tell the driver to stop the car. *I* will shoot *him*. Then you must take the pistol from me and kill me. Then go immediately to the *dacha* and wait for the women you just saw pass us on the motorcycle. The redhead and the other one."

"Shoot *you?*" Vladimir said.

"Yes. It's the only way. They must believe that I was on *their* side. If you leave me alive, they'll suspect that I colluded in your escape, and then *my* network will be in danger. I cannot let that happen," the general said.

"But. ... There must be another way," Vladimir said.

"Comrade Vladimir; the Gehlen network murdered my daughter years ago. I vowed revenge. My wife is dead. I've no family left, now. I'm all alone. Please do

350

what I ask of you. ... I've lived a good life, Comrade, and it's been all in the service of the Revolution and our motherland, and I have no regrets. It's time for me to go ... I expect to see my wife and daughter in heaven. I will finally be at peace." The General looked at him squarely. He had blue eyes, and even in the twilight Vladimir could make them out. The General threw his cigarette out into the mud of the verge. "Do you promise to help save us from the Nazis, Comrade? It's no different than before, back in the Great Patriotic War. It's a fight for freedom for our Russian people."

"I'll try. Yes," he said. "Yes, I'll do my best."

"Good. *Good.* Now, let's get on with it, shall we?" Maximovna said. He turned around and motioned for the car to halt behind them. Vladimir glanced toward the west across the field of winter wheat where the sun was now starting to set. He turned back and watched the General take out his pistol and shoot the driver, firing three times into his chest at almost point-blank range. A flock of geese suddenly lifted off the pond, *en masse,* frightened by the sound of the gunfire. The General then turned and looked at him.

"I can't do it—not like *this,*" Vladimir said.

"Don't be afraid, Comrade. Do it for my daughter's sake. Please. I won't beg you, but the future of Russia is at stake, and I mean that literally."

Vladimir took the pistol from his hand. An instant later, he was trotting briskly down the road, the car lost behind him in the mist from the pond and the failing, gone-to-gray light, and the General lay dead, face up, in the middle of the muddy road.

*   *   *

Malcolm had to use a cane for two weeks while he walked around George's house, because of what they'd done to him. It was an embarrassment to him to have to depend on it, and every time he grabbed for it, something went off in his head—a kind of hatred and a refusal to lose this fight. The house had a typically large English garden, and he would go out in the morning and stroll around it, coming in a bit later and eating breakfast with George and his wife. The nanny had usually already taken the children to a nearby posh private school. He'd gotten to like George's wife a lot. She never asked him any questions, and instead treated him as if he were an old friend of hers as well as of her husband's. She'd invited him to play gin rummy the evening that George had left for Germany.

"Your play," George's wife said. She and Malcolm were still playing cards, and it was quite late. She was a very good player, had played bridge competitively, and especially

351

enjoyed beating her male opponents, as most of them were arrogant about their imagined male superiority in all things, and she knew they were mentally denigrating her as they played; or at least they were *at first.*

"I'll be in Rome in a week with your package," George had told him. He'd been wearing a Catholic priest's garb and was still standing by the cab's door outside the entrance to Paddington Station, where Malcolm had dropped him. He was singularly unconvincing as a priest, Malcolm had thought. There was something just a little too rakish in George's smile for him to really bring it off, in Malcolm's opinion. Malcolm had given him the name of a key man who had worked the ratlines during Operation Paperclip immediately after the war—a Monsignor Karlo Petranović—a Croat and a Franciscan, who was still alive and active as a minion of the Central Intelligence Agency in Italy. The Monsignor was now in his sixties, and was the chief economist and a vice president of the Vatican Bank, as well as an important advisor to the Bank of Italy. He had been an ardent Fascist and member of the Ustashe Party in Croatia during the war, despite his "marriage" to the Church at an early age, and he'd participated in the wholesale murder of "foreign elements" in Croatia during the War. He'd secretly had three sons with a French woman, and all three were now involved in the world of international finance: two in New York at Chase Manhattan Bank, and one in Paris with Union Bank Of Switzerland.

"I know that George has gone and done something he probably shouldn't have," his wife said. George's wife had grown up in Kenya, as the daughter of the Eleventh Earl of Sackville. The family had made their money in coffee first, and then from banking and insurance. "He's easy to read, my George," she said.

Malcolm looked up. He had a good hand, but he was feeling like he should let her win, because she'd been so gracious to him since he'd come to stay there at their house.

"On the other hand, some of his friends aren't as easy to read. You aren't a drug fiend at all. I knew that right away. You see, I grew up in Happy Valley. My parents' crowd was chock-*full* of dope fiends." She said all this while apparently studying her cards. Then she suddenly looked up at him. "Besides, you're much too bright in the morning. For a drug addict, I mean," she said. "No, I think you're some kind of spy, and you're hiding out here. George took you in after a scrape, is *my* guess. You see, I know all about George's past. He's told me all about it. I have a brother in the spies. It's how I met George, in fact."

"Me? A spy? No," he said. "Far from it."

"You're lying; he's told me all about you. ... Is George going to be all right?" she asked.

"Yes, of course," Malcolm said. "Sorry, I didn't know. ..."

352

"So, is he on some kind of mission for you? He was very tight-lipped this morning. Said he would be back in a week. ... I love George very much. You aren't going to get him killed, are you? He likes you. I'm trying to understand exactly why," she said. She put down a winning hand. He'd misjudged the play, by quite a lot, really.

"There's someone coming by here tonight. A man named Wally," Malcolm said. "Look, I promise you that George will be fine and be back in a week."

"You spies all lie so much," she said. "Don't you ever get tired of it?" He looked at her and put down his cards.

"I'm sorry."

"So am I. He really misses it, George does. That's the tragedy of it all. He's never really grown *up*, my George. Not really. I know all this: the little family, Bayswater, and the lot of it. Well, that's not what he *really* cares about, is it?"

"No, this is his life," Malcolm said. He was lying because he had to. He knew lots of men like George Cummings. The problem was that they'd never really come back from the War. Not really; and their families and their friends never understood that about them. In George's case, he knew they both shared that feeling of having never come back.

"He's fine, and he'll be back in a week. ...This man who's coming over. ..."

"George told me that you might have a visitor," she said. "When he comes back and has done whatever it is you've got him doing, will you leave us alone, *then?*"

"Yes," Malcolm said.

"Do you promise?" she asked.

"Yes. Yes, I promise," Malcolm said.

"I'm arranging it all now. I had to wait. Go to Bern and wait for my signal," Malcolm had said as he walked George into the station. "You'll have to go dark until you get to Rome; don't contact me until you're actually *in* the Vatican. Do you understand? You'll have to trust Petranović and his men to get you inside the Vatican with the Hauptmann after you arrive in the city. Once you're there, they'll contact me, George. Stick to the ratlines, old man, or I'm afraid the people who want the Hautpmann will catch you, too."

"Right," George said. "I'll stick to those priests like glue."

"It may still be dangerous. I don't know," Malcolm said. "I can't be a hundred-percent sure you understand all this. Each stop will have a handler who'll then pass you off to the next one."

"Yes, I understand *that*. ..."

"You just have to trust the ratline. ..." They'd reached the steps that looked down on the enormous station platform. Malcolm remembered how the place had looked during the war. It hadn't really changed much. "... Thank you, George. Now I'll tell you where to find the Hauptmann. He's with someone I sent. A man called Birnbaum. They're staying at a hotel in Bern called the Belle Époque. It's on *Gerechtigkeitsgasse* in the Old Town. Check in under the name of Father Alphonse. They're in Room Ten, waiting for you. It's important that you use the Vatican passport that I gave you. You *must* turn it in at the desk of the hotel." They shook hands, and then he watched George disappear into the morning crowd at Paddington Station.

37

■ **LOS ANGELES**

The day was like most June days in Southern California—warm and clear in Agoura Hills there wasn't a cloud in the sky when Lorie Talbot's alarm went off at six A.M. Her husband, Detective Warren Talbot, had gone to work hours before, having been called to a homicide in Topanga Canyon in the middle of the night. She was used to calls coming in at any time, day or night, that would take Warren away. When the call came, she had instinctively reached for him and rolled his way, holding him for a moment before letting him go, comforted by the feel of him, his broad shoulders, his stomach pressing up against her. It was something they had done—embrace silently—since he'd been a rookie cop. She'd met several wives who had lost their husbands, shot down in the line of duty; some of them had lost their lives in the most odd circumstances. A husband of one of her good friends had gone to check on an old girlfriend while he was off-duty—she'd called him to complain about her new boyfriend, who she said was beating her regularly. The boyfriend had shot the cop dead as soon as he'd rung the doorbell, shooting through the front door of her apartment and killing him instantly. The shooter's family had been wealthy: they'd gotten him a good lawyer and he'd only been convicted of manslaughter, doing a mere five years for the killing. He was already out of prison and selling real estate in Hollywood.

Lorie still reached out for her husband when the phone rang in the middle of the night; it was an instinct with her now. Morning breath or not, they'd kiss, and then she'd feel him slip out of bed and go to the bathroom to pee and run the shower. He always dressed in the guest room so she wouldn't wake up again. That morning, she'd fallen asleep and dreamed, as she often did, of children. In her dream-world she always had the same two young children, a daughter and a son, one white and one black. They were always sitting with her in the car as she drove them to school. In a new dream she was with her husband and they were trying to find a certain classroom in an elementary school, but the doors of the classrooms were all unmarked. In the dream she kept opening the doors and seeing other parents, white and black, with their children, but she couldn't find the door to the room where *her* children were waiting for her. She'd turned to look at Warren, who she'd thought was right behind her, but he was gone, too. She woke with a start as she was standing alone in the school's hallway, completely lost.

Her alarm rang at six A.M. sharp. It was a Thursday, and happened to be the last day of the regular school year. She had taught at the same junior high for the last ten years. For a moment after she opened her eyes, and after she looked at the clock, she'd laid back on her pillow and thought about her life. No one had ever expected her to marry a white man. No one in her family had *wanted* her to marry Warren, the tall, thin Marine home on leave from Vietnam. No one in Warren's family came to the wedding, because she was black. No one in *her* family came to the wedding, because Warren was white. It was as if they had not existed at all, but were wraiths, two people without families, without friends, without anything, as they only had a hundred dollars between them on the day they were married. They had "tied the knot" in Reno, and when they'd just left the church, a redneck drove by them yelling *"Nigger-lover"* out the window of his car as loudly as he could. They were both only twenty years old. Three days later, Warren left for another tour in Vietnam.

She lay there for a moment thinking of her mother. Her mother had been a maid in the Saint Francis Hotel in San Francisco for forty-three years. Her father had been a longshoreman. She had grown up in San Francisco's Fillmore district. Fillmore itself had been a wonderful and prosperous black-owned street. Her father had been a steward in the union. Why she was thinking of her parents and her wedding day, all so long ago, now, *this* morning, she wasn't sure. Both her parents had been dead for years, now. The family home in San Francisco had been sold long ago, and was torn down during the "Urban Renewal" period in the 1960s, which her father had called the "New Apartheid." Lorie finally slid out of bed at a quarter to seven and got ready for work, still feeling odd. She told herself that it was always an odd day—the last day of the school year—a kind of reckoning and summing up. The students were moving on to high school and leaving childhood behind forever.

In the garage, she'd stopped a moment and looked at a *Biedermeier* dresser that she and Warren were refinishing. It had cost them a thousand dollars. It had been their first major find as amateur antique collectors. According to their reference books it was probably worth thirty-thousand dollars, restored. They'd found it at the home of a deceased woman in San Diego, who had come to the U.S. from Germany in the 1920s. They'd gone to her estate sale, which had been advertised in the *LA Times* one Sunday, and discovered what they suspected was an actual circa 1850 Josef Dannhauser dresser in the bedroom of her small, 1930s-era bungalow. They'd gone out to their car twice to check their antiques reference books, finally deciding it was probably the real thing, and ended up buying the dresser, in spite of its appearing to everyone else there as an ugly-looking—and very expensive—broken-down piece of furniture, with several missing pulls to boot.

Lorie ran her hand over the damaged top of the dresser. They had taken off the remaining pulls and were trying to come up with a way of reconstructing the top of the piece. Without understanding why, she went to the nearby pile of tools, picked out a hammer, then came back and started smashing the dresser top; beating it until it was completely splintered and broken, anger pouring out of her in a way she didn't understand: anger about her wedding day, anger about the way people *still* looked at her and Warren in restaurants, as if they were circus freaks, looks made even worse by the fact that they were middle-aged, and anger about her childless life. The truth was, she had once had an abortion, not telling her husband about it, because she was afraid to bring a "mixed raced" child into the world after suffering so many random insults herself; so many that she and Warren no longer even heard them, really. Hatred had become something they just ignored. She was putting the hammer back in its place on the wall when she was shot dead. She never knew what ended her life.

Someone identified later only as an "intruder with long brown hair" had shot her in the back of the head. She never heard the sound of the pistol's discharge or saw the gunman, who immediately crossed the garage and placed the barrel of his gun fast against Lorie Talbot's forehead. The man was going to fire again, but quickly realized that the bullet might very well ricochet off the concrete floor, and that was something too dangerous to risk, right there. He looked at her lying there, blood now flowing copiously from her head wound and, instead of shooting her again, he knelt over her and felt for a pulse. There was none. He checked twice just to be sure, and felt nothing either time, so there was no reason for his usual *coup de grace*. He tucked the revolver into the waist of his jeans at the small of his back, then turned and walked out of the garage and down the long driveway. He got onto the motorcycle he'd left at the foot of the drive, and left the way he'd come, rolling through the empty suburban streets of Agoura Hills. Lorie didn't die immediately: the shooter had been wrong—she wasn't dead yet when he'd felt for her pulse. She'd had a pulse, but it had just been too weak for him to detect. She had one last dream before she crossed over: Warren was going to pick her up with their two kids, and they were going to leave for a new home in San Francisco. Their new house, she dreamed, was on the same block where she had grown up. She was packing things up for the move—her children's toys—when she finally died.

By pure chance, Warren Talbot caught the call of a murder at his own address. He listened to the dispatcher relaying the address a second and then a third time without believing it could be his wife, because he knew that she must be at work. It was just not possible that Lorie had been murdered. The victim must be one of the gardeners who came on Thursdays, he thought; they'd probably gotten into a fight over something trivial—maybe they were drunk and on speed—things had gotten out of control, and one of them had ended up killing the other over nothing, as was usually the case in these types of senseless murders. *Lorie is at work.* He immediately called the school to tell his wife what had just happened at their house, and ended up speaking to the secretary, who immediately asked him why Lorie hadn't called in sick that morning. He'd put down the phone and driven home in a daze, speeding through the suburban streets near their house, numbed and stunned, not emotional at all. He saw the cop cars in the driveway when he arrived. Several patrolmen wrestled with him to stop him from running into the garage. The situation had gotten so bad that they'd had to handcuff Warren to a patrol car and call for a doctor to hit him up with a sedative. He'd screamed at them like a madman, yanking on the cuffs until they'd cut into his wrists. The neighbors could hear him screaming all up and down the street.

Warren Talbot had been suspected of murdering his wife until he was cleared by the DA, who'd given the case to a colleague in the department to investigate. They'd concluded that the murder was "random," and may have been committed by a transient who'd reportedly been seen in the neighborhood that morning. It was suspected that the killer had been "living rough" in the hills above the house. The transient had never been found, and so far no real suspects had been developed in the case.

Six weeks later, after the funeral and the leave he'd taken, Warren had decided he could finally walk into the garage. His first instinct had been to sell the house immediately, as he was sure that he couldn't take living there anymore with memories of Lorie at every turn. They had lived in the house for almost twenty years. He felt strange; he hadn't been sleeping much, and had been watching TV late into the night, but hadn't really been paying much attention to what was on the screen. He'd tried reading, but he couldn't keep his mind on the text his eyes were scanning—his thoughts would wonder back to the murder and what could have happened. He'd have strange thoughts about why he hadn't been home that morning. Why had there been a call for him that particular day?—it was supposed to have been his day off, but another officer had been injured the day before while apprehending a suspect, and Warren had caught the call in the middle of that night. If he'd been home, Lorie would still be alive. *If he'd only been home that day, as he* should *have been.* He was sitting at the kitchen table eating breakfast when the phone rang one Saturday morning. He thought it was going to be the cop shop or his partner, but it was neither.

"Your wife's death was a hit ... not a murder. Your wife wasn't murdered by a transient. *You* were the target. There *was* no 'transient.' That was bullshit—all of it," the voice said. Warren was sure that he'd heard the voice before, but he just couldn't place *where* he'd heard it right then.

"Who are you?" Warren said.

"A friend. ... Watch your back. Let the Capri Motel shooting go," the man said.

The man on the other end of the line hung up. Warren held the phone for a moment, the dial tone buzzing in his ears. He finally put the receiver down again in its cradle. He tried desperately to recall the voice that he'd just heard on the line: he remembered hearing it *some*where fairly recently, but it just wouldn't come to him. It finally came to him the next day in the shower. He remembered the DEA officer at the Capri Motel. It was *his* voice—Perrys'—he was sure of it.

Butch Nickels had read about Talbot's wife's murder purely by accident in an *LA Times* edition he was idly browsing through on a plane he was taking down to El Salvador, and he had put the probable scenario together right then. He knew how it worked: Talbot's investigation had pushed against the secret machine and the machine hadn't liked it. But Talbot was a fellow Marine, and Butch had felt somehow responsible for making the man aware of the true situation, after he'd read the story by chance. He'd called Talbot from a secure phone in the American Embassy in San Salvador, El Salvador. Talbot's phone had been listed, and Butch had decided to call when he was half-drunk—his standard mental state most days, now.

After Warren put down the phone all the pieces fell neatly into place in his mind, and he got up, put his coffee cup into the sink, and walked out to the garage. *It was a hit ... my God, it was a fucking* hit! He'd actually *known* it, instinctively, subconsciously, but he'd suppressed it. Now it was somehow comforting to know that the murder of his wife had *not* been a random act of violence, because knowing that removed a type of fault for her death that he'd imposed on himself: now, however, he had *another* type of responsibility for her death to deal with, but it didn't affect him the same way emotionally, because he might actually be able to *do* something about it. He had seen enough of the "random" types of murders to know that they happened, in fact, every day: serial killers, desperate dope fiends, and flat-out insane people committed them all the time. Those types of people, he knew, were always "out there." But his wife's murder was different—it had felt different from the beginning, because nothing had been stolen, not even the cash in Lorie's purse.

He opened the garage door with a spare opener he kept in a drawer in the kitchen. He had refused to go into the garage since the day his wife had been killed. He stood in the driveway and watched the door move upward; the motor that hauled it up was noisy and old. For some reason he ran down the driveway when he saw the dresser smashed to pieces. He ran along the street in the early morning heat; not fast, just a steady jog in his pajamas, the tears running down his face. He didn't show up for work that day or for several days afterwards. Because of the circumstances his bosses let it go; everyone covered for him. He came back to work two weeks later and began again to ask questions about the shootings at the Capri Motel. It was those same prying questions that had brought him to the attention of the cabal inside the FBI in the first place. He had not wanted to give up on the Capri Motel case for the dead girl's sake. *Now*, he was determined to understand why his wife had been murdered instead of himself, if indeed he had been the target of an actual assassin. He'd decided to go after the truth—whatever it turned out to be—and make whoever was responsible pay for what they had done to Lorie.

                        *   *   *

There was a helipad on the roof. One tower of the castle had been reconstructed for that very purpose. They could see the tower as Marie drove toward the Count's castle. The Count—once called one of the world's sexist men by *People* magazine—had just flown in from his house in Rome, where he'd been meeting with various important people in the international drugs trade, as well as squeezing in a meeting at the IMF, where he represented the Bank of Italy and the Vatican Bank. In fact, he sat on the Board of the Vatican Bank and was responsible for its active use in the laundering of drug money on behalf of the Sicilian Mafia. Cici had gotten a call in Rome from Sonny Delmonico—one of the few people in the heroin business who actually handled the product who could reach out and contact the Count personally. The two went back to the old days in Palermo during the 60s when the Count was young and ambitious and was helping to push the Corsicans out of the heroin business on behalf of the Sicilian mob. Sonny had been used as a messenger and cut-out by Sicilian interests and the Bonnano family. He'd reported directly to the Count in those days, and the Count knew him well and liked him.

Count Cici's family seat was the castle outside the town of Gigliotto, the town named after the family. The family's castle had been built by crusaders in the twelfth century and from there passed down through various tenants until the Cici family acquired it as booty in a local war in the fourteenth century. The family had owned the village and surrounding countryside for the last 500 years. The family coat of arms was ancient: the black Sicilian eagle, on one side of a Crusader shield, facing a lemon tree on the other side. It was common knowledge in certain European ruling circles that Count Cici was the CEO of the Sicilian Mafia's heroin operation and had been for years. After all, only someone in the drugs business—and at a very high level— could afford the hundreds of millions of Lira to restore the hulking medieval ruin and turn it into a modern twelve-thousand square-foot mansion with the "latest gifts of modernity" as the cardinal said as he blessed it. The parties held at Cici's for royalty and other European dignitaries were on a scale unimaginable to most people, and something that the Count enjoyed very much. Some went on for days. The Count's wife, a former Asian supermodel, preferred to stay in Rome because of their sybaritic nature and the presence of so many prostitutes that were rolled out on the second day after the wives had been sent packing.

The trio were directed by the security men as they drove into the castle's garden. Sonny had called Count Cici before the police came looking for them at the hotel and he was expecting them. Marie looked at the interior courtyard of the 13th century castle, completely rebuilt to *look* old. It had been a surreal day so far and this experience was only adding to that feeling. She'd never seen anything like it. The castle looked both modern and ancient at the same time.

"Who the fuck is *this* guy, again?" Butch asked. He was sitting on the back seat next to Sonny with one of the automatic weapons resting on his knees and his suitcase of money.

"Count Cici di Gigliotto," Sonny said. A guard in a tailored black jacket pointed to where they were to park. Marie, driving, slowed the car to a crawl and they slid to a stop in front of a huge, orange bougainvillea-covered stone wall.

"Count?" Marie said. "The count of ice cream."

"Yes. He shits ice cream and Lira. ... And you can leave the weapons in the car. You won't be needing them anymore," Sonny said, "we're safe now."

There was no one in Europe as politically connected *or* as compromised as Count Cici de Gigliotto. He stood at the crossroads of a tremendous amount of political intrigue, and had also managed to ride the heroin tiger now for over twenty-five years, which might have been some kind of world record, had such records been kept. He was one of the richest men in Europe, and was said to be the tenth-wealthiest man in the world; at least according to *Forbes* magazine in their yearly list. They listed his assets every year, and at the top of that list was the steel business that his grandfather had bought in the 1920s and built into one of the largest producers in Europe before the War. Now, the family sat on an empire that included pharmaceuticals, banking, real estate development—they owned the luxury *Sparta* hotel chain with locations throughout the world—and industrial-scale agri-businesses, which had been the foundation of the family's fortune, as their estate in Sicily was one of the biggest producers of citrus fruits on the island. What *Forbes* magazine failed to say—and of course couldn't know—was that Count Cici di Gigliotto was a "made" member of the Sicilian Mafia as his father and grandfather before him had been. They had helped Italy become a fascist state in the 1920s, and had profited tremendously from the Second World War in every manner imaginable. Most of their steel production was sent to Hitler's Germany. Due to the famous German efficiency, they were still receiving regular payments from the Reich for rolled steel as late as the summer of 1944. The payments had been made in gold to the Union Bank of Switzerland, because the family didn't trust paper money. Where the gold came from they didn't ask. Most of the gold had in fact been stolen by the Nazis.

"Sonny, I'm afraid you can't go to Switzerland right now—it's impossible in the present situation. You *must* go to Rome and met with this American. He's anxious to meet you," the Count said.

"I'm afraid things are rather complicated as far as that goes," Sonny said. "Thank you for taking us in, truly, though—we were a little out of our league in *this* game, so to speak."

"Sonny ... of course. I'm sorry about the problem you had at the hotel. I've already spoken to General Bastico about it. There was a miscommunication, that's all. It won't happen again; you'll be free to travel now without any trouble at all from any of the authorities. I'll have you flown to Rome tomorrow," the Count said.

"Yes, I'm sure there was some kind of "miscommunication." I'm afraid there were some casualties. Some policeman were shot and killed, in fact—that kind of thing," Sonny said. The Count waved his hand as if the dead policemen were a mere trifle.

Sonny looked across the polished walnut desk at his friend. There was a Miro painting above the Count's head, one Sonny especially liked, very bright and lively. They were sitting in the Count's intimate wood-paneled office: the interior of the castle was chic and modern and unexpectedly bright.

"Sonny, you have to remember that these chores we do for the Americans. ... They're part of our *duty*, aren't they?—it's the price we pay to live like we do," the Count said. He was sitting at the elegant desk wearing only a swimsuit and a designer-type terry cloth "cabana" jacket.

"Yes, I understand. I've heard from Wally about the situation. He's warned me off this young American."

"Nonsense." The two men looked at each other. Sonny had known the Count since he was a young man working for his father's company. They had always gotten along well, and Sonny had been very important in the establishment of markets in areas where the French Corsicans had tried to compete with the Sicilian mob. He had spearheaded a takeover of Corsican heroin production, in fact, and, after many bodies were buried, had succeeded in his task.

"It seems that the CIA wants me dead," Sonny said. "They sent this man I've come with to kill me last week in Spain."

"*Really?* Yet here you are, still alive!" The Count smiled.

"You could say that I convinced him I was worth more alive than dead—to him, *personally,* that is. ... I'm just saying that I think perhaps this American Tucker isn't what he seems to be."

"Well, after all, who *is,* old boy?" The Count smiled at him again. They both laughed. It was the first time Sonny remembered laughing naturally in days.

"Well, I'd rather not be murdered outright—just in case there *is* another miscommunication. ..."

"The American girl, she's very pretty, eh?" the Count said, abruptly changing the subject.

"Yes—she was Joe B's *goomah* up until just yesterday."

"*Really?*" Cici said.

"Things have been moving rather fast lately," Sonny said.

"Have they? I always wonder what it's like to be Sonny Delmonico. It must be very exciting. Not like me, stuck in meetings with fat men all the time," the Count said. He genuinely respected and liked Delmonico, and understood that it was men like Sonny, the especially cunning and brave, that kept the Sicilian mob on top.

"Yes: In the space of a week I've lost my house and I've been close to death twice. ... And now, I'm back here with you. And I'm broke, as the suitcase the American is carrying is full of *my* money. My life savings, in fact," Sonny said.

"Do you want me to? ..."

"No. No, I don't," Sonny said.

"Why not?"

"I think he can be useful to us. I know he's a CIA officer, but he's well-trained and I like him. I think he's looking out for himself first—right now, anyway—and if he stays in the Agency, he might be able to do us some real good in the future. It's hard to say exactly why I like him, really; I just do. ..."

"You *like* him? Wasn't he sent to kill you?" the Count said.

"Yes—but he's a charming bastard, and that counts for something with me," Sonny said.

363

"Certainly—charm counts for *some*thing." Cici smiled. "But he *did* come to kill you, *nicht wahr?*"

"Yes, but he didn't. He *could* have taken all my money and then shot me, but he didn't. He's lived up to his word," Sonny said. "I think he can be trusted to live up to it in the future, too. I just have that feeling about him."

"I see."

"He's the kind of person we can use—I'm sure of it," Delmonico said.

"All right then, fine—for the time being, anyway. The Americans have sent me a message that they want you to meet this Tucker. They've called off their dogs for the present. Apparently they were angry with this Perry fellow that you're with. I insisted they not bother you or your new protégé again, at least on *our* turf. I've spoken to Wally and told him to leave this Tucker fellow alone as well. He was very anxious about you, by the way. I didn't know Wally cared so much. But he *insisted* that you be protected. I was actually moved by his loyalty," Cici said.

"Wally and I go *way* back—we trust each other," Sonny said.

"Trust in our business is everything, isn't it?" the Count said. Sonny leaned forward: For the first time in a long career he was truly afraid. It was a feeling that had been with him since the lobby of the hotel. He'd realized that things were no longer predictable and quiet. In the old days things had been under control; most of the time, anyway. But not now. The DEA and the Americans were really dangerous. Or perhaps he was only fearful because he was now in his fifties and didn't want to die as he'd seen so many others die—stupidly and needlessly and only because of money. Right there and then, sitting in front of his old friend the Count, he realized that he, Sonny Delmonico, after all the work he'd done for years now in the underworld, was flat broke. He'd lost the one thing he really cared about—his home. The house he'd built for himself was gone forever. Just simply gone. He was not only afraid of dying—a new emotion for him—he was also angry in a way he hadn't been since the day he'd landed at Anzio Beach and had quickly realized that he might be killed right there for no good reason at all.

"Why is this American, Tucker, so damned important? He's very new to the business, as far as I can tell—our friends in LA tried to have him killed, too. He's reported to have robbed product from people. I'm asked to kill him one day, and now you're asking me to *meet* with him. *Why?* Does anyone know what the devil is going on?" Sonny said.

"Sonny, my good friend, sometimes in life much is denied to us. ... Dinner is at eight." The Count smiled again. "Now I must make a call." Sonny looked at his friend and nodded. He stood up and left the office. The Count waited for the door to close and then he dialed a number in London. Malcolm Law picked up the phone in a hotel room.

"I've done what you asked. I'm going to play the middle game with you."

"And that is?" Malcolm said.

"You have your war with Mary Keen and her bunch—if you want it, that is. Personally, I don't like them. They want more and more from us every day. I'm sure that soon they'll be after me, too. If you win this, fine. If you loose, I never spoke to you. ... Do you understand?" the Count said.

"Yes. ... Thank you," Malcolm said.

"Not at all, Malcolm. You have a month to get done whatever it is that you're going to do—I'll be watching with great interest," the Count said, then hung up before Malcolm could reply to him. A moment later the Count was getting up from his desk when there was a knock on the door.

"It's me—Sonny."

"Come in." Sonny walked back into the office.

"I need a favor," Sonny said.

"Yes?"

"I want you to fix my problem in Ronda. I want my house back."

"What happened?"

"The American killed two priests at my house there. The police will need to blame someone. I'm convenient for them. I'd like that to go away," Sonny said.

"Done," the Count said. "What're a couple of priests ... among friends?"

38

■ LONDON

"Why did you save me?" Bridgette asked him. "I thought you were going to kill me, baby! I really did—I'm still shaking ... look!"

It was pitch-black in the bedroom because they'd pulled the blackout curtains closed; they were drawn tightly against the big picture windows that all gave onto views of the Thames. Wally had trouble sleeping, and he always needed absolute darkness to fall asleep. She'd never gotten used to it, herself. In Jamaica it wasn't ever totally dark like this, and cold; it could be both in London, any time you wanted it to be. There was always light in the sky at night in Jamaica even if it was only starlight.

Bridgette felt her heart beating within her chest. She knew she'd just screamed. She'd woken with a start from a terrible nightmare. The kind of nightmare that you see in vivid color. In the dream she was sitting in the apartment playing solitaire. The playing cards were out in front of her on a black table top. The apartment walls started to move in on her, as if she were still in the car-crushing machine—it was like a movie she'd seen of an Edgar Allan Poe story when she was a little girl, and she'd dreamed about the room where the walls came in to crush the guy to death for weeks afterwards—now, all these years later, the man she loved had almost done that very thing to her. The dream-walls of the apartment took on a bizarre metallic-yellow color, identical to the sides of the car-crusher. In the dream, she'd run for the front door to the apartment, but it was locked. She'd frantically pulled on the door-handle. She'd screamed for Wally to open the door, somehow knowing that he was standing just on the other side, listening. She'd finally backed away from the door after hearing him laughing in the hallway outside the room. She'd run back into the living room of the apartment, with its views of the Thames. She could see the sluggishly-moving river clearly: the new buildings going up on Canary Warf; the huge cranes outlined by the sun, standing there aggressively against the sky. She looked out of the big picture windows and saw Wally's face as if he were a giant looking in at her—like in the old *King Kong* movie. Wally was holding an ace of hearts and he was laughing. The ace of hearts turned into a white dove and Wally bit its head off. Like some kind of a voodoo priest, Wally had sprinkled the headless bird's blood against the big windows. The blood darkened the window in front of her until it was solid red. When she turned around again the walls were only inches from her body—in mere seconds she would be crushed to death. She'd woken up screaming, and Wally had to calm her down—he'd gone to get a brandy for her. He'd flipped on the nightstand light and now the room appeared *chiaroscuro*. The black-lacquered headboard reflected the light and the white satin sheets glistened under it. She pulled herself up onto the headboard pillows behind her and tried to calm down. She was sweating, and the room felt fuggy and warm.

"Because I'm in love with you," Wally said. He was shirtless, lying there just in the blue silk pajama bottoms that she'd bought for him. He had the word "Harold Hill" tattooed on his left arm. He was strong-looking, a Taurus type—like a country bull, her grandmother would have said.

"... But I betrayed you—you were going to kill me for it," she said.

"Yeah, I really was. People make mistakes, though. I have a terrible temper. I hate myself. I do things when I see red that I regret later. I'm sorry, baby. I told you." She looked at him. He did in fact looked pained by what he'd almost done to her at the crusher. She wanted to believe that. How could anyone do something that horrible and sadistic to a fellow human being? She had been in the car and seen the walls start towards her. It was something she'd never be *able* to forget, even if she really wanted to.

"You'd kill me if? ..."

"If you do it again? *Yes*. I'd have to," Wally said.

"I love you, baby. I mean it. When I was in the crusher ..." she said. Wally looked at her. He'd poured himself a drink, too, and he took a sip. He looked at the clock on the nightstand. It was three in the morning. It was a beautiful modern clock, made out of solid silver and with a black dial. He liked to buy things for their apartment and bring them home to her. He seemed strange to her in that way. He was interested in things that she wouldn't have thought a gangster would be interested in. Sometimes he brought flowers and actually arranged them himself. He'd stand in the kitchen and look for just the right vase to display them in. He was a budget of paradoxes to her.

"I thought I was going to ... I thought you were going to kill me, Wally."

"I thought I was going to, too," he said. "I *wanted* to, really, *then*—I won't lie to you. Part of me—the "Wally" I don't like—wanted to see you crushed to death—for a moment, there. But I couldn't, finally, don't you see? The part of me that loves you stopped me. *That* "Wally" is stronger than the other; when it comes to *you*, anyway. I tried to kill you and I couldn't." They looked at each other. "You know what I am," he said. "I've never tried to hide that from you."

"I can't love a *monster*, Wally."

367

"I'm not *that* ... I'm not." He made the statement in a tone that was different from his usual brashness. He *must fear the monster, too*, she thought.

"I've known ever since the day I met you in that knocking shop that I love you," Wally said. "I had a dog like that once. He would bite me sometimes, but I still loved him. You know how you are when you're a kid. ... It was a German Shepherd. He got hit in the head by a bus and lived, but he wasn't quite right after the accident. He would bite you out of the blue, but I couldn't have him put down," Wally said. He reached over and touched her face and then he kissed her. "I put up with it, because I truly loved that dog."

"I'm afraid of you," she said. "That you'll turn on me—that you'll kill me."

"Don't be afraid of me, baby," he said. She sat up higher and cradled her drink. The phone by the bed rang, and she expected him to pick it up, but he didn't. He ignored it.

"Aren't you going to answer it?"

"I know who it is," he said.

"Who?"

"It's my wife," Wally said. "She's lonely. She's been calling late at night." Bridgette put down her drink, and he watched her ass as she leaned over so she could put it on the nightstand, setting it alongside her. He grabbed her from behind and they made love. At first she resisted, still upset by the dream, and not sure anymore about anything.

The phone rang again while they were doing it. She was afraid of the man she loved and she didn't understand why she didn't run away from him; just go *home* to Jamaica and forget about everything she'd been sucked into these past few years. Afterwards, before he drifted off to sleep, he told her again that he loved her and was sorry for what he'd done at the car crusher, and begged her to forgive him. She did. She stroked his head; something she knew he loved for her to do. He looked like a boy to her at that moment. But her own life seemed totally out of control, as if she were helpless to stop it careening into the abyss. Wally finally fell asleep. She thought again for a moment that she should just get out—bolt—disappear. Go back to Jamaica. Never come back. Later, she opened her eyes in the pitch darkness. She knew somehow that this, right *now*, was her last chance to escape him, but she did nothing, deciding that in fact he did love her, but that he was not altogether sane, either, and she just didn't care.

*　　　　　*　　　　　*

368

He heard a bell. It was an old fashioned Swiss sleigh bell that was attached to the door, so that when a guest entered the paneled lobby—full of antique cuckoo clocks—it would ring, day or night. It was the bellboy bringing in George's one suitcase. He'd walked George's suitcase to the desk and put it down next to him. The lobby smelt slightly musty and sweet, like a cold fireplace. It was snowing outside and his black raincoat still had snowflakes on the collar from where he'd stood paying the cabbie off.

"Yes, Father?" the desk man said, looking at him.

"I'm here for just the one night," George said. He smiled, but the desk clerk, a man his age with a big forehead and a shock of jet-black hair, didn't smile back. He nodded instead, giving away nothing.

"Passport, please," the clerk said. George took out his Vatican passport and handed it to the man, who opened it and looked carefully at the page with his details. When he was finished reading it he looked up at George and gave him a meaningful look.

"Did you say just one night, Father?"

"Yes," George said. "A quiet room, please. I'm to meet some friends for dinner here."

"Yes," was all the clerk said. Then the clerk took his passport and put it under the counter and began to fill out the necessary registration card. He waited as the man carefully filled out the card and finally had him sign it at the bottom.

"I have to keep the passport, of course," the man said.

"Of course. There should be a package for me," George said.

"Yes—I'll get it," the man said, finally smiling "Welcome to Switzerland. I trust you had a pleasant trip?" He came back in half a minute and handed him a small package, then rang for the bellboy, who had stepped to the front of the lobby to look out the big window at the dusk traffic. There was a red wet shimmering smear of brake lights reflecting in the mirror. Several cuckoo clocks in the lobby went off simultaneously: it was exactly six o'clock.

"I will help you with your bags," the bellhop said. When they got to the room the bell-hop walked in front of him and put down his bag. The man seemed tired. George got out his wallet and began to count out ten Swiss francs.

"I'm Hauptmann Neizert," the bellboy said. George looked at him. He'd barely noticed him, before the man's sudden announcement. He was wearing an absurdly ornate old-school Ruritanian bellboy's uniform.

"*You?*" George smiled.

"Yes. They thought it best since the Jew was taken."

369

"The Jew, Birnbaum—the American—was taken?" George said.

"Yes ... Birnbaum," Neizert said.

" 'Taken?' ... How?" George asked.

"He went to the international calling phone at the drugstore and they captured him. He wanted to call his wife. They have no phones in the rooms here. ... He will talk. So they hid me in plain sight. No one looks at the bell-man," Neizert said. "I was told to look out for a priest, and here you are."

"No tip required, then," George said, putting his wallet back into his pocket.

"How long can the Jew hold out do you think?" Neizert asked him.

"I couldn't say, really—I don't know him," George said.

"They will torture him. To find out where I am," Neizert said.

"Probably," George said.

"We are to wait for them now to take us into the mountains. They should be here tonight," the Hauptmann said.

"The man at the desk, when I checked in, is he with us?"

"No, he's new. He's the weekend man. The manager is with us, though. He's gone to get the priests. He's the one who suggested I wear the bell-man uniform," Neizert said.

"Does the new desk clerk know you're Hauptman Neizert?"

"No—only the manager knows. He was once a priest. Back in the War."

"We'll leave in the morning, then," George said.

"But the priests ... they know the passes ... the ratlines. We *have* to use the rat lines," Neizert said.

"I'm changing in the plan," George said. "I don't like the looks of your pal downstairs. He's a military man if I ever saw one. Anyway, it's always good to change the plan. I learned that long ago. The Japs didn't like it when you wandered off the trail," George said.

"We have to trust the priests," Neizert said.

"Listen, old man—the man they've picked up is going to talk. Maybe in an hour, maybe in a day—but he *will* talk. Do you under*stand* me? The plan has to change," George said. "Can you ski, at all?"

"What?

"It's a simple question, Herr Hauptmann—do you know how to ski?" George asked.

"Yes."

"Cross-country style?"

"Yes. As a boy."

"Good. Let's relax, right now. We'll leave in the morning—early."

"Are you sure you know what your doing?" The Hauptmann asked. He seemed fit; about a hundred and forty pounds or so, with no visible fat or pudginess. His hair was grey but his face was still youthful. He'd obviously kept himself in decent shape over the years.

"Listen: we Brits won the War, didn't we? You fellows didn't. Now go find some clothes that make sense for our change of plans. Do you have some here at the hotel? We can't have you out in *that* getup."

"Yes—in my room ... thirty-four."

"Were you really an SS man? Is that true?"

"Yes," Neizert said.

"Can you use a weapon?"

"Yes; but I think we should keep to the plan, Father," Neizert said.

"Don't call me "Father." My name is George. I'm not even Catholic. Church of England, in fact—they're actually *worse* than Catholics, you know. ..."

"George—I think we should stick to the plan. The rat-lines have never failed us before. I trust the priests who were here. I've spoken with them about our trip."

"Yes—Stick to that plan and you won't survive another day. Is *that* what you want, Herr Hauptmann?"

"Of course not—I have to get to Rome. I have something very important to tell Malcolm Law. I *must* get to Rome, and then America," he said.

"Well then, shut up and let me think this thing through. In the meantime, go on and get some other clothes on."

"Yes, okay. The Jew, he was very good to me," the Hauptmann said.

"Yes, I'm sure he was. I don't think they'll be discussing his love of Germans in general, though," George said.

The first thing George did after washing his face in the bathroom sink and looking at himself in a slightly chipped mirror was to open the package that Malcolm had sent to him. It contained a Walther pistol with two clips. He took the gun out of the box, carried it over to the desk, then swept the Bible and various tourist-oriented detritus off onto the floor with a casual brush of his forearm.

He took the Walther apart and made sure it was clean, examining the interior of the barrel in the reflected light from a wooden match held up close to a piece of stationery. He saw the clean grooves of the rifling inside and was satisfied. He took all the ammunition out of the two clips and examined the bullets one by one until he was satisfied that there were no foreign objects adhering to any of them that would obstruct the action of the spring in the magazine. He then replaced one of the clips, jacked the action to send a round in the chamber, then sat the hammer back down. He slipped the other clip into his back pocket. Then he called down to the desk and ordered a *Financial Times* and a pot of coffee and just simply waited. It was so quiet in the room that he could easily hear the cheap travel clock he'd set on the bedside table ticking away like the mad automaton it was.

It was that same clock that he checked in the middle of the night when he heard a knock on the door. He turned on the bedside light and stood up. He'd been sleeping fully dressed. The Walther had remained in his hand the whole time he'd been asleep. He pulled the hammer back and got his bearings. Whoever it was had just knocked again. He'd pushed a desk chair under the door handle so that no one could open the door without a great deal of noise and trouble.

"Yes?" he said, moving to the side of the door "... Who is it?"

"Father?"

"What do you want?"

"Father, I've come to take you to them."

"I didn't catch your name. ..." George said, moving to the corner of the room after he spoke. He leaned hard up against the wall. An intuition told him to move, and he did so just in time to miss a hail of gunfire that riddled the door—the bullets went cleanly through it to smash and embed themselves in the antique desk across the room, with some of them hitting the window and shattering its glass. He watched the fire from an automatic weapon eat through the door around its lock, then the door was violently kicked in. The chair he'd placed under the doorknob had held for a moment, though.

He strained all his senses, waiting and listening as carefully as he could. He heard someone fumbling with the clip of a weapon. He walked up to the door and emptied the Walther through it at chest-height, counting his shots and making sure that he kept them to the center area of the chinked door. He pulled the chair away from the bullet-smashed door and looked out into the hallway. He saw a man crawling toward the elevator. An automatic weapon lay abandoned on the rug. The man was obviously badly wounded. George walked out of his room and caught up with the man. The would-be assassin was using his hands to pull himself forward on the rug. He was young, maybe twenty five or so. He'd been hit square in the chest and was bleeding horrifically. He suddenly stopped moving and lay still. As George walked up to the man, he pulled the fresh clip out of his back pocket, racked the action on the Walther, then knelt down and turned the man over. His eyes were open.

"Who sent you?" The man just looked at him, unknowing, almost gone. His eyes were blue and he had short blond hair.

"Heil Hitler!" the man said weakly. He turned himself back over and tried to crawl down the hall again. George just stood there watching him for a moment, stunned by the fanaticism behind the remark, and the man's animal ability to still keep crawling, trying to escape, with so many vital organs obviously shattered beyond hope of repair. He walked behind the man for a moment as he crawled slowly towards the elevator door. Then George passed him and stood in front of him, blocking his way. The man's head stopped against George's shoe.

"Are you with Gehlen?"

"Heil Hitler," the man said. His voice was barely audible. George suddenly heard the elevator bell go off and realized the man probably had accomplices who had been waiting for him in the lobby. He started to move down the hall toward the stairs but quickly wheeled around and put a bullet in the back of the man's skull for good measure.

*   *   *

They had been electrocuting various parts of his body in the basement of a mansion owned by a manager at UBS. The man was name Uri Von Misen. He had once been a colonel in the Waffen SS, and had narrowly escaped the gallows at Dachau via one of Gehlen's infamous rescues. Somewhat ironically, Von Misen was now in charge of the largest gold depository in the Western financial world, and was in daily contact with his peers at the Bank of England and the Federal Reserve's New York District bank.

The six men in the room had been chasing Hauptmann Neizert across Europe, using all their contacts inside police departments from Sweden and the UK to Italy and various North African regimes to help them find him. The team, except for Misen, had all been called in from Argentina and all of them had Argentine passports and worked for the Argentine intelligence service. Most of them were in their fifties. They were the hardest-looking men that Sal Birnbaum had ever seen, and he knew from the moment they'd snatched him off the street corner exactly who they were. All of them were Eastern Front combat veterans. They had brought a younger man with them to Bern—an Argentine intelligence officer who they were training. Gehlen had been careful to recruit new blood into the network over the years: young ex-military men and would-be career intelligence officers from Greece, Argentina, Brazil, England, and even the U.S., where ex-Green Berets and Navy SEALS had been recruited straight out of the jungles of Vietnam and Cambodia into the burgeoning Gehlen organization.

The man who was clamping him right now had been a corporal in one of the *Einsatzgruppen* and still had boyish looks despite his age. He now worked for Volkswagen and was one of their most important executives, charged with running assembly plants in Brazil. Adolf Eichmann, too, had been given a job with VW in Argentina. Eichmann had been actively assisted by Gehlen and higher-ups in the Volkswagen Corporation in Brazil until he was captured by Israeli agents and taken to Tel Aviv, where he'd been tried and executed.

In the car, the man had been solicitous and even kind to Birnbaum. The corporal had gone with Eichmann to Argentina, had been assigned to him as a bodyguard, and was a wanted war criminal. His name was Rudy Obberstein, and he was using a U.S.-made tractor battery to produce the shocks, clipping jumper cables to Birnbaum's testicles and penis and nipples. He'd actually learned the battery technique from a French Army officer who had worked extensively in Vietnam torturing the Viet Minh. At times, the former SS corporal would examine Birnbaum's agonized writhing to see if there might be an adjustment he could make to produce a higher level of pain. He was a perfectionist, of course, just like so many of his countrymen. The clamps themselves had already injured Birnbaum's testicles, just from their pressure alone. Rudy Obberstein, the sadist, expert marksman, and able corporate executive, was now eagerly engaged in clamping the cables onto Birnbaum's ears, but just then a man walked into the basement room and interrupted him. The three other men in the room immediately stood at attention, two of them clicking the heels of their boots as he walked by them. The man said something to Rudy in German and he unclamped the jumper cables and stood aside. The presence of former SS colonel Hans Kamptner, now serving as a member of the West German intelligence service, showed just how much the Gehlen network wanted to catch Hauptmann Neizert.

"My name is Hans. ... You are the Jew Birnbaum. Can you hear me, Jew?"

"I can hear you," Birnbaum said. It had only taken a few minutes of being in the custody of these men before Birnbaum the lawyer and family man started to disappear and Birnbaum the combat veteran seemed to come to his rescue. It was almost as if all the years since the War had suddenly not existed; as if he were not a middle-aged father and husband. The soldier was back. For whatever reason all of that other life left him. What he was left with was the anger and hate for the enemy that he had felt before he'd worked so carefully to rid himself of his wartime experiences. The experiences which had left him an emotional wreck, and angry as hell at the world and everything in it. Angry in a way that "normal" civilians could never, never, understand, and that had scared him. He wanted to get up from the chair where he was now handcuffed and kill each of the men in that room with his bare hands—see them die and be personally responsible for their deaths. He prayed to God for some kind of miracle that would allow him to somehow slip from the cuffs and kill them, even if he should die in the process himself and never see his wife and daughters again.

"Go fuck yourself," Birnbaum said. "Can you hear *that* okay?" He had to mumble it because they had punched him in the throat and it had affected his ability to speak. His voice seemed to come from somewhere below his normal voice-box.

"*What* did he say?" one of them asked. Sal couldn't see very well, as one of his eyes had swollen shut from the beating he'd taken. But he turned his head to look at the man who had spoken. He had a burn mark on his face; his cheek and nose had been scarred from a *Panzerfaust* that had blown up in his face when he'd fired it at a Soviet tank.

"He called you an *ashlock*," one of the men said in German, and then laughed.

"*Ja*; okay. I want to know where the Hauptmann is," Hans said. He signaled for quiet. He moved closer to Birnbaum so he could better hear his quiet responses. He looked at the naked man, with his face swollen and one side of it already blue-black, his penis bleeding from where they'd clamped it. "Do you understand? We have very little time. We understand someone else has come in to help you move the Hauptmann. Is that correct?"

"I'm going to fuck you up," Birnbaum said. Even to him it sounded funny, because he still couldn't get his words out correctly.

"... What did he say?" No one could understand him because none of them were native English speakers, all of them were foreigners and that particular bit of American slang was lost on them. They all got closer so they could make out what he was saying.

"The Hauptmann ... which hotel?" Hans asked.

Birnbaum tied to speak, but something was wrong with his jaw and it hurt like hell. He remembered feeling his jaw give-way when one of the men had stood on it right after they'd first brought him here. It had enraged them that he'd fought back and they'd made him pay for it. Birnbaum had hit the driver with his elbow, pushing the man's nose bones up into his brain and killing him. The others had at first not believed it possible.

"He killed Klaus Mattie," one of them said.

"He did?—How?" the man Hans asked in German. It was explained to him that he'd driven his elbow into the man's nose. Hans looked back at Birnbaum with a strange look.

"These Jews can be tough. *Ja. Gut.*" They spoke in German for a moment discussing what they should do, now. Hans listened to the men talk and Birnbaum watched Hans looking at his watch. He was wearing a blue suit with a white shirt and colorful tie, and wore a handsome leather trench coat; all of it impeccable, as if he'd just stepped out of a store. Birnbaum watched him from his half-closed right eye, as his left one was completely swollen shut from the beating.

"I want to tell you ... about the Hauptmann," Sal said. But the Colonel didn't hear him: instead, they pulled his tongue out of his mouth and clamped it with the battery clips. They stood back and watched him move against his restraints, jerking this way and that while they watched impassively with professional curiosity.

"*Ja; das ist gut,*" Rudy said. He had forgotten about the tongue. And he should have known better.

39

■ GSTAAD, SWITZERLAND

Sandra White, a tall, strikingly beautiful blonde in her early forties, had been a popular English model in the Sixties, and a friend and flat mate of that era's ultimate "It Girl" Twiggy. Sandra had met George Cummings at one of the many parties the girls threw in their shared flat. Sandra and George had had a brief affair. She'd also been a girlfriend of George Best—the famous footballer—but had left him due to his overindulgence in the booze and consequent inattention to *her*. Sandra had moved to Brazil in the 70s to get away from London and the drug scene that had taken over her life. From Brazil she'd gone to New York and married an English heart surgeon. The entire time she'd kept in contact with George, who'd originally spotted her as a possible asset for MI6. At times, especially while living in New York, she'd done favors for MI6, and George Cummings in particular, acting as a kind of high-class madam; helping them to pick up working models who were willing to sleep with important men, either simply for money, or, in some rare cases, just because they loved the idea of acting out "Bond Girl" fantasies, and truly believed themselves to be "patriotic".

Sandra divorced the surgeon after he struck her one night in a drunken rage. He'd told her that she was losing her looks and that he was "fucking tired of her." She'd gone to Switzerland and opened a girl's school in Gstaad, modeling it on the nearby Le Rosey school, which was quite famous among the world's elites. She used the money she'd saved from modeling to start her school, and made the most of her New York and London society connections. Unfortunately, the school failed because the European and American society people found her background a little bit too "exotic," and were afraid some of her former lifestyle might rub off on their daughters. She *was* able to secure a job at the Le Rosey school as a counselor, though, in part because of George and his "friends," many of whom had attended Le Rosey and lobbied for her. It was George himself, though, who made sure she was hired as a counselor and "talent-spotter." She'd stayed on at Le Rosey and had eventually become one of the most liked and admired staff members in the entire institution.

"Ms. Contreras." They were speaking in Sandra's office at Le Rosey. The student sitting across from her shared a significant secret with her about George Cummings.

"Yes?" The student's full name was Carmen Contreras. No birth certificate had been issued at her birth, so her exact age was unknown. Officially, she was listed as seventeen, but was in fact somewhat older. The Catholic nun and nurse at the country hospital in the mountain village near Bogotá, Colombia, had given her the name of her mother, a girl who had only been fifteen when Carmen was born. Carmen's mother had had the bad luck of dying in child birth, a not uncommon occurrence in those parts, as the hospital had few medicines available. She'd died of a simple uterine infection that in the United States would have been easily treated.

Carmen looked much older than her schoolmates. Men in the town of Gstaad—some very *very* rich men, in fact—all stared at her when she passed by on the street with the other girls from the school. She had the voluptuous figure that girls from Colombia often have at a young age. She had coal-black hair, olive skin, and was tall like her father, who she'd never known, who knew about her birth but had never come forward to claim her as his daughter. She and another girl from her village had gone to Bogotá with a pimp when they were only thirteen, and he'd put them out on the streets together in that cocaine-fueled metropolis of the Andes.

It was George Cummings who had happened to pass by Carmen, and she had solicited him as he walked into a five star hotel for a meeting with an agent he was running—a prominent Colombian journalist. He'd stopped and stared at the young girl, shocked by her appearance, and by the proposition she'd just made to him in pidgin English. He'd seen her on that block every day that he'd been in Bogota, working the hotel row. He had tried to ignore her. But she was sporting a black eye that particular day—given to her by an Italian customer—and he'd finally stopped and asked her name, and had been moved to help her.

"You want fuckie-fuckie?" the young girl asked him. She had been sniffing glue earlier in the day, and her eyes were red and unfocused. It helped to give her an otherworldly look. That question, coming from a mere child, dressed as she was in a dirty T-shirt that featured a cartoon of Snoopy lying atop his dog house, her hair needing to be brushed, had simultaneously frozen his blood and broken his heart. It was a grim country, Colombia, and he'd thought he'd built a fort around himself by staying half-drunk most of the time, but his emotional fortress had been blown to smithereens by that awful question.

"I want you to come with me," he'd said. She'd followed him into the hotel. The bellhop had smirked, expecting the worst. George walked to the desk and had them give her a room. Then he'd called a friend in the Colombian intelligence service, saying that he'd just taken a girl into protective custody and that he wanted a guard posted at her door. He gave them the room number. "There'll be some kind of pimp who'll come along soon enough. Can you make him just disappear?" Two weeks later, after having been spirited around Bogotá by George's secretary, the little girl had been put on a plane for Switzerland and the Le Rosey school. They never found her pimp. He'd been picked up by the police and was simply "disappeared". Not a single person missed him.

"You're in trouble again, dear?" Sandra asked.

"Yes, Sandra ... I'm in trouble again," Carmen said.

"You went to the Biathlon meet in Turin without telling the school, didn't you," Sandra said.

"Yes, because I knew they wouldn't let me go. It was during the week."

"Your roommate says that you're smoking marijuana in your room. Ms. Wang was caught while you were in Turin."

Yes ... sometimes *Sally* does. I've warned her about it," Carmen said. "But she brings it into the school. She's seeing someone in town who sells it to her. Her allowance is too big." That was definitely true. Her roommate's father—a Chinese real estate developer in Hong Kong—was said to wear a dinner jacket covered in diamonds. His daughter was probably the most promiscuous girl Carmen had ever met, and gender was of no importance to Ms Wang. If it had a pulse she would seduce it.

"You know I'll have to tell your ... benefactor. They're threatening to kick you out *again*. I've spoken to the headmistress," Sandra said.

"George? ... He's not my father is he? So what do *I* care" Carmen said. Carmen's English had a French accent because when she'd first come to the school she had only spoken Spanish. Her English teachers at Le Rosey were French, and couldn't help imparting their accents to their students.

"What's wrong, Carmen?"

"Nothing," Carmen said.

"You're a gifted athlete and a very beautiful girl. Why do you risk being expelled *now*, so close to your graduation? I've been pulling strings to get you into Cambridge, you know. George has been writing letters like mad on your behalf. You know you could have a place on this year's Swiss Olympic team. You would give that up, too ... if you're expelled."

"I don't care," Carmen said in French. And she meant it. She was wearing the same all-white ski-outfit that she wore on the biathlon course. Her current lover was her shooting instructor. They'd been sleeping together for a year, now. They had tried to keep it a secret, but Carmen was almost certain that Sandra knew, but just wasn't bringing it up in their talks. He was a German, ten years older than her. She was actually the better shot. It was a gift she had; a naturally low pulse rate, and when it became elevated during biathlon competitions, she didn't have the tendency to jerk the trigger that other shooters with higher pulse rates had. She had "the squeeze," as competitive shooters called it. That was the ability to see the target, focus, and then hear the shot go off without actually having felt yourself squeeze the trigger. No one knew that she was mentally going to the zone where she had lived as a child prostitute when she pulled the trigger. She had learned the trick of disconnecting her mind from her body; to exist completely inside her own head when the Johns and tricks were having at her. The ability to put that distance between mind and body made her a terrifically accurate shooter. Because she was tall, the cross-country skiing part of the competition wasn't as difficult for her as it was for shorter people. She had a long, elegant stride, and was known as "the animal" by her Le Rosey teammates because of the way she could herringbone like a machine up the steep, icy hills of late winter.

Her tuition was paid yearly by George. On several occasions George had come to see her. Whenever he came, he would take her out to dinner in Gstaad and act "fatherly" to her; or, at least, what *his* version of "fatherly" was. He always sent her a terrifically expensive Christmas present that made her cry. She would spend her Christmases with Sandra White, either in Sandra's London apartment, or at her house in Gstaad. George had kept her a secret from his new wife, thinking it best to do so, never realizing that Carmen needed more than an expensive education to be happy.

Carmen had run away when she was fourteen and tried to track George down in London, but had failed. There was a time between the ages of thirteen and fourteen when she was desperate for a "father." She'd escaped from the school and had used her allowance to buy a train ticket to Paris, and from there she'd gone to London, where she knew George lived. She only had his first name and no home address, though, which made the chances of her finding him in the City virtually impossible. But still she had gone–driven with a burning desire for what she'd fantasized as a "normal family life." Sandra had come to take her back to the school when she'd run out of money. Sandra White—with no children of her own—was the closest thing to real family Carmen had ever had.

" ... George is coming very soon," Sandra said. "He needs our help."

"I hate him—I hate George," Carmen said.

"He cares about us—you know that. And you always say that just before he arrives."

"I hate him," she said. "I *do*."

"I don't believe you," Sandra said. "Not really." Carmen looked at her. She smiled at Sandra. It was true that she always said it, and then spent the rest of the time waiting anxiously for him to arrive. She couldn't help herself; it was like some hopeless Hollywood story about a poor girl and her rich uncle, except in her story George always left without taking her back home to London with him. And there was no beautiful music or laughter in the end. Only George getting into a taxi and leaving her alone again.

"When will he get here?"

"In just a few hours, I think."

"What does he want? ... It isn't Christmas. Or any other *official* time," Carmen said.

"He wants you to guide him to the border with Italy. ... On skis."

"What? ... You're joking!"

"No I'm not. Sometimes, dear, we shouldn't ask too many questions. Will you help him? He's bringing a friend, too."

" ... Yes, all right." Carmen put on a brave face. The fact was that she loved George Cummings like a father because of what he'd done for her. At the same time, she also hated George Cummings for what he'd done for her, but she just didn't know which of the two powerful emotions would finally win out.

"Good," Sandra said. "Now go on and get ready, dear."

*   *   *

George knew that Sandra and Carmen were his best chance of getting the Hauptmann out of Switzerland alive, given the events of the past few hours. Even with their help it would be a pretty iffy situation at the best. "Why are we going to Gstaad?" Neizert said. He'd changed into nondescript clothing: running shoes and a faded-blue windbreaker. He seemed thinner and older in his street clothes. They were on the train to Gstaad. The route to Gstaad, via Spiez, had spectacular views of lake Thun and the Alps. The sky was very clear that morning.

"Because I have a friend there and we can't do this alone," George said.

"This is not part of the rat-line," Neizert said. "We should be in the care of the priests, and you know it. We should be in Montreux." The Hauptmann had now become suspicious, and had only agreed to board the train for Gstaad because he knew they were going to be followed when they left the hotel, and it would be certain death for him to stay in Bern by himself. They'd gotten first class tickets and were in a private compartment on a train designed for the well-heeled—mostly tourists and skiers.

"If you're so bloody sure about the priests ... go on, then," George said. "But it was the priests who were in charge of security at the hotel, and you saw what happened *there*. I'm afraid that sometimes it's best to throw away the playbook." George lit a cigarette and gazed out the window—they were looking down on a classic Swiss valley, complete with large ski chalets with A frame roof lines, each with its huge old dark wooden barn. All of the buildings in the valley were snowbound, and the scene looked like something off a postcard. "Relax, old boy—the worst they can do is kill us. ..." George mused.

"Is that supposed to be funny?" the Hauptmann said.

"Yes, it is, actually," George said. "Have a drink or something in the dining car—just to take your mind off things for a while. ..."

"And where are we *going?*" Neizert asked.

"To Gstaad, of course." The Hauptmann looked away for a moment, then stood up.

"Do you understand what's at stake here?" he said, looking down at George. *"Do you?"*

"Not really—I'm just a soldier in this war," George said. "I leave all the morality and high-talk to the others. Now let me get some sleep. We're going to need it. Can you ski, really?"

"What?" Neizert said, his hand on the compartment door.

"It's a simple question: I asked you before, and I want to make sure you weren't lying to me." George closed his eyes. He had not really slept since the gunfight in Bern.

"Yes; I said so. I'm not in the habit of lying—about anything."

"Cross-country?" George asked again.

"Thirty years ago I was quite a good skier, actually," the Hauptmann said.

"Really? Excellent," George said. The Hauptmann left their compartment and went to the dining car for coffee. George—his eyes closed, now—wondered if the man might not get off at the next stop. He very much doubted it.

*　　　　　　*　　　　　　*

Catherine Birnbaum heard the phone ringing. She hadn't heard from her husband in over two days. She'd called the number at the hotel in Bern he'd left for her and been told that no such person was registered, or had ever *been* registered there. She had argued with the person on the phone and insisted that he put her through to her husband.

She snapped on the light and lifted the receiver.

"Hello."

"Is this *Fraulein* Birnbaum?"

"Yes—who is this, please?"

"I want you to say something to your husband," a foreign-sounding man's voice said.

"Hello. ... Who is this? Hello." She stopped for a moment. She heard a rattle on the other end of the line, and a voice that sounded distant and strange—as if it were coming from a metal box. Yet she instinctively knew it was Sal. She screamed. It was a big house and she was on the second storey, but her daughter heard her very clearly and ran half-undressed up the stairs from the ground floor, straight to her parents' room. She saw her mother clutching the phone to her breast. Then she finally put the phone down. Her hand was shaking.

"He said we should run?" Catharine said absently.

"*What?*" her daughter said. She looked around the room, thinking they'd had an intruder.

" ... Your father said we have to run—right now, this instant—that they'll kill us if we don't."

"Mother, what's going *on?* You were screaming just now." Her mother looked up at her and then started to sob. She slid off the bed and onto the floor on her knees. It took a good five minutes for her daughter to understand that her father had been on the telephone and that he was asking for help. They both looked frantically for the number of Malcolm Law—the man who had mysteriously come out of the past.

*   *   *

The over-sized tractor battery had finally gone dead; but Sal Birnbaum—for some reason—had not. Although most men probably would have by now. He had long ago passed into a strange state that was beyond pain; perhaps it was simply pure hate that kept him going, now. He had watched the proceedings from high above his broken body, looking down on himself, as he'd read in the tabloids that some people said they'd done during near-death experiences, lying on a hospital operating table while surgeons were operating on them. But Sal wasn't in a hospital. He could see the men gathered around this bloody naked body below him. He could hear the man called Hans screaming at him, but it no longer mattered. Then, transported into a dream world, he was sitting on the couch at home with his wife and they were reading. He looked up at her and saw how beautiful she was. They often read together in the living room after dinner. It was something he loved to do, to be physically near her. She was wearing a black sweater with a turtleneck and her red hair looked beautiful. He sat there realizing how lucky he was that he'd overcome all the obstacles to his own happiness. He was thinking that he *could* have been someone else entirely. He'd come home from the war and walked into a pool hall in downtown Baltimore called "The Shack"—a place where he'd hung out as a kid. At noon it was full of unemployed combat veterans like himself, their young faces as intent over their pool games as if they expected an attack from the enemy. He could spot them all very easily. He'd stood in the doorway near the cashier—a big black woman named Alice who recognized him. The place was owned by the Jewish mafia, and he could have had a place there if he'd wanted it—he'd felt that as a certainty. But he'd suddenly turned around and never gone back to the place, not even once. It had been his first victory in his personal war against despair. In his dream state, he was walking down the snowy street towards Catharine, toward his daughters, toward the future. The war finally—and for the first time since he'd come home from Europe—seemed to belong to the past. He'd carried a gun with him everywhere since he'd come home. He tossed the revolver into the snowy street and turned the corner, glad to be rid of it.

Hans was screaming at him, and suddenly he was back in the chair. They'd thrown something at him; something sticky and cold. His wife looked at him for an instant and smiled, and then she was gone and only Hans was standing in front of him, surrounded by the other ones, the ones who'd broken both his arms and his legs so that he wouldn't have been able to stand up even if he wanted to.

"Jew Birnbaum, I will light you on fire and burn you up right here if you don't tell me where the Hauptmann is—do you understand? You have run out of time." It was as if he had not been tortured for an entire 24-hour period. His senses came back to him and he could focus on Hans, on the other, now weary, men in the basement of a non-descript house in the outskirts of Bern, Switzerland. He saw that he'd shit himself copiously, and that all the toes on his right foot were gone, mangled first by a pair of pliers, then finally cut cleanly off by a straight razor that Hans carried.

"Okay, buddy," Sal said in a hoarse whisper. " ... Okay ... you win. I'll tell you." His voice was suddenly clear enough for Hans to put down his lighter. He'd thrown a can of paint thinner on Sal and the thinner was making the man's skin turn red, as it oozed into the cuts and burn marks. Birnbaum signaled with his head for Hans to come in closer. Hans handed his lighter to the corporal and came up very close to Birnbaum, putting his right ear right next to Sal's mouth so he could hear as clearly as possible what he was going to say.

"Go on—where is the Hauptmann?" Hans asked.

Sal saw the man's ear; he could see it very clearly, as if he were looking at it under a microscope; he could see the hairs sprouting wildly out of its edge; and the sight of those hairs suddenly nauseated and disgusted him. He opened his mouth and bit down on the ear as hard as he possibly could, feeling his teeth cut into it as he shook his own head violently from side to side like a mad dog while his prey struggled in vain. Han's ear was torn from his head and Sal—feeling it go—knew he'd won. He held the ragged and bloody prize in his teeth for a few seconds as the men stood and gaped at him while their comrade howled in pain. Hans, enraged, put the palm of his hand over his now torn and bleeding ear-hole—his expression incredulous not able to believe the Jew had got to him. The German immediately reached for his pistol with his free hand. Sal spat the ear flap onto the floor; he smiled at them all, and began to laugh manically—ready to die.

While he was burning alive, after having been doused with paint thinner and set on fire by Hans, Sal really didn't feel very much. Before they trooped out of the smoky basement, the other men all thought that the Jew was in terrible pain as his body twisted and burned. But they were wrong. He was not even there in Bern anymore. Sal Birnbaum was in Chicago, sitting in his living room next to his wife, who was on the telephone with her mother. They were speaking in Gallic, a language he always enjoyed hearing spoken, although he knew only a few words of it himself. Sal looked over at Catharine, who smiled at him, then he turned back to reading the *Tribune's* sports section—feeling very content with the way things had worked out for him, in the end.

40

■ ROME, PARIOLI DISTRICT

"So, how are we going to handle this?" Butch asked. He and Alex were having breakfast on a veranda with a view of an English-style garden below. The pre-War Roman apartment was walled off from the street outside, so it seemed as if they were not even in the city. Butch, Sonny, and Marie had been flown to Rome aboard Count Cici's helicopter and had been left at the Rome airport. Butch and Marie had been detained at the airport by the Italian police, who had been on the lookout for Butch. Sonny had disappeared into the crowd before the police spotted him. Another phone call to Count Cici by Sonny did the trick, and Butch and Marie had been released.

"What do you mean?" Alex said.

"I mean, being undercover. Is that still ... you know. Are we still in the dope business? Delmonico kind of knows who I am. I mean, I was sent to *kill* him, you know, by your father. And then shit just happened," Butch said. It was cool on the veranda. Alex had been told not to tell Butch about the Hauptmann—*anything* about him, in fact. He'd been briefed by his father, who'd come to Rome on a night-flight from London and explained his plan directly to Alex: Delmonico would bring Neizert to the U.S.-Mexican border at Sonoyta using the mafia's drug pipeline as a cover. It would appear as if Neizert were just another gangster in Sonny's employ. No one special. To make sure that Neizert was well-guarded, Alex and Butch would be the drug buyers who were there to receive their shipment of heroin at the border, taking Neizert into "custody" and arresting Delmonico, who would later "escape." The heroin would be turned over to the DEA there at the border and the case closed. Neizert would be kept in DEA custody as a low level drug trafficker and brought by a DEA plane to LA where Malcolm would take over.

Alex's father had confessed, for the first time, that there might be people who would try to kill Neizert, at any time, in Mexico, or while he was being taken to L.A. He and Butch were to guard Neizert and take him from the border to the Capri Motel, where Malcolm would meet them and debrief Neizert.

The Agency—Alex was told—would not be able to assist in any way, as his father was determined to keep Neizert's existence a secret from everyone in the CIA for the time being. He'd decided that hiding the operation out in the open—as a DEA operation that was focusing on the Italian Mafia's infiltration of governments both in Europe and South America—was the perfect cover story. He would get the DEA to protect his man until he was finished debriefing him. If he was lucky, the story would hold up long enough for Neizert to tell him what he'd come to the USA to reveal about the penetration of the Gehlen network into the CIA.

"You know, since L.A. ... my father doesn't trust you," Alex said. "He thinks you're the devil incarnate or something. You were supposed to kill this fucking guy Delmonico, Butch ... not go into *business* with him!"

"No shit!? But ... " Butch started. Alex decided he didn't want to hear what had happened in Spain, for his *own* good, and held his hand out to stop him from any further explanation.

"Save it—I don't want to hear anymore bullshit," Alex said. "Save it for the suits, later."

"Okay ... I got to go make peace with your old man, though; he's at the Embassy waiting for me right now with the Head of Station. I don't know if they're going to fire me or what. ..."

"They aren't going to fire you; I guarantee that—I won't let them," Alex said. They were having a late breakfast and the huge apartment was empty except for them. The two girls, Gemma and Marie, were out shopping. They had hit it off immediately, and Gemma had asked Marie to go out with her, as she was getting ready for Mexico, and had no luggage or traveling clothes.

"I like your girlfriend," Alex said. "By the way—she's pretty."

"Yeah. She's no joke," Butch made a sign, holding his hand like a pistol.

"Yeah? What's that mean?" Alex said.

"She's in the game," Butch said. "She's—*you* know—connected. ..."

"And ... that makes her the perfect girl for you?"

"Yeah," Butch said. *"Most definitely."* Butch smiled big in a way Alex had never seen before.

"If I tell you something ... you have to keep it a secret. Do you think you can do that?" Alex said.

"Yeah—do you have to ask, after what we've been through together... ?"

"Gemma ... She's a Communist ... I think—I'm pretty sure. ... And she saved my life there in Palermo."

"No shit? Really!" Butch said. "I had an uncle that was a Communist."

"Yeah—I think so," Alex said. "She thinks I'm a drug kingpin in LA."

"Wow. Holy fuck. An open-minded Communist, huh? Aren't they like our sworn enemies and shit? That's what they kept saying in Vietnam. I remember that part—

they pounded it into us all the time. But I've never met one that good looking before, I must admit," he joked. "All the ones I ever met dressed funny, in black pajamas—and tried their best to kill me, too!"

"Yeah. I wanted you to know that, just in case it means something, down the road. ..."

"Maybe she's a real spy?" Butch said "You never know. She's good looking enough to be a spy."

"Yeah, sure. She was just waiting for me in a basement in Palermo," Alex said.

"I'm just saying," Butch said. "Be careful."

"There's something else. ... In Mexico ... there's someone coming *with* the heroin—someone that my dad needs to be in the States. That's what this has been all about since they sent us to L.A. I thought you should know that," Alex said. "My dad doesn't want you to know about him, but I'm telling you anyway."

"Well, I figured we weren't *really* in the dope businesses, all along—it just didn't make any sense. Who is the guy?"

"Some old Nazi," Alex said. "That's all I know."

"Old *Nazi?*"

"Yeah."

"What the fuck; *that's* what this whole thing has been about? I thought we won that war a few years back. ... "

"Apparently we didn't, according to my father," Alex said. "I want you to come to Mexico with me. My old man didn't want you to come along. He's still ... he doesn't trust you. He was going to have you arrested after what you did in Spain. For dope, no less, *and* murder, and have you handed over to the Spanish police. He was hoping they would throw away the key, and he'd never have to see you again."

"*Really?*"

"Really," Alex said.

"Damn. Thanks for the look-out on that, pal."

"Anyway, I've finally gotten him to agree that I'll need you. I also had to agree—in exchange—not to shoot Delmonico myself. He fucked me over bad, you know—that's how I got in that dungeon in Palermo; he *sold* me to those mafia fuckers, and they were going to just kill me—not ransom me—I have no doubt about *that*—until Gemma showed up. ... So, go to the Embassy, smoke the peace pipe with my old man, and come to Mexico with me and Gemma. I want you there with me," Alex said. "My father said that there are people that want this old guy dead in the worst way, and they're very well organized. They might even try to kill *us,* too. Imagine that."

"Kill *us,* eh? That's not very nice. ... Sure. I got to bring the girl, too, then—Marie. She's worth her weight in any kind of ammo you want to talk about."

"Why the fuck not?" Alex said. "The more the merrier. *I'm* bringing a girl. They're good cover, anyway."

"There's something *you* should know about ... I made a deal with Sonny," Butch said. Alex held up his hand again.

"I told you—I don't want to know. Keep all that shit to yourself, now. Don't tell me *anything.*"

"Wait. You *got* to know about this," Butch said.

"Look, man, I don't want to know about any side-deals. I don't want to hear the details. I don't really care what you do on the side. Just don't tell me shit about it, okay?" Alex said. Butch looked at him, nodded, took a swallow of coffee and got up from the table.

"This shouldn't take too long, then, now that I know the score," Butch said. And he left for the U.S. Embassy.

*   *   *

They'd met Sonny Delmonico in the bar of the Hotel Majestic at 5 P.M., when all the elegant people of Rome were slipping in for cocktails.

"Sorry about the misunderstanding," Sonny said. "You have to understand that in our business things can be—how should I put it?— notoriously confusing? I want to apologize for what happened in Palermo. And our horrible misunderstanding." Sonny extended his hand for Alex to shake, holding it out as if the misunderstanding had been about a simple thing; not murder and acid baths and dying in horrible agony.

"You see, he's *sorry,*" Butch said enthusiastically. "I *told* you Sonny wasn't a bad guy, really!" They'd gone to sit at the end of the bar. There were two barmen on duty; both were wearing snappy green jackets and had slicked-down hair.

"Would you shut the fuck *up?*" Alex said. *"Please."* He looked at Delmonico. For a month he'd fantasized about what he would do to him if he ever caught him. The most satisfying scenario was to stab Delmonico in his one good eye. He'd replayed that over and over in his mind, while hiding out in Sicily with Gemma.

"They were going to throw me into a vat of *acid,*" Alex said, still nonplussed at having just sat down for a drink with a man he'd been obsessively fantasizing about killing in a horrible way, not reaching for Sonny's outstretched hand. He looked straight at the older one-eyed man, who was now dressed in a beautiful new fine-wool blue suit; straight into his one good blue eye.

"Monstrous," Sonny said. "The business is changing, totally. I keep telling this to everyone. It used to be much more ... civilized. Those men were animals. We wouldn't do things like that, not in the old days," Sonny said. He kept his hand out, still expecting Alex to shake it. "There's no excuse for that kind of behavior."

"*Acid*," Alex said. "... I shit my pants." One of the barmen looked over at him, as he'd said it louder than he should have.

"I would have, too," Sonny said quickly. "Like an elephant. ... But look ... here you are, old boy! ... All's well that ends well. And I *tried* to stop it."

"It's not healthy to keep a grudge, Bruce. *You* know," Butch said. Alex looked at both of them. "Go ahead and shake. It was a misunderstanding. Get over it." Alex realized that he was talking to men who had already factored-in the worst possible deaths for themselves, and simply weren't getting his resentment. In some ways they were very child-like. Nothing mattered to them but the right here-and-now. If you escaped death, why worry about it? He found himself reaching for Sonny's hand to shake it—the last thing he'd ever expected to do. But he understood their attitude now, at least somewhat. "An hour ago I wanted to kill you, and here I am, shaking your hand," Alex said.

"As I said, it's a strange and confusing world we live in," Sonny said, shaking Alex's hand and patting him on the shoulder as if they were old friends.

Butch was wearing a grey sharkskin suit he'd bought on the Via Venito. He'd had to go into the U.S Embassy and meet with the Head of Station and Malcolm Law. Law had barely spoken to him, and it was clear to Butch that he hated him. He'd gotten a haircut and a new grey suit and looked entirely different; as if he were some kind of straight businessman, not a bent CIA officer with a mafia girlfriend. It had been Marie's idea that he look the part when he walked into the U.S. Embassy.

"Okay," Alex said. "I'll forget it."

"You see? I told you Tucker is a reasonable guy," Butch said.

"I'm leaving for Mexico City in the morning. I want to be sure that you're bringing me what I'm going to need," Alex addressed Sonny.

"Yes; absolutely," Sonny said. He believed that the young American sitting in front of him was a major heroin dealer with big-time protection, reaching into the government itself in the United States. He spoke over the top of his wine glass. It was obvious that Butch, the man who'd been sent to kill him, knew everything important there was to know about him. That fact didn't surprise him, as he was used to the relationships between intelligence services and the mafia, in all the countries of the world. Perry was a corrupt CIA officer and Tucker was his connection to the American underworld. It seemed consistent with what he knew of the world and very much in line with what he'd experienced first-hand in Italy.

"We'll meet in Sonoyta. ... I'll have what you need—fifty kilos. I've put it all down, in here." Sonny tapped his head. He didn't mention the Hauptmann, or having met with Malcolm Law—a meeting arranged by Count Cici. Malcolm Law had told him that the Hauptmann was to remain a secret. Whatever the truth was, Delmonico had left the meeting with Cici and Malcolm Law uninterested in anything other than staying alive and still being in business.

"If you somehow fail to bring me what we're buying, I'm going to hunt you down and kill you," Alex said. "I will not forgive you a second time. I will bury a hatchet in your face. Is that perfectly clear?" There was a new tone in Alex's voice that Butch had never heard before. It was very gangsterish, and he realized that what had happened to his friend in Palermo in that basement, probably really *had* forever changed him. He was a much harder man, now. He was a little nuts, too, now, maybe. Butch understood that kind of madness and was impressed. He immediately felt a new respect for his partner. He shot Sonny a look like that said: "You see—he's one of us."

"No need to worry, old man," Sonny said. "I won't fail you."

"I was told to make a payment of two-hundred-and-fifty-thousand dollars. It's here," Alex said. He slid a key across the bar. It was an old fashioned hotel room key that was attached to a fancily-decorated, heavy metal ball; the type of key used at the Majestic to keep the guests from taking their room-keys out into the street with them when they left the hotel. "Room Sixteen. In the closet," Alex said.

"Excellent," Sonny said. He took the key off the bar-top and put it in his coat pocket.

"So ... Mexico. How long will it take?" Alex asked.

"It shouldn't be more than two weeks at the latest. There's a hotel called *El Presidente* in the center of Mexico City. It's a good place to wait before heading north. Pleasures of the flesh can be had there, young man ... for a song. ... When I was your age. ..."

"Let's say the 15th in Sonoyta, okay?" Alex said, cutting Delmonico off.

"Excellent! Will do!" Sonny said in a cheery tone of voice. He stood up, and Butch stood up with him.

"Where the fuck are *you* going?" Alex said to his partner.

"I need to speak to Mr. Delmonico in private," Butch said.

"We don't have to go to Switzerland, now," Butch said. He closed the door to the hotel room. "He said it was in the closet."

"Excuse me?" Sonny said.

"You know ... you owe me ... two-hundred-and-fifty-thousand dollars," Butch said. "For not *killing* you—remember?"

"I thought ... I thought perhaps we could renegotiate," Sonny said.

"Can't do that," Butch said.

"Well, God, man, I thought. ...You know—we were mates, now."

"We are," Butch said. "I like you. You introduced me to Marie."

"Look—I've told my associates that you might be someone that we could employ in the future. For the odd job, you know. Things we'll need done. In the States and elsewhere, too," Sonny said. Butch looked into the empty hotel room. There were two twin beds with new-looking, yellow bed spreads. He had a quick fantasy of seeing Marie on the bed waiting for him.

"I don't know about *that,*" Butch said.

"It pays *very* well, old man. You'd be part of an elite group of men that see the world in a certain way. I see that you've already made connections."

"But I need money right now—I want to get married," Butch said.

"Sit down; I want to confess something," Sonny said. "Go on—please." Butch sat down on one of the perfectly-made hotel beds.

"Yeah?"

"I was lying," Sonny said, still standing.

"About what?"

"I have no money in Switzerland. That was a lie. Obviously I was under duress."

"Shit! I thought you might be lying about that shit! God damn you!"

"If you take this money I've just been paid by your friend, I'll be in a great deal of trouble with my people. In short, they'll think I stole the money and they'll kill me," Sonny said. "And don't forget that you *did* get about ninety-thousand dollars of mine, *and* the girl. Don't forget about Joe B's *goomah*. If you would have killed me you would never have met your future bride," Sonny said, brightly taping him on the knee.

"... Okay. All right. If you fuck with my pal again, though, I *will* have to kill you," Butch said.

"I understand completely," Sonny said.

"Neither one of us can be trusted," Butch said. "That's funny, isn't it—a fucking stalemate." They both broke out laughing.

"That's the problem with having an alternative lifestyle," Sonny said.

*   *   *

■ SWISS ALPS

They were sitting in a mountain "warming" hut that had been built for cross-country skiers, near the small Swiss town of Obergons. As the crow flies, they weren't far from the Italian border.

"Those were called Kutar carbines back in my day," George said. "Where did you get it?"

"From my boyfriend. Sandra said that I should be prepared for trouble. That's what you told her, wasn't it?" Carmen said. She'd leaned the CAR 15 against the wall. It was one of the weapons she'd learned to shoot. It was quite different from the semi-automatic .22 she used in competitions. But her boyfriend, who was on the Swiss National Biathlon Team, was in the Swiss army, and he'd lent her his weapon, which had been designed especially for alpine troops.

"Yes," George said, "I did."

"I'm glad you did—that you thought of me ... 'that girl in Switzerland that I send money to,'" Carmen said, sarcastically

There was a small fire burning in the hut's fireplace. Hauptmann Neizert, although a decent skier, had been exhausted by the ten kilometer trek in the snow and wind, and was still shivering from the cold, even after Carmen had built a fire. His face was haggard and he was clearly terrified. They'd spotted a party of three men behind them—all of them dressed in black, and skiing with terrifying precision. Carmen had guessed that they were seven or eight kilometers—perhaps less—behind them. She looked intently at the Hauptmann: with his day-old beard, and grey plastered-down hair, looked like some especially old and wizened war refugee.

"Will they catch us?" Neizert asked.

"Don't ask me, old man," George said, looking at the girl. "*She's* the bloody expert."

"Do you think they'll be here soon?" George said. He looked tired, too, Carmen thought. She realized George was getting older, now.

"What's that?" she said.

"It's a pistol, dear. I thought you could use some help." George took out the Walther and dropped the clip onto his lap. She turned and looked at the rifle she'd brought. She had gone to her boyfriend's apartment and asked him for it without any explanation.

"They'll be here in about twenty minutes," she said, turning back to look at George.

"Well." George stood up and opened the door. There were completely white-out conditions the small valley they'd skied into, which was split down the middle by a frozen river. Carmen had warned them about the small river. She'd skied out onto it knowing that she was fast enough to ski to the other side if the ice began to give way. George watched the tall figure in all-white ski quickly across the river to the other side. There wasn't much snow on top of the river-ice, and her skis took her quickly and smoothly across, but she made quite a bit of noise doing it. Once she'd made the other side, she whirled around, the CAR15 automatic rifle strapped to her back.

She signaled to them that it was okay to cross. George looked back across the valley and saw the long run they'd come down. The girl had been able to Telemark down the hill, but he and the Hauptmann had been forced to take off their skis and climb down the run in knee-deep powder. It was there that the men chasing them had gotten close enough to see the three through their binoculars.

"It's nothing," Carmen said to him. "You didn't drink enough liquid, that's all." It was snowing heavily and she could tell that the snow was just the prelude to a very bad storm that would be upon them within the hour. She'd spent six years hiking and skiing all over the Alps and because of those experiences was more in tune with the mountains and their fickle weather patterns than most of the native Swiss. The fact that her mother had been a full-blooded Indio may have had something to do with her being so in touch with Nature. Reality, for her, had been the discovery that the physical act of sliding down a snow-covered mountain on a pair of long, oddly-shaped pieces of wood and glue, called *skis,* brought her the first true happiness she'd ever experienced in her entire life. The first real, unadulterated *joy* she'd ever felt. Before skiing, life had been only a hardship; something to be gotten through—endured, not *lived.* All the bad things that had happened to her growing up in Colombia were finally addressed and dealt with on those long, cross-country ski runs. It was as if Nature, in the form of the dense pine tree forests, the rocks, the great alpine vistas, could pull all the poisons out of her soul and make her believe in life again. Her physical body got stronger every year, so that now, at almost eighteen, she was very, very fast, indeed.

"My boyfriend skis for the Army. ... He's taught me a lot, really." She looked at George. They were sitting in a the small hut that had been built by the Swiss government to shelter cross-country skiers in case they ran into bad weather; a scenario that often killed people who came out in the morning under a perfectly clear blue sky, but only a few hours later were faced with white-out conditions, struggling to just stay alive in the middle of a sudden blizzard. She had made love with her boyfriend in the same hut where they were now camped out. She knew the valley well, and wasn't afraid of the men who were chasing them.

"Are you in love with the owner of that weapon?" George asked.

"None of your business, *George,*" she said. He had taken out the clip and was ejecting the bullets into his boot, making sure that if there *were* a gunfight in their immediate future, everything would be as in order as he could make it.

"Do you actually *know* this girl?" The Hauptmann asked, half-incredulously. The hut had a hole in the top, so that fires could be built within it, and the inhabitants wouldn't be smoked out in the process. They had a small fire going, and had boiled water and made hot chocolate, lacing it with sugar. That was all they had with them for sustenance.

"Yes," George said.

"She's too young to be useful in a fight," The Hauptmann opined.

"Who *is* this man?" Carmen asked.

"An old friend of mine," George said.

"You're lying," Carmen said, staring hard at him.

"I'm not sure I like him though," George said. "And I don't think those fellows on their way here like him, either."

"How can a *girl* stop them?" the Hauptmann said, looking over at Carmen. He took a sip of his hot chocolate.

"Those men are nothing," she said. "You don't know what danger even *is*. When I was on the streets of Bogatá, once a man took me home and put me in a hole in the floor in his basement. He worked for the police. He said that I belonged to *him*, and that no one would know or care what happened to me."

The two men looked at her. There was a weird expression on her face. "It was very dark in the hole. He would only turn on the light and look down at me when he brought me food or when he was ready to lift me out. He had a chair all rigged-up down there like in a movie. He would lower the chair down and tell me to sit in it, and then he would lift me up out of the hole. There was a cat that lived in the hole with me, too. ... I left a week later," she said. "He didn't make it to the next Sunday. I pushed him in front of a bus—I killed him. ... Right outside his own house. ... Those men that are following us—they never lived in a hole in the floor like that," she said. "Right, George?"

"Right," George said.

"I care about George ... a lot. So I'm going to go out and kill those men," she said. "You will have to do very little, but you *will* have to help me, just a little bit. Can you do *that*, old man?" Carmen said, looking over at the Hauptmann. "Or are you too tired to save yourself?"

"I want you to adopt me," Carmen said. "*Officially*. Will you do that, George? I want you to be my father, George Cummings." Carmen walked over to the wall behind her, her shape bathed in the dim firelight, and picked up the submachine gun.

"All right," George said.

"I want to move to London and live with you and your new family."

"If that's what you really want," George said.

"If it's what I *want?*" she said. "It's what I've *always* wanted, but you were to stupid and indifferent to see that I needed a father," she said. "I love you, George." She looked at him. "Do you want me to be your daughter? That's what I want to know," she said.

"Yes. I'm sorry, baby—I was selfish and stupid," George said.

"You thought that the money was enough. That putting me in Le Rosey was enough."

"Yes. I loved you, but I was ... I didn't think I'd be alive for very much longer, to tell you the truth," George said.

"Because you're a spy, that's why—Sandra told me all about you," Carmen said.

"Yes. I didn't want you to have to go through all that."

"Let's not talk about it anymore. ... Father." Carmen smiled. It was a very clipped and frightened young girl's smile, and it signaled that she was vulnerable to his emotions and state of mind again. She pulled the clip out of the CAR 15 and pushed the first bullet down to check the spring tension, more out of a reactive anger at the conversation they'd just had than because of any concern she had about the readiness of the equipment, which her boyfriend kept spotless and one-hundred percent functional at all times.

"We must go now. *Vamonos,*" Carmen said. "We have to set ourselves for what's coming." She looked at her newly-minted father, then grabbed her skis and walked out into the strange, white world of the building blizzard.

What he would never tell her or anybody else, was that on the day he'd first seen her on the street, standing in front of that hotel, he'd recognized a fellow soldier—one with combat-hardened eyes and a thousand-yard stare—who needed his help. Very few people would have understood *that* attraction.

"Women," George said. "Can't live with 'em. ... And it seems, truly, that we can't live without them."

41

■ MEXICO CITY

Walking across the *Zócalo*—directly opposite the Presidential Palace in Mexico City—he was no longer Vladimir Putilin. He had created a separate, carefully-constructed stand-alone identity to frustrate the KGB's efforts to find him, should his own people ever turn on him. Over the years, he'd seen too many of his friends disappear into the bowels of Lubyanka prison and never walk out again. They'd been charged with "Crimes Against the State" or "Treason;" or they'd been killed simply because they had failed to satisfactorily perform in some way. Their bodies were never even returned to their families for a proper burial, but instead were dumped in paupers' graves at the state-run Moscow Cemetery Number #17. His fellow officers had just simply been "disappeared" and their official KGB files were destroyed after their deaths. When that little bureaucratic detail was completed, it was as if they had never existed at all, at least "officially."

Now he was among their possible future number, and on the run. He was literally being sought by every KGB officer in the world—a very dubious state of existence. Every Soviet embassy and every KGB front organization across the globe had been instructed to find him. They'd all been given his university graduation photo to help identify him. A special team trained in hunting down fellow KGB men had been deployed from Moscow. They were very tough characters, and presumably knew how he would think, and how, and where, he would try to hide. Two of them actually reported directly to the Gehlen network. The Gehlen organization had just established a new headquarters in New York City after years in West Germany. The organization's cover was a private investment bank called Troika Capital, located just one block from Wall Street. All organization employees were required to be tattooed under their left arm with Troika's corporate logo—the Knight's Templar cross—women included. It was a holdover from the old Nazi days and Gehlen had insisted on it just before he died.

Vladimir was traveling as an American businessman named Michael Lerner on a forged U.S. passport he'd had fabricated in Marseille. The chaotic streets of Mexico

397

City's downtown area were comforting to him, because he knew how difficult it was for Europeans to hide on Third-World streets. He knew that he was being hunted by a special team, but that it, too, was handicapped by being Russian and white. He was taking every opportunity to confuse his hunters, making sure not to stay *anywhere* very long, and barely sleeping when he did. He'd bought a pistol and ammunition from an upper-class Mexican woman who ran a famous brothel near the Presidential Palace—she'd been a long-time KGB asset and didn't know about his present situation.

Vladimir walked the three blocks from the upscale brothel to Mexico's principal Catholic cathedral and straight to the building next door that housed the offices of the Archdiocese. He examined the lobby index board and saw the name he was after: one Monsignor De Leon, who, the index board proclaimed, had an office on the third floor. The lobby was cool after the heat of the street outside, its floor made of ancient-looking black and white marble tiles. Even the office building had the distinct smell of a Catholic church. He rode the elevator to De Leon's office and was informed by his secretary that the monsignor was busy taking confessions next door in the Cathedral between two and three o'clock. After Vladimir explained that he was an old student of the monsignor's, and only in Mexico for a short time, she gave him the number of the confessional booth.

"Dmitri sent me," Vladimir said as soon as the wooden confessional gate slid open. He could see the monsignor's ruddy-hued European face. The man wore heavy black glasses and bore a remarkable resemblance to the famous film director Martin Scorsese. He was an agent of U.S. intelligence and had been known to the KGB for years as being a contact for the CIA—a kind of gatekeeper to a backdoor into the U.S. Embassy if you were on the run.

"In the name of the Father, and the Son, and the Holy Spirit. My last confession was a week ago, father," Vladimir said.

"Yes, my son. God will forgive you," De Leon said.

"Dmitri sent me, father. I want to be forgiven." Vladimir repeated the code word he'd overheard while listening to a tape from the interrogation of a Russian defector to the U.S. who'd been recaptured by the KGB.

"... Are you a sinner?" De Leon asked.

"Yes; I've sinned countless times in Hungary." Vladimir gave the counter-password that he'd heard the defector give on the tape. CIA officers had given the countersign to would-be Russian defectors, along with the instructions on how to contact De Leon in Mexico City. "He said I could find help here with you. I am a KGB officer and want to make contact with the CIA. I want to defect to the West," Vladimir said. "Can you help me, father?"

"What is your name, my son?"

"My name is Vladimir."

"Are you sure you want my help, my son?" Vladimir saw—through the metal lattice that still separated them—De Leon turned his head around so he could get a better look at him, actually leaning in and peering at Vladimir through the lattice.

"Yes, father. Yes—I want to defect to the West."

"How can you be contacted? Where are you staying?"

"10012 *Avenida de La Santisima*. There's a hotel there called *Hotel El Polanco*. I've checked in under the name Hector Mares—Room 214. He pushed a card from the hotel through the wooden grate separating him from the monsignor. "I've written the room number on this card."

"They will send someone to collect you," the priest said, still looking at him. His nose was large, and the black horn-rimmed glasses dominated his face. He moved his face close to the metal lattice separating them. De Leon was close enough now that Vladimir could see that the man's brown eyes were small and his expression hooded.

"You must answer some questions for me so they can verify your story."

"Yes, of course."

"The number the KGB used for you in cables?"

"987-1100," Vladimir said.

"What year were you born?" De Leon asked.

"1952," Vladimir said.

"Where?"

"Leningrad."

"On what street did you grow up?"

"Navsky."

"What was your mother's name? And is she alive?"

"Svetlana Lebed. No, she has passed."

"Leningrad, city, street Navsky, mother's name, Svetlana Lebed: is that all correct?"

"Yes, father."

"May God go with you, my son, and forgive you your sins." He saw De Leon reach up close the gate over the lattice, ending the interview. Vladimir got up and walked out into the massive, sweet-smelling church. A young Indian woman—on a pilgrimage from some faraway village—was on her knees, rosary in her fingers, ambling toward the empty alter with a pained expression on her brown face.

"I want room 211."

"Across from the other room?" the desk clerk said.

"Yes."

"Are you filming in 214?"

"Yes," Vladimir lied.

The cover story normally employed by the KGB was that room 214 was used to produce blue movies. The owner of the hotel had a standing contract with a front organization called *Peliculas Educacionales SA*. Room 214 at the *Hotel Polanco* had been equipped with a special one-way mirror—directly across from a brass bed—that hid a filming booth used by a KGB camera unit, which would film politicians and other famous people, including quite a number of Americans, in bed with prostitutes. The films and stills from them would later be used to blackmail individuals targeted by the KGB. The films were often passed around among KGB officers and played at their drinking parties; especially one taken of a world famous American religious leader known all over the world as "Pastor to the Presidents."

"We haven't seen you in a long time," the desk clerk said. He slid the key over the counter and smiled.

When he worked at the embassy in Mexico City—one of the most important KGB stations in the world—he'd often used the *Hotel Polanco* to film diplomats in bed with whores. It was an old and useful method of getting *to* people who would otherwise not cooperate; to help them to suddenly find the Soviet Union and its "great patriotic cause" very worthwhile. It was a choice of either becoming a soviet agent—and reporting to a KGB handler—or facing the humiliation of being seen cavorting with whores on film, in what was jokingly referred to at the embassy as a "star performance." Once made, the films *always* worked. What he'd learned as a young intelligence officer, in fact, was that the most responsible politicians and family men could never refuse the offer of free sex from a young woman. They seemed to be physically and mentally incapable of refusing, or of even being suspicious of what were known in the intelligence world as "honey-traps." The type of men who had what it took to claw their way up into those powerful positions were always so egotistically self-centered and arrogant that they thought they were actually *attractive* to young women. They literally couldn't conceive of themselves otherwise.

*　　　*　　　*

For some reason George Cummings was dreaming of the first time he heard Frank Sinatra's version of "Blue Skies." He was sitting in an officer's club in New Delhi, India, and someone had put it on the record player. He had just cleaned up, and was having a cocktail to relax. He'd finally gotten a short leave after a solid year of fighting in the jungles of Burma. He'd been trying to decide what exactly he would do that evening. He finished his drink and nodded to the barman, who happened to be a Sikh. He could hear dice being tossed and the sound of the barman shaking his second cocktail.

"Been on safari?" a woman's voice asked. George looked up. She was a good-looking strawberry-blonde wearing an American WAC's uniform, and she looked a little like Veronica Lake, the movie star.

"Light?" She had a cigarette in her hand, and held it up for him to light.

"Yes, indeed. ..." George said, brightening up and fishing for his lighter.

Then a branch broke and fell not far from him. He heard it crash to the ground, and then he was back lying against a tree in the Swiss Alps. The snow was falling hard, and he couldn't see more than ten feet straight in front of him.

As he opened his eyes, he saw the Hauptmann lying in the snow directly in front of him. He was trying to stay low to the ground, shifting his weight back and forth in an attempt to dig himself into the snow. George could see that they had been there long enough for the falling snow to have begun to cover his pants.

He'd followed Carmen out of the hut and they had begun putting on their skis. He remembered Carmen in her white outfit, with the rifle slung over her back, and he remembered the sound of the wind and the distinctive crack of the bullet that had struck the hut's door. They all three immediately instinctively crouched down. He lifted his weapon and looked into the blinding snow, seeing nothing but pure white and the vague shapes of tall pine trees; dark hazy specters. There were several more shots fired at them in quick succession, which he thought had come from two different locations. He turned and saw Carmen falling. He quickly ran to her side and pulled her behind the hut, dragging her up against the back wall and checking her body for wounds. She was in shock; mentally anyway. She was staring at him wide-eyed—terrified at having almost been killed so suddenly and so arbitrarily.

"You're all right," he said without knowing if it were in fact true yet, trying to calm her. Neizert came bounding around the side of the hut and looked down at them.

"Two men," the Hauptmann said. He pointed to the front of the hut "I saw both of them." The wind was blowing very hard, making Hauptmann's words almost inaudible, and they had to strain to hear him.

"Get down," George said. He made a downward motion with his hand. He had a quiet voice that he only used in actual combat: a very different voice and different George entirely from the ones that were so recognizable to people who only knew him from attending parties and soirees. It was a clipped and very precise voice; a voice that carried the authority of Death itself behind it. He saw the Hauptmann slump to his knees and thought for a moment that he'd been hit, too, but quickly realized that he was just allowing himself to fall where he stood. He turned back to Carmen. He saw now that a bullet had exited out the front of her shoulder near her right breast. There was a clear exit hole in her jacket. He unzipped the coat and saw that the back of her nylon pullover was stained with blood. She was looking straight at him, in shock.

"Don't let me die here, George. Please."

"Do you have an extra clip for the rifle?"

"Behind me ... under the jacket," she said.

"You're going to have to help *me*, now. Do you think you can still shoot? You're going to be okay—you've been shot but it's not a bad wound, and it'll stop bleeding by itself—I've seen that kind of wound many times, and I *know*, so don't worry about it, you're not going to die out here. The main thing is—can you still hold a rifle and shoot? Or do you have too much pain from the wound?"

"Yes I think I can still shoot."

"You have to try, Carmen." All the bravado of youth was gone, now. Paper targets were not armed men trying to kill you, and now she understood what that meant in the only way that a person really can "understand" something that horrible; by having it actually happen to them.

He looked around the corner of the hut and tried to spot her rifle, but he didn't see it. He'd dragged her so quickly away from the front of the hut that he'd forgotten to pick it up. He still had his revolver, but that was all. He knew that it was useless against long rifles.

For a moment he didn't know what to do. For an instant, everything seemed hopeless to him. He could tell from her wound that she was losing blood, but it wasn't coming out the exit wound so he leaned her forward and saw that it coming out the entrance wound, but he couldn't really tell how fast, and how quickly it would clot-up, or how weak she'd be from moment to moment. He laid her gently back up against the rear wall of the hut. He looked behind him and saw that the hut was situated at the side of a frozen lake—probably Lake Lugano. They hadn't even been able to see it, before; but now, because of the higher winds, he was able to catch glimpses of it, about seventy-five yards away.

"Is the lake safe to cross?"

"Yes," she said.

"I'm going to treat this wound right now. I think I can stop the bleeding ... it isn't that bad, really ... You have to go on out there. As far out as you can get on the lake. And you have to take the Haupmann *with* you. Set up out on the lake. You'll be able

402

to shoot them from that position when they come for you. I'll get the rifle."

"Wait." The Haupmann had crawled to the corner of the hut and was looking out around it. "There are three of them, not two." He turned back. "I see them all three right now. They're above us. Not that far. Three men. Yes." Neizert came back to them and looked at the girl.

"Can she still ski?"

"Yes," George said. "I'm going to get her rifle and the skis; then you help her out onto the lake—understand? When they come, help her set up. She's a good shot and we'll have a chance that way, because they won't have any cover to hide behind out there." George took off his coat, then his shirt, and even pulled off his T-shirt. The Hauptmann saw the scars from a Japanese sniper's bullets etched into the flesh of his stomach. They were pink, and looked as if skin there had been replaced with smooth plastic plugs of scar tissue. He handed the Hauptmann his pistol and told him to go to the corner of the hut and fire at the figures if he saw them. That would slow their approach a little bit, at least. Then he turned back to Carmen. He unzipped her coat. He cut around the bullet's exit hole in her nylon shirt and exposed the exit wound itself. He took his T-shirt and wiped the blood from around the dime-sized hole. If she were going to die from the wound she would have already bled-out, so he guessed that no arteries had been hit. He knew then that she could live, maybe even help them in the coming fight. Looking now at the entrance wound, he saw that her overall condition wasn't nearly as bad as he'd first thought. The bleeding had slowed to almost nothing at this point. He placed the wadded-up T-shirt against the entrance wound and pressed down, watching the blood ooze out at a very slow rate. It was a good sign. An excellent sign, really, even in light of the fact that they were being hunted down like wild game animals by three assassins who knew what they were doing. Over the years, he'd seen countless wounds like it: bullets hitting the back going through the scapula and exiting the upper chest with no major bleeding.

"Now—you're going to *live*—do you understand me? You have to help *me*, now. You have to take this man to Turin. You have to live; and we have to kill these men today—right *now*, in fact. Can you help me do that?" She nodded weakly.

"I love you, George," she said.

"I love you too, dear." He smiled at her "You snotty little girl. Do you remember?"

"I remember. That day you found me. ..."

"It was a winter day—cold as Hell—and you had snot on your face." She smiled a little.

"You said your name was George, like the monkey. ... You had a handkerchief and you handed it to me," she said. They heard the Hauptmann fire twice. The shell casings ejected from the Walther hit the snow just in front of them.

403

"Papa? ... You'll be my papa," she said. He could tell she was fighting her fear now, and could probably overcome it, even if the situation became untenable.

"Yes, I will. Okay—now I'm going to go get that rifle of yours," George said. He pulled the cord from her parka and managed to tie his wadded-up T-shirt to the front of the entrance wound. He zipped up her stained parka and looked her straight in the eyes. "Now I want you to get up. Because you're fine. Do you understand?" He stood her up and she hugged him with her good arm. He held her for a moment, then.

"I'm sorry I brought you here, into all this," he said. "Will you forgive me?"

"I *wanted* to come. I wanted to help you the way you helped me that day."

"Okay. As soon as I come back with the rifle you start out across the lake," George said. He leaned her—still standing—against the hut.

"They're coming," The Hauptmann said. He said something in German to himself, under his breath.

"You have to help me get the skis, old boy," George said as he turned to him. The Hauptmann looked at him.

"They shoot us," Neizert said.

"Nein. We're going to shoot *them*—but they'll kill us very soon if we sit here and do nothing."

"Ja. Okay."

George kissed the girl's forehead and took his pistol back from the Hauptmann, ejecting the spent clip and tossing it and ramming his extra home, all in the same motion. Then he picked his overcoat up and put it on over his naked chest.

"You saw *three* men?—You're *sure?*" George said.

"Yes," Neizert said.

"All right, then. When you hear me begin to fire, I want you to get our skis and the rifle. Understand? Wait until I start firing."

"Ja."

"*George? No!*" Carmen suddenly stumbled towards them. "No!"

George ran across the snow toward the tree line, crouched over and staying as low to the ground as he could get. The wind had started to blow snow around again and it covered his escape to a large extent. The Hauptmann grabbed Carmen as she tried to follow George, tackling her and falling with her at the corner of the hut. "*George!*" Her yelling actually helped, because the young men watching the hut saw the two struggling bodies and missed George slipping into the blowing snowy mist.

The two gunmen had decided to wait on the rise above the hut, having sent the third to circle to the right and come up behind the hut from along the shore of the lake. They would close the door on their trap as the third man would simply have to fire on the back of the hut from the lake and the trio would be forced to flee in *some* direction, and they would be cut down as they did so by one group or the other; or, if they got lucky, the three would be captured alive without a fight.

The two had a good view of the front of the hut about a hundred yards below them, as well as the alpine lake, now that the wind had suddenly died down. There was nowhere the fugitives could *go*. The trio they'd chased for hours now were trapped. All three pursuers were young and excited by the hunt. All were expert skiers. One was an American and two were French. They were being paid a fabulous sum of money to kill a group that they considered to consist of only two old men and a girl. They had laughed about it. They planned on capturing the girl alive if at all possible so they could enjoy her before they killed her—something they'd decided between themselves, outside the purview of their employers, after they'd seen her near the Le Rosey campus. While they waited for the other man to ski down to the lake, the two young gunmen discussed the things they were going to do to the girl. The weather broke as they talked, their rifles resting between their legs and their backpacks used as cushions. There were even moments of blue-sky brilliance, when the ice on the lake below was hit by an astonishingly bright post-storm sunlight.

George was totally out of breath, his legs freezing from slogging through the deep snow, his rented ski boots wet inside, and he had to stop as he came down the hill behind the two. His lungs were burning so badly that he thought his heart would stop at any instant. At his age, and because he smoked, it was no longer possible to run in heavy snow without stopping every twenty yards to catch his breath. He bent over and tried to breathe. He knew that with only the pistol, he had to be almost directly on top of them before he could be sure of killing them. The sound of his rasping breath was so loud to him that he was sure that the men below would hear him coming. He finally looked up and tried to quiet his breathing. They were still seventy-five yards away, and it seemed like a mile. He was still trying to control his breathing. The sun suddenly popped out and he felt its rays hit him. It was that warm. A blue patch of sky opened over the lake and he could see that it was miles across. He started off again, walking with difficulty through the knee-deep snow towards the two men.

42

■ CUERNAVACA, MEXICO

Alex was reading a history of Mexico that Gemma had bought him; he put it down now and got up, ready to jump into the hotel pool. He had chosen this hotel because he remembered staying there as a teenager with his parents. It had a huge pool that had been perfect for ogling girls as a teenage boy. He walked to the diving board and dove into the water, remembering those days when he'd been sixteen and sexually frustrated *in extremis* until he'd met a girl here. His skin was oily and he was very warm, having sat in the sun reading for thirty minutes or so. Gemma had said that she was going back to the room to take a shower and get ready for lunch—they'd found a Moroccan place in town that they liked, and often went there in the mid-day heat. They had a beautiful suite overlooking the hotel's garden. There wasn't much to do in the town once you'd seen the Rivera murals and visited the market, so they would usually come back from breakfast and read, inevitably make love in the room, then go for a swim before lunch. They'd played tennis twice and he was surprised that Gemma was an expert and beat him badly both times. She said that she'd learned to play in New York at a high school she'd attended as an exchange student. She'd seemed distant since they'd come to Mexico; not unfriendly, but preoccupied, as if she were working on a problem of some kind; one where the solution was of mythic proportions, but always just out of her reach. He would catch her standing on the veranda and looking down on the garden for what seemed like hours to him.

She'd asked him if he was going to take her to Washington, D.C., where he'd told her his parents lived. He said he wasn't sure, because he didn't really like his parents and thought that she wouldn't like them either. At dinner the night before he explained that his mother was a snob and that she thought only girls from "old" families would do for him. Gemma had joked that she was from a *very* old *Stalinist* family. They'd laughed, but she seemed to understand that he was embarrassed by his family and thought them backwards.

"I just don't want you to be uncomfortable," he'd said.

"But your mother speaks Italian."

"Fluently; her father was ambassador to Rome before the War. She used to call

Mussolini 'Uncle Mussi.'" Gemma had raised her eyebrows.

"I don't believe your mother is as formidable as you make her sound," she'd said.

"If you insist, I'll take you up there, then."

"I insist." Gemma smiled. "Why am I here ... in Mexico?"

"I wanted to be with you," Alex said.

"Why?"

"I'm in love with you," he confessed.

"You know that we are too different, you and I. ..."

"Are we?"

"Yes. Of course we are," she said. "Are you a gangster?"

"Yes," he said.

"Is that really what you want to do with your life?"

"I'm not sure. ... Does it matter to you?" Alex said.

"Yes."

"Why did you agree to come with me?" he said.

"I don't know. I like you."

"You *like* me," he said.

"Yes. Very much." She looked down at her little squares of watermelon.

"I hate you for being so good at tennis, you know. I thought I was finally going to be able to impress you. ... Will you marry me?"

"No, Bruce."

"Why?" She just shook her head as if he were crazy.

"I'm sure you would be the worst husband in the world," she said.

"Probably. Probably." He laughed, but he was hurt. She'd said no immediately, without even thinking about it.

He climbed out of the pool, their breakfast conversation still on his mind. He was finished with the CIA, he decided. He would do this assignment for his father and then he was getting out. He wanted to be married and have someone to take care of, he thought. He looked around the pool area. It was Wednesday afternoon and there were no other guests in sight. They had had the place to themselves pretty much since they'd checked in Sunday night. He walked back to the lounge chair and picked up his wrist watch and checked the time. It was exactly 12 noon. They'd left Italy three days ago and he had no idea how long he would have to wait for the signal to move. He looked towards the veranda where he'd caught Gemma standing looking out on the garden earlier that morning. There was something wrong, he thought now. He'd felt an emotional distance from her since they'd arrived in Mexico; she'd grown very quiet, too, as if she were keeping something from him. *Perhaps she's never really loved*

me. But why had she agreed to come? ... Because she'd been unable to break it off in
Rome?

Maybe, he thought, she was using him in a way that wasn't obvious to him yet, although there was nothing in her personality to signal that she was that type. In fact, he knew that she was just the opposite—she had not seemed eager to come to Mexico at first. But she'd come for some specific reason, he decided. He had thought it was because she was in love with him. Now he suspected she might not be, and it was something else. He gathered up his things—the bottle of suntan lotion, the book that was boring him a little, the wristwatch his parents had bought him when he'd graduated from Yale—then walked back toward their room.

Gemma had managed to call and leave a message at the German language paper in Mexico City before the first bout of morning sickness hit her. It came late in the morning because they hadn't eaten breakfast until late. Alex came back to the room while she was in the bathroom. She lied and told Alex it was just something they'd eaten that had disagreed with her, and that she was fine, now. The desk called and Alex picked it up.

"The line for Mexico City is open again," the clerk said, "if the *señorita* would like to place her call?"

"Fine, yes," he said.

"Who was that?" Gemma said as she stepped out of the bathroom.

"You wanted to call Mexico City?" Alex said, looking at her.

"Yes," she said.

They looked at each other. If she hadn't been so pale and fragile-looking he might have been more inquisitive.

"Are you all right, baby? You look terrible," he said

"A friend of mine lives there . ... We met in New York while I was at school. ... the call. ..." she said, still obviously queasy and unsteady on her feet. He knew then—for the first time—that she was lying to him, but he let it go. He simply nodded.

A half-hour later, while riding the bus into Cuernavaca, she blacked out. They had to wait to get to the bus station in town before an ambulance could be called.

*   *   *

Just before he shot them both dead, George was able to hear them talking over the sound of his ragged breathing—an awful raspy wheeze which was very loud to him, although he knew that they probably couldn't hear him yet. He had gotten to within twenty yards or so of the seated men, and he felt that if he aimed at their torsos he could make both shots. The sun was full on his face when he stopped moving toward them, the lake and hut were in plain sight below them. He decided he'd have a better chance of hitting them both if they were standing or rising up, so he threw a snowball. He gathered up some snow in his gloveless hand, red and going numb, and tossed it to their right. It was a risk, certainly, but long ago his pistol instructor had told him that the more silhouette, the better, in any shooting situation. The two men rose almost simultaneously. He fired at the one on the left, aiming directly between his shoulder blades, then swiveled slightly and saw that the second one was turning to his right, so he waited an instant for him to get fully turned and begin to swing his rifle up. He had plenty of time, and the man saw him clearly. He fired, and the man fell back, caught in the throat with a lucky shot. The second man landed on his back in the snow and didn't move again. George heard his own donkey-bray breathing and waited a moment more. He held his pistol out and waited for either one of them to move. The snow glistened in the sunlight. More and more storm clouds were being blown clear as he stood there above the downed men. It was as if he were suddenly standing in an entirely different place: as he'd struggled down the hill in the moments before he'd reached the men, he'd been in a grey and cloudy world—now he was standing in bright sunlight. The men were just lying there, either wounded or dead. Their bodies were just dark spots on a brilliant white background. The first man he'd shot was groaning, but didn't move. George walked heavily—pistol held out in front of him—toward the two. He was sinking up to his knees in the deep snow, it was difficult for him to reach them. He saw they had snowshoes. The first man now tried to get up, but was moving very slowly. George shot him in the head from ten yards. The man's head literally blew apart: the bullet had found a seam in his skull. Half the man's skull was suddenly just gone, the contents having splashed out onto the brilliantly glistening snow.

He slogged his way towards the second man, his donkey-wheezing loud again in his ears, and when he reached him, he put the muzzle of his Walther against the man's temple and squeezed off two more rounds. He knew that the man was already dead, but his training overrode everything else and made him do it. Then he stood up and glanced down at the two bodies and managed a tight smile. It was a smile that his men back in Burma would have seen many times, and which would have scared civilians, or been misunderstood as bloodthirsty, but it wasn't. It was simple. He had lived and someone else had died, once again.

George looked down the hill and saw that the Hauptmann—as good as his word— had run out from the corner of the hut and was scrambling towards their equipment. He lowered his pistol and pulled a pair of snowshoes out from under one of the dead men and strapped them on. He took another pair from under the other man's pack.

He'd slung both of the dead men's rifles over his shoulder, and made sure he found all the extra clips. He began the long tramp down the hill towards the hut, his wheezing better now, the going much easier on snowshoes. The sun was out now, and great stretches of blue ripped across the clouds. He saw the great white-painted alpine peaks in the distance.

He heard a shot as he neared the hut, dropped everything he was carrying, and snowshoed quickly around the building. The Hauptmann was gone. Carmen was lying face down in the snow. He threw himself down and began to crawl towards her. He saw that the white parka had been taken off her and was now being worn by the Hauptmann, who was crawling toward the third gunman.

*   *   *

It was a small, private clinic, as the ambulance driver had taken one look at Alex and decided that he could afford Cuernavaca's better emergency facility. They'd put Gemma in a private room and sedated her. The staff had kept him waiting for four hours while she slept, after they'd taken a blood sample and had it tested. A young female doctor would occasionally come out and tell him that she thought Gemma was probably just dehydrated, but that she wanted to make sure there weren't any other problems. The blood test would give them an indication of any kind of infection or any other serious condition that might have been lurking in the background. In the meantime, the doctor said she wanted Gemma to sleep, as she seemed exhausted and sleep would do her more good than anything else.

He'd spent his time looking at weeks'-old Mexican newspapers and thumbing through an English-language *Time* magazine that a tourist had left in the bare-bones waiting room. He'd read the *Time* twice, cover to cover. The doctor finally reappeared around dinner time and told him that his wife was pregnant, and that there was nothing seriously wrong with her other than dehydration.

"She's young and should be fine after her rest. You can go in now," the doctor told him. He suddenly felt as if his feet had been nailed to the floor.

"*Pregnant?*"

"Yes. You already knew that, of course? ..." the doctor said.

"No, I didn't." The doctor looked at him and smiled. "Well, you do now."

"Does *she* know?"

"She must," the doctor said. She led him down the corridor to Gemma's room, opened the door, and left him standing there in the doorway.

Gemma was sitting up and looked normal again, now. Her hair was pulled back in a pony tail and she looked a little thin to him, but much better than just a short few hours ago.

"Sorry," she said.

"Why?" he said.

"It's all a big mess—I just fell out," she said. "It's never happened to me before."

"Did they tell you?"

"Tell me what?"

"That you're pregnant," Alex said. The room had white walls and was very clean. The metal hospital bed was from the 1920s, and looked like it belonged in a museum. The floors were very clean and clinical in feel: it was a place where people were *examined*. He looked for a chair, found one, and brought it over to the bed.

"Am I free to leave, now?" she asked

"Yes; I think so. ... I still have to settle up the bill." He stood up.

"Bruce ... sit down." He sat down again. She drew her legs up.

"Yes, it's true; I'm pregnant," she said.

"Okay. ..." he said.

"I was going to tell you. ..." It was the second time that day that he'd thought she was lying, but he said nothing.

"It's mine?"

"Yes—of course," she said.

"I want to keep it. If that's what you're wondering. I want a family. We can get married as soon as ... "

"You're a *gangster*—I'm not sure this would be the right place to ..."

"I'm *not* a gangster," Alex said. "... I want the child. Please, don't ... You know—do something. ... Something you might regret later," he said.

"I don't understand?" she said.

"I've been lying to you ... from when we first met in that cellar, in Palermo," Alex said. He said it without any forethought at all.

"Lying?"

"Yes. I'm an officer in the U.S. Central Intelligence Agency. I've been undercover for almost a year. My real name is Alex Law. Nothing I've told you up until today has been the truth. It's all been lies," he said.

"... The CIA?"

"Yes."

"Why were you in Palermo?"

"It doesn't really matter. But I'm not a gangster. And I want to have the child and marry you." She looked at him, drawing her legs up under the sheets.

"I don't know what to say," she said.

"If you want to, we can get married right away. I'd like that. There's nothing *to* say, really. I've got money. ... I want to leave the Agency. We can go back to Italy if you want to. We can have the baby there. I don't care where we go."

"What are you doing in Mexico?" she said.

"I can't tell you that. And it doesn't matter anyhow, really, not now."

"All right. ... Alex Law. That's your *real* name?"

"Yes. Alex. ... All right—what?"

"I'll have the child if you want it," she said.

"I'll go and settle the bill, then. Are you *sure* you're all right?" She nodded her head, yes. He picked up the chair and carried it back to exactly where he'd found it, then went and paid the bill. When he came back she was dressed and waiting for him, sitting on the bed. He kissed her. She held onto him and wondered where Vladimir was. She didn't love the American; she knew that. But she felt connected to him now, and oddly protective of him. He pulled away from her and smiled. It was a smile she'd never seen before on his face; a smile of relief, and of course, care. He loved her, there was no doubt in her mind about that. It had all gone so wrong, she thought. All the fine ideas she'd thought were so important seemed oddly trivial and *un*important, now.

"Will we be here long? In Mexico?" she asked.

"No. ... A week, maybe—two at the most." He helped her to stand up, even though she felt fine, now. Her weakness wasn't physical, but emotional. She felt desperate to hear Vladimir's voice again, to ask for help, to have him come and take her back. She wanted no more to do with this charade. She didn't want to hurt this man who was now no longer her enemy.

"Do you love me?" Alex said, stopping. The smile was gone from his face. "You don't have to lie. ... Just tell me the truth."

"Yes ... I love you, Alex Law," she said.

43

■ LONDON, HEATHROW AIRPORT

The driver's side of Wally's new Rolls Royce had been badly damaged by a bomb. There were hundreds of pellet holes in evidence from a blast targeting the car earlier in the day; ugly chinks in the metal from when Wally had been unexpectedly attacked while driving the Rolls to his counting house that morning. Sonny stared at the car—windows blown out—as it pulled up to the curb at Heathrow, looking like it belonged in a Middle Eastern war zone.

"Spot of bother this morning ... Sorry. ... I'm late." Wally said, bounding out of the car and helping his friend put his suitcase in the trunk. The front of Wally's coat was covered with splotches of dried blood. His arm was in a sling, and his face was heavily bandaged. He was wearing sunglasses as well, so his entire appearance was terrifying. Fatigued-looking travelers, passing by on the sidewalk, stared at them. A large family of Turks, waiting for the bus to central London, looked on in horror at the two men. The father had caught a glimpse of a double-barreled sawed-off shotgun lying on the passenger seat when Wally had gotten out of the Rolls. The barrel had just been cut off—the hacksaw marks were fresh—and two gray-steel circles had stared balefully straight out at the Turkish patriarch, sending a chill down his spine. Wally slammed the trunk shut and then walked quickly to the open, driver's-side door, ducked inside the car, and came back up holding the wicked-looking shotgun, holding it out to Sonny.

"What happened—did you stand up Shirley Bassey?" Sonny asked, gob-smacked, trying to joke with his friend, who was now brandishing a shotgun in a *very* public place.

"You'll have to take this. ... I *am* smiling, old man, but some gentlemen might come along and try to kill us; should they—please don't hesitate to *use* this," Wally said, handing the weapon to Sonny. Sonny took it and looked around him for any coppers who might be watching. "Colombians," Wally said "If you see any, mate—bag'em."

"Right," Sonny said. "... Is it loaded?"

"Don't be a plonker ... Are you coming, then?" Wally asked. He climbed behind the wheel and slammed the driver's-side door. It wouldn't close properly because it had been damaged in the bomb attack, so he had to slam it again, even harder.

Sonny walked around to the passenger door, carrying the shotgun, and slid in. He noticed the passenger seat was heavily blood-stained, as was its headrest: Wally's bodyguard—sitting in that exact spot—had been rudely decapitated by the bomb blast. Wally checked the rear-view mirror and pulled out into traffic. "You'll have to keep a look-out while we're driving, I'm afraid—for any dubious-looking Latino gentleman, I mean."

"Right," Sonny said.

"They're a new element in the game ... the Colombians, I mean," Wally said. "I don't understand them at all—their motives—they torture and kill people just for grins, it seems. It's the way everything's heading now, I suppose."

"All berks,[1]" Sonny said. It was very late, and the streets near Heathrow were all nearly empty. He slid the pump-style shotgun's action open a tad to make sure there was actually a shell in the chamber, then closed it, and fingered the safety to the off-position. Satisfied that it was ready to fire, he laid the shotgun across his lap.

"... It looks like it's just you and me, again. ... We're down to the last nubs now, old man. They killed two of my men out in the old neighborhood yesterday. And one today." Wally turned and looked at his old friend. Gunmen had tried to shoot him down in front of his brother's house in Harold Hill the day before. "Bridgette was across the street buying a package of cigs and screamed at me when she saw them pull up. They have a contract out on you, too, no doubt," Wally said.

"Really?"

"Berks," Wally said.

Sonny had known Wally since they were kids, and he was one of the few people in the game that he could be frank with.

"Where are we off to, then?" Sonny asked.

"Elephant Road," Wally said. *"If* we can make it there, of course!" He turned to look at his old chum, and winked. His red-stained, bandage-covered face was disconcerting, even to Sonny.

"Who's Bridgette?" Sonny asked.

"A byrd I met since you were last here." Sonny nodded. Wally, even as a teenager, had always been known as a ladies' man.

"The septic tanks[2] have given us orders," Wally said "They've had enough of some MI6'er and want him put down—by us, no less."

---

1   pussies
2   Americans.

"And how are we supposed to do *that?*" Sonny asked "*And,* is it wise?"

"Use the loaf[3] ... we've got no choice, mate. A big yank, someone who knows you from the old days, wants curtains pulled on this prat[4]," Wally said. "How's your mum, by the way?"

"Mutton,[5] now," Sonny said.

"Sorry to hear it," Wally said.

"I've got to get to Mexico in a day or two," Sonny said, "so there's no time for the long way around town, I'm afraid."

"I want you to see Max—he's in town. We'll see him right now," Wally said.

"Max Salinsky. ... Now *there's* a loaf," Sonny said. He checked the side-view mirror, but didn't notice anything suspicious.

"Mexico?"

"It's a special job for the Yanks," Sonny said, turning to look at Wally again.

"That Bill Burns wanker?" Wally asked.

"I don't know that name."

"What's happened to us? Look at us!" Wally said. "Just look at us: Fucking Colombians trying to kill me. ... Yanks bossing us around. ... Queens at MI6 ... DEA plods hiding in the shrubbery everywhere. ... It's a pig's breakfast. I can't concentrate on business until I take care of this mess," Wally said.

"The old days were better, no doubt about it," Sonny said, checking the side-view mirror again.

"All that's over, now," Wally said. "Still sticking boys in the rear, are we?" Wally said, trying to joke. Sonny smiled.

"Do we have time for a drink, Wally?" Sonny asked. "I'm parched."

The place on Elephant Road was a one-storey counting house that was used to store and account for cash of all kinds until the money could be sorted and the American dollars weighed—640 twenty-dollar bills equaled one pound in weight. The cash, after being sorted and counted, was then sent on to New York by various means, including cash-mules, Federal Express boxes, and carry-on suitcases taken by airline hostesses for a fee. More recently they'd employed Eastern Block UN diplomats, who, for a hefty percentage, used their diplomatic pouches to smuggle money without fear of detection.

3	head / as in using your head
4	fool
5	deaf

Max Salinsky was waiting upstairs for them. There were several gunmen standing on the sidewalk out front of the counting house to provide security since the attack.

"I've started up with Jamaicans, now," Wally said, "because of Bridgette. She's Jamaican, and she pointed out to me that they're a hard-working bunch," Wally said, pulling up to the front of the warehouse. A huge, coal-black Jamaican opened the Rolls' door for him. Sonny could see the butt of an automatic pistol protruding from a leather holster strapped under his long black overcoat. The guard was wearing clean white Adidas running shoes, a black velour jumpsuit, and sporting dark glasses even though it was four in the morning.

"Hey, boss-man," the Jamaican said to Wally.

"Go fuck yourself," Wally said. The man laughed. It was Wally's way of being friendly, and they all knew it.

"Hello, Max. Long time no see," Sonny said. They'd gone upstairs, and were now in the large high-ceiling room that had several long tables with various piles of currency spread out on them being worked on, talking to the Main Man, Max. Pound notes, Deutschmarks, Swiss Franks—all were in plentiful evidence. Wally's main enterprise was selling heroin all over Europe, and he was using London as a shape-up point for all the cash-money that came in, arriving at all hours of the day and night. Laundering the cash was actually his biggest problem. Because of the recent attacks on him, the lights were off, and the workers, who were weighing and bundling the cash, were using flashlights. It was a very surreal scene: the cash, piled in heaps on the large wooden tables, once used for cutting cloth, now held millions of dollars, or pounds sterling, or Deutschemarks that were being carefully sorted by mostly very young black women, organizing the bills and preparing to load them into cash-counting machines placed on each of the tables. After the cash had been sorted out it was fed into the counters. Stacks of currency were automatically tallied—incessantly flipped by the machines—with a frightening accuracy. The distinctive sound of fanning bank notes, and machine gears whirring never stopped.

"Boys—how are you? ... Sonny! ... Come over *here*—let me look at you," Max said. He looked like a disheveled and slightly rakish Rabbi. He had a grey beard, and wore a flat-crowned black hat with a wide brim.

"I love this man," Max said, with genuine affection "You look good, Sonny."

"You mean, compared to *me*," Wally said.

"Did you see what these animals did to our Wally?" Max said with real horror in his voice. "Look at him. *Oy!*"

"Max. ... I want to talk in private," Wally said. "Sonny and I have a problem—I don't want everyone to hear the details." Max made a sign to a head girl and told her to get everyone out of the room.

"Come back in twenty minutes," Max said to the small black girl, who appeared to be no more than seventeen. "Do you know that we've lost money in just the past *hour?* You want to know how much?" Max asked, turning back to Wally.

"No, Max—why don't you tell us," Wally said. "I'd like to know ... just to add to the festive feeling. And the beautiful day I've had so far."

"A million nine-hundred thousand dollars. It's a nightmare!"

"What?" Wally said.

"Do you know *why,* boys?"

"Why?" Sonny asked.

"Because your queen is a *cunt,* that's why—this whole country stinks. The pound sterling fell through the floor today in New York. I got a fax from my cousin Mel who works at Bank of America." Max took the fax out of his coat pocket and handed it to Wally.

"How can we get rich, boys ... if your fucking *queen*—that whore—keeps screwing with our *money.* Huh? Really. *Farkakt Malke,*" Max said in Yiddish.

"Sorry, old man. ... Come again? Wally said, clueless as to the meaning of the last comment.

"DE ...VAL ... U ... A ... TION, you call it in English," Max said. "The almighty British pound. Today, in New York, *schtupped* by twenty percent. ... Maybe still we have a good year. But it can't go on like this. I'm moving everything into dollars. Yeah, as of today no more of these shitty English pounds—that *cunt!*" He picked up a stack of ten-pound notes. "Only good for ass wipes!"

"... Where's Bridgette?" Wally said, looking around. He'd left her there when he'd gone to the airport, afraid now to even be in the same car with her, driving around, since the Colombians were definitely out to kill him in any way, shape, or form they could get away with, and at any opportunity.

"... I sent your girlfriend home," Max said. "She looked terrible. She's worried sick about you. She loves you, quite obviously. You should get a divorce and marry her. She's a good girl." Wally turned and looked at Sonny.

"What is it these Colombians *want,* anyway, Sonny?" Max asked. "You've dealt with them before, haven't you?"

"It's quite simple, really—they want *everything,*" Sonny said.

"Just like the fucking Nazis," Max said. "I see. Okay ... I get it, now. ... They're not really businessmen, the way we are."

"The Americans want us to kill someone for them," Wally said. He went to an old refrigerator they kept stocked with soft drinks and pulled out a soda, knocking the cap off against a corner of a table as he turned back to Max. Then Sonny reached in and took a soda, too.

"And? ..." Max said.

"This someone is an MI6 officer," Wally said, wiping his lips. He'd picked an orange soda, and a little of it dribbled out of his mouth down onto the bandage covering his chin.

"MI6?" Max said.

"Yeah," Wally said. "If I don't agree to do it, they'll probably kill *us*. At least that's what the bloody Yank I talked to insinuated. And I think we have *enough* problems right now without adding *that* into the mix—don't we?"

"What happened to our 'special relationship?'" Max asked. Sonny could tell that the old man was truly shocked.

"It's not so special anymore. They came to my house and tumbled it. Pushed my wife around. I can't have that. We had a deal—the Specials and us—but apparently not any more," Wally said.

"But they didn't touch our *business*—and they easily could have," Max said.

"I think this is personal," Sonny said. "The hit, I mean."

"Personal?" Max seemed even more shocked.

"I *think* so—it just doesn't make sense to me any other way," Sonny said.

"Personal or not, we've got a very big problem. How do I kill an MI6 officer and not burn down our operation?" Wally said, looking straight at Max.

"You ask *me* to figure this out?" Max said.

"Yes," Wally said. "I'm asking *you* to figure this—if you can—because I can't come up with a way; not yet, anyway." He put his pop bottle down. Max looked at him a moment, contemplating the entire matter.

"Call a meeting with this person; this MI6 cunt. Tell him you want out of the business. ... That you're retiring."

"Call a meeting?"

"Yes. *Then* you shoot him. If Sonny is right, the other MI6s won't really care, because they'll find out he's dirty. That you wouldn't have killed him otherwise. Wouldn't *dare* to, otherwise, of course. Then you walk into Scotland Yard and tell them *you* did it."

"... It's a *she*. One Mary Keen of her Majesty's government—a very old-time and very high-up MI6-er," Wally said, finishing the soda. He'd been impressed with the old Jew's logic. He tossed the empty *Fanta* bottle across the room into a big metal can they kept for money that was torn and therefore couldn't be deposited. It made quite a loud noise as it hit the side of the can and dropped onto shards of bank notes.

"I'll do it," Sonny said. "I doubt that she'd meet with you, alone. She can't take that

chance, if she knows there's a possibility that you know the Yank."

"*You'll* do it?" Wally was surprised, as Sonny wasn't one to volunteer for such work—normally, anyway: he usually kept his business to himself, and didn't get involved in larger machinations in "the game," such as the one they'd currently been more or less forced into being part of.

"Yes, I know Mary Keen. We go way back. To Hungary, in fact. Why didn't you tell me it was *her,* of all people!?"

"... There. Have Sonny do it. Then go tell them *you* did it because she was trying to blackmail *you,* personally. ... If I understand the normal police mentality, they'll back down because *they* need us, too. How many times have we done *them* favors? Anyway, it's the only way I can think of to do it. ... Now, can I go back to work?" Max said. "I've got to get this load of cash to New York before we lose any more on the fucking exchange rate!" Wally looked over at Sonny, but he was preoccupied in still trying to knock the cap off his *Fanta* bottle.

"Here, give me that. ... I didn't tell you it was Keen because you just got here—and how the hell did *I* know you knew her. ... All right. ... If you actually *know* the byrd, and think you know how she'll react," Wally said. "Fuck it—let the Beer Monster do it, then." Sonny didn't mention that Mary Keen was personally very well known to *him* as well. He'd realized just at that instant that the Americans and English were having some kind of secret war, and he and Wally were smack in the middle of it. Why, exactly, he didn't completely understand, but he was *starting* to. After his insight, his first reaction was to keep it all a secret until he understood it better, more thoroughly, coming at it from different angles—all the angles he could think of, in fact. Wally knocked the cap off the bottle and handed it back to his old friend.

"Grape?" Sonny said.

"Yeah—so? ..." Wally said.

"Nothing. It's fine," Sonny said, taking the bottle. "It's just that I like orange better."

"Did you hear that, Max? ... He likes orange better."

*   *   *   *

Hauptmann Neizert crawled through the snow toward the lake. Everything seemed to stand still; the wind had finally stopped blowing and the storm seemed to have passed. The crows, that had come out and landed around the area while they'd been waiting for George, had all flown off when the shots hit the side of the hut. Being trapped inside the warming hut had gotten him thinking about his time in Russia, and quite a different type of hut that he'd walked into in the winter of 1943, soon after the German defeat at Stalingrad.

Three Russian children had been left hanging from the rafters of that hut—it all came back to him in a rush. The open road, the snow, the look of exhausted looking German *landsers* using horses to pull half-tracks through the semi-frozen mud, the forest being cut to provide logs so the mud roads—horrible quagmires—could be traversed by their equipment. Thin horses were pulling men and matériel on these roughly-hewn log-roads, Russian prisoner-of-war work gangs were dragging tree trunks into place as their command car worked its way west on this strange timber roadway, part of the German 4th Panzer Army, that was fighting to retake Kursk late that winter. Their retreat had been through seemingly endless dark pine forests, a snow and mud-filled Hell.

The children had been hung in reprisal for partisan attacks on the German supply lines. It had been only an hour ago that they'd been alive—maybe less than that, even, he'd thought, looking numbly at their small hanging bodies. There had been a fire going in the fireplace, a few embers still smoldered. ... There'd been a wooden table with scattered plates and half-eaten scraps of food, or what passed for food in those days among the Russian peasantry. The SS troopers had scoured the hut of anything useful or edible. The children had stared down at him in death, their wide eyes accusing. A little girl's face was horribly twisted, her tongue protruding like a devil-mask from South America that he'd seen as a child in a world geography book, one of her small hands caught in the noose where she'd unsuccessfully tried to free herself from Death's grip. She seemed to be looking straight at him—they all did. The hanged-children had been discovered when he and his comrades had sought refuge from the bitter cold. The children had been summarily executed—hung—because of a recent standing order to hang any, and all civilians, that were encountered, in reprisal for the partisan attacks, which were daily becoming more numerous and brazen. Starting at that moment, Hauptmann Neizert decided to work *against* the Nazis. It was in some very real way the childrens' terror-riven faces, so horrific and ghastly, that had profoundly sickened and changed him. From that moment on, he'd sworn to himself that he would help end this madness in any way he could. He'd begun looking for a way to contact the NKVD. A week later he allowed a Russian soldier to escape with a message detailing Nazi anti-aircraft positions along the Dnieper River. Later he would be become part of the Russian's famous "Lucy spy ring" operating from Switzerland with great effect.

The Hauptmann had seen Carmen fall, screaming in terror, when the shooting started again, coming this time from the direction of the lake. And, without thinking, he'd torn the white jacket off the girl and had taken her rifle and gone after the gunman, firing in bursts at the man as he snaked his body through the deep snow. They had been well trained in his Division about the importance of camouflage in winter warfare, and also on the absolute necessity of returning fire, no matter what the overall situation might be. His response to seeing the girl fall had been automatic.

The top of the snowpack had started melting in the sudden sunlight, but immediately turned to a crust of ice as the slightest wind passed over its surface. Each time he pushed his soaked body forward, he heard the crunch of the icy-snow beneath him. He'd worried suddenly that the rifle's safety might have been pushed to the on position while he'd been crawling, so he'd stopped, found it, and thumbed it on, then back off, having seen the red dot appear that signaled the safety was indeed off.

He'd been a good marksman in his Division, having received commendations twice during training. But he knew that that had been over thirty years ago. His eyesight now was not nearly as good. But he'd instinctively taken the rifle and the white coat as if he were twenty. Ambushes on the roads of Russia were common. It was as if he were back on the Eastern Front again, a traitor to his country, yet nonetheless forced to fight for his life.

Neizert crawled on out into the brilliantly-sunlit snowy emptiness, an area that was fringed on all except the lake side by impenetrable dark pine forest, to look for the gunman who had just fired at them from a kneeling position. The bullet had passed through the girl's palm, and she was definitely no longer capable of helping them in any way in this fight. If the Hauptmann hadn't returned fire immediately they both would have been killed by the gunman's next shots. The first thing they'd been taught as young officers at the SS Academy was to return fire at any cost, or die! The gunman's position had been too exposed, and he hadn't expected the old man to muster any kind of defense. But the Hauptmann *had* responded, and the gunman had almost paid with his life right then and there. The gunman had been forced to duck and crawl back towards the lake shore, and he was now lurking out there somewhere along the shoreline. Neizert knew he would have to find him first, if he were going to succeed in killing the man. The Hauptmann kept crawling, only now he was not the old man, but the young man of forty years in the past. It was as if the combination of adrenalin and pure, unadulterated *fear,* could take away the years and bring him back to that moment in March of 1943 where his command car had been stopped by a lone sniper. Their driver had been hit in the face and was dead. They'd all jumped out of the crashed and now undrivable Mercedes and into the snow banks that towered ten feet high on either side of the muddy road. He would be the only one to live through the incident, having crawled a solid half-mile through the deep snow, found the sniper's lair, and killed him; but not before the rest of his group had been picked off by the Russian, one by one. The sniper had turned out to be a young boy no older than sixteen. He'd been a very good shot.

The Hauptmann's glasses started to steam up with condensation from his breath, the glass nearest the metal rims of his spectacles grew cloudy after each exhalation. His fingers were going numb, too. He was almost sure he would be shot and killed, but he suddenly realized he was no longer afraid. Then he remembered a partisan trick, and used his hips to cut a wallow in the snow, so that he quickly disappeared from horizontal view, the girl's white parka covering him. The rifle's barrel was sticking just out in front of him. He waited, remaining as motionless as he was capable of, listening for the crunch of boots in the snow. It was a risk, because the man would have to be *very* close for him to be able to hear the gunman approaching.

A few minutes later, the Hauptmann heard what he'd been listening for. He didn't know that the gunman was already wounded. When Neizert suddenly popped up almost directly in front of the man, lifting himself onto one knee and firing as he did so, the gunman was truly shocked. He had stupidly slung his rifle over his shoulder, thinking that the old man was dead somewhere in the deep snow. For a moment, after his first burst of fire, the Hauptmann waited for the man to stand up again and fire back; but he didn't. Neizert's glasses began to clear up slightly, now that he was out in the open, and it was much easier for him to see. He realized that he *had* been firing almost blindly. He stood up and walked towards the dead man, who was sprawled out in the snow, facing the sky.

"I need to dry myself out," The Hauptmann said after he got back to the hut. George had watched the whole thing. The way the Hauptmann had sprung from his hiding place, the way the young gunman had fallen without being able to fire back. He'd been taken completely by surprise.

"Good work, old man," George said.

"I dry off. ... " the Hauptmann said.

"Right," George said. The Hauptmann looked at Carmen, propped up against the back of the hut.

"She can't ski, now," George said. "She's too weak. And her hand is ... She simply can't pole." The Hauptmann stopped. He had Carmen's rifle slung over his shoulder. His face was dusted with snow; his trousers appeared stained, dark and wet from lying in the snow. He had a very strange look on his face.

"We can make a *schleppen schlitte* ... a drag-sled," the Hauptmann said. "To get to the lake. We pull her. We did it during the War. Don't worry—it will work." He walked on by them, around to the front of the hut, without waiting for an answer and went inside.

"Are there ... are there any more of them?" Carmen asked. She had her head against the hut and was shivering uncontrollably, now. Her left hand had a bullet hole through its palm and it was obviously terribly painful to her, although it appeared that it had stopped bleeding of its own accord.

"No—I don't think so," George said. He walked over to her and picked her up, carrying her in his arms.

"I thought he was just an old man," Carmen said.

"Yeah—me, too. Obviously, we were wrong." George carried her inside, and they built a fire in the fire pit without worrying that pursuers would see the smoke, this time. The Hauptmann stripped naked in front of the fire and laid his clothes on the floor directly in front of the flames.

"Where did you get the *matches?*"

"From the dead man," the Hauptmann said, his naked and bullet-scared back turned to them as he answered. They noticed that a small Iron Cross had been tattooed on his left shoulder.

44

■ SWISS ALPS

The Hauptmann made the sled for the girl to ride on. He'd made them before for the wounded and dying soldiers who were being dragged, sometimes by horses, but more often by their comrades toward the Dnieper River after the battle of Kursk, his Division in full retreat across the seemingly endless dark Russia forests, their long columns of retreating men harassed from the air the entire time.

The Hauptmann had cut nylon strips from the dead gunmen's jackets and used them to make two harnesses, then he'd tied them to the crude drag sled that he'd cobbled together from two small pine tree "rails." He'd constructed a crude platform over the rails using stout pine branches interwoven in a crosswise manner, tied to the rails with shoelaces taken from the dead men's boots. The sled was an almost perfect replica of what he'd used thirty-five years earlier in Russia.

When they reached the lake he planned to attach the girl's cross-country skis to the rails. The Hauptmann did all of this in less than fifteen minutes. While he worked outside, George talked to Carmen lying in the hut, trying to keep her mind off her pain and the difficult journey they all still faced. They held hands and talked about London. He told her he wanted her to come live with him and his new family. She didn't speak; she just listened to him talk, kneeling there in front of her.

"Woden's Men are here ... more storm clouds," the Hauptmann said "It won't be easy until we can put the skis on the sled when we get to the lake. Five hundred yards will be very difficult in *this* snow." Neizert looked at the two of them. George saw that the man's hands were red, and that he'd cut himself using the knife that he'd found on one of the dead gunmen.

"Are you all right? You're cut. ..." George was genuinely concerned about his charge, and very grateful now for the Hauptmann's efforts on their behaves

"*Ja. Ist* nothing," the Hauptmann said. George noticed than that one of the Hauptmann's hands was maimed from some former accident. For some reason he hadn't noticed it until just then. Two of the man's fingers were partially missing, and his palm was missing a chunk from its center, as if the flesh had been scooped out with a surgically-sharp kitchen scoop or similar instrument.

"An old Christmas present from some of Stalin's friends," the Hauptmann said, holding his injured hand up after he'd seen George staring at it.

"Right, then—we're off." George helped the Hauptmann lift Carmen up from where she was sitting back against the wall of the hut to a more-or-less standing position, supporting her on each side. He saw how pale and weak she looked. He knew that she was probably still bleeding, and that she very well could die soon if the bullet had hit a vital organ or vessel—something he couldn't tell from a cursory examination, but that he now suspected was the case, because of her extreme physical weakness; but her condition *could* simply be due to the shock of being shot like that, unexpectedly. It just wasn't possible for him to tell, so he felt even more anxious about getting her to some kind of medical help, wherever he could, and damn the rest of the "mission" at this point. "How far is it ... across the lake, dear?" he asked. George held her more closely and stroked her hair as he spoke to her.

"I don't know," she said. "I've never crossed it."

"Is it safe, do you think—the ice, I mean? Will it hold our weight?" he asked.

"I don't know ... Papa." she said. He noticed that she was calling him Papa now, and it was affecting him in a way he hadn't expected. He had become agitated—very nervous and jittery, in fact. Always since the war, when he'd been in tight spots, he'd never really cared about the outcome, and that had been a secret weapon of his that had made him fearless. But now he suddenly cared about having the chance to make it all up to the girl—for not having understood that sending her to some cold place in Switzerland to school was not what she'd needed. The realization of what he'd done to her had just hit him, hard. She'd been forced to spend her life among strangers, and on top of that, to have been a brown girl in a white world.

"We never used the lake to ski on," she said. She took his hand and held it tightly. He'd taken off his coat and laid it on top of her, then wrapped it around her as best he could, but she was still shivering. George looked over at the Hauptmann. He thought the man looked exhausted. Neizert had wrapped his main cut with nylon but it was still dripping blood onto his right ski boot. George watched another drop of blood hit the toe of the Hauptmann's boot but made no comment about it.

"All right. It's going to be all right. ... We'll be in Turin, soon," George said. But he didn't really believe it, now. *And if it starts snowing again?*

They had carried Carmen out of the hut, laid her down on the sled , then began to pull her down towards the lake through the heavy snowpack. Carmen was holding onto all their skis, which they'd piled on top of her. George looked up into the sky.

It had filled with clouds again—grey clouds that were oddly human-shaped; what the Hauptmann had called "Woden's Men." He looked back down and saw that with each step forward he sank into the snow to knee-height as he leaned hard against the harness that was starting to cut into his parka, and felt like it was already cutting into his flesh as well. The whole situation suddenly seemed horribly desperate.

"*Papa!*" They stopped and he turned to look down at Carmen.

"It's ten kilometers ... across the lake. I remember, now. To Italy." She was looking up into the sky and her face was very pale.

"All right, then ... it won't be long now," George said, trying to sound cheery, starting to pull again. He closed his eyes and pushed with all his might again through the knee-deep snow and prayed to God that they could at least reach the shore of the lake before he collapsed. He looked at his wristwatch: it was a little after four P.M.. The day already seemed to have lasted an eternity.

*   *   *

"Do you like him?" Bridgette asked. "Is he a mate, then?"

" ... The Beer Monster? ... Yeah," Wally said simply. She noted the anxious tone in his curt reply. "We both came up on Harold Hill."

"Is the bitch in there with your pal the one you want dead, then?"

"Yes. ... Old Mary's part of the Colombian's move," Wally said. The bandage around his mouth was gray and saliva soaked. Bridgette noticed and thought it needed to be changed.

"She's a dirty copper, then?"

"Yeah," Wally said.

They were parked out in front of an Italian restaurant named Lulu near London Bridge. It was trendy, and the current "in" eatery with journalists and actors. People on the street glanced askance at Wally's shot-up Rolls. He suddenly realized that he would have to buy a new car, as this one was knackered and obviously beyond salvation.

"... I'm frightened, Wally," Bridgette said.

"It's always hard the first time," Wally said. "You'll get over it."

"No—not about *this*. And it's not the first time, either," she finally admitted to him. He looked at her for a moment, then decided not to ask exactly when or what the 'first time' had been—at least right now. "I'm frightened for *you*, baby!"

"Oh ... Yeah, well, you never know what to expect from these Colombian gentleman, that's certain. They're quite a nuisance," Wally said with obviously false joviality. He looked toward the street, watching the front of the restaurant again. He could see Sonny and Mary Keen at a table that was situated at the front of the dining area. Sonny had arrived first and had managed to get a table next to the window. The "L" of the sign giving the restaurant's name blocked their view of Mary Keen's face. But Wally had seen her arrive and enter the restaurant a few minutes after Sonny had been seated. He turned to look at Bridgette—she was wearing trainers, and she looked almost like a teenager because her hair was pulled back into a ponytail and she had no makeup on.

"You should go to a doctor," she changed the subject again. "I can't stand to see you looking like that." It was quite true: his heavily-bandaged face made him look very Frankenstein-ish.

"Don't worry, I will—as soon as this is over," Wally said. He looked at his watch again. "Are you *sure* you want to do this, then?"

"Yeah—I want to do it—she tried to *kill* you, the fucking evil bitch."

"Sonny showed you *everything* about how to do it—you're positive, now? ..." Wally asked.

"Yeah. Close up."

"And he told you exactly what to say when you go in?"

"Yeah—yeah," she said.

"Okay. We just have to wait a bit, then," Wally said. Max was right, he thought—she was a good girl.

*   *   *

"So how's our Barrow Boy these days?" Mary Keen said. She'd come to the Italian restaurant alone.

"Mary, dear. ... Long time no see," Sonny said.

"Ten years, actually. It was Istanbul," Mary said.

"More like eleven," Sonny said. "... if we want to be exact." Sonny had put on a clean suit and dressed "up" for the occasion. He'd bought a pink carnation and put it in his lapel in memory of the boy who he'd once loved and who Mary had had murdered.

"Right. ... Fun times in the old days," Mary said. "You did the right thing in coming to me, now."

"Did I?" Sonny said.

"I expected it, really. I knew Wally would dig you up. ... He always does. ... We'll let bygones be bygones, if you can do that ... I *hope* you can. ... Shall we? It's how the world works—you know that," Mary said. Sonny just smiled back at her noncommittally.

427

The waiter came over and she ordered a cappuccino. Sonny was already nursing a half-finished glass of Calvados—Wally and Bridgette could see the liquor shining a beautiful gold even through the restaurant window. "... I was very fond of the boy. Do you remember him?. He was a very beautiful boy," Sonny said.

"Yes—I'm sure you were. ..." Mary said.

"He was an innocent. He didn't know our world. He wasn't any part of it, in fact," Sonny said.

"He was a prostitute ... if I recall correctly," Mary said. Sonny looked at her then straight in the eyes. Her eyes were stone-cold and very blue.

"Right—a prostitute. ... Aren't we *all?* ..." Sonny said. "But he had his charms. He was child-like, really. He was from the country. He took me to his village, once. It was terribly poor. A lot of mud buildings and donkeys."

"We don't really have time to reminisce," Mary said.

"What is it you want from me, then?" Sonny said.

"There's a package that the yanks want taken care of."

"And?"

"It's one we'd rather not see delivered at all."

"I see. Is that why you called *me,* then?"

"Yes."

"And the Yanks ... They'd never guess it was *you* behind everything if *I* took care of it, eh? After all this time and *still* up to no good, aren't we, Mary?"

"They won't, unless you tell them," she said. "But then, that would ruin our friendship," she said.

"And in ex*change* for this service?" Sonny said, lifting his glass. Through the tawny light of the liquor, he saw the face of the Turkish boy he'd fallen in love with—the boy this filthy, ice-cold, murdering, upper-class cunt had had killed because he'd overheard them discussing business one night, completely by accident. Something that would have had no consequences whatsoever in regard to their business. The boy had been in bed in one of the other rooms of the suite, and Mary had been talking about her future plans to Sonny while they were sitting in the living room of the suite. Sonny had actually been quite shocked to learn about her real reason for being in Istanbul. She'd gone over to the dark side, she'd said, and wanted a steady supply of heroin for persons she wasn't at liberty to name: "very important persons, though." "I want it delivered in Canada," she'd told him. And then the boy had stepped out of the bedroom and walked by them on his way to the bathroom there in Sonny's suite at the Gellert Hotel where Sonny was keeping him.

"You have friends in high places. You and Wally go on, steady. Stay in the game. It's all very normal."

"It's *our* game, though, isn't it? Yours, too, if I recall? ..." Sonny said. "And if I were to say 'no?'"

"Sonny, you're hardly in a position to do that. One word, Sonny: Colombia," Mary said. She must have had plans for the evening because she had an evening gown on under her raincoat.

"The boy was in love with me. Did you know that? He had no guile at all. He had been working in a shoe factory, but they'd closed it down and he was sleeping rough on the street, and he happened to walk by my hotel totally by chance. He was brand-new to the game. Not a young, seasoned street-hustler—he wasn't really very good at it at all, like a pro would have been," Sonny said. "I was taking the waters. I'd gone out on the patio for a smoke."

"I'm truly sorry about the boy, but you surely understand that he couldn't possibly be left to simply walk away after what he'd learned, listening to us. There are *rules* in our game, you know, and they have to be followed, even if they don't concern one of 'us' directly."

"Learned? What did he 'learn?' He was a kid from a village in the back of beyond and only had a little schoolboy English." Sonny slid his drink away from him and signaled the waiter that he wanted a fresh one. "Anyway, I fell in love with him and promised him I'd take care of him. It was pathetic, really, looking back on it from now. The old faggot in Turkey shacking up with a cherub who thought that our queen Elisabeth was wonderful. I promised to take him to England. I was going to show him the sights," Sonny said.

"I need an answer on this," Mary said. "Yes or no?"

"Of course, dear ... I'll do it. Of *course*," Sonny said.

"I thought so: I want this package to be lost, *totally*," Mary said. Sonny nodded.

"Do you know what it's like to be an old queer with no family? *Wally* has a family. He goes home and he sees his children, and I think he must feel something. I don't know ... what do *you* think he feels? I go home and ... well—home; I've lost that, too, now. So really, I'm like a stray dog someone should shoot and put out of its misery. Just a really pathetic old faggot. There's nothing worse than that, you know. We're very self-indulgent, us fags." Sonny turned towards the window and lit a cigarette. That was the sign. He turned back to look at Mary and pulled a clean glass ashtray a little closer to his side of the table. The very young waitress brought his fresh drink and set it down in front of him.

"I've always loved Calvados. My parents used to make it in our basement. Hush-hush, it was." Sonny looked at the woman across the table from him. Mary was writing something down and was apparently no longer paying him any attention at all. He took a sip from the very full highball glass as he watched Bridgette walk up to the bar and say something to the bartender. She suddenly pulled out a pistol and started yelling.

"It's as hold-up," Sonny said. Mary, who was in the process of tearing off the note page from her Day-Runner, looked over her shoulder.

"God—you're *kidding*. London, these days," she said. "Everything's gone to the dogs. *Someone call the bloody police*," Mary said in a very loud voice. The person with the gun was wearing a hoodie, and turned to look at Mary. The hooded figure came bounding down the aisle past the few other early diners.

"*What did you say?*"

"Kill her," Sonny said. Mary Keen had been looking at the slight young woman brandishing a gun, but she quickly turned to look back at Sonny.

"I *said*, someone call the police," Mary said, staring hard at Sonny. Everyone in the restaurant heard the shot. It was extremely loud in the confines of the dining room. Sonny saw the side of Mary's skull explode outward. The force of the bullet's impact knocked her entire body sideways and into the window. The bullet's path was deflected by Mary's head and missed hitting the glass, however; it tore, instead, into the wooden window jam. The young girl in the hoodie quickly ran from the restaurant and out into the street. Sonny Delmonico then calmly stood up. He took the carnation out of his buttonhole and threw it on the table in front of Mary's startled and very dead half-face; then he calmly left the restaurant. The evening papers said that a botched robbery had cost a diner her life. Mary Keen's name never appeared in any press accounts. The assassination put MI6 on high alert status. The broadsheets all had to bury the story on orders from their owner, who was a very politically well-connected citizen, and personal friend of Margaret Thatcher.

*　　　　　*　　　　　*

The snowstorm had come at them across the top of the mountains from the Italian side of the lake. He and the Hauptmann had stopped in the snowy gloaming and yelled at each other over the wind. The Hauptmann said that the conditions were so bad that maybe they should turn back. George shook his head no and they had skied on into the falling snow. George knew they were moving incredibly slowly, and if they could have seen a film of themselves they would have seen two small, pathetic creatures pulling a sled, with a girl supine and unconscious behind them. The high winds were constantly buffeting them from all angles, trying, it seemed, to stop them from moving forward at all. When a prolonged gust hit them head on it took all there strength just to stay upright, forcing them to lean forward with all their weight just to ski in place.

430

The Hauptmann's face was plastered with ice and his hair looked wet where his breath came into contact with it. Suddenly, he fell to his knees. George watched him vomit onto the ice. He could see that the ice they were passing over was thin enough to have turned a blown glass-like blue color when a gust of wind blew the snow off its surface. He took hold of the Hauptmann's arm to help him up, but the man didn't move. He was obviously stone-exhausted. The German looked up at him and said something.

"What did you say?" George yelled back at him.

"I can't go on!" The wind ripped the words away from the Hauptmann's mouth as soon as he spoke them.

"Get up!" George yelled. But his words, too, were torn from his mouth and were no match for the raging wind. George turned and looked at Carmen. Her face was covered with bits of ice, now, and her eyes were closed. He wondered if she'd died. He was so tired that he had to strain just to keep standing. His cross-country skis were sliding on the ice beneath his feet—another indication that the area they were crossing was exposed and thinner. He moved closer to the Hauptmann and pulled roughly on his arm.

"You've got to move on," he yelled, "... or die right here." The Hauptmann allowed himself to be picked up. George helped him with his poles, and suddenly, like two cogs in an icy machine, they set off again, pushing and jabbing their ski poles at the ice until they could get some momentum up again.

Carmen was no longer on the sled. She could see George and the Hauptmann pulling valiantly in the raging wind as she looked down on them from a great height, and then she was back in Colombia, a child of eleven, on the chicken bus as it wound its way toward Caracas. The pimp had lied to her about everything, but at that moment, looking out the window as the higher elevation changed to banana trees and cane fields, she believed it was all going to get better; that she and her new friend would be going to school, and that there was a future with other children in it. There would be a schoolhouse with nuns and regular meals waiting for her; all the things she'd been promised.

"I can hardly wait to get there," she told the other girl that the pimp was bringing to the city . The other girl was named Matilda Cruz and was twelve and was very pretty—much prettier than Carmen. She and her two children would die in an explosion as she walked the streets of Caracas ten years later, no longer pretty, because she was a glue-sniffer. The bomb that killed her had been intended for an important lieutenant in the drug trade. She and her children were vaporized instantly and returned to the air from which we all come. No one even knew that she had been killed because she and her children were unknown and uncared-about street people, modern-day Untouchables.

"It's all going to change." Her new friend—Matilda—said that to Carmen as she held her hand. "We'll get to go to school, now."

"I know," Carmen said, smiling. "It's all going to change for us."

"... Will you be my little sister?" Matilda asked. "I have no one in the city."

"Of course," Carmen said. Matilda gave her a little kiss on the cheek and squeezed her hand. "I will be your sister because I have no one, either."

"Good ... good," the older girl said.

Carmen saw the two young girls riding on the bus and wanted to call out to them to warn them about the future, but she was suddenly back on the sled, and her face was being touched.

"Are you all right?" George asked. "... *Carmen?*" She couldn't answer but she felt his hand holding hers. It was almost dark when she was back on the bus, and then she was gone for good.

"*Töt,*" the Hauptmann said. He had skied back to the side of the sled. He'd seen so many people die during the War in the East that he knew the look instantly. Something changes in the human face, and it had changed in hers and she was gone. It was in the milky-looking eyes. George looked over at him.

"We have to go," the Hauptmann said. "You have to leave her, now."

"*NO!*" He looked hard at the Hauptmann "*No*" He took out his pistol and stood up, holding the gun loosely at his side. "We take her on to Turin."

"But she's dead," the Hauptmann said. "*We* might die, too. I can't pull her anymore." He saw a look come over the Englishman's face then. It was as cold as any look he'd ever seen in his life and he knew what it meant: he would pull or he would die, right there. He turned and skied back to the strap he'd let fall on the ground and slung it back over his shoulder. In a moment he saw the Englishman lift his strap and slide it over his chest. In another moment they both—after leaning into it with all their might—started to ski again, very slowly, through the penumbra and toward Italy. Their ski poles made strange sounds on the ice.

45

■ NORTHERN MEXICO

There were high cirrus clouds, distant but not-quite-discernable shapes stamped onto the January sky. It seemed to the Hauptmann that they were literally in the middle of nowhere, the landscape itself adding to the abject loneliness and physical exhaustion he suffered after spending weeks on the road.

In the late afternoon their bus reached an ancient and weird cardón cactus forest, comprised of surreal looking multi-armed cactus-men marching across the desolation in their chaotic headless battalions. The forest went on for miles and then just as mysteriously petered out, revealing The Great Emptiness of the Sonoran Desert. The horizon abruptly flat-lined. Nothing stood to give relief but a few mean looking black volcanic outcroppings signifying nothing. The rocks became a dumb silent trope that was repeated again and again—only one idea—flashing by his window. In that ugly repetition, the Hauptmann recognized the physical embodiment of his own appalling despair.

Their bus passed through randomly appearing squatter's hamlets of cardboard and rusted tin, built over the sand. Their no-street rough communities were full of half-naked brown children milling in flimsy doorways. A few times, in a completely surreal indication of a larger Humanity, a Mexican Red Cross worker in a white blouse with a large red cross embroidered on it, would be standing by the side of the two-lane highway soliciting donations. The bus sped by, leaving the man standing in a cloud of dust and making his efforts seem paltry and ridiculous. At sunset the winter sky turned blood crimson and the day was finally, and mercifully, over. The Hauptmann, who'd barely spoken all day, felt completely alone and vulnerable. He doubted he'd survive the Mexican leg of the journey. He thought of his wife of thirty years who'd died in their apartment in East Berlin the year before, just after New Years Day. In his mind that day was called "the silent day."

When the bus slowed down, Sonny Delmonico got out of his seat and walked carefully to the front and spoke to the driver in Spanish. The Hauptmann looked at his watch; it was four in the morning, and he could make out the dawn starting to peel back the edges of what would become day in another hour or so: bits of mountains came into view, but just by virtue of their blue edges. The driver applied the air brakes and the bus finally came to a complete stop. The driver opened the door and Sonny got out.

The Hauptmann was frightened by any interruption in their progress toward the border, and he stood up and looked out the window, watching Sonny as he walked in the sand at the edge of the highway. He could make out a Mexican police checkpoint. He saw a lantern and two policemen standing there with the collars of their green nylon jackets turned up around their necks to protect them from the cold. They walked casually toward Sonny, each of them with an automatic weapon slung loosely over his shoulder. The Hauptmann became too afraid to watch the encounter, remembering all the checkpoints he had to pass through in Germany coming back from the Eastern Front, so he sat back down and gingerly touched his Stage-One frost-bitten face. A female Italian doctor had treated him for frostbite after he and the Englishman finally arrived in Turin with Carmen's body.

His face was still healing. She'd had to cut a square inch of flesh out of his left cheek to prevent gangrene from setting in. Most of the flesh on his face had frozen solid on their way across the lake. Sitting there lost in thought, the Hauptmann heard the big doors to the luggage compartment open, and then, after a moment, close again. He turned and looked at the stewardess sitting in the back. She was awake and looked evenly at him, not averting her gaze when they made eye contact. She seemed very young to him, but already as hard as if she'd never been a girl at all, but had instead skipped that part of her life and gone straight to middle age.

"They had to check the luggage," Sonny said as he sat back down across from the Hauptmann. The bus had left Guadalajara's main bus station eight hours earlier that evening. The station had been quite lively at the time. The Hauptmann had been brought to the bus station in Mexico by two Venezuelan men who'd been guarding him since he'd first arrived in Caracas. He'd been hidden in various cheap hotels in Caracas, always on the move. His guards never allowed him to stay more than one night in any of them, afraid to keep him in any one place too long. Then, very early one morning two days' ago, they'd woken him and he'd been driven to the Caracas airport and they'd taken a flight for Mexico, casually, just like that. He didn't meet Sonny Delmonico until he walked into the bus station in Guadalajara. The two men brought him to Sonny, who was waiting for them and already had the Hauptmann's ticket. The two men who'd been with him up to that point only spoke Italian, and he'd communicated with them solely through gestures and the few words of Italian that he knew. His two protectors disappeared, and he was suddenly left alone with the well-dressed Englishman who wore a patch over his eye. Then they had lunch. Delmonico had introduced himself as Simon Lee. The two Italians from Venezuela reappeared, sat down, and ate lunch with them. During the entire meal, the two spoke in Italian to Mr. Lee and acted as if the Hauptmann weren't even present. He and Mr. Lee boarded an empty bus at five p.m. and left the city. The fact that the bus was empty of any other passengers struck the Hauptmann as very strange.

"Why is there no one else on the bus?" the Hauptmann had asked.

"It's a special bus—" Sonny commented dryly, "—reserved." The fact was, there were 85 kilos of heroin locked in the luggage bay—one of two large shipments moving across Mexico under Sony's control at that particular time. The bus company had long been owned by an outfit called *Productos del Norte,* which was in turn owned by one of the Sicilian Mafia's many front companies.

"Special?" the Hauptmann said.

"That's right," Sonny said. They were sitting in the middle of the bus. It was a first-class bus bound for Tijuana. It smelled strongly of the disinfectant normally used in hospitals. There was a pretty young girl, a stewardess, who was sitting in the back. It was her job to bring them soft drinks and sandwiches. There was also a machine pistol in the locker by her seat that she was very familiar with. There was a chase car a kilometer behind them with several ex-Mexican Special Forces soldiers in it, should there be any problems en route.

Sonny lit a French cigarette and offered the Hauptmann one. Neizert refused it, but nodded a 'Thank you.'

"You're German?" Sonny asked.

"*Ja wohl,*"

"I thought so," Sonny said. "What happened to your face? If you don't mind me asking," Sonny said.

"Frost bite," the Hauptmann said. "In Switzerland."

"*Really.*" Sonny lit his cigarette and glanced out the window. For a moment they rode on in silence. Lights from ranchos sitting isolated and alone in the desert could occasionally be seen off in the distance. Sonny looked at the Hauptmann's face in the reflection of the interior light on the window glass. He had Band Aids over the spot on his cheek where the doctor had cut out the dead flesh.

"I don't like Germans very much," Sonny said. "Were you in the War?"

"Yes."

"What division?"

"*Deutschland.*" The Hauptmann said it with pride. To this day, and despite

435

everything the Hauptmann believed in now it was still something he was proud of: having been trained by some of the best military tacticians on earth and the *espirt de corps* that training had created in his division.

"Was it a *combat* division, then?" Sonny asked. "... Or did you sit in bathtubs in Berlin sipping champagne with *der Führer?*"

"Combat ... on the Eastern Front. ... Most of my men were killed ... or taken prisoner and died in Russia. ... Were *you* in the war?" the Hauptmann asked. His answers had been curt and quietly spoken.

"Yes," Sonny said.

"Is that how you lost your eye?" the Hauptmann asked.

"No. I lost that in a different war," Sonny said. "I'm a homosexual. Life's always a battle for our kind."

"I see."

"*Do* you? I doubt it. ... Or then again, maybe you *do*. I heard that Hitler was queer and liked the boys. If your tastes run our way, *please* do let me know. There's little opportunity till we get out of this country, though. The Mexican's take a dim view of us, too—for the most part, anyway."

"I don't think so. I was married," the Hauptmann said.

"Hitler, I heard, used to fuck fat-boy Röhm in the ass while Goring watched and jacked-off. ... Is that true?" Sonny asked. He was throwing rocks at the German now and enjoying it. A murderous look came into in his eyes. He didn't want it to, but it had suddenly come over him, the hatred he had for the Germans—*any* Germans. The last month of travail, that had started with the moment Butch and the priests had broken into his house in Spain, was all coming out now, finally, here on the bus, and all his pent-up fury was pointed straight at the old German.

"You're angry at me—why? I've done nothing to you. ..." Neizert said.

"Am I?"

"I hate the Nazis, too," the Hauptmann said, and he obviously meant it. He was thinking that it was the War that Sonny was reacting to, and he was used to defusing these types of situations.

"*Really?*" Sonny said, sitting back in his seat.

"Yes. Of course. I was never a *Nazi*. I was a soldier, and that's all," Neizert said.

"That doesn't make me like you any better, Fritz," Sonny said. "Not really. It's the uniform, you see. It's hard to describe, really. I've tried before, and words seem to fail me. But I'm not educated, really. I'm a Harold Hill boy at heart. But you wouldn't have heard of it. ... Harold Hill. ... Fancy a game of cards to pass the time? Strip poker, perhaps? The way Adolf and the boys played it? Just kidding." Sonny dug into the seat pocket in front of him and pulled out a new deck of cards and unwrapped them, but then put them back down again.

"Why were we stopped by the police?" the Hauptmann asked.

"Why do the police do anything, old man? To be paid off. It's always the same, the world over," Sonny said.

"Are there drugs, then—on the bus, I mean?"

"Clever chap, aren't we? But you lot still lost the War, in spite of your cleverness, didn't you?"

"No, ... it ... we've been in two cities and two major bus stations and yet no other passengers have gotten on," the Hauptmann said very matter-of-factly.

"Do you know, I don't care if they catch you or not. Whoever it is that's after you," Sonny said, ignoring the Hauptmann's questions, as his observations had been true enough.

"You don't like me *just* because I'm German, is that it?"

"That's the problem with Germans ... they all understand everything perfectly. That's what I used to tell my mates in Italy. We would ask them, when we finally had them in front of us—that was always the hardest part, you know. Are you fellows *Germans*, then? Do you understand the question? And usually, at least one devil would pipe up in the Queen's English, and say: "*Ja*, we understand," and then we would shoot them," Sonny said. "Are you sure you don't want a cigarette? ... No, I suppose cards might not be the right game. Chess probably is more in your line. Being an *educated* man and all. ..."

"No thank you," the Hauptmann said. "Are you in the mafia, Mr. Lee?" For some reason Neizert couldn't help himself. He'd slowly become terrified of the man sitting across from him, as their conversation had progressed, understanding by now that this Mr. Lee was probably deranged in some way, and that he'd unknowingly pushed the wrong buttons on the man. But he was interested, too, curious. For three weeks he'd been shut up in various hotel rooms, alone with his thoughts most of the time, reliving the crossing of the frozen lake, or different incidents from the War, or his years working in East Germany, with no one to talk to but an occasional maid or waiter. He spoke no Spanish, so even when he had a chance to converse with someone, there was little he could say. He just wanted to *talk* to someone, even if it was this one-eyed, obviously insane gangster.

"Why? Do you want to join? A little old for that, aren't we?"

"No, I didn't mean. ..." Neizert said.

"I'm afraid we don't take in strangers—and it's strictly an Italian organization, you could say. Although I've heard rumors recently that we've got some Germans in with us, now." Sonny looked at him very carefully. "Have you heard that, too? Just rumors, mind you. I think for some reason that's why I've been given you to babysit. ... All

437

these new faces keep cropping up in the trade, lately."

"...Where are we going?" the Hauptmann said.

"The place is called Plata. A veritable Shangri-La," Sonny said. "If Shangri-La is made of tin, and has more whorehouses and bars than Hell itself. It won't be long now and we'll be there. ..."

"Why do you hate me?" the Hauptmann asked again. He asked the question without any guile or hidden motives, as he was truly curious. Sonny looked at him a long time. He drew a revolver from his ankle holster and put it up against the Hauptmann's forehead, centering it just-so, then pulling the hammer back. It was obvious that the man was insane and was going to blow his brains out right then and there. Now it came down upon him with the force of inevitability—the Hauptmann knew he'd somehow gone too far by repeating his last question. He closed his eyes and prayed. He'd seen that look on men's faces many times on the Eastern Front—the man sitting across from him was in the semi-aware, killing-without-thinking zone; where most otherwise "normal" people had to put themselves in order to do such things to their fellow human beings. He waited for instant death to come, his heart shrunken now, unable to even breathe.

"*Perdon—Estamos a punto de dejar la carrettera. Algo durro, el camino de tierra,*" the girl said. The Hauptmann opened his eyes. The stewardess was standing in the isle looking strangely at Sonny. But Sonny Delmonico was lost somewhere in the past, seventeen years old again with both eyes open and wanting to kill every German that stood between him and going home to Harold Hill. The stewardess's voice brought him back, though. He very quickly brought the gun down from the Hauptmann's forehead. He kept pressure on the hammer very carefully with his thumb and slowly returned it to the uncocked position. Then he bent over and slipped the pistol back into the backup holster on his ankle.

"Right. *Gracias.* My girl," Sonny said. He now looked *at* the girl for the first time since she'd spoken, and he suddenly had a completely different expression on his face—he was no longer the mindless murderer of a few seconds ago. She calmly nodded to him—she'd had to deal with coked-out *pistoleros* and their like many times during the years she'd spent doing this particular job, and Sonny's lapse was more or less a routine incident for her to diffuse—then she turned around and walked back to her seat at the back of the bus.

"There's rough patch in front of us, she says," Sonny translated her remarks for the Hauptmann, smiling at him as he spoke. "These dirt roads are truly awful, you see. ... It's a filthy country, really."

■ LONDON

They met in Green Park near the Playboy Club, and began to walk together without talking to each other. It was raining slightly and George had brought an umbrella, a golf-style one that he held over both of them. He'd lost one finger to the frostbite, and Malcolm noticed it almost immediately.

"I'm sorry," Malcolm said. "I didn't know anything ... about the girl."

"My daughter, really ... adopted. I'd rather not talk about it if you don't mind," George said. "Of course, Mary Keen is dead, now. She was shot down in a restaurant yesterday. I'd imagine that's no surprise to you, though? ..."

"I can explain exactly what happened if you want the details," Malcolm said.

"Please don't. I'd rather *not* know, really. Of course, MI6 are all on full alert now and have closed the drawbridges around the world. It seems they believe she was set up, and that it may have even been the KGB that was responsible. No one knows *what* to think, really, because murder isn't what our lot normally do, as you know. Not like *that*, anyway. Professional courtesy and all that rubbish—we don't generally go around shooting the other side down in the street."

"I couldn't stop them—it was *their* way of dealing with her," Malcolm lied, because now he realized that he had to protect his old friend from the truth.

"Well, now you have our side out looking for her killers," George said.

"Do they know about the Hauptmann?"

"I can't say that they do ... or that they don't, for that matter. They know that the KGB is turning over heaven and earth trying to find someone *they've* lost, an officer called Vladimir Putilin. The KGB came up with *that* little tidbit. It's really confusion's masterpiece over on their side. He's been spotted recently by our people in Mexico City. He apparently tried to get in touch with *your* lot down there," George said. "It seems that the KGB have blamed Mary's death on him. They're calling him a 'rogue element.' They had one of their attachés go to Whitehall for a meeting, actually, just yesterday. It's unprecedented, really. It makes no sense. And a KGB general named Maximov was just killed outside Moscow. They're trying to keep that one quiet, though. ..."

"George, it *does* make sense if Vladimir has been sent out after our man by the Gehlen people. Think about it: Maximov was working for us—he ends up dead. It was Maximov who got the Hauptmann out of East Berlin. I can't explain everything right now, but MI6 has been compromised—I'm sure of that. Maybe fatally. My side has been, too. It's worse than I've ever seen it. Only God knows now what the truth is.

Even the KGB is being used."

"I see," George said.

"The Hauptmann will know a lot about the Gehlen network, and how compromised the chain of command is at CIA. That's what I'm hoping, anyway. Whatever happened in Switzerland ... If it still matters to you. ... It will make a difference."

"Well, we like to be of help when we can," George said.

"Can you try and find out what they know at your old shop? And what about Sal Birnbaum?"

"He's dead. He was found in the basement of a home in Bern. Not at all pretty, I'm afraid. He'd been severely tortured. I got a call from a friend in Swiss intelligence. Off the record. There won't be an investigation—the Swiss would rather just sweep it under the rug because he was a foreigner."

"I see. ... " Malcolm said. They walked on. George noticed then that Malcolm was showing the strain on his face for the first time. It was suddenly printed all over it, for anyone to see. He guessed that they had both just lost someone who was close to them.

"Have they actually taken over, then? These Gehlen people? Is that it? What you were talking about before I left?" George was angry now, Malcolm could tell. He wanted payback, because of what had happened to the girl.

"Yes," Malcolm said, "I still need your help. Will you come to Mexico with me? Please—I can't do this alone." He stopped and took hold of George's elbow. "I've no right to ask you to do this after what you've just been through, but I'm going to anyway."

"Right. Give me a two days. I have to see the wife and kids and explain myself— tell her I've managed to lose a finger in the Alps." He smiled, but Malcolm noticed he'd aged a little, and the smile was very tight, even for George. "Where will you be?"

"I'll call with the name of the place," Malcolm said. "In two days, then. This Vladimir person could have been sent by them—by the Gehlen people, as a ruse. I mean ... That's what *I* would do," Malcolm said.

"Perhaps they want you to lower the drawbridge and let him in," George said.

"I think that may be the case," Malcolm said.

They walked on until they reached a town car that was waiting for Malcolm. He got in and went straight to Heathrow for a flight to Mexico. He turned once as the car left, and saw George crossing the road, concealed by his big black umbrella.

*   *   *

440

■ CUERNAVACA, MEXICO

Vladimir had watched the gunmen fire into the mounds of pillows he'd carefully placed on the hotel Polanco's bed. Two Europeans had burst into the room and immediately opened fire with automatic weapons. He'd watched it all from the secret viewing room the KGB had created to make films of whores and politicians for blackmail purposes. His own answer to the question about the CIA being compromised, as the General had feared, had now been answered. He'd waited a few minutes and then left the hotel via a fire escape while the gunmen were discovering that they'd just assassinated a collection of pillows and bolsters he'd crammed under the bed covers, having taken the light bulbs out of the overhead light so that when they'd turned on the lights in the room they would have been disappointed and not had a brightly-lit, presumably sleeping, target. His plan had worked, as they'd opened fire instead of crossing the room and turning on the light by the bed to see if he was really in it.

He'd gone by taxi to the German-language newspaper offices that were used by the KGB as a front. It was dangerous for him, but it was the only way he knew to collect the message from Gemma. There were scores of front organizations that the Soviet government sponsored in Mexico, and he knew it would be difficult for his hunters to approach them all quickly enough to figure out which one, or ones, he was using, or even to have a list of them all, in fact. He'd decided to take his chances.

"You shouldn't have come here," Gemma said

"I had to," Vladimir said.

"I can't go on with this—you have to get me out of here," she said. He looked at her a moment. She looked older to him for the first time; not like a school girl any more. They had found a place in the hotel garden that she thought would probably be safe. She'd told Alex that she wanted to go down to the restaurant for a coffee. He'd been busy talking to Edward Perry the other American, who she'd met in Italy. Perry had shown up at the hotel in Cuernavaca with his girlfriend in tow.

"*You* have to help *me*. There's been a change," Vladimir said.

"I can't talk here for long," Gemma said.

"There's something I need to explain," Vladimir said. He'd come straight to the hotel where she'd said she was now staying in the message she'd left for him at the newspaper, desperate to tell her that the Hauptmann must not be harmed in any way. He had to explain to her in person that everything had suddenly changed, after his meeting with Maximov. He'd called her room directly, taking the chance that Tucker might answer the phone, but luckily she answered, and he told her that he was waiting for her in the lobby.

"The other one has arrived. He's here now, with Tucker," Gemma said.

"What 'other one?'"

"A man called Edward Perry. ... He was in Rome, with Tucker. He's an American and he's brought a woman with him. They're all armed. They're waiting to leave as soon as they hear something, but they won't say what, exactly. I suppose it's the same Hauptmann that you're after? ..."

"You have to help me get the Hauptmann to the other side—to the U.S.," Vladimir said.

"*What?*"

"I don't have time to explain it all now, but you must not hurt this man Neizert," Vladimir said.

"Why ... Why am I even here, then?"

"I had to escape from Russia. The KGB is looking for me, too, now. They don't know about you. They've been penetrated by a group. I can't explain it all right now. ... But it's very important that the Hauptmann makes it to America."

"I'm pregnant," Gemma said. "I tried to tell you in Italy. And I'm in love with *you*." She put her hands to her sides as if she were a child in a school yard blurting it out.

"... Is it his? ... Tucker's?" he asked, dumbfounded.

"Yes. I can't stay here. He knows. He believes I'm in love with him. I'm not. It's too cruel to both of us for me to stay. I've got to leave. *Now.*"

"All right," Vladimir said. "I understand."

"I love you. ... Do you understand *that?*" she said.

"... Yes, I understand."

"I only did all this for *you*," Gemma said. "Because I thought you would fall in love with me if I did what you wanted."

"... I'm married, Gemma."

"I don't care. ... Leave her. Do I have to beg you?"

"No."

"Will you leave her?" she said.

"Yes."

"Do you love me?"

"Yes, I do. I tried not to, but I can't help myself," he said.

"What is it you want?" Gemma said. "I'll do it. Whatever it is."

"I want you to help them get the Hauptmann across the border and into America. ... Tucker and Perry will need help, I'm sure. The kind you and I can give them."

"Is he that important?"

"Yes," Vladimir said.

"What about you and I?"

"We'll be together after this is all over, I promise you. ... Go back to Tucker for now," Vladimir said. "I'll be close-by. When you know where you're going, call that number again at the newspaper and leave me a message."

"You promise ... when this is finished ..."

"Yes, I promise you, my darling, we'll be together forever, after this is over," he said.

"... They're waiting for someone called Sonny Delmonico to arrive in Mexico with the Hauptmann. Delmonico is to take the Hauptmann to a place called Plata and hand him over to Tucker. ... It's near the border, I think," she said. "I overheard them talking about it this morning."

"All right. I'll be there in Plata, waiting for you. Now go back and pretend you love *him* for just a little while longer. ..."

46

■ CUERNAVACA, MEXICO

Gemma was sitting poolside holding the history of Mexico tome unopened in her lap.

"God, it's *hot!*" Marie said, calling to her.

The American girl had walked down to the hotel pool wearing just a gold-colored bikini and carrying a large matching beach bag. She was barefoot, and wearing very dark sunglasses. The sunglasses somehow made her blonde hair seem even more lushly perfect. Marie seemed like a beautiful female creature from the planet "America" to her—a totally alien world full of big shiny cars and buxom movie stars. It was just *that* America, with its relentless images of mass consumption and physical perfection, that had been projected worldwide for decades by American movies and television, which Gemma resented on some very deep level, and this beautiful young girl—now walking casually towards her—personified all of it so perfectly.

Despite the fact that they were almost the same age, the two hadn't really connected—they were simply too different. Gemma had realized that when they'd first met. In Rome, they'd gone shopping twice together to buy clothes for their trip, and Marie had tried to strike up a friendship; in fact, she'd been genuinely warm and open. But Gemma couldn't bring herself to respond in any real way, knowing it would be dangerous to let her guard down, even slightly. A few times she'd been tempted because she liked the girl, and probably was also even a little jealous of Marie's classic type of beauty. Gemma knew, watching her approach, smiling at her as if they were just normal girls, that she had to continue to keep her distance. She prepared herself by putting her book aside and emotionally locking herself down. Then she looked up and finally smiled back at her would-be friend.

"It's like a fucking bath," Marie said, after briefly sticking her toe in the water, then retreating from it to look for the right lounge chair.

Gemma glanced up at her from where she was sitting. All the waiters and bus boys in the restaurant where they'd eaten breakfast that morning couldn't stop staring at Marie. She'd worn a beach dress that she threatened to spill out of with every movement of her body. Her boyfriend, Perry, was a true Neanderthal, Gemma had thought when they'd met in Rome, and her initial opinion had been confirmed and even intensified ever since. Perry seemed to love the attention the girl got from other men—the more lascivious the looks they gave her, the better it seemed.

"It's delicious to be here all alone. Like, who gets to have a pool like this all by themselves?" Marie said, dragging a lounge chair over next to Gemma's. "... You're Italian, aren't chew?"

"Yes," Gemma said.

"Yeah, I didn't think you were American," Marie said. "I'm really homesick ... *you* know—for America. I even missed Christmas this year. In Bensonhurst—New Jersey. It's great there ... Christmas time." Gemma smiled, not knowing what to respond. "I speak a little Italian," Marie said, giving her a coy smile.

"Your parents are Italian—*from* Italy?" Gemma asked politely. She'd wanted to be alone and quietly forget everything for a while by losing herself in the book, but that obviously wasn't going to happen now.

"Yeah ... Sicily. Everyone in the neighborhood where I grew up seemed to be from some little town in the Old Country. Everyone knew *everyone*, there—and all your business, too!" Marie stood up and dragged her lounge chair even closer to Gemma's, finally sitting back down when she was satisfied that she was sitting close enough to her—their pool chairs were practically touching at this point. She pulled a bottle of suntan lotion out of her beach bag and proceeded to squeeze a wide white ribbon of the lotion out onto her thigh.

"The guys are sure nervous about *some*thing," Marie said. "Have you noticed that with Alex?"

"No, not really," Gemma lied.

"I'll tell you, Butch is a *trip!*" The girl used his real name even though Gemma had been introduced to him as Edward Perry in Rome. Gemma pretended not to notice.

"I like him, though—a lot. He's different from all the other guys I've known. Kind of nutty, but I like it. And he's a tiger in bed." Gemma smiled. She looked around the pool area, hoping to see Bruce, thinking that he might save her from another forced conversation with the girl. "I saw you with that other guy. ... He's cute," Marie said. "Yesterday, I mean. *You* know, the big, tall one?"

"Pardon me?" Gemma said, completely taken aback that Marie had seen her talking to Vladimir.

"Yeah. ... over in the hotel garden—yesterday." Marie looked at her and winked. "Don't worry, I won't tell." She shook her head a little and smiled rakishly. "Look, I get hit on all the time. Even by these Mexican guys. As soon as Butch is gone and I'm alone they're all over me. *Jesus.* It's like I got guys all over the place—like ants at a picnic!"

"He was ... Oh, I remember now. Yes. The tall one," Gemma said, trying not to act surprised that the girl had seen them speaking briefly.

"Did he ask you out?"

"Yes," Gemma said. "But of course I told him no. Just a tourist . . ."

"He *was* cute, though."

"Yes, very cute—but please don't tell Bruce. ... He's ... you know ... he can get *so* jealous over nothing. ..." Gemma looked at the girl. There was a kind look on Marie's face, as if she truly understood Gemma's predicament.

"No ... I wouldn't do that. Some of these guys ... they get *violent*—you know, if you even *look* at another guy," Marie said. "Back home it's *crazy* that way."

"Yes, believe me, I know!" Gemma said. "Thank you."

"Us girls have to stick together sometimes," Marie said. She suddenly reached over and grabbed Gemma's hand. "You want some lotion?" Gemma smiled, finally realizing that the girl was probably incapable of being anything but affable and unguarded with most people. She had now, whether she liked it or not, a reason to be friendly back now. The fact that Marie had seen her with Vladimir the day before and hadn't said anything about it to Alex or Butch made them co-conspirators, now, too, of a particularly female stripe. A "real" friendship would cement that, Gemma thought, so she started to initiate further conversation, instead of just responding to Marie, as she had been up to that point.

"I *love* Christmas, myself," Gemma said, trying to change the subject back to the more mundane. It was December, and they'd seen the streets of Cuernavaca decorated in "American" style, with strings of colored lights draped over everything.

"Yeah ... Me, too," Marie said.

"We always had very beautiful Christmases in my village. They light bonfires in the streets all over the place," Gemma said, finally letting her guard down and motioning for Marie to hand her the bottle of lotion. Marie gave it to her and then laid back. Her stomach wet with sweat and sparkling.

"Yeah. But where *I'm* from, you never know what's going to happen at Christmas time. ... Even Jesus would be surprised!" Marie said.

* * *

1970 ■ NEW YORK, BENSONHURST CHRISTMAS DAY

The Anastasias' house was on 79th Street, just up from Colombo Avenue in the heart of Bensonhurst. Every Christmas the family put up a spectacular manger scene in the front yard that was one of the biggest and best lit in the neighborhood. The traditional donkey and Wise Men were nearly life-sized, and the stable that housed them was so heavy that it had to be lifted and carried by Tony Anastasia *and* his two brothers from the garage out onto the lawn. Marie had always been the one to carry the Baby Jesus into the manger, placing it in the place of honor in the straw-packed crib. There was a photo that Marie's mother had taken one year, of Marie posing with her father, both of them holding the Baby Jesus and smiling very happily at the camera.

Marie hadn't heard the phone ringing over the sound of the music coming from downstairs. She was busy talking to her Ken and Barbie dolls, telling them that sometimes they could run into the basement if there was any trouble, or go over to their grandfather's house. *"Nobody* messes with *nonno,"* she'd told her Ken doll, giving him a very serious look.

Her dad, Tony Anastasia, was playing a new Dean Martin album he'd just gotten for Christmas from his brother Joey. "Ain't That a Kick In the Head" was playing very loudly on the living room stereo, just next to where the family's pink-flocked Christmas tree—all seven feet of it—was brilliantly lit up. In fact, Tony had barely heard the phone ring himself, with the caller warning Tony that two Chinese guys were on their way to his house to kill him at that very moment.

The brand-new, console-type RCA stereo—one of those that had legendarily "fallen off a truck"—was turned up almost as loud as it would go, and you could hear Dino's voice in every room of the house. The new stereo had been delivered to Tony's house two weeks before by two very large men dressed in grey track suits who were part of Tony's regular crew. Tony had been talking on the phone when the new Hi-Fi arrived. He was finalizing a contract he was going to take in Chinatown, not bothering to try to keep the conversation from the ears of his men as they struggled with the stereo. Tony really regretted getting involved with the "Chinks" later on. They always wanted a discount, and they were slow to pay, too. And *now* it seemed that they wanted to cancel the debt altogether—*And at Christmas time, no less,* Tony thought, yelling up to his daughter from the living room. *Fucking chinks!*

"Hey, Marie!"

"*Yeah!*" Marie yelled back over Dino. Both she and her father had very loud voices.

"*Can you come down here for a second?*" Tony heard the telephone ring again and picked it up, but forgot to turn down the music first. He told his brother Joey to hold for a minute.

"*I'm watching Johnny for Ma!*" Marie yelled down to him.

"*I know that!* Listen, Joey, I know. ... Two chinks. Ah ... they don't respect nuthin'. I *did* do the job for those cocksuckers. Hold a second. ... *MARIE GET MY SATCHEL, WILL YAS?*"

"*Okay!*" Marie yelled as she jumped into action, because she knew that if her father wanted his *satchel*, it was not good, and there was going to be a *job* of some kind, and probably right *now*. *But it's Christmas*, she thought, looking at her little brother napping in his three-hundred-dollar Macy's crib, an item that had also shown up late one night, stuck in the back of the white Cadillac convertible her father had bought with the proceeds from killing two Cuban guys in Florida in an ice cream shop. Marie had been waiting in the car during the Florida job, and had watched the whole thing go down, from the moment her father walked in the front door of the shop, setting of the little bell, to the moment he arrived back at their car, having left two bodies on the floor inside, lying there, dead meat, in spreading pools of blood.

Marie had been happily playing that morning, and had been quite content to stay upstairs with Ken and Barbie keeping an eye on her little brother until her mother got back from her sister-in-law's house two doors' down. Her mother had taken her aunt Jenny (a non-Italian) a *frittata* because her mother's brother, Michael, had disappeared two weeks ago, and *everyone* in the neighborhood was thinking that he was never coming back. Marie ran out into the hallway, smelling the scent of the Christmas tree mingling with the Italian herbs that her mother had ground up that morning in preparation for that night's big meal, which Marie was so looking forward to.

"*You* sure *you want the satchel, Papa?*"

"*Yeah, bring the satchel ... and hurry up, Marie! Come on down here. And bring your little brother, too. I want yous to take him over to your auntie's house.*" Tony said.

"*Yeah?*" Marie said.

"*Yeah .... now hurry up, honey. We don't got all day here.*"

Marie came down the stairs dragging the satchel and leading her little brother by the hand. The old leather satchel—actually a vintage doctor's bag—contained two .45 automatics and a hundred rounds of ammunition for each of them. Her father, who was still a very handsome man at forty with his jet-black hair combed straight back, was barefoot, wearing a wife-beater and dark slacks, and was sitting by the Christmas tree loading two twelve-gauge sawed-offs. He had a twelve-pack of shells; about 500 rounds at his feet. Tony bought ammunition in bulk.

"It's *Christmas*, Papa. ... Why do you need the satchel?" Marie said from the foyer letting the bag drag on down the last steps and then onto the floor at the foot of the stairs.

"Yeah. ... Well, someone forgot to tell these guys that're comin' for me right now, honey. Just bring me the satchel, will you please, Marie, and take your brother over to your uncle Michael's house. ... And tell your mom to stay *there* ... till I come get her in a little while. Uncle Joey is coming over right now. We got a little problem wid some guys...." Her father was sitting in front of the Christmas tree loading the second shotgun; sitting right in the middle of all the wrapping paper and ribbons that had been torn from that Christmas morning's presents, including what she'd torn off the Ken and Barbie dolls' boxes. The Christmas-morning detritus was scattered all over the floor of the living room. The whole scene was a mess of shotgun shells and gold wrapping paper.

"*But it's* Christmas, *papa!*" Marie said again, stopping just short of the arched living room entryway.

"Yeah, I know what day it is, Marie ... but *these* guys ... they don't celebrate like us. They're *Chinese* guys—see?" He looked up at her and shrugged, like he didn't understand it either, but it just was what it was. "Now hand me that satchel."

"You want me to come back and help?" Marie said.

"No! I want you to stay with your mom and your aunt. And no matter what you hear going on over here—you stay *there*, okay?" He shoved two rounds into a second shotgun—one that she'd seen her father throw into the back of his Cadillac countless times. The barrel was slightly dented-up, close to where it joined the stock, in the place he'd had to use the weapon as a club more than once when the SOB just wouldn't die. She'd never seen the other shotgun before: she supposed that it must have been hidden somewhere around the house, in an area she wasn't yet privy to.

"Well, go on, Marie!" her father said.

"But—it's *Christmas!*" Marie said for the third time. Then she ran into the living room and handed her father the old leather satchel, half dragging it because she still had hold of her little brother's hand, pulling him along behind her. Tony stopped what he was doing. Her father gently held her wrist for a moment and looked into his daughter's eyes. She was his favorite and he could never hide it.

"Hey, Marie . . .You like the Barbie kitchen we got you, huh?"

"Yeah," she said. "Yeah." Her father had the bluest eyes she'd ever seen, and she loved him more than anything in the world.

"Good. Now give me a kiss and get out of here. And don't come back until I call youse guys. And go out the back, don't go out the front door."

She looked at him a moment, suddenly terrified, as what was going to happen finally sank into her child's mind, because she knew exactly what the satchel meant, then kissed her father's cheek. She hated the satchel, but she knew somehow that it was part of her family's business, and it was very important. That didn't make her like it any better, though. She turned and ran toward the kitchen, her little brother still in tow, and then straight out the back door of the house and onto the snow powdered back lawn. She heard her father spill the contents of the satchel out onto the floor as Dean Martin sang "Ain't That A Kick In The Head," as she left the house.

Marie ran into her aunt's kitchen. It smelled of coffee and fruitcake. Her aunt was crying and her mom was holding her hand. Marie's two cousins—two little boys—had looked up at her when she ran through the front door. They were sitting in the living room playing with a train set that they'd gotten "from Santa" that morning. They thought that Marie, as they heard someone coming through the front door, might be their dad, finally coming back home. But when they saw it was just their cousin from down the street, they went back to watching their model train move around the little circular track.

"Momma, Daddy says that you shouldn't come home right now. And he wanted me to bring Johnny over here, too. He says he'll call you on the phone when we can go home again." Marie stood there breathless by the time she'd disgorged all that info for her mother.

"*What!?*" her mother said. Her mother was tall and very thin; she'd run track in high school, and made "All-City".

"That's what he *said,* Ma. ... Hi, Auntie C," Marie said. Her aunt was still weeping, but she nodded hello to Marie. Then she began to ball even harder, really wailing it out, very loudly. It seemed like she couldn't stop even if she wanted to. Her mother suddenly let go of her sister-in-law's hand and turned toward her daughter.

"You better not be making this up, young lady, just so you can go over to Angelina's house to play—I swear to God!"

"*Ma*—I had to get the *satchel.* And it's *Christmas,*" Marie said. Then a very strange look came over her mother's pretty young face.

"*But it's Christmas ...*" her mother repeated, *sotto voce,* unconsciously parroting her daughter.

"I *know!* Papa says Uncle Joey's coming over—*right now!*" Her aunt suddenly burst out crying even more loudly, as if she were alone in some distant place where no one could hear her; then she got up and walked over to the little restaurant-style booth that she and her husband had had specially built in their kitchen just two years' before.

Marie liked that booth a lot because it remind her of going out to dinner in a restaurant, only it was in a house, and in her *auntie's* house to boot, so she could go there and sit in it practically any time she wanted to, within reason, and pretend that she was eating in a fancy restaurant. They'd even had the booth upholstered in red leather, and as far as Marie was concerned, it *was* just like a restaurant booth.

"Here." Her mother reached for her brother.

"What are chinks, Ma?" Marie asked.

"*What!?*"

"Papa said that the chinks didn't respect Christmas."

"... Oh, God," her mother said. She held her son more tightly.

"Momma—what *are* they?" Marie said. Suddenly she was feeling like the world had gone crazy and was starting to spin faster—*too* fast for her to keep up with it, in fact—and that "chinks" might be *anything,* even real *monsters* of some kind, although she thought that believing in monsters was something she'd out grown by now.

"'Chinks' are Chinese," her mother said.

"Why do *they* want to come over to our house on Christmas anyway?" Marie asked. "We ain't Chinese—we're *Italian!*"

"I don't know, honey," her mother lied.

"I mean ... if Papa needs the satchel," Marie said. She watched as her mother's face turned very pale. "The chinks are *bad*—aren't they? ... Are they going to try to do something bad to Daddy?"

Her mother could only nod. Hearing her sister-in-law in low-grade hysterics was bringing home to her exactly what her husband did for a living; something she always tried to keep on her mind's back-burner.

Then, without really thinking about it, Marie ran upstairs where she knew her uncle kept *his* satchel. She ran through her aunt and uncle's bedroom. The big queen-sized bed was unmade. She dove under it and found a satchel very similar to her dad's, and saw a Winchester .30-.30 lying next to it under the bed. Her father had shown her how to load and fire that exact rifle—moving the weapon's lever back and forth, up and down—earlier that summer, up in the Catskills, where both families had gone for a long vacation. The two families had shared a big summer house in the country for an entire month.

What the two Chinese hit-men saw—or thought they saw—was a little girl of about twelve walking down the sidewalk with a toy rifle of the type that little kids get as Christmas presents. They'd just gotten out of a green Jaguar and had asked Marie if Tony and his family lived in that house.

Marie didn't even answer, verbally, anyway. She just opened fire on them. Her

451

Uncle Joey was just pulling around the corner in his yellow Lincoln, and saw the whole thing go down. *"Holy shit, Marie,"* was all he said when he took the rifle from her.

"But it's *Christmas*, Uncle Joey. ..." was all that Marie had said. Her father came running out the front door, jumping straight over the two Chinese gunmen, both of whom had instinctively run for the "safety" of the manger and had knocked it over when their bodies were slammed into it by Marie's barrage of fire. One of them was now lying there badly wounded in the stomach, and the other lay dead on the lawn next to one of the terra cotta Wise Men. The Baby Jesus had rolled down the lawn and out onto the sidewalk, losing his head somewhere along the way.

The Chinese guy with the stomach wound was still alive when Marie's father went into a red-rage and clubbed him to death with the ceramic donkey, right there on their front lawn, in full view of a number of witnesses—people who'd come out of their houses to see what was going on after they'd heard the shooting. Neither the gunfight nor the two dead bodies were reported to the police, who had been paid off and been given strict orders—in any case—to keep off that block *no matter what happened*, unless they were called first.

Well before they had Christmas dinner that day, the two dead bodies had been removed via Uncle Joey's Lincoln, and had been driven to a farm in upstate New Jersey to be disappeared.

Christmas dinner was a traditional one, of breaded Italian-style fish smothered in fresh herbs, with an apple tartin for dessert. Everything tasted wonderful, as Marie's mother was a very good cook. Because her mother and father were so relieved and grateful that everyone was alive, including Marie, the whole family had the best and loudest Christmas dinner they'd ever had; the house full of family and friends almost none of whom were aware of what had happened earlier that day.

Marie's mother never treated her daughter the same way after that Christmas, and they never once spoke about what Marie had done that day. She caught a lot of respect in the neighborhood after that, too; especially from the older people, who would whisper about her and nod knowingly to each other. In Italian they would say, *"She's got balls ... just like a man."*

*   *   *

Detective Warren Talbot was wearing what he normally wore when he was off duty: blue jeans and a plain white T-shirt, with nearly worn-out New Balance brand running shoes. Ever since his wife had been murdered, he hadn't been exactly right in the head. He'd run out of the house very early that morning, forgetting to shave, because he was anticipating the long drive to L.A. He had a hammerless five shot Remington .38 in his front pocket that morning; a gun that he always carried when he was off-duty. He'd set it on his dead wife's side of the bed the night before and tried to mentally piece together what he actually knew for certain about her murder, and it wasn't very much. He'd studied and re-studied the official case file of his wife's murder by the light on the nightstand since about a week after it happened, lying there on their bed, unable to sleep from the frustration of it all: She'd been shot in the head by an unknown assailant. Robbery was apparently not a motive. There had been a report of a strange motorcycle in the neighborhood, but no one had taken down the license number. His wife's case, like so many he'd investigated himself, was seemingly hopeless, as there *was* no viable suspect, or even a motive. Murders like this happened every day in LA. People were murdered by complete strangers, and a lot of the time there was very little or nothing the police could come up with to serve as even a far-fetched explanation as to why exactly the person had been killed.

Two weeks after her death he'd gotten that mysterious call from one of the DEA officers he'd arrested the month before at the Capri Motel in Malibu, telling him that his wife's murderer had been in fact looking for Warren himself, in all probability. The man on the phone had told him to stop looking into the murders at the Capri Motel as well. "You're out of your league with these people, my friend. I'm trying to help a fellow Marine, here."

"Who *are* they?" Talbot had asked Edward Perry—the DEA officer he'd met at the Capri. But Perry had already hung up on him. He was hoping Perry would call back, but he hadn't—yet, anyway. When he tried contacting the man by calling the DEA office in Los Angeles, he was told to call Washington, D.C. The man he'd talked to in D.C. had told him to call LA. He'd finally just given up.

Warren was sitting in a run-down Denny's down the street from the Hollywood bowl. Since his wife had been killed he had changed considerably. At times he found it very difficult to talk to even close family members. Both his family and Lorie's had made it a point to stop in and check on him, though. They always brought him food; dishes they knew that Lorie had cooked for him. Lorie's brother had invited him to watch the Super Bowl with his family, so Warren had gone and sat in a living room with Lorie's brother and his large family and watched the game, with everyone, down to and including his nephews and nieces, being very sweet to him—careful to include him in any conversation they were having. But it had been an absolute agony for him. The fact that he and Lorie had not had any children bothered him now more than ever before. Seeing his brother-in-law's kids only made the pain of Lorie's death that much worse. At least if they'd had children maybe he would still have had a reason to live; someone to love who could understand how he felt. His grief had cut him off even from those in his family who were reaching out to him. He found their well-intentioned visits awkward, and never knew what to say to them. He preferred to be alone when he wasn't working. At work he just felt numb, but at least he could forget, for a brief periods, anyway, that he really wanted to kill himself. He'd finally called up Lorie's brother and left a message asking him to stop coming around; that he couldn't take it any more—*any* of it. His brother-in-law had called back immediately, truly worried now that Warren was going to do something horrible to himself, but Warren had not picked the phone up when he heard the man's voice. Instead, he'd put all his weapons—three pistols and a shotgun—out onto the kitchen table, and had proceeded to clean them, very meticulously. Twice he thought he heard Lorie speaking to him from another room—her voice was as clear as day. He'd answered, knowing it was crazy, but needing to talk to her more than anything in the world. She'd appeared to him one evening while he was cooking fish tacos—a favorite of theirs. He'd run out of the kitchen in a blind panic, scared stiff of what was happening to him. He was certain by now that he was losing his mind, but he had no idea what to *do* about it.

"Are you Flaco?" Warren asked.

"Yeah," the Mexican kid said.

"Okay ... Good," Warren said. The Mexican looked very thin, and was obviously a drug addict.

"You're a cop?" Flaco said.

"Yeah," Warren said.

"DEA?"

"No. ... No—Sheriff's department," Warren said.

"I got a call from Cambell."

"Yeah ... We're friends."

"He said you would pay," Flaco said.

"I will," Warren said.

"What's this about?" Flaco asked.

"A girl was killed in a shootout at a motel in Malibu ... A month ago—remember it?"

"Yeah ... I heard about it," Flaco said.

"You knew her?" Warren said.

"I want a thousand dollars for my info. ... Like we agreed on the phone," Flaco said.

"Okay," Warren said.

"Now, man—I need it up front," Flaco said. Warren took the cash from an envelope and laid it out on the table. Two old ladies looked over at the two men from a booth across the aisle and down one. Both of them were wearing winter coats despite the warm weather. They looked quickly away when they saw the pile of money lying on the table: after all, they were only there for the Grand-Slam breakfast and the Senior Discount. Flaco proceeded to count the cash very slowly—twice.

47

"So you knew the girl who was killed at the motel? Patty Montgomery?" Warren Talbot asked.

"Yeah, I knew her. ... Can I have something to drink? A Coke or something?" Flaco said, taking the cash he'd been paid off the tabletop and stuffing it into the front pocket of his jeans.

"Sure. ... Who was she?" Warren asked.

"Just a squeeze, from what I could tell," Flaco said. "A good-looking *huerra*, though."

"Did you know her boyfriend?"

"Yeah. ... The skinny white boy."

"Bruce Tucker?"

"Yeah." Warren signaled their waitress.

"And the other one—Perry? What about *him?*"

"Perry's a *mother*fucker—he really is. ... The faggot little white boy called him Butch. Perry's crazy; stone *loco*," Flaco said. Warren thought he was probably stoned, the way he was talking.

"Why do you say that? ... Faggot, I mean?"

"The blond boy just vibed queer to me—always talking shit. ... But I guess he wasn't, really."

"What were you doing for them?" Warren asked.

"I was their guide through Indian Country, man. Out *there*. ... Like in the movies, *vato*." Flaco pointed out to the street in front of the restaurant. It was eleven o'clock in the morning and a dull, bright sunlight was reflecting off car windshields, making them all look the same. L.A. had a haggard, witless feel to it that morning, as if there were no point to any of the asphalt and concrete except to look ugly. It was the face of an imbecile.

"They had lots of enemies—or so I've heard," Warren said.

"Mother fucking right!"

"They ripped people off, too?" Warren said.

"They did." An ancient waitress brought a bottle of Coke to the table along with a tall red plastic glass with lots of ice and set it down in front of Warren. Flaco reached for it and slid it over in front of himself. Warren thanked the woman. He watched as Flaco's dirty and grimed hand, his fingernails slightly yellowish from the speed, reached for the plastic glass. The detective caught a whiff of something rank-smelling that he'd encountered before, and realized that Flaco stank like crack-house—he steamed off a kind of cat-urine smell mixed with bleach—extremely foul decomposing-human smell.

"Two sheriffs were shot dead right after Perry and Tucker got to LA. ... Did *they* do it?" Warren said, ignoring the stench.

"How do I know?" Flaco said. Warren thought he was lying because he looked down into the top of his Coke as he answered.

"Someone called LAPD from the scene with the license plate number of the shooters' car. It was a DEA undercover car. A new Mustang, in fact. The caller fingered two shooters."

" ... Mr. Lucky—that was his street name. The guy they shot first," Flaco said. "I knew the dude. They fucking flat killed his ass, colder than shit, man."

"Mr. Lucky?" Warren said.

"Yeah. A black dude. A hustler and dealer. They shot the motherfucker dead in a gas station the morning I set up the deal."

"Why?"

"How the fuck should I know *why?*" Flaco said.

"Did you know they were DEA special agents—Perry and Tucker?"

"Hell, yeah. ... I was already working for the DEA—they hooked it up. I was facing a felony—ten to fifteen years of getting corn-holed by some toothless Aryan Brotherhood motherfucker. No way was I going to pull *that* time."

"Didn't you think it was strange that they were killing sheriffs and drug dealers?" Warren said. "And nothing happened to them? ... No heat from the cops?"

"Fuck *no.* The DEA does whatever the fuck they want to do out here, man. Where you been, Jack? Who do you think is going to protect people like me from *them?* Huh? ... The *cops?* You think they care about people like me? *Shiiiit.* Wake the fuck up—this is L.A., Homes."

"You mean they were bent—Perry and Tucker?" Warren said.

"Fuck, yeah ... some of them are. Sure. The sheriffs that got hit were bent, too."

"You're sure?"

"Fuck, yeah, man. Everyone knew about those cats. They were some mean motherfuckers, too."

"What were they into. The sheriffs, I mean?"

"Heroin," Flaco said.

"They sold it?"

"Yeah."

"And did Perry and Tucker steal from them?"

"How the fuck should I know? I told you I *wasn't* there. I don't know. And do you think I'd tell *you* if I was!"

"Who did the sheriffs work for?"

"... That will cost you another five-hundred dollars," Flaco said. Warren looked at him a long time; it was a strange, blank look. Flaco noticed it and it bothered him because he couldn't read it.

"Okay, sure. ... I'll have to go to the bank for it, though."

"Go on, then. I'll wait here. I got nothing better to do."

"... No, you'd better come with me," Warren said. It was the way he said it that made Flaco suddenly realize the guy was dangerous. He had gotten a crazy look in his eye.

"You sure?"

"Yeah," Warren said, "I'm sure."

*　　　　　　*　　　　　　*

■ MEXICO CITY

Monsignor De Leon was handcuffed to a chair in the living room of a large, cold, and moldy-smelling mansion that the CIA kept in the hills above Mexico City. All the lights were on in the cavernous concrete and glass living room that had spectacular views of the sprawling mega-city. It was a very modern house, and had been built by a famous Mexican architect who'd worked on the original ideas for Brasilia, and had also once been featured on the cover of *Time* Magazine because Clare Boothe Luce, the famous wife of the magazine's owner, had loved his work.

"You can leave us," Malcolm said. The two men who had brought the priest in were from Mexican intelligence and were unaware of what the matter was about. The two often did favors for the American embassy unbeknownst to their nominal bosses—any cop, of any type, was for sale in Mexico. A trusted source inside Mexican intelligence—a woman—had called Malcolm and told him that De Leon had been picked up and sent to the address that Malcolm had requested. The safe house was in the *Pedregal* district.

"Where is this place?" De Leon asked, obviously frightened.

"Does it matter?" Malcolm said.

"I'm a friend, Malcolm. ... You know me—you've known me for years. And you, George ... You know me, too." The monsignor was starting to hyperventilate as he spoke to them.

"Yes, I do, Monsignor," Malcolm said.

"George is very angry with you, Alberto." Malcolm used the monsignor's first name.

"I don't understand? Why?" De Leon said.

"He wants to know about the Gehlen organization, and I think you know a great deal about it," Malcolm said.

"I don't understand. ... *What* organization?"

"Gehlen. We know you work for them, now. You see, we've checked your bank accounts. You received a deposit of five-hundred thousand dollars just a week ago; wire-transferred to your account from New York. *We* don't pay you that kind of money and I know the Brits don't, either. Nobody does—but Gehlen's people pay that much for information when it's *important*, don't they, Alberto?" Malcolm said.

"I'd like a glass of water. Please." De Leon said. Malcolm got up and went into the house's enormous and totally empty kitchen. While running the water, he heard a loud slap. The sound was quite distinct as it echoed through the house.

"George hit me," De Leon whined after Malcolm had come back to the room holding his glass of water.

"*George!*—did you hit a priest?"

"Yes, I did," George said.

"I told you, Alberto, George is angry," Malcolm said, as if talking to a child who had misbehaved.

"But I haven't done anything *wrong*." De Leon said, a pleading tone to his vice now.

"What did you do to *earn* that money, Alberto?" Malcolm asked.

"I'll tell you if you promise that you won't hurt me," De Leon said.

"Don't promise him that," George said. George made the request in a very strange tone of voice. "Do you know what we did with Japanese prisoners when we were lucky enough to catch one?" George said. "I haven't told this to many people because, well, it's not very pretty. But I want to tell you now, Alberto. ... I think you should know what we did. Are we completely alone here, Malcolm?"

"Yes; quite alone," Malcolm said. He held the glass of water against De Leon's lips and let him drink. When he was finished the monsignor looked at him. He'd been picked up coming out of church and was still wearing his vestments. His eyes were wet-looking from fear.

"... Malcolm, my friend ... George has gone mad. I've known him for years. I've been a friend to British intelligence—what's wrong!? Why am I here? Please tell me!"

"The money, Alberto? Five-hundred thousand US dollars wired into your account at Citibank? Where did it *come* from, Alberto?"

"Will you keep George away from me, Malcolm? Promise me that," the priest said.

"Yes. All right. ... Will you behave, George? At least until we hear what Alberto is going to tell us?"

"If I recall correctly, Alberto has a fondness for the good life," George said. George took off his jacket and put it neatly over the back of a chair, then he went into the kitchen and came back out with a boning knife he'd found there in a drawer—a wicked looking devil of a knife which had a blade that had been sharpened to almost the thinness of an ice-pick. When he saw it, the priest screamed like a woman for several minutes, twisting in the chair as if he'd already been stabbed and cut-up. They let him howl, since there was no one there to hear him, or care, either, for that matter.

"What's wrong, George? Why are you *treating* me like this? So mean. I'm a man of God," De Leon said, raggedly sniffling after he'd calmed down somewhat. He'd simply exhausted himself with his hysterics. His fat cheeks were red and wet from crying. All the time he'd been blubbering, George had been telling him in great detail just exactly what they'd done to their Japanese prisoners out in the jungle in Burma, going through every torture step by step, starting with pegging them to the ground so that all the jungle bugs could feast on them, just as a preliminary.

"I lost someone who was very close to me and I want to know *why*. I want to know exactly who was responsible for her death," George said very calmly.

"I told you he was angry, Alberto," Malcolm said.

"... ... I'm sorry, George. But, please—you're scaring me."

"Tell us, Alberto. This is the last time I'm going to ask you," Malcolm said.

"It was for making a simple call," the priest said.

"To *who*? About *what*, exactly?" Malcolm said.

"I was told by a man who said he worked for West German intelligence that the German's would pay me for any information about a certain KGB officer if he should contact me looking for a way to defect to the West. Anyone who said he wanted to make contact with the CIA, in fact."

"What was the KGB officer's name, Alberto?"

"Vladimir Putilin. He came to my church and asked for a pass through to your side. Just a week ago. So I called the man in Germany and told him this Vladimir had contacted me. That's all I did, Malcolm. ... I'm sorry—I have expenses and debts; I have a family, a wife—my children need things."

460

"A priest with a wife and children?" George said. "Do you have a daughter?"

"Yes, George, I do," the priest said.

"Well, good for you," George said. "Frankly, I didn't think you had it in you."

"And you told this man in Germany where this Vladimir was staying?" Malcolm asked.

"Yes."

"I say, that wasn't very nice of you, Alberto," George said.

"Right now I wish I hadn't—I wish I hadn't gotten involved at all."

"Who was the man in Germany?" Malcolm asked.

"His name is Hans. Hans Kamptner. I checked with people here I know in the West German Embassy to make sure that he was with the BND in Bonn. He's one of them, no question about it. I thought it was all right after that."

"You didn't wonder why an *ally* of the United States would be trying to interfere with a KGB officer who was trying to defect to the U.S.?" Malcolm asked.

"Only God knows what kind of double-dealing goes on with you people. I suspected he'd worked for the BND and they didn't want him to leave their employ. All of you people keep secrets from one another, don't you?" De Leon said.

"Did you know that the BND was headed by Reinhard Gehlen?" Malcolm said.

"Yes," Alberto said. "I'd heard various things about him over the years."

"You'd better leave now," George suddenly said to Malcolm.

"Why?"

"You should just go, Malcolm. I'm going to send a message to the Devil," George said. He took the knife and held it against the priest's neck. He heard Malcolm leave the room. The priest looked at him and began to sob.

"I'm going to give you two seconds to save yourself," George said.

"George, *please!*"

"One second. ... This Russian? Where is he? You've kept track, *haven't you?* Your job is to reel him in, isn't it? That's what *I* think, anyway." George placed the point of the knife on the man's neck and depressed the fat flesh to a depth of about one inch—any more pressure and the blade would sink in, and not just a little way, either. "It works very quickly, actually—the body empties *itself,* really," George said.

"Cuernavaca," the priest said. "George ... please! ... Cuernavaca. Hotel Mirador."

*   *   *

■ PLATA, BAJA CALIFORNIA

Here, this far north, the Sea of Cortez took on a strange, magnetic presence—night *or* day—as if it were alive and conscious of itself. It was a flat cerulean blue and slid in small waves towards Baja's forlorn black-sand beaches. The hundred-foot long grey jetty sat alone over the water, directly across from a rustic beach-side restaurant, and seemed to shimmer like a mirage. Or a giant bug that was caught in the surface tension of the water. This early in the morning, the water was still mercurial, and reflected the jetty's hoary and rotting pilings. A few rag-tag fishing boats sat randomly anchored along the beach. The end-of-the-world feeling of the seaside desert town was completed by an old, partially-sunken fishing boat that sat just offshore where a storm had stranded it the year before.

"My boat will be here at four," Sonny said. "There was a message from the skipper that came in via the doctor's CB radio a little while ago." They were sitting at an outdoor restaurant in the small town of Plata, State of Sonora, Mexico. It was a godforsaken village that had been founded solely to service the La Sangre silver mine a few miles inland to the west. The silver mine's refinery was belching a yellow, sulfurous-looking and -smelling cloud into the clean blue sky of Baja California del Norte. La Plata sat just fifty miles south of the Arizona border. The mine was owned by an American company that kept an airstrip near town so their executives could visit the mine on a regular basis.

"In the meantime, we have a problem," Sonny said.

"What?" the Hauptmann asked.

"Someone broke into my room at the hotel—they completely tossed it."

"When did this happen?"

"This morning," Sonny said. "While I was in the can, showering. Cheeky fuckers, weren't they?"

"I don't understand," the Hauptmann said. A young American, shirtless except for a jean jacket with the Vagos' "rocker"—the club's name embroidered on the lower back of the garment—rode his motorcycle by the restaurant, followed shortly by several more tough-looking young men, also on motorcycles. The loud roar of their engines disturbed the otherwise idyllic morning silence in the small village. Sonny had been told when they'd checked in at the hotel that there was some kind of motorcycle club there for the weekend, tripling the size of the town's population overnight. Since Sonny's company owned the hotel, rooms were made available for the two of them, despite that weekend's crush of visitors. As soon as Sonny learned that the motorcycle club had come to Plata, he was concerned that they were there

462

to rip him off. He knew the Vagos had an Italian connection, and also that the club was linked to the Italian intelligence service—an organization that was notoriously corrupt, even by *Italian* standards.

The Hauptmann looked at him.

"I thought you said this was a 'safe' place?" Neizert stated, with a strange look on his face.

Sonny shrugged. "Maybe it's changing—I don't know. ... Anyway, I'm not sure what to do, now, exactly. ... I can't very well call the police, now *can* I?" Sonny said.

"I'm afraid," the Hauptmann said.

"Don't worry about it: Tomorrow, you'll leave for Sonoyta with the good Doctor," Sonny said. "I'll fly out to Tucson with the old couple and meet you on the other side. You'll be in Tucson in just a few hours. They'll be waiting for you there ... the American agent, I mean."

"I won't go," The Hauptmann suddenly said. "They're here—Gehlen's people—I'm sure of it."

"*Who?*" Sonny had no idea what he was talking about.

"Gehlen's people. That's who sacked your room."

"Who's Gehlen?" Sonny asked.

"It doesn't matter who he is, really; it only matters that they won't let me leave here alive. They're here to kill me," the Hauptmann said.

"*Really.*"

"They've been trying to stop me ever since I left East Germany," the Hauptmann finally confessed to him. He didn't like this Delmonico gangster, and hadn't trusted him. But he was suddenly terrified for his life, and he wanted to confide in *some*one. He *needed* to, if he were to survive what he was sure was coming for him. "You've got to get a message out to Malcolm Law," the Hauptmann said, very tensely, leaning in toward Sonny over his breakfast.

"Who? I don't know any 'Law,' old man," Sonny said.

"*Malcolm Law,*" the Hauptmann repeated.

"You mean, the American?"

"Yes, *him!*"

"The man I know as Tucker?" Sonny said.

"The American who hired you to bring me to the states, yes—*him!*" Neizert was getting more and more agitated. He suddenly pushed the plate with his breakfast away from him. He had hated the ambience of this small, filthy, third-world town as soon as they'd stepped out of the Doctor's jeep the night before. The few dim electric lights; the miserable looking shopping strip with its dingy bars; a few ramshackle, fly-infested restaurants; the two brothels that served the miners and the American tourists who came there to fish—all of it repelled and disgusted him. The whorehouses blared Mariachi music all night. The constant sound of diesel generators reverberated through the fly-specked sea-stained Sodom and Gomorrah. Ribs-exposed curs snuck around the edges of old buildings eating shit if they found it. It was a truly horrible place, the Hauptmann thought—a place they could find him very easily. He'd had a recurring dream in which he died before he got to America, and his end always came somewhere in an anonymous desert in Mexico, a place he'd always associated with death and Indians and dirt. In his nightmare, he was walking toward the border in his bare feet through unbearably hot sand. Suddenly, out of the blue, he was shot by someone he never saw. In the dream he didn't die immediately, but laid there looking up at the blue sky and the circling vultures like he was in some cliché-ridden Hollywood Western.

"You can't stay *here*," Sonny said. "I have to leave with the old couple on the plane."

"... Call the American and tell him that *they're* here—in the town—Gehlen's people," the Hauptmann said.

"Nothing will happen to you if you go with the Doctor," Sonny said.

"The Doctor could be stopped by the police," the Hauptmann said. "I don't trust him."

"There are no police on the road to Sonoyta, and if there are, they know him," Sonny said "That's why we use him. He's got a Ministry of Health pass. He's allowed everywhere. You'll be fine. I'm sure of it. They'll wave you through."

"*I won't go alone with the doctor.* Call the American and tell them that they have to come and help or I won't cross at all," Neizert said. The Hauptmann got up then, his heart pounding, remembering his dream and truly afraid for his life. He didn't want to die here in Mexico, in this particular shit-hole. The idea of it scared him in a way he hadn't expected. It wasn't the fear of death, really—it was the fear of death in *this particular* godforsaken town. No, he wouldn't accept it. Not here, and not like this.

"I'll have to wait to use the pilot's radio. And that might not even work," Sonny lied. He had access to both a CB and a long-distance phone line but didn't give the German that information.

"Do you want to die here, too?" the Hauptmann asked.

"Not particularly," Sonny said. He looked down the beach toward the south; the direction his boat would come from. There were a few ATV's already out, racing down the huge, empty beach that seemed to lead nowhere but to other beaches that were even more solitary. The Hauptmann stood up and was obviously about to cross the beach and walk to the jetty. The rickety dock attracted him for some reason, but suddenly they heard gunfire in the distance and he froze before he could start across the dirt road that separated the restaurant from the beach.

They'd already made countless stops because the Mexican doctor's routine had to be followed exactly in case he was being watched by the DEA. The doctor made a circuit that covered the Sonoran coast from Guaymas to Puerto Penasco. Every day of his rounds, he was expected to be at either a different government *Ejido*, a particular small fishing village, or a certain mining town. Poor fisherman and miners had no money or transport to get to the hospital in Guaymas or Hermosillo, so they would simply wait for the traveling doctor to show up. Sometimes he came in time to save someone and sometimes he didn't. Many people died while their families watched anxiously for the doctor's jeep, or the hopeful sign of dust cloud in the distance, as the roads that far up the Gulf were all dirt, and any approaching vehicle could be seen from miles away. If the doctor didn't come in time, the dead would be carried back and buried in an anonymous desert cemetery and the doctor would only hear later that so and so had waited for him, but in vain.

From Guaymas they'd driven to Plata at night—something that was normally dangerous and ill-advised. The young Mexican doctor drove as if the devil were after them all the way to Plata in almost pitch blackness, because it was a new moon that night. The town was a back-of-beyond rathole and perfect for Sonny's purposes because it had a landing strip for small planes and a jetty for the boat that came up from La Paz. And, it was in striking distance of the U.S. border. The boat from La Paz was a Pierce Seiner, and it would sail up to Plata and unload the heroin with no problem at all because there was no authority controlling the dock at the small village. No DEA, no one at all. Sonny's men—the Plata police force—unloaded the heroin in full view of the fishermen, all of whom pretended to not watch the police loading green plastic-wrapped bundles into a pickup truck.

The police in Plata had been bought-off long ago, and acted as security. About a year before, when the newly-minted DEA landed agents at the airstrip, to do a general investigation of the area, they were told that the town was too far from Tijuana to be of any use to anyone in the drug business. The DEA agents, having come in with their Mexican government handlers, had taken one look at the miserable, fly-infested town, and had left immediately, sure that they were hearing the truth. It had helped that it was mid-July and a hundred and ten in the shade with no ice to be had anywhere at any price. The new DEA prided itself on its instincts, as they told their new Mexican friends, who had been paid off by Sonny's people, too.

"That's the mine. ... We're close, now," Sonny had said, seeing the lights of the La Sangre mine; an enterprise that went full-tilt 24 hours a day. "It's about ten minutes to town, now." Sonny's face and jacket were covered with a fine gold-colored road dust—the Hauptmann could see his dust-smudged face lit by the dashboard lights. "We've arrived, Herr Hauptmann. Welcome to Plata, Mexico—the devil's armpit," Sonny had said, glad to have finally arrived. He nodded toward the few miserable lights of a small desert town on the coast of the Gulf of California—the Sea of Cortez—just north of Nowhere. "Don't die here, old man, because you can't go to heaven from Plata. Saint Peter won't be able to find you." Sonny laughed at his own joke and took a hit off a beer before tossing the empty can out the window. The Hauptmann just looked at him. He was exhausted and his ass hurt from the constant smashing of the jeep's weak suspension as it bucked horribly over every rock and rut that had plagued them since they'd left the asphalt road twenty miles back.

They had all ended up drinking warm beer to keep hydrated, because they were out of water and there were no stores or gas stations this far north—only subsistence fishing villages that had nothing at all to sell. Most of the villages didn't even have a generator for intermittent electricity. It was still well over eighty degrees at ten P.M.. The sky was full of stars, the Milky Way in its full splendor. All the windows in the Jeep were open. All of them were a little light-headed from the beer and the constant pounding and careening of the jeep along the sandy road. The sand very deep at times and forcing the jeep left or right, as if the front end were being slapped. The young doctor was a good driver and maintained a constant forty-five miles per hour regardless of the obstacles in their way. The Jeep's headlights reached forward into a pitch-darkness that seemed solid and barely penetrable. On occasion they had to brake for horses and cows that were roaming wild in the unfenced brush, but the doctor took it all in stride and never let up on the gas.

The young Mexican doctor had chuckled under his breath at Delmonico's description of Plata.

"It is truly a place far from any God," the doctor said. "He's right. Even the whores in Plata don't want to be buried there. No one seems to have actually been born here, either."

"Everyone is a foreigner in Hell," Sonny said. He wiped his face. He'd been here countless times, knew the town well, and, oddly enough, actually liked the place. There was something about its being so perfectly forlorn and corrupt that made him appreciated the town the way a young priest might relish walking into *Notre Dame*. And, in fact, the town had been good to him for years since it was a completely safe transshipment point for his product. He loved to jump aboard the Peirce Seiner as it slipped into position at the dock, just to take a peek at all the bales of heroin that had come such a long, long way. It always excited him to cheat the devil one more time.

The doctor's redheaded French wife, only twenty-two, was asleep in the back of the Jeep. She seemed to be able to sleep despite all the horrible rattling and bucking. Nobody—not one single car or truck going either direction—had passed them for fifty miles. It was as if they were on a course to the center of Hell with a blue-black

466

void constantly looming on their left—the Sea of Cortez. Its salty breath and watery mass had been omnipresent throughout the trip. At times the headlights caught flashes of silver off the water as the phosphorescent crests of small waves broke on an isolated stretch of beach. If any of the occupants of the Jeep noticed either the beauty, or strangeness of their present situation in Nature, they made no comment: the vehicle simply pushed on through the blackness toward its destination.

The Jeep was pulling a trailer, and at times it swung back and forth behind them in a crazily unsafe fashion. The trailer actually belonged to the doctor, personally, although he was employed by the Mexican Ministry of Health. The trailer served as a mobile clinic-cum-waiting-room, all in one. There was a picture of the President of the Republic hanging on one wall of the trailer, just across from a stainless steel examination table that was bolted to the floor. The doctor had performed many major operations in the little trailer: everything from childbirth to a ruptured appendices; and of course he'd treated many cases of shark-bite, which were among his worst challenges, because usually the patient had already lost a great deal of blood by the time he finally saw them. According to what he told them en route, bullet wounds were actually the easiest to treat, normally; unless there were complications of some type. For as young as he was, he was a very good doctor. He'd gotten so much experience in just one year of traveling around and treating every kind of emergency that he seemed considerably older than his twenty-seven years. His dark eyes were now those of a veteran care-giver. As they drove along, he mused out loud that gore and guts no longer had any effect on him, emotionally-speaking. Of course he was a totally corrupt young man, but otherwise very intelligent and certainly not heartless. He carried the heroin shipments from Plata to the border, after picking them up off the Pierce Seiner from La Paz. He'd met his French bride in an upscale bar in Santa Monica, California, and had married her shortly thereafter because the desert and his job were both very lonely and he felt that he'd needed a wife to keep him company. She'd come to Mexico with him after deciding that she hated living in the intellectual and cultural desert that was L.A., and that she might as well try living the real thing for a while—it was bound to be more interesting, no matter the hardships. So far, she hadn't been disappointed in the latter.

They'd pulled up to an ancient hotel called Las Palmas. It looked like it belonged in a vintage Western. It was a two-storey bungalow with a large wooden front veranda that hadn't been painted for decades. What little paint remained on the outside was heavily blistered, and of an indeterminate color. The hotel had twenty rooms, all infested with bedbugs, which the maids tried their best to control by spraying continuously with "Flit." creating a terrifically poisonous DDT fug that managed to keep the bedbug infestation somewhat under control. The same couldn't be said for the cockroaches, that were legion.

"Well, here we are: Home sweet home," Sonny joked, getting out of the Jeep and knocking the dust off his pants and jacket with both hands, the way he'd learned to do in North Africa during the War.

48

■ PLATA, MEXICO

Sonny heard the loud and very familiar sound of swarming horse flies as he trudged through the sand towards the immobile Ford pickup truck. The truck's engine was still running possibly because there was no one left alive inside the bullet riddled cabin to turn it off. He reached for the driver's side door handle and noticed that the truck's windshield was completely blasted out, with only a milky white ring of glass left around the edges of the frame. The heavy truck door swung open to reveal a grisly mass of two bleeding, bullet-raked bodies, everything caked with a bluish-colored powder from the windshield's pulverized style safety glass. The gunfight had smashed every window in the truck.

He reached in and pushed the driver—a young police captain who he knew quite well—into an upright position. The captain's head lolled back against the seat's headrest and Sonny saw that the captain's eyes were now vacant fly-encrusted obscenities. He'd seen this kind of thing during the war in North Africa, but it still shocked him. The man's horrible death mask made his zeroed-out, mouth-open gaze into nothingness just that much more repellent. Sonny let go of the captain's shoulder ruefully watching his head fall back onto the steering wheel.

The police unit had been ambushed just east of town, on the sandy road heading to Plata's dirt airstrip less than half a mile away. Two of his subordinates had also been killed in the gunfight. One of them had jumped out of the truck and tried to run, but he'd been cut down only a few yards from the rear of the pickup, and had bled-out lying face down in the sand. The man sitting next to the captain had attempted to return fire, but he was now hanging out the window of the Ford sporting a gaping black hole in his face where his nose should have been, the back of his skull gone. The rest of the Plata police force—only two other men—had already left Plata, escaping their probable fate by commandeering the town's only other police vehicle. Sonny had driven out to the airstrip when he'd heard the shooting.

The inside compartment was a bloody mess. Sonny reached in and unsnapped the Captain's holster and took out the automatic pistol that he'd been unable to use. He took the key from the ignition and killing the still-idling engine. He walked back

469

to the enclosed bed of the truck and examined its contents. There were three AK-47s lying inside. He took the weapons out of the truck and put them in the welded-on basket that was attached to the ATV. He then started the ATV's engine, turned around, and drove back towards town. Everyone in town had heard the shooting quite clearly, but only Sonny had been brave enough to venture out to the airstrip.

On the way back to town, Sonny decided that the Hauptmann had probably been right, and he'd better call the Americans for help, a.s.a.p. He looked at his watch. The boat was expected to arrive at four that afternoon, with one hundred kilos of Sicilian heroin aboard. He had no police to temporarily safeguard it, now. He briefly pretended to himself that things were not as grim as they suddenly seemed and drove on into town, the weapons making loud rattling noises just behind him as he wound his way over the dunes. He drove straight to the police station and saw immediately that it had been abandoned. He went inside the building and picked up a white desk phone, placing a call to a switchboard operator and standing there tensely looking out onto the street as he spoke. He explained to the Mexican operator that he wanted to call Great Britain. The operator took the number and told him to hold the line. He sat casually down on the edge of the dead police captain's desk and waited, with the door to the office standing wide open, not sure at all what would happen next.

"Wally—is that you, old man?"

"Beer Monster, you sound like you're talking from down the hole of a Turkish crapper."

"It's Mexico. It's all gone to shit here in P."

"Really?"

"Yes. I'm sure things can't go the way we've planned, now."

"Right. Okay. ..."

"Better call the Yanks on this one, in fact."

"And the old couple, then ... did they fly in?"

"No. And they probably *won't*, now, is *my* guess," Sonny said.

"I see," Wally said.

"If they don't see our boys on the field—which they won't, now—I doubt that they'll land."

"What happened to them—our boys?" Wally said.

"Had a problem they couldn't resolve," Sonny said.

"I see."

"So that means I've got to use the doctor," Sonny said.

"Well, it could be worse; I suppose—you could be married to the wrong boy," Wally joked.

"... *Wally*. I'm afraid there are others that would like to wipe up our drippings." Sonny said this in a very serious tone of voice, so Wally would understand that he was not kidding, at all, about things having gone south.

"We can't allow that to happen," Wally said. "Yanks it is, then. Don't move, old man. In P., are you?"

"Yes. I'm waiting for the boat. It will be here soon."

"Right. ... Hold onto our goods, Beer Monster," Wally said.

"... I'll do my best," Sonny said. "I do believe I'm finally too old for all this shit." But Wally had rung off before he heard his final comment.

Sonny put the phone down and looked outside at the dirt street in front of the police station. He noticed a very old lady, walking barefoot, her skin the color of worn mahogany, carrying a blue ceramic pail that contained a lunch she'd packed for her husband, a fisherman who'd soon be back in port, and would be expecting to see her waiting there for him with the other wives. She was looking curiously into the police station at Sonny, with what he interpreted as the look that comes over a person's face just before they raise an alarm. Sonny raised his hand and waved at her, but his hand happened to have a gun in it. She quickly hurried on off down the dirt street toward the dock. Sonny slid off the desk and proceeded to unlock the station's weapons room, using the dead police captain's keys. He looked for hand grenades, found them, then filled up a desk drawer with them. He took the drawer and walked out of the building, then carefully filled the side basket of the ATV with grenades. He went back in and found some extra clips and boxes of ammunition for the AK 47's, then came back out to his green four-wheeler. A group of children had gathered around the vehicle and were watching him.

"*Policía?*" a young girl asked. She was barefoot and wearing a bathing suit that was tattered and filthy. He could see where the sea salt from an ocean bath she'd taken earlier in the day had dried on her legs, leaving traces of white crystals on her brown skin.

"*Si, policía especial,*" Sonny said as he got onto the four-wheeler and took off, having forgotten to shut the police station door behind him. It now stood wide open for the children's inspection. He drove on out to where he'd hidden the Hauptmann. *Why were they* waiting *to kill the Hauptmann?* The only possible answer to that question became clear to him as he drove: they were waiting for someone else to arrive. Someone who wanted to speak with the Hauptmann before he was killed. He suddenly sped up. Gusts of the warm afternoon air were hitting him in the face like a closely-spaced series of random slaps with a wet rag. His one eye was stinging fiercely from the sweat dripping down his forehead.

471

*　　　　　　　　　*　　　　　　　　　*

The DEA agent pilot called Alex into the cockpit of a Beechjet 400A. Malcolm was on the radio and wanted to talk to him. The pilot handed Alex the earphones. His father's voice came over the ether.

"Alex—there's a Russian KGB officer on the way to Plata to either kill or capture Neizert, I don't know which, at this point, so we have to assume he's coming to *kill* him. You have to kill *him* before he gets to our man. He's alone right now, but he might be meeting with help there in Plata. His name is Vladimir Putilin: I don't know what name he's traveling under, though." After the end of their conversation, Alex took the earphones off his head, gave them back to the pilot, then walked back to the passenger cabin.; the sound of the corporate jet's engines very smooth sounding. They flew directly over Mazatlan as he slid back into his seat next to Gemma, who was still reading the book on Mexican history that he'd bought her at the hotel.

The DEA plane had picked them up in Cuernavaca and taken all four of them on a three-hour flight up the Pacific coast. Sonny Delmonico had met them at the dirt airstrip in Plata and taken them to a godforsaken hotel in a local taxi. So much had seemed to have happened in only the last hour that Alex was sure it was a bad dream, and that he would suddenly wake up lying in the hammock back in Cuernavaca, where he'd hung around in just a bathing suit reading pulp fiction for a solid week, sleeping whenever he felt like it, making love to Gemma whenever the notion struck him, and going to the pool or downtown for lunch.

Sometimes he would think back to his time with Patty. He missed her very much. The four of them were living at the hotel like they were rich college students on vacation. It had been a very carefree time, and the knowledge that Gemma was pregnant with his child making him feel about as good as he'd ever felt in his entire life. He really loved her, though, in a different way than he'd loved Patty. He and Patty had been very similar in most of their thinking—Gemma was extremely different in that respect, and strange to him in many other ways as well. He had secretly begun making plans for his new family. A wife, children, a house somewhere, all the fantasies and daydreams that belonged to youth that he'd missed out on while he'd been a miserable soldier in this coldest of cold wars, the one in his head. It had all changed for the better, now, he thought. He had an actual, real, *purpose,* now; a clear direction in which to take his life. He'd felt like new man, in fact—until Gemma had sat him down and confessed everything to him just a moment ago.

They had checked into the hotel. Their room had neither air conditioning nor a bathroom. It smelled of Flit and stale sheets that were yellow with age.

"Where is he *now?*" Alex asked. He felt as if all the blood had been suddenly drained out of him, his body a husk suddenly, totally sapped of any strength.

"I don't know. ... I hope he's on his way here," Gemma said.

"So, it's not mine. ... The baby?" Alex said.

"... No ... it *is* yours. The baby is yours," Gemma said, telling him the truth.

"But you love this Russian?" Alex said, trying to take it all in, suppressing the urge to just run out of the room, or worse, grab her and, somehow—and no matter how pathetic—force her to love him the way he wanted her to.

"Yes," Gemma said. "Yes, I love him. I've been in love with him for a long time. I had to tell you—I just couldn't let this go any further."

"So all of it was a lie. ... You were part of a KGB intelligence operation."

"Yes," she said. "I told him where we were going. I'm sure he'll come here."

The idea that he was going to be a father had been crushed to death inside of him. Again, he wanted to bolt from this room that smelled of bug spray and leave her behind forever. He looked for the shoes that he'd taken off, wanting to lie down and rest.

"He's really a KGB officer?" Alex asked again, still not really believing what she'd just told him. He saw a cockroach slowly climbing the wall by the door to the hall. He reached over and slapped it with his open palm, leaving bug guts smeared over the palm of his hand.

"Yes, he really is."

"I see. ... Brilliant work of them, actually. A fabulous ploy. Based on solid knowledge of human frailty. My respects." He spoke while looking at her and wiping his hand on his jeans. "So all of it was ... the time in Sicily ... everything was a lie—the way you acted, what you told me you felt for me, everything? ..."

"Yes," she said. "I don't know what else to say. I'm terribly sorry. Bruce, you're a good man. Alex ... I mean. I couldn't lie to you any more. I like you; a lot. I *care* about you, Alex. That's why I just couldn't do it any more" He walked out of their room, then stood hesitantly for a moment in the narrow hallway feeling completely lost. He could hear voices speaking in Spanish downstairs at the front desk.

Delmonico came up the stairs. When they'd landed and he saw Butch deplane, he'd felt much better about whatever was coming. Just the man's presence instilled confidence. Now, looking at Tucker, he wondered what kind of man *he* was. Sonny had a Kalashnikov slung over his shoulder. His white coat was filthy, covered in the gold-colored road dust from riding on the four-wheeler.

"Where is he ... Neizert, I mean?" Alex said.

"I've hidden him in a safe place," Sonny said. "He's out of harm's way, for the present, anyway."

"Do you have a *plan?*—I've got to get him out of here, somehow," Alex said.

"I need some help down at the jetty first," Sonny said.

"*What?*"

"I've got to have some security for my product," Sonny said.

"You mean the heroin?"

"It'll arrive here shortly. I'm afraid my regular security has been delayed— *indefinitely* delayed. There could be trouble. It seems that some fellows are sitting around just waiting for my boat to arrive. I can't have that. If they want to take it, I suppose now is their best time to make a move."

"I don't care about the heroin," Alex said.

"Then I'm afraid you can't have your Hauptmann," Sonny said. "You see, I *thought* you might not want to help me."

"Is that the way it's going to be?" Alex said.

"I'm afraid so, old man," Sonny said.

"... I'll get Perry to straighten this out, then," Alex said.

"You mean Butch. There's no reason to hide anything from me, now," Sonny said. "His name is Butch. And I know that you two work together and that he's an officer in the CIA. ... None of that matters to me. I've got some four-wheelers that I've organized out in front. It's the quickest way to get through the dunes around here. I don't think we should take any of the streets now, frankly, unless we want to get shot." Sonny looked at his watch: it was almost four P.M., and he expected the boat would be close to arrival. Alex walked down the hall and banged on Butch's door.

"Hey. ... There's been a change of plans, dickhead. Open the fucking door."

*   *   *

"What about our informant, the Mexican kid ? ... He could be helpful." Muller was watching the door to the golf club's restaurant very closely, hoping to see someone he knew and could signal to help him out of the bind he suddenly found himself in. He knew Talbot's pistol was pointed at him under the table. *The man is obviously insane,* Muller thought. He was the chief of the DEA's Los Angeles field office and thought that he was the last person in the *world* who could be assaulted in this manner.

"He's disappeared," Detective Talbot said. It was a calculated lie that Warren had decided to tell his superiors and anybody else connected with the investigation of his

474

wife's death. "Did you have him killed? ... Did you? You know, I'd like nothing better than to blow a hole in you right now," Warren said.

He was using a tone of voice that was very gentile and would not be overheard by someone at another table. Warren's quiet tone made him seem doubly crazy to Muller. The detective reached over and took the glass of ice water from in front of Muller and took a long drink from it. "I'm not sleeping well, you see, and I get irritable. Small things. Just small things do it to me. Guys on the freeway who look at me funny. ... DEA fat-cats who lie to my face. I just want to blow a hole in them, and watch them die right there. It's not my fault. ... You see, Uncle Sam sent me to Vietnam when I was nineteen. I killed a lot of people over there. ... It's nothing to me. Killing you would mean nothing to me. My wife, she got me to change; you know, relax a little. ... Live a normal life. I think it's losing the one person in life I truly loved that changed me back. It's not good for you. It puts a lot of stress on a man—thinking all day about that, what happened to her I mean. Was she scared? Did she call my name and I wasn't there?"

Warren put the almost empty glass of ice water against his cheek and closed his eyes for a moment; the pain of his loss obvious on his face. Muller thought about jumping him right then, but held back; actually, he was terrified. He'd never been a brave man and he was paying for it now. His fear of being shot dead was overpowering a frantic desire to act. Instead, he'd had the coward's typical reaction—a lame hope that things would somehow eventually resolve themselves in his favor.

"I see. ..."

"What is it you see? You bent fuck," Warren said. "Do you see yourself dying here in on the floor of a fancy golf club? Do you see *that*, asshole?" He put the now empty glass down in front of him.

"Don't be unreasonable, Detective."

"I'm not being 'unreasonable,' *moron*. ... Right now, the only things I want to know are: *who* killed my wife, and *why*? That's all, *Mister* Muller. That's *all* I care about, really. When I find the answers to those two questions, I'm going to kill the people responsible for my wife's death, so you'd better convince me right *now* that you're not one of them!"

"I don't know anything about it. ... Your wife's 'murder.'"

"... Really? But you personally covered up the killings of two L.A. County Sheriff's deputies, for starters. That's what I heard, anyway."

"You're way over your head here, Detective—believe me," Muller said. Warren pulled his chair closer into the table speaking even more quietly, as if they were just two businessmen discussing a secretive deal.

"I really don't give a shit if you think I'm 'over my head' or not—I'm going to get the answers to those questions; either from you or somebody else, so you'd better start talking, and telling me the truth or I'm going to shoot you right here in this fucking restaurant, right now."

"Detective: if I were you, I'd just turn around and walk out of here. I would just go *home*, while you still can. I'll forget I ever saw you here, I promise," Muller said, pretending he wasn't terrified.

"So you can have *me* killed, too, later this afternoon?—or maybe you'll even give me the courtesy of waiting until tonight? ... Nice club, man. Very expensive, I suppose," Warren said. They were sitting in the dining room of a very elite golf club where, to even be considered for membership, another rich member had to recommend you to a board of other, yet *more* important, members. They were the kind who sat in the new air-conditioned, imperial, corporate big-dick office towers on Wilshire Blvd. or in downtown LA. *Men in tasseled Nordstrom six-hundred dollar loafers and glamour suits, with The Big Job, who looked down on everyone and everything below them,* Warren thought. He stared a hole through the golf-attired professional pencil-neck desk-jockey sitting across from him who he knew was terrified of being shot, and who he very much *wanted* to shoot. *He's no soldier. He's just a scared fucking rat.*

"Who *are* these guys, Tucker and Perry? They somehow managed to *not* have their mug shots taken after they were arrested. How can *that* be, eh? When I call the DEA and try and contact them I was told to call Washington headquarters. When I call Washington ... I'm told to call *you* here in L.A."

"They're DEA special agents," Muller said.

"I don't think so," Warren said. "DEA agents can be gotten on the phone. They're not *ghosts*. These two guys are *ghosts*—I don't get that."

Warren had walked into the exclusive golf club unannounced and without an invitation, and because he was white man of a certain age group, no one gave him a second glance. He'd found Muller exactly where the man's wife had told him he'd be after he'd called him at home, but she'd answered instead of her husband. He'd gotten Muller's home number from a friend of his who worked for the DEA in San Diego—a guy by the name of Vincent Calhoun who'd been in the Marines with Warren and was now heading up the DEA's Tijuana operations.

"You tell me why my wife was murdered and I'll leave you out of this. You can start with the killing of the two deputies. I'll shoot you right here if I have to—I'm not kidding, at all," Warren said. Muller looked around him. The place was full of entertainment lawyers, movie agents, and TV executives—not cops with guns. It was the kind of place where Talbot knew he could drill Muller in the head and walk out clean, with everyone giving a different description of the shooter later because they'd been busy shitting their pants at the time. He suddenly kicked Muller in the shins under the table. He watched Muller flinch from the pain, and was now sure that he'd finally gotten the man's attention in a serious way.

"I'm going to shot you in the balls first. I promise you that's going to hurt a lot because I've seen it happen and heard the people scream. I guess it's all the nerves and shit there in your nut-sack. ..."

"COINTELPRO," Muller blurted.

"What's *that?*" Warren said.

"It's a Defense Department channel that we use to cooperate with the CIA in domestic situations, when they ask us to."

"So you're saying what?" Warren said.

"Perry and Tucker are CIA officers," Muller said.

"And they were allowed to *kill* L.A. County Sheriff's deputies and get away with it?"

"Yes. The two sheriffs were crooked as hell," Muller said. "I understand there was even a gunfight involved."

"What do you mean, exactly, by 'crooked?'"

"The sheriffs were selling drugs for a gang out of Bakersfield."

"What's that got to do with the CIA?" Warren said.

"I don't *know*—and that's the truth. Look: If you want to get along, move up in the DEA, you have to play ball with the CIA when they call on you to do something for them. It's as simple as that. I didn't ask any questions about it. I don't *know* who killed your wife, Talbot. That's the God's honest truth."

"Who were the deputies working for, *exactly?*" Warren asked.

"As far as I know, it was the Vagos motorcycle club."

"Those *bikers?*"

"Yes," Muller said.

"Are you going to call the CIA now and tell them about me?" Warren asked.

"No," Muller said. "I don't want to be involved in your problem, at all."

"Fair enough. I'll kill you if you do it, and I *will* find you. ..."

"... I'm sorry about your wife, detective, truly I am." Muller said.

"*Everyone* is. That doesn't help me, though—being sorry. This COINTELPRO ... what's it about, anyway? Who actually runs the fucking thing?"

"Here in LA the FBI field office runs it. They're the ones that provide the manpower, anyway. They *use* us, but they don't actually *trust* us. So we never get told shit about anything important. We just do what they tell us to do, and that's it."

"You mean the FBI doesn't trust the DEA?"

"That's exactly right."

"That's fucked up," Warren said.

"It's just the way it is."

"Why is my wife dead?"

"I truly don't know, Detective. I would tell you if I did, believe me."

"Is it because I was looking into those shootings at the Capri Motel?"

"Yes, I think that's the reason. The Capri Motel case—the shootings, I mean—has been completely taken over by the FBI—we've been frozen out of it since about day two. It's now marked COINTELPRO. I was told not to follow up on anything related to it. They know that the L.A. County Sheriff's Department is trying to investigate."

"So that's why we were told not to bother; that the FBI was on it and *they'd* solve it."

"Correct. You should have left it alone, Talbot."

"I was curious as to how three people could be shot down right in the middle of Malibu and no one wanted to investigate it," Warren said. "The FBI didn't do shit."

"Now you know why."

"Not really."

A Latin waiter came over and asked if Warren would care to order lunch. The detective abruptly stood up and walked out of the dining room. He located his grimed-up Ford "Country Squire" station wagon in the middle of a parking lot that was full of the new Mercedes and BMWs that all the entertainment-industry types drove. He drove out of the parking lot and headed back to his office so he could use the National Police Computer Network before they could lock him out of the system.

*   *   *

■ PLATA, MEXICO

"Where's our German, Sonny?" Butch said.

"He's put away for safe-keeping." Sonny pointed down the street. "You've seen the motorcycle gang that's here for the weekend—fun and games isn't all they're here for. Right now, they're all partying down there in those two taverns.

"Say what?"

"They've already killed all the police that were in this little shit-hole—working for me, by the way, three of them, anyway—and now they're waiting for my product to get to the jetty so they can steal it," Sonny said.

Butch walked to the window. He'd come to Sonny's room to discuss a deal he wanted to try. He looked out through the fly-specked glass of the hotel window to the dirt street. There were forty, maybe even fifty, bikes parked in front of a saloon called

Mr. Frogs.

"They want my product," Sonny said. "And probably your Hauptmann, too, although I'm not sure just why yet."

"Who?"

"Your German, man—they want him, too."

"And you want me and Alex to help you do what?"

"I need to get my product to Sonoyta," Sonny said. "I'll make you a deal. I'll pay you five-hundred thousand dollars to help get the heroin to Sonoyta," Sonny said.

"I think that the odds on doing that are definitely *not* in our favor, from the way things look out there right *now*," Butch said, turning away from the window.

"They usually aren't in this business," Sonny said. "But there *are* four of us." Butch laughed at Sonny's warped sense of humor.

"What are we supposed to do—throw rocks at them?" Butch said.

"I've got some weapons: Some AKs, some grenades, and some pistols," Sonny said.

"Five-hundred thousand—no shit?" Butch turned around again and looked down on the street.

"Yes, that's the amount," Sonny said.

"All right," Butch said. "For that, we'll do it. Where is it—the money?"

"You have to trust me on this one, my friend. I'll pay you when we get to the States. I promise. You can even have it in cash if you want. It's all there in Tucson." Butch rubbed his chin. He hadn't shaved in a few days.

"Okay, then," he said, studying the layout below and down the street from where they were standing in the room. "Okay why the fuck not? But where's the German? I've got to get him. That's what they want ... *my* guys. If I give them the German they'll be happy."

"He's stashed in a well," Sonny said.

"A *well*?"

"Yeah—fifty feet down, where it's nice and cool," Sonny said.

"No shit," Butch said, impressed once again with Sonny's improvisational abilities. Just then he saw the girl he'd almost shot in the Vagos club house— the sexy redhead—come out of the bar across the street with another man, an older man who was obviously not a biker. He looked like an intelligence officer—he was nondescript, but had a certain air of authority about him.

"He's as safe as houses," Sonny said from behind him. "... No one will find him— including you, if you want to waste your time looking."

"Let them *have* the dope ... when the boat gets here," Butch said.

"What?" Sonny said.

"Let them *have* the dope. Let them take it off the boat."

"Why?"

"Because I got an idea," Butch said.

"Is it a really *good* idea? ... Because I've counted quite a few of them, and there are only four of us," Sonny said.

"I don't know, yet," Butch said. "If we're still alive tomorrow then it was a good idea." He was watching the two talk as they stood out in front of the bar just across the street from their hotel. *I should have shot that bitch when I had the chance back in L.A.*

"I see," Sonny said.

"I need you to get a message to the boat that's bringing the dope. Tell them to hold off coming here to Plata for a little while. Can you do that?" Butch said.

"I thought you said you wanted them to off-load the product here," Sonny said.

"I want them to *think* they're off-loading the stuff, is all," Butch said. "Do the bikers know what the boat looks like?"

"No, I don't think so."

"Okay, then. Good. You said there was a working silver mine near here, right?"

"Yes. The old La Sangre mine. That's why they call the town Plata. It means silver."

"Okay. Let's go to the mine. I'll explain my plan on the way. We better take everybody along with us. And we'll need another boat," Butch said. "Let's go turn some sliver into gold," he said, then he turned around and walked out of the room.

*　　　*　　　*

The sky far above the Hauptmann's current location was a blue, stationary circle, twenty-five feet above his head. At times, during the day before, he'd seen distant clouds passing overhead. Two scorpions had crawled down the wall of the well, but he'd been able to kill them with his shoe. At night he assumed there would be more coming down. That morning there'd been several moving around his feet when it was light enough that he could finally see them. He'd killed six altogether. The stress of waiting for more of the creatures to climb down the dry walls of the dry well was starting to get to him. He'd had no food and water for over a day, and he'd reached an hallucinatory state.

The previous night, the temperature had dropped into the thirties at the bottom of the well, and he'd nearly frozen to death. The Hauptmann had seen a boy and then a donkey, and that was *all* he'd seen since Delmonico had lowered him into the well the previous afternoon. The well was located on a government *ejido* that had failed years before. The entire *ejido*—thousands of acres of desert—had never bloomed with anything more than government promises. The buildings that still stood presented their hoary, concrete faces to the world, with open-doors for mouths. There was nothing left but empty and blistered concrete-block buildings, rusted-out tractors, and a lingering sense of forgotten lives and abandoned hope. The water the government had promised had never been found. There was no aquifer under that barren land. The one well that the men had dug had come up dry.

The boy had dropped a red plastic bucket down the well and had almost hit Neizert on the head. He'd been asleep on his feet at the time. The well was dry, but the boy, who was helping to dry fish at the *ejido,* was from Tijuana and didn't know that fact. He looked down the mouth of the well after he heard the bucket hit the sand and the Hauptmann's groan.

"I'm sorry Señor—are you okay?" the boy had asked.

"Yes."

"Has caido, Señor?" the boy asked in Spanish, putting his hands on the edge of the well. "Did you fall?" he'd asked.

"No—forget you saw me here, boy," the Hauptmann said in English, not understanding. "Go away!" The boy looked down at him a moment longer and then disappeared. Two or three hours later, near noon, a donkey looked over the edge of the well in hopes of finding water, having smelled the faint trace of moisture that had wafted up into the desert air from Hauptmann's open canteen. The two stolidly regarded each other until the donkey finally lost interest turning away to continue his search for water else where. A half-hour after that Hans Kamptner looked over the edge of the well.

"This was your idea, Hauptmann?"

" ... Yes," Neizert said.

"You learned it during the War, didn't you?" Hans asked, looking down at him.

"Yes, again," the Hauptmann said

"On the Eastern Front, eh?" Hans said.

"Yes."

"I did, too," Hans said, and smiled. "I was thinking back to that time just this morning while I stirred my coffee. I started to realize that we had had many of the same experiences. I was in the *Liebstandarte* Adolf Hitler, too, you know."

"Are you going to kill me now?" Neizert asked from below.

"Not right away, no," Hans said. Then he disappeared from view. The Hauptmann heard the sound of a four wheeler. He sprung onto the wall and began to climb towards the opening by placing his feet on either side of the concrete tube. But each time he tried to move up, his feet gave way and he fell back to the sandy bottom, still littered with dead scorpions.

49

■ LOS ANGELES

Warren counted the number of motorcycles in front of the house twice. There were seven in all. Three were parked in the driveway. Three were parked on the dead lawn, and one was parked illegally on the sidewalk.

The Vagos' safe house, located in the seething suburban morass of the San Fernando Valley, looked like most of the other outlaw motorcycle gang safe-houses that Warren had seen—and even raided—over the years, while working in the Vice Squad. It was a nineteen twenties-style bungalow with a wide porch, a shingled roof, and white trim around the windows. It was a nice family house in a lower middle-class neighborhood, in fact. Seen from the street, the safe house was framed by a newer six-unit apartment building to its right, and a similar bungalow to its left. Warren wondered what the neighbors had said to each other the day the Vagos had moved in.

He'd been assigned to the Vice Squad right out of the Academy, working the prostitution and strip-club scenes, and he'd quickly found out that most of them were run by outlaw biker clubs: the Vagos, Mongols, and Hell's Angels were the major players in that underground world. They all had "safe" houses like the one he was now looking at—places where gang members could crash and keep a low profile if they were on the run from either the authorities or other outlaws that they had beefs with. The houses also provided legal, verifiable addresses for parole officers to visit; officers who otherwise could, and oftentimes did, revoke paroles if they couldn't account for the whereabouts and/or actions of their charges.

The employment status of most of the parolees was normally written-up as "bartender" or "bouncer," and was also legally verifiable because the businesses were, in fact, owned by the Vagos' business organization. Usually houses like this one contained little or no furniture—just a few mattresses casually strewn around on the floors of the different rooms. This house was typical in that way, and shared the general derelict quality that all these places had in spades. Looking the place over Warren realized that he'd always hated outlaw motorcycle clubs on principle alone. Lorie had called them "The Klan on bikes" once, when a large group of customized hogs and their studiedly grimed and disheveled riders had passed them on the freeway. They'd both laughed about it at the time, he now remembered. Thinking back to those very, very good times with Lorie at this particular moment served only to feed the red-rage and bloodlust that had been building inside him for the past few days; a desire to mete out a very painful vengeance for her death on anybody he found to be even remotely connected with it. He'd decided that there were at least seven men in the house; probably more.

It was only eight A.M., and he imagined that they were all probably still asleep. He'd gotten the last known address of the man who he suspected was Lorie's actual assassin off the police computer at work. The guy's street-name was "Fat Joe." He'd gotten out of San Quentin just six months ago, and for that reason, had to keep a permanent address on file with his parole officer, and this particular house was it. He now felt pretty sure that Fat Joe was sleeping inside the house at that very moment, and with that feeling, the adrenaline had started to flow through his veins in a way that portended considerable ill for Fat Joe.

Warren sat there in his car listening to a local AM radio station, where the DJ was enthusiastically, and with demographically-verified and market-driven panache, delivering the weather report for the Greater Los Angeles Basin: according to the slick DJ It was going to be another official "Spare-the-Air" day in the Southland. The woman's voice segued to a up-beat and very saccharin jingle—the backbone of American AM radio—a catchy ditty about the "Carpet-Hero" company's ability to magically zap your pet's poo-poo stains and make them vanish without a trace.

Then Paul Harvey's program came on, Warren reached over and switched Harvey off immediately, turning the dial to find another station—the old announcer's obviously fake, cob-assed, pseudo-folksy delivery had always annoyed him, ever since he could remember first listening to the old-wingnut bigot, back when he was still in high school. Maybe it was just the muggy weather that morning. Or maybe it was the fact that, whenever she'd heard him, Lorie would make fun of Harvey's outrageously-stagey delivery. But his wife wasn't there now to make Paul Harvey's trademark pauses funny anymore. He suddenly turned the radio off. He knew now he stood at the edge of an abyss: *Maybe, if I'm lucky, in thirty minutes, by the time Paul Harvey has wrapped it up for the day, Fat Joe and I will both be dead.*

"I miss you, baby," Warren said out loud. He turned and looked over at his wife. She was smiling at him. He had starting seeing her more and more, lately. She looked absolutely real to him, as if she were still alive and sitting next to him in the car.

"What are you *doing*, Warren?" she asked.

"I'm going in there and find out who killed you."

"Why?"

"Because I have to. *They* know who ... you know ... shot you, when they actually meant to shoot *me*."

"It won't do any good, honey," she said.

"Yes, it will. Anyway, I have to either do *something*, or. ..."

"Or *what*, baby?" Lorie asked him. She reached for his hand and held it and looked at him "Why are you suffering so?"

"I'm sorry this happened," he said. "I don't have anyone to talk to, now. Nobody. And I don't *want* to talk to anyone, really. That's the worst part. The loneliness. And I know it's never going to go away. You're the only one whoever made it stop, and now you're gone. ..."

"You should let that Mexican boy in the trunk go, Warren. Stop all this foolishness right now."

"I can't let him go. ... I can't stop it."

"But he's suffering back there," Lorie said.

"So am I, up *here*," Warren said.

"Still, he's somebody's son, Warren," she said.

"How come we ... you know ... didn't have any kids?" She didn't answer him. She gave him a penetrating albeit ambiguous look, then she was gone. He thought a moment about letting Flaco go, but he was sure the little Mexican would tell the Vagos—or someone connected to them—that he'd given Fat Joe's name to him. The Mexican kid would immediately connect Warren to the killing that he planned on doing in that house.

"Shit!" Warren again said out loud. He picked up the tire iron from the floor of the passenger side of the car and got out. He went to the trunk and opened it. He'd put the little Mexican snitch in a long, burlap cotton-picker's sack that he and Lorie had found on a trip to Georgia, and had kept for hauling things to the dump. The Mexican was small, and he fit into the sack quite easily. Warren had tied the top of the sack closed with a wire-tie after he'd handcuffed Flaco and made him crawl into it.

"Let me out." Flaco spoke to him from inside the sack. Warren raised the iron bar over the already badly-stained old sack, intending to smash it down on the kid's head and kill him right then and there.

"You're going to tell them all about me, aren't you." Warren stated it as a fact, not a question.

"No, I won't—I promise," Flaco said from inside the sack, not realizing he was about to be killed.

"You'll tell the Vagos, or *some*body," Warren said. "You're a fucking dope fiend; you couldn't keep your mouth shut if your life depended on it."

"I'm finished with all this kind of life," Flaco said. "Let me go, man! I've had a enough—I'm not kidding you, *ese*." Warren held the tire iron up above the sack, poised to brutally smash it down, for what seemed like an eternity. He knew the kid was lying but he just couldn't do it; not that way. He couldn't kill him in cold blood and he knew it. Instead, he put the tire iron down and undid the wire-tie, then he pulled the sack down from around the kid's head so they could see each other.

"I've decided to let you go," Warren said.

"Okay," Flaco said, a tremendous relief obvious in his voice.

"Don't tell anyone I was here—Understand?"

"Okay, I understand," Flaco said.

"Give me your hands." Flaco moved his cuffed hands up through the bag and Warren proceeded to unlock the cuffs.

"Where *are* we, anyway?"

"We're at a Vagos safe-house. Fat Joe is in there right now," Warren said.

"*Jesus,* Warren!" Flaco looked around. "Fuck man, that's crazy!"

"Get out. ... Go on home. ... You *got* a home, kid?"

"Yeah, I got a home." Flaco climbed out of the trunk. "Fuck, Warren—I thought you were going to kill me. Damn, man. I pissed myself in there. You put a human being in a sack like a fucking chicken, Warren."

"I *was* going to kill you, but I just couldn't bring myself to do it," Warren said.

"... Go on. Go home. Stop taking drugs or you're going to kill *yourself.*" He suddenly felt compassion for the kid. And a real sense of horror at what he'd almost done to him. He realized now that he wasn't right in the head. Not really. He'd gone crazy and he knew it, now.

"... What are you *doing* here, man?" Flaco said.

"Fat Joe is in there. ... The guy you said probably killed my wife is *in* there. That's what you told me."

"Yeah. ... But you can't just go in *there.* They'll kill you, man. You're just one old white guy to them."

"Maybe ... but I'm only forty three," Warren said, defensively. He turned around and walked off towards the door to the house. Flaco watched the balding older white man walk up to the house and climb the steps to the porch. He rubbed his wrists where the cuffs had been.

"Warren!" Flaco saw him turn around and look back at him. "Don't do it, man!" Warren looked at him and smiled. It was the smile of a crazy man, Flaco thought. "Motherfucking *white man!* You crazy, *carnal!*" Flaco turned and was going to walk down the street, as quickly as he could without attracting attention, to get away from that place. Then he felt himself stop. It suddenly occurred to him that his whole life had somehow been summed-up to this one particular moment—everything he'd ever done—and he'd finally reached the last crossroad. He knew that if he took one more step away from that house, he would never change; he'd be Flaco-the-dope-fiend for the rest of his life. It was as if a powerful force were gripping him and twisting him inside, both mentally and physically. He sagged to his knees and looked up at the sky. He remembered looking up at the sky as a child and wondering about all the great things he was going to do with his life—important things, he thought back then. He would have a family, and he would be a doctor or a lawyer or an astronaut. Never once did he think he would become what he had become.

"Mother fucker!" Flaco said. He looked down at the sidewalk a few inches from his nose and saw a trail of ants marching resolutely along, carrying tiny pieces of mysterious things. When he closed his eyes he saw his mother wiping the kitchen counter, pouring hot water on it to clean it. She was a clean-freak and ants drove her crazy.

Warren Talbot knocked on the front door. He was only armed with the hammerless Smith and Wesson .38 revolver that he'd put in his front pocket when he got out of the car. His sole idea was to shoot Fat Joe dead, right there, and forget whatever happened after that. That's all he wanted to do, and then he could die, too, for all he cared. He wanted to die and have the pain go away. It had all become just too much for him to mentally handle anymore. He looked at the small fake-pearl doorbell button. There was a bumper sticker stuck to one of the windows just to the right of the front door that said: "When in doubt / knock 'em out." He pushed the button and held it down. He could hear it going off inside the house. He listened to chimes build, drop off, then build again, but no one came to the door. He turned around and saw Flaco standing behind him holding a police shotgun. He had taken Warren's out of the back seat of the car. Looking at the weapon itself, Warren finally realized that he actually wanted to die right there, or he would have taken the weapon to the door himself.

"What are you doing?" Warren said.

"I don't know, man. You know. ... I really don't. You stupid fucker," Flaco said. Warren looked at the skinny Mexican kid for a moment then reached for the door knob and turned it. It was unlocked. He walked in. He heard Flaco coming up the wooden steps behind him.

"What the fuck?" Flaco said. Warren put his finger up to his lips. He was looking at the body on the stairs. It had practically been cut in half. The man had been shot in the stomach with a shotgun. He was lying at the bottom of the stairs with his intestines pushed to the right and falling out of his corpse where his kidney's had once been.

"Is that Fat Joe?" Warren whispered. Flaco shook his head, no.

Warren looked down a hallway and saw that it ended in a little breakfast room. He turned into it and walked on down to the end. He had the revolver out now, and Flaco was following him. Warren entered the little breakfast room. It was an abattoir; and the blinds were peppered with buckshot. There were six people lying naked and very dead on the floor—two woman and four men. The men were in their underwear. They had all been executed with a bullet to the back of the head. Warren rolled over each of the men and asked Flaco if any of them was Fat Joe. Flaco, his eyes big, shook his head, no.

"Shit," Warren finally said.

"What happened?".

"An execution, evidently," Warren said. He walked on into the kitchen. Someone had been making hamburgers, and not too long ago, either. The raw paddies were all pressed out on the counter and they'd barely started to turn dark from being out of the refrigerator. There was a package of white bread and a Safeway bag on the floor with two heads of iceberg lettuce still in it. He walked over to the Safeway bag and looked into it. He took out an unbroken bottle of pickles and carefully put it down on the counter.

"I think someone wants Fat Joe dead besides me," Warren said. He looked down at the hamburgers. There were nine of them on the counter. One of them was child-sized. They found a stack of handbills announcing the "Run" in Plata, Mexico, that weekend. It boasted that every Vagos member and chapter in the Western United States was going to show up in Plata.

While the men of the house were being rounded up to be executed, one of the women had had the presence of mind to hide her little daughter from the killers. Warren learned that much from the little girl they found upstairs hiding in a laundry shoot. The mother had been smart about it—she'd stuffed in sheets from the bed, wedging them into the shoot, about three feet down. Then she'd put her seven-year old daughter atop the sheets and closed the access door. That's where Warren and Flaco found her as they searched the house.

"What's your name, honey?"

"Bonnie," the little girl said. "Where's my mommy?" Warren just looked at her, nonplussed. She was very blonde and tiny. She was wearing jeans and a pink T-shirt that said "Big Girl" on it, but no shoes. "My mommy said I was s'pose to play hide and seek. But no one came and I got scared," the little girl said.

Warren looked at Flaco. Warren and the child were sitting on the bed's now-bare mattress. The little girl suddenly hopped off. "Mommy? Have *you* seen my Mommy?" she asked Flaco.

"Honey, your mommy sent us to take you to her," Warren said.

"She did?"

"Yes. She's going to take you to Disneyland, but she had to go do a few things first."

"Disneyland." The little girl smiled. Flaco wiped at his face. He was sweating profusely and looked junk— or some other kind of dope-sick—or maybe he was just physically sickened by what they'd just seen downstairs; Warren couldn't tell.

"Yes. She's waiting for us, right now. So let's go see your mommy. Where are your clothes?" Warren said.

"In my room. What's *your* name?" the little girl asked Warren.

"My name is Warren."

"Who's *he?*" the little girl asked, pointing at Flaco.

"That's. ..."

"Flaco," Flaco said. He smiled weakly at the little girl and then looked back over at Warren. *"Now* what, Warren?"

"We have to take Bonnie to her mom, don't we?" Warren said.

"How we going to do that, Warren?"

"We're just going to take her." Warren looked at Flaco. Flaco rubbed his face again.

"What's that?" Bonnie said, pointing at the shotgun Flaco was holding.

"That's for doing magic tricks," Warren said.

"Magic tricks?" the little girl smiled.

"Okay, let's get your clothes and then we'll take you to your mommy," Warren said as he stood up.

"You told me you had people near here," Warren said.

"Yeah—My mom and dad," Flaco said.

"Let's take her there," Warren said.

"Why?"

"Just because," Warren said. "Remember 'just because?'"

"We should call the cops," Flaco said. "Give the girl to *them.* ..."

"I don't want to," Warren said

"Why not?"

"Because. ... I just don't," Warren said.

"You want me to take the little girl to my parents' house?" Flaco said.

"Yeah. Whoever killed her mother might come looking for her if they find out she's still alive—she might-could identify them, even. If we give her to the cops, it's a cinch they'll find out; it'll be in the newspapers tomorrow—*you* know *that.*"

"I still think you should just take her to the cops, Warren."

"I. ... I want to keep her. Maybe," Warren said.

"What?!"

"Yeah, that's right," Warren said, "but I have to get to the run down in Plata and kill Fat Joe first. You're going to help me do that by keeping the girl at your mother's place and watching over her until I get back. Is *that* your parents' house?" Flaco had given him an address a few minutes before. Warren had pulled up in front of a nice stucco house that was located in what appeared to be a decent neighborhood just south of LAX; he could see clothes drying on a clothesline in the fenced backyard.

"The kid isn't *yours*," Flaco said. "She's got a family, Warren. Someone is out there, and they're going to be wondering what happened to her." Flaco was holding the little girl in his arms; she'd fallen asleep on the drive over to his parents'. They'd carried her out of the house after first moving the body on the stairs out of the way so she wouldn't see it.

"It was meant to be," Warren said. "That's the way God wants it."

"Why? Because you happened to walk into a house full of dead people?" Flaco said. "*That* isn't right and you know it, man."

"Yes it is. I *found* her, didn't I? I'll love her better than anyone else ever could," Warren said. "I know that as sure as I'm sitting here." Warren turned and looked at him. It was a pleading look that went as deep as the need Flaco now had for changing his own life, and he understood it. It was completely crazy, yet it wasn't crazy at all.

"My mom's name is Victoria. My pop's name is Horacio," Flaco said. Warren turned off the engine and the three of them, with Flaco carrying the little girl, got out of the car and walked up to the house.

*   *   *

■ PLATA, MEXICO

"There's a man down there ... in the well." Hans said, walking toward Sonny Delmonico's four-wheeler.

"*Is* there? My word," Sonny said. He had just driven off the road and up to the well, and had seen the stranger standing there looking down into the place he'd hidden the Hauptmann.

"Yes, there's really a man down there," the stranger said.

"Is that your car?" Sonny asked the man, looking at the new Jeep that Hans

Kamptner had driven to the *ejido*.

"Why, yes," the man said.

"And may I ask what you're *doing* out here?" Sonny questioned the man over the sound of the ATV's engine.

"I'm a mining engineer. My company bought this *ejido* and I was sent over to take a look at the property, and I just found a man here trapped down the well," Hans said. He was feeling in his pocket for his straight razor and smiling as he walked slowly toward Sonny. "Shouldn't we *call* someone? ... About the fellow in the well. I'm sure he's hurt and needs help."

"I don't think so," Sonny said. He watched as the older man, about his own age, in fact, walked toward him, keeping the smile on his face all the while. But he also noticed the mans's right hand slip into his pants'pocket, and he suddenly put the four wheeler into reverse and backed it up twenty yards just to be on the safe-side of whatever might now happen. That maneuver made the man stop dead in his tracks, but he maintained the stiff smile on his face nonetheless.

"Would you be German by nationality?" Sonny queried him, over the sound of the idling engine.

"Why, yes, I'm German," Hans said. He'd stopped moving toward Sonny, now. He took his hand out of his pocket very slowly. The razor was now hidden in his palm. He'd had the same razor since he'd left Berlin for the front in 1943 and knew it well; just how to flick it open at the last instant and slash, before his opponent had time to react. He glanced over at his Jeep. There was a pistol there, but getting to it was out of the question at this point.

"Perhaps we can get him out together," Hans suggested.

"You think so?" Sonny said, watching the man's slightest movements very carefully.

"I'm sure we could." They both heard a buzzing-type rattle, then. A very *loud* rattle, in fact, in the silence of the desert around them.

"I would not move if I were you," Sonny said. "There's a snake just behind you. A sidewinder, as the Yanks call them." Hans turned to see a large diamondback rattlesnake coiled just behind him, just slightly to his right. "I've heard that they get agitated very easily," Sonny said. "Don't make any sudden moves—I'll drive over it and kill it."

"Excellent, thank you," Hans said, eyeing the snake. "I'll stay put, then. ... It's very kind of you."

"Don't mention it, old man," Sonny said. He drove slowly toward the engineer with his eye on the coiled snake, aiming the left front tire of the ATV straight at the reptile. He'd decided that the engineer was harmless, not a threat to him or his plans in any way; plus, it was time to pull the Hauptmann from the well and he could use some help in performing that task.

Hans Kamptner watched as Sonny drove slowly toward him. He was a lucky man and always had been. After all, he'd survived the entire Second World War without a scratch, hadn't he? As Sonny approached closely enough, Hans swung up and out with the razor, slashing Sonny in the shoulder and just missing his neck. Hans started to run along side the ATV, holding his razor up and ready to strike again, when he suddenly saw a *second* snake—at that time of the year, diamondbacks were always found in pairs. The second snake struck hard at him but missed his flesh, hitting instead the heel of his shoe with its fat head, and causing him to trip over the its partially-extended body as he tried to dodge it.

The unexpected slash had cut Sonny's shoulder to the bone, but he had no time to react to the new situation, and the ATV roared forward and ran over the first snake, smashing it flat, as he'd originally intended. He then glanced at his wounded shoulder. The sweat was rolling down into his one good eye, but he could immediately see that he was badly wounded and arterial blood was rhythmically spurting out of the bone-deep gash. He'd seen wounds like this one in the War, and he knew for a fact that he could bleed-out and die from it in a very short period of time. He drove back toward the well, steering the ATV with his one good hand and staying well away from the man with the razor, not yet realizing that his attacker had fallen down, until he glanced in the rear-view mirror and saw the man stretched out on the sand, just starting to get up again.

Sonny quickly turned the four wheeler around and gunned it, full throttle, going straight at the man, who had stood completely up and was staring at him. Hans tried to run and dodge the vehicle bearing down on him, but the ATV's front tire caught his right leg and ran over it, crushing his ankle in the process. Sonny managed to turn the machine around again, but he felt himself starting to lose strength. The ATV was now headed straight *at* the well, and Sonny had to somehow brake hard and steer the four-wheeler away from it with just his one good arm straining to turn the handlebars with a quickly-diminishing strength. He managed to turn and slow the ATV just in time, missing the well by mere inches.

The man who had attacked him was sitting in the sand, holding his broken ankle. Then Sonny saw him manage to stand on his one good leg and begin hopping toward his Jeep. To Sonny, his goal was obvious—to get back to the vehicle; and if he made it, Sonny was certain that he personally wouldn't survive another minute afterwards. Sonny gunned the ATV and ran at the man again. He watched the German try to speed up his pace, but he suddenly tripped on a rock and fell down a few yards in front of Sonny and the barreling ATV. It was all a sweaty blur to Sonny as he closed in on his would-be killer. Sonny felt the big front tire roll directly up and over the man's back and head. The tire broke a vertebra up near the German's neck as his body was slammed-down onto the ground by the tire, paralyzing him instantly. Sonny stopped the ATV and looked hard at his wounded shoulder. He quickly stripped off his shirt and saw the exposed white bone with his blood still shooting out of the ugly wound in pulsating bursts. He dismounted and dizzily staggered the two steps to the rear of the ATV, then dropped to his knees and leaned his naked wounded shoulder fast up against the vehicle's red-hot exhaust pipe, instantly cauterizing the flesh wherever the pipe came into contact with it; holding his shoulder there against the blue-colored pipe as long as he could stand it. He screamed uncontrollably from the exquisite pain as he forced his shoulder against the pipe. It was a very loud scream; a scream that held the fear of imminent death in its decibels, as they radiated away through the empty desert air.

Deep inside the well, the Hauptmann heard the screams; but he had no idea from what type of creature they were issuing—human or non-human—nor, indeed, what events were transpiring above, at all.

50

■ PLATA, MEXICO

Vladimir had never experienced a desert like this before: the burnt horizon at 2 P.M., the cardón cactus forests, the engine noise of the taxi as it raced towards Plata on a seemingly endless perfectly straight dirt road. Everything in the physical environment made him feel lost; an alien. He found himself in a surreal setting that reflected and highlighted his actual predicament. He knew that the Gehlen people were close-by; he'd become aware of that situation in Mexico City. He'd left the Capital after receiving a warning from Gemma that she was leaving with Tucker by plane and heading to a town called Plata in the state of Sonora. She told Vladimir from the hotel in Cuernavaca that she was going to tell Tucker the truth as soon as they arrived there. He begged her not to, afraid of what might happen to her, but she was adamant. She was going to tell him the truth, period. She'd told Vladimir on the phone that she simply couldn't stand it anymore. She'd told him that she was in love with him, and that she'd wait for him there in Sonora.

"Plata, Mexico, *Señor. Ya pronto llegaremos,*" the taxi driver said. They'd driven past the local silver mine, that was belching yellow smoke from a single tall, red-brick stack. On the ride from Sonoyta he'd had a lot of time to think about his life, and how he'd lived it up to now. He'd finally admitted to himself that he was totally in love with the Gemma, and now all he wanted was to be with her. He'd never felt that way about his wife, although he had loved her, and he still did. His feelings for Gemma were in a completely different category, though, and overpowered everything else he'd ever known, emotionally. That's all he knew for sure, really. He'd made a promise to General Maximov that he'd help get Neizert to the United States, and he was still going to make good on that promise unless keeping it would somehow hurt Gemma. If he saw or thought that anything to do with this smuggling of a man across the border would affect her—would affect *them,* their future together; well, then, he'd simply walk away from it. He would have to tell his wife the truth as soon as he could talk to her—that he'd fallen in love with another woman. He realized that the life he'd known up to now was over; he understood that completely. He had no idea about what would happen from here on out; he just knew that it would happen with

493

Gemma at his side, as his partner.

"I need to buy a weapon." Vladimir spoke to the driver from the backseat of the old Ford taxi. "Can you help me get one?" He made the universal hand-symbol for a gun by using the index finger and thumb of his right hand, holding the imaginary "pistol" up in the air so the driver could see and understand him. "I can pay very well for one." The taxi driver looked at him in the rearview mirror.

"I speak English, *Señor.* You can put down your hand," the driver said.

"... Right," Vladimir said, suddenly feeling foolish.

"What *kind* of weapon do you want, *Señor?*"

"An automatic pistol of some kind. ... " Vladimir said.

"It shouldn't be a problem, *Señor*—this is Mexico."

"Thank you," Vladimir said.

"Don't mention it," the driver said. "Where are you from, *Señor?*"

"Sweden," Vladimir said.

"Ah—snow. We have none here, as you can see. ..." An ATV suddenly pulled up behind them. It was a strange sight: there was a one-eyed man behind the handlebars, driving. Neizert—Vladimir was immediately certain that the man was Christophe Neizert—was riding on the back, holding onto the one-eyed man around his waist. The man driving the ATV had a horrible burn mark on his shoulder, and his pants were freshly stained with blood—they looked to be still wet with it, in fact. The driver looked as if he were just leaving Hell itself, out for a short joy-ride before returning to his torments. They rode alongside the taxi for a moment, then finally pulled ahead and passed. Vladimir watched them go by in frank shock. The taxi driver made the sign of the cross and kissed his thumb as he slowed a little to let the ATV pass.

"The Devil never rides alone, *señor,*" the driver commented wryly.

*　　　　　*　　　　　*

"Marie and I will do it," Butch said.

"You're sure?" Sonny said.

"Yeah—why the fuck not?" Butch said.

"Well, I can think of a lot of reasons. The biggest one being that you might both end up dead," Alex said.

"Maybe, but I doubt it," Butch said.

"You're sure?" Alex said.

"Yeah. Somebody has got to take that guy to Sonoyta. It might as well be you," Butch said. "You can go on ahead with the doctor and the drugs."

494

"But *you're* more interested in the dope, aren't you?" Alex said.

"Maybe so. I made a little deal with Sonny, here," Butch said, nodding at Delmonico, who was lying on his bed, half-loaded. The Mexican doctor had given him Vicodin for the pain after he'd performed the minor surgery that was necessary, and Sonny had also drunk several beers while the doctor was operating on him. He was now obviously feeling no pain, at all.

"Is this 'little deal' worth dying for?" Alex asked.

"I don't know, man—maybe it is, for *me*. The money is ... a lot ... to me and Marie; we're going to get married as soon as this is over. Start a family," Butch said. Alex saw Sonny smiling at the three of them from the bed.

"I would say that Mr. Nickels is the least likely groom I've ever met," Sonny observed, with a marked devil-may-care sluggishness from the alcohol and opiates, both fueling his wry comment.

"Congratulations," Alex said to Butch.

"Yes, indeed, congratulations, old man," Sonny said from the bed. "I've heard the first year is always the hardest. Try not to shoot each other, okay?"

Before the operation to sew him up, the doctor had given Sonny a stronger opiate than Vicodin for the pain from the second degree burn on his shoulder, so he was still more than a little high. The young Mexican doctor was an expert at treating the worst kind of wounds, and he was able to suture the artery, which had been cleanly severed by the German's razor, using a stint that he'd had at hand amongst his normal supplies. He'd told Sonny that if he hadn't cauterized the ends of the artery the way he had, he would have bled-out and died out there in the desert, and he congratulated Sonny on saving his own life; or in saving it to the point where he, the Doctor, could finish up the job.

"I'll give the Hauptmann to you, then, if Butch stays. Go ahead, Tucker, take your German on to Sonoyta," Sonny said.

"And just how do I do *that?*" Alex said.

"There's a bus at six; it leaves everyday for the border. It's four hours from here to Sonoyta. Take a good book with you," Sonny suggested.

"Take *him* on the fucking *bus?*" Alex was flabbergasted and outraged simultaneously, apparently.

"Why not?" Sonny said. They were all sitting in Sonny's hotel room. The Hauptmann was in the hotel restaurant eating a meal, angry at Sonny for leaving him in the well overnight where he said he'd almost died of exposure, even though it had been his own idea to do so.

"I just get on the bus with him?" Alex said.

"That's what *I* would do," Sonny said. His arm was bandaged up now, and you'd

495

never think to look at him that he'd almost been murdered a short time before. Delmonico seemed to be indestructible, like some kind of old car that just would not quit. Alex was looking at him now in a new light: he'd developed a strange admiration for the man's fortitude and attitude, given all that had happened to him up to this point. "Just go to this address—I'll write it down. You'll be met there by a colleague of mine and then taken to Los Angeles. A coyote will cross you at Tijuana. You can trust the people who'll meet you there." Sonny stood up, gingerly holding his left arm, then walked to the desk and opened it. He took out a Gideon Bible that could be found in the bedside table of all the rooms in the hotel, tore out the first page, and wrote down an address on it with a cheap ball point pen. "*I will lead the blind ... by ways they have not known ... along unfamiliar paths I will guide them ... and I will make the rough places smooth,*" Sonny quoted, from a passage he still remembered from his Catholic school days. He handed Alex the page with the address in Sonoyta and smiled.

"Speaking of the bus, it just dropped off an L.A. County Sheriff's detective," Butch said, looking out the window. He watched as Warren Talbot stepped off the bus from Sonoyta. Talbot looked around; first at the bar across the street, then at the hotel. He saw Butch in the window looking down at him. The two men exchanged glances for a moment. Then Warren walked toward the hotel entrance. Alex walked to the window and looked down at the detective.

"Fuck," Alex said. "What's *he* doing here?"

"I'll go find out. How's that?" Butch said.

"His name is Fat Joe," Warren explained. They were sitting in the hotel's dusty restaurant at a red Formica table drinking *nescafe,* which didn't taste like coffee at all, but some kind of 'health drink' you wouldn't even give a donkey, or so Butch thought to himself. He drank a cup of the stuff and then asked for another, putting tons of sugar in it after the waitress set it down in front of him.

"You came all the way here *because? ...*" Butch said.

"I'm going to kill Fat Joe—it's that simple," Warren said. "What are *you* doing here, Perry?"

"It's a very long story," Butch said.

"I bet," Warren said.

"Are you sure you want to do this?" Butch said. "Maybe you should just go back home."

"Yeah, I'm going to do it—he killed Lorie, my wife." Butch looked at him. It had finally just dawned on him that the detective wasn't right in the head. "How are you going to do that? Kill him, I mean?" Butch asked.

"Just shoot him," Warren said, sipping his coffee. "I think he's across the street in the bar right now."

"Okay. ..." Butch said.

"Yeah. Well, that's the plan anyway, amigo," Warren said. "He won't be the first motherfucker I've sent over."

"Okay," Butch said. "He may be the last, though, the amount of other bikers there are in this little shit-hole right now."

"Is all this because of what happened in Malibu? What really happened there? Is *that* why my wife was killed, Perry?"

"Probably," Butch said. "I think so, but I can't be sure of it. I told you to leave it alone that day in LA."

"Is it important—what you guys do? I mean, for the government?"

"To tell you the truth, I don't even know, really," Butch said. "I just show up for work. You're a cop; you know what I mean."

"You called to warn me, didn't you?" Warren said.

"Yeah," Butch said.

"Well, thanks for doing that, even if it is belated! That's twice you tried to warn me."

"*Semper fi,*" Butch said.

"If I hadn't stuck my nose in all this *shit,* my wife would be alive right now and I'd be in Agoura Hills," Warren said. He looked across the street. "Funny, the mistakes we make in life." He was suddenly wistful, staring out into space.

"Well, we all make mistakes, man. ... You just didn't know," Butch said.

"I was just trying to do my job," Warren said. He turned back and looked at Butch. "That's all it was." Butch looked at him.

"It's not worth it, Warren. ... None of it. Not really; that's what I've learned. If you go over there you probably aren't coming out the other end. You know that, though, I guess."

"His name is Fat Joe," Warren said, again looking out the dirty window at the bar across the street. "He's the one that did it. ... Killed my wife, Lorie." He put down his coffee and got up. "I want to thank you for what you did, calling me and everything," Warren said.

"Don't mention it, man," Butch said.

"I'll see you around, then," Warren said. He put a five-dollar bill down on the table.

"Yeah. See you around," Butch said. He watched the detective walk out of the hotel and cross the dirt street, heading toward the bar. There were over fifty motorcycles parked in front of the place. Alex walked into the restaurant.

"Have you seen Gemma?"

"No," Butch said.

"Where's *he* going?" Alex said, watching Talbot cross the street.

"Agoura Hills," Butch said. "... Okay, let's go get that boat."

*　　　　*　　　　*

"And the girl? She doesn't know who you are yet?"

"She's an American," Gemma said. She walked up to Vladimir and put her arms around him, hugging him tightly. It was the first time she had ever embraced him.

"Where's Tucker?" Vladimir asked, holding her.

"Here somewhere. In the hotel, I think," she said.

"In the hotel?" Vladimir said.

"Yes." She kissed him, then. It was a very long kiss. She went to the window and pulled the shades and pulled off her shirt, unbuttoning it quickly. He watched her undress in the soft-yellow coral-colored light.

"I'm going to get a divorce," Vladimir said, looking at her. He watched her take off her shirt and drop it to the floor. She had a pistol stuck in the back of her jeans, which she took out and laid on a chair by the bed. She undid her hair and brought it forward onto her shoulders. They looked at each other for a moment.

"He could find us," Vladimir said.

"I don't care," Gemma said. "I don't care anymore." He nodded and took off his shirt and put it on the bed. She walked up to him, and then he could feel her breasts pushing against his chest, her narrow waist, the warmth of her skin, the warmth of her breath. She pushed him backwards onto the bed. When he tried to speak she covered his mouth with hers and made love to him. He could see the ceiling. There had once been a fire in the room where the flames had gone all the way up the wall, and the high ceiling still bore the black char-marks from that blaze. He looked at them as he held her and felt her hips slip into the man-woman place; the place that joined Heaven and Earth. The room was quiet, with just their breathing and a few errant sounds drifting up from the road below as the four o'clock bus pulled out at for Sonoyta. There was a kid who rode with the driver, he called out the bus' destination; something they still did in Mexico. They could hear him call out: "S O N O Y T A" in a loud voice, making sure any potential passengers could hear it along the street. They both heard the boy's voice crying out almost in concert with their own. ...

Afterwards, after night had fallen, they lay together in the bed, neither speaking for a long time: it just wasn't necessary.

"He'll find us if I stay here with you," Vladimir finally said.

498

"Yes, I know," Gemma said.

"I could speak to him. Explain that we now both want the Hauptmann to reach America," Vladimir said.

"His father told him to kill you. He told me that on the plane."

"His father doesn't understand the situation—how it's changed," Vladimir said.

"*I'll* tell him," she said. "I'll explain that you want to help the Americans, now."

"He most likely won't believe you," Vladimir said. It was very dark in the room now. He could feel the warmth of her lying there beside him. She'd felt so small and delicate when he'd held her.

"I'm pregnant," she said. She reached for him. "Please don't be angry." He didn't immediately respond to her revelation.

"Is it Tucker's?"

"Yes."

"I understand," he said. "Is the Hauptmann actually *here*—In the hotel?"

"Yes," she said.

"Do you know where?"

"Yes. There's a room behind the desk. They're keeping him hidden in there," she said.

"*We* have to take the Hauptmann to America. I made a promise and I have to keep it," Vladimir said.

"Tucker will kill you," she said. "Explain to him that you want to help—that you're on their side, now. ..."

"Come on, get up," he said. "Go back to him. Don't say anything at all about us. I'll meet you in Los Angeles," Vladimir said. "It's best this way."

"*Where* in Los Angeles?" Gemma asked. She looked at him. "Tucker talks about a motel there all the time. In Los Angeles. He's mentioned it many times. It's called the Capri. It's right *on* the ocean," she said.

"All right ... go there, then. I'll find you there. Tell Tucker that he can pick up the Hauptmann at the Motel Capri in three days. Tell him that if he does anything to you in the meantime I'll kill the German. Tell him he gets the German, and I get you in exchange."

"Are you sure this is the right way?" Gemma said.

"Yes," he said. "I've thought about all the ways this could go forward, and for us, my love, this is the best; there's no doubt in my mind." He reached across the dark room and felt for the pistol he'd bought earlier that day. He didn't say he'd kill Tucker if they saw each other before the rendevous in L.A., but he knew he would have to if they happened to run into each other at any point along the way.

"How can you get Neizert out of here?" she asked.

"I don't know, but I will," he said. Then he stood up and got dressed in the dark.

A few minutes later, the sounds of a shooting melee across the street allowed Vladimir to slip into the room behind the desk downstairs while everybody else had immediately hit the floor in the hotel lobby, fearing that their lives might end right then, and there, from a stray bullet.

51

■ PLATA, MEXICO

The old shrimper's bilge-pump was hammering out a quick and staccato beat as it sucked up sea water and pumped it out of the boat's "head" where there was a persistent leak; two inches of fetid diesel-slicked salt water was pooled around the base of stained and broken toilet.

They were less than one nautical mile from Plata now, heading due north, sailing along a desert coastline that resembled a moonscape. The boat's main cabin smelled like diesel fumes and shrimp—a truly nauseating mixture. The boat had been neglected for years and was filthier than a pig-sty. The boat's large cabin—a luxurious space in 1935—was now a complete shambles. The very loud sounds of the diesel engine—the sounds of old engine-rods loosely clattering and banging within their confining steel space—hurt the ears of anyone unfortunate enough to be spending time aboard the floating derelict. The flathead style engine's exhaust pipe went from the hold directly up through the wooden cabin, then stove-piped out onto the deck. The thick black diesel exhaust roiled out of the pipes, and if you had been watching the low-slung white fishing boat from the beach as it sailed by, it would have looked like it belonged to an era that had ended years ago.

They'd rigged the boat with dynamite from the silver mine, placing bundles of the explosive all around the cabin—five sticks of Hercules-brand dynamite per duct-taped bundle. That had been the easy part. Now Butch had to crimp each blasting cap with a fuse of an appropriate length.

The mine where they'd commandeered the dynamite had only older-style pyrotechnic blasting caps—the type with fuses. The mining engineer had explained that the old-style "blasters" were best for their work—*if* you crimped the heads correctly. Crimp them the wrong way and they could ignite and take your hand off.

Butch was smoking a cigar and wearing surfers' baggy swimming trunks with a T shirt that had an fluorescent image of the Virgin of Guadalupe hand-painted on it. The cigar was a small and thin Mexican one that helped cut the stench of the shrimp. Butch looked at a remaining stick of dynamite sitting there on the cluttered galley countertop. The brand-name 'Hercules' was stenciled on its side, along with the words "Safety First." in Spanish He smiled to himself, because he didn't expect what they were planning on using the explosive for was what the company had in mind. He taped the stick to the last bundle—each bundle contained five sticks—with some duct tape that they'd taken from the tool room at the mine. He placed the last bundle next to the dummy stack of dope they'd created on the cabin floor. The dummy stack was made of decoy bundles that were really just heaps of fishing nets piled under a heavy, green-canvas oilcloth. The dummy stack of dope was about three feet high. By the time the Vagos got down to the cabin it would be too late for them to turn around, Butch thought, so he judged his job to be good enough. At least that was the plan.

Butch stood below deck surveying his handiwork. There were small bundles of dynamite nested all over the place, such as those that might be found on the set of an old Western movie, and that scenario made him smile. He saw the fuses as being so many paths leading into the maw of a TNT Hell that he was building.

The mining engineer had explained that the fuses were waterproof and that, once they were lit, a fuse would burn at 2.5 seconds per foot. The engineer—a tall and very animated Spaniard—explained it all to them in almost unaccented English, while Alex held a gun to his head. He'd been very careful with his English, as he wanted to live through this robbery. He used his hands a lot when explaining how the blasting caps were to be crimped "just-so."

"Okay ... the big question, boys and girls: how long should I cut the fuses?" Butch asked, as he came back up on deck. He looked over at Sonny, who had decided to come along, too, not trusting Butch and the girl to pull it off without his help.

Sonny was observing Butch from the boat's wheel house. Marie was sitting in the old boat's captain's chair. Once, years before, it had been a rich man's a yacht. They'd bought it down in Ciegos, another fishing village, not far south of Plata. The "fantail"-style, sixty-foot yacht-cum-shrimper was christened the *Argosy*, and it had cost Sonny ten-thousand dollars cash. It was an all-wooden boat, built in a Seattle shipyard back in 1929, long before the invention of fiberglass. The Argosy had somehow ended up in Mexico and was currently on her last legs, being kept afloat solely by bilge pumps and "hot-tar" patches. But there had been a residue of dignity still about her that they had all three noticed when they pulled her out into the Sea of Cortez, away from the surprisingly modern quay at Ciegos, with Sonny at the helm barking instructions. Her big flathead Cummins engine reverberated loudly off the dock when they fired her up.

The former owner was an old Mexican fisherman, and he helped them untie her. He stood there waving at them from the dock as they pulled away, very glad to see the last of the *Argosy*, which he expected to break up at sea in the first bad weather they'd hit.

"Well, if you leave too *little* fuse, we won't get them on board in time for the festivities," Sonny said, having apparently thought it through. Butch looked at Marie, who stood there holding an AK- 47 that had recently belonged to the Plata police; its worn canvas strap slung casually over her shoulder. She was wearing shorts and a tank top, and was barefoot. She seemed completely at easy with riding on top of a floating bomb, and with Butch lighting the fuses and then inviting the Vagos on board as *they* would somehow then get off the boat and watch their enemies be blown to Kingdom Come from the comfort and safety of the beach. That's how, sitting in bed that morning after a vigorous bout of sex, Butch had described his plan to her, anyway.

"Ten minutes should do it, I think," Butch said, looking over at Marie and winking.

"That's too much time," Sonny said, over the noise of the engines, turning toward Butch as he spoke, so he could hear him.

"*Five* minutes, then?" Butch countered. "We want *them* to take a real good fucking, not us!"

"Too little." Delmonico smiled. "Let the young lady decide!" They were now about a hundred yards offshore and heading due north, straight for Plata. They could see the yellow smoke billowing out of the brick chimney at the La Sangre mine up ahead. Marie had casually walked into the silver mine's compound and held her AK-47 on two half-dressed guards who were in the middle of eating lunch, and had been unarmed at the time. Then Alex, Butch, and Sonny had driven on over to the engineer's office. Sonny had been there before once, to play cards with the engineer, and knew the layout of the place. The mining engineer was a voluble Spaniard, and he walked out of his office smiling, thinking that Sonny had come for a social visit. He stopped smiling when Butch told him they needed to take away some dynamite.

"What for, *señor*?" the Spaniard asked. A worried look suddenly appeared on his long face.

"The Fourth of July," Butch said.

"We'll pay, of course," Sonny said.

"I'm afraid, *señores*, that we need all of our current stock of dynamite. We use it every day, here, you know." The engineer was still trying to sound friendly.

"I would reconsider that response," Butch said, pointing the hand-cannon at him.

"... Yes—I see. It's a question of urgency," the Spaniard said, getting the point. "Right this way gentlemen."

"Seven and a half minutes, then," Marie said, smiling. "Seven is my lucky number. ..." She pulled the clip out from her AK-47 and took out all the rounds, one by one, laying them out on the top of the cabin's roof, so that the bullets rolled slightly—back and forth—with the gentle rocking of the boat's progress northward.

She inspected them for flaws and made sure they were all clean. Butch loved to watch her doing soldierly things.

"Okay, kids, you get seven-and-one-half minutes to get your asses off this here boat," Butch said. "... Isn't it shallow here Sonny? ... Shouldn't you be out a little further?" Butch asked, trying to change the subject now because even he was scared by what would happen if they misjudged the timing of the explosion.

They were close enough to the shoreline that he could see flocks of Marbled Godwits wading in dark spots that were crisscrossed with rocks, creating big tidal pools. Huge flocks of them stood in eddies of tidal backwash. The shorebirds moved as one entity when they occasionally lifted off the beach, only to circle and land again en masse, in what appeared to be almost the same place they'd taken off from before. The three boaters could hear hundreds of wings slapping the air as they circled overhead.

"Don't worry, we're fine right here," Sonny said. "I took up sailing in Brazil and I've loved it ever since—I know what I'm doing. I should have my own boat, really. Some day, I will."

Butch was enjoying the bright sunshine and the feel of the air, which smelled very clean to him after being down below deck. He looked far past Marie working on the rifle's magazine and stared for a moment at the reddish-brown coast, which appeared quite jagged at times as it moved slowly along behind her bent head. The Cummins engine seemed to have found its stride, now, like a runner who was fully warmed up. He noted that the sky was clear; not a single cloud to be seen anywhere. Butch went back down below deck and started to cut the fuses to the right length. There were eight bundles of TNT, and each one needed a fuse. He worked at cutting them with a penknife, just the way the mining engineer had showed him. He crimped each fuse into the head of a blasting cap, and then attached a fuse-ready cap to the center stick of each taped-together bundle. He wondered what might be left of his hands and face if a blasting cap were to go off by accident while he worked. For a brief moment, he saw himself trying to grab the ladder leading up to the deck with bloody stubs where his hands had just been. He quickly put the image out of his mind, chomped down hard on his cigar, and got on with the business of fusing another cap.

Butch's idea was that they would take the boat to the quay at Plata, then light the fuses and walk off while the Vagos' boarded her thinking she was carrying the heroin. Sonny's boat with the actual heroin shipment was already anchored near Plata but had not docked yet. It had been Butch's idea to blow up the dummy boat and kill everyone at once—or as many as possible, anyway, since they'd probably have to fight their way out of town through any survivors. He wondered now, as he cut the fuses, using the top of his thumb as a rough measuring gauge, if they themselves would all live or die. He wanted now to live more than ever. He wanted to get married and get started on a completely new life with Marie. He decided that his luck was going to hold, so he smiled and smoked away as he worked, unafraid of anything now, and sure of success.

"No guts ... no glory," Butch said out loud, talking to himself as he crimped the first fuse into place. He saw the copper throat of the blasting cap flatten when he crimped it, just as the engineer had showed him. He re-taped one of the bundles after inserting the fuse into it, then trimmed it down a little. After he put the fuse into the last bundle of dynamite, he placed it on the floor with the others next to the phony pile of drugs; then he climbed up the ladder and left the cabin area, back out onto the deck. It was just four in the afternoon and beautiful.

"We're late," Sonny said.

"Good—let them get antsy," Butch said. He walked over and put his arm around Marie's waist and drew her close against him.

"Look ... dolphins!" Marie said. She ran to the side of the boat and Butch followed along. He saw two dolphins in the crystalline water of the Gulf that were apparently leading them towards Plata. Marie said it was good luck and excitedly kissed him on the cheek. That morning in bed she'd told him she'd marry him, and she was as happy right then as she could ever remember being. She was absolutely sure she was doing the right thing. She told him then that he was going to love her family.

The two-storey bar across from the hotel—Mr. Frog's—was an infamous one. The owners bought ads in the University of Arizona student newspaper and put up advertising flyers in nightclubs and college student hangouts in Tucson. Mr. Frog's in Plata was touted as having the longest bar in the world. The ads showed skimpily-dressed young Mexican girls holding a giant papier-mâché frog with the come-on: "Get Stupid ... Get Frogged-Up."

The advertising was all a lie, of course. The longest bar in the world was actually located in Tijuana, but Mr. Frog's ruse worked to pull down frat boys to Plata for weekends of drinking parties where no one would be carded and the most extreme behavior was tolerated by the police including drunken public fornication. As long as they paid for their drinks and sex in cash, everything would be all right. This particular weekend, though, the frat-boy crowd had been run out of Mr. Frog's by the entire Vagos' motorcycle club. They had literally taken the place over, to the point of having their own members tend bar, along with the scantily-clad Mexican girls—the male bartenders had been told unceremoniously to just walk out the door and not come back until Monday.

Warren had looked into the place through the bar's big front window, and had seen, at that time of the afternoon, the typical scene that he'd expected. Gang members and their girlfriends crammed the main barroom. He didn't know that the run had been paid for by the Gehlen organization, or that the bikers were there expressly to deal the Sicilian mob the first serious blow to its domination of the heroin trade. It was time for the Gehlen network to send a message: things were about to change, and the Colombians were now the Gehlen network's go-to guys. In the future, the international heroin trade would no longer be owned by the Sicilian mob, who wanted too much of a cut. Simultaneously with what was happening in Plata, in various places in Sicily, and everywhere else the Sicilians had heroin production and/or transportation facilities, the Gehlen organization was attacking them. They were making a point of stealing most of the Sicilians' product currently en route to the U.S. as well. The shipment coming through Plata had been part of this heroin *blitzkrieg,* to take over from, and if possible physically eliminate, the Old Guard Sicilians, replacing them with various Colombian-centered organizations.

"Don't go in there." Warren heard a voice. He looked to his right and saw Lorie standing there, ethereal.

"I *have* to go in," Warren said. He turned back around and looked into the crowded bar again.

"No, you don't! ... Go back home, Warren," his late wife told him.

"I can't go home until I do *this*," Warren said.

"Why?" she asked.

"Because I just have to. I can't just let him go free."

"It won't do any good," Lorie said. He turned sideways and looked at his wife again.

"I miss you. I don't like eating alone. And I don't like the way the house feels—it's so cold there without you," Warren said. "I'm more than just pissed-off."

"It still won't change things. What you're going to do," she said.

"I want to be with *you*," Warren said.

"Are you sure about that, Warren?" Lorie said.

"Yes," he said. "You know I am."

"I'll go with you, then—inside," she said. "If you're absolutely *sure*."

"Do you remember when we first met?" Warren asked. He loved the story.

"Yes." Lorie smiled at him because she loved the story, too.

"I thought you were so beautiful," Warren said.

"You did. That was a long time ago. I was skinny then," Lorie said.

"Yes. I've always thought you were beautiful. I loved you the minute I laid eyes on you. Something happened—something clicked, and I was really happy, for the first time in my life," He said. *"You* know."

"I was, too," she said.

"We lived in our own world, didn't we?" Warren said, fully realizing the truth of it for the first time. They'd just ignored everyone who hadn't understood them.

"Yes, I guess we did.

"I'm sorry we didn't have kids," he said. He was crying, but he didn't realize it. Then he noticed that she'd disappeared from the boardwalk. *"Lorie!"* He was yelling her name but didn't realize that, either. A Vago suddenly grabbed him by the arm and tossed him into the barroom before Warren knew what had happened to him.

"Hey, look here ... what I found," the young man said. He had long blond hair in a ponytail. Warren wiped his eyes and looked around at all the faces that turned to look at him. The Rolling Stone's "Midnight Rambler" was playing on the juke box.

"I think this guy wants to join up," Ponytail said. The kid was wearing just jeans and his motorcycle jacket; a jean-jacket with the arms cut off. Warren, wiping his eyes, could see that the kid was strong—had big "guns"—and was taller than he was by a couple of inches. He'd tossed Warren into the bar like he was a rag-doll.

"He could be a cop," someone from way down the long bar commented. Everybody laughed at that. Warren didn't look like a cop. He looked like a mailman or a junior high school English teacher, maybe, but definitely *not* a cop.

"Buy him a drink," a girl said. She was sitting on the bar. She was only seventeen or eighteen, and was examining Warren like you would a bug that had unexpectedly dropped into your lap.

"Pull his pants down and make sure he's not a cop," someone further down the bar piped in. Someone came up behind him and poured a pitcher of beer over Warren's head. The beer-drenching had taken Warren completely by surprise and he looked behind him to find another biker—a smaller guy about his own size—standing there, holding the empty pitcher of beer and grinning a shit-eating grin from ear to ear. The beer was stinging his eyes, and for a moment everyone in the bar seemed to fade away, time slowed down, and he was suspended in between the beats of existence for an endless instant.

"Go. Leave, Warren. Now." Lorie was speaking to him again. He saw his wife standing across the bar over by the wall.

"I can't ... not *now*," Warren said, talking to her as if they were back in their living room in Agoura Hills.

"This guy's crazy; man—he was standing outside talking to himself before! He's a crazy old motherfucker—SEE!" Ponytail said, pushing Warren again, moving him further up the bar. Suddenly, Ponytail pushed him as hard as he could with both hands. Warren stumbled backwards, trying to stay on his feet. One of the other bikers, sitting at a table near the door, put his foot out and Warren tripped and fell hard onto the barroom floor. He could see only motorcycle boots and a woman's black leather clogs. He tried to get up, but someone kicked him from behind and his head was slammed into the bar, and he was momentarily knocked unconscious.

While he was unconscious, he saw Lorie again for the first time, at the campus of the community college where he was picking up his brother. He was wearing his Marine Corps uniform and kids on the campus were looking strangely at him. He had arrived there early, and had decided to get out of his parents' Rambler station wagon and take a walking tour of the campus, just for the hell of it. He also did it because he'd been thinking that, when he got out of the Marine Corps, maybe he would try going back to school for awhile, although he didn't know what in the world he'd major in.

He was sitting on the steps of the library watching the girls walk by when Lorie came out of the building, walking with two other girls. She was carrying an armful of books and they briefly locked eyes as she passed him. She was wearing a yellow miniskirt that day. Most of the kids had looked away when he'd walked by—uniformed soldiers weren't popular on campus during the Vietnam War. But she'd smiled at him as she passed, making eye contact, and maintaining it longer than he'd expected her to.

"Hi," he said.

"Hi," she said back.

"My brother's in the Army, too," she'd said.

"Yeah," Warren had said, ignoring her mistake as to the branch of service he was in.

"Yeah," the stoned beautiful girl affirmed, and she seemed to want to keep talking to him, or at least he *thought* she did, and that was good enough for him.

He stood up and introduced himself.

"My name is Warren. I'm a Marine, actually, not an Army guy like your brother."

"Hi—I'm Lorie."

"Do you need a ride home," he blurted out, not knowing what else to say at the time, "or *anything*?"

"I live on campus," she said. "But thanks." He was standing there looking into her brown eyes. Her hair was done-up in a huge Afro. He couldn't keep his eyes off her, not for an instant. She was taller than he was, and she had great legs, and he'd always been a leg and ass man.

"I'm here on leave." The moronic inanity was all he could come up with right then, standing there mesmerized by her African beauty.

"So's my brother," she said. "He just got home."

"Yeah?"

508

"Yeah." The other girls had walked on, not waiting for her to catch up with them.

"Could I call you sometime?" Warren asked. She looked at him and cocked her head to the side, really *looking* at him, now.

"... Say *what*?"

"Call you—maybe we could go out sometime? My parents live here in Claremont."

"Mine live in San Francisco," she said, as if San Francisco were the other side of the Moon. She also answered that way to put him off—to see if he would *be* put off—wanting to treat him like a crazy white boy with a lot of nerve, to ask *her* out like that, so casual and all. Was he *color blind*?

"Do you like to bowl?" Warren forged ahead, not picking up on any of her not-so-subtle messages. He glanced down at her legs again—he couldn't help himself.

"Do I like to *bowl*? ..." The girl asked him, truly astounded.

"Yeah, why not?" Warren said. She burst out laughing, suddenly disarmed. *He really doesn't get it,* she thought.

"Yes, I do," she said, "the few times I've been."

"It's a date, then," Warren said, pushing it as far as he could. She gave him her number at the dorm, all her reluctance suddenly gone. He'd charmed her, and all the big "race" issues magically disappeared, and they started acting as if they were the only two young people on Planet Earth. He was unconscious and dreaming all this as various men kicked and stomped him. He was looking at Lorie again as she gave him her phone number. He watched himself write it down again on his open palm with a pen he'd just borrowed from a shocked white boy he'd stopped while the guy was walking up the steps to the library.

Warren's brother had been watching him from across the quad, and when they hooked up he asked Warren what he'd been talking to that "nigger" about.

"Why do you call her that?" Warren had said. Any racial prejudices he'd had had been quickly obliterated in combat—many of his fellow Marines were black, and he'd come to really love their culture and various attitudes about life in general as they'd rubbed off on him over the past few months.

"Call her what?" his brother said.

"*Nigger,*" Warren said. "That's a nice girl, there. You don't have to call her something like that."

"I don't know, really," his brother had said, suddenly sounding sheepish.

"... *Asshole,*" Warren said. "Has anyone called *you that*?" His little brother decided right there that the war had changed him, from the Warren that *he'd* grown up with, and thought he knew. He wasn't the same easy-going Warren who'd left for Vietnam just a year ago. Not the same at all, and it really puzzled him.

When Warren regained consciousness they had stopped kicking him. Several of his front teeth had been broken and his jaw was damaged—probably broken—and his right eye had broken open like an egg as the result of a particularly well-placed and vicious kick. But he was still alive. They'd left him there on the floor of the bar, having finally lost interest in him. He shakily stood up, with Lorie helping him. He saw the world with only his left eye, now—the right having closed up— so the room seemed as if it had been folded in half, with only one side showing.

"I want to kiss you," he said to Lorie. No one could hear him because he was bleeding profusely out of his torn-up mouth—the blood coming from his gums where the teeth had recently been. The blood came out like a slow fountain. He braced himself against the bar. Someone came up to him and punched him in the stomach and he fell down again. A young girl from Fontana decided to try her luck, and kicked him in the side of the head while he was trying to get up and he went out again.

Lorie was the only black person in the bowling alley on their first date. People stared at them, but they ignored them until they just couldn't anymore, then they left and went for a walk on a lonely road Warren knew of; a road that was very near his parents' house in the foothills of the San Gabriel mountains. It was a narrow road lined with oak trees. It was very quiet and they could hear a brook running nearby. Lorie was telling him about her mother working in a hotel. A Redtail hawk flew very close to them, and Warren pointed it out to her and told her he used to ride his bike up there with friends after school. She told him he was lucky, but he didn't quite understand what she meant at first. He finally kissed her at the end of the road, near a horse rental place that had a muddy road running into it. She kissed him back, passionately and hard. They were married in Palm Springs just two months later. Everyone in both families went completely nuts. He told a friend back in Vietnam, on his second tour, that it was quiet there, in-country, compared to what he'd been through at home after he'd told his parents he was marrying a black girl. It was the same for Lorie. Her father refused to go to the wedding. He was ashamed that his daughter was a "traitor to her race." Much later, Lorie realized that her father had literally been driven crazy by living in America.

When Warren stood up again there was an argument going on between two Vagos down the bar, so, in spite of sporting a face that was swelling up monstrously now, he was ignored. He tasted fresh blood and spat out a tooth that had lodged under his tongue. He touched his lips and found that they were split and bleeding. Lorie had him by the arm and was trying to hold him up.

"I'm not finished," Warren said. "I'll be there soon—don't worry, baby." He stumbled past the two belligerents at the bar, but they only gave him a brief look, then

510

went back to their argument. He continued down the bar, but stopped in front of a girl with red hair who was wearing black leather pants and a black leather vest.

"I'm looking for Fat Joe," Warren said. He had to say it three times before she could understand his garbled speech.

"Fuck you," the girl said. She was looking at the door and checking the time.

"Can't you help me?" Warren said. The woman pushed him away. He stumbled backwards and a Vago caught him and actually stopped him from falling over.

"I'm looking for Fat Joe," Warren said to the man who'd caught him.

"*Who?*" It was hard for him to articulate words now, with his lips swelling up and his teeth gone.

"Fat Joe." He tried to say the words very slowly tasting blood as he did so.

"Fat Joe?" the man said.

"... Yes," Warren said, nodding his head up and down. He could only focus on part of the face of the guy he was talking to because of his swollen-shut left eye.

"Anybody seen Fat Joe around here?" the man asked.

"He's busy. In the back," someone yelled. "Getting his crankshaft adjusted."

"He's in the back, amigo. But I'm sure he'd love to speak with you," the man said. Unseen hands shoved Warren toward the back of the bar. Someone turned up the jukebox and replayed "Midnight Rambler" so that it was suddenly *very* loud. Warren felt himself being propelled forward again by people who were laughing at him as he was physically passed down the bar like a broken and useless toy. Warren's face looked like a watermelon had been smashed into it, and red bloodstains ran willy-nilly down the front of his torn-up T-shirt.

Warren wiped his good eye and saw a very tall, overweight man heading out of the brothel that was connected to Mr. Frog's by a discreet stairway. The man appeared to be heading for the bar's restroom. Warren walked in just behind him. Fat Joe pulled down his pants and sat on the toilet. The stall was minus its door. He looked up at Warren and whistled.

"What the fuck happened to you?" Fat Joe asked from his station inside the doorless crapper, as Warren heard the plop of a pinched-off turd hitting the water.

"Are *you* Fat Joe?" Warren asked. He was fishing in his pocket as he walked up to the stall. He'd asked the man twice already if he was Fat Joe, but the man sitting on the toilet couldn't understand him because of all the swelling in his mouth—even his throat was swollen up, now.

"You never seen anyone take a shit before, buddy?" Fat Joe asked him.

"Are *you* fat Joe?" Warren leaned in and spoke very slowly. The blood was bubbling from his smashed mouth.

"Yeah, I am—so what?" Warren pulled out his little thirty-eight and put it against Fat Joe's forehead. Then he pulled the trigger and blew his brains out. The bullet painted the white tile wall with blood and grey-matter, as Fat Joe slumped over dead.

"Good," Warren said out loud, looking at the dead man's flaccid face: "Good."

He turned around and walked out of the bathroom and out the backdoor of the bar into the sunlight of the alley. He stumbled once, but caught himself on the corner of a parked ATV. He passed a young Mexican woman who was smoking a cigarette; taking a break after fucking a fat guy for ten dollars, nine of which she had to give to the house. She screamed when she looked at what was left of Warren's face.

52

■ PLATA, MEXICO

"I'm you're best hope to get to the States," Vladimir said.

"I don't believe you," Neizert said. The Russian had forced him onto the Sonoyta bus at gun point, just as the boat blew up out on the water. They were sitting in the very back of the bus and had felt the impact as the blast rocked the vehicle sideways on its worn-out suspension, almost tipping it over. Everyone in the bus had turned and seen the fireball shooting up along the quay. The whole long quay was suddenly on fire, with pieces of boat and human parts landing in flames on the beach and burning debris descending onto the surface of the water.

"You see?" Vladimir said, as the bus windows glowed, reflecting the fire.

"I see that you are a *Russian*," Neizert said, terrified that he had been captured and was finally going to die at the hands of the KGB after all he'd gone through. A young woman on the bus began to scream. She made the driver stop the bus so she could get off. The passengers watched her run towards the burning quay.

A motorcycle came roaring up the street at ninety miles and hour—straight down the middle of Plata's main drag. The bike's driver was obviously wounded, leaning forward over his handlebars. He passed the bus but failed to make the turn in front of him and crashed into a parked car. The rider's body flew like a puppet over the hood of the car and straight into a wooden storefront. The bus driver was an elderly man, and he seemed totally confused by the explosion and its aftermath. He hesitated a moment to collect himself. Then, after a short pause, he finally put the bus back into gear and pulled on down the street towards the turn off to Sonoyta. They passed the motorcycle, now lying on its side, completely totaled, its front forks smashed, its back wheel still spinning, the engine still running. The rider's body lay crumpled and broken, hanging suspended, lodged halfway through the wooden façade of the building he'd been thrown against when his bike had hit the parked car.

"I won't tell you what you want to know," Neizert said, nervously squirming in the bus's worn-out seat.

"There is nothing I *want* to know," Vladimir said. The Russian held the pistol in such a way that the passengers in the adjoining seats couldn't see it. But it was pointed straight at Neizert all the time.

"Are you going to turn me over to them in Sonoyta?" Neizert asked.

"No," Vladimir said.

"You're a liar," Neizert said. He was angry at himself for being caught this close to the border; this close to success. He looked out the window and tried to imagine a scenario wherein he could escape. This man was thirty years younger than he was and obviously in good shape—a trained KGB officer. He decided that there was no way he could win a physical confrontation with him. If he suddenly wrestled him for the gun right there on the bus it was barely possible, but highly unlikely, in reality, that he'd come out on top, so he gave up on the idea.

"How did Gehlen manage to do it?" Vladimir said suddenly. Neizert turned and looked at him.

"What do you mean?"

"How could he ... I mean, how did the Americans let him get so *far*?"

"Don't be stupid," Neizert said. "... That was what the *Americans* wanted. Gehlen was very knowledgeable about the Russians. Of *course* they wanted him to work for *them*. Many of America's top families were sympathetic to the Nazis. You surely know that! Joe Kennedy got some kind of medal from Göring, even. Many other Americans did, too."

"And the KGB? Was it, too, infiltrated?" Vladimir asked. Neizert looked appraisingly at him for a moment.

"Yes."

"How?"

"Because the NKVD was already compromised. The Nazis were good at penetrating it, *during the War*. Remember; Germany was *winning* the war at one point; or so it seemed to us at the time. We had reached Moscow, even. The Nazis had scores of double agents in the Kremlin—Nazi agents were hidden in all sectors of the government back then, in fact," Neizert said. "Who are *you*?"

"I was sent here by General Maximov," Vladimir said. "To help get you to America."

"This is another KGB trick, isn't it? ... *Pretend* to be on my side. ... I won't speak to you again," Neizert said.

"He was a very brave man—the General," Vladimir said. The bus slowed. There was a checkpoint run by the Mexican police twenty-five miles from Sonoyta. Vladimir looked out at the empty desert. It was dusk, now, and a beautiful crimson light shone on the distant mountains along what he assumed was the border, but their blue peaks looked cold to him, in spite of their desert setting.

"That must be America," Vladimir said.

"What?"

"There—those mountains over there, on the horizon ... America," Vladimir said, pointing. Then he turned his attention to the police, who were in the process of boarding the bus.

"If you say one word, I'll shoot you," Vladimir said. He had no intention of being stopped by the Mexican police, knowing that they would sell him back to the KGB without fail.

*   *   *

"Where is he, Gemma? You have to tell me," Alex said.

"He's gone," she said. Alex was pointing a gun at her.

"Are you going to kill the mother of your child?"

"You're really a bitch—you know that? Where *is* he?" Alex said.

"I won't tell you," Gemma said. He'd kicked in the hotel room door and found her still in bed. He could tell that she'd been with the Russian. Both the look on her face. and the look of the bed told him, without her saying a word.

"Is he *here*? In the *hotel*?" She sat up. She was frightened because she understood that he loved her, and that he might just go crazy from grief and kill her and the baby in a red-rage.

"Alex. Stop it."

"Stop *what*?"

"Threatening me," she said.

"I love you," Alex said.

"Then put the gun down." He did, letting it fall to his side.

"Where is he?"

"He's gone," Gemma said, covering herself up with a sheet.

"Where? *God damn you!*"

"He's taken your Hauptmann and gone," she said. They heard the explosion then. It rocked the hotel room, making the windows rattle. He ran over to the bed and lay down and put his arms around her and held her, wanting to protect her. She glanced out the window and saw the fireball rising up, orange and black, and wondered what it was. When it was over she saw that Law was crying, sobbing like a child. He suddenly let her go, stood up and wiped the tears from his eyes, then walked out of the room without saying another word to her. After he left she got up and showered. She stood there with the slightly salty-tasting tepid water running over her body and wondered what would happen to her now.

*   *   *

Flaco watched the little girl eat. His mother had made pancakes for breakfast. There was a large stack of them piled on a yellow platter that she'd set down on the old red Formica table. It was the same table that their family had owned since he was a little kid himself. He remembered when his mom and dad had bought it at a yard sale for five bucks and put it into his father's broken-down Chevy pick-up and brought it home. His brother and he had been given the task of keeping the chairs—all six of them—from falling out the back of the truck. He was in pain, both physical *and* psychic, from dope withdrawal. He was sweating, and his hands were shaking like he had palsy. His father was looking at him. The father who now looked like an old man to him; wrinkled and wizened from his years of working outside as a gardener. His father—judging from the look on his face—understood that his son was hurting.

"*¿Que te pasa, Tomás?*" His father used his Christian name and it brought him up short. He was very rarely called Tomás by anyone except his immediate family.

"*Gripe,*" Flaco said in Spanish, saying that he had the flu.

"*¿De quien es la gringita?*" "Who does the little girl belong to?" his father asked in Spanish. As a child he hadn't liked it that his parents didn't speak English. It bothered him. It seemed weird that they could live here and *not* speak the language that was on the TV and that was used by his teachers, and that in fact their own children spoke at school and with their friends.

"My friend, Warren, the gringo," Flaco said in English. His father understood English but didn't speak it much, or well, even now.

"*¿Y quanto tiempo la vamos a tener aquí?*" His father asked. "And how long will she be with us?"

"Until my *amigo* gets back," Flaco said.

"Okay," his father said. "You okay?"

"Yeah, I'm okay, Pop," Flaco said.

"*¡Horacio! Déjalo, por favor. Y la muchachita puede quedarse aquí. Me gusta mucho tenerla en la casa.*" his mother said. He knew that his mother liked the little girl—that was obvious from the moment they'd brought her into the house. His mother's face had lit up the first time she'd seen her. She'd always wanted a little girl and hadn't gotten one from her marriage.

"Is she your friend's child?" his father asked in Spanish.

"Yeah," Flaco said, again lying. He picked up a fork and stabbed a pancake and

516

brought it to his plate. They all watched his hand shaking as he did it. Even the little girl noticed, looking up from her food to stare at him.

"Why don't you people learn English, anyway?" Flaco said. He picked up the syrup and opened the top and poured a lake of it onto his pancake. "How do you think I liked going to teacher-parent night with you two? *Huh? Huh?!*" He suddenly started to shake uncontrollably like he was having apoplexy and was going to die. He stood up, then sat down again and just looked at his food, sitting there shaking in his chair. His mother came over and held him from behind. She took the paper towel she was holding and wiped his sweaty face, paying no attention to his string of insults.

"Mom, I think I'm dying," Flaco said. She didn't understand, but kept on holding him. Later, she took him up to his old bedroom and had him lie down. He asked her to go out and score for him in a very quiet voice—delirious from being junk-sick. He woke up twenty-hours later from the pressure of a gun that was being shoved into his cheek muscle by a big white man.

"My name is Stuckie. This is my partner, Special Agent Van Steeps." Flaco looked over at a huge black man with no neck who was standing there filling up the doorway. Van Steeps looked at him with the expression of a stone-cold killer. "We need your full cooperation, amigo. Do you understand what I'm saying?" Stuckie said.

"Yeah," Flaco said, finally coming completely awake.

"Your parents' lives depend on it. And the kid's," Robin Stuckie said. He pulled the gun out of Flaco's face and sat down on the side of the bed. "Now, we work for some people that need you to do something very important."

"Yeah." Flaco knew they were cops. They smelled like cops and they looked like cops, he was sure of it.

"Leave my folks out of it," Flaco said.

"We can't do that," Stuckie said.

"What do you want me to do?" Flaco asked.

"I want you to kill someone," Stuckie said.

"I don't want to do *that*," Flaco said. "I'm trying to clean my shit up. Turn over a new leaf and everything."

"Okay. Then I bring your nice old moms up here and shoot her in the face. How would you like *that*?" Stuckie asked.

"What the fuck is this all *about?!*" Flaco demanded.

"That, my friend, is for me to know, and you to find out, as my mother always used to say," Stuckie said.

"*That's right, you little dope fiend motherfucker!*" the black cop chimed in.

"You don't look so good, *vato*," Stuckie said.

"He sure don't," Van Steeps said.

"Where's my mom and dad?" Flaco said.

"In their bedroom, keeping company with another friend of ours. He's not a nice man at all—our friend. He saw way too much violence over there in the jungle. In fact, I personally think he's fucking crazy," Stuckie said. "I'm afraid of him my own self."

"As crazy as they get. He gets *off* on killing people," the black guy said. Flaco slid up on the bed. He looked at a family picture that had been taken years before at his first communion that sat on his dresser. It showed the four of them: Flaco, his younger brother, and his mom and dad. The black guy saw him looking at it and he walked over, picked it up off the top of the dresser, then threw it, face-down, hard onto the dresser, breaking the glass. Stuckie picked Flaco up out of his bed by the neck and threw him bodily towards his closet.

"Come on, you stinking sack of wet donkey-shit. ... Get dressed—you got *people* to see."

*　　　　*　　　　*

"Will he live?" Alex asked. He'd found Warren Talbot lying in the alley behind the bar. It was almost completely dark. Warren had passed out again from the beating and was lying face-down in the dirt of the alley. Alex saw Sonny and Butch in the ATV coming back down the street from the beach. He'd wondered where they were, or if they had even lived through the blast. He didn't see Marie with them. Delmonico stopped the four-wheeler in the middle of the street. Alex had been dragging Warren, holding him under the arms, towards their hotel.

Butch got off the four-wheeler and picked the detective up, carried him to the back of the ATV, and placed him gingerly in its small truck-bed. Alex got onto Sonny's ATV behind the Englishman and Butch climbed into the truck-bed with Talbot. Delmonico drove on off down the street. No one was talking. They drove like hell toward the end of town, with its multiple trailer courts that all faced the beach. Delmonico pulled into one of them, headed down to where a jeep and trailer were parked and then pulled to a stop. Butch jumped out of the truck-bed, then lifted the detective out of it and started running toward the trailer, carrying Talbot like he was a little kid, yelling in English for the doctor. The young French girl opened the door to the trailer and moved quickly aside to keep from being knocked out of the way.

"Where's Marie?" Alex asked, sitting there behind Delmonico. Sonny didn't answer. He turned off the motor, slid off the seat, then lit a cigarette without saying

518

a single word. The force of the blast had ripped the eye-patch off his face and singed both of his eyebrows completely off.

"Yes. He'll live, but he'll probably lose the sight in that eye." The young doctor was speaking to Butch. He'd stitched-up the detective's various lacerations and managed to stop the bleeding in Talbot's mouth. He'd given him a sedative and the detective was now sleeping quietly on the short examination-room table, his legs hanging over the side. Butch was looking at him with a strange, distant look on his face.

"Where's the old Kraut?" Butch asked.

"Gone to Texas," Alex said.

"Great,." Butch said. "Where the fuck *is* he—do you actually *know?*"

"Sonoyta, I guess," Alex said. "The KGB got him; from right under our noses." Delmonico looked over at Alex. The doctor tore off the silicon gloves he'd been wearing while stitching up Talbot. He pretended he hadn't heard any of what had just been said.

"I've got a boat coming," Sonny said, getting out another cigarette. He had dark circles under both his good *and* bad eyes. The bandage on his arm was now wet and filthy. The doctor walked over to him and lifted it off his arm and then whistled.

"You sit down right here," the doctor told Sonny.

"I've got to go," Delmonico said.

"Go, and you'll shortly die from gangrene. Bacteremia. ... Do you know what *that* is, Sonny?"

"Yes. But it can't be worse than losing the load." Sonny ignored the doctor's warning and proceeded to walk out of the trailer.

"Where's Marie?" Alex asked.

"... She didn't make it," Butch said. "We had some bad luck."

*   *   *

Marie had come down to look at what he'd done. Butch was thumbing through a tattered old book that he'd found—*Hunting the Grizzly Bear*—in one of the cabin's built-in cupboards

"Sometimes you eat the bear. ... " Butch quoted.

"And sometimes the bear eats *you*," Marie finished the quote for him. "My father always says that." Marie had the AK strapped to her back. She walked across the cabin to kiss him.

"All set?" she asked.

"All set," Butch said.

"Are you going to light it?" Marie said.

"Yeah, in a minute. How far are we from the quay, now?" Marie went over to a starboard porthole and looked out. Butch could now see the rusted metal roofs of the town through the portside portholes. They were very close.

"They're out there, right?" Butch said.

"Just like you said ... a bunch of them are waiting at the end of the quay," Marie said.

"How many, do you think?"

"... At least ten—No, more. ... Some chick with red hair is with them, too," Marie said. Butch lit a Blue Diamond match and re-lit his skinny Mexican cigar, hot-boxing it to get the end burning hotter, making it glow a bright orange.

"We're about fifteen feet from the quay right now," Marie said.

"Okay. ... Here goes nothing." Butch lit the first fuse with the end of the cigar.

"I love you, baby," Marie said. She pulled the rifle off of her shoulder and went up to the deck.

"Okay. Give it up when they brace you. Just toss the rifle in the water and walk off the quay. Just run right on by them," Butch told her as she climbed the cabin ladder and disappeared.

By that time, Sonny had piloted the boat right up to the quay, and Butch could see from the porthole that they were docking. He felt the boat hit the rubber truck tires along the edge of the quay and heard Sonny kill the engine. He waited one more minute, then began to light the fuses on the other bundles of dynamite with the end of his cigar. He'd made each successive fuse shorter than the last, so the last bundle he lit had only a five-inch fuse on it. When he was done he walked to the ladder and turned. He could see the bright white light of the fuses traveling up toward their respective bundles of impending death—all lit now, and burning well. He tossed his cigar on the floor and climbed up on deck.

As Butch came up on deck he saw Marie toss the AK-47 into the water and put her hands up. The redhead—the one Butch had almost shot months before—was coming down the quay with several men in tow. The Vagos were all armed with automatic weapons. Sonny finished tying up the boat's stern, then put his hands up. The redhead stopped in front of him.

"Everyone off," the redhead ordered. She walked toward them with a pistol in her hand. Butch stepped carefully along the railing of the boat, then jumped down onto the quay near Sonny and put his hands up. He nodded to Marie, and she slid over the side and onto the quay and stood behind him.

"Get the fuck out of here," the redhead said. "This is *ours*, now." Butch walked down the quay toward the redhead. When he got in front of her she looked directly at him. He felt Marie bump into his back.

"Let's go," Marie said. "Let them have it—it's not worth getting killed for." Marie looked at the redhead. Butch started to walk on, his hands still up. He heard a gun shot. He turned and saw Marie's head go back violently and her body falling into the water.

"I remember *you*—asshole," the redhead said, smiling and pointing the pistol at him. "Go on," she told her men. "Get our shit." The men walked past her, and then past Delmonico, who was looking down in the water at Marie. Sonny passed the redhead, who didn't give him a second look.

"Was that *your* bitch? ... I hope so," the redhead said. Butch involuntarily jumped as she pointed the pistol at his head. Four of the Vagos had stepped up onto the boat and were looking for the cabin entrance when the thing blew. The blast killed everyone near the boat instantaneously. The redhead was decapitated by a porthole cover on the spot. Her body still reflexively "lived" on for a few seconds, though, and the headless corpse actually fired her pistol at the place where Butch had been standing, but he was already in the water and gone. The quay's underpinnings had been blasted out from under his feet and that was what saved him. He was two feet under water when flaming pieces of the boat's cabin and superstructure started landing on most of the group of men who had escaped death in the initial blast. Now, however, they found themselves burning to death in searing agony as they ran away from the conflagration, most of them temporarily mad with terror, unable to respond in any rational way to what had just happened to them. The shock wave had knocked Delmonico face-down onto the beach as he trotted toward the road. He could still run pretty well despite his age.

Butch came up with Marie, but she was dead. He was too experienced with death to fool himself into thinking differently. Delmonico stood up and watched Butch come out of the water and walk up onto the beach—patches of the water on fire behind him—still holding her body. Butch walked right by him and crossed the road, still holding her. People ran by him towards the flaming debris and burning bodies on the beach. wondering what the hell had just happened in their sleepy little town of Plata.

No one noticed a new purse-seiner roll in and anchor a half -hour later, just down the beach from Plata's main drag. The boat was unloaded by two leathery old Mexican fisherman plus Delmonico, using two rowboats. The heroin was taken via ATV through the streets and put in the doctor's trailer while he was working on

Warren Talbot. The last and heaviest of the loads capsized the rowboat, and Sonny had to jump in the water and carefully swim through the oil slicks and body parts left from the explosion until he'd gotten every single bale of heroin back aboard the small craft. He was tireless in doing so. Ironically, the salt water made his wound burn like hell, but it temporarily cleaned the bacteria out of the now-infected arm and kept gangrene from setting in and killing him before he could get a proper dressing back on the wound.

Before they left Plata, Butch buried Marie. He took her body in an ATV down the beach, driving past flocks of geese that had landed there on their way north. The geese scattered and he drove on up the empty beach onto a bluff: a place that overlooked both the beach and a small water-fowl-filled lagoon. Butch dug the grave and laid her down in the sand. He covered Marie up, one shovelful of sand at a time, until she was buried. He didn't say a word the whole time, until the very end, when he'd finished. He remembered that she was a Catholic—like he was—and so he recited the only prayer he could remember. He'd recited it during the Tet offensive, too, when he'd run out of bullets and was hunkering down by the front of the American Embassy searching dead Marines' bodies for more ammo. He'd said it to himself without realizing it, back then. Now, he said it again, remembering the words. Only the migratory birds stretched out along the sand at the water's edge could hear him speaking.

> Our Father, who art in Heaven,
> Hallowed be thy Name;
> Thy Kingdom come;
> Thy will be done on earth
> As it is in Heaven.
> Give us this day our daily bread;
> And forgive us our trespasses
> As we forgive those who trespass against us;
> And lead us not into temptation,
> But deliver us from evil.
>
> For thine is the kingdom,
>
> And the power, and the glory,
>
> For ever and ever.
>
> Amen.

When he was finished, he looked down at the place he was going to leave her, the love of his life, forever. It didn't seem good enough, somehow. It bothered him that there would be no marker there, ever. He thought for a moment of her looking out at the sea on the way to Plata that afternoon, so full of life. The way she'd smiled like a little girl at him. Then he got on the ATV and left, driving down the lonely beach. *Markers don't matter,* he said out loud.

He would never find another woman that was as right for him as she had been. You only get one chance to have *that,* he realized much later in his life—there was some kind of rule about that that was written in the stars. There's just one chance for most of us to connect. The strange thing was that—later in life—he would always expect to see Marie if he was in trouble. He would look for her, too, in strange places back home: malls, restaurants, almost any random place at all; always when he was lonely, which he was for the rest of his life.

53

■ US / Mexico Border

Vladimir found a coyote who worked out of a convenience store he owned in Sonoyta. The Russian and Neizert left that same afternoon for the trip across the border. They departed the flat and ugly town in a caravan of three new white Chevy vans, each one chock-full of illegal immigrants. The illegals were mostly from Guatemala and central Mexico, and all of them looked lost and scared to death to the Russian—not unlike prisoners he'd seen back home in one of the several gulags he'd visited over the years. All of the illegals riding in the vans knew that literally *anything* could happen to them during the next forty-eight hours—up to and possibly including a horrible dirt-eating death; a death that would be due to acute dehydration, a state that they all knew could drive a lost, desperate, and delirious person to try to actually suck water from sand and rocks, the result of which action would be to finally choke to death in a feverish and frenzied seizure. They'd all left the vans behind at midnight and had struck out on foot through the desert toward the U.S. border, guided by two very hard-looking, middle-aged Mexican men, both of whom were wearing brand-new thick down-filled coats.

Three short young Indian women dressed in layers of odd-looking, mismatched jackets and sweaters were walking in front of Vladimir and the Hauptmann right now. The girls were each carrying a gallon jug of drinking water. The young women had been kind to the two white men, who were at the very end of human line that stretched for a quarter of a mile through the moonlit desert. The white men had paid the coyote just like everyone else; but they obviously didn't fit into this world of the Latino young and poor, heading to Tucson on a Friday night under a full, cold-hearted moon. The young women carried the extra water because they'd made the trip before and understood that it might very well save their lives. There were seventy in their party, and two older women—only in their forties—had already been left behind to die because they'd been unable to keep up with the rest. In fact, they did die together just the next day, from exposure. The two armed Mexican men who guided their party spoke very little and were feared by all. No one spoke, in fact, unless it was absolutely necessary. All Vladimir could hear was the sound of boots hitting the ground—a sound that traveled well through the still, cold air.

The Hauptmann had turned his ankle in Sonoyta when he blithely stepped into a hole in the sidewalk—such holes were common in all Mexican towns, and the natives knew to look out for them. After that incident, Vladimir had to help him walk. Now that they were out in the open desert, he was forced to support the Hauptmann by holding him up around the waist, as the man's ankle had gotten much worse, having now turned a nasty bluish color and swollen up considerably. Twice, one of their armed handlers had warned them that they would have to speed up their pace or be left behind. The three young teenaged women in front of them expected the two white men to fall out of line at any minute and be left, stranded in the middle of nowhere.

"I had a dream that I would die out here," the Hauptmann confided. He was wincing with every step he took. "I'm sorry—I have to stop. I just can't go on. Let me be. Let it end here."

"No—we have to keep up with them," Vladimir said. It was very late at night now, and the stars were out, brilliant in the dry desert air, the Milky Way ribboned across the sky in all its glory. It was much colder than Vladimir had expected. He'd thought the desert was an habitually warm place, even at night, but they were both almost freezing, not having even brought light jackets along. An hour later they finally saw the faint lights of Ajo Arizona in the far distance. The Russian was very strong, but he had been literally forced to carry the Hauptmann on his back for the last several miles. At times, when it got to be almost unbearable, Vladimir thought of what his mother had endured in the War, and how she must have suffered during the battle for Stalingrad, and that kept him going.

*   *   *

The motel in Sonoyta was just outside of town. They could see blue-colored mountains on the US side of the border looming aggressively above a pan-flat desert.

"Where's your friend?" Alex said.

"I don't know," Gemma said.

"Has he left you?" Alex said.

"Maybe," Gemma said.

They were waiting now for the DEA to come and arrest Sonny and find the heroin. It was two in the afternoon and the room was cool because Alex had turned on the air conditioner, a hulking, rusted affair sticking out of the wall near the bed.

525

"What happened to Marie?" Gemma asked.

"She was killed," Alex said.

"For what?" Gemma asked.

"Does it matter? ... She wasn't a Communist. Not a comrade. Don't you people just care about each other? What is it you believe in, anyway?" Alex asked.

"Life," Gemma said.

"Life?"

"Yes," she said.

"What does *that* mean?"

"It means we believe in people, not money," Gemma quickly answered him.

"You believe in *people?*" Alex said.

"Yes. My father taught me to believe in the basic goodness of people and not money," Gemma said.

"What's wrong with money?" Alex asked.

"It's dirty," Gemma said. "It makes people crazy. Look at your friend, Perry." She was sitting across the dark motel room from him, not sure what was going to happen, no longer privy to Alex's thoughts. She'd confessed to Alex that Vladimir was going to deliver the old German to Los Angeles, to the motel Alex had once mentioned to her, thinking that telling him that would somehow make him feel better about the whole situation.

"Are you going to marry him?" Alex asked. He was bitter and angry and wanted her to know how he felt.

"I hope so," she said. "Yes; I want to."

"Are you going to live in Russia?" Alex asked.

"I suppose. ... I don't really know," she said.

"I love you," Alex said, surprising her.

"I'm sorry, Bruce. I am, but I don't have any control over who I'm in love with, I really don't, and it's Vladimir," Gemma said, and she meant it

"You're still a bitch," Alex said. She didn't answer him. He was sitting on the edge of the bed and had a pistol lying on the bed next to him. He put his hands through his hair.

"Is he good in bed?—is *that* it?" She still didn't answer. "What *is* it then? Why don't I affect you the way *he* does?" She realized then, at that moment, that Tucker had never been refused anything in his entire life, and really didn't know what it was like to deal with something he couldn't have; either buy outright or connive somehow to "possess." At first she thought it almost amusing, the rich boy without an explanation for his defeat. But then, and because she *did* care about him, she felt guilty, knowing that she was hurting him.

"You should leave them—all of this. The CIA and everything to do with it," Gemma said.

He walked to the front of the room and saw the doctor and Delmonico standing outside in the parking lot. The two were leisurely removing the kilos of heroin from the secret compartment in the doctor's trailer. He watched them carrying bundles of heroin into one of the adjacent motel rooms.

"My name is Alex Law. I'm not Bruce Tucker. You know that; and I'm *not* a gangster," Alex said, watching them work, his back to her.

"Alex, of course," Gemma said.

"I'm *not* a criminal; I'm an intelligence officer," Alex said, speaking as if he were trying to convince himself. "... I want the baby Gemma. Please don't do anything to it."

"I wasn't going to," Gemma said. Alex turned around. They looked at each other. They both realized that they would always have this connection if nothing else. The child that was coming would always belong to both of them.

"I want to know the kid," Alex said. "I want to be a father to him or her."

"Yes, I understand," she said. "I'm sorry ... *Alex.*"

"Law," Alex said, and turned around to face her.

"Yes, of course," Gemma said. "Alex Law."

"All right, then." The door flew open and Butch was standing there, dead drunk. He pulled a pistol out and waved it around. He had a bottle of tequila in one hand and a .45 in the other. He could barely walk.

"Is that the Commie bitch?" Butch said.

"Get out of here," Alex said.

"*Is* it? ... She killed Marie, The fucking *bitch*," Butch said. He walked into the room and lifted the pistol and fired. The bullet hit the pillow next to Gemma's head and Alex jumped on him. Another bullet went off and hit the floor at their feet as they fought over the gun. Butch was much stronger, even dead drunk, and finally wrestled free and punched Alex viciously in the face. Alex flew backwards and hit his head on the room's small desk, collapsing. He lay there unconscious. Butch turned and looked at Gemma.

"I kill commie bitches. You wouldn't be the first." He teetered closer to her.

"I didn't kill Marie—you *know* that," Gemma said.

"You *did* kill Marie. She's dead because of you and that old man and because of *me*," Butch said. He slapped his chest with the .45 and walked towards her. He pointed it directly at her and stood only a few steps from where she was sitting on the bed. He had a horrible tortured look on his face.

"*I'm pregnant.*" Gemma said, suddenly pleading with him, no longer able to hide her fear. She'd seen that look on mens' faces before, and knew she was in mortal danger. *"Please God ... It's his. Tucker's. Alex's."* Butch wobbled. He finally lowered the pistol and walked out of the room. She watched through the open motel room door as Butch fell down in the parking lot and lay there immobile. Delmonico ran over with the doctor and with great difficulty they both picked him up and carried him toward the doctor's trailer. Alex still lay there unconscious. She ran to his side and screamed for help, as loudly as she could.

*   *   *

"Do you remember me?" Malcolm Law asked. Malcolm was standing at the foot of the bed. There was vomit on Butch's pillow, and the smell of shit and vomit permeated the room. Butch had been so drunk that he'd simply turned his head and puked on the bed when he got sick, then later rolled in it—he'd also shit himself in the bed. It wasn't a pretty sight, to say the least; but Malcolm Law had seen and experienced worse. In fact, he'd been *responsible* for much worse, so he just ignored it. Butch's T-shirt, face, and hair were covered with pinkish-colored dried vomit. Malcolm nudged Butch's foot with a pistol. George was standing behind Malcolm with a bemused look on his face, obviously breathing through his mouth, trying to ignore the stench in the room.

"Do you, Nickels?—*you piece of shit."* When Butch opened his eyes, he saw several men standing above his bed, and raised himself up with a start. He heard the unmistakable click of a pistol's hammer being pulled back and suddenly felt the weight of a gun barrel pushing against his vomit-covered face. His eyes were almost completely stuck shut, and he could barely see who was speaking to him. He reflexively pawed at them with his right hand, trying to wipe his eyes while he propped himself up in bed with his elbow as he strained to get them open. He looked like a bear, or some other wild animal, waking up from a long hibernation. The sight of him wallowing in his own filth truly disgusted Law. Malcolm stood up, maintaining the pistol barrel's pressure on Butch's dirty face, then forced the barrel down *hard* into his cheek.

"Do you, asshole?"

"No, sir. I can't see very well right now, sir," Butch finally recognized Malcolm Law's voice. He was still drunk, and he had no idea why Law was there, or what he'd done to deserve his wrath. He rubbed again at his eyes. He began to see things now, a little at a time, but at first, everything was in triplicate. Eventually, Malcolm Law came into focus, and Butch saw an older-looking man with black hair standing behind him. The man was very tall and quite well-dressed, and even in his still half-drunken state, Butch was sure he'd never seen him before in his life. "You piece of *shit,"* Law said again. "I should just shoot you right now and get it over with—I'm serious, Nickels."

"*Please* don't, sir," Butch was whining, now.

"Look at you," Law said.

"Looks like a pig shit all over his face," George said.

"You've got chunks of *shit* on your face, Nickels." Law said.

"Yes sir. ... I've got to puke right *now,* sir," Butch said.

"Go ahead." They watched Butch stagger unsteadily up from the motel bed and try to make it to the bathroom, using the wall for support. Law tripped him and he fell. Malcolm then kicked him in the ribs, hard, stepping back out of the way as Butch, between grunts of pain, puked all over the dirty nylon motel rug. The rug was an ugly "Amazon"-green, and yellow bile-saturated vomit spewed out of Butch's open mouth in waves as his stomach spasmed repeatedly, leaving a several-foot-square area of stinking, alcohol-tinged and half-digested food chunks mixed with his own blood to slowly permeate the carpet.

"You are the worst piece of shit I've ever met," Malcolm said. He was teetering on the brink of kicking him again. After months of being literally at his own, personal, breaking point, Malcolm had finally gone over the edge into uncharted realms, and was about to kick Butch Nickels, one of his own operatives, in the head. Malcolm would probably have stomped Butch to death right there in the motel room if George hadn't stopped him by pulling him back before he could complete his next kick—he'd already drawn his leg back when George grabbed him from behind and dragged him away. Butch got up, first to one knee, then the other, his chin still dripping puke onto the pile in front of him. He put his hands down in the pool of vomit and finally managed to stand up.

"I'm going to *kill* you, Nickels. Do you *understand that?* I'm going to *have you killed.* DO YOU UNDERSTAND ME, YOU WORTHLESS ASSHOLE!" Malcolm yelled. Then George took charge and forced Malcolm out of Butch's room, pushing him into the parking lot.

Butch sat on the floor in front of the toilet with his head resting on the rim of the seat for what seemed to him like hours. It was Sonny Delmonico who finally got him up and put him into the shower-stall, clothes and all, and turned on the cold water tap, trying to sober him up.

"You've got a job to do, mate. ... It's time to wake up," Sonny said. Butch sat there on the floor of the shower for a long time, the cold water hitting him and soaking his clothes, not *wanting* to sober up because of the pain he knew would come back when he was clear-headed again. He dreaded that psychological pain more than anything

Malcolm Law could possibly do to him. Finally, almost sober now, he stepped out of the shower still fully dressed, only to see Malcolm Law still there, staring at him again from the bedroom.

"My son has a concussion, that *you* gave him, in your drunken stupidity," Malcolm said. He'd come back to Butch's room after having put Alex on a helicopter to the Naval Hospital in San Diego. Butch looked at him oddly; he didn't remember the fight with Alex at all, or pulling the gun on Gemma. Butch, standing there drenched, his clothes still sopping, his thinning hair looking funny on such a young man, glanced around the room, nonplussed, first at Malcolm Law, then at the tall man he'd seen earlier, while Malcolm detailed to him what he'd done.

"I don't understand. ..." Butch said.

"You don't *remember* what happened?—you were *that* fucking drunk?" Malcolm said.

"No, sir."

"You have no idea, then?" Malcolm said.

"No sir, I truly do not," Butch said.

"You and Alex got into a fight yesterday. ... Now Alex is in a fucking helicopter on the way to the hospital, with a serious head injury."

"I don't remember *any* of that—I really don't, sir," Butch said. He looked around the room for his weapon, but didn't see it.

"Looking for *this*, old man?" George lifted up Butch's .45.

"Okay. I ... I'll go see him—right now," Butch said. He started to walk toward the door.

"Not like that," George said.

"Okay, piece of shit. This is how you are going to stay out of the federal penitentiary. Are you *listening* to me?" Malcolm said. "I've got a Russian KGB officer in Mexican police custody along with my German. You are going to go to Tijuana, Nickels, and *get* them for me. Should you happen to die in the process of doing this, I don't care. In fact, I hope you *do* die, Nickels, after what you did to my son. Don't think about coming back to us if you fail. Keep right on going. ... But I will catch you and I will kill you *myself* if you fail at this. How's *that* sound to you, boy-o?" Malcolm said. Butch merely nodded, still half out-of-it, but trying to take it all in.

"To Tijuana?" Butch said.

"Yes. They're holding my German and some KGB asshole. The Mexican police are trying to extort money out of the Russians—they're holding them both for ransom. I want you to kill the KGB fuck if you have to, but go get me my German back. And I really hope you don't fuck this thing up," Malcolm said.

"I'll need help," Butch said. He'd started to shiver involuntarily.

"Do you? Take that broken-down LA detective along, then," Malcolm said.

"What about Alex?" Butch said.

"Did you *hear* me? He's on the way to the *hospital* in San Diego—a helicopter took him away about half-an-hour ago. ... You're going on a *suicide* mission, Nickels. I don't think I'll send my son along with you," Law said.

"Tijuana?" Butch said again, trying to get it all straight. He tried to remember fighting with Alex, but he still couldn't remember anything about what the elder Law had told him he'd done the day before.

"They're moving them at four. I've paid the ransom. The *problem* is that the Mexican police don't plan on giving me my German. They're planning on selling him a few more times first, now that they know how valuable he is. They also plan on killing *me* when I try and leave with my man. The Russian got a spanking and talked, you see. He's told them everything, so naturally they see him as a big profit-maker," Malcolm said. "Get the German. ... Bring me the fucking Russian, too, if you can. I want them both. They'll leave the police station sometime after four this afternoon to supposedly meet me. I'm going to be watching them, though. I've been able to use the NSC to listen to the Mexican police's calls. Have you *got* it? The main police station in Tijuana. Even a fuck-wad like you, Nickels, should be able to find a place like *that*. Can you stay sober long enough to do this?"

"Yes, sir. Just the two men, sir? It'll be difficult," Butch said, standing at semi-attention and feeling just like he was back in the Marine Corps. He tried to stop shivering, but couldn't control his body.

"My hope is you'll be killed in the line of duty," Law said. "I will pay them their money and I will get my German anyway, finally, in the end. Do you understand?"

"Is he going to be all right ... Alex?" Butch asked. "I think he's going to have a baby?"

"*What did you say!*"

"I think the Italian girl is pregnant," Butch quickly said. He'd suddenly remembered hearing Gemma tell him that she was pregnant, sometime the day before, but he couldn't place the context of the remark. Alex's father just looked at him for a moment, then walked out of the room without saying another word. George walked up to him and handed him back his pistol.

"Good luck, old man. ... If it makes any difference to you, he's at the end of his rope. It's all about this German. He's sure he's going to lose him, now. He's been quite a bother, this old German." Butch nodded stupidly, still in an alcoholic haze, and feeling sick again. He watched the tall man leave his motel room and very carefully close the door behind him. Butch looked down at the puddle of water that had dripped off him and formed at his feet. The motel's rug was soaked where he'd been standing.

"What the *fuck,* man," Butch said to himself out loud. He looked up and saw his reflection in the mirror across the room. It was as if he were looking at another, much older, version of himself. He was brought up short by the filthy, hard-beaten low-life staring back at him from the world of the mirror.

*   *   *

The cell in the Tijuana jail was a very special one. It had a new, white-plastic table, with a chair, and the walls were also painted white. It was very clean. It was the cell that the Mexican Federal Police used for show and tell; when the UN or the U.S. Consulate people came to check on American or European prisoners. There had been lots of reports recently of mistreatment of prisoners, especially of American college-age girls, who, after being arrested for public drunkenness, had been molested by the police while in custody.

"My name is Capitan José Delgado. Your name is Neizert. You are a German scientist," the Mexican police captain stated.

"I want to see someone from the American Embassy," Neizert said. He'd been saying the same thing all morning, but no one was listening to him.

"I'm sure you do, but first you will answer my questions," Delgado said.

"I will not," Neizert said.

"Sit down, *señor.* Let me explain something to you," Delgado said. His English was perfect. He'd gone to school at San Diego State—his mother was an American. Delgado had completed his degree in Business Administration, but had chosen a career with the police force in Tijuana because he could make a lot more money working across the border, from graft and corruption, than he ever would have been able to laboring in a "legitimate," U.S.-based company. "Let me explain your situation to you—*exactly.*"

"Explain what?" Neizert said.

"I'm going to explain the facts of life in Tijuana to you. Please, sit down." The captain pulled a chair out for him in a very courteous way.

"You were taken from among a band of illegals who were attacked by thieves," Delgado said.

"You mean police," Neizert said. The truth was, a squad of *Judiciales* had come across the party of illegals and had tried to extort money out of their two guides. They'd ended up murdering both the guides, who'd refused to pay them, and then had shot several other men to make it look like a criminal gang had been ravaging the area. The police had raped two of the young women while the rest ran away out into the desert where, without guides, they would soon die of exposure.

"This is Mexico—do you understand that?" the policeman said.

"I do," Neizert said.

"Good. Then you understand that *I* will decide when you can leave here. Your companion, the Russian, has told me that you are traveling to the United States illegally and that you are a German scientist of some importance. Is that correct?"

"I will not speak to you," Neizert said.

"*Ollye—Pablo, Juan, trigan al Ruso,*" the captain said in a loud voice. The guards dragged Vladimir Putilin down the hallway and into the "nice" cell. The police had attached leads from a car battery to his testicles, and had shocked him repeatedly with the apparatus, while buckets of cold water were occasionally thrown at him to keep him from passing out. When that treatment didn't elicit any favorable responses, they'd trotted out a plumber's acetylene torch and literally fried his flesh in various places on his body—including under his arms—until he finally confessed both his identity and Neizert's. Two uniformed policeman dragged the Russian into the cell and held him up against the bars so Neizert could see him and the condition he was in. He looked like a completely different man altogether at this point.

"I'm sorry," Vladimir said weakly.

"Now ... I can repeat this performance if I have to," the captain said. "But you don't look anywhere near as strong as this young Russian, my friend."

"My name is Christophe Neizert. I am a citizen of East Germany, and a scientist," Neizert said, staring at Vladimir, who was looking at him vacantly, heavily sedated now.

"Good. Now we are *getting* somewhere!" Delgado said happily. "We can speak like friends. ... I feel like you have a much better understanding of the present situation. *Bravo*. Take the Russian back," the captain ordered. "I've hurt my ankle," Neizert said. "It needs to be treated."

"Are you a Russian, too?" the policeman asked.

"No. I've just told you! I'm an East German citizen. What do you want with me?" Neizert said.

"Where does it hurt? Your ankle?" Delgado asked. He looked down at the injury.

Neizert sat down on a wooden chair in the corner of his cell and rolled down a filthy sock. His leg was very dirty from their long trek through the desert. He exposed his ankle, and the injury looked serious. "It's a ligament. ... I'm sure of it," Neizert said, looking up. Delgado looked at him with curiosity and concern. He suddenly kicked the Hauptmann, hitting his injured ankle dead center with the heel of his cowboy boot, hard. Neizert screamed, falling off the chair and holding his ankle, trying to protect it from any further assault, writhing in pain on the concrete floor of the cell.

"I'll ask you again—are you an important Russian?" Delgado said.

54

■ TIJUANA, MEXICO

It had been raining very hard for the past hour in Tijuana, Mexico. Buckets of water had come down all over the city. The hotel had a direct view of the street. Outside one window was a funkadelic car-jammed parking lot, with an old yellow sheet metal sign from the 1950s hanging on a bashed-up cyclone fence, which read: SAFE PARKING ... NEAR ALL THE GOOD BARS ... NO REASON TO WORRY HERE."

Because the hotel was very close to "The Line," everything around it looked surreal or weird: whorehouses-cum-bars operated around the clock right next to spotlessly clean pharmacies that sold pills without a prescription to American junkies of all ages and walks of life. Leather goods stalls were crammed with out-of-date '70s' fashions. The streets were lined with college-age bars. Laced in through all the seething mass of "legitimate" businesses were narrow alleys where "special," usually sexual, treats were sold. Out on the main drag, teenaged hawkers cajoled passersby 24/7, trying to get them inside the whorehouses or the dance clubs. The scene was starting to come to life again after having gone through the quiet time between six A.M. and three in the afternoon, when Tijuana took a long breath before starting up its Sodom-song all over again. Rain ran in the streets, and cabs splashed through the intersection across from the parking lot, drenching anyone unfortunate enough to be standing there waiting to cross the street. Most of the pedestrians seemed to have been freaked-out by the sudden monsoon-like downpour.

Butch kicked the chair that Warren was sleeping in. It was getting late; almost three-thirty in the afternoon, now. Because of his injuries and the medications he was taking for them—Valium and pain killers—Warren was completely conked out. He'd been asleep since shortly after coming back from lunch, sitting there in the chair all afternoon with his feet resting up on the bed. Butch had been laying out and cleaning their weapons while Warren slept. The oppressive feeling that Malcolm Law—the Big Boss Man—personally wanted him dead had finally angered him. He didn't want to die—not like that, anyway. The suicide mission order from on-high had sparked a savage defiance deep inside of him. He was really angry about it by this time, and he

535

wanted to prove something to himself, too, in carrying out the mission successfully. He wasn't a *dog* to be kicked around like that, goddamn it!

"Time to draw straws, amigo," Butch said. "We only got forty minutes."

"We're doing the 'Dead Man,' then?" Warren asked, finally waking up. He opened his eyes. He was so marked-up and swollen from the stomping he'd taken in the bar in Plata, that the little kids—the tough ones that begged near the whorehouses—had made way for him because he looked so fucking *scary*—like a monster out of a B-movie come-to-life.

"Yeah, it's best that way. ..." Butch said.

"That makes sense, I suppose. ... How do I look?" Warren asked. He'd come to Tijuana straight from emergency treatment at the motel in Sonoyta, a trip that even the young Mexican doctor had said was crazy. He'd told Warren that he'd suffered a concussion and should go to a hospital immediately—that he was in no shape to be going anywhere but a hospital bed.

"It's funny," Butch said, "but you look great. Kind of like a toothless eggplant that got beat-up."

"I always want to look my best when stepping out, you know," Warren said, in a false, prissy voice.

"It's raining, Butch said.

"Yeah. ... Does it *rain* in this burg?" Warren asked. "This is Southern California, after all."

"How the fuck should *I* know? ... But it is," Butch said. Warren moved around in the chair a bit, but finally got up, obviously trying not to show that he was in pain. He walked over to the bed and saw the weapons they'd decided on earlier all laid out in a row. The "Dead Man" tactic was something that Warren thought was probably not going to work, so he figured that his face, just a short time in the future, was going to stop hurting for good. That part of his anatomy, along with his ribs, and every other part of his body, too, because he would be dead in just less than an hour. He thought about death for a moment, and frankly didn't care one way or the other. The sooner the better, actually, he decided, looking down at the assortment of pistols laid out on the twin-sized bed.

"What do you think it's like? Being dead, I mean?" Warren asked, shuffling past the bed and on into the bathroom. His khaki pants were filthy. He picked up a grease-stained towel and dabbed at his face, which still hurt like hell despite all the painkillers he'd taken. *"Fuck!"*

"I guess it's like sleeping," Butch said "That's what I hope, anyway. Of course, that's if you're on your way to Haven." Butch smiled, enjoying his own joke.

"You think so? *Really?* Dead people don't *look* asleep. ... They look like they've left town," Warren replied from the bathroom.

"Thanks for helping out," Butch said, wanting to change the subject.

"Don't mention it, pal. I didn't have anything better to do. And I owed you a favor, too," Warren said. He ran the cold water tap in the tiny sink, waiting for it to get as cold as it was going to, then splashed handfuls of it onto his swollen face. His torn-up and bruised face hurt so much that he wanted to yell out loud, so he began to whistle a Marvin Gay song instead. Butch watched him with a mildly curious detachment.

Their hotel stood on the corner of *Revolución* and *Benito Juarez,* just a block from the city's main police station. The police station building took up half a city-block, and was protected from the street by a No-Man's Land of rolls of ten-foot-high razor-edged barbed-wire. It looked more like a battlefield headquarters in a war-zone than a city police station.

"So we'll be doing the 'Dead Man?'" Warren asked again from the bathroom. "Like out on good old Route One in Nam?"

"Yeah," Butch said. "That's the one."

"You think it will work? A dead man in the *city?*"

"I hope so. I got no straw, so how about we toss a coin?" Butch said, digging in his pocket for some change he'd gotten when he went out to case the police station and had bought a watermelon drink from a stall across the street. The extremely sweet drink tasted great to him, and he'd sat there and enjoyed it directly opposite the place where he thought he was probably going to die. He tossed all his change on the bed and picked up a *centavo.*

"Shit, yeah ... fine," Warren said, still working on himself in the bathroom. Warren patted his face with the dirty towel again, then looked at himself in the cloudy mirror. He'd been given some sterile bandages by Sonny's doctor in Sonoyta; but wrapping his cuts up in the gauze made him look even worse. Butch pretended to toss the coin. He tossed it but didn't bother to look at how it landed on the bed. He'd already decided he was going to give Talbot the easier position in the 'Dead Man' ambush no matter how it landed. There was the smallest possibility that Talbot wouldn't be killed. He didn't hold out much hope for himself, because he really didn't expect the 'Dead Man' to work, but it was the only idea he could come up with, and he had to try *something.*

"You won," Butch said. "You're the Dead Man. ... You won. Fair and square."

"Okay," Warren said. "It's my lucky day, then." He'd moved over from the sink to the toilet bowl and was taking a pee. "How much time we got left, trooper?" Warren asked over the sound of his pee hitting the porcelain. "Hey, man—it looks like somebody had a bad tamale dinner in here. *Jesus.*"

"... Thirty minutes," Butch said. "Yeah, that was me; I'm *still* fucking hung-over. You want a weapon? Just in case?"

"Naw ... I'm the 'Dead Man,' right? I don't really need one," Warren said. He walked out of the bathroom zipping up his fly.

"Okay, let's roll," Butch said. He stuck two handguns down his pants: a U.S. Army .45 in the back of his jeans, and the .357 Magnum in the front. He pulled out his shirttails so neither of the weapons could be easily seen.

"The Dead Man" was a tactic first used by the Viet Minh, and later adopted by the Viet Cong. It had been used against the French, and was still being used when U.S. troops were relatively new to Vietnam. The idea behind it traded on human sympathy: ironically, the desire to be of assistance to others who were in distress was hard-wired into most human beings. Warren had mentioned it to Butch when he'd been lying on the doctor's table, saying that he would make a great Dead Man. He'd been joking, but later the tactic came to Butch as a possibility. The template was simple: someone would lie, pretending to be injured, on a country road. A French patrol, or later on an American patrol, would roll to a stop, thinking that there had been an accident of some kind. Men in hiding on the side of the road would ambush whoever had stopped, usually waiting for them to walk up right next to the man lying in the road, who *looked* dead, but wasn't. In many cases, the Dead Man was able to get away with his life. Sometimes the Dead Man was accidentally killed by his own men in the ensuing crossfire. The Viet Cong never tried it in Saigon, though. It stopped working soon after the Marines landed and learned the hard way just what it was all about. Also, the Marines weren't that interested in helping out *any* Vietnamese after spending only a few weeks "in-country." The young soldiers had quickly learned to drive right over the 'Dead Man' at a high speed, and keep right on going.

*　　　　　*　　　　　*

It was a beautiful day, and Flaco had decided to take the little girl to the park with his mother. His father had gone to work as usual, and had not said much of anything after their "visitors" had left. The men had been well-dressed and had come in a new white Ford. Because his parents were illegals, they didn't argue with whatever the police wanted, or did to them. The three burly men, all sporting crew-cuts, had come to the front door and showed their police IDs, asking to speak with Flaco. One had taken his parents and the little girl to a different part of the house. His parents were used to this kind of drill, as Flaco had been arrested countless times by the LAPD.

Flaco took the little girl by the hand and they walked the two blocks from his parents' house to the park. They'd bought the house in 1969, only ten years after

538

crossing the Rio Grande one fine October morning, with almost no money, but full of hope for the future. Before she'd stepped into the dirty water of the river, his mother had said a prayer for her son, for their future, for her husband, and for herself, and then they'd gotten on with it—along with about fifty other people that had nothing left to lose. His mother had been only sixteen at the time; his father nineteen. Flaco had been a baby, exactly 9 months-old when he was carried into this new country, where the young couple had heard life was very good for everybody.

As he walked with the little girl, who was still convinced that her mother was coming to pick her up, Flaco caught waves of greetings coming from the older women of the neighborhood, most of whom were out "taking the air" in front of their houses for their morning talk and gossip sessions. They all knew Flaco and his younger brother, who was now a resident in a hospital in Boston and had married a white girl named Buffy Hamilton. Buffy's father was a corporate lawyer with nothing *but* money. They never came to L.A. to visit because Buffy was obviously embarrassed by her husband's parents; by the smell of peppers in their kitchen; by their brown skins; and by the hokey photos of the family taken at Disneyland that hung all over the house in cheap, second-hand frames. Buffy was embarrassed by the broken-down cars in the neighborhood, too, many of them up on blocks with no tires. She came from Money Land and was terrified of the whole brown-skinned Mexican down-at-the-heels, Poor-America-That-Don't-Smell-Right experience. Even his brother seemed embarrassed by the place he'd come from, and acted like his name was "Smith" rather than Cruz.

Flaco had once told his younger brother, right after he'd gotten married, that his new wife didn't love him. Not really. Flaco had said that she'd married him because he was a winning dog, and that was all. That she would look down on his brown ass the rest of his life. His little brother responded by saying that Flaco was just jealous because he'd bagged a "white girl." At the time, Flaco was selling dope but not taking it himself, and was making more money than his brother and twenty guys just like him. He had white girls coming out of the woodwork wanting to "ease his way," and he knew the type very well. There was something cold and machine-like in their eyes. They were like cash registers, only with pussies. He stopped at a place on the corner, still holding the little girl's hand. A big bush with red bottle-brush flowers grew there. The little girl looked up at him. He was looking down at an old stain on the concrete sidewalk like it was a ghost.

"Is that the park?" the little girl asked. Flaco didn't hear her. He was listening to the distant past. To a day when his brother had been jumped by two black kids from around the corner; kids who were pounding his brother like they were professional boxers. His little brother was catching fists from all sides—most of them straight to the head. Flaco had run down the block from his parents' house like a lightning bolt, yelling in Spanish for any of the other Mexican kids on the block to come and help, but nobody else came. He ran into one of the motherfuckers with a steak-knife and left it sticking out of his gut, the kid stunned at the sight of the brown wooden handle sticking out of his stomach. Flaco had become a legend in the neighborhood that day because he'd plunged the knife into the bigger of the two brothers—a guy who was known in the neighborhood as a real asshole—right smack in his belly button, and *left it there.* It was the first one of the BIG THINGS he'd done that made him who he was now. He regretted most of them, but not that one. He'd loved his little brother, but his brother had never really understood that. Not really. His brother was "smart" in book-learning, but he was dumb, too, in street-smarts, Flaco mused as he stared down at the old red stain. He looked down at the little girl, then picked her up and held her in his arms. They had to cross a busy street, and he didn't want anything to happen to her. Right at that moment she seemed so innocent and perfect to him. He knew he'd fucked up his life as royally as any human being possibly could, and it came crashing down into his consciousness, as he crossed the street with the little girl: *I should have had a family like my mom and dad.*

"Your ass belongs to us," one of the policemen had said to him. They were sitting in the back seat of the new white Ford. "You understand that, don't you?" The men—Stuckie and Van Steeps—had come back, and now had specific instructions for him on the hit. The first time, they'd taken him to the county jail for a day, just to make their point—charging him with selling an ounce of heroin. He was taken in and held, and no one seemed to give a shit that he was innocent, or had even looked into his case at all. Then, just as suddenly, he was released "on his own recognizance."

"Yeah," Flaco said. He'd gone into street-mode, and was playing the dope fiend for them now, but he was, in fact, completely straight. His mother had given him some herbs she'd gotten from a Chinese woman on the block, and she'd made Flaco stay in bed for two whole days, taking them regularly. She'd been right there with him during the worst stages of the withdrawal. Holding his hand when he wanted to get up and run out to get some crank, sweating like a pig and twisting and turning in the bed, crawling out of his own skin with anxiety. He called her every name in the book ... he swore at her and her religion that she clung to so fiercely. He said horrible things about Jesus and God, but she just sat there with him until the torment finally broke and he was "clean" again, at least for the present. It was the kind of clean he'd never known before, or hadn't known for so long that he couldn't remember what it felt like. It was a clarity of soul that he'd never experienced before as an adult.

"So, not only will we kill everyone in that house, but we will kill that kid, too," Stuckie said. "Yeah—that's right. *Remember* that. So don't fuck this up, kid."

"No problem. Whatever you want, officer." Flaco replied to them in a very quiet voice.

"That's it, boy. Now, it's very simple: you kill this motherfucker at the hotel and you'll never see us again."

"Sure," Flaco said. "Sure."

"Now—have you seen that fuck-wad Talbot since we were here last?" Stuckie asked.

"No, sir, I haven't," Flaco said. The two men looked at him. They were wearing cheap suits just like the two men who'd arrested him after he'd stabbed the kid in the belly—the ones who'd driven him to the California Youth Authority lock-up. It was while he was doing his time at CYA in Tracy that he'd really been schooled about the world; had seen the contours and hillsides of human cruelty in all its splendor. Every gang-banger from every important ghetto in the state, from Compton to Oakland, was up there at Tracy with him. There was no God. There was no help. And there was certainly no mercy—for anyone. It had been an Education. His little brother, who'd been leaning towards the street-life, heard his stories in the visiting room. Flaco's stories about life on the yard had changed his brother's mind about what he was doing with his life. He started to go to school regularly after Flaco went to Tracy, and he'd left off running on the streets for good.

When they got to the park, Flaco took the little girl to the line of swings. They were the same swings his mother had pushed him on when he'd been a little boy. The same ones he'd swung on while he'd watched Los Angeles change all around him. The city had become a monster—an aspect that was never shown on the TV sit-coms. It was a gigantic death-house that had blue skies and innumerable alleyways behind old houses where kids shot each other dead several times each and every day.

"Do you think my mom is coming to get me today?" the little girl asked him.

"I think so," Flaco said. "Definitely—I'm sure of it."

"My daddy has a motorcycle," the little girl said. "*Higher*, uncle Flaco. Push me higher. ...." She had started calling him uncle Flaco straight out of the blue that morning.

"You're going to get a call," Stuckie had said to him. "Then you do exactly what the guy on the phone tells you. This meeting never happened. You never saw us. You tell anyone about this and we'll be back. Now get the fuck out of the car."

"Yes, sir," Flaco said, and got out of the white Ford and went back into his parents' house, not even wanting to look at the car as it backed out of the driveway and drove off.

* * *

Warren and Butch were waiting for a streetlight to turn when an ancient ambulance went screaming down *Avenida Revolución* towards the border, red lights flashing and siren blaring, adding to the chaos of the people-packed intersection. Despite the momentary distraction, pedestrians entering the intersection boldly stared at Warren as if he were a carnival exhibit. He and Butch walked into a liquor store nearby and bought a pint of brandy, then split it, drinking it down on the sidewalk right out in front of a shoe store. Butch said that they were still a little bit early to start their set-up.

"What are you going to do ... You know, when we get back?" Warren asked.

"Me? Same old shit I guess," Butch said.

"You like it?" Warren asked.

"It's okay. You don't get bored ... I can tell you that much, anyway." Butch took a slug off the pint. "What about you?"

"I'll go back to the cops, I guess. I just have to do about eight more years and then I can retire," Warren said.

"That sounds good," Butch said. They watched people walking by on the sidewalk. They had gone into the alcove of a shoe store entrance that had very clean windows, and were nicely tucked away from the lines of sight of all the people passing by on the sidewalk. Butch looked at his watch. It was almost time. "Well, I guess it's show time, buddy," Butch said. He took what remained in the bottle and poured the brandy over Warren's shoulders and shirt. "You sure you want to add this twist?" Butch asked him.

"I think we got to," Warren said. "It's more dramatic this way." It had been Warren's idea to light himself on fire.

"What if I can't put out the fire?" Butch said. He looked at Warren. Warren didn't seem to be nervous or concerned, or scared at all about being lit on fire.

"Just make sure you get the flames out *first*. ... I'll be fine. I can roll on the ground, too, if there's a problem," Warren said. A speaker that was located just inside the store started playing "Blue Skies"—the Frank Sinatra and Tommy Dorsey version. The owner of the shoe store was a big Sinatra fan and played his records in the store all day long.

"Okay, let's do it, then," Butch said, putting the empty pint bottle down at his feet. He turned around to look at the Mexican police station directly across the street. A

Federale, attired in the signature white cowboy hat, armed with an automatic in a rakish holster that was strapped to his waist, walked out through the No-Man's Land of razor-wire, unlocked the massive hinged-gate to the driveway, then, holding up the free-swinging end of the gate with both hands, managed to swing it around until it was fully open. Butch tapped Warren on the shoulder and he started walking towards the street corner. They were about twenty feet apart as they simultaneously stepped off the sidewalk, then both of them walked out into the traffic, Butch was now trailing just slightly behind Warren. They hesitated three or four seconds, until they saw a car pull out from the back of the station, then Butch quickly used a Bic disposable lighter to carefully light the back of Warren's T shirt on fire while cars pulled around them in the curb-lane of the street. Then Warren Talbot dodged the traffic and ran across the busy street with his back on fire, screaming bloody murder as the flames climbed up the back of his T-shirt. By the time Warren got to the section of the street in front of the gate, his whole shirt was on fire—front *and* back. He raised his arms and faced the unmarked car that was coming down the driveway with flames haloing his head.

"*Help! Help me!*" Butch yelled as he knocked Warren to the ground and beat on the flames with his hands. The police car kept coming at them "*Help! Help!*" Butch yelled, trying not to look at the car. He finally glanced up at the approaching car. It came to a stop with the bumper only a few inches from Butch's head. Butch heard someone exiting the passenger side. A middle-aged cop in a white suit was facing him. The man looked suspiciously at Butch.

"*Please, help me—please.*" Butch said. The Mexican cop walked slowly toward the front of the car.

"Get the fuck out of the way." The cop spoke perfect, unaccented English. He suddenly bent over and grabbed Warren by his belt and started dragging him face-down out of the driveway. When he'd finished hauling Warren's smoking body out of the way, the cop turned back toward the driveway and the open car door. Butch shot him in the back of the head. It was a shot he could have pulled off in his sleep, as he was only ten feet away. The other cop—the one who'd opened the gate—was walking towards him and reaching for his gun, but Butch was already running at him as he fired at the man several times, killing him almost instantly. Warren had gotten up—his T-shirt a smoking-ash ruin, his belly exposed, but he now ran toward the driver of the car—something that was not in their plan. The driver tried to back up, but Warren had already reached through the open driver's-side window and into the car. The driver floored the vehicle, and the moving car picked Warren cleanly up, so he decided to jump into the driver's lap to keep him immobile, pinned to his seat. The car was moving as fast as possible in reverse now, and as it passed Butch, he reached for the .357 magnum. Warren could feel the driver moving beneath him, trying to get

543

at *his* gun. He could feel him squirming violently under his weight. Warren turned around and saw two white men in the back seat of the car at the same time as he got his elbow going, hitting the driver several vicious blows in the face. His feet were hanging outside the car, and he felt them repeatedly bouncing off the fence that abutted the entrance to the station's driveway. The car abruptly stopped. The driver had slammed on the brakes because Warren was now choking him with one hand while holding himself in the car by the steering wheel with the other. As soon as the car stopped, Warren got his feet on the ground and continued to choke the man, violently shaking his neck, causing his head to whip back and forth. He could see the cop's eyes go back in his head, but he kept on shaking and squeezing, shaking and squeezing. Warren was tangentially aware of more shooting, but didn't pay attention to anything else that was going on until he saw the two men in the back seat get out of the car, and Butch leading them down the driveway. Warren finally let go of the now broken-necked and very dead driver to follow them. There was an American Embassy Chevy waiting for them at the bottom of the driveway with a black Marine guard, in plain-clothes, behind the wheel. The kid was only about twenty or so and looked scared shitless. Butch knocked him out of the way, got behind the wheel himself, and took off driving. Warren had to run the last few feet in order to jump into the back seat, and one of the men in the back literally yanked him inside the car. At the border checkpoint they were expected. A Border Patrol agent in the booth waved them through immediately. No one in the car had said a word.

"I'm supposed to tell you to go to the San Diego Navy base," the black kid said.

"*Fuck* that. ... We're going to L.A. Tell that asshole Law that we'll be in touch," Butch said. He had the black kid get out in San Ysidro at a random bus stop, then drove off into the night.

*   *   *

They were talking as if Gemma weren't even in the room with them.

"Where's Butch?" Alex said. He was lying in bed in the San Diego Naval Hospital.

"He's taken my German to LA., apparently—is that girl pregnant?" his father asked.

"Yeah," Alex said.

"She's a KGB asset," Malcolm said. "Just so you know." Malcolm looked at the girl who'd insisted on flying with Alex to the hospital, genuinely concerned for him. Something had happened inside her when she'd seen him injured like that, lying on the floor unconscious. She wanted to protect him then, and still did. Even Malcolm

544

had sensed that her feelings for his son were genuine.

"*Is* she? So what?" Alex said. His father looked at Gemma again. They were in a Navy medical center on Balboa Island in a private room with a view of the ocean.

"She was recruited in New York. I'm guessing she's in very deep cover and that this Vladimir character is running her." Gemma's eyes lit up at the mention of Vladimir's name.

"Where is he?" she asked.

"He's in L.A. with my German. I don't know where exactly, yet. Maybe *you* can help me there?" Malcolm said, looking at her. "Everything she's told you is a lie." Malcolm said to Alex, who was now sitting up in the bed. He still had a terrible headache from hitting the desk back in the motel in Sonoyta. He'd been told he had a severe concussion and that they wanted to keep him under observation for several more days at least.

"I'm taking her to the brig here for questioning," Malcolm said. "Then to Virginia."

"No, you're not," Alex said.

"I don't believe she's pregnant," Malcolm said.

"She is," Alex said.

"You're absolutely sure?" his father said.

"Yes."

"Is this your father? The famous Malcolm Law?" Gemma asked from across the room. Malcolm looked at her. The fact that she knew his real name shocked him. "Vladimir is actually trying to help you," Gemma said.

"Is he?" Malcolm said.

"Yes. He's the one that brought the old man to Sonoyta," Gemma said.

"You're telling me that the KGB is helping *me*?" Malcolm said.

"Yes."

"You're lying. He's going to kill my German when it suits him to do so. He probably wants to kill me, too, when I pick him up. That's my guess," Malcolm said.

"He could have killed the German in Sonoyta." Gemma said.

"It's true," Alex said. "He could have. *Easily.* Here's the deal. I'll bring in Butch. You leave Gemma alone. ... She goes back to Italy," Alex said. "And you leave Butch alone. He was drunk. He didn't mean to hit me," Alex said.

Malcolm looked at his watch. It had already been four hours since Butch had crossed the border with Neizert and the Russian. They were all still at large, somewhere in Los Angeles. He was getting reports of KGB consular officials coming to Los Angeles on a flight from Mexico. He couldn't stop them because they had legitimate credentials from the Russian foreign service, but he had a horrible feeling that they were after Neizert, too.

"All right. ..."

"She goes to Italy. She's left alone there. I want your word on that," Alex said.

"All right," Malcolm said. "Where's Butch?"

"He's probably going to the Capri," Alex said.

"That motel in L.A.?"

"Yes. I'm pretty sure that's where he'll go. He'll want to hide out until he thinks he'll be able to cut a deal with you. You've scared him with your threats," Alex said. "He wants to keep that money we made dealing."

"Okay. ... Go get him. And get *Neizert,* for God's sake," Malcolm said.

"I want you to promise me you'll leave Gemma alone," Alex said again.

"*All right,* I promise," Malcolm said, looking over at the girl. She seemed very small; fragile and very young. She was just the kind of girl he would have tried to turn himself. He was impressed. She gave him a very hostile look. It was obvious that she hated him. Malcolm suddenly turned and headed for the door. "I'm going to be watching," he said, with his back to them as he left.

*   *   *

The ambulance that had passed Butch and Warren with its lights and siren going, went straight to the border checkpoint. A man inside holding an American passport had only one good eye. The young doctor attending him was very nervous. The driver was an experienced mule, a Corsican, who had the biggest balls, according to Sonny, of any Frenchmen he'd ever met. The ambulance had passed all the cars in the queue at the border at San Ysidro and drove right up to the check point—the cars courteously moved out of its way.

"What the hell is going on?" the border patrol agent started questioning the driver as soon as he pulled up to the booth.

"An important American ... He's had a heart attack ... he can't be treated in Mexico." the driver said. The border patrol agent walked out of the booth, went to the back of the Mexican ambulance, then opened the door.

"This man will die very soon if we can't get him to a *real* hospital," the young Mexican doctor said, sitting on the gurney next to Sonny, who looked to be in real agony.

"Is he an American?" the border patrol agent asked. The Corsican had kept the siren on and the lights flashing the entire time they were stopped at the checkpoint. The sound of the siren was making everyone's heart race, including the border patrol agent's. The doctor held up two phony American passports and offered them to the man.

"Yes. Here are our passports. ... Here." the doctor said, holding them out. The agent took the passports and then took a second look at Sonny Delmonico, lying there with an IV in his arm. He handed the passports back to the doctor without even looking at them.

"Fuck it—go on, then," the agent said. "If he's an American—go on!" He slammed the ambulance's rear door closed. And—with fifty kilos of Sicilian heroin hidden inside, just under Sonny's gurney—they crossed the border with lights and siren going, as if to warn all the junkies in L.A. that they were on their way, and to get ready for Paradise.

55

■ SAN DIEGO FREEWAY

A grizzled old Navy doctor had prescribed Vicodin for his pain, but Alex hadn't wanted to take any, afraid the pain killers would dull his senses, which he felt he needed now more than ever, as this whole thing came to a head. His own head felt like a thin metal clamp had been wrapped around his skull, and was being slowly tightened down, bit by bit, millimeter by millimeter. At times he had to squeeze the car's steering wheel to cope with the pain. He and Gemma had only spoken about trivial things in the car; so far, anyway. He'd barely paid attention to what she was saying, until she started to speak about her Russian.

Alex's expression was grim. They drove northward on the freeway through downtown San Diego, through a glaring sunlight reflecting off the tinted windows of massive glass-clad skyscrapers. As they passed the airport exit, Gemma started speaking in a very quiet, trance-like voice, chronologically detailing her entire life to him; her life since she'd fallen in love with Vladimir as a high school student in New York. She told him how they'd met at an NGO party, and how she'd only gotten involved with the KGB because of Vladimir, and not because of any political feelings of her own. How she'd lied to everyone, including Vladimir, about that; and how she'd lied to herself, most of all, she said. Alex was taken aback by her confessions, as he'd thought that she was a real believer in the Socialist Idealism that she'd constantly talked about in Italy. But it turned out she was only a girl in love. It actually deeply shocked him, and somehow made him feel worse about the whole situation; his own lies to her, and everything that both their strings of lies had led to.

"I convinced myself—lied to myself—for a long time that it was all about politics, about the Revolution, about winning the 'class-war'—I really did," Gemma said. "But I don't care about politics, now. Not anymore. I just want to see Vladimir again, and be with him for the rest of my life. That's *all* I want. I want to see him *alive*." She said it in a very pathetic way. Her current tone was hard for him to equate with what he knew about her being a brave woman, and what he'd seen her do with his own eyes, back in Italy, to save his life. Her love for Vladimir seemed to have made her a coward now. Or maybe it wasn't really cowardice; maybe it was a state of intense and abject need that he'd never encountered before.

He intuited that much, at least, so he didn't say anything back to her, about any of it. They drove on up the freeway in the light-grey U.S. Navy Ford, his head aching like hell, and with the dawning realization that his future life would not include her, ever, or even their child. As he silently drove on, it finally sank into his emotional being that he was going to lose Gemma, but he also knew that he still had to help her get back with Vladimir, because, even if just in a very small way, he wanted her to "love" him, if only for getting her what she wanted and needed; to be reunited with her true love. The fact was that he still loved her, despite everything, and would do anything for her because of that. The state of being in love, requited or not, had turned them both into pathetic and hapless people.

"So you'll go to Russia with him?" Alex asked her. The idea of his own child, who would be the grandson of a famous capitalist mine-owner—one of the richest men of the Gilded Age—growing up *there*, of all places, seemed a bit *more* than just surreal and ironic to him.

"No, I don't think so. Not now, anyway. ... In Italy, I hope," Gemma said. They were passing a long, open stretch of hills with the ocean to their left that reminded him of their time in Sicily. He had a premonition about his future life just then. He would be unfulfilled, emotionally, which was the only way that really counted, when all was said and done. It was very startling to him, because he had always believed that he *could* be happy, that happiness would someday come to him, no matter what intervened along the way. Even when Patty had been killed, he'd been hurt, agonizingly in fact, but he didn't believe life was over for him in that particular and most-important way. Now he knew, instinctively, that it really was. He would be married to the Spies for the rest of his life. There would be no way out for him, now. Just a bottomless future without happiness or relief from the way he felt right at that moment. There would be drinking and spying and certainly other women, but no Love. He would not experience that feeling again.

"Your father frightens me," Gemma said later, when they were just south of L.A. Alex didn't bother to answer her.

*   *   *

"This is where you get out, old buddy," Butch said. He looked over at Warren with a genuine smile.

"You *might* still need some help, ranger," Warren said. They'd bought him a new T-shirt at a flea market in San Yisidro. There was a photograph of a smiling Groucho

Marx stenciled on the front of the shirt. Warren's pants were as filthy as ever, but the T-shirt was very clean indeed.

"No, I don't think so—I think I can handle everything myself from now on in," Butch said. He turned and looked at the old German and the Russian sitting together in the back seat. "You can get out now, too, if you want, Boris," Butch said to the Russian.

"No, I'll go on with you," Vladimir said.

"You sure?" Butch asked. "They won't be nice to you when we get there—that I can promise. I know these assholes; hell, I'm *one* of them still, I guess. ..."

"Yes, I want to go with you," Vladimir said.

"Okay, then. But *you* got to get out," Butch said, turning back to Warren. "Go home, Warren. It's time. The game's over for you—you got your man down there."

"Okay, Butch," Warren said. "Somehow I don't think we'll be seeing each other again, though, and I'm kind of sorry about that, to tell you the truth."

"No I don't think so either, *amigo*," Butch said, "but act like we might, anyway. Go home and get some rest right now, man. Go back to being a cop if you want to. Maybe ... Maybe you can find someone—you know ... like your wife. I think it's possible. Maybe you can start over again."

"Yeah, sure," Warren said. "Okay, then." Warren opened the car door and got out. They'd stopped in the health food restaurant parking lot just down the coast highway from the Capri Motel. Warren closed the door and looked back inside at the three men through the open car window. They all looked very tired, and it felt to him like they all understood that their journey was almost over.

"Keep the rubber side down, then," Warren said. He reached through the window and shook hands with Butch, then he watched the car pull out of the parking lot and head on up the road to the Capri Motel. He thought for a moment of going there; of following Butch, to join in on whatever they were going to be a part of. He knew that he didn't really have a life to go back to; just empty nights and long meaningless days stretching in front of him. At least with Butch he'd been a soldier again, if only for a little while.

Warren sat down near the bottom of the wide wooden steps that led up to the health-food restaurant. Three pretty young surfer chicks looked down at him as they walked past him up the steps. One of the young girls handed him a quarter, thinking he was a bum. He took it and nodded mutely back to her, embarrassed. He knew he was scary-looking. She'd quickly turned her head away when he'd reflexively smiled at her.

For awhile, he just sat there watching the surf roll onto the beach, straight across Highway One. Watching the waves made him feel better, somehow, about life. Lorie came to him while he was sitting there and told him to go back to work, because he was an honest cop, and people of all kinds would benefit from his doing his job the *right* way. He took a deep breath.

"Okay, baby, if you say so," he said. Warren placed the quarter on the step and stood up. He crossed the highway to the beach. Once on the beach, he stopped and took off his shoes, then walked south towards Santa Monica, shoes in hand. As he walked, he disappeared from sight, merging with the incoming cool marine layer of pearl-grey fog. Warren Talbot became just a speck fading into the horizon, like so many others.

"You—sit down *there*," Butch said. The motel was empty. The front office had been shut down and wasn't operating at all, but he figured that the motel was probably still owned by the Agency, and would be a safe place to hide until he could figure out his next move. Butch had more or less counted on that as being the case, in fact. He'd kicked in the door to room 16, on the second floor, and had told the old German to go inside and wait. He'd stopped the Russian from going in with him, though.

"You and I have to talk, Boris—and right now, if you know what I mean," Butch said.

"Okay," Vladimir said. "My name is Vladimir," he said. Butch pulled the door to room 16 closed and walked Vladimir down to the motel's office. He broke into the still-working Coke machine and lifted out two Cokes for them. Then he used the butt of his pistol to smash the glass of the motel's office-area's backdoor, which allowed them to enter the Capri's front office undetected. He wanted to talk with Vladimir and have a view of the highway in front at the same time.

"What's your game, anyway, amigo?" Butch said, handing Vladimir one of the Cokes.

"I want you to bring me the Italian girl—Gemma," he said.

"What? What are you talking about, man?" Butch said.

"I want that girl brought here," Vladimir said. Butch scratched his chin and looked at him.

"Why? What's your angle?" Butch thought that maybe the KGB officer was, like him, a kind of freelancer, looking for various side-opportunities to make money in the course of his "regular" work for his government.

"I don't have an 'angle' at this point. I promised someone back in Russia—someone very important who's dead, now—that I would make sure Neizert got here to the States safely. That's all over, now, obviously. *Now*, I have to think of myself," Vladimir said.

"Okay; that sort of makes sense to me ... in a way, anyway. But ... who *are* you, *exactly*, man? In terms of what we both do for a living, I mean," Butch said.

"I told you that back when I first got in the car—remember? I'm the same as you— or I *was*, anyway—an intelligence officer working an assignment for my country. To *you*, the 'other side,' I guess," Vladimir said. "But things have happened to me recently that've made it so I don't see it that way anymore. We're both on the *same* 'side' as far as the German goes—you know that from what you've seen me do yourself."

"Is there money to be made out of this girl?" Butch asked. Vladimir smiled and shook his head.

"No. ... No, there's no money in the girl," Vladimir said. "Nobody wants her but me."

"What are you going to do to her?" Butch said.

"Take her away, marry her, and, as you Yanks like to always say: 'live happily ever after'—I'm not kidding you about this, at all."

"Well, right now I still need your help. I don't want anything to happen to that old man," Butch said. He went into the bathroom and lifted the lid off the tank of the office toilet. He'd hidden a 9mm automatic inside the toilet's small cistern month's before, when he and Alex had used the motel as their base of operations, secretly keeping it there in a waterproof bag for the duration of their stay, just as backup. Now, he pulled it out of the bag and brought it into the office, laying it down on a desk in front of Vladimir.

"Here—make sure nothing happens to the old man," Butch said.

"You'll give me the girl? Gemma?" Vladimir asked.

"Maybe. ... Okay," Butch said, "I'll do my best to get her for you."

"Okay, then," Vladimir said, either consciously mimicking one of Butch's stock replies, or not—even *he* didn't know. Then he went back out to the parking lot and on up the stairs to the room where they'd left the Hauptmann: number 16. A minute later, the phone rang in the office, and Butch saw that the call was from one of the rooms. He walked over to the switchboard, studied it for a moment, then picked up the call.

"Yeah?" Butch said.

"You get me Gemma, or I kill the old man," Vladimir said, and immediately hung up. Alex drove up with Gemma just as Butch was putting down the phone. Butch wasn't at all surprised to see him *or* the girl.

*   *   *

Malcolm Law and George were arrested as they were getting onto a Navy helicopter in the parking lot of the Naval Hospital in San Diego. Malcolm was told that he was being placed under arrest for suspicion of spying on the United States of America. The young FBI field agent, who had been waiting hidden inside the helicopter, handcuffed him. Malcolm was told he was in the custody of the FBI's counter-intelligence division, and nothing more. George and he were immediately separated. The FBI took Malcolm away in the very same helicopter that he'd been trying to board. He looked down from the open door as the chopper took off, and he could see George being hustled toward a line of cars. Then they were flying over San Diego Bay, the harbor chock-full of sailboats and Navy ships of various kinds. When they got over the ocean, the chopper turned north and headed up the coast toward LA.

*   *   *

The Corsican driver had turned off the Mexican ambulance's lights and siren almost as soon as they were on the other side of the line. Sonny had gotten up off the cot in the back and was now riding sitting up. He was in a very good mood. He'd beaten the Devil once again, and he always enjoyed that feeling. There was something about cheating Fate, no matter how old he got, that still excited him. The adrenaline rush was still there. He joked with the doctor about their going into the movie business, because their performances at the border had been Academy Award-quality. The young Mexican doctor smiled at him and patted him on the back in congratulations.

"You have nine lives, amigo," the doctor kidded.

"But I've used them all up on *this* particular trip," Sonny said, still smiling.

"Where to now?" the doctor asked.

"London, I think. Back to Harold Hill for a nice, long rest," Sonny said. He felt the ambulance slowing, and heard the clicking of a turn-signal indicator. They'd just moved from the center lane of the freeway, and right away Sonny knew something had gone wrong, because they were supposed to meet up with a new group of bikers in downtown LA. No stop had been scheduled in San Diego.

"It's not lunch time yet, is it?" Sonny said. The young doctor shrugged his shoulders and pointed a small woman's-sized pistol at him. It was a little .38 he'd kept hidden in his pocket. Sonny looked at it almost amused, as if it were all a joke.

"I thought we were friends, Ricardo," Sonny said.

"I'm truly sorry, Sonny," the doctor said. "It's just business."

"I don't understand," Sonny said.

"There's been a change of plans," the doctor said. He went and sat down on the

553

floor and rested his back against the ambulance doors, still pointing the gun at Sonny.

"Bloody hell ... The Colombians again!" Sonny said. The doctor smiled and nodded slightly. "It's always *some*thing in this business. Just when you think you get a downhill patch ... Is it the merchandise they want?" Sonny asked.

"I'm afraid it's *you* they want, amigo," the doctor said.

"I see. It's time for a close-up, then. You know, like in the films. To catch my good side," Sonny said. The doctor smiled again, realizing how much he actually liked the Englishman.

"Sonny, I like you; it's not personal," the doctor said. "Please forgive me."

"No. I understand. Sicilian rules," Sonny said "I understand. What if we came to some kind of arrangement, old man? You and I?" Sonny asked. He gave the doctor a fey look.

"I'm afraid not, Sonny. You just can't do that with *them*. They'll find me and kill me if I fail. *You* know *that*. These Colombians are tireless—they never sleep," the doctor said. "It's a new world, now." Sonny just nodded.

"I've got an account in Switzerland, you know. Numbered, of course," Sonny said. The young doctor shook his head, "no."

"Well, then," Sonny said, sitting up straight. He put his hands on his knees. "I've got a little Spanish, you know. We'll have a talk with these gents. There's always time to sort things out between reasonable men." They rode on into a commercial district and the ambulance finally stopped in front of a roll-up door to a tire repair shop. Sonny heard the metal door rolling up from inside the ambulance. They moved forward. He heard the rolling door come back down and slam shut. He braced himself. He heard the sound of a Messerschmitt, and smelled the salt air of the sea over Anzio beach ... he was seventeen again for just an instant. Then the doors of the ambulance were pulled open.

*   *   *

Gemma had run up the stairs as soon as Alex told her that Vladimir was in the motel room. Later, she remembered running up those steps very vividly—the texture and look of them, in fact, for the rest of her life. She would remember running up those stairs after she'd had her baby in Rome in a Catholic hospital where her name had been changed. She'd remember how she felt when she opened the door, so happy, and saw Vladimir standing there. He looked tired, but his smile was intact. It was that smile that she would always remember. It contained every single thing that she hoped for in the future. They would have a life together. There was hope and safety in it—there *was* now, in fact, a future. He held her for a moment without speaking. The old German stood there looking at them from the bathroom door.

"Are you all right?" she said, finally breaking away from him. She glanced at the old man; he had taken his shirt off and was washing up. She saw the scars on his back. He turned to look briefly at Gemma, then turned back to the sink with a very distant expression on his face.

"Have you seen the American? ... Law?" The Hauptmann asked over the sound of the running the water in the sink.

"Yes," she said. "Today—a few hours ago."

"Good," the Hauptmann said. He put the towel back down carefully, draping it over the towel-bar. "Good."

She'd left the door to the room wide open. It was very bright out. The Hauptmann could see the ocean over the motel's dark rooftop, a line of blue water on the horizon. He realized just then that it was the Pacific, and that he was finally safe, and he relaxed just a little bit for the first time.

"The Russian guy wants your girlfriend," Butch said.

"I know," Alex said.

"You *know?*" Butch said.

"Yes. Gemma told me," Alex said.

"What about the kid? The baby?" Butch said.

"My father should be here soon. He's going to take the old German to Washington with him. Then we're done with the whole thing," Alex ignored Butch's question about the baby.

"And the Russian?" Butch asked.

"He gets a free pass. They can leave. Both of them." Alex looked out on Highway One. It seemed like old times seeing the beach, surfers on the water, and the great weather.

"What a ride, huh?" Butch said from behind him. *"Fuck."* He put his pistol down on the counter.

"I'm staying ... in the deal—with the Agency, you know," Alex said. "I *want* to stay, now."

"Yeah ... I know. Me, too," Butch said "There's good money in it, after all." He laughed. Then they heard a helicopter approaching. It suddenly got very loud as it managed to land in the motel's empty parking lot, behind the office. The sound of the helicopter drowned out the sound of gunshots coming from Room 16.

"That must be your dad," Butch said.

"Yeah," Alex said. Butch thought he saw Flaco running across Highway One right then, towards the beach, dodging traffic as he made for the sand. Several cars almost simultaneously turned off the highway and entered the motel's parking lot. Alex turned around and looked strangely at Butch.

Alex walked out of the office and looked at the helicopter as it sat down in the parking lot. FBI agents—some wearing nylon jackets—were suddenly everywhere. A car pulled up in front of the office and men sprang out of the back. Alex was shoved against the Coke machine and told to spread his legs.

"Is anyone inside there?" an agent asked, standing behind him.

"No," Alex said, lying. "Who are you?"

"FBI," the man said. Alex felt handcuffs close around his wrists. When the agent turned him around he saw Gemma running down the stairs from the upper rooms toward him, hysterical. One of the FBI agents grabbed her and threw her against the hood of the car, face down. Alex tried to go over to her but he was viciously shoved back.

"Where's Neizert?" the agent asked him.

"Who?" Alex said stalling, trying to look at Gemma.

"Where's Christophe Neizert, *asshole?*" the agent said.

"What's going on?" Alex said. The agent punched him hard in the kidney and he fell to the ground, coughing.

"I'm going to ask you just one more time. ... Where's Neizert?" the FBI agent demanded, standing over him. The agent pulled a pistol out of his holster.

"Alex! *Alex!*" Gemma was screaming his name and trying to break away from the two men who were holding her down on the hood of the car. Alex was dragged away toward the helicopter, then bodily thrown into it, and it immediately took off.

What Gemma had seen before her life changed forever was a silhouette in the doorway of the motel room—a young Latino man, hovering there, spectral, wearing a white T-shirt and jeans, stood in the doorway. He had dark hair and was looking in at them. His body was outlined by the setting sun. The young man suddenly ran by her into the room and fired at the old man, who was just coming out of the bathroom, hitting him twice, once in the chest, and once in the head, killing him instantly. Then the young man turned and pointed the gun at Vladimir as he walked quickly back toward the door. Gemma tried to stop Vladimir, but he reached for the man's gun. She saw the fear in the young man's eyes for just an instant before he fired at Vladimir. She screamed, but by then the sound of the approaching helicopter was very loud, and her screams weren't heard by anyone. She held onto Vladimir, who fell toward her, badly wounded. She laid him down on the floor and ran out of the room to get help.

Vladimir, gut-shot, crawled across the motel's blue rug. He could hear the helicopter taking off. The sound of it was tremendously loud in the confined space of the room. He moved slowly across the floor and finally reached the Hauptmann. He reached out for him and touched his neck. He was dead. Then Vladimir tried to get up. The sound of the helicopter was still very loud because the door to the room was wide open, with bright orange sunlight streaming through it. He tried to stand up, but couldn't make it. It was as if he had no legs. But he was able to roll away from the dead Hauptmann using just his arms. He saw his mother, then. She was standing in the corner of the room looking at him. She was wearing her partisan uniform and smiling at him. She was just a young girl.

"Mother?" Vladimir said, confused. He closed his eyes. He could feel the blood, warm and wet, running between his fingers, which were intertwined—he'd been unconsciously pressing both of his hands hard against his wound.

An FBI agent ran into the room and saw immediately that the Russian he'd been after was lying wounded on the floor. He thought the man was dead until Vladimir suddenly opened his eyes. The young FBI agent immediately walked up to him and spoke: "Vladimir, Vladimir Putilin?"

"Yes," Vladimir said with his eyes wide open. He could clearly see the man standing over him.

The man shot Vladimir twice in the face, then went to check on Neizert. When he was sure that Neizert was dead, he went out on the balcony and yelled down to the others that he'd found the German, and that he was dead.

It was at the exact instant that the helicopter took off that Butch Nickels chose to calmly walk out the front door of the motel's office, shoot an FBI agent down who tried to stop him, and disappear.

George had finally been released by the FBI because of pressure from Kroll International and the British Embassy, and he found Butch two weeks later, hiding in Panama, where he managed to get him onto a Royal Dutch jet bound for Europe. The stewardess brought Butch a note just as they took off from a private airport near Panama City. The Gulf Stream Seven lifted off easily, the flaps lowered slowly, and it headed east over the Atlantic. Butch watched rusted-tin roofs of all shapes and sizes pass underneath them, then he saw the ocean suddenly appear. He'd taken the note from the woman, but hadn't opened it right away. First, he looked at his bankbook. He'd opened an account in a Panamanian bank while he was there. He tucked the bank documents into his shirt pocket and just sat there for a while, listening contentedly to the plane's engines. He looked around the plush cabin, which was almost empty of other passengers, and looked very clean and tidy. Then he finally tore open the envelope the woman had handed him and read it.

Go to Hotel La Carmen. Madrid. Do not move from there.
Await further instructions.

George C.

56

■ CALIFORNIA, AGOURA HILLS

Warren caught the call when he was cleaning out the garage, finally able to go into it and start back to work on the Biedermeier dresser that Lorie and he had been working on when she was murdered. His beeper went off and he called in. An hour later he pulled up in front of a typical LA bungalow that was located out in the flats of a neighborhood that was made up almost exclusively of Mexican Latinos. Most of the former Mexican nationals had moved there in the 1960s, buying their houses from white people who were fleeing the city and moving out to the San Fernando Valley. Warren had been to this house before. The day was hot and the air felt dirty because a bad inversion had settled over the city: a hot spell had locked-down the LA basin that May and it didn't seem to want to let go its smoggy death-grip. There were already several L.A. Country Sheriff's deputies at the scene, milling around the area of what had been called a "gang-related" shooting at the address in San Pedro.

"Hey, Warren." One of the officers at the scene, Dennis Connelly, was an old friend of Warren's, and gave him a shout-out when he pulled up. The man said it was good to see him back on the job, and obviously meant it. Warren nodded and smiled. The Department had allowed him back because of his officially-clean record, and because the FBI—whose counter-intelligence divisions were now within the purview of the Gehlen Network—had decided to leave Warren Talbot alone. He was no threat to them, and it was easier just to ignore him.

"What we got here, Dennis?" Warren asked the officer who'd called out his name.

"You got a Mexican kid who went off on two DEA agents. We didn't want it out on the radio. Someone has been here from the DEA and said that the press wasn't to be allowed in on this. Some kind of special operation that went wrong."

"Okay," Warren said.

"The shooter lived. The lucky little fucker. I think he set up on them. Shot both of them as soon as they walked into the house. I don't think they expected it at all."

"Well, shit happens out here in the Big World," Warren said. His attitude was more jaded and street cop-like now than it had been before his wife's murder and Mexico;

he was much more protective of himself, in fact, in general. The beat-cop gave him a "it sure does" smile and lifted the incident tape that had been strung across the front of the porch so Warren could duck underneath it and go on into the house through the open front door.

"Hello, Flaco," Warren said.

"Hello, Warren," Flaco said back, and then smiled. Warren glanced around the living room. It still appeared very neat and orderly, just as it had the previous time he'd been there. The sawed-off shot gun Flaco had used to kill the two DEA agents had been carefully placed on the clean dining room table.

"How you been, Warren?" Flaco asked.

"Good, I guess. No complaints, really. How is ... you know ... the little girl?"

"Yeah—she's okay, no worries. I sent her with Mom and Dad to Disneyland this morning," Flaco said. "Real early."

"Right. And these dead guys?" Warren said, nodding towards the foyer where the men had been gunned down.

"They came for a visit," Flaco said, "but they decided not to leave. Unfortunate, really." He mimicked a pseudo-British accent at the end of his reply.

"You had a disagreement, or what?" Warren asked him.

"Yeah, you could say that. It seems they weren't going to live up to their end of a bargain we made a while back. I didn't *think* they would, actually," Flaco said. He was sitting at the dining room table and had a family photo-album open in front of him. He'd brought it out of his parents' room after he'd shot the two men who'd come to kill him and his parents—and anyone else who happened to be in the house at the time. Those were their orders from the FBI's counter-intelligence unit. Robin Stuckie and Agent Van Steeps hadn't questioned their orders, or asked why. Since the "New Day" had come, and was moving through the FBI and the DEA organizations, it was best to just do what you were told, and *not* ask any questions. Stuckie had called Flaco the day before, and told him they just wanted to come by and check-up on him—make sure he was okay, and would still be an "asset" to them if they needed him in the future.

"Is that you?" Warren said, looking down at a picture in the album. It was shot of a family visit to Disneyland years' before.

"Yeah ... That's my little brother. He's a doctor in Chicago, now. A real big shot," Flaco said. "A neurosurgeon."

"Yeah? No shit. He made good, huh?" Warren said.

"Yeah," Flaco said.

"I think maybe they'll be back in an hour or so. Can we wait? I'd like to say goodbye to my parents—you know, Warren," Flaco said, turning the page in the album.

"Yeah, sure," Warren said, "why not? There'll be tons of paperwork with this anyway."

"I'm glad it was you that came," Flaco said.

"Yeah, I caught the call at home," Warren said, sitting down from him across the table. He glanced at the two dead DEA agents, lying where they'd been surprised by Flaco, who had hidden in the hall-closet, letting them come fully into the house and turn towards the kitchen before he shot them down.

"Nice work," Warren said. "Clean."

"Yeah. They didn't expect it. I was in the closet," Flaco said, then smiled, looking at a picture of himself standing in front of the Matterhorn at Disneyland with his brother, their arms around each other.

Later, after Flaco had been processed at the L.A. county jail, Warren was supposed to take the little girl over to the county facility for abused and abandoned children, but he didn't do it. He just drove on home with her and didn't tell anyone. She started calling him "Dad" about a year later, one day at the supermarket. Just out of the blue, and it surprised him. Warren had told everyone who asked that he was just taking care of the girl until his sister got back from her stint in the Peace Corps. Then Warren sold the house in Agoura Hills and moved out to the San Fernando Valley, buying a nice place with a pool for the kid. Sometimes he and Lorie would have long talks, sitting out by the pool late at night. She would sit on the end of the diving board and let her feet play in the water. No one even thought to ask him about the little girl—everyone just assumed that she was his daughter. Some of them even remembered reading in the newspapers a few years before that he was the cop whose wife had been murdered, and that it had never been solved, and wasn't it a shame that he had to raise his daughter without her mother around. By that time, every aspect of life in the Valley was pretty anonymous; everybody lived in their own cocoons, insulated by the consumerist TV-marketed culture that they'd been spoon-fed since *they* were the little girl's age. Of course, it helped that everyone knew he was a policeman. The forged paperwork he submitted to the girl's Catholic school was never questioned.

Warren drove up to San Quentin to visit with Flaco one more time, just before he was executed. They talked about the little girl's progress in school and in life in general, and, of course, the Matterhorn ride at Disneyland.

Market Street Books

"Only the best in new fiction"

The Rat Machine is intended by the author as the first book in a three-book series. Look for part II coming soon. If you have any questions, or comments, or would like to receive Kent Harrington's newsletter please contact socialmedia@kentharrington.com.

If you enjoyed this title, please look for other titles by Kent Harrington online, or at your local bookstore. Or please visit Kent Harrington on the web for more information and schedule of appearances: www.kentharrington.com.

Kent Harrington's available titles

Dark Ride *(available soon from Market Street Books as an eBook)*

Author's first novel. Set in the Napa Valley. A classic Jim Thompson-type noir and as hardboiled as they come—sex soaked. Lush vineyards, Big Money, a beautiful young wife, an ambitious all-American boyfriend, a very rich and kinky older husband, who has to be gotten rid of. Now, add meth to this explosive mix of Lust and Love ... in the same vein as *The Postman Only Rings Twice*.

Dia De Los Muertos *(available as an eBook)*

Set in Tijuana Mexico, during the Day Of The Dead, about a rogue DEA agent, Vincent Calhoun, who is suffering from heavy gambling debts, and Dengue fever. He has one last chance to pull his life out of the fire ... and then Celeste, an old girlfriend, gets off the bus. A hyper-modern version of *Casablanca*.

The Good Physician *(available as an eBook)*

A Graham Greene-style thriller about the war on terror. Set in Baja California. The story of a young idealistic doctor working as a CIA officer in Mexico City, thrown into the deep end of an ugly and dangerous world.

Red Jungle *(available as an eBook)*

Set in Guatemala; it is the story of an American newspaper reporter who takes after the "The Red Jaguar" a mythical treasure buried in the deepest heart of the jungle. It's a mix of *Treasure of Sierra Madre* and *Under The Volcano*. It's violent; it's sexy; it's Harrington at his most thrilling.

Satellite Circus

(available soon as an eBook and trade paper edition from Market Street Books)

The world's press has landed on the small Caribbean island of Tortola to report the disappearance of American college student Mary Waters. Among the crowd of journalists is 33-year-old Stanley Jones, on his last chance as a reporter for the Royal, a London tabloid. Stanley's editors have told him he must manufacture a lurid story about an innocent blonde ravaged by a" local savage", or don't bother coming back. The novel exposes the vicious face of Tabloid Journalism, and its typical twenty-four hour death-grip news cycle. It's a dirty high-stakes game where well-paid foot soldiers, and even spies, called "journalists," trample the truth on their way to the hotel bar.